WINTERWODE

- BOOK THREE OF THE WODE -

Being a tale of Robin Hood (a.k.a. Robyn Hode)

J TULLOS HENNIG

FOREST PATH BOOKS

WINTERWODE
Published by
FOREST PATH BOOKS

Stay informed on our releases and news!
Join the reading group/newsletter at:
https://forestpathbooks.com/into-the-forest/

Cover & interior design by Mahli (*bookdesignbymahli.com*)
Cover content is for illustrative purposes only, and any person depicted on the cover is a model.

Map illustration © 2013 by J Tullos Hennig
Pi Rho Runestones font © Peter Rempel (licensed for use)
First published in North America by DSP Publications, 2014

Library of Congress Control Number: 2019918720
ISBNs:
978-1-951293-58-1 (trade paperback)
978-1-951293-36-9 (hardcover)
978-1-951293-04-8 (e-book)

READERS LOVE THE BOOKS OF THE WODE!

"Hennig's Wode series continues to reinvent the legend of Robin Hood . . . Thick with conflict and intrigue, this retelling turns a well-known legend into a fresh, earthy tale of human passions twisted by politics and ancient powers."
—*Publishers Weekly*

"There's nothing quite so exciting as an author taking an overused traditional narrative and breathing full and rich life into it the way that Hennig does with her retelling of the Robin Hood/Green Man stories in her *Greenwode* series. I was smitten, right from the beginning."
—*Charles de Lint*

"Hennig expertly weaves the threads together in seductive, evocative prose that put me in the scene as few others have ever done . . . An enthralling transformation of folklore and legend into something wonderfully original from start to finish."
—*Susan R. Matthews*

"An intensely emotional, breathtaking version of the Robin Hood legend . . . Beautifully showcases the cultural and religious upheaval between peasant versus nobility, oppressed versus oppressors . . . Highly recommended."
—*Bella Online*

"A complex, meticulously researched, and vividly realised re-imagining of the Robin Hood myth, which depicts Robin and Guy as lovers instead of sworn enemies."
—*A Swimming Pool Library*

"I can't recommend this book highly enough. The prose is poetic, powerful, insightful. Hennig has a masterful command of weaponry and battle-speak, as well as of wode magic. This is a soul-plumbing, life-changing experience."
—*Historical Novel Society Review*

"It felt like discovering a fine wine. There was incredible tension: romantic, character-driven, and plot-driven. This isn't a light sip of a read."
—*Queer SciFi*

"Given the author's innate ability to take classic lore and make it new again through works of fantasy, fans of other genres or literature in general are sure to enjoy these."
—*Amazing Stories Magazine*

"With The Wode books, Hennig weaves Welsh mythology into the classic tale and reimagines Robin Hood and Guy of Gisbourne as lovers and Maid Marian as Robin's sister–and all three entwined by magic and fate. The world-building is intricate, the language is gorgeous . . . and the characters are achingly flawed. It's the best Robin Hood retelling I've encountered."
—*Kathy Shin, Pages below the Vaulted Sky*

- BOOKS BY J TULLOS HENNIG -

The Books of the Wode
(Tales of Robin Hood, a.k.a. Robyn Hode)

Greenwode
Shirewode
Winterwode
Summerwode
Wyldingwode

1. Main Keep
2. Curtain wall / wall walk
3. Chapel of St Nicholas
4. Motte stair & bridge
5. Motte ditch
6. Kitchens
7. Dye shed
8. Well
9. Wing bastion
10. Wall bastion
11. Smithy
12. Lord's armory
13. Sally port
14. Wet moat
15. Barn
16. Postern
17. Stable

18. Practice field
19. Garderobe
20. Granary
21. Dovecote
22. Kitchen garden
23. Gatehouse
24. Drawbridge
25. Great hall
26. Guard hall / armory
27. Servants' quarters
28. Craft stalls

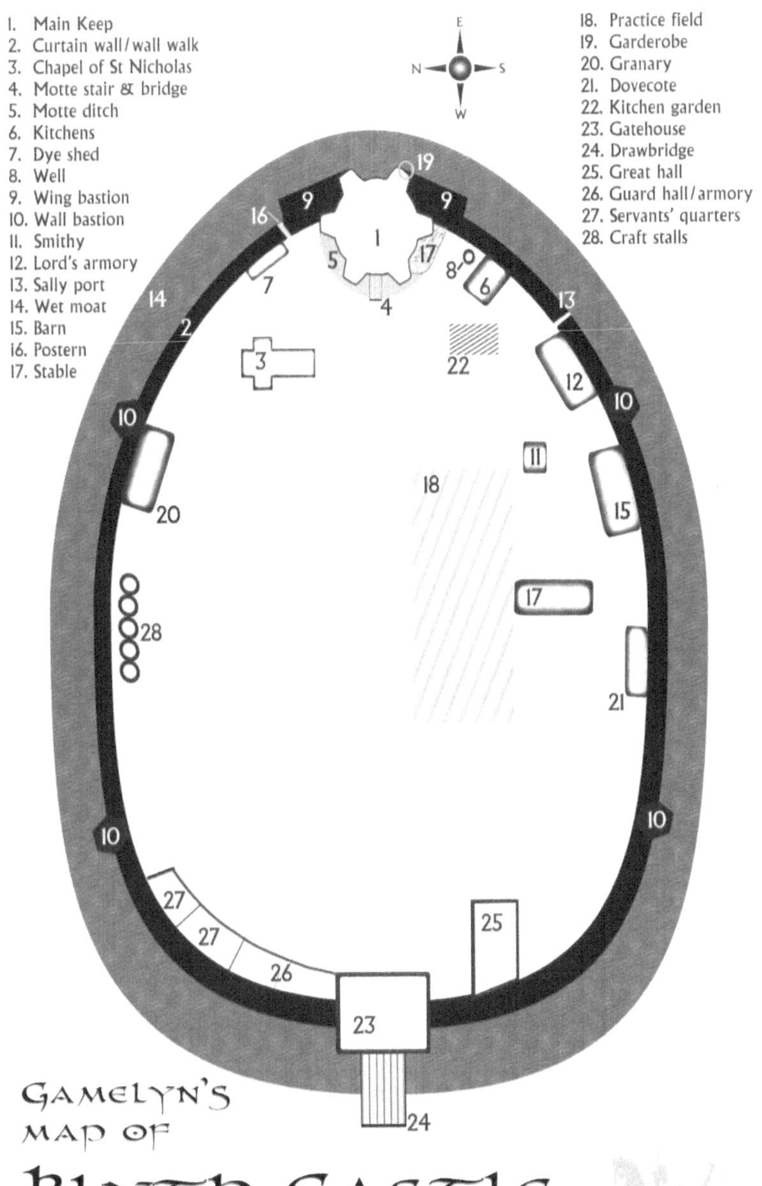

GAMELYN'S MAP OF

BLYTH CASTLE

LATER KNOWN AS TICKHILL

For Mary Virginia
Whose absence wounded, yet left me feral-strong,
and always, always wondering:
What if?

WINTERWODE

- PRELUDE -

Deep in the Shire Wode
Waning of Samhain, 1193 CE

Fire.

Sculpting shadows in the trees. Singeing a dour, angry glow across the horizon. Sparking into a vast night sky, falling stars and embers. Setting shimmers of copper and indigo into the waters of a green-shrouded lake, old when his people were young.

Fire kindles the heat of thaw and change and passion. It is a desert simmering in his heart, with *mizmar* drone and *darbuk* beating. It is what he sees when he looks in the mirror.

Even there, you were mine. Hariq aljinni alshier al-ghaba, *the fire-haired* djinn *of the forest. . .*

Ice is his shield, but fire is what he covets. Fire is what he *fears.* What he surely will find when death finally demands its due and spins him back into Hell.

Back? Nay, this *is* Hell.

It slaps his sunburned face with all the molten power of a stoked forge, grinds and gristles in lungs labouring for breath. It sears through the thin-worn soles of his boots, heats the metal of his sword pommel into a scorch against his hip, dries the blood leaking onto his shoulder into a hard, thick crust.

Guy stumbles, nearly drops his burden. With a growl and grit of his teeth, he hangs on. The small *waha* is close, so close.

"Nearly there," he murmurs, and the weight slung across his back shifts as Much utters a faint groan.

Ahead, a small well and a patch of green in the unforgiving sun. Behind, the bodies of two good horses and five goodly skilled Saracen soldiers. The ambush had been clever, but not clever enough.

They reach the *waha*, pitching stunned and grateful into the sparse shade. But not for long. Guy forces quivering, exhausted limbs into movement. Much is sorely wounded and needs care.

The well is small, but deep; the water is sweet, and cool. Much gulps it down and asks for more, relaxing in Guy's hold. His pain-clouded gaze wanders past Guy's shoulder, sharpens with acute warning.

Guy wastes no time in asking. The searing-hot pommel of his knife fits to his hand as he whirls and strikes, swift as a desert viper and just as venomous. The attacker is bowled over. A shout: his name.

Only it is not his name, *not his name*, not any more . . .

"Gamelyn, wait. Gam—?"

And the name chokes as he grinds hard fingers into their attacker's windpipe. He knows the voice—*knows it*—but this . . . it cannot be! It is a lie, all of it a lie to weaken him, so he brings the lethal curve of knife across the pale throat, teeth bared for the kill—

Gamelyn.

It is a shiver-bolt of heat lightning, with enough power to chase the sun away and fill his eyes with darkness.

Rhyddau! the voice hisses, a tangle of unfamiliarity merging into the familiar. *Release it. Now.*

Behind those words implodes pain and bliss and pain again, as if a hand sinks into and then twists at the brain matter within his skull. With a huge gasp and shudder . . .

Gamelyn woke.

He was atop Robyn, snarling-silent. The oasis—indeed, the desert and the sunlight—all were gone. Gamelyn had one hand shoved white-knuckled into Robyn's shoulder, and the other held his quillion dagger to Robyn's throat.

The dagger twitched. A thin line of scarlet gathered beneath the bright edge, then trickled down into a thick, glistening bead to quiver upon ebon curls.

Breath escaping in a tiny groan, Gamelyn started to draw back. Robyn's hand darted out, snarled in his hair, and stayed him. Awareness expanded, then; a click of tumblers in a costly lock, instinctive tally made—and nigh too late—of heat and menace. Of the night, and shadows surrounding, feral. *Waiting.*

Something flitted through those shadows: the gleam of steel half-drawn at Gilbert's belt, as if he truly didn't want to use it—but would. Little Tess growling—growling!—on his shoulder, ready to launch in ferret defence of her favourite human perch: Robyn.

Robyn, whose throat pulsed beneath Gamelyn's fingers and against his knife. Whose other hand was down Gamelyn's braies—and not for anything resembling amorous play. Nay, those fingers wrapped brutal-tight in the thin braid girdled around Gamelyn's hips. *That* had shocked him awake, was perhaps how he'd not felt Will's thick fingers twisted in his tunic, ready to wrench him back to meet Arthur's raised and ready axe. John crouched beneath it, weaponless . . . ah, but John *did* have a weapon, and Gamelyn was damned sure he knew how to use it. Hand splayed at the small of Gamelyn's back, John too had hold of the braided cord: Gamelyn's measure—marked with blood, seed, and sweat—and a true weapon in the hands of one with the magic. These two could indeed stop him with it.

Could likely kill him with it.

Truly a standoff to impress any war-hardened Templar.

Ebony eyes bored upwards into Gamelyn's. Then Robyn said, very soft, "Another bad one, aye?"

Deep in the Shire Wode
Waxing of Winter Solstice, 1193 CE

Before the dawn, Marion had, accompanied by David and the vigilant shadow of Much, trodden deep into the fens for some late-season additions to her medicinal kit. They'd left a banked hearth and a peaceful, fur-buried lot of sleeping outlaws behind.

They returned to wide-awake tension, unfed and silent. Robyn was trying—and mostly failing—to rescue a boiled-over pot of porridge. David's ferret, Tess, rode Robyn's shoulder, scolding all the while. Gilbert hovered behind Robyn, as if making to help despite the likelihood of getting clouted for his pains. Will and Arthur sat by the fire, noticeably out of range and glaring at Gamelyn, who just as obviously took no notice. Staring into space, he leaned against the elm as if someone—likely Robyn—had propped him there and he'd not bothered to shift himself since.

Without a word, Marion marched over and smacked her brother's pate, careful to avoid Tess. Ignoring his offended yelp, she plumped herself down beside the hearth and rescued the mess Robyn had made of the porridge. Then, with a meaningful glance at Gamelyn, Marion set herself to heating a brew she'd of late had all too much reason to use.

Thankfully, this time it took only a glare and an insistent tip of the drinking horn towards Gamelyn's mouth to make him surrender.

Marion felt the tiny tremor in his fingers, brushing hers as he took the small horn.

Afternoon came and went, along with the rain, leaving its chill behind but no longer tapping and rolling at the tarpaulin stretched taut overhead. Marion sat by the fire, waterproofing her boots and enjoying that roof of well-oiled deer hides. It was lovely, quiet. The lads had gone hunting, thank the Lady. All except Much, over by a well-concealed little shed, busily splitting wood with a great mother of an axe, and David—Tess restored to his shoulder—making an audible, if invisible, periphery to gather more wood, as well as . . .

"God." A rusty growl. "What is *in* that brew you give me?"

Marion smiled and didn't stop oiling her boots. Sliding her eyes sideways, she took in Gamelyn, whose copper hair spilled, lank and untidy, over his face. From beneath that, a glint of green caught the light as he tilted his head.

Pushing up from his facedown sprawl beneath woollens and furs, Gamelyn steadied himself on his forearms for a moment. This made him grimace and settle back onto his bent knees with an unthinking reach to his ribs; he flicked a furtive glance towards Marion, aborting the gesture. But she had seen and, worse, he knew it. With another growl, this one soft and resigned, Gamelyn heaved himself upright—carefully. Clad in nothing but braies, he tottered off into the trees, breath trailing in hanks of mist.

Marion shivered and put her stockinged toes closer to the hearth. Winter might be late in coming this year, but it was coming, if this chill and wet bore any clue. It remained a constant marvel to her, how Gamelyn and Robyn both didn't seem to feel the cold until they were turning blue.

Much left off swinging his axe—to follow Gamelyn, Marion guessed. Instead, Much threw a glance in his master's wake, then unearthed several substantial dry splits from the shed's back corner, brought them over. Sparks flew as he tossed the wood onto the coals, where it simmered, then leapt and licked into flames.

"I can do that," Marion protested.

"Aye," Much acknowledged and kept on with it.

Marion smiled again, put her toes closer, and kept up her oiling. "I've been lazy, left this too long. Serves me right if me toes freeze whilst I catch up. Not that I'd know 'twere cold by the looks of you lads. Gamelyn canna be arsed with a tunic, and you're down to nowt but undertunic and hose."

"We've been blessed with mild weather 'til now," he demurred. "An' wood-work's warming, methinks."

"Mm. *Methinks* life en't fair. Whilst we women shiver, you menfolk have your own built-in heating rods."

Much couldn't stop a snort, but his cheeks darkened and he dipped his chin, extra attentive to placing a few more splits on the fire, just so.

Altogether fine-looking, he was—strapping and sturdy and just the way she liked, though she did prefer a full head of hair on a man. Much seemed to follow Templar custom more than Gamelyn, there. But as if to make up for it, Much's dark beard lay longer and thicker, tending to curl. Marion inched her toes even closer and huddled into her cloak, kept working—and looking. The two-finger scar tracing from Much's left temple to jaw didn't mar his looks, only the beard, sparse in the scar's wake. His neck and arms were brown and corded beneath the rolled-up sleeves, and the thin linen clung to the small of his back, damp with sweat, and . . .

And here she was, nerves humming from neck to knees, gawping like a bairn hoping to steal a taste of sweet. With a rueful smile, Marion reattended her oily hands and boots and did not let herself imagine what that oil would look like on his bare chest.

Not much, anyway, and she snorted softly to herself at the pun.

It had been too long since she'd had a man, that was all. Not that she hadn't found herself amongst an abundance of them—and one in particular eager to do her service.

Will.

Marion frowned, fingers stilling at her work. She peered at the fire but did not see it.

Abundance had its own problems—more subtle, but there all the same. Marion recognised both her awkward position and her good fortune. A lone woman, surrounded by men—good Heathens all, and respectful—but the Heathen world was being undercut as if 'twere a rotten old tree. The old morals of woman-right and choice were being forgotten. Not here in the Shire Wode of course, where her brother exacted a straightforward code of Heathen customs. Some called them "ruthless," but Marion would have added "chivalrous," even if Robyn would have laughed and said chivalry was a rich man's luxury. Nevertheless, Marion remained uncertain as to how far to test that code.

She'd be in some straits without it: a renegade nun, a pagan peasant of a wortwife with no man to protect—own—her.

Aye, and the Christians were altogether proud of their subjugation of their women, of the way they'd tamed their goddess into an untouched virgin on an unreachable pedestal. Their women fled to convents for protection and what power they could find. A poor choice, to Marion's mind . . . yet how was she any different? Here she sat, finally back amongst her kind with memories all her own again—yet cloaked in celibacy as if she had remained in convent walls. Even Gamelyn, who'd both flourished and suffered beneath the proscriptions of his Christian upbringing, gave her a distant respect that made her want to snog him senseless just to see his expression.

Mayhap she should set up shop at the old temple stones nigh to Barrow Mere, like her mam had said they did in the old times, and take a man every other fortnight in sacrifice to the goddess's ways. That should set everyone, including herself, to some satisfaction. She smirked, but it started to fade.

Everyone, that was, except Will.

"You've a nice smile. We en't seen it enough, of late."

Marion blinked and looked up. Much had bent over the hearth, tending it into a cheery blaze. Wiping the sweat from his upper lip, he gave her a cheeky grin. But as their eyes met they held, chance meeting by firelight, thinking to expand into distinct possibility . . .

It was Marion's lot, this time, to flush and turn sudden attention to her work.

Her choice, here, should she lie with anyone. *Her choice.*

But neither was she stupid. Robyn thought to set the Old Ways back aflame, hot and strong . . . but the new ways were insidious, taking advantage of human frailties with a startling cunning. For Marion to stand anywhere other than upon a pedestal of older sister and avatar of a remote and fierce Lady Huntress was to court trouble. Even here. And they'd trouble enough for twenty at present—and just as tied to sex and claiming. Robyn Hood's band of outlaws roiled with change. A former adversary bided amongst them, openly courting their leader.

Pack rights had shifted amongst these wolves, and none of them knew quite how to manage.

Any road, she was being ridiculous! Daft and quivery as any wilting damsel in a silly courtly romance. Gratitude, it was, nowt more and that being plenty; she should be grateful to both Much and Gamelyn, freeing her from Nottingham's gaol by stealth and arms. But where with Gamelyn the ability to dismiss any lingering interest stayed a habit familiar, and effortless . . .

With Much, it was not so easy.

So Marion focused on another topic. "What was it like?"

Much didn't answer right away; she tilted her head, and found him frowning. It smoothed as he noted her gaze upon him.

"Much?"

"What were what like?" he answered, slow.

"Brother Dolfin said it. War is a horrible thing. Is he right?"

Much ruminated on the fire. "'Terrible' don't begin to describe it." He gave a savage poke to the flames, blue eyes lit nigh yellow as sparks flew. "But when it's all you know?"

"Surely it canna be *all* you know," Marion said, muted.

"Mm." Another poke, somewhat gentler. "A soldier's ways're all has mattered since I first came up Tica's hill—"

"Tica's hill?"

"Aye, and I forget." Much's grin was sudden and rueful apology. "'Tis what locals have allus called Blyth Castle. Since me great-granddad were a wean and they raised it."

Marion considered this. "How old were you, then? When you came to a soldier's ways? Up Tica hill."

"Not sure." A laconic shrug. "Old enough to sass me da, not old enough to know he were makin' sense. Likely eleven 'r twelve, when all lads need be nailed in a barrel and fed through a bunghole. Couple of years after, they assigned me to Himself."

"Himself," Marion murmured, scrutinising her boots. A dry spot begged oil; she dipped her hands in the tallow and started rubbing. "Gamelyn wanted to be a monk."

"He is, en't he?"

"You tell me," she replied, soft. "He wanted to be a scholar, not a soldier."

"Well, he carries enough books, at that. Even on campaign." Much shook his head, sent sparks with another jab at the fire. "Him and Master Hubert both."

"At least he had them. But, still . . . " As the flames started to lick higher, she bent forwards, closing her eyes against the heat on her cheeks.

"Still?" Much prompted.

"Still," Marion repeated, slow, and opened her eyes to stare at the coppery blaze. Ventured, still careful, "I think some days Gamelyn doesn't know where he is."

Much was still watching her; she could feel his gaze, burning her cheeks no less than the fire. As he turned back to repair the damage his injudicious poking had done, she could all but hear the shrug in his voice. "He knows where he is, aye, an' well enough."

Marion snuck a glance. Much was now looking the way Gamelyn had gone, a frown twisting his brow. Curious, she waited. Much had none of Robyn's quicksilver nor Gamelyn's detachment, but Marion had come, over the past moon's waxing, to appreciate his deft prudence. She was fairly sure he'd not finished.

And he hadn't, though his next comment was audible only to her: warning, and lament. "I think he en't sure *who* he is no more."

"A mad dog, is what that bloody Gisbourne is! And one what needs to be put outta *our* misery!"

Robyn had been waiting for it. It had been building for some time, brewing like fens rotting in summering heat—and wasn't that apropos? Because since that horrific night over a fortnight ago, spent sleepless and wondering if Gamelyn's wound would end up killing him or no, then after, as Gamelyn had finally begun to recover, merely to slide into nightmares altogether sudden, and violent . . .

Will had never been one to hold his tongue. Robyn was surprised it had taken this long.

At least he hadn't risked frightening the game for miles around. He'd waited until they'd tracked and taken the deer to start his daft objections.

But now wasn't exactly the best timing, either. After a fair stint beneath the tether pole from which they'd slung the dead buck, Robyn and Will had traded lading with Gilbert and Arthur. A heavy buck meant good eating, but it made for just-as-substantial tempers when camp were a-ways.

"This en't the first, aye? But one morning could be t' last."

Behind their yoked companions, John kept pace at Robyn's right elbow, weighted down with a sling of hare carcasses as well as Gilbert's bow and his own. He nudged Robyn, caught his gaze in a resigned look.

Robyn rolled his own eyes in answer and kept walking, glad enough to be out from under the yoke for now. Rain had blown through during the night, and it made his scarred left shoulder ache like damn. They were finally nigh to camp, with an afternoon of relaxation ahead once they'd broken the carcass. But, like any good ox freed from the furrow before he'd been proper worked, Will was striding point and spoiling for something to further whet the edge.

And he wasn't finished, not by a long shot. "Mark me words, but that mad Templar'll have you before this is done."

"You think he en't already had me, and more'n the once?" Robyn drawled. "Bloody hell, Scathelock, here I thought you were paying attention."

Gilbert snorted what was meant to be a laugh but, beneath Will's glare, became a cough.

"An' there's proof of what brain you're thinkin' with!" Will retorted.

"Aye, and you're a ripe one t' talk, when y' canna keep yer own eyes off me sister!"

"An' *there's* another cause to be spoken to, how you let that Templar's lackey shadow Marion on 'er wanderings, 'stead of one of us."

"'Stead of you, you mean?" Robyn laughed as Will flushed. "Sweet Lady, Scathelock, but she'd have me for lunch, did she know I were sendin' anyone to ride herd on her as 'tis, and you about as subtle as an ox-horn up the arse!"

"It's allus arses with you, aye? Sweet Lady, Rob, are you that bloody besotted? Look at you—wearing the sod's clothes!"

John started to protest, caught Robyn's eye, and desisted.

"A cloak en't clothes. Happens this one's warm, t' boot." Robyn switched it over one arm, defensive and defiant both. "An' changing the subject wain't change me mind. Or me sister's, if you keep actin' the ass."

"Huh. At least yer sister's one of us. While that . . . that *nobleman* en't, and never will be if 'twere mine t—"

"It en't yours to say. And it sure en't yours to say who I lie with. Happens last time I checked, you weren't interested in my bed." Robyn smirked, but there was little humour in it. "Are you telling me you've changed your mind?"

Will flushed again. "I'm telling you t' ginger bastard'll be your death, he will, an' see if he wain't."

"'Tis more likely I'll die right here and now. Of boredom."

"Damn it, Robyn—"

"I mean, listenin' t' you. *Tellin'* me. Going on and on. And on. The same song and dance, Will, and y' canna so much as carry a tune in a really well-plugged bucket."

"You en't taking me serious—"

"Nay." Robyn's voice dripped sarcasm. "Y' think so?"

Will stopped, turned, and opened his mouth again. The path was narrow, so Gilbert almost ran into him.

Arthur gave a mild curse. "Give over or have it out, but get outta the way, man!"

With a grimace Will stepped into the bracken. Gilbert and Arthur continued on, Robyn in their wake as well as John, unstopping.

Will lurched in behind. "I'm not the only one who feels this way, you know. Arthur—"

"Don't bring me into this mess now," Arthur warned.

"David's had a few things t'—"

"David isn't here," Gilbert interrupted, "so you've no rights to speak for him."

"David were only on about that 'un's masters coming after him, 'tennyrate," Arthur pointed out. "I think none of us want a lot of flaming Templar Knights storming t' Shire Wode."

Let 'em try, Robyn thought but did not say. *He's here with t' Wode, now. The Wode and me, and the sooner all of you and those be-damned monks realise it. . .*

John was peering at Robyn as if parsing his thoughts, a rueful smile tucked into one cheek.

"You keep forgetting, Scathelock," Gilbert continued with no little sarcasm, "the slight matter of Guy—um, Gamelyn—taking an arrow in the back? *For* Robyn?"

"He did that," Arthur admitted, albeit unwilling.

"So? It don't mean he en't out t' skewer you in your sleep *now!*" Will made a grab for Robyn's arm.

Robyn deftly avoided it, kept walking. "It en't a-purpose."

"It don't matter. He's dangerous!"

"Of all the nonsense being spouted, that's something I do have to agree with," Gilbert ventured.

"Living's danger." Robyn gestured, palms up and fingers spread.

"He's an expert killer, Robyn." Gilbert gave a grunt and shifted the pole on his shoulder. "Hold up, Arthur, eh?" Arthur nodded gratefully at the respite; as they both nudged out from under the yoke Gilbert eyed Robyn and continued, "Not only one of the mostly highly skilled knights in the Christian world, but Siham told me he also trained with the Saracen Assassins—"

"How would she know?" Robyn snorted.

"Because she's a Saracen too?"

"Gilly, I swear, a lass takes hold of your knob—in truth or the wishing," Robyn clarified as Gilbert shot him an injured look, "and you'll heed anything she says! If you fancy the lass so, mayhap you should hie yerself t' Pontefract and go a-courtin'."

"Robyn, do you even know what an Assassin is?" Gilbert persisted, very quiet, and peered round at the others. "Do any of you?"

"Happens I know more about this than you might think," Robyn snapped back.

Even if he didn't. Not as much as he'd like. Not that it bloody *mattered.*

"And *happens* he could take you out in a heartbeat and not even know he'd done it until you were bleeding at his feet!" Gilbert shot back. "*That's* what worries me."

"You can only tie a mad dog fr so long, Robyn," Arthur put in.

"He's *not,*" John snarled from between his teeth.

"Johnny, you'd excuse him owt and I en't about to understand it," Will growled. "That poncy ginger nobleman is bellying what's *yours,* and you en't—!"

His voice yipped and choked as Robyn whirled, grabbed him by the throat, and shoved him backwards against a tree.

Silence. And Will had the brass to look *surprised.*

"No man belongs t' another," John said, hushed but iron-hard. "Not in *our* Wode."

Will started to reply; Robyn tightened his grip, leaned closer until he could see his own eyes, reflected in Will's like fire-laced coals.

More silence.

"Go have a shit," Robyn finally growled. "Cause you're proper full of it. Even to your bloody mouth"—his fingers tightened—"which you canna. Keep. *Shut.*"

He loosed Will. Will lurched away from the tree trunk and, cursing beneath his breath, retreated into the trees.

Away from camp, at least.

Robyn turned his back to the tree, slid down it to his haunches with a choked noise, half snarl and half sigh.

Gilbert started forward; Arthur looked torn between following Will and staying put. Before Robyn could say a word, John stepped forwards with an adamant shake of his head and gestured, plain: *Go on, back to camp.*

Somewhat reluctant, they hoisted their share of the burden and obeyed.

Robyn dropped his head, took in a long breath and let it out.

A hand came into view beneath his black forelock, flipped it aside, and cupped his jaw, the pressure steady, asking.

"Go on, love," Robyn told John, gentle but brittle. "I'll come anon."

Breath and lips caressed his forehead, then in another soft breath, John departed.

Gamelyn didn't, at first, go very far from camp; just enough to tend to the morning's needs and not foul a good site. But once he finished, he stood retying his braies, taking in the quiet.

For it was quiet. The only sounds were of the damp, and the forest in that damp, and his own breath wafting a hazy exhaust into the stillness. Even the trees slept, surrounding him like stark, grey spirits, with only a soft underground thrum to hint of life, burrowed warm-deep, within them.

Sleeping, aye. Was he still half-asleep, still so tangled in dreams as to imagine it possible he could hear them? Hear the life in trees— feel their breath, as Robyn would say, or their souls, as Marion would—as if it were not the greatest of blasphemies that anything other than man should have a soul?

He'd have thought himself well inured to blasphemy by now. A wry smile touching his lips, Gamelyn took in the lovely, moisture-laden air and held it in his lungs, counted to five before he let it escape.

Take this from me. Instinctive, the plea, and always, always unspoken.

I can only take what you will give, proud one.

The Lady Huntress was a constant presence now. Shadowing him. Speaking his name. Waiting . . . aye, She was waiting for something. He could all but taste it. Sweet as the mead Robyn had shared with him several nights ago, and the kisses after. Bitter as the foul-tasting—and necessary, so it seemed—drug with which Marion plied him, to quiet a snarling, vicious beast that refused to die.

If only they would quiet the dreams . . .

Dreams recognise what yearnings will not. There are things still undone, my Knight—but mayhap not the ones you think.

Things undone, aye.

He should have returned to Temple Hirst by now.

I don't want to go. It burst from Gamelyn like the last flare of sunset: the singular truth of his present existence, yet also tinged with treachery, falsehood. He shook his head, negation against the betraying heat working its leisurely way from neck to cheeks. *You said I belong here, with them. With* him. *You said I would be. . . whole. It is all I've ever wanted, prayed for.*

Yet to whom do you pray, my Knight?

Gamelyn hesitated. He reached out, traced fingers over the rough grey bark of the tree closest to him. It was chill, but he barely felt it, wondered if his fingers were that cold. Ventured, *I don't know.*

When you do, then you shall.

And the Lady's presence sucked into darkness, leaving Gamelyn shivering in truth—not with cold, but an inexplicable emptiness.

He should go back to camp. At least fetch a cloak. An overtunic. Something.

But he didn't. The wandering started with a real enough goal, to be sure. Marion's draught gave sleep and a modicum of temporary peace, but Gamelyn always woke tasting bird dung and dust, with only fresh water to slake it.

He found that soon enough, in a small hollow bordered by willows and rocks tall as his own head. There was a small rise beyond, the rill at his feet clear-running over grey stones, narrow enough to leap over, did his injuries allow. Gamelyn knelt and drank, splashed the chill water over his flushed face for good measure. He remained there, crouching, for a while, bare toes digging into the bank and face dripping.

He should go back to camp. Marion would have at him for chilling the wound. But it was well bandaged, the hole left by a Nottingham crossbow bolt nearly closed and finally clean of infection. Marion—and David too—had spent far too much time in the tending of it these past fortnights, draining, swabbing, and packing it with herbs and unguents. The fever had been the worst of it, but the Saracen doctors with their civilised medicaments could not have done better. Gamelyn had endured those, and more than once. He also well knew the healing of ribs; his were improving at a goodly pace, no longer exacting as severe a punishment for movement, only warning twinges and stabs when he unwisely twisted, or bent over as he now was.

Something resounded above the rippling stream, a harsh echo into woodland calm. Gamelyn slung the wet hair from his face and rose—a bit injudicious, for his ribs seized tight. Eyes crossing, for moments Gamelyn heard nothing more than his own rattling attempts at breath.

Discomfort ebbed, gave way to sounds. Voices. At first faint, then growing closer. Head cocked to one side, hand reaching by instinct for the short, elegant dagger strapped to his bare right calf, Gamelyn focused on the sounds.

Recognised them. Particularly one voice, a baritone both common and powerful. Robyn had a tilt of speech straight from his Welsh mother, overlain with the ever-present shire-bred purl that gave an improbable length to some vowels even as it discarded others.

Closer and closer, from up the rise past the stream bed. Gamelyn crossed the shallow stream, heedless of the chill water darting up his ankles, intent upon the conversation as it grew more heated. Another slow burn suffused its way from chest to cheeks, sent Gamelyn's breathing shallow. Made him draw, slowly, his dagger and reach for his sword. The latter, of course, wasn't there. Foolish to leave it behind—or fortunate. For, as he listened, he wanted nothing more than to use it.

On Will Scathelock.

A deep laugh: Robyn's, derision lurking beneath the humour tickling its edges. More back and forth, voices drifting and snatching through the trees; argument but not quite, coming closer until they coalesced into speech. Gamelyn started up the hillock and out of the stream hollow. As they came into view, Gilbert's voice halted Gamelyn in his tracks, made him seek cover and remain unseen.

"—could take you out in a heartbeat and not even know he'd done it until you were bleeding at his feet. *That's* what worries me!"

"You can only tie a mad dog fr so long, Robyn." Arthur—no surprise, coming from him. From Gilbert, however . . .

Yet Gilbert was right, was he not? Because Gamelyn hadn't known, *hadn't* realised.

John said something, brief-soft as ever. The hunters passed Gamelyn's crouch, boot tops first, then the glassy eyes of their quarry—a young, fat hart.

"Johnny, you'd excuse him owt and I en't about to understand it."

Will, again. "That poncy ginger nobleman is bellying what's *yours*, and you en't—!"

A yip and a curse, strangled silent. A full stop of the small party, and more murmurs, vehement and unintelligible, then a heavy silence. Gamelyn started to rise. A sudden crashing of brush stayed him. It suggested more a wounded buck than any outlaw whose life depended upon stealth—but it proved the latter. Will came stomping through the trees, not a stone's throw from Gamelyn's own hiding place, curses following his retreat into the hollow.

Gamelyn's attention returned to Robyn. The others departed: first Gilbert and Arthur, laden with their catch, then John, not so laden with his own burdens that he wouldn't try to ease Robyn's. But John also retreated—not willingly, to be sure—and when Robyn felt himself alone, he flung his arms and gaze upwards.

What Gamelyn then saw on Robyn's face thwarted what he wanted to do—chase down Scathelock and give him a damned good thrashing—and made it clear what he had to do.

It should have been difficult for even a *hashishin*-trained Templar to sneak up on the Green Man in his own Wode. But it wasn't until Gamelyn was nearly upon Robyn that Robyn looked up and saw him.

Robyn's first thought was to ask what in bloody damn Gamelyn was doing out here in nothing but a bandage and his braies. Then he saw the set to Gamelyn's jaw, the flame in his cheek and the white around it, and he knew. *Knew.*

"You heard," Robyn said.

And when the coppery head tilted to one side, more shrug than verification, an almost frightening hot fury filled the back of Robyn's throat.

Then he longed to strangle Scathelock.

Instead, Robyn's gaze sought Gamelyn's, sought and found the tiny, irresolute flit of emotion, quickly smoothed into cool jade even as Robyn watched. Robyn's heart gave another lurch and twist—not fury this time, but an odd shame. He had to look down, away, anywhere but those eyes. They would no doubt greet a headman's axe or an avenging army with the same taut disconnection.

Robyn hated that expression and everything it meant. Everything it had *always* meant.

Gamelyn held out a hand. Robyn took it, allowed himself to be pulled upright. Trying to speak, though the words caught, tangling and stuttering his throat even as John had once said his own had.

Not that John needed words, never really had done—and neither did Robyn, here and now.

So Robyn used the handclasp to pull Gamelyn close. Kissed him, hard. And when Gamelyn thought to duck away, Robyn merely followed him.

Only Gamelyn was just as determined to back out of it.

Not this time. Robyn followed.

"Rob—" Gamelyn broke off with a curse, nearly went down. They ended up half sliding, half stumbling over rocks and tree roots, tangling in bracken and each other's flailing limbs.

Robyn found himself grinning. Gamelyn wasn't so amused; Robyn was sure that one swipe at his head had been aimed. They'd gone halfway down into the ravine before Robyn halted their descent—first with an uncanny twist, then a grunt and a halfhearted shove to send Gamelyn on his arse against an upswell of moss and earth.

"*Damn* it, Robyn!"

A tiny tinge of culpability stayed Robyn as Gamelyn grimaced. But the moss was soft, and the light in Gamelyn's eyes suggested more *Give me a chance and I'll knock you another one* than *Ow, you're breaking me, you stupid sod.* So Robyn gave another push—gentler than usual, granted—against Gamelyn's breastbone and straddled him, snarling his fingers in the rumpled copper hair.

"Robyn, are you out of—?"

"Just shut t' bloody fuck *up*, will you?" Robyn growled.

Bent in.

No words. *This* was all the language they needed—all they'd ever needed, really. Body and breath and sweet, sweet fire . . .

This time Gamelyn shivered as Robyn rocked his hips, ground down, began to trace a line of nips from mouth to cheek to neck. Gamelyn's head tilted with the beginnings of compliance, a faint smile ticing at his lip.

"My arse end is getting damp," he murmured.

"You're proper fussy for sommun who's like to find 'imself spread out and shagged 'til he screams."

Gamelyn was silent, then whispered against Robyn's ear, "Promise?"

Robyn licked a heated line along Gamelyn's jaw, gave a satisfied sigh as he felt another shudder runnel down hard muscle. "Not many promises I can be keeping, but that one? Aye."

Likely there was no better place to curl up, dozy in the aftermath of a satisfying and hard tup, than the Wode's gentle bed. Particularly if one had a cloak to spread a lover out on, nubbled soft as a hare's fur, yet spun tight enough to keep the chill and damp somewhat at bay.

"You stole my cloak," Gamelyn accused.

"'Twere cold this morning," Robyn defended. "I en't a cloak so fine as yours. Anyways, y' lie with thieves . . . "

Gamelyn laughed, in a rise and hiccup Robyn oft loved to tease from him. He was lying half atop Robyn, braies unwound about his thighs. Robyn's own garb was in similar dishabille, sated anatomy nestled, as if hopeful for another round, against Gamelyn's freckled haunch. Robyn's forehead also rested against pale, freckled skin—Gamelyn's shoulder—and his callused fingers traced, lightly, the bandaging just beneath.

Not that Gamelyn let it stop him overmuch. Robyn's lip twitched in appreciation, and he ghosted a kiss along the expanse of scabbed-over flesh beneath the linen, lingered to trail both hair and breath across it, grounding the magic they'd made.

"It's better," Gamelyn insisted.

"Mm. Several of those gasps you treated me to weren't nigh pleasurable," Robyn countered.

"Sure of that, are you?"

"Aye, well, no question but there's a fine line draws the two with you." Robyn smirked, bent close, and nipped at Gamelyn's neck. He was not gentle, and was unsurprised as Gamelyn sucked in a quick breath, let it out in another soft chuckle.

"Ah. You have me there."

"I'll have you anywhere." Robyn nipped him again. "And look there, but if that longbow of yours en't stringing itself for another round."

"It's as eager for something to do as I am," Gamelyn growled.

Robyn chuckled. He reached down and cupped soft flesh, felt it quiver and further stiffen against his fingers. "Make no mistake, I'm glad to see you all eager again," he purred, with a leisurely stroke that had Gamelyn leaning back and pushing into his hand. "But take your rest as y' find it, pet. A bad day of layabout and shagging's better than a sunny day workin' fields on your knees."

"And no doubt your next comment would consider how I've never worked fields in my life."

"Aye, there's that . . . but I weren't about to say." Robyn grinned. "Not when you're so bloody eager to say 't for me."

"I could, of course, point out how you've never been on a hard campaign across a desert waste, sunburnt and bloody with chainmail nigh molten to your skin in the heat."

"No doubt 'twere uphill both ways t' ploughing, as me old grandda allus claimed." Still grinning, Robyn began to nuzzle a trail of kisses down Gamelyn's pectoral. "And it made you proper hard. En't as hard, I'm thinking, as I fancy you are here and now in me hand. Aye?"

"Aye." Gamelyn nuzzled against Robyn's forearm, murmured a string of words—Frankish, from the sound of them.

"So far I've learned how to say *shit, bloody fucking hell,* and *fuck me* in Frankish," Robyn ventured once Gamelyn had lapsed into quiet. "Also there's *please*—which sounds a lot like *shit,* if you ask me—and *faster,* and aye, the most important one, *oh god, harder.*" This with a coy slide of eye and an impenitent grin. "So care to translate what you just said?"

Something that distinctly looked to be a flush was gracing Gamelyn's cheeks and neck. "Um. Not terribly."

"You might have just called me 'limp and useless in the furs' for all I know."

"Oh, I think you know of all the things I might call you, 'limp' would definitely not be amongst them."

"You've no fair call sayin' things to me I wain't understand."

"Says the man who gibbers Barrow talk at me all the time."

"Hoy, it en't gibbering!"

"I'm not sure what else you'd call a language that encompasses that many sounds in one breath. Though it has its uses, to be sure— I'm reasonably sure I know from whence came that agile and talented tongue of yours."

Robyn snorted up a laugh that would put a she-ass to shame. "Now you're just trying to distract me with poncy English. Whilst not a breath ago you called me sommat peculiar in Frankish."

Gamelyn sat up. "It wasn't . . . peculiar. Or uncomplimentary." Insistent. And . . .

Bloody damn, but he *was* blushing.

Robyn reached out, tangled his fingers in the thick, ruddy hair, and gave a yank to pull Gamelyn back against his chest. "What, then?"

"No."

"*What?*"

"*No.*"

Robyn drew in breath for another try; instead, a low whistle filled the quiet. Almost—but not quite—a bird's call, it was followed by a footfall so soft it could have only been heard by Robyn. As its bearer no doubt intended.

Gamelyn stiffened against him, didn't relax until Robyn half sat up and said, "John?"

Another soft whistle, mere confirmation as a slight, familiar figure rounded the rock leading up from the hollow. John's brown eyes danced as he took them in; half rueful apology and half amusement. He carried a well-stuffed bag over one shoulder, but even that couldn't deny the silent grace of his approach. Well, John could sneak up on a hind and slap her haunch before she'd so much as smelt him.

Robyn entertained a fleeting hope—mayhap John could join him in teasing the truth of the Frankish phrase from Gamelyn, mayhap even another tup and tangle on Gamelyn's fine-woven cloak. John's expression, however, upskelled that.

Leaving Robyn with another hope: nowt or owt, let it not be Will. Again.

John settled on his haunches beside them, reached out to give a fond pat to Gamelyn's bare thigh, then brushed a kiss over Robyn's mouth. "Company."

And that perked Gamelyn up almost as much as Robyn biting his neck. Aye, well, they were all getting bored. Very few travellers had braved the Shire Wode of late. None would soon forget how Robyn had called down nightmares upon Nottingham, clothed in the spectres of the Wild Hunt.

Gamelyn lurched upwards, pulling up his braies as he gained his feet. "It's about time we saw some action."

John rose, treating Gamelyn to a lift of brow and a return of his sly-shy grin. The *I should think you have done* remained unspoken, yet all too plain. An expression like to John's teased at Gamelyn's lips as, eyebrows still raised, John reached into the bag at his hip and pulled out first a tunic, then boots, then leather chausses—all Gamelyn's.

"Has anyone told you you're brilliant?" Gamelyn extended his hand and ran his fingers along John's cheek with . . . well, Robyn would say it was shyness if Gamelyn wasn't some notorious Templar assassin.

Of course, both Robyn and John knew this Templar assassin had been—and still could be—not quite sure what to do with his affections.

Robyn peered up at the two men, knew the smile on his face was proving him a besotted git and didn't care, contemplating slow burns beneath stone façades, and how true power wasn't all in hew or height. He twitched at his own tunic, steered his thoughts back to business. "Company. Mm. What sort, John? Where?"

John kissed Gamelyn's hand with a grin, then handed over the tunic and pointed north, towards the cart path that wound north-east through the Shire Wode's uppermost reaches, and elaborated, "Singing."

Well, it was elaboration for John, anyway.

"*Singing?*" Gamelyn burst out, somewhat muffled by the fabric over his head. "What in hell?"

"Happens Gilly knows." John shrugged again.

Which, since Gilbert was the only one of them who knew the Frankish tongue—outside Gamelyn, Marion, and Much, Robyn amended—it likely meant their singing intruder wasn't common. Which likely meant a full purse.

Robyn rose, tucking himself back into his braies, and paused with laces in hand to eye Gamelyn. "I'm wonderin' if you're up for this?"

"One man, singing?" Gamelyn stepped into one legging with a roll of his eyes.

"'Tweren't just over a month ago you had a crossbow bolt in your back," Robyn persisted, still quiet.

"One man." Gamelyn's riposte was flat. "Singing."

John stayed out of the small dispute. He busied himself making sure Gamelyn was properly garbed, then, with a repeat of his half smile, shoved Robyn's hands aside and started lacing Robyn's braies.

"Bloody mamma hen," Robyn started to protest, then submitted to the inevitable.

"Happens"—Gamelyn aped the common-speak—"*I* en't after fetchin' me dinner guests wi' tackle out, Robyn 'ood."

Robyn laughed.

John smiled wider, kept lacing.

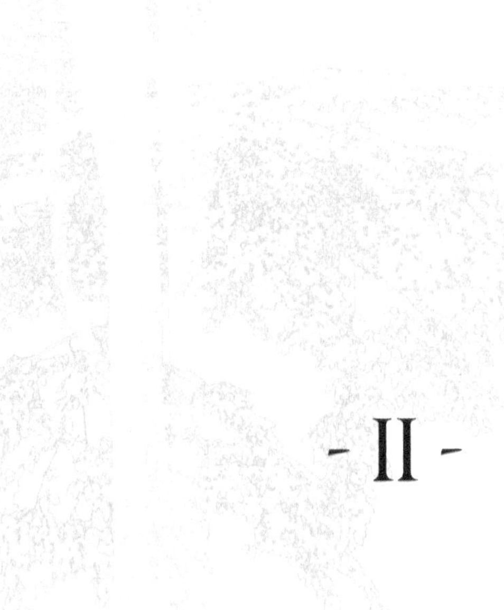

- II -

The sun had long since trimmed the treetops and disappeared into a thick veil of mist. It wafted upwards, swirling about the outlaws, both greeting and cloak.

Of course, finding their mark was no hardship, and tailing him easier still. The fellow started, stopped, started again merely to nudge his horse on. Once he turned around and went back the way he'd come. The tale was easily enough told without him singing it: the fellow hadn't sense to know a clear, chill day often began with thick mists. He was lost.

The rest of his tale wasn't so easily parsed. He was dressed loudly as any common minstrel. Those clothes, however, had an uncommon sheen, and the pale blue cloak over them was just as fine. The lute slung at his back was also no commoner's instrument. Not to mention, the fellow sat comfortably upon a fine palfrey, a flashy bay roan that would bring a goodly price at market.

The most uncommon, though, was how the man kept *singing*.

Robyn had for some time intended to signal his people to close in, but found himself mute. He was proper upskelled, to put it mildly. Was the man looking to be waylaid by outlaws—or just too daft to imagine he would be?

"I've not heard that lay in years." Gilbert's whispered, wistful sigh came from behind Robyn.

Arthur gave a derisive snort and aimed a swat to the back of Gilbert's head.

"At least he *can* sing it," Gamelyn murmured from Robyn's other shoulder, sliding Arthur a look as if daring another swat.

The dare went unchallenged. Arthur, unlike Will, didn't underestimate the Templar.

"No common minstrel or jongleur, this," Gilbert murmured. "He's a troubadour."

"Nay," Gamelyn corrected. "A trouvère. Listen."

Gilbert frowned and cocked his head, then started to grin. It was a distinctly wolfish expression, of which Robyn fair approved. "Oooh." Gilbert nudged Gamelyn, who cocked an eyebrow, bemused, as Gilbert continued, "All the better!"

Robyn's puzzled look demanded an explanation; again, Gilbert nudged Gamelyn.

Still somewhat bemused by the show of camaraderie, Gamelyn offered quiet explanation. "He's a fancy court musician from the north. Of France," he furthered. "There'll be money."

Good news. Robyn mightn't be sure what the fellow was singing—but one thing was bloody damn sure: the fellow *could* sing. He'd a fine, clear tenor lifting and falling, vibrating against the damp tree boughs as if inviting songbirds to rival him. Mayhap that was the reason Robyn kept holding off. It was proper agreeable just to listen.

Robyn cast a quick eye over his companions. It was a different mix than any previous raiding party, not only considering who'd refused and who hadn't. Will was still off somewhere—sulking, no doubt. Marion remained firmly entrenched with brewing some noxious—and useful—potion of hers, and David had stayed behind with her, avid to increase his own herb lore. Much, who'd until now seemed torn between self-inflicted duties—not only to his lord but to the woman he'd helped steal from Nottingham—had found this choice easy. He kept a protective hover at Gamelyn's elbow.

Robyn smirked again. Much was as itchy for action as said lord. As Robyn himself, truth be told.

And this promised some fun. Mayhap this rich tosser would agree to keep his purse in exchange for lowering his sights from Frankish courts to an outlaw camp. Mayhap he could sing for his supper. Too sombre, Marion was, after what all had happened in Nottingham—though she'd said little enough to it. Which, to Robyn, gave it away too plain.

Of course, there'd be no merry-making did this daft fellow keep wandering. He might end up warbling himself over a steep crag. If they were careful enough, made proper sure the trouvère couldn't place their most valuable campsite—well, the fellow was lost, after all, and Robyn would give his bow arm to see his sister dancing about the fires again . . .

Nay, Archer. The mellifluous voice nipped eagerness close as a rope snugged about his neck.

He tugged at it, nevertheless. *But Marion—*

It is a loving impulse, but this one could lead to danger. You indeed bide close to things which lie precious to Our ways. . . and there is more to this wandering singer than meets even your canny eyes.

Robyn tensed, waiting for more. But the Lady's voice faded away as quickly as it had risen—no surprise there, truly. She seemed as discomfited in his skin as he was in having her there.

The Horned Lord, on the other hand, gave a heated growl of warning against Robyn's nape.

The trouvère went abruptly silent. As one, the outlaws dropped to earth—save Robyn, still a bit skewed out of time from the Lady's voice, and Gamelyn, who had slid against the tree beside which Robyn stood. Thankfully it was stillness and silence that mattered in this fog, not shadows stark against winter-naked woodland.

Sure enough, their mark's nervous restlessness gave audible betrayal, its message carried upon wafting mists. The horse's footfalls, heading north, checked with a stumble and prance in place to contemplate the smaller path Robyn knew to be there. Then a grunt as the horse was turned, more scattered-damp beats of hoofs on loam and moss as the main path was found again. Horse and rider headed, this time at a quick amble, back where Robyn and his men waited.

Robyn's lip quirked. He slid his gaze to meet Gamelyn's and found a like expression there, eager ferocity lighting those juniper-green eyes.

And bloody damn if *that* only made Robyn want to shove him up against the tree and snog him senseless.

A smirk to answer Robyn's own suddenly tilted Gamelyn's mouth. He leaned forwards, nuzzled into Robyn's cowl to breathe, nigh soundless, against Robyn's ear, "Do you want the mark, or do you want me?"

"It's a hard choice you're giving me," Robyn murmured, just as silent. Gamelyn smirked.

"Mayhap, since we're trailing some minstrel—"

"Trouvère."

"Whats'mever. But since we're trailing some stroppy Frank, happens you'll tell me what you were saying earlier?"

"Happens I won't." Stubborn clot.

But Gamelyn's next tactic was not at all disagreeable. He slid a hand into the small of Robyn's back and nipped at Robyn's ear. The open demonstration was testament to how thick the concealing fog lay. But company had never thrown Robyn off his game, and he was proper ready to fling to Gamelyn's hell anything but a hard rut against this tree, here and now . . .

The hoofbeats came to a halt not a stone's throw from where they were. Robyn froze. Gamelyn's hand clutched, protective.

A heavy sigh, then a muttered curse. From his crouch at Gamelyn's calf, Much started to slowly rise; Robyn sent a silent, urgent signal by eye and Gamelyn dropped his free hand to Much's shoulder, stayed him. Of the others, only John moved, with a slow reach of his hand upwards from where he knelt beside Robyn. A question marked across Robyn's palm, and Robyn curled his fingers into John's, answered in kind: *Wait.*

Eerie quiet, as if to spite how the trouvère had been so heedless before. Listening, Robyn kenned, and closed his eyes to See what wove itself from the moment and the silence. Dark and light, then and now, strands of future possibilities . . . fate . . . *tynged,* vibrating as if some hand had plucked it like strings. Not danger, not quite, but no lack of it, either. Robyn let out a soft breath along the skeins, found them pliable, biddable. Ran thought-fingers along them in another, invisible breath. Saw the next sunrises dawn upon their campsite, running past him like ripples in a deep pool: nights spent in keeping watch—one in company with Will, which gave Robyn respite from a disquiet he'd not yet acknowledged—spent in sleeping, hunting . . . waking between his sister and his lover, or at times two lovers—not much difference there from the past fortnights . . .

Winter cold and warm cavern, surrounded by a people and a place both strange and familiar . . .

The nights passing again, time stretching nigh to snap; beside Robyn lay John, wrapped all desperate-tight, and the men so close, as if unsure. Gamelyn gone, as well as Much and also Marion, and an ache filling the space where they should be . . .

Fires rising into the night, full moon's tide of Beltane thrumming through his veins . . . the hunt ridden and the horns lying upon the altar. Marion bending to pick them up, an offering, and Gamelyn walking from the firelight, solitary and sombre, to accept them, heft them skyward . . .

Then, nothing. Only Robyn himself, wandering solitary in a foreign, darkling woodland.

Time receded, leaving Robyn's knees weak but unwilling to buckle, and consciousness once again consisted of his own heartbeat, of John's fingers quivering in his palm, of Gamelyn's palm hard-hungry against his back and Gamelyn's breath held in his hood, and Robyn Hode's outlaws lying in wait like a pack of wolves in the mist.

A loud, tenor *harrumph!* came from the road, breaking the uneasy stasis. Hoofs danced upon the path once more. With another grumble in the Frankish tongue, their mark started north. As the horse steadied into a quick amble—*ke-tump-ke-tump, ke-tump-ke-tump*—the trouvère's voice once more rose into song to match the rhythm, bold and lovely.

Answers were never given nor obvious, but Robyn thought he understood the Lady's warning: the risk to their camp, Barrow Mere and their sacred places, his covenant—everything that mattered. It was then Robyn's knees betrayed him, and only Gamelyn's hand against his back saved him from a noisy—and foolish—gaffe.

"Robyn?" Gamelyn whispered.

Robyn propped himself, gave his head a slight shake to clear it. Then he leaned forwards and nipped at Gamelyn's earlobe. "Later, pet."

In answer to Gamelyn's frown and John's silent query, Robyn stepped away, hefting his bow and pulling an arrow from the trio stuck in the knot of hair tangling over one shoulder. A soft click of the tongue—it could have been a tree branch breaking, or a burrower's warning—gave the awaited signal.

John rose from his crouch, tickled an arrow to string. A ghostly swirl in the mist became a hefted axe, and Arthur; another described Gilbert's bow, arrows ready. After giving Robyn a piercing look more felt than seen, Gamelyn drew his sword, silent and unasked. As Much followed suit, Robyn backtracked, leaned against Gamelyn.

"'Tis grand," he whispered, "to see you proper eager. No killing t' poor sod, mind."

Gamelyn rolled his eyes. Robyn grinned, then again clicked his tongue—orders, this time. John circled back to flank, only a roiling of mist to betray his passage, his weathered grey cloak merely another hank of vapour and winter-bare bark. Arthur pulled a woollen cowl over his close-shaved pate and, axe at ready, disappeared to steady-silent point. Gamelyn and Much were sent on, twin shadows flitting across the road barely two ells behind the trouvère. A pretty sight, worthy of any true green Wode creature; their quarry didn't so much as break his song.

The next bend would be the place, where a thick stand of hawthorn provided ample cover. The mist was that, for now, and Robyn slid through it in Arthur's wake, lacing his own black leathern hood close about his cheeks. As the trouvère's song announced his approach, Robyn contemplated the arrow he held, then shrugged and tucked it back into its knot. Instead, he swung his bow up onto his shoulders and strode, bold as rubbed brass, onto the road.

Robyn didn't say a word, but the trouvère's voice warbled quiet and he checked his mount with a jerk. The palfrey lurched and tossed her head.

A pretty mare. If there was anything truly disagreeable about their present way of life, it was the lack of steady equine companionship. Robyn kept an eye on the fellow, sensed his men gathering into their places. Still, he didn't speak. A raid's beginning was the most unpredictable. Robyn always saw too many possibilities playing out behind his eyes, skeins of slow-time twisting, then untangling. His instincts rarely played him false, and they held true this time. The unpredictable passed.

Silence. The trouvère held to it for longer than Robyn would have given him credit, then finally spoke—in Frankish, of course. Robyn gave a slow shake of his head. The man frowned, tilted his head. His gaze raked Robyn up and down and plainly found him wanting. Then the trouvère switched to English. Sure enough, it was clipped flat; more of a lord's hall than any peasant croft. "Let me pass. I've nothing you want."

"I'll be judge to that." Arthur appeared from the mists, nearly atop their visitor's left stirrup. The palfrey wheeled an eye but stood more solid than her rider, who started and tottered sideways. At the last moment, the trouvère snatched at the saddle. It did little good, as Arthur grabbed his fancy cloak.

"I say—oof!" The trouvère clutched harder. Neither did that do him any good; Arthur only had the one arm, but it was corded thick with muscle.

"Off your horse, man!" he ordered, with another jerk at the velvet cape.

The trouvère resigned himself to the inevitable, saving what could have been a hard tumble with a frantic but nimble twist. The lute tottered sideways; as it smacked the saddle cantle with a discordant, hollow thud, the trouvère curled a protective arm about it.

"I'm lost." It was more defence than any plea.

"I'll say you are." Gilbert's voice drifted from opposite Robyn. "Lost and noisy."

The trouvère spun about, blue eyes wide for the source.

"An' frightenin' every deer for miles about," Arthur ventured, with a gentle push to one velvet-clad shoulder. Well, gentle for him, anyway—the trouvère staggered against his palfrey's shoulder, once again shielding his instrument as Arthur continued. "We don't half care for going hungry."

"Mm." Robyn trod closer, bow still slung, lazy-arrogant, over his shoulders. "Hungry men, a lost and lone guest for dinner, and no game?" He shook his head, *tsk*ed. "I fear 'twill cost you, man."

The trouvère frowned, peered at Robyn as if he'd only just then seen him. Those blue eyes took in the enormous longbow athwart

Robyn's shoulders, then the more common, if no less powerful, statement made by the dark cowl, and widened even more.

"You're the one they call Robyn Hood."

"I am that," Robyn said. "And yourself?"

"I am called . . . Alundel."

Tiny, but telling, the way his lips wanted to shape another name. Robyn narrowed his eyes, let Sight obscure sight, however brief. This time he was knocked for six by the responding surge, all the tangles and strands of future/present/past that spun inward, then out.

"What do you See, lord?" A familiar hand at the small of Robyn's back, and John's whisper nudging Robyn back into thisnow. He must have been "gone" longer than he'd thought; Gamelyn had also come into view, green eyes sparking worry.

Aye, Gamelyn knew, even as John did. Even if the knowing didn't always come, and even if he wasn't quite sure what to do with it when it did.

Robyn narrowed his eyes on the trouvère. A liar, and understandably so, given circumstance. But the lying came altogether easy, with more working here than one untruth could account for.

Gamelyn's concern found abrupt outlet. Rounding on their quarry, he snapped out something in Frankish. It wasn't near poetry, from the sound of it. The trouvère— Alundel—gave a start, hand slipping against his lute with another hollow thrum, and Robyn realised what else Gamelyn had seen: a small sheath within the lute's strap, and Alundel's fingers drifting towards the dagger surely there.

This Alundel might be a decent liar, but Robyn would warrant him no great shakes at dice.

Alundel gave Gamelyn a terse answer. Of course, to Robyn's ears the Franks constantly sounded either pissed up or brassed off.

Nay, definitely the latter. Gamelyn snapped another clutch of words and stalked over. The bay roan shifted sideways, wheeling her eyes. Gamelyn's sword was angled behind him but no less ready to use. Alundel stood his ground—bloody daft, that—and kept protesting in rapid, angry Frankish.

"He says he's no time to tarry." Gilbert, arrow still to string, murmured against Robyn's shoulder. "That he's on king's business, and—"

The menace rippling Gamelyn's voice needed no translation, and neither did his sword, which he flipped just that much too close to the trouvère's nose. Much hovered at Gamelyn's shoulder; he had taken hold of the palfrey's bridle and was an adequately large roadblock. Not to mention he had purposefully—aye, quite purposefully—dropped his own sword point-first into the moist ground between himself and the trouvère.

A grin tilted Robyn's lip. The two Templars worked a mark with more poetry than any fancy singer.

Alundel paled but held his ground. His eyes frantically sought Robyn's, voice rising in a slight, breathy squeak of English. "If you are indeed Robyn Hood, I can ransom my passage!"

"Can you, then?" Robyn's answer was bland.

Alundel made a grab for his belt; Arthur started forwards, but Gamelyn had already given a swift, false-gentle tap to the offending hand with the flat of his blade. Alundel froze.

The mare shifted. Much *tsk*ed and shook his head, gave an absent tuck of the mare's forelock beneath her browband.

Arthur shot Robyn a wounded look: *Are you going to just let this bloody Templar keep doin' my job?* it said, plain as plain.

"I can," Alundel insisted. Robyn had to give the trouvère this much—he was a cheeky little bugger. "If you will kindly call off your *garde de corps écarlate?*"

Gamelyn stiffened, and Gilbert gave a soft snort.

"Care to translate that?" Robyn murmured from the side of his mouth.

"Not on my life," Gilbert retorted.

"I'll find out later," Robyn threatened.

"You do that."

Bloody damn, but Robyn was going to have to bloody learn Frankish himself at this rate. Robyn treated Gilbert to a half-lidded glower, then turned it on Alundel, who seemed much more impressed. "I'll call off nowt 'lessen it suits me. Just to make it plain, though—we speak English here in t' Shire Wode." This last with a reproving look towards Gamelyn, who rolled his eyes and muttered a very English— and foul—epithet. "You have to excuse my friend, here, messire traveller. He en't killed anyone in far too long. I wain't answer for what might happen if you make another try for that dagger of yours."

Alundel, whose fingers had indeed twitched towards his dagger as Robyn advanced, went still. "*Mon Dieu!* I tell you, I cannot tarry!" It held more frustration than anger. Nevertheless, Robyn heard a bowstring creak taut. John, from his hiding place across the road, expressing displeasure with their visitor's cheek.

"Your mouth will earn you trouble, trouvère," Gamelyn added, ever so soft, and Alundel paled.

"Not t' mention you've 'tarried' long enough to've gone to Derby thrice over, man." Robyn shifted the bow on his shoulders, gave a shrug. "Seems to me you've time to spare if you've enough to keep y'rself lost."

"Please. I will pay you whatever you ask," Alundel said.

"Whatever we ask?" Arthur leaned in and tilted his axe, clearly aggrieved Gamelyn had usurped his role of Bad Sheriff to Robyn's Friendly Captain. "That's more like it, then."

Alundel was plainly encouraged. "I can promise even more for your coffers should any of you do the kindness of pointing my way from this curst place—"

"My Wode en't curst," Robyn growled. "Cept, happens, to your kind."

"Good silver doesn't tarnish under the skim of ill-chosen speech." Gilbert reminded from his own hiding place.

Alundel's gaze flitted to every compass point, worried but calculating. "Have you gathered a damned harvest fairing in the trees?" he blurted out. "How many of you *are* there?"

"Enough," Robyn hazarded. "Even a few with a bit of poetry to 'em—and wisdom. Not that those two things come mated, like, but show us the colour of your money. Mayhap we can be persuaded to see you on your way."

Alundel started for his instrument again; again, Gamelyn gave a silent, light tap to the offending hand. Alundel gestured, affronted, to a small purse upon his shoulder strap, and was allowed to unwind it.

Robyn dipped a nod to Arthur, who took Alundel's purse and tossed it to Robyn. Robyn in turn tossed it to Gilbert as he came into view, bow and arrows in one hand. Hefting the purse, Gilbert peered inside and raised his eyebrows to Robyn.

"Enough?" Robyn asked.

"To let him go on. To guide?" Gilbert shrugged. "Twould depend on where."

"I'm headed for Pontefract. I've come from Blyth—"

Arthur laughed outright. "Man, you're miles out of your way in the wrong direction!"

Gilbert was chuckling as well. But Robyn's gaze riveted to Gamelyn.

Blyth.

Gamelyn waited until the laughter had ebbed. "And your business at Blyth?"

Casual, almost pleasant. Save to Robyn, who remained silent. Watching.

Alundel's eyes narrowed. "It is of no matter."

"King's business, you said," Gamelyn riposted, smooth-quiet. "Important, you said." He cradled his sword in his arms, almost musing. "Important enough, it would seem, to arm a trouvère with the mettle to sass a band of notorious outlaws."

Alundel flushed and muttered something. Somehow, Robyn considered, it sounded different than anything he'd said thus far.

The guess was proven for truth as Much gave another of his

aggrieved *tsks*, and Gamelyn tilted his head, a light behind the green eyes Robyn well recognised.

"You might be talented, but you're not altogether brilliant," Gamelyn purred. "So you're able to tell Queen Eleanor your troubles?"

Alundel went very pale. He sought Robyn's face, hopeful of rescue. Which just made Robyn want to chuckle.

"I'll wager I know about any language you should choose to grouse in, my singing friend," Gamelyn furthered. It was not the least bit friendly; in fact dipped just south of threatening.

Robyn layered that atop one more undeniable fact: Gamelyn sliding into Dangerous Templar was something Robyn fancied. Quite.

But it also meant they'd lost the opportunity to learn anything else by chance—and that proper calmed any tight-sprung anatomy.

"Milord here," Robyn drawled, walking forwards and laying a purposeful hand on Gamelyn's sleeve, "would like nothing better, methinks, than to beat the truth out of you. But"—Robyn held up a chiding finger as Alundel started to protest—"we en't allus fetching what we fancy out of this life. You offered up some coin for guidance to . . . Pontefract, you say?"

The muscles beneath Gamelyn's brown woollen tunic were tense, quivering—in control, but a chancy one, merely waiting for the leash to be slipped. His gaze slid to Robyn's and held, defiant.

Aye, their world had changed, but here lay proof: they were still what they were, and all the better for it.

Robyn merely smiled, tightened his grip and, very slightly, shook his head. The staredown continued—another breath, mayhap two— then Robyn leaned in and laid a kiss to Gamelyn's temple.

He wasn't quite expecting the reaction he received—though really, he should have. Gamelyn jerked as if he'd been slapped; nostrils flaring, his eyes flickered, then dropped.

Alundel's expression had also slackened, no doubt wondering if the notorious Robyn Hood had gone quite spare. The outlaws, on the other hand, were well used to their leader's unpredictable ways of going about life and everything; they'd their focus on the prize.

"Two silver marks, a shilling or two, and tuppence," Gilbert said into the odd lull.

"Mmm," Robyn said, with a light pat to Gamelyn's arm and an eyebrow lifted Much's way. Much mirrored the eyebrow, his face holding its own mix of apprehension and bemusement as Robyn sauntered over and halted just that much too close to the trouvère.

"I thought you said this 'un should have more than *this*," Arthur accused Gamelyn.

Gamelyn merely peered at Arthur and crossed his arms.

"Now, Arthur," Robyn chided, then said to Alundel, as if an aside, "Mind you, we've stripped a few bishops and seen 'em to Nottingham for less."

Alundel paled further- . "As I said, I can obtain more."

"And how'd you go about doing that?"

"In Pontefract I've allies. Contacts." Real fear threaded through the words now. Mayhap Gamelyn's threats had worked their own magic after all.

"Fancy that." Robyn gave a quick gather of his men by eye. John was still hiding in the mists, bow ready, but Robyn knew exactly where he stood. Arthur was half visible a bow's length away—the mists were finally starting to lift—and Gilbert was spilling coinage back into the proffered pouch. Gamelyn had reassembled his composure into something akin to a stone cairn. Much still held the mare, still radiated fair menace.

And the strands of future/past/now, writhing into the black just behind Robyn's eyes . . .

Abruptly, Robyn wanted nothing more than to be done with this fellow, be rid of him and whatever trouble he surely carried.

"We en't guides for hire, we're outlaws. We'll have those silver marks and shillings for the trouble of taking you back to the North Road nigh to Blyth, since 'tis where you come from."

"I cannot go back th—!" Alundel bit it back.

Gamelyn exchanged a look with Much, who had started to speak. They held each other's gazes, then Much glanced Robyn's way, offered, "There's an inn near Worksop. I know it well, can take him so far and help him find a guide."

"I can hardly hire decent guidance for tuppence," Alundel muttered.

"But you'll leave our Wode alive, man," Robyn purred, leaning into the trouvère's face. "Were I you, I'd be thankful for that much."

"So, what were *that* in aid of?"

The mist had begun a lingering retreat, giving visibility of farther than a few feet. Gamelyn had also retreated, to lean against the tree where he and Robyn had taken refuge not long before. Arms crossed, eyes contemplating the naked branches above, Gamelyn didn't answer until Robyn came to stand beside him. "What was what in aid of?"

Which, by Robyn's sigh, wasn't the answer sought. But Robyn didn't speak again; at least, not right away. He'd waited until Alundel and Much had disappeared down the path; now he waited until the rest of the outlaws had dispersed as well. Then he paced the rest of the distance to the gnarled old elm and leaned against it, his right shoulder brushing Gamelyn's, looking up as if curious upon what Gamelyn saw or sought.

When Robyn did speak, it was light, almost teasing. "Are you playing your own game, milord Templar?"

"Your lack of trust wounds me."

Robyn snorted, repeated, "Are you?"

"Not everything's a game, Hob-Robyn."

"Aye, well, you do seem proper serious about this. Which means I've the right to know what you're up to."

"True enough."

"And the right to say who takes the minstrel—"

"Trouvère."

"Whats'mever." Robyn lifted one arm and rolled to his right side, chin digging into Gamelyn's shoulder.

Gamelyn shifted—even with the padding of beard just long enough to start a distinct curl, Robyn's chin was bloody *sharp*. "You made the choice. Much offered, and you agreed to it."

"Because it were bloody obvious you and he had come to some conclusion . . . and don't be tellin' me you said nothing," Robyn furthered as Gamelyn started to speak, "cause you 'n' I both know better."

Gamelyn's mouth twitched with the urge—no, the *need*—to smile; sheer admiration for this ragged, bloody impossible wolfshead. Instead, he crossed his arms and peered at Robyn. And Robyn was worth the look, sprawled all lean and lazy against the tree, hood flung back and hair fingering across his face. But those equally impossible eyes, sloe-dark in the dim, belied indolence, alight with tiny sparks. Cunning, aye, and all too aware.

"I thought on sending Gilly," Robyn ventured, "stead of Much."

"Much knows Blyth better than Gilly and you know it."

"Well, then"—a grin began to scrawl itself across Robyn's mouth—"*you* know Blyth better than Much, Gamelyn Boundys of Blyth."

Gamelyn let an answering smile tip his lip. "And I'll wager John knows it even better than I. Which is, no doubt, why John headed off in the opposite direction of camp?"

"Mm. No doubt."

They were silent for a while, then Robyn prompted, "So. The not-game?"

"Information. Something's up."

"The Lady been talking to you too, then?"

Gamelyn frowned, slid a glance towards Robyn, who was peering up into the mist-topped trees. He looked . . . unsettled. "I didn't think," Gamelyn ventured, soft, "She talked to you much."

Robyn shrugged, and a short silence made it plain he wasn't about to elaborate.

"No . . . other means to this," Gamelyn continued. "Just how the man acted. What he said."

"What *did* he say?" Robyn suddenly asked. "What is a . . . uh . . . 'garducor'?"

Gamelyn had to think hard on that for a moment, then snorted. "Bloody cheek, was what it was. He called me your scarlet body-guard."

Robyn laughed. "Scarlet, were it? Aye, well, I prefer ginger."

"I prefer neither, but scarlet is preferable. Scathelock takes entirely too much pleasure at calling me your 'poncy ginger paramour' as it is."

Robyn fell silent; musing, no doubt, on the Problem of William.

"I'm slipping, Robyn."

"Slipping? On what?"

"On my own feet, it seems. Six months ago, I'd have known what a sodding fool of a court singer was on about. You said game, but I've been *out* of the game just a little too long."

"And likely to be yet," Robyn retorted, with a sharp, three-fingered prod that sent shards of pain through Gamelyn's still-healing torso. "Aye, see?"

"God *damn* it, Robyn—"

"Damn with any god y' fancy, I saw you cradling your sword like a bairn. If you canna hold a sword aloft for longer 'n it takes to count thrice, you en't ready for *any* games."

"Are you going to let me finish, or are you going to keep torturing me with your bloody poky fingers?"

Robyn smiled. "Depends on what you call torture, milord."

"If you call me that once more, I'll show you torture."

"Mm. Later. Tell me what you're up to."

"I'm *trying*, you chatty tosser!"

"Try harder." Robyn merely grinned wider. "Seems to me you want Much to keep an eye on the minstrel."

"Trouvère."

"Whats'mever."

Gamelyn rolled his eyes. "Seems to me you wanted the same thing, or you wouldn't have agreed. And sent John after. But Much speaks several languages other than Anglic; he can fetch information John can't. Tell me, do you really think Alundel was going to Pontefract?"

"Mm. If so, he were proper bloody lost." Robyn shrugged. "It's a good thing, Much and John tailing the minstrel—"

Gamelyn rolled his eyes again and abandoned further correction.

"—but what else are you thinking? I'm thinking there's too much trouble wrapped up in the fellow. I'm glad to be rid of him."

"Trouble." Gamelyn frowned. "Aye. That trouvère knows too much."

"His like, they feed off knowing, aye?" Robyn pointed out. "For their songs and stories."

"The man could well have Queen Eleanor's ear," Gamelyn reminded.

"For fashion sense, if his cloak's any guess."

"And on king's business, he said."

"King's business!" Robyn shoved away from the tree. "So?"

Gamelyn tried another tack. "King Richard does make the forest laws, you must realise."

"And a fine job he's done so far," Robyn sneered. "Hoarding 'em, then selling 'em off with no regard for proper management. The head forester knows sod-all from what I've seen!"

And another. "A land without a king is a land without justice."

"I've seen precious justice *with* a king."

"But if he's being held prisoner—"

"So?"

"So, what laws hold the head forester in check?"

"*My* law, of late."

"God grant me patience!" Gamelyn also heaved up from the tree—not without a grunt as his body made sharp protest. "While the King is so openly powerless, others move in, take that power. What do you think the taxes you're so intent on stealing are meant for? Richard's ransom from prison. Bloody hell, Robyn, weren't you paying attention when Count John tried to suborn you into working for him?"

"I understand nowt when it comes to nobles' thinking!" Robyn growled back. "Happens I don't read so well as you or me sister, and happens I en't 'understanding any language you care to speak'"—and, yes, mayhap Robyn did have the right to sound brassed off, but the mockery he put into aping Gamelyn's noble-born accent stung like a clutch of bees—"but I en't stupid!"

"I didn't—"

"That sodding bum boil Count John wanted the same thing his brother wants—the same thing all your like wants! Land. *Money*, made off the backs of *my* like. Why d'you think I take it from them? Because it's what they want the most! I'd as lief melt it down and piss on it for all the good it does me—I have what I want, here. In my forest. And it *is* mine, blood and bone, heart and soul of a magic any Motherless sod of a . . . *Christian* king canna even dream of. His like sees nowt in the green Wode—our Wode—but sommat to use as prizes for his nobles and surety for his wars!"

For someone who feigned such ignorance over politics, Robyn nevertheless had a keen grasp of what they were about. "Robyn—"

"Why should I care?" Robyn shot back. "What sort of king has he ever been to me and mine? What blood has he spilled here, for our land, our forest? And why should *you* care, after the hell that bastard put you through in Saracen lands?" There were tears in Robyn's eyes, now, liquid-dark. "Aye, let whoever-it-is lock Richard up 'til he rots, and well done t' ones as put 'im there. If the gods smile on us, then happens he'll have a taste of what me sister had done to her!"

That didn't just sting; it put a knife into Gamelyn's gut and twisted. Moreover, he'd strode forwards and put a hand on his sword hilt before he recognised what he was doing.

Gamelyn lurched to a halt. Peering down at his hand, he flexed it, fixed upon it a scrutiny suggesting the hand belonged to someone else.

At times like these he felt he *was* someone else.

Robyn hadn't moved. There was still colour in his cheeks, more from his outburst than anything Gamelyn had done. And his *eyes . . .* still awash, only this time with a strange and sympathetic grief.

Well, they each had their own ways of dealing with pain, aye? Each equally as dangerous.

"And this," Robyn said, soft. "*This.*"

All Gamelyn could voice was "It's all I know how to do, anymore."

"Not nearly like," Robyn countered. "Or I'd be in two neat pieces."

This time the shudder went to his bones. Still looking at his hand, Gamelyn said, "He's not dead, you know." It was wooden. It made him feel nothing. *Nothing.* "Gisbourne. He's still here."

"You're the only one as wants him dead, *anwylyd.*"

Only Robyn would call him "beloved" with tears running down his cheeks, and mere moments after hurling a veritable fury of indignation; a backdraught of fire up a turret stair, just as quickly sucked back into the depths.

"*You* wanted him dead."

"Never. Though," Robyn reflected, "twere a time I thought I would have to take him out."

"Like a mad dog," Gamelyn whispered, and thought *Will's right. God help me, but he's right.*

He leapt like a startled hare as Robyn's lips brushed against his cheek, but didn't move. Just closed his eyes—pain, this, but sweet and gentle and lacking any reaction, only reception. Submission. Robyn was also the only one who could sneak up on him so, and if there were other lives as the Heathen claimed, then in any life Gamelyn had perhaps lived, he was fierce-glad of it.

Robyn's mouth lingered, traced a breath that raised and prickled coppery beard.

"You're here now. With me," he whispered. "With us. 'Tis all that matters." Then he turned and started to walk away.

Gamelyn's hand shot out, grabbed Robyn's wrist—hard. "Why did you kiss me, in front of a mark?"

Robyn chuckled, twisted his wrist free. "Well, it confused the bloody hell out him, aye? And"—he turned away, voice floating behind him—"twere the only way I could think to distract you without getting a right cross for me pains."

$$- III -$$

Marion refused to worry when Arthur and Gilbert came back alone. She scooped heated cider into pots, passed it all around, then kept tending to her brewing. She listened, curious, as David queried their comrades as to what had happened with their singing mark.

But when Robyn finally returned to camp alone, all those protective instincts rose up in her throat and nigh throttled her: *Is it all right? Are you all right? Is he all right? Is. . .?*

It was an odd type of panic, she had decided some time previous. Undeniable. *Infuriating.*

Nevertheless, with shaking hands she turned from her attention to the brewing pot, shoving stray, damp curls back into the confinement of linen kerchief, and poured a pot of warm cider. Forced herself to walk—not hurry, not *run*—to her brother, hand over the drink, though she did snug an arm tight into his.

Robyn, of course, noticed her agitation, but merely accepted the pot with the briefest of frowns her way and a nod of thanks. He sipped the cider, saying nowt to that notice, and thank the Lady's grace for at least *that*.

"I'd say sommat smells good, but I'd be lying." Robyn nudged her. "Even cider under me nose fetches itself lost in the fray of all those concoctions. You're tryin' to scare the marks from the Wode, then?"

Marion nudged him back. "Better now than when we have to retreat to the caves."

Midswallow, he grimaced. "Hoy, there's that."

"Is Gamelyn coming soon?" She made it casual, but Robyn wasn't fooled.

"Soon enough, I should think."

"I keep telling him he's not to chill that wound."

"Mari." A small shake of her arm, and Robyn began pulling her back towards the fire. "I don't think you came here to be nursemaid to the lot of us."

"I'm not. I mean, I don't mind pitching in. We all need t' be doing as we can, and . . . " She looked away, uncomfortable. *I have to, don't you understand? I don't know why, but I do, and. . .*

Marion tried again. "Rob, I've been thinking."

Robyn snorted. "Aye, you and himself *both* think too much on things."

"Don't be daft." She shoved against her brother and he pretended to stumble. "Gamelyn's doing well enough to come to the Mere with me."

Robyn flicked her another frown; this one stayed. "And have you asked *him* about this, pet?"

"I have. Several times."

"Mm."

And with abysmal timing—as if their naming had charmed entrance—Gamelyn emerged from the trees. His expression warmed as he saw Robyn and Marion, but he didn't intrude, merely unbuckled his sword belt, then started rummaging in his tidy pile of belongings. After finding a small pouch, he unsheathed his sword and spent a few more moments looking for something, then espied it: his cloak, which Marion had hung close to the fire for drying.

"I thought," Marion murmured with a nudge to Robyn's ribs, "you might help me out here, little brother."

"Mari." It was both sigh and warning.

Laying sword and pouch on the peripheries of the circle, Gamelyn then pulled the cloak from its stook of wooden staves and flung it around his shoulders. The scarlet cross upon the cloak flared and caught in the sparse grey light—its own special, oddling beacon. Between that, and the careful berth he gave the others at the fireside as he sat . . . surely the fierce pang it gave Marion was simply overwrought, out of place. *Thinking too much*, Robyn would say.

Well, aye. "You know Her will in this."

"And what of *his* will?" Robyn countered.

Marion took a sharp breath to answer, found it whistling past her teeth, unused, as Gamelyn settled on the ground. Taking cloth and whetstone from his pouch, he gave a critical peer down his blade. Gilbert said something and leaned over, offering Gamelyn a pot of steaming cider. Gamelyn accepted with a brief and grateful smile, took several sips, then set it aside and started to drag the whetstone down the curved edge of his sword.

The rasp of it filled the small clearing, commingling with the murmurs from the others, a soft retort off the hide stretched above that fled into dark green and naked grey.

Marion turned back to her brother, saw only his profile and his dark eyes fixed on Gamelyn. "Rob—"

"I have him back." It was set, fierce. "He's here, with me. *That's* what matters."

Marion tried again. "I know. I *know*," she insisted as Robyn finally turned to her, brows furrowed. "But he canna shrug it off forever. Any more than you can, love."

A soft curse, foul and vehement. "Aye, well, the Lady might want his magic alive and aware and being wielded . . . but I know better than most what price it'll have."

"And I know what price is spent in just letting it lie, wasted."

"Bloody damn!" Robyn growled. "You womenfolk—goddesses, renegade nuns, or scullery sluts—you'd all shake the straw tick 'til the vermin go scuttering, but vermin just go burrow somewhere else, aye? 'Tis what they do."

"You menfolk, thinking everything can just be slaughtered or stuffed into some hole, but the bodies pile up and fill the empty spaces 'til they overflow, aye?"

"'Tisn't just men who do that, pet." It was low, and purposeful, and made her eyes burn with something she didn't want to inspect too closely.

The sound of steel against whetstone had paused; Gamelyn was peering at them, aware of something amiss, but without surety.

Robyn snugged Marion close, both arms about her, chin resting atop her head. Sweet Lady, but he'd grown so *tall* these past years . . . and stronger, she amended, as her bones nigh cracked. "I know," he murmured. "And 'm sorry. 'Tis a proper strangeness we've found ourselves in, but we're in it together, en't we? Finally."

She nodded against his chest, not trusting her voice.

"As to Gamelyn . . . leave 'im be. He'll come 'round in time."

Marion pushed back slightly, peered at him. "How much time d'you think he has?"

"How much time do any of us have, pet?" A smile curled Robyn's lip, but his eyes were dark and knowing. "Mind me in this and leave it, Mari. Let him curl up in the darkness a while longer. He's only just come into thisworld, and at that 'twere bum-first and screaming."

Marion held silent, remembering. Gamelyn's survival had ended up taking all her healing skills and every available scrap of magic—not only hers, but her brother's. A rude awakening, indeed.

"He's *with* us," Robyn said again, fierce-soft. "He's alive. Spring comes. And t' summering."

Marion peered at her brother, at the conviction stark in his black eyes, then ducked her head against his chest. "I saw you born. Swaddled and rocked you to sleep . . . How's it now you're so much t' elder?"

A chuckle, and Robyn drubbed the top of her head. Then he released her and paced over to the fire.

"Leave enough cider for the rest of us!" Robyn challenged as Arthur dipped his pot in.

"'Twere only me second!"

"Third," David pointed out, and little Tess, curled up on his shoulder, chittered in ferret agreement.

Above the others' heads, Robyn aimed a swat at Arthur's shaved pate, then lifted a teasing eyebrow at Gamelyn.

Well enough, then. Whatever he and Marion had been so earnest about, it wasn't altogether serious.

Or was, Gamelyn reminded himself, and Robyn had shrugged it off, intent on fresh game. Sneaking a glance at Marion, Gamelyn found his instincts true. She was lost in thought, contemplating . . . something. Peering off into the trees.

He followed her gaze, saw a shadow he still wasn't quite used to: a silhouette, half man and half beast, great sweeping tines burnished against the trees with mists hanging from them like scraped-away velvet. It stirred all sorts of emotions deep within, and the most powerful of those a small, fiercely devout child who staggered back, averting eyes and mind from the very real terror of demons and Hell.

But the man had seen both demons and a very real hell on earth, and had long possessed the ability to overcome any terror—save for that small, nigh-instinctive shiver and cry. Gods became men, in the end, and men made their gods, treacherous and manipulative, and if there was any hell past this one they now trod, then better to burn in a lover's arms.

If only he could so easily catalogue what he kept hearing. It wasn't any presence he'd grown to know amongst the green Wode Heathen; not a horn-crowned god or moon-clad goddess. This was an unintelligible murmur, one just out of hearing: an echo, or a persistent ghost's whisper in the night . . .

Gamelyn gave a slight but vigorous shake of his head, and wielded his whetstone with renewed enthusiasm as Robyn knelt behind Arthur and Gilbert.

"Has anyone seen Will?"

"Not yet." Gilbert leaned over to dip his pot and brought it out dripping. The cider kettle, nestled into its embers, hissed as the droplets trailed over its belly, shivered, and dried.

"Best to leave 'im be." Arthur shrugged. "Y'know how he is."

"Aye, I do, and more'n most." It was soft, a slightly bitter edge to it that made Gamelyn want to wince.

"In this?" Arthur lowered his voice but raised his gaze to Robyn's. "Mayhap there's more simmering in Charming William than you *want* to know, lad."

"Then happens Charming William and me 're even, aye?" Again, the soft bitterness.

"As you said," Arthur allowed, "you know 'im. So you know damn well things never bide 'even' with our braw lad—'lessen he thinks 'tis his own doing."

Robyn gave a growl, propped elbows on knees, palms against his chin, and stared into the fire. Arthur sighed and turned his gaze to Gamelyn.

Gamelyn dipped his head just in time, forelock concealing his expression; he could, nevertheless, feel the man's eyes burning against him. *I know you're listening, Templar,* they said, *and likely this en't your business.*

And that's where you're wrong. Gamelyn tilted his head to let his own gaze impact against Arthur's. *I'm thinking likely it is.*

Will returned just before sunset, as Gamelyn was taking his shaky turn at a practise clout set up in the meadow nigh to their camp.

Just loose the bloody thing, aye? was Robyn's silent plea. The bow was the lightest recurve they had; still Robyn couldn't help but wince at the shimmy and shake of Gamelyn's shoulder as he pushed. It was the weak side, to boot. But the stubborn git had insisted.

It was during his wince and glance away that Robyn saw Will approaching. Will was being proper cautious—nigh silent, in fact— until Gamelyn had his arrow at full nock. Then Will let out a great sneeze, one to be heard over fifteen leagues away in Nottingham.

The arrow spanged wild from its loose and sailed sideways. In the very next breath, Gamelyn had whirled about, shiv to hand and poised to throw.

Will's bark of laughter throttled itself midthroat. Robyn hid a smirk against the hands clasped on his own longbow—served the arsy bugger right.

Gamelyn was the one to break the stare-off. With a slight,

mocking dip of his head to Will, he flipped the little shiv and slid it back into its forearm sheath.

Robyn's smirk widened; one day, anon, there was a proper game to be had in a slow strip-search of Gamelyn for all those blades.

"*William!*" Marion growled into the silence.

"Aw, no harm done!" Will blustered, sauntering over to where Marion stood next to Gilbert—both waiting their own turn at the archery practise. "But I'm thinking 'tis a good thing I didn't come in from the east. Or"—Will tossed a smirk at Gamelyn—"*southeast*, the way *you* aim."

True to form Gamelyn gave an eye roll, then went to fetch the ill-shot arrow.

"A few arrow holes in you might let in some sense," Robyn drawled.

Will had the grace to look abashed. Tilting sideways, he slung a well-filled leather pouch from its place over one shoulder and tossed it at Robyn. "Well. Um. Here."

Robyn snatched it midair, frowning at Will as he opened it. A rich, loamy smell wafted up, and frown turned to grin. "Mushrooms!"

"Naw," Arthur said.

"Aye," Will insisted.

"'Tis too late!"

"Naw," Will again insisted.

"Happens not. And not just any mushrooms," Robyn continued and, as the others gathered around, unlaced the bag to display them: quite ordinary-looking, actually, small and dark-skirted with a pale nipple atop.

"Lovely!" David crooned.

"Aye, well, Scathelock," Robyn stated, "you've done better penance than a nobleman throwing money at his bishop."

Will chuckled, sauntered over, and gave Robyn a clout on the arm. Being Will, the blow was, naturally, staggering.

Robyn elbowed him back, straight to the chest.

"By an outlaw throwing brown fungi at his Heathen priest?" A soft curl of sarcasm announced Gamelyn's arrival; with eyebrow cocked, he eyed the revealed loot, plainly dubious.

"Ah, but these are indeed special offerings," Marion pointed out, lacing an arm through Gamelyn's. Which, obviously, didn't best please Will. "Better than good wine. Not as strong as the agaric."

"Ah. A drug, then."

"One t' fly you higher than a little falcon a-wing." Robyn met Gamelyn's gaze and winked. "Where'd you fetch 'em, Will?"

"I've a special place," Will boasted. "In a hollow, well sheltered, where it stays warm longer."

"And you've never shared it before this?" Gilbert demanded.

"Well. Um—"

"Greedy sod!" Arthur accused.

"More like he got lucky." Robyn laughed.

"Aye," David said, and Marion pointed out, "There's been no frost yet to kill mushrooms. No question you fetched some luck, Will."

"Life's nowt but luck, pet." He shot her a smile and wink. "Care to share some of mine?"

"I'd say you're pressing that luck. And that you've already had a few of those beauties."

"I had to make sure they were good ones!" Will protested, then blinked, looked about. "Hoy. Where's the monk's lackey?"

Gamelyn lifted his gaze skyward. Robyn wanted to do the same; instead, he gave Will another clout, this to the back of his head.

Will yipped but persisted, "And our little John?"

"You're too pissed up to pay attention did we tell you!" Marion retorted. "We should fling you in t' brook to sober up."

"Mayhap better to join him?" David asked, a hopeful grin starting on his face. "In the piss up?"

Robyn pondered the bag. "As long as we save a fair share for our mates, as we should. They shouldn't miss out just because I sent 'em to do some dirty work."

The stars were coming out to dance upon the small stretch of meadow between the trees. The moon had already retreated past the black horizon, and most of the outlaws had stumbled back to the camp proper. Marion and Robyn lay, heads touching, contemplating those stars in companionable silence.

"Getting cold, nights," Robyn mumbled. "Gots to think . . . um. Think on moving into . . . "

"Caverns," Marion supplied.

"Aye. That." Robyn sighed, started to shove himself up. "I s'pose I should head back, make sure t' lads en't set fire to themselves."

"You'd just trip and fall in y'rself." Marion grinned.

He peered down at her, flashing his own grin. "Bloody show-off." It must be some odd blessing—or curse; sometimes Robyn wasn't sure—but just as sure as it took a pitiable amount of any drug to do Robyn in, Marion's constitution could quadruple it. She seemed satisfied but awake, while Robyn felt as if he could kip out, belly to the fire. Or better yet, he amended with a grin, belly-to-belly with Gamelyn, and after, sleep this buzzy feeling off for several days.

Pleasant, for a change, to not have some god nattering between his ears. No cares. Not even when a broad, dark shape loomed up over them, because the brilliant starlight betrayed that shape's identity, almost courteously limning russet into frost.

Gamelyn was also remarkably steady. Poncy git.

"I've smoked better," the git said, reiterating his poncyness.

Robyn mulled over what he'd said. "Smoked? You've *smoked* mushrooms?"

Marion giggled like a young lass—a lovely sound, and he'd not heard it enough of late.

Gamelyn's voice also betrayed a smile as he answered, "Nay, not mushrooms. But the vices of the East are quite . . . potent. Work as well as Marion's brew. Unfortunately, they taste little better."

"Hoy!" Marion warned.

"Truth is oft painful, fair Maid." Another grin, this one very visible. "Mayhap we *should* try to smoke a few 'shrooms."

His Poncyness might have "had better," but seemed remarkably mellow for all that. Of course, Gamelyn had refused his full share, said someone besides Marion had to have their wits about them . . . which was preposterous. Robyn had more wit about him even dead drunk than His Poncyness had in one sullen pinkie finger. Another, was Gamelyn, who needed to laugh more.

"I think," Robyn drawled, "you're essa . . . exag . . . exagerry . . . hoy, fuck me. You're lying."

Gamelyn put a hand to his breast. "'Struth, and no exaggerations. Next time I obtain some, I'll have to show you."

"And me," Marion added.

"And you." Gamelyn turned as if to pad off, hesitated. "Are you going to lie here pie-eyed and star-drunk all night, Hob-Robyn?" A quaver underpinned the soft voice. Even compromised, Robyn kenned the query beneath, both wilful and willing.

Robyn was also beginning to ken a mushroom-gentled Templar might just prove a fine thing.

"Go on." Marion gave Robyn a shove. "I en't sleepy. And happens he en't likely offering sleep straight away."

"Happens not," Gamelyn's voice drifted over his shoulder, slurred-soft. "Come to bed, Robyn. Now."

Everyone had been long asleep. Only wise, this waning time of year, to curl in and make an early night of it, fall into lazy, cosy sleep by the fire-coals.

But it was nigh to midnight, and Marion's inner timekeeper, primed by several years of a novice nun's schedule, was not so ready to relinquish old habits. She half missed and half hated it both; the waiting for an abbey bell calling her to prayer and observance, or the sound of her mistress's step . . .

Her enemy's step.

Enough, she growled to herself. *She's dead. I'm free. It's over and I'm here with the ones left to me.*

As if to punctuate that, she scooted closer to her brother's back. He gave a soft, sleepy grumble into Gamelyn's hair—curled up beside Robyn, of course, and Marion was glad of it. Gamelyn could outheat a damp pile of compost, and the night had turned bloody cold.

Will had picked those mushrooms just in time. And Robyn was right—they'd soon have to move to the caverns.

Gamelyn was also quiet. Too quiet. Marion would wager he lay as wakeful as she—and just as in thrall to the anticipation of chapel bells. Surely his preceptory held the Hours no less sacrosanct than any order, despite what rumours might fly as to Templar rituals.

Whilst Robyn, damn his black eyes, lay between his wakeful bedmates, deep in the slumber of the uncomplicated and unfettered.

But then, whatever fetters Robyn might possess weren't so recently made. It was still difficult to wrap her thoughts around the reality of it; her baby brother passing through his own desolation and despair. And death, according to John. The ultimate initiation for the ultimate purpose: to wear the god's form. Robyn had never spoken of it, but then, Robyn had always been a creature of the moment, more so than Marion ever could be—or truly wanted to be. Had she been so bespelled by a moment when she'd been thrown in Nottingham's gaol, with everything she'd known thought long dead and all hope lost? She shivered. Might she have retreated into some inner oblivion? Or dashed herself to pieces against prisoning rock, in thrall to the passion of one horrific moment?

It was one of the things that terrified Marion about her brother: for him, and of him. She'd sooner cut Robyn's throat herself than see him taken, imprisoned.

Stop it! she ordered again. Robyn had survived his own horrors, and if time had blunted their sharp edges, so it would for her. Anyway, she knew full well what brought on such thoughts. It wasn't fungi-induced muzziness, though she wished it were that simple. Nay, it was this midpoint between dusk and dawning, the Night Offices, where she felt as if she were choking, couldn't draw a decent breath. It had ever been so, since Loxley. Her body's memory taking over, even during the years her mind had no place for any memory:

the sun setting into Beltane, a wild ride behind her brother into Loxley's fiery ruin, an arrow in the back robbing her of breath . . .

The midpoint between May eve and morn had seen the destruction of all she'd ever loved and known. Before the black curtain had fallen, shrouding memory into oblivion.

But no matter how painful the waking, Marion never prayed for the return of that oblivion.

With a soft grunt, Gamelyn stirred. Marion closed her eyes to tiny slits beneath the coverlets of woollen and furs, watched him push himself to hands and knees. Ever so careful, Gamelyn extricated himself from Robyn and the furs piled atop them all, started to rise. Hesitated, half kneeling, to peer down at Robyn. Then Gamelyn reached out and smoothed fingers over Robyn's temple and cheekbone, flicking back a lock of unruly dark hair.

It was so gentle, so . . . pensive. Marion's heart gave a shiver and cracked, just a little.

Taking up his cloak, Gamelyn gained his feet and padded over to the fire. Marion shifted, as if in sleep, to watch him stoke the dying embers—a methodical stacking and framing by one used to doing with less fuel than any English woodland offered. Crouching there, eyes gleaming, Gamelyn waited to ensure it caught, then rose. With the stealth of any born to the Wode, he wove a careful path through the sleeping outlaws, slipped from the dim light of the circle, and disappeared into the trees.

Marion waited for a while. Then, just as careful—and silent—she took up her cloak, wrapped it about her, and followed.

He should have heard her coming.

Even had she been the nigh-silent bitch fox of five years ago, he was a Templar Knight. A weapon, one honed into a fierce, ascetic edge by his Order and the Assassins of Outremer . . . and it just brought everything all the more home.

Including the feeling they were, somehow, running out of time.

The magic. . . roils in our Knight, the Lady whispered.

That was it. All that power, trying to claw its way out, pinned up and wailing like a bairn forced into a small, sunless box with its only outlet fury and regret.

Aye, he should have heard her coming. But Gamelyn remained lost in some reverie, leaning back against the old, gnarled oak guarding the Barrow Mere. Arms raised overhead, his hands were clenched on a branch twined with mistletoe, his face lifted to the night sky. The moonlight kept escaping thin hanks of clouds to spill molten silver down over him. His eyes were closed, as if bathing in it.

All that denial, all that *will.* All the times Gamelyn had refused—so polite and diffident—to accompany her, yet here he was, seeking refuge in one of the Wode's deepest wells of magic, drawn on his own.

But then, did any of them have the choice, really?

"Canna sleep?" Marion pitched her voice soft, yet nevertheless watched the dark-clad body tense, rope-taut, then just as quickly unknot. He opened his eyes, dropped his arms, and turned to her—but didn't leave off his lean against the tree.

Aye, he knew, not with any conscious thought but with a clear, deep instinct: oaks were protection, and strength.

"I'm not the only one, 'twould seem." His voice was soft, light, faraway; as Gamelyn turned to her, a small smile quirked his lips. But what he said next betrayed the smile for what it was—another dodge, another renunciation. "Night Offices. When we were squires in Normandy, we'd call them the Knight Orifices."

Marion chuckled.

"So this much hasn't changed, eh? We still prefer to roam the night hours. Just think what trouble we could have made, you and I, if I'd been allowed to stay the night upon those long-ago summers? And our Hob-Robyn snoring, left out of the midnight prowl. It would have made him spare."

Still chuckling, Marion walked over to lean on the tree beside him.

"I don't know how he sleeps the way he does. I've at times groped him to make sure he's still breathing." It was purposeful, the grouse—another distraction, and yet more proof the lad she'd known was still there.

Perhaps there lay part of the problem, as well. The mask of Guy de Gisbourne had directed Gamelyn's killer instinct from inward maiming to outward objects. Now that the mask was . . . disfigured . . .

"Surely 'tisn't the only reason you give 'im a grope," Marion chided, playing along.

Gamelyn snorted and pushed away from the tree, but didn't walk away. He seemed to consider the breeze-rippled water for several breaths, knelt. Still contemplative, he ran two fingers along the tree's mossy base, then put those fingers to his lips and tossed a kiss across the Mere's black surface. "'Twas here, you know."

More than magic—the making of it, she realised. It had been here, after all, where two lads' passions had met and matched, teased and tested, for the first time.

"I was . . . worried. I think." His gaze followed the kiss. The moon's frost-gilt ghosted them into snow over juniper, remote and too deep. "I'm not sure what I was, really. Only he'd a life I had no part of, one that fascinated me. I wanted to take a little of it with me, like a small coal from a sacred fire. And every time I reached out to warm my hands, he'd shove me away."

"And it made you all the more determined."

"It must have." He peered up at her, brows quirked. "Each time you wanted me. Welcomed me. Why?"

"I liked you. Why not?"

He kept peering at her, the question plain—and he deserved a better answer, surely.

If she had one. Marion put a hand against the oak, thought for a moment, said, soft, "I'm not sure. Mayhap I always knew, somehow, what you are."

His gaze slid away, then returned. Just as drawn as he'd ever been, seeking even if he feared the search. "What I am," he repeated, softly, and rose.

Aye, Summerlord. Our sword of iron and shield of Oak, sorcerer-King.

It was soft, faded, this not-whisper. Yet not unintelligible, as the others that had, more and more, penetrated Marion's own senses when the Lady Huntress spoke to Her Knight. And, not for the first time, Marion wondered if, when the Lady spoke to her, Gamelyn heard it also? As if the two of them somehow shared Her possession—not fully, but closer than Gamelyn liked, Marion was sure.

Gamelyn ducked his head and leaned against the oak once more. One hand rose to his face, shielding any expression from moon, Mere, and the Maiden coming to stand beside him. "I think . . . those mushrooms have rendered me a little less in possession of my wits than I realised."

Marion reached out, tried to put a hand to his shoulder. Without thought, he avoided the touch. She stood there, hand still outstretched, even as he stopped himself, shook his head.

"Sorry. Habit."

Marion tried to meet his eyes, but he wouldn't let her. Instead, she turned and leaned into him, aligning with some care along his ribs, her head nestling against his good shoulder. Another hesitation, then one arm stole about her. An awkward, oddly shy quality always edged his affection, as if Gamelyn wasn't sure what he should permit or what she would.

It was no longer the artless, animal comfort of two youths lying together in the grass and making pictures in clouds. With death and fire and helplessness had grown awareness in the space between. Without full heat, it quickened spirit and breath but nothing more;

any more primal reaction had been subjugated by both habit and frosty purpose.

It was . . . comfortable. For both of them.

"Aye, and at one time we both were covered in habits."

A rueful joke, true enough, but Gamelyn didn't respond, save for a small huff of breath into her cinnabar curls. "Yet," he mused, "mine is still with me."

"Only if you clutch to it."

Leave it, Mari.

He started it, she said to the small memory.

"Is it clutching, to honour an oath?" he replied. "To feel shame at even contemplating abandoning it?"

"Is it shameful to cast away shackles?"

Again, he shook his head. "You don't understand."

"You're so sure of that, are you?" Marion deliberately put her hands on his chest and looked him in the eye. "I were as long in my abbey as you in yours. Months . . . *years* . . . locked away from every instinct, every natural thing born. A chapel fancies locking those things away, aye?"

"And make you fear the finding of the key," he murmured. "Marion, you had no memory of your former life; you truly were prisoner. Whereas I . . . it . . . the Church was always where I thought I'd go. Be a scholar, a dutiful monk, a good third son to my father. Even after . . . Loxley . . . well. I took all the oaths of my own will. I made a life in those oaths, with all I had remaining to me. And now?" A shrug of shoulders and, against her palms, bones shifting, too prominent, beneath his breast.

The silence stretched out, made Marion's stomach sink. But when she would have spoken, Gamelyn continued, slow. "I should have returned to the Templars before now. I've been well enough for the travel for weeks, thanks to you. Every day I'm capable of returning and don't, I'm foresworn."

"And what of Robyn? What of"—she gestured, encompassing the Mere, the woodland, the moors beyond, all of it—"this?"

"I cannot deny," he said, slow, "the Wode holds my heart. It always has. But I owe Hubert my life, Marion. He . . . the Templars . . . they gave me my *mind* back, don't you see? It was all I'd ever possessed, the only thing I could claim, make mine. Whilst my heart . . . " He suddenly kissed her forehead, lingered there. "It was taken from me before I'd a chance to . . . become used to it."

"Gamelyn—"

"Even that *name*, Marion. My own name, more cause to be foresworn. Gamelyn never lived at Temple Hirst. It was always *Guy's* province. *Gisbourne's* place."

It might have been a scourge upon her flesh, iron-tipped. "Guy of Gisbourne is *dead*."

"Is he? Is he, really?"

"Don't say that!"

"Oh, he's mortally wounded. But it seems where sweet Robyn Hood hacked Gisbourne's traitorous head from his shoulders, two more are growing in its place." A smile tilted his lip, held no mirth. "The Lady told me, not long ago, how I was a serpent in my own garden."

"To our people, serpents are not of evil. They are of the Wise."

"I have no people, save the Temple."

It was the mushrooms, Marion knew, and nowt more, to make him spew this nonsense. "*Gamelyn—*"

"Here's some wisdom for you, O forest priestess. You can't kill the serpent lying in the roots of the World Tree." Not nonsense, this, setting deep-dark in green eyes. "You can't kill grief and hate, Marion, nor undo what comes of them. It's like some chancre that won't be cut or burned away . . . mine. *Me*." His voice dipped. "I prayed for absolution, traded it for a promise. I carried it like a banner into battle and never let it drop. *Beauséant*—to be whole. The promise of my master and my order, but I never felt it, not once. And now I *do* feel it, begin to understand it . . . only it's not so easy here, lying naked with what I was, what I still am . . . *God!*"

He took in a breath, then; halted the flow of thick, edged words with a clench and grate of teeth and jaw. Tried to push away, humiliation obvious.

Marion didn't let him, clenched her hands into his tunic and stayed him from escape. "What you are," she growled, "and whats'mever you were and will be, it's part of *us*. Wain't you see that?"

"I see too much, some nights. Enough to appreciate . . . " This time he did win free, in a negligent twist altogether reminiscent of the strength waiting in battered flesh. He turned from her—fled, really, only to halt at the banks of the Mere and crouch there once again. "We've come back to the garden, haven't we? Only Eden is long gone." There was a wistfulness to his voice, underlain with a low, thwarted tremor. "We've seen too much. We know too much. We've tasted every fruit of a deceptive tree. And we're fools to want that garden back . . . but still, we are. Fools."

An odd peace settled between them. Only the burble of the brook feeding the dark pool, only the soft, dense *silence* all but hanging in spiky evergreens and naked, winter-drawn trees. Only Gamelyn's fingers, tracing in the moss thickened at the tree roots. Only Gamelyn's breath, quickening against the damp soil, and her own, snatched away by the chill breeze. She wrapped tighter in her cloak, shoved her spine hard against the oak.

"You once said," Gamelyn finally said, slow and heavy between his teeth, "there might be a way. An understanding."

The breath went taut in her lungs.

"I can't continue to . . . exist like this. This waiting." Gamelyn hesitated, frowning. Tried again. "You said this place held answers. Answers to . . . *dreams*, and . . . " Once more, the hesitation. His gaze flitted sideways, gleaming across the water.

"Gam—"

He didn't rise, brought a slow finger to his lips. No idle gesture, no fond-mocking kiss to toss into the air; it stayed, demanded silence. Gamelyn slowly lifted his chin, eyes flitting first one direction, then another.

Marion heard it, then. First a stirring to the east, then another, closer. Shadows— aye, there were more than one, slipping nigh to the rocks where a riverlet ran with cold, clear water into Barrow Mere.

"Come." The summons was impatient. Gamelyn held out a hand. "Help me up."

A bit puzzled, Marion nevertheless did as he asked. With a catlike ease belying any pretence of needing that help, Gamelyn grasped her hand—with his good arm—and gained his feet. In the next motion, he pulled her close, bent as if to grace her cheek with a kiss.

Instead he whispered—"Take the knife from my belt"—and buried his face in her hair, nuzzling even closer. Steel nudged against her hip, shielded her grasp of the fine-carved hilt with the cover of their close bodies.

Another rustle, this one to the south, silenced as Gamelyn whipped his head that way.

Then, even more improbable, what seemed little more than a soft, mocking chuckle, wafting across the mists of the Mere . . .

Where, moments before, there had been no mists.

Summer comes, warming to Winter's touch, waxing 'neath the breath of the Hooded One's power and realm. Things shall wake, my own. It is inevitable.

"Things," Gamelyn muttered, and pushed back from Marion as she kenned they had both heard the Lady's words, plain. His hand still held to hers, tight; sword in his free hand even as she still clung to his dagger. "What . . . *things?*"

Things from the hearts of men. . . and not.

The Lady's voice faded beneath another sound, which echoed across the water. Laughter? A sigh? Marion saw more shadows, then lights—tiny golden flickers, bobbing and weaving in some improbable dance.

"Fireflies," Gamelyn murmured, as if bemused. "Did you . . . ?"

Another rustle sounded, louder, and a huge, pale stag glided from the trees to drink.

Neither of them moved. Gamelyn's hand twitched in hers; Marion slid her eyes to meet his profile, wide-eyed but lower lip set, pursed.

The stag drank, ears twitching with each swallow, the tiny fireflies darting about him, gilt streaks against his crème coat. Through some trick of light, the stag shimmered into shadow, nigh invisible save for the fireflies.

And the glimmers of light, behind him. More fireflies, surely . . . ?

Or not. They looked to be eyes. Animal eyes, reflecting the green-gold of the fireflies' illumination, the ebon and aubergine of night.

Marion found herself shoring up against Gamelyn, her hand shifting, ready, upon the dagger. His hand twitched in hers again, then set hard as stone, vice-tight. With his other hand, Gamelyn twirled his sword and stuck it, point-first, into the damp earth.

A shiver pierced Marion, as if the earth had shot sparks from her heels to her nape.

The eyes went out.

The stag alerted, but did not start, or flee. He merely lifted his head to peer at Marion and Gamelyn, water dribbling from his muzzle. Fourteen ebony tines branched from his poll, sculpting furrows into the mist. The fireflies scattered in their wake, made irresolute return in twos and threes. Presently they crowned the stag with hundreds of tiny sparks, pulsing darkness and light. The stag's eyes flared with gold and green, as if the fireflies had taken refuge there, and the great head shook.

Then the stag's form . . . *spattered*, somehow, shedding uncountable and tiny darts of light. A stagger, which became a blur and shimmer, then a shift in some arcane flux: changing, reshaping . . . *transmogrifying.*

A shadowy man-form rose upon the banks of Barrow Mere, horn-crowned, lean and black with eyes burning upon Marion like Bel-fires. The antlered god of the woodland shifting into thisworld, expressing all He was, with what forms were His, through His avatar, through dreams and shades . . .

Robyn. The form was his—yet not. And those eyes, pale and green-gilt, were also not his.

They were Gamelyn's. Beside her, he let out a soft gasp.

"*Arglwydd,*" Marion acknowledged, barely above a whisper. "Why come you to this place?" For the woodland was His, but Barrow Mere belonged to the Mother.

Your brother, the Lady breathed on Marion's nape, *has opened the door.*

Aye, he has. The Hooded One has called the vow, and the Scarlet Knight needs give his answer. Time draws nigh to see it joined. The man-stag raised whipcord, woad-traced arms, and the fireflies danced between his hands.

The Ceugant has entered thisworld. The Lady of the Wild Things shall bring the gifts of Spring, coax the victorious Hunter from warrior to a gentler role. And so shall Summer rule the coming dawn whilst Winter falls into the dead leaves, to sleep his time and make the bargain.

"What bargain?" Gamelyn had recovered composure; the query was more a growl.

A chuckle, but no answer. The fire-opal eyes never left Marion. *Your scarlet Summerlord thinks too much, and your darkling twin—my soul's mate and avatar—does not dwell past the moment. However will you tame them, Maiden? Surely 'twill take a wild dance to call the wind and kindle the flame, a wild goddess to claim the unclaimed.*

Whatever those lights were—beings, mayhap?—seeming more eyes than form, they were returning. Wary, clustering behind the Horned Lord as if for protection, first the gather then the retreat, inward and outward.

They stayed far away from the sword.

But, ah!—your chosen shall weave the spiral back around, ground it strong upon My altar. Our tynged *will be paid in the binding of your powers, the truth of your hearts, and the blood you will, all three, bear to it.* A smile, fanged-sharp and hungry. *Aye, there will be blood. But first there will be vengeance, and betrayal.*

"There will be," Gamelyn gritted out, "no betrayal."

You. Those eyes—Gamelyn's own, in his lover's form and edged with bronze flame—turned upon him, making him shudder with the impact. *Aye,* you, *My ironclad Oak. . .*

And the words trailed into silence—or so it seemed. Marion heard nothing. But Gamelyn's shoulders shook and his jaw roiled, betraying the clench and grit of teeth. He gave a sudden stagger backwards, hand pulling from hers, eyes white-edged with . . . surely not panic, not wholly, but panic was there, spawning first disbelief, then fury, then a fierce, hot-eyed defiance.

Slowly, as if a hand had snarled in his hair and dragged him down, Gamelyn was forced to his knees.

Marion started to lurch forwards, was pinned in place by the firestorm flare of the Horned Lord's gaze. *Do not,* He growled, *interfere.*

The command stopped her feet, but it could not keep Marion from a silent entreaty: *Do not give way, Gamelyn. Do not let Him take you.*

Gamelyn's chest heaved, rapid-hard, panting into the dark and the chill even as the Horned Lord's own breath—hex and invocation and command—echoed harsh upon the water. And across . . .

The forms lingered in the shadows, restless, witch-lights winking. Compelled, perhaps, to stay close enough to watch but daring no closer. And Marion's gaze— instinct, no more or less—riveted to the blade Gamelyn had thrust into the ground. Remembered the sharp, strange shiver it had given her when he'd done so, and how the eyes had winked into darkness.

The old magics grow bolder, the Lady whispered to Marion. *The Horned Lord grows all the more restless.*

"I will *not.*" It was guttural, forced out from between Gamelyn's clenched teeth.

You will, the Horned Lord rumbled. *Or risk losing all.*

Silence. Gamelyn kept staring at the Horned Lord. Then he laughed.

Marion winced; it was that harsh, that full of mockery.

Laughter choking itself into stillness, Gamelyn tried to lurch up. Once, and failure, then twice, and finally he gained his feet. Hunched beneath forces both arcane and of physical limitation, Gamelyn swayed in place. Held to it by sheer tenacity, and spat, "Really? Haven't you already tried that?"

You have but a meagre concept, the Horned Lord rumbled, *of what can be rived from that heart of yours. What can be forever lost, or found. Or*—the uncanny gaze licked verdigris flame into pure darkness—*gleaned from dreams.*

Fists clenched, Gamelyn had opened his mouth as if to speak; with the last words he tottered back, shaking his head.

Then he turned on one heel and fled.

There was no other word for it. Marion watched him, her own mouth hanging open, unable to so much as make a sound to stay him. The Horned Lord and the Lady did not move, or speak. The Wode hung silent, as if it too lay stilled in the wake of a flight that should not be.

Slowly, small noises began creeping back into Marion's consciousness: the whirr of a bird's wings, the *shuss* of damp loam from a burrowing animal. Dawn had begun to finger its way across the darkness—Dawn? How could dawn have already come?—and the sullen, roseate light beckoning mists anew, glancing off the cold steel thrust into the banks of Barrow Mere.

Gamelyn had left his sword.

Marion took a deep, considered breath, then headed towards it. Her head felt heavy, her eyelids thick, her legs and feet foreign. She put a questing hand to the pommel of Gamelyn's sword, gripped then pulled it from the earth. It made a strange, harsh sound as it came free. Metallic, aye, but also oddly akin to the sound of flesh, and a slick of loam rimed the curved blade, like blood.

He is not being ready, Maiden. Do not be bringing him here again.

It was not the Lady, or Her Lord. Marion spun, sword in hand. Panicked whispers rose, echoing into the naked trees, and shadows fled into the grey. There were several darting splashes into the water—fleeing no less than Gamelyn had, seeking refuge.

Barrow Mere went silent. And the Horned Lord was no longer there.

- Entr'acte -

He saw the Templar rise, when the fire was sullen embers, and was satisfied to see the Templar had enough sense to tend it.

But then the Templar turned and retreated from camp, and every sense Will had hummed warning.

For aye, the Templar had nightmares to plague the damned—a proper punishment, that, as far as Will was concerned—but the man hadn't so far gone off in the middle of the night on his own. Not been able to, truly, either because of Much-the-lackey keeping a tight leash, or because he'd only recently improved enough to gad about in the damp and cold with a hole in his back.

Will wanted him gone, aye. But he didn't want him dead—well, mayhap at the odd moment, but nay, gone was better than Robyn's sorrow should the man up and die. And within Will the hope rose with every day of improvement: the Templar would go back to his bloody-minded kind and leave them all *be*.

And now the lackey wasn't here to jerk the chain—at least that was a relationship Will understood, having to occasionally slap sense into one's leader—and it went against Will's sensible grain to just lie here and let the Templar wander their Wode as if he'd the right.

Then Marion got up and followed the poncy ginger-haired nobleman, and warning swerved into straight-up anxiety.

Will lay there for a while longer, willing Robyn to wake, to get up, to *follow*.

But Robyn slept heavy as a bairn—like usual, unless sommat were up, the git—so Will decided he'd better go after.

He was careful and silent on the track, undeterred . . . until he kenned where the Templar had gone and where Marion followed. Will halted, a different caution raking his nerves. This place lay sacrosanct. True, he and a young Rob had, as ignorant lads, used it as meeting place more than once. But Rob's blithe comfort had matured into more awareness of what paths he trod, and Will was no longer a heedless boy-novice but fully bound and blooded to the Wode covenant. He was *dryw*, but he was not Robyn. He knew, deep down, Barrow Mere was not a place he had the right to carelessly tread.

Will stayed there, hesitant, for some time. Anger, however, began a slow replacement of any trepidation. This place *was* sacred, after all, and no Motherless Christian should foul it. Surely when Marion found the Templar there, she'd run him off.

And Will himself would be there to help, should she need it.

What he saw when he arrived to the outskirts of the clearing didn't best please him.

Marion wasn't running the Templar off. She was shored up all cosy and close, her head lying in the crook of the Templar's shoulder.

Will had to turn away, grit his teeth. Remind himself it was something Marion would have done with Robyn, how she often treated the damned Templar more as another brother than anything else, but . . .

But.

Will looked again, and it was there; the tension beneath. The most ancient of snares. And aye, Will knew this hunt well: the small smiles, the laying out of baits, one by one, the waiting and readiness and small hints, the unspoken language of a girl deciding to be courted.

And that . . . that ginger-haired, fish-cold, boy-buggering monk was *responding* to it. Awkward, slow—no doubt his like wouldn't know what to do with a woman if one crawled atop him naked and willing, but *something* in the bastard knew. Will could all but smell it.

Women're funny things, Arthur had said, one night he and Will were out hunting alone. *Give 'em sommat to cosset and they have kerwhallops of the heart. An' if some braw lad manages to sweep 'em off their feet?* A scratch of his shaved pate and a smirk at Will. *Lad, that Templar's a double threat, he is. He's been sore wounded—an' saving* our *lovely lad, mind you.*

Will had snorted derision.

Well, he did. And for that alone he deserves the care she and David have been giving him. But women like caring for things. No surprise she fancies him.

He's a monk.

And you and I both know people want all the more what they think they can't have. His like en't s'posed to so much as touch a woman, remember?—though I'm guessing poking lads en't against his rules, because that 'un's *tight-arsed enough to not show th' weakness of breaking 'em.*

Again, Will had snorted his opinion.

You'll take that Templar too lightly once too often, Will, Arthur growled. *Don't be forgettin' how he saved our bonny lass from gaol, he and the lackey.* A smirk. *Methinks you worry too much about the Templar, lad. Milady eyes up the lackey all the more.*

It should have been me to save her! Will had thought. But what he had said had been nigh as worse. *The lackey I can fight, fair. 'Tis that greedy, noble-bred bastard. He en't satisfied with takin' Robyn from us— now he wants* her *too.*

Arthur had cocked an eyebrow at him and risen, patted his shoulder. *I hope you en't daft enough to say such things to anyone but me, lad.*

Nay, Will wasn't daft. He saw it, plain. He'd keep his mouth shut, even if his tongue burned with wanting to make Robyn see.

He felt sick. Woozy. As if his head and his heels weren't in agreement of which was sky and which was ground.

He wanted to turn around, stomp into the clearing, just bloody well challenge the damned Templar and be done with it . . . only . . .

Only.

It was *Barrow Mere.* The Mere of the Barrow folk, of which his mam had told tales of deep magic to frighten any small boy: of dragons lying submerged to snatch the legs of unwise children; of the ghosts of the Barrow folk, burnt and drowned by the conquerors so long ago, their bones fertilising the lake bottom; of tree spirits and shadows to draw unwary travellers into another wood; of that wood, the one between thisworld and the otherworld, where Time stood still and the *cwn annwn* waited in the dark for the Horned Lord to call them to the Wild Hunt.

Will had seen the Wild Hunt, had seen a young man—his oldest friend, the Horned Lord made flesh, the *dryw ardhu* of their covenant—clothe himself in the Horns and the madness not merely once, but twice. Once to bring a bounty hunter down, and the second when that same murdering bounty hunter had been brought down by others. And Robyn had lied about it to them— well, if 'tweren't exactly a lie, he'd certainly hid the truth of who Gisbourne was for far too long, and all after some senseless boyhood passion for a damned *nobleman.*

The Templar was of their greatest enemy, the Church—he wore their cursed bloody cross on his breast! The Templar's fathers had

crossed the sea and swarmed Britain like ants, had made slaves of
the people and taken Her stones to build their fortresses. Had
raped and murdered Will's mother when Will was but a tiny lad,
had whipped a thirteen-year-old Rob like an animal for standing
up for another girl they'd tried to abuse. Bloody damn, the Templar's *own kin* had, in the name of their White Christ, burned
Loxley to the ground. How Robyn could even stand to touch the
bastard was beyond Will's comprehension . . . and to lie with him,
laugh with him, say he *loved* him? Why? *Why?*

A dark-clad form came hurtling through the trees, swift and
strangely silent, and Will juddered back to himself to find the
Templar retreating—running!—through the trees as if demons were
stooping upon him. *Why?* turned into *how?* and *what the hell?*
before it swerved around to *Marion!* and the impulse to chase the
bastard also fled beneath the ultimatum: *what has he done to her?*

Will headed for the Mere, expecting the worst.

He found the Horned Lord's shade wisping into nothing, Marion
standing at the water's edge with the Templar's sword in her hand,
and a rosy-grey dawn beginning to streak the eastern sky . . .

Dawn? When he'd left, it had been closer to midnight, he'd swear
it, and the nights too long to be seeing the dawn this soon after.

Marion turned, saw Will. Her face, pale, began to flush with a
myriad of emotions: alarm, then humiliation, then an unmistakable
fury.

And she held that sword like she damn well knew how to use it.

Will beat a very hasty retreat.

-IV-

"What do you mean, *this en't the first time?*"

Robyn was still half-asleep and a bit tender behind the eyes from one too many mushroom caps; he'd been minding his own business and warming a pot of mulled cider. Amidst shivering. He'd woken up to a bloody cold, very empty bed.

Then Will had shown up, in a very bloody hurry, with his shoulders hunched around his ears, and had he a tail to tuck, it would have been tight-wrapped somewhere between his knob and his navel.

And right after *that* had Marion shown up, wielding Gamelyn's sword like a stony-eyed angel threatening parishioners from the corner of some cathedral of the Christ.

However, instead of lighting into Will as she'd clearly wanted to do, she'd flown at Robyn and begun bloody *chasing* him all over camp with Gamelyn's sword. All because Robyn had been half-asleep, and when she'd asked him if he'd set a watch on her, he'd been daft and told the truth.

He'd not even had a *piss* yet.

"What do you think I'm supposed to do? Let you wander the forest on your lonesome?" Robyn retreated to the other side of the fire, snatching at both his unlaced shirt and the fur nigh dragging it off his shoulders.

Not that it did any good; Marion just followed him. "Let me? *Let me?* Who do you th—"

"Mari, pet, if you'd just—"

"Don't you 'pet' me—and what were you thinking? On second

thought, you *weren't* thinking! You were just assuming! Like you've t' rights! Putting minders on me as if I were some child!"

David had already scooted out of the way, taking his precious iron utensils with him. Gilbert and Arthur dodged right, then left, then scattered as brother and sister darted around the hearth-fire, first one way, then the other.

"You en't no child, but you're a woman, and in case you'd not heard, these parts are filled with outlaws—*Ow!*" Robyn skipped sideways as she swung, and the flat of the blade smacked his thigh. "What're you trying t' do, geld me?"

"You en't using 'em, anyway!"

"I *am!* Just 'cause I en't after making a bunch o' bairns—"

"The likes of more of you is *all* we need—!"

"—like me goolies just where they are!" This time Robyn leapt over the fire. "What in hell are y' doing with Gamelyn's sword, anyw—Bloody *damn,* woman!" Robyn yipped as she swung again, too close for any comfort. He changed tactics. "Put that sword down! Right now, before y' really do cut someone!"

"Stay still so I can whack you another one, you bloody great"—a lunge— "arrogant"—another dart—"*knob!*" Marion overbalanced and the sword nearly went flying. Robyn skittered sideways, took refuge against the huge trunk of the hazel sheltering much of the camp, and snatched up the only weapon he could muster—a staff.

Marion glared at him for one breath. Two.

Robyn raised the staff, glaring back.

None of the others dared to so much as twitch.

Marion stomped over, hefting the shamshir over her head. It came down, a glittering, curved arc. Robyn went staggering back against the hazel's trunk, his staff cloven in two, and the sword's curved blade rebounded against the root-laced ground with a sharp, nigh painful ring.

"Hoy! What in bloody hell are you *doing* to my sword?" It was Gamelyn's voice.

Marion spun around, snapped out, "So, were *you* in on this too? Either of you?"

Robyn took part of his attention—only part, mind—from Marion. Gamelyn stood on the camp's edge, fists clenched, and beside him stood Much, dusty with road dirt. Both seemed baffled.

Join the ring, mates. Robyn barely had time for the silent reply before Marion turned back on him and growled a curse surely no novice nun should know. In the next moment, Marion flung the sword down, turned on one heel, and stalked off.

Gamelyn cringed as his sword once again made contact with the hard, root-tangled ground.

The outlaws—those who happened to be in the wake of Marion's passage—wisely scattered.

Robyn wasn't considering wisdom or anything else; he lurched upright, started after. "Mari!"

Marion kept going, and Robyn kept following, and just before she reached the camp periphery, she whirled. Robyn nearly ran over her, halting just in time with the aid of some creative arm flailing and despite some clumsy foot sliding.

Silence. Then:

"Do *not*," Marion growled, "bloody *follow* me!" And she stomped off into the trees.

More silence, punctuated by a huge sigh of relief from Will.

It was a mistake.

"I told you!" Robyn rounded on Will. "Told you this would happen, did you not mind what I said and go aft—"

"I en't the one as is allus going after, and you know it!" Will snapped back, with a venomous look in Much's direction. "This weren't *my* fau—"

"It never is, Scathelock, but you followed her this time, aye? And just like I said, you were a great lumbering pillock and she *saw* you."

"She never saw me," Much said, low. "I know she didn't."

"Or mayhap she prefers you to follow her!" Gilbert tried to joke.

That was a mistake as well. It was Will's turn, this time, to round on Gilbert and hiss, "Shut your gob!"

"Bloody *fucking* damn, William." Robyn stalked over and shoved at him. "It's not like I en't had eno—"

"You followed Marion?" Gamelyn interrupted. It was soft, almost colourless in tone—which was no doubt why it penetrated Robyn's growl of accusation. "Tonight? To Barrow Mere?"

An uneasy silence followed; none of the outlaws took that place lightly.

"Aye, I did!" Will broke it, defiant, and tucked his chin not unlike an angry bull. "What of it? I should think I've more rights there than any bloody *Templar!*"

Barrow Mere. Robyn narrowed his eyes, put off and puzzled. Will was on the defensive, no question, and Gamelyn . . . well, *he* was proper brassed off, because when Gamelyn did get that offended, you'd never see it in those flat eyes, but the blood would rush beneath his skin until all the freckles disappeared and his face turned into a bloody coppery *idol*.

"You'll push too far one day, Scathelock," Gamelyn snarled.

"I'm waitin' for 't, believe me," Will snarled back.

Robyn decided that was enough of that, here and now. He strode into their sight line—Gamelyn was still having a cold-blooded seethe at Will, whose own glare surely belonged on the business end of a crossbow—scowled at both of them, and crossed his arms.

"Right, then," Robyn said to Much. "Where's John?"

Much's gaze darted to Gamelyn, then he tipped Robyn a reassuring nod. "He's well enough. No doubt having a bite and flagon of ale at the inn. We thought it best he stay near the trouvère, considering."

"Considering."

"Aye. There's a few more branches to this tree. As we figured." Much flicked another glance at Gamelyn, now peering into what seemed to be thin air, then Will, red-faced and muttering at the ground, then the others, still scattered in Marion's wake. "Looks to me like we could all use a good stiff drink, at that."

"The man's sent a message, you say?"

"Aye. Several. Parked himself down at the inn, pulled out his lute, and started holding court." Much shifted his position, cross-legged on a flat rock, scratched at his beard and ventured, "Mayhap we should fetch Marion? Likely she knows Worksop better than any of us."

"True, but *I* en't after fetching her," Robyn declared. "Anyone else game?"

There were no takers. Not even Gamelyn, who'd obviously had some sort of encounter with Marion during the night. Nay, that one had refused hot cider in lieu of giving his sword a careful inspection, on the outskirts of Much's perch and the listening outlaws.

And bloody damn, but Robyn *still* hadn't had a piss.

"She wain't like it," Much murmured.

"I'm thinking she'll like it less do we follow her th' now," David said.

"Aye, leave it," Robyn said. "We'll fill her in soon enough . . . wait up." He rose; that last sip of cider had done it. Normally he would go off a ways; this time he angled over to where Gamelyn was obsessing over his bloody sword and watered a respectful distance off the back side of the hazel tree. He was of a mind to ask what was going on, even if Gamelyn's face did not invite so much as a fond look.

Nevertheless, he tried. "Gam—?"

The green eyes flickered to his for no longer than a breath, then returned to the sword.

Robyn finished up, laced his braies, and considered how he'd been given flat notice over something. Whats'mever that something were.

Much kept hazarding a glance their way. And bloody hell if Will wasn't watching after them too—but openly, furious as some murderous mamma bear.

With a tiny snarl, both at intemperate stone-faced Templars and sodding overprotective pillocks, Robyn returned to the fire.

"—nothing more than earning some coin," Gilbert was saying. "We did rather force his hand to it, if he meant to hire a guide. He's the means for a good meal in his voice, why wouldn't he use it?"

"Worksop's a goodly town," Arthur offered up. "More than a few make their way to the abbey, and there's an inn for those as en't staying in abbey walls. It's first-rate, an inner courtyard and everything."

Much shrugged, with another glance to Gamelyn. "This un's no mere jongleur, and Worksop en't no noble's hall. Seems odd he'd bother, like."

"Well, *that* sort thinks anything's beneath 'em, 'less it's given with a lot of arsepadding cushions," Will sneered into his cup.

"You're makin' absolutely no sense, Scathelock." Robyn crouched down, forearms across his knees. "Did you save a few mushrooms for this morning, then?"

"Mushrooms?" Much's query was mild, if puzzled.

"Later," Robyn said. "Did you find out where the messages went?"

Much grinned. "We did that. One were to the old one at Blyth's stables, of all things. Well, that one weren't written on parchment, like. Brand en't readin' more than his name. A lad went to tell it."

"Brand, Blyth's stable master?" This snared Gamelyn's attention. "He's still alive?"

"'Twould seem so, milord. And if that weren't a puzzle, t' other were proper interesting. Sent directly to milord Baron of Pontefract."

Sword still in hand—as well as a whetstone he plainly meant to use—Gamelyn was edging nigh to Much. "Pontefract? What would a trouvère want with Roger de Lacy?"

"De Lacy." Robyn peered up at Gamelyn. "En't that the Sheriff's brother? The one as recognised your claim when you defeated *your* brother?"

"And who argued for our right to go free after Nottingham's archery contest." Gamelyn's gaze met Robyn's, inexplicable frost beginning to thaw about the edges. "I would call Pontefract a friend."

"Well, aye, you can afford to," Arthur pointed out.

And the green eyes went cold once more. Robyn contemplated smacking Arthur halfway across the camp; fortunately Arthur's next words had more sense and less bait.

"More, why's this minstrel calling him friend?"

"Trouvère," Gamelyn countered, with a tiny-quick smirk in Robyn's direction.

Arthur frowned.

"Sending a message doesn't mean they're friends." Gilbert grabbed a water skin from behind Arthur, took a long drink.

Arthur was giving a covert go at sounding out the Frankish word, lips tracing *troovair*. Robyn hid his own smirk.

"You didn't fetch a look at the note, then?" Robyn asked Much, who answered with a puzzled look.

"Much reads less than you," Gamelyn revealed, and Robyn's eyebrows climbed into his forelock. He had surely guessed Much for the reading type.

"I canna stand it, neither," Robyn confessed to Much, who gave a soft chuckle. "Me mam tried to learn me, but it makes me head spin. Well, that's that, for 'tis sure our little John makes charms and runes better than any letters."

"Which is partly why I'm back," Much added. "If the trouvère fetches up a reply from his 'contacts,' 'twould be good to have sommun there as knows what it says."

"And more, what he does between now and then," Gilbert added, passing the water skin to Arthur.

"Aye. And also, why he's asking so many questions." Much peered at Robyn. "About you."

Robyn shrugged. "Surely he's cobbling a bunch of nonsense for his tales."

"He asked me questions along the road, as well." Much leaned in. "Wanting to know what interest we had in the castle." He looked up at Gamelyn, who'd come to stand beside Robyn. "*Your* castle, milord."

Gamelyn's eyes narrowed. "First off, it isn't mine. Count John has the honour of Tickhill, given to him by the King, but Blyth Castle itself is still administrated by de Lacy's seneschal, unless . . . "

Much was nodding. "'Tis all a bit too neat, like."

What satisfaction Robyn normally gained from watching those two work all clever in their tandem harness was muted; his own thoughts were milling about, trying to find purchase. And roiling beneath, the odd-tense jangle of nerves that always signalled: *This is important. This matters.*

"What did you tell him?"

"I told him nowt," Much assured. "He were fair clever at trying me, but I've been . . . questioned before. By experts. Of which he weren't one."

Robyn's ears were humming; he closed his eyes. Much's last statement flitted before Robyn, a sweat-soaked, torch-lit glimpse of cruel captors and endless questions; he shook his head and the vision spattered into darkness. In the next instant, the darkness had once again coalesced, spun itself into colours, corded and quivering. Like lute strings plucked by a careful hand.

Robyn brought his palms up to his face, let out the strands into a breath that tickled across his palms and trickled between his fingers. Behind closed eyes, the cords combed themselves out, glittering . . .

A peacock's tail, folded then fanning, quivering . . . nay. A fancy peacock-feather fan, fluttering in one well-manicured hand, lowering to reveal kohl-marked, slate-grey eyes . . .

Stone walls, heavy about him as he pursues a familiar copper-haired shape up an unlit, narrow stair, and the hem of Gamelyn's cloak brushes his cheek as draughts puff downwards . . .

More copper, and crimson, and a nimbus of heat and sparks as the blaze reaches for treetops and stars, limning silhouettes dancing, singing, *making* . . .

The tat of a horn, and galloping hoofs pounding through the Shire Wode . . .

And the trouvère, sitting across an ill-lit tavern board, saying, almost breathless, "So it's true—"

"Robyn?"

The trouvère's voice drifted away on strands of disappearing *tynged* as a firm hand took hold of Robyn's shoulder, shook him back to his hearth and his outlaws. It was Gamelyn whose hand pinched his neck tendons, whose voice gave a slight tremor as he said, again, "Robyn."

"We need to go to Worksop," Robyn said. "We need to see what this"—he cocked his head, grinned up at Gamelyn's concerned frown—"this *trouvère* is on about."

Better, that one.

Marion hefted another stone—she had at least ten of them gathered in her overskirt, carefully chosen for heft and balance and surface—and took aim.

The sun streamed, insistent, through the mists. A small glade, this; no eerie silhouettes, no dark fens surrounding it. Just grass suitable for grazing cattle, and a clear pond uncomplicated by any myth or legend, sunny when there was sun to be had, and spring-fed by a rocky, cold-clear brook from which Marion had more than once gathered drinking water. Just a normal, unremarkable, suitable-for-stone-skimming pond.

"Bugger!" This as yet another projectile flipped midflight and sank with a small *blurp*. That made six to not so much as skim the surface past a count of three or four.

"You're throwing too hard, y'know."

Heart lurching up into her throat, Marion whipped around. At the same time, she dropped her skirt edge and all the stones she'd so carefully selected spilled onto the rocky bank. "*Now* look what you made me do!" she snapped.

Much ambled into the little glade—gingerly to be sure, and so he should, she thought with a sniff. Several angry retorts gathered on her tongue as she bent to her dropped stones, muted as Much reached her side and started helping her retrieve them. What ended up escaping was "I suppose you could do better?"

Much regarded her with mild blue eyes, and Marion had the sudden wish to kick him in the shin, just to see if those eyes would bloody well show *something*. "Sweet Lady, but you are just like your master!"

"I'd normally be considering that a compliment," Much replied, dropping his gaze to his task. "But I'm thinking you weren't exactly meaning it as one."

"I'm thinking you might just be right."

Another glance upwards and . . . was that a tiny smirk?

Damn him. Damn all men. What in hell was she *thinking*, coming to live with a herd of them? Useless, high-handed, arrogant, bossy, bloody-minded sods!

Much rose, handed Marion a few of the stones he'd gathered. It was in her mind to comment how they weren't the ones she'd gathered, but they were good ones. The one Marion hefted and aimed fit into her palm quite nicely, in fact.

Unfortunately, it too sank before it could skim across the pond's surface. Only two, this time.

Much considered the one still in his palm, then shrugged. Aimed. "You wain't fetch nowt from this sort of thing by ridin' your fury like a mad horse."

"My brother wouldn't agree with you."

Much hesitated, then shrugged again. "Mayhap it works for him. I'd hazard it en't working for you, about now." His gaze met hers. "You want to be chilly, like, when you strike the blow."

"Hm. You and your master certainly know a bit about *that*."

Much hung his head, didn't quite hide the smirk tugging—again— at his mouth. Taking a deep breath, he aimed again and let loose.

The stone danced across the pond like a crane fly, lighting only to recoil again, and again. And again.

Fifteen! Marion let out a sudden laugh. "Well. You *are* fairly brilliant!"

"Aye, well, what else is there to do, in the dam above the mill?" Much shrugged. "Though if me da caught us at it, he'd tan our hides." He tossed another stone; it skimmed the water's surface and Marion counted nineteen, this time. "Said stones 'twould likely cock up t' wheel."

"Your father, he were miller, then." Marion hefted another stone. "To Auckley."

He blinked.

"It's what you said at Nottingham. I had one of my . . . flashes. Well," she shrugged, "what I call 'em, leastways. It were the memories, they kept trying to break through. You kept me from a nasty tumble down the stair. I had our cloaks, mine and my . . . *hers*. Abbess Elisabeth. You introduced yourself as the Templar's paxman, whose people were of Auckley Mill."

This time, when Much grinned, his eyes smiled as well. "Fancy you remembering that."

"I have a memory, now." That sobered him for a moment, but she returned his smile and aimed another stone. "Some things still aren't so clear, but more and more— aye, that's more like!" The stone flitted across the water to the count of eleven.

"See? The pond likes your smile as well."

As well. It gave a semisolid flutter to the pit of her belly; she negated it by saying, "I did ask not to be followed."

"You asked your brother not to follow you, were my take on that."

"You're quibbling, Much the miller's son."

"I en't sure what that word means, Marion the outlaw's sister."

"I think you do." She snorted. "But 'tis true, I am little else now."

"Nay," Much murmured, as if to himself. "Nowt little t' you." Then, louder, "Where did you learn to handle a sword?"

"Gamelyn taught me, a long time ago." It was a memory with another smile. Gamelyn had begun carrying a second sword—a spare, as he had explained to a manipulative elder brother who had stalked his doings like a carrion bird. Robyn had scorned it, but Marion, despite sparse tutorials, had taken to it well.

Much was examining another stone, chuckling. "I think you quite surprised that stroppy lot."

It reminded Marion of her anger. "They'd no right."

"When you're anxious after sommat, rights never seem to enter into it, do they?" Marion slid him a look, captious but curious.

He dropped his stone, knelt on the ground looking for another. "Look. Your brother's worried, is all. And to be fair, you started it, like."

"*I* started—"

"You're the one as came to him with talk about the Mere. Of seeing all manner of strangeness about."

"How did you know that?"

"I listen."

"Mm. Do you, then?"

Much found one stone, frowned over it for a moment, then discarded it, kept looking. "Your brother knows you can defend yourself, like. But he also knows you've spent the last years . . . not yourself. He knows you're . . . you're still looking. For lost . . . things." Much fell quiet, tumbling a stone in his fingers, gaze fixed to it.

Marion stared at him, somewhat dumbfounded.

"Sometimes, when people are searchin' that hard for sommat," Much continued, slow, "they en't paying attention to what's around 'em, like. I understand. More, Robyn knows I understand. Me master . . . well. Let's say, when we first went into battle, milord weren't too careful about his back. But 'twere my charge, see? Mine, and more *Her* charge upon me, to care for our Summerlord."

It made Marion's throat fill, close up. Much stood, made a try with the new stone in his hand. Only it didn't skim as far, and when he picked up a second, it was worse.

He was angry, his words skimming flatter than the stones as he continued. "Scathelock, he wanted to be the one. I ken he's dear to you and your brother both, but he's about as subtle as a pikestaff up the bum. And Robyn . . . well, he figured enough about me to ken *I* wouldn't be walking the hem of your skirts."

Sweet Lady, Marion thought, staring at the rock she still held, *no wonder Will is furious.* And abruptly she was just as furious. As if he had any right to *be* furious. To assume upon what might have been, once.

Eden is long gone from us, Gamelyn had said, with that strange, wistful-cheated throb in his voice. *We've seen too much. Know too much. And we're fools to want it back. . . but still, we are. Fools.*

Will was decent, loyal to a fault, forthright with his loves and his hates. He would die for Robyn, the outlaws, and Marion as well . . . but such love came with terms, soft shackles that, nonetheless, were shackles.

Marion was of a beaten people, but she had been loved. Been as free as one of her kind could, never fully appreciated shackles until she'd woken from nearly four years of them in the hands of her family's murderess.

And now, the least thought of them was loathsome.

Much seemed uneasy by her silence; he kept skimming stones, which kept sinking closer and closer to shore, and his words came quicker, as if he had to say them but wasn't sure he wanted to. "I never meant to intrude. Robyn Hode en't my master, not like milord is. But he bears the horns, is the face of our god just as you're the Lady's own. Robyn never said I should stalk you, like. I kept meself private, and you more so, didn't watch or listen to what weren't proper. Robyn figured, could I keep me master safe and sound in the Holy Land and not make 'im resent me for 't, likely I could keep you the same here, and never let on 'less you needed me."

Marion reached out and grasped one of Much's hands, turned it over. Placed the stone she held in his palm, closed his fingers about it. "You were good." It was a bit grudging. "I never knew you were there." He shrugged, peering at the stone.

Hardly believing what she was doing even as she did it, Marion grabbed hold of his beard and angled his face to meet hers. "Don't do it again."

Much regarded her for a long moment, then ventured, soft, "One thing a soldier knows—if his disguise is burnt, he'll play hell fetching another one as good."

"That's no answer."

"Aye, well then." Much unclenched her fingers from his beard, closed his eyes, and laid his cheek upon her open palm.

He didn't so much as nuzzle her hand. No kiss even attempted, nothing remotely erotic about it. Nevertheless Marion's gut warmed, gave a twist, and lurched down into her pelvis, laying a trail of heat through her loins. Abruptly she wanted nothing more than to push him back into the grass, find out if that broad body fit to hers as well as it fit against his tunic. She wanted to undress him, kiss and caress him rigid, hike her skirts and ride him until they were both spent and senseless.

Instead, Marion firmed her hand against his cheek. "Don't do it again."

Much hadn't looked up. Surely if he felt anything akin to what she was, he would at least look at her, at least try to look? His cheek twitched—a quiver of a smile against her palm, and he merely stood, looking out across the pond.

Said, quiet and thoroughly, wretchedly unaffected, "I'd not dream of it, milady."

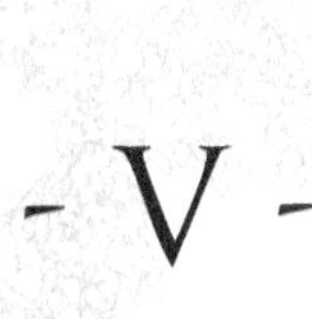

"No fights."

Will started laughing.

"I mean it, Scathelock. No fights. No starting 'em, no—"

"You seldom start 'em, Rob, but you oft end 'em." Still chuckling, Will nudged a grinning Gilbert, who shrugged.

"He has a point, Robyn."

Robyn slid a glance over to Marion, just out of reach. There was a distinct twinkle in her eye. Much and Gamelyn were just beyond; Much avoided everyone's gaze, but his lip twitched, whilst Gamelyn heeded none of it, engrossed in the jumble of mud-and-wattle buildings hunched outside Worksop Abbey's walls.

And here Robyn thought this would be a good idea. Will had suggested—more insisted, like—Robyn should bring more backup. Not that there was likely to be need of any more backup than two bored-as-hell Templars; myriad reasons squirmed beneath Will's insistence, and Robyn fancied he knew most of them. Nevertheless he'd agreed. Always good sense to have a backup plan.

Just as it made sense Marion should come. They'd all worn their cleanest and best for this bit of work, but she looked proper lovely all kitted up in woman's garb—the finest woollen overtunic and kirtles thievery could provide, of course—with her shoulder-length hair respectably plaited and veiled beneath a grey linen that matched her eyes, and a braided cord fillet securing it against the fitful breeze. They'd thought to dress her as another lad, which had failed miserably now she'd gained some of her weight back. Well,

Robyn considered with a quirk of lip, no doubt his sister tended a wee top-heavy.

There was also no doubt she knew every inch of this place.

"There'll be *no fightin'*," Robyn insisted. "We're here to find what this fellow's about. Nowt more."

"Nowt?" Will wheedled. "An' here I were hoping for an ale pot or three."

"A try at the dart pricks would be fine," Gilbert put in his bid, furthered with a grin, "or Emmie, at that."

"Do you know *every* whore within shouting distance, Gilly?" There was admiration as well as exasperation in Will's query. Gilbert just grinned.

Much also had a distinct smirk starting into one cheek.

"Hot bread." Marion made it an invocation.

"Some decent wine," Gamelyn added, proving he was paying attention despite his gaze still strafing the village.

Robyn had to laugh; he couldn't help it. "Aye," he said when he could, "all that too."

The inn was as first-rate as David had claimed. And the scrumpy was even better. Robyn propped his feet in Will's lap, tilted the pot to his lips, and spared a thought for Arthur and David. The latter was out of sorts with some mild ague, and Arthur looked to be starting it as well. Robyn didn't fancy keeping too many rules in his band, but this one was inflexible: sickness was not to be fooled with.

Another reason to be thankful his sister stayed with them. David had a way with simples, but he hadn't been taught wortwifery by Eluned of Loxley.

Robyn beamed at his sister; she sat next to him, mumbling praises amidst bites of the hot loaf the innkeeper's wife had brought to their board. "Mayhap we should order another?"

Marion wrinkled her nose at him and, when Will reached for a piece, slapped Will's hand.

Will was definitely a braver man than Robyn. Or stupid. Robyn had learned, long ago, not to get between his sister and hot bread.

He took another drink and let his gaze wander, albeit with purpose. Gamelyn and Much had taken a table against the far wall; conspicuous in their dark habits with the scarlet cross, they were being given the wide berth of both fear and respect. What corners of the inn Robyn couldn't see from his chosen table, those two could, and all four exits—not counting the arch leading to the courtyard— were covered: one through an alcove to Robyn's left shoulder, another hallway nigh to the Templars, the third being the innkeeper's private one, and the last nigh to the dart pricks, where—

"Gilly's winning again," Will said, wiping foam from his upper lip and giving another longing look towards the bread.

Gilbert was. Robyn frowned.

"Emmie must be busy." Marion chuckled.

"Mm. I told him to not brass 'em off—hoy, that's more like it." Robyn nodded as Gilbert missed his sixth throw. The others commiserated with Gilbert on his throw and took his money—only half what he'd already won, Robyn noticed, but enough to restore good humour in the competitors.

Will tossed down the rest of his ale, shoved Robyn's feet off his thigh, and went to join Gilbert. No easy task, that, weaving amongst the crowd; the inn was packed.

For there was an entertainer in their midst.

The outlaws had glimpsed him when they'd first arrived, and if they were in adequate disguise, Alundel also looked nothing like the bedraggled vagabond lost in the Shire Wode. Well-garbed, fair hair falling down his back smooth as a dove's wing, he amused the innkeeper's three youngest children with some sleight-of-hand tricks in between bites of a sumptuous meal. Alundel was making a point to charm the innkeeper's wife—and also spent some time chatting up the teenaged son.

Robyn's ears nigh pricked. He knew flirting when he saw it.

But when the trouvère began his first song, the clear tenor would have given him away had the clean and natty appearance fooled them. What a voice Alundel had!—and the watchers responded to it, realising they'd not often have the chance to witness such talent. Mindful of his listeners, the trouvère made only small forays into the Frank tongue, using it for colour or emphasis and not without explanation. First a ballad, one with a heart-wrench at the end that had more than a few cheeks glistening. After, Alundel began a round to take the sad edge off, fun and familiar questions that convinced every person to sing out just-as-familiar answers.

The innkeeper must be ecstatic—he and his family were serving all manner of folk. A minor lord with his wife and servants and paxmen took their ease in the sunniest part of the courtyard. A few peasants had wandered in for the singing, and some soldiers— Robyn propped his feet back on the extra bench, denying the hunch that wanted to claim his shoulders as the latter passed—and plenty of yeomen class, likely pilgrims to the abbey. The two Templars, of course, in their corner. There were several nuns. Marion was less successful at concealing her own reflex—wide eyes and a too-quick turn away—but in time she'd learn.

Where was . . . ?

"Hoy, there he is," Robyn murmured, thankful, as a slight figure in worn woollens slid from behind a huge chestnut at the courtyard's end. John's eyes glinted amber as he winked at Robyn, then leaned back against the tree, lifting his face to the sky.

Just another peasant lad, enjoying some fine storytelling and a welcome day of sun. And a hunk of cheese, which he took from his tunic, unwrapped, and began to gnaw.

"Ha'penny for the bread and sausage, pet, and I'll fetch your fine husband there another bit o' scrumpy." The innkeeper's wife, after seeing the colour of their money, had been a convivial host.

"Husband?" Marion blinked, looked up at the innkeeper, then at Robyn. "Oh. But he's—"

"Quiet in his beer, that's the best sort," the wife approved, setting down a fresh jug and several pewter plates filled with the promised victuals. Robyn tipped his head, smiled thanks. "And my, he's pretty t' boot, en't he? When he en't scowlin' like a surly boy."

A surly . . . boy? Robyn tried not to look offended.

"'Tis sure that bairn'll be a fair one."

"Bairn?" Marion repeated, with a helpless look at Robyn, who shrugged a quick *How the hell should I know what she's on about?*

"Aw, lass," the wife chided with a smirk. "I've had nine meself. You think I wain't be recognising a breedin' woman's appetite?" Her glance towards Robyn was coy. "Aye, the menfolk don't know until you pitch 'em out of bed and leave 'em to their own devices."

Robyn tried to smirk right back, couldn't. Surely his own expression must be as blank as Marion's.

The wife continued, albeit softer, "Aye, poor lass, and you c'n only pray it en't redheaded too. It well could end up like that nasty monk ower there." She tilted her head over to where Gamelyn was leaning his bench against the wall with pot in hand, looking—one had to admit—thoroughly and murderously grumpy.

Robyn did laugh this time. Marion's boot made a sharp impact with his shin, and he gave a yip—but couldn't stop chuckling.

"Lad, lad," the wife said, shaking her head and turning away at another summons. "Must be his first, aye?"

"She just called me and Gamelyn redheaded!" Marion hissed his way and threatened another kick.

"Well, you *are* redheaded." Robyn wrinkled his nose at her, then furthered, knowing he was likely to fetch more than a threat for it, but unable to resist, "Why didn't you tell me you were breeding, wife?"

Marion did kick him. Damned hard, too.

Will and Gilbert were both playing the darts now. Gamelyn was watching the game; Much leaned over and murmured something in his ear. One eyebrow lifting, Gamelyn slid his gaze towards Alundel. Both eyebrows drew together and his head tilted, sliding a ginger lock across his cheek.

Bugger daft people, anyway; Robyn loved Gamelyn's hair, like silk and copper spun together all fine. Even Marion's, thick and curly as his own, was just as pretty, more fire embers than gilt . . . but Robyn wasn't about to say such a thing. The teasing was half the fun. Despite what temper seemed to go with red hair, Robyn considered, wincing, with a drub at his dented shin. He took another sip of scrumpy. Gamelyn kept scrutinising the trouvère. Not so odd, perhaps; the *way* he was looking, on the other hand?

Alundel's lute gave appropriate emphasis to every turn: a stirring minor chord as the hero found trouble, a fierce strum and tap as the confrontation rose . . .

Then Robyn heard the words "—met a young knave in a hood—" and kenned what had so claimed Gamelyn's interest.

> *"When crossing Sherwood's finest rogue,*
> *The knight was stricken dumb;*
> *He'd heard the tales, you see,*
> *The hints of sorcery become*
> *As living things, the trees as ghosts,*
> *The mists as foul and hellish breath.*
> *He feared that with his boldness, he had but met his death."*

With a vigorous pop of strings, Alundel's voice wavered into a hiss and stop. The audience murmured, gasped. Leaned forwards, eager, as the pause lingered.

Alundel's eyes, blue as the clearing sky above, had by chance or purpose met Robyn's.

Too late now, to conceal or deny. Robyn let a hint of a smile tilt his lip, angled forwards. Resting his chin in one hand, he prompted, silent, *Aye, well, go on, then.*

This seemed to take the trouvère aback. His lute went silent, hand poised midstrum. The audience started to murmur again, this time with puzzled impatience. So reminded of his task, Alundel broke from Robyn's gaze and, running his fingers in an elaborate arpeggio across the strings, continued:

> *"Still a purpose filled the knight; he said: "I cannot tarry here,*
> *"My purpose was to dine this day, at Blyth or Doncaster. . ."*

Blyth. Again. The remainder of the tune faded into the lute's belly, into the strings vibrating, dissipating into an advancing distance, beckonings of Sight curling about the edges. Robyn shook it away with a soft oath—not now, *not now*—and made a gather of his cohort by eye and gesture. They weren't betrayed even if he was, and no telling if Alundel had his own collection of allies. Likely; being a nobleman, after all, and in his own element.

The Templars' corner was already vacant. Robyn caught a glimpse of Gamelyn pulling his cowl over his head as he and Much disappeared into the far hall. Will was heading for Robyn, casual but ready.

"What's happening?" Marion murmured. Robyn had a fierce surge of pride; the undeniable quaver of voice refused to show in Marion's hands as she broke off another hunk of bread. "He knows it's you, aye?"

"He knows. We'll see what he does about it. Remember t' stick tight to Will or our Temple lads if it comes to trouble, aye?"

Marion nodded, kept chewing at the bread as Will leaned up against the wall behind Robyn. John's gaze met Robyn's, chased away again as he ventured closer, ostensibly listening to the story. Gilbert was laughing, paying off the last game he'd lost, and pocketing his winnings. Glancing Robyn's way, Gilbert sauntered over to the tavern board and ordered a refill for his pot.

Robyn cogitated over his own drink, leaning back against the scarred, wooden wall.

"What's the man on about?" Will stood beside him, only the slight clench and release of his free fist betraying any tension. "Y' sure he marked you?"

"Aye. He knows."

Will took a noisy drink from his pot and growled, "Tis Sherwood's finest *fool*, you are. I thought the plan were t' stay hidden."

"Aye, well, can I help it if he en't following the plan?" Robyn nudged him, grinned. "Did never a one tell you how handsome you are with those indignant eyes and ready muscles? For an auntie type, leastways," he temporised.

Will snorted and flung the chaff-coloured forelock from his brow. "Did never a one tell *you* how black-eyed tossers who fancy pullin' danger's whiskers mightn't live to see the next sunrise?"

"Aye, you have done. Many a time." Robyn nudged him again. "So why do you stay with me, Auntie William?"

"Someone has to keep you clear of trouble."

"My hero." Yet another nudge. "What's life without a bit of living?"

"Living's the *point*, Rob."

A snort. "You *are* an old auntie. Everyone dies."

"Fancy that, for 'tis killing me slowly, you are."

"Aw, you do love me." Robyn snorted, then winked up at him. "Happens you'll fancy a fuck wit' Sherwood's finest?"

"Happens I don't love you *that* much."

"If you two are finished slobbering ower each other?" Marion jerked her head towards the trouvère.

Alundel had finished his last stanza with a flourish and a smattering of approval, was calling for a drink. He stood, stretching; clearly this act was over, to the disappointment of more than a few. Then, with another look Robyn's way, Alundel slung his lute 'crost his back and started over.

The trouvère wasn't a total git; he took his time, visiting other tables and accepting praise—and coin. But that he was meandering their way left no doubt in Robyn's mind, and puzzlement and admiration were tussling for the win beneath Robyn's foremost thought: *What to do now?*

"Rob?" Marion's voice quivered tight, unsure.

There was no sign that Alundel was accompanied. None watched the trouvère's passage save with admiration or thanks, none spoke to him save in offer of that admiration. Even the clutch of soldiers—most of them gathered at the largest table, several others wandering the courtyard—gave no sign of alert, merely bestirring themselves for another drink and further applause.

And all the while, the trouvère advanced ever closer to their table.

"Robyn?" Will this time, with a tilt to his chin and a glint in his eyes. The others were also beginning to rouse, flustered. Of Gamelyn or Much there was still no sign.

Robyn had no true answers, within or without. It was one of those moments of fraying threads and unsung *tynged* waiting, and nothing to do but be *in* it. So Robyn took in a breath and propped his feet once again in Will's seat, one hand at the hilt of Gamelyn's quillion dagger and the other in a tight gesture that ended, flat, on the board in plain signal: *Wait.*

Then Robyn exhaled, took a pull at his drink, and followed his own orders.

Surely it didn't take as long as Robyn fancied, but by the time Alundel reached their table, it had been long enough that people were turning to their own pursuits. Prettily done—skilfully done, Robyn mused. Alundel paused, peering at Robyn as if to ensure guesses were indeed truth. Smiled.

He turned, bowed to Marion and ventured, "Good day, milady. How does a maid fair as the moon find herself companied by so . . . ah . . . notorious a fellow?"

Marion sought Robyn's gaze; under the table, his knee touched hers, warning and negation. In the next breath, her eyes lit with challenge and she turned to Alundel. More fierce pride filled Robyn as a smile curved his sister's lip—and bloody charming it was, too.

"You do me honour, messire trouvère, but I fear I am no lady. I'm yeoman-bred, here in pilgrimage t' Worksop Abbey with my kinsmen, in memory of a friend." Soft and formal—and careful, giving nothing away—Marion could well have been of any class in the shire. "Struth, I'd not thought to hear such fine music in this little village. Such things are for larger towns . . . Blyth, or Doncaster, for instance?"

Alundel nearly frowned—nearly. It quickly widened into a smile to match Marion's. "And now you do me honour." His eyes slid to Robyn, gauging. "Is this, then, your husband? Or"—he eyed Will—"mayhap this doughty, fair-haired fellow?"

"Nay, both brothers, but enough of me. Will you allow us to stand you and your excellent voice a drink?"

Not for the first time, Robyn wanted to hug his sister 'til her ribs cracked. She'd little timing as of yet, but she'd the instincts. No better place, after all, to keep the fellow nailed down than a seat at their table.

Alundel hesitated, then eyed the bench holding up Robyn's boots. "I will gladly take your offer if your sloe-eyed, um, brother will allow me a seat."

Robyn smirked, tilted his head with no little pretence at courtesy, then pulled his feet off the bench. "Be me guest."

Alundel tossed his hair back and swung his instrument into his lap, busied himself with the tuning pegs. It was an absent gesture; his attention stayed, wary, upon Robyn. "I've been your . . . guest before, I fear, so forgive me if I keep tight hold of my lute. And my purse."

"Mm." Robyn took a sip from his pot. "You seem so sure we've met. And that I'm . . . notorious, were it?"

Alundel plucked a string, grimaced, then set to tuning it. "Indeed, your reputation precedes you."

"You sing of a hooded knave," Marion posited. "Surely 'tis he—not my brother— who is this notorious one from your singin'?"

"Your brother wears a hood."

"As do many. It keeps away the damp, aye?"

"That it does." The trouvère gave Marion a broad smile—no hesitation, it seemed, at flirting with lasses as well as lads. That well-groomed length of flaxen hair might appeal to Marion, but it merely finished the picture of Alundel as a bit too fussy-pretty for Robyn's taste. He wasn't young, but neither was he old; no question but he'd like to have had an easy life, with that smooth, clean-shaven boy's face.

"Flattering," Marion acknowledged, "to sing of him as dangerous and charming both. 'Twould surprise me anyone would have courage t' dare sit with such a knave."

"Courage bows to necessity." Alundel ran quick and silent fingers down the neck of his lute, then leaned forwards, confiding, playing the game Marion was dealing. "This, ah, *brother* of yours, with his dark hood and his darker eyes . . . those eyes are quite the give-away, if I might say so. You don't often see such a hue west of the Levant or south of the wild Welsh hills. All the shades of night and gleaming like a desert cat's when he's intent on something."

Robyn snorted. "Aye, you're quite fancy wit' words. Seems t' me night is dark and me eyes are black. No more, no less."

A tilt of Alundel's fair head and a crooked smile. "Some speculate how black is the absence of colour, yet a night sky contains so *much*, eh?—should one bother to look . . . ah." Alundel sat back, crossed one leg beneath his lute. "Now those eyes have a metallic sheen to them. I'll warrant you've a knife to hand."

"I'll warrant he en't the only one," Will said, from his post by the wall. "I'd be taking some care, rilin' such a notorious man. Or his comp'ny. It might see you dragged back into the forest and strung up like mutton on the spit."

Alundel's diffident pose faded. "You daren't harm a musician. I could have soldiers upon you in a heartbeat."

"Go ahead, then." The mild, familiar voice came from the alcove behind Robyn's left shoulder.

Robyn hid a smile behind his drink as Gamelyn stepped from the shadows of the alcove near their table. Dipping his head in parody of a bow, Gamelyn straddled the near bench and lowered himself to sit beside Marion, flipping his cloak back to reveal the crimson cross upon his tabard. Much was, of course, behind him, crossing powerful arms, mute sentinel.

"We're waiting," Gamelyn prompted as Alundel kept staring, unspeaking, at the Templar sigil. "Call the guards."

If Alundel had been pale before, now all the colour had drained from his expression. "So," he whispered. "That tale, too, is true."

Every sense Robyn possessed went a-prickle at the words. He had to clench his fist to stay the dagger he'd half drawn; even more, needed the pain of metal jabbing his palm to banish insistent Sight, spiralling outward from the utterance.

And what came of it. Another voice wafted through his forelock, drifting ebon across Robyn's right eye. The Lady but a mere echo, a whisper he could sense but not fathom . . . and beside him, Marion gave a shiver—she heard. Heard it and seemed to understand, with another shiver and a quick, sucked-in breath. At the bench's end, Gamelyn had gone as rigid and impenetrable as any donjon wall—had he, too, heard? Mayhap understood?

Or mayhap Alundel's words drove the reaction, for in the next breath, Gamelyn tucked his chin, eyed the trouvère, and asked, deadly-soft, "What do you mean, 'it is true'?"

Will's hand descended to Robyn's shoulder, undecided upon the greater threat: Templar or trouvère.

Alundel bent over his lute once more, running noiseless fingerings up and down its neck. His words, when they came, were timed with the motions, subdued beneath the common room's roar. "The *garde de corps écarlate.* I should have guessed." He didn't look up, didn't see the slight, irritated flare of Gamelyn's nostrils. "But your true . . . calling . . . was quite obscured when last we met. I'd never have known you were the same man—save your voice." A mild strum, the lute responding like a woman singing a lullaby. "So controlled. Seeming so gentle, so woman-soft—but in truth neither—the telltale to give you away. And now"—his fingers ran faster, in a nervous, low trill—"the cross upon your breast, vastly more powerful than any rumour."

"Rumour." Gamelyn looked bored, tossed the hair from his forehead.

"I'd heard tales, you see. Spreading from Nottingham, drifting upon the wind like embers, to set every cot and village aflame. Tales of madness, of magic, of ghosts and demons to serve a pagan king . . . and *quean.*"

Gamelyn's nostrils gave another slight, offended flare—Robyn was likely the only one who saw it, and wasn't sure he understood; merely an old inflection, giving proper due to the goddess of the ancient temples. Though, aye, proper odd a noble should know it. Singer or nowt.

Mayhap Alundel had, after all, seen the signs of Templar pique. He continued, somewhat hastily, "Trifles of superstition, some might say. Tales of derring-do and fancy. So many . . . whilst those many seem little more than poetic nonsense."

"Fancy you objecting t' that" was Robyn's dry comment.

"No doubt gossip makes a good tale," Marion put in. Her expression was daunting as well, but she was nervous, the soft, common drawl of their birth creeping back into the speech she'd kept so carefully formal. "But surely a learned man as y'rself wain't put stock in such?"

Robyn put a hand on her thigh and gave a pat and caress, slight but soothing.

Alundel's smile was genuine, albeit wary; the soft fingerings upon his lute hesitant. "Your pardon, maiden, rumours are grist to my song-mill."

Nor did Robyn like how Alundel called her "maiden." It held no respect, yet hinted at more knowledge than any singer of the White Christ was like to have by honest means.

"But this? This rumour, set in scarlet, is as particular and peculiar as what others surround a maiden's black-eyed, ah, *brother*."

Robyn also didn't like the inflection beneath that.

Gamelyn showed adequate contempt: a slight yawn, then the blasé comment, "You're becoming tiresome as a street-side jongleur."

Aye, well, and didn't *that* crawl up Alundel's well-dressed pipe. A discordant *twang* escaped his lute.

"And"—Gamelyn leaned forwards, his voice dipping into the threat—"unless you leave off all this nonsense, I'll make you sing, all right. Like a neutered boy from . . . the Levant, was it?"

The fingerings stopped, and Alundel's gaze flicked nervously at Gamelyn, wide and very blue indeed beneath that well-groomed fringe of flax. Still, he didn't back down. It was another inexplicable reaction amidst a host of them; they swarmed Robyn's brain like angry bees.

The fingers once again began their nigh-silent dance. "Singing is my trade, *Chevalier*," said the trouvère who was altogether too savvy to be a simple trouvère. "And my delight. Mayhap you will first do the honour of sharing something with me? How has it come to pass a Knight Templar should owe fealty to a pagan peasant?"

"Templars owe no fealty but to their oaths and their Master," was Gamelyn's riposte. "Mayhap you'd do better to tell me how a trouvère with the birth-tongue of Picard has the ear of an English Queen Mother."

"Ah, but did not this selfsame Queen Mother once hold the finest court of all in the country of *her* birth? The Aquitaine is truly a rare and perfect rose amongst the flowers of grace and style."

"Noble ideals blossom outside the pretences of civilisation—just as base things are oft dreamed in the hearts of courtly men."

Will gave a sigh, small but telling: *Why are we lettin' these two poncy bastards run this chat, anyway?*

Ah, but it takes poncy to know poncy, sweet William. Robyn stayed silent, watching the verbal sparring match like Tess crouched at a warren.

"And so," Alundel was saying, "you would bring back the rites of Saturn, where facile peasants dethrone their betters and crown themselves with wreaths coarse-woven."

Gamelyn's eyes glittered and his lips curved to reveal a gleam of teeth; Robyn knew it more snarl than any smile. "*Honi soit qui mal y pense.*" The lute let out a cacophonous groan.

And the words laved a tongue of black at Robyn's nape: the blood-thick, darkling shiver of an oath, or curse. He'd no idea what Gamelyn had just said—didn't need to know, as threat further parcelled and wrapped itself within the soft, furious waver of Gamelyn's voice.

Robyn glanced about; none else had so much as twitched. He was the only one who'd sensed the power running beneath the phrase—and also sensed, plainer than plain, he'd best interrupt. Or this verbal bout might end up with a spitted trouvère and more trouble than they could manage.

A shame, truly—he was having a fine time watching.

Reaching past Marion, with a hand still concealed beneath the table board, Robyn laid that hand on Gamelyn's thigh. A tiny jerk of disbelief met his fingertips; green eyes slid his way, bewildered, tension broken. Robyn smiled, and there was no question the expression twisted to a snarl as he leaned in, addressed Alundel.

"You en't called the guards yet, *milord*. Likely you'll need 'em, should you keep on thinking you can kick and kiss me both and I wain't do owt."

Alundel tensed, and Robyn wondered for a moment if the man was cheeky enough to call this bluff as well. Gamelyn seemed to think no guard would interfere if a Templar was involved—but then, he'd been wrong before on *that* count.

Instead Alundel slumped, as if all the air had left him. "I cannot. I don't know whose side they're on, and from what I've gathered so far?" He hesitated. "Many are of certain . . . factions."

"Factions?" Will asked. Neither hand had left Robyn's shoulder or the hilt of his broad skinning knife.

Robyn had already seen the tabards; seen and recognised them from his own experience. Yet he knew the limitations of that experience, knew who amongst their party wasn't burdened with the same. Robyn slid Will a quick and silent chide—*keep quiet.* With a soft, grumbling sigh, Will obeyed.

"Nottingham and Worksop both are in flux now." It was Marion who spoke, muted. "Who knows who will rule those?"

Alundel looked . . . confused? Surprised? As if he'd not expected a woman to know such things—likely, Robyn scoffed to himself, particularly if he was of the Church. Women and peasants, like dogs in their eyes, nowt more.

Meanwhile Robyn's fingers, responding to his ire, had begun to burrow into Gamelyn's thigh muscle. Said muscle was still iron-hard from years of riding and combat, but inactivity had taken its toll, and Robyn's fingers were just as powerful in their own fashion. Gamelyn gave a nigh-imperceptible wince, then reached down with negligent fingers, tapped at Robyn's in clear admonition: *Let go.*

Meanwhile, Marion was clearly enjoying Alundel's discomfiture. "The question is," she ventured, "who owns *your* loyalty, messire trouvère? And why you believe we should trust it?"

"I see more of Nottingham's colours a-wander here," Gamelyn put in, steepling both hands before him, "than any of Blyth. There are reports, of course, that Nottingham's sheriff has been replaced with mere castellans, and therefore his soldiers are more at liberty of late. But I know for a fact the soldiers of Blyth used to often journey here for leisure. Those would, as a matter of course, include Pontefract who is now Blyth's overlord. Which could mean several things, not *all* of them foul." His green eyes narrowed. "Instead, I find myself with one abiding query. Why would a trouvère, an honoured and noble talent with free access to the highest halls in our kingdom, hesitate to trust royal soldiers?"

Robyn had been the recipient of the implacable gaze more than once. He didn't envy Alundel—well, mayhap he did, though the reasons for it were entirely different.

"That word. *Royal.* It can mean so *many* things." Alundel was still gazing down at his lute, his fingertips brushing the strings, pulling soft, broken murmurs from it as if the instrument were tuned to the shifting of his thoughts. "A king's ransom, an ambitious count, a queen's loyalty to sons or crown. Dilemmas fall from the sky."

"Only a dilemma if you're amidst it," Marion pointed out. "Are you?"

Alundel peered at her, his regard no longer surprised, only sombre. Seeming to come to some decision, he put a deliberate hand to his breast, reached inside his tunic. Everyone stiffened. Alundel regarded their caution with his own hesitation, then slowly withdrew his fist, closed over an object too small to be any serious threat. He extended the fist across the board towards Gamelyn, though his attention seemed thoroughly upon Robyn.

"I but suspected you and yours might be hope of help to me. Now I'm sure of it."

"Suspected," Robyn repeated, flat.

Gamelyn frowned, curious, tilted his head, then slowly reached out. Alundel covered the outstretched hand with his own; Gamelyn's eyebrows rose as he saw then accepted whatever it was.

"It is no rumour, is it?" Alundel didn't take his eyes from Robyn's. "That a Templar saved a renegade novice nun from being burnt at Nottingham Castle." He inclined his head to Marion but still spoke to Robyn. "It is no rumour, is it, that a hooded archer did not in truth behead the bounty hunter Guy de Gisbourne, but saved him from a witch's pyre and sent a legendary Hunt of Wild madness across the ground of his enemy, the Sheriff of Nottingham. And it is not rumour, then, that the bounty hunter Robyn Hood saved was that Templar, also once youngest son to Sir Ian Boundys, mesne lord of the honour of Tickhill and the castle known as Blyth. Or that this Templar's paxman and, indeed, at least one of Robyn Hood's own men, were villeins to that castle."

Robyn gave no answer, slid his gaze to take in Gamelyn who had closed his eyes—and also his fingers—upon what had been transferred to his palm. Robyn tensed; behind him, Will did likewise. Across the courtyard, John was fairly vibrating and, closer, Gilbert stood ready, watching.

But in the next moment, Gamelyn opened his eyes, met Robyn's. Within them lay an extraordinary gleam of . . . well, Robyn would say it was the same Gamelyn-type ingenuous wonder Robyn had taken such intense delight in years ago, had he not imagined the power of that expression long perished from his lover's gaze.

Beneath cover of the table, Gamelyn put his hand in Marion's lap, uncurled his fingers. Marion looked down, gasped.

It was a ring, a bloody big one, with an intricate seal. The carving upon it gave Robyn a strange chill-thrill up and down his spine—there was deadly power in the flamboyant bit of gold with a goddess's visage—or near as like—crowned and draped in Norman finery, surrounded by tiny marks. The way Gamelyn held it, as if it might bite him—aye, Gamelyn felt its power, and Marion as well; her fingers were trembling as they reached for Gamelyn's.

Somehow Robyn didn't think Alundel was offering them this pretty and deadly bit of jewellery. This would buy and sell the Shire Wode, more like.

"Eleanor," Marion translated, barely above a whisper, "by the Grace of God Queen of the English, Duchess of the Normans."

Gamelyn still held Robyn's gaze with his own. He said, very low, "It's real."

Not that Robyn doubted that for a moment. He slid his narrowed glance back to Alundel and said, hoarse, "What do you want, singer?"

This time, Alundel spoke to Gamelyn. "'Tis said at Nottingham, beneath trial by battle, you proclaimed your name and birthright, and further claimed both were taken from you false." Only then did Alundel meet Gamelyn with gaze and words to hold there, intent.

"Well, my disseised lord of Blyth. Would you like that honour back?"

- ENTR'ACTE -

S he could hardly believe her eyes.

It was over two months ago, now, the world had changed. When word had come roaming and truth had come a-horse: Abbess Elisabeth dead, felled by a peacock-fletched ebon arrow. Nottingham cursed. Templars riding into the aftermath like furies of Hell, and the Shire Wode swallowing decent people whole, spitting them back out with nightmares to haunt the damned.

The Wild Hunt, called by a witch-spawn wolfshead known as Robyn Hode.

She knew the breed well. Had been one of them. Had worshipped their demon and drunk of their rites like poisoned mead. Yet even now she could scarce believe what she saw, sitting at a table in one ill-lit corner, drinking and eating, listening with no little interest to the minstrel's cunning tales.

So homely quiet, as if the scum belonged here, at the inn serving her mistress's abbey of Worksop. Unremarkable, almost.

Deirdre, however, was marking them well.

Abbess Elisabeth's brothers had disagreed upon who had killed her. Deirdre had heard them, a quiet yet vehement conversation after her mistress had been blessed and interred in the walls of Worksop Abbey.

Never truly know, the baron of Pontefract had reasoned; *let it go, Brian. That cursed outlaw*, Nottingham's sheriff had insisted, *has dogged me from the start. He had her killed and has been the ruin of me. He will pay, I'll see to it. Somehow.*

They were both wrong. They didn't know who had killed Abbess Elisabeth.

But Deirdre knew, now, who had done. The murderess sat there, brazen and undeniable clue as to the identity of the man seated next to her—and if she had the devil's hair, then the hooded outlaw had Lucifer's own eyes, flat and dark with no hint of light. They sat just that much too close, smiling and intimate—*free*—reeking with power gained from the blood of a devout woman.

Deirdre slipped from the small cluster of nuns gathered to listen to the minstrel, moved silent and furious to where the enemy sat, next to her demon consort.

When the red-haired girl had first come to the abbey, her demons purged by fire and her soul cleansed by a miracle, Deirdre had been chary. Morning and night, Deirdre had watched the girl, and felt the corruption caged beneath the sweet, blank face. Deirdre had warned her Abbess: the girl was curst twice over, born of a Welsh witch-priestess and a devil—and, therefore, inheritor to a pagan goddess's power.

But her Abbess had scorned such fears.

No doubt Abbess Elisabeth had been a very holy woman—one to emulate and adore—but one also blinded by a tender-hearted pity for what she saw as an innocent soul in jeopardy. And she had succumbed to something even more heady: the belief that pious and gracious weapons alone could defeat such bone-deep evil.

But Deirdre knew the power of evil, knew its temptations. Had herself felt the power of it: sharp-sweet ichor coursing through her veins, the wanton, mad abandon of the Dance. She had recognised the evil clothed in the novice's lovely face and body; had more than once wished she could slip poison into the draughts meant to give only sleep, summon death to still that breast.

If only she could do so now.

But nay, now she could only give notice. And wait.

You. I will poison everything you love, and turn it to hate. I will take it from you, as you took my Abbess from me.

At the table, Marion gave a start, looked up.

Deirdre met the clear grey eyes, smiled and nodded, then passed by the table, unspeaking.

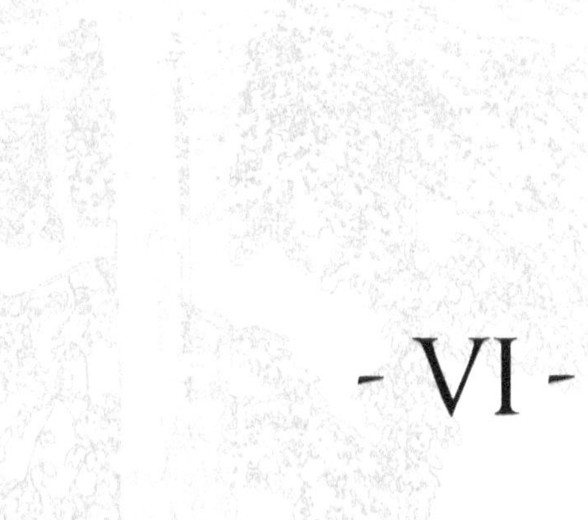

- VI -

Do you know the south transept of the abbey? Then come there, just after Vespers. I will stay and pray alone; none will question others who do as well. There I can explain more, beyond the reach of expectant audiences and prying ears.

Gamelyn sat at the table, rubbing his fingers together. He could still feel the weight of the seal in his palm, the undeniable power of it, like a benediction, or a curse . . .

" . . . curse?" A firm nudge into his shoulder—and it merely spoke to Gamelyn's chancy mental state, how Robyn had exchanged places with Marion without Gamelyn so much as noticing.

Odder still—or perhaps not, knowing Robyn—how Robyn should speak to his thoughts. Gamelyn angled a curious glance, found the dark eyes just as curious upon him.

"Well, what?"

Gamelyn frowned, peered at his fingertips. He would swear they vibrated with some faint . . . something. "What?"

"You cursed him. Or near like as . . . bugger me sideways, did y' truly feel nowt?"

"Feel nothing?" Gamelyn took in a long breath, glanced at Robyn. "It's what I'm good at, after all."

Ah, that was more like it—a spark of annoyance diverting Robyn's expression. Gamelyn wasn't altogether sure he wanted to drag this . . . this whatever-it-was out before Marion, and Much, and—particularly—Scathelock to frown at or paw over.

"Woolly-headed ass," Robyn accused, then leaned closer and

murmured, "I en't about to let you swear in Frankish without asking what you've charged . . . particularly when you set the otherworlds to vibrating with it."

"Other worlds?" Gamelyn was still muzzily contemplating that signet ring and what it had meant. "What are you talking about?"

Robyn's brows were pinched tight, dead giveaway to his growing irritation. "I'll bide still when you're all arsy at likely mutterin' some soppy Frank love-talk t' me, but this?" Not only twisty brows, but those eyes beneath; they would be better suited beside an arrow's nock. Robyn was getting more brassed off by the moment. "Winter's tide en't yet faded, my lovely Oak, and you en't in proper control of Summer's reign. I'll peel the bark from you in strips before you'll set, all careless-like, sommat *that* powerful a-fly."

Ferocity, challenge accepted and tossed back, with the spark and quiver of longing set . . . then flame doused, abruptly, by a fleeting sensation of hot breath and stabbing tines, a whirl and eddy of elemental rage. It flung Gamelyn back a few days' time, to the bank of Barrow Mere, and how the Horned Lord had forced Gamelyn to his knees in a mortifying mix of denial/desire/defiance . . .

Strangely enough, both brought reality back, cool water in desert heat.

And *God*, but Robyn's furious whisper sounded so akin to accusations with which Hubert had struck him. It wasn't the first or only time Gamelyn had touched his own . . . whatever-it-was, by rare chance and little else, hurling up something from depths he was unable to plumb save in mere blind instinct.

Control it! Are you a Templar, or a puling child?

Even the memory was a two-edged dagger—the one avenue of failure, yet also the sole disobedience left to him.

Robyn seemed to be coming to his own realisations at the same time; wrath was fading, fierce glower becoming replaced by a quizzical quirk of brow. "Marion's right, by damn."

Keeping up with the Thief of Sherwood's twists and turns of thought was beyond Gamelyn at the moment. Nevertheless, he peered to the table's end where Marion was sharing a second loaf of bread as well as good-natured bickering with Scathelock— situation normal there, so what was Robyn on about now?

Gamelyn turned his focus to what he believed had started all of this: the oath he had growled at Alundel. Nay, not only oath, but curse. Reminder. Promise.

Honi soit qui mal y pense.

"'Evil to he who evil thinks.' That's what it means. Roughly."

"And the other?" There was a tease in the low baritone, now. "Those sweet whispers from our last tup?"

Gamelyn gave a barely audible snort. "I think not."

Robyn's smile widened, a flash in the dim, then faded. He went silent, kept peering at Gamelyn.

Gamelyn made his own verbal counter. "What is Marion right about?"

A shrug of long-broad shoulders, shifting Robyn's dark hood in a slight, sideways tilt. "More'n I'd fancy counting."

Over in the sunniest part of the courtyard, Alundel was tuning again. Both Much and John, albeit apart, were amongst the listeners. Alundel had to be aware of at least Much's presence, dauntingly close and observant, yet he laughed and hummed, indulged in both song and banter with his audience as if he hadn't just made a precarious bargain with renegades.

"We are, you know," Gamelyn said, watching the trouvère.

"We are what?" Robyn's question was soft. Patient.

"Renegades. Thieves, nuns, monks—"

"Aye. Yet he says a queen would bargain with outlaws. With *you*, renegade monk."

It surpassed understanding that Gamelyn should so hate it when Robyn called him what he was. Even if he wasn't a very good monk. "Many argue we aren't. Monks. We fight. We kill. We don't close ourselves up in our cloisters and hide from the world."

"Sure of that last, are you, pet?"

Gamelyn rubbed his fingers together, said nothing.

"And you want it, don't you?"

It was even softer, even closer; a breath upon his shoulder and a long-fingered hand surreptitiously curving beneath his knee. The intimacy was jarring, displacing Gamelyn for precious moments into wondering exactly what Robyn was asking, and why *here*.

Then Gamelyn heard what quivered beneath the breath, sweat-soaked and just short of desperate. No illicit magics here, no extraordinary senses he himself half feared and Robyn wore, unashamed, as slicked upon his being as skin and breath.

Nay, this desperation—this *fear*—Gamelyn thoroughly, wretchedly understood. He opened his mouth to speak . . .

Robyn started, the shudder and crouch of a deer caught by wolves in a meadow. Gamelyn's own instincts flared even as Robyn's took hold; one hand went to his sword as he swept the room. Saw.

Soldiers. A goodly handful of them—ten, twelve—advancing from the entry. A few abbey paxmen, but most were wearing the tabards of Nottingham and the sheriff's guard.

"Bloody hell," Scathelock swore beneath his breath, and for once, Gamelyn was in complete agreement with him.

Robyn had gone from crouch to a coil not unlike a drawn

trebuchet; one hand to his dagger, the other reaching for Marion. Not many had noticed the soldiers' intent, too caught up in the entertainment. Alundel saw what was happening; he looked a hart poised to flee. Much, John, and Gilbert had disappeared into the crowd. No doubt they'd reappear exactly when they were needed.

"The damned minstrel's done us," Will muttered.

"Nay," Robyn said, low. "But we're nicked, one way or t' other. Mari, are y—?"

"Don't nag, little brother."

A smile ticced Gamelyn's lip at this, smoothed away as Robyn started to rise. Gamelyn's own hand shot out, grabbed the back of Robyn's tunic, and held him in his seat.

"Gam—"

He held Robyn's gaze for a moment, making sure. Robyn's nod was all but imperceptible. Gamelyn released him and stood, flinging his cloak back over one shoulder, exposing the blood cross upon his chest.

"Arrogant tosser," Scathelock grumbled, with a glance that begged scorn but instead expressed pained appreciation.

The innkeeper had gathered his wife and one of the lads behind the bar; they stared, all dubious, after the backs of the soldiers. Alundel's music twanged to a halt. Any number of shocked and excited mutters filled the place.

Just as Gamelyn expected, the abbey paxmen halted as they had a good look at their adversary's telltale garb. But Nottingham's men kept coming. Seven . . . nay, eight of them. Swaggering, stiff as fighting cocks.

Fools.

Gamelyn met their advance with a deceptively mild "Is there a problem?"

The leader of the small group wore the markings of a guard captain. How he'd achieved that was questionable; Gamelyn recognised the type all too well. Capable enough in his own tiny sphere—where a bully's tactics were easily swallowed by already-cowed serfs—but flat useless in any true campaign or pitched battle. Save, mayhap, as arrow fodder.

Gamelyn couldn't help the tiny quirk playing at his lip.

The leader advanced well within easy reach—first mistake—rolled his full weight onto one hip—a second one—then tapped the flat of his sword against his free palm—a blustering, idiotic third and fourth mistake, possibly fatal. Gamelyn could have the daft bastard's head before he could so much as offer defence.

"This en't your fight, Templar," the leader sneered. "Out of our way."

"If you mean to harass my companions," Gamelyn ventured, "there won't *be* any fight."

Several more of the guards looked uncertain, but the leader was more bluster than sense. "Mayhap you en't understan—"

"It seems to me you're the one lacking understanding."

"I've word these are outlaw scum. The Crown will pay well for a bunch of murderers and thieves."

The Crown. No mention of Nottingham, who would indeed pay handsomely for Robyn's head.

"Your information is faulty," Gamelyn replied, soft. "These people are with me. You have absolutely no authority over me or mine. Unless"—Gamelyn put his hand on his sword hilt—"you think to countermand Church rule and take upon yourself the power of the Holy Father?"

The tavern had gone deathly silent—so much that from behind Gamelyn, Robyn's soft snort was quite audible.

Shut up, Hob-Robyn. "Are you so welcoming of Hell, then?" Gamelyn persisted.

A murmur passed itself around the tavern. Most of the impromptu posse crossed themselves. Several more lost heart and melted into the tavern's crowd. The leader snarled at them, to no avail. His cohort had winnowed down to two: one a beefy fellow with a squint, the other towering and glowering.

Well, at least the odds were improving.

"Your like don't heed any Church *but* Hell!" the leader snapped.

Ah. This one was bringing his own baggage to the fight. Fifth mistake. Definitely fatal.

"Aw, fuck me but if I en't heard enough of this!" Agile as any cat, Robyn leapt onto the table board and began pacing down its length—within striking distance, Gamelyn noted with a quiver of trepidation. Immediately his brain kicked in, gave lightning-swift consideration to all possible scenarios and outcomes.

Another murmur around the tavern, just as anxious and pervasive as the one Gamelyn himself had inspired—but there was something else, too. Rising and rounding the walls, settling in with a mix of fear and awe as the lean, hooded figure stepped slow—oh, so slow— to the edge of the table and put his booted toes there.

Will half sat, half crouched on the table's other end, hand on knife.

From within Robyn's cowl the words came, sweet and sibilant. "You en't afeared of your hell, then? Neither am I. Happens I've been there, and brought it back with me." And in the silence, the murmur became a hiss, and the hiss became a name: *Robyn. Robyn Hood.*

"It's him, I tell ye."

"Robyn Hood—"

"It's *him!*"

A smile flashed in the dark hood, but Robyn's gaze didn't leave the guards. They were, slowly but surely, inching back, their faces slack and ashen. Clearly they remembered what had happened in the autumn, how Count John had thought to burn a Templar and the Sheriff had meant to hang a wolfshead. Aye, they remembered what had happened after: an endless, hag-ridden night of Hell.

"Take me, then." It was a purr. "Take me and me merry lot of outlaws to your little gaol. See how long it holds us." Robyn leaned forwards even more, perilously over the edge, and for the first in a long time, Gamelyn prayed: *Don't fall.*

Because ghosts and ha'nts and wild Green Men didn't trip and mop a grubby tavern floor with their faces. That was for mortal men.

"See how long you'll sleep sound in your own cots," Robyn continued, looking down at them with black eyes gleaming, "when the Hunt comes a-lookin', all Wild."

And more than just the remaining guards crossed themselves. The spellbound impulse even claimed Gamelyn, albeit brief; he did flinch as a hand slid against the back of his thigh. It was Marion. She had crept closer, silent and quick as a mouse. Her free hand, splayed flat against the table, slid forwards. A moonsilver bow was shimmering beneath her lowered lashes. Waiting.

Swords and twisted symbols are not the only way to stand down an enemy, the Lady whispered, then was gone.

The leader of the guards abruptly snarled defiance and put hand to sword. Gamelyn tensed.

Robyn dropped to a crouch. It was so sudden, all the whispers choked into silence. The guards, to a man, gave an involuntary stagger back. And Robyn, still *smiling,* all but daring them to come for him.

"Or you'll be *witness*"—the hiss of it echoed into the silence and curled about the tavern walls, a singsong power sending Alundel's rhymes to shame—"when the Lord of the Shire Wode decides to take what's his . . . and mayhap you as well." He looked a crouching predator, leaning out even farther—though it should have hardly been possible.

The guards dragged backwards another slow and fearful step.

"Aye. *You as well,* partial teind for all the taking, the breaking. For every rope you've shackled to your own, you'll reckon. For every penny you've beaten from my people, for every soul you starved by bein' what you are." Robyn drew clenched fists before his face. Sucked in a soft, growling breath.

It was answered by another growl—this from the crowd. The leader of the guards stood frozen; he seemed only then to take notice of what Gamelyn had all along sensed:

The taverngoers, shifting from scared to angry, closing in. Silent menace—and not towards any wolfsheads or Templars.

Careful, deliberate, the leader took his hand from his sword hilt. His two compatriots had visibly deflated.

"Nay?" Robyn let his hands drift down and cocked his head, seemed to be gauging them. "Mayhap I should turn you into toads and feed you to a ferret? Or just let those you've bullied give you what you deserve?"

The guards' retreat was stepping itself up. Quailing, not only beneath Robyn's eyes, but the menace of the people with him.

Marion, her eyes once more the normal grey of a stormy sky, pulled her hands into her lap and slid Gamelyn a tiny quirk of lip. He couldn't help but answer it with his own.

"*Go!*" Robyn thundered, and like puppets with their strings yanked, the guards fled.

"You're too big for your boots, you are."

"I'd think me boots are big enough, Scathelock!" Robyn was grinning as he linked arms with Will, swung around, then loosed him. He then grabbed Gamelyn's arm and pulled him the rest of the way into their impromptu camp.

Gamelyn was grinning as well. "Daft sod. Though you nigh put the Old Man of Alamut to shame, the way you make a crowd into a mob."

"I'm hoping that's a compliment?" Robyn tossed back, but the gleam in his eyes suggested he knew, and he leaned in, kissed Gamelyn on the mouth.

Will scowled just before he turned away—well, sod that, Robyn wasn't about to rein in his own glee because Charming William disapproved. Much, on the other hand, seemed pleased, particularly as Gamelyn suddenly chuckled and kissed Robyn back. Of course, the sun was still shining, not even a hint of clouds and just now midday.

John and Gilbert also were cheery, though John threw Will a look—warning as well as concern. He and Gilbert had been waiting for them, having slipped away once it had been obvious the potential fight would be turned into a bloodless rout of their enemies. They'd had time to start a fire worth cooking on, with a pottage started and awaiting Marion's special touch.

Yet Marion seemed . . . odd. Of course, Robyn had felt her at his back, like a waiting, deep well, and it had nearly upskelled him there and then, the knowledge she'd been *with him*, mind and heart and lovely power, in ways he'd never before grasped.

But this—it wasn't the lax nerves of *tynged* strung too tight then loosed. It was something different.

Well, it had been her first real set-to. Not that his sister'd ever backed down from a fight if it had to be fought, but this was different. Too akin to war, and the first taste of a blood spatter upon the lips.

But still, Marion seemed steady enough. She gave her own kisses, first to Gilbert's, then to John's cheek in thanks, and started to ponder the pottage.

Which was just short of all right. He was famished.

"I just wish I knew who." Will was shucking the fur over his shoulders into a comfortable seat.

"Who?" Gilbert tossed him another fur, then passed several more all 'round.

"Who nicked us at that tavern," Will answered. "Someone had to've."

"But just outlaws," Gilbert agreed. "They didn't know who, it seems."

"They knew soon enough." Robyn grinned and nudged Gamelyn.

"You will be too big for those sizeable boots," Gamelyn murmured against his hair. Aye, nothing like a row to mellow a fellow.

"You know what they say," Robyn murmured right back. "Big feet, big . . . ?"

Gamelyn snorted.

"I think I know," Marion said, from beside the hearth. "I think I'm t' one as nicked us."

Well, the uproar had been less than she'd thought it might have been, at that.

"I *am* sorry," Marion repeated. "I should've let you know the moment I saw her. But I didn't think owt of—"

"Owt or nowt, pet, there's no doubt but that bloody nun's the one as set those dogs on us," Robyn said. "And now you're more the liability."

"Which *you* knew was possible from the moment we decided I should come!" Marion retorted. "You said it yourself, little brother: my knowledge of Worksop outweighed any risk. And still does if we are indeed going onto abbey grounds."

Robyn growled a curse and looked down. Marion took in a quick, relieved breath and bent over the small kettle where she'd begun stewing a pottage from the venison, carrots, and swede they'd brought along. Robyn's nostrils twitched and he tried—unsuccessfully—to hide his interest as she keeled a wide spoon through the pottage and let the smells waft over their makeshift camp.

Aye, better to sweeten bad news with the promise of a proper meal, their mam had always said—and like with so many things, Eluned had been right.

"You weren't exactly keeping it mum, Robyn." Will came to her defence with a smirk. "Threatening to hex those soldiers."

John grinned, pulled a straight face as Robyn eyed him.

"But now we know the people of Worksop love us!" Gilbert put in, triumphant, then mugged a pout. "And we missed it, John."

"Leastways this time y' weren't having to hand over damages, Gilly!" Will leaned over the fire, jiggling at the small kettle.

Marion smacked his hand. "Have patience, you greedy sod!"

"Oh, whats'mever, I'm with Will." Robyn flashed a grin and gave his own peek into the pot. "A good row makes me hungry, y'know."

"We can have another, mind." Marion warned him off with the upraised spoon. "Row, that is."

Robyn held up his hands, mock surrender, and lowered himself on a fur next to John. Asked, all innocence, "How 'bout a bit of cheese?"

Will chuckled, reached over, and snagged a linen pocket from their bags. "He'll faint away, he will," he protested at Marion's look, and pitched the pocket at Robyn.

Robyn caught it midair and dove in. As he chewed, he told Will, "I love you, you know."

"I know. Belt up—you're spraying curds everywhere."

A deep, sonorous clang and hum from the village: chapel bells. Robyn winced, tilting his head and rubbing at his chest—it was that close and piercing. John didn't seem best pleased either with the racket; he leaned against Robyn, fingers in his ears.

Marion hesitated in her motions; Gamelyn and Much did the same, and the three of them said, about the same time, "Sext."

"I'm allus up for being sexed," Robyn suggested, purposeful misunderstanding.

Marion threw the spoon at him; Robyn yipped and ducked. "It means noontide," Gilbert said. "Aye?"

Much chuckled. "I'm a decent Heathen and I know that much."

"One of the things I gladly put behind me was the Church," Gilbert defended, grinning. "All that eternal kneeling. There are much better things to do on one's knees."

"See?" Robyn offered. "Sexed."

"Would you give *over*, already?" Will groaned.

"Fetch the spoon, and this time you've me blessings in breaking it over his curly, pointy head," Marion suggested.

Robyn stuck out his tongue at her. Unfortunately, there were still bits of cheese curd stuck to it, so the effect was not what he'd surely intended.

Gamelyn had a hand over his face—groan or giggle, Marion wasn't sure.

"Anyway," Gilbert furthered, "don't you think it's absurdly self-centred to imagine some all-powerful god would heed one person's beggings above all the others?"

Gilbert might act cavalier, but then he'd pop up with something like that. Marion smiled. "Sext is midday prayer—*do not* say it!" she warned Robyn as his eyes lit up again.

"I'd say it's allus a prayer."

Had Much just really said that? Marion rounded on him, mouth agape. Much merely peered back at her, all *who, me?* innocence.

Men.

"Nice to have such expertise in our ranks." Gilbert included Much and Gamelyn with his smile.

"Know thine enemy?" Gamelyn offered, wry.

"Some knowledge is too close fr comfort." Will poked at the fire with a stick.

"I think we can all agree on that," Gamelyn said, flawlessly polite. "Marion?"

"Aye?"

"Shall supper be awhile yet?"

She nodded, retrieved her spoon, and tapped her brother's cheek with it as she returned to the hearth. She passed Much, already gathering weaponry, his eyes lighting at the prospects unfolding. Marion hid a smirk in her sleeve.

Boys.

Gamelyn slid his gaze to Robyn, questioning.

"Aye." Robyn was nodding, following the unspoken query. "You and Much should have a shufti at t' bloody church. See what we're up against—*what?*" This as Gamelyn kept peering at him, query turning to an exasperated frown.

"I've the same question," Gamelyn replied. "What did you just say? Have a *what?*"

Robyn waved a hand in the direction of Worksop. "You say it all the time. Wit' your desert talk, when you're about having a look at sommat."

Much's lip twitched—so quickly Marion almost didn't see it. As if to hide it, he bent over, took up Gamelyn's sword, slid it from its sheath for a quick inspection, then resheathed and tossed it over. The gesture was accompanied by a soft spate of Arabic.

And likely an explanation, for Gamelyn's lip also twitched as he snatched his sword midair, not once taking his eyes from Robyn. Said, mild, "It's *šufti.*"

"Whats'mever."

Marion didn't bother to hide her grin this time. "Was I having a . . . um . . . look about? I'd suggest a try at the east walls first"—a sniff of the pottage—"and the nave entry."

From exasperated eye roll to all business; Gamelyn nodded, snugged his sword belt about his hips, and jerked his head at Much.

"Take care, aye?" Robyn added. "No more growlin' at guards."

"Pot," said Gamelyn, "meet kettle."

And just like that, he and Much were gone into the trees.

"Damn," Gilbert watched after, "but they're proper trained. They could teach us a bit."

Will snorted. "Hardly. 'Lessen it's foreign ways as have no place here."

"Pin your lip," Marion said, curt, "else one of us'll trip over it, it's flapping so bloody loose. And you, little brother. Don't spoil your dinner with all that cheese."

"Aye, Mam." Robyn grinned. "But when do I ever refuse your pottage?"

Marion grinned back—had to, realising she was indeed acting like their mother. Met her brother's black eyes—those also so like Eluned's—and thought again how much she missed her mam. Always would, and no help for it, but Robyn knew just how she felt, and he was here, after all.

True enough, Robyn threw her a kiss and tossed the bag of curds back to Will. "Twill be dark soon enough, and time to go in."

"The bells will announce Vespers." Marion took another taste of the pottage, poured in a libation of ale, then began tearing up some wild garlic.

"How long after, you think?"

"They'll close up when they're done, since the light goes so soon now."

"Aye, then." Will tucked the cheese away and leaned forwards, eager. "What's our plan? I'll make sure—"

"You'll make sure we've backup in case we need it."

"Backup?" Aghast. "Rob, you en't seri—"

"I am. *You* en't going, and neither are John or Gilly."

"*Rob—*"

"That's me final word on it, Will. I'm taking Marion because she knows the place sideways, Much is going because I know he wain't hesitate to protect Gamelyn, and the reason I'm taking Gamelyn should be obvious if you arsed yr'self t' pay attention."

"Obvious you're thinking with your knob. *Again.* Goin' in with nowt but that bloody Tem—*ow!*" This as John reached over and thumped Will in the back of the head with a knife pommel. Hard. "Sod you, John, that *hurt!*"

John merely raised an eyebrow. *Nay, really?* it said, plainer than plain.

Marion stayed out of it, though she wouldn't have minded a few licks in. But that was Will—just as you wanted to snog him silly, he made you want to smack him.

"Right, then." Robyn lurched into a crouch. "Both John 'n' me've been looking for an excuse to pop you one for a while, now. Shall I have my turn, then?"

Will growled a low curse. "You're too fond of trouble. You should at least leave Marion behind, *outta* trouble!"

All right, then, that did it. Marion started round, spoon raised.

Will leapt to his feet, scooted out of reach.

"Or happens"—almost lazily, as Robyn once again lowered himself beside John—"I should just save me strength and let Marion take your ears. Too bad she canna take your mouth with 'em."

Noiseless and swift as shadows, Marion led Robyn, Gamelyn, and Much through the walled labyrinth of nighttime Worksop. The moon had already climbed halfway across the sky, three-quartered against the clear night with stars flanking—their only illumination. The domiciles were mostly dark, the occupants bedded down with nightfall, either unwilling or unable to indulge the cost of lamp or candle. The abbey itself was lit more generously; a fitful flicker and spatter against the narrow window ledges.Even in starlight, even for eyes used to green Wode darkness, it comprised a chancy path; a winter day's-worth of sun wasn't enough to dry out the puddles of the previous week's rain or the slick of mud beneath a layer of firmer soil. And, of course, another sensory challenge to woodland dwellers: the sharp reek of body waste and wood-rot and stagnant water, the constant and furtive motion of other strays traversing the dim streets—those, mostly four-legged.

Unable to help a shudder and hop sideways as a rat came close to her skirts, Marion gave herself a muttered chide and curse, bumped against Gamelyn. His supportive hand upon her was all business, brusque. Conversely reassuring. Odder still was a memory, not words Gamelyn had spoken, or even Robyn, but Much: *Y' want to be chilly, like, when you strike the blow.*

Marion resisted the urge to steal a peek his way, tucked her chin, and went on.

They were across from the chapel, ready to dart across the muddy street. Marion ducked beneath the shadow of a shop's eave as light spilled from the dark maw of the chapel's front doors. The men followed, silent and graceful predators.

A pair of nuns exited. One held a torch as the second, with a small grunt, closed the double set of doors behind and bolted them. The mechanisms were well-oiled but heavy, and gave a sharp report against the half-dry ground, the walls of surrounding buildings, and the low-hanging clouds. Looking neither right nor left, the two nuns headed around the chapel's far side and towards the abbey cells. Marion knew the routine; it had once been amongst her duties to secure the abbey's valuables within the sacristy and close up the chapel.

The chapel itself was rarely locked, open to pilgrims. But instead of broaching the front doors, Marion had suggested a little-used side entry. It would take them directly to the south transept.

Would, and did. The door was smaller, unbolted, less noisy. Marion pushed inward and glided through the doorway with Gamelyn close upon her heels. At the latter's nod, Much took up his agreed place by the door, holding it from swinging shut as Robyn hesitated.

Peering first at the door, then about the deserted street with wary eyes, Robyn gave a tiny shake of his cowled head. "I should keep watch," he whispered, then winced as the hiss of it echoed against the chapel walls and sucked inward.

Marion peered at him, uncertain.

"Nay, Much will. Keep to the plan. Better all three of us hear what the trouvère has to say." Gamelyn also seemed puzzled, nevertheless kept his words half-swallowed, no harsh consonants to bounce off smooth stone. And when Robyn seemed to further hesitate, Gamelyn leaned closer. "You'll hear what we can't."

Which was simple truth as Marion saw it. Yet Robyn still hesitated.

"I'll hear nowt in this rubble," her brother muttered, his dark eyes scanning the walls—an arrow's half flight upwards—then narrowing into the entry and the darkness beyond. But before either Marion or Gamelyn could question, he shrugged and nodded them on.

Worksop Abbey was not as magnificent as some, but it was cared-for, stately; a grand and well-dowered woman. The grey walls were familiar and, in their own odd way, home. Marion supposed she should feel horrified by the concept—again, her mam came to mind. Eluned certainly would have been horrified. Mayhap she would have come to understand, as Marion herself had. Uncomfortable, but impossible to deny; this cold place had in its own way been shelter, a den of retreat for a tattered soul to find some healing.

Even if the abbey's sovereign had sought to stymie it.

Marion leaned against a near pillar, peered across the main chapel. A figure knelt at the altar, flaxen head uncovered and bowed—it looked to be Alundel. Turning to her companions, the *what next?* died in her throat—not upon sight of Gamelyn, who was scrutinising the altar with all the affection one might give a body insect, or Much, a silent silhouette in the doorway, but the one just inside. By chance or will, Robyn had come to stand in a shaft of moonlight philtring down from one of the high, narrow windows. It spilled over his slender frame, through some trick of light reflected off his drawn dagger to dance in black eyes—despite the hood pulled so far forwards.

He looked eerily like the figure by Barrow Mere, divine and dark . . . and by decree of these sparse, cold walls, wantonly damned.

"I'll be back," Gamelyn muttered and disappeared into the shadows towards the entry. Stray airs caught his cloak, sent it swirling behind, the last thing visible before it too vanished.

Marion leaned harder against the pillar. Between the silent, strange avatar standing behind, and Gamelyn's exit, she felt oddly—shamefully—bereft.

Gamelyn reappeared beside the font, pulled the cowl from his hair, dipped his fingers in, and knelt. Another habit, ingrained so strongly he couldn't enter the chapel without it—yet perhaps more, as Gamelyn made the sign of the cross not only upon his own breast, but in the air before him. A priest blessing a congregation, or an endeavour.

Well, he was, wasn't he? In more ways than he wanted to admit.

Then Gamelyn ambled, silent, down the nave to the altar. Knelt, not too close but not altogether far, from . . . surely it was Alundel. Who else could it be?

"I hate these places." Robyn's voice sounded behind her, subdued.

Marion peered over one shoulder, saw Robyn had moved from the narrow luminous shaft. No doubt concerned it made him a better target. She'd come to realise, now more than ever, her brother's instincts were as much a part of him as his longbow.

He kept watching Gamelyn.

"This is his," Robyn murmured. "All of him, and none of me. He was born here, was marked with their prayers and incense. Was raised in these walls, taught to walk and run and fight with the steel rendered from their stones and fire, and he . . . he *feels* sommat here, sommat powerful t' fill him. But all I hear are the stones . . . *weeping.*" A glitter brimmed his black eyes, and as he looked up to the wood-and-stone vault, tears spilled, twin snail-tracks down his cheeks. "It's old, this cry, a pain nigh old as our people . . . D'you not feel it, pet?"

Marion tried. Tried but couldn't, somehow. Mayhap she'd been closeted here too long, dulled to anything but sleep and stasis.

There was, to her, only a heavy sense of . . . waiting. An endless patience, and the sharp bleed-over from Robyn, *tynged* expressing itself with silent waves and sharp-edged shudders.

"'Tis resigned, they are, to their place in men's plans." Robyn was staring at the walls, white-eyed as a hart run to ground, his voice a shaky whisper echoing against the cold wood-and-stone buttresses. "But resignation is not submission. Nay, they remember their Mam and bide patient . . . always, *always* ready for the day when they return to Her. And they will, one day. They will . . ."

His head bobbled, ever so slight, and Marion lurched forwards, took hold of his arm.

The touch brought him to her in more ways than one. His nostrils flared, and he covered her grip with his, eyes closing. "All this time, I blamed meself for not knowing . . . for not feeling you were still alive, in thisworld, here with me."

"Rob, I—"

"No wonder I'd no sense of you. You were here, kept silent . . . sleeping . . . *buried.* This place could still a beating heart." His hand upon hers shook; his eyes finally opened to meet hers, still brimming. "Oh, Mari, how did you *bear* it?"

She still wasn't sure. But instead of pondering further, Marion acted on her own instincts. "Because She's here." Marion slid her hand around, fingers lacing into his—as if he were the curious toddler who'd wanted to walk through the fire, or the stripling who'd tried to fly from the thatched roof. "Come, just a little farther, and I'll show you."

His hand went lax as she turned inward; she squeezed and led him to the far end of the corridor, just off the altar, to an alcove containing one of the most valued artefacts Worksop possessed.

It was large, unable to easily remove, lock away. There was no need; none would touch Her.

Robyn's breath escaped him, a gout of mist into the surrounding stones. It wafted on another fae lift of air, spread to curl about ebony cheeks, to caress a veil of indigo stone. The babe, held close at suck, was just as dark. Both of them, clad in midnight.

"'I am black and lovely, O daughters of Jerusalem. Like the tents of Kedar'—"

Robyn started—only slight; he knew the voice, as did Marion.

"—'the curtains of Solomon'," Gamelyn continued, soft but powerful, sliding into the alcove beside them. "'Ah, but the sun has burnt me . . .'"

Alundel lingered just behind him, frowning. Nervous.

"I fear I'm very well versed in Solomon. Hazard of my order." The words were light, almost mocking; as he spoke them, Gamelyn gave

Marion a shrug. Yet his gaze was fixed on Robyn, brows faint-drawn with disquiet.

Robyn's gaze chased away.

"And this Mother is no shackled Virgin," Gamelyn mused, still light, and dropped his own gaze. Kissing his fingertips, he knelt to touch them to the dark Madonna's feet.

It was so curious . . . so detached. Yet sombre, almost reverent.

And so, the Lady whispered: a glint of moonsilver from the Mother's black visage, and a satisfaction that sent another shiver down Marion's spine. *Our Knight shall be no Virgin Hunter.*

Robyn breathed something that drifted, slowly, into an audible murmur. "Aye, well, we all go to Her in the end."

Marion slid a troubled look to Gamelyn, unsure how to respond to this, to any of it. She had never seen her brother so . . . so unnerved. Gamelyn paid her no heed; once again he was peering at Robyn, a steady, odd light in his eyes. Marion was no more sure of how to interpret it than she understood Robyn's inexplicable frailty.

Then Gamelyn reached out, cupped Robyn's face with one hand. Robyn ducked into the caress as if it were shield, or shroud.

"Go," Gamelyn said, soft.

And without another word, Robyn went.

- VII -

"Is he ill?"

"Does it matter?" Gamelyn whirled on the trouvère, had a little satisfaction as the man shrank back against a huge pillar. Only a little; his thoughts were still with Robyn . . . that, and the sharp stitch claiming his side without warning, making him realise he'd also put hand to sword. The twist of body had been instinctive—and unwise, he concluded as his lungs seized, fleetingly refused to expand, let him breathe.

But pain also banished the odd, muted wail of a . . . mêlée, was the only word Gamelyn could come up with, despite the fact that finding the proper word seldom proved difficult. But this he'd heard—sensed—like a far-off battle.

One being lost.

Gamelyn gritted his teeth, clamped his forearm against his ribs, and just as surreptitiously throttled the desire to hurtle after Robyn, pull him close, take this whatever-it-was from him. Both pain and wail dwindled, even as Robyn vanished into the darkness.

Much hovered at the door, frowning. Gamelyn jerked his head and, when Much would have hesitated, reiterated it with a hand sign that left no room for doubt: *Follow. See him safe!*

With a tight and tiny sigh, Much obeyed, easing the door shut between them.

Marion's hand came to rest upon Gamelyn's tight forearm, making him start. He let inner silence suckle dry the remainder of his discomfort, was able to meet her concerned gaze with bland surety. *I'm fine, actually, and you?*

She didn't seem reassured, but let it go.

"The peasants are full of the stories," Alundel mused, peering after Robyn's departure, "of how wild Robyn is son to demons, can darken the door of no church."

Gamelyn started to speak; a bristling Marion gave him no chance. "The only devils in thisworld are the ones as killed our family—and those, the Church made."

Alundel turned to her, frowning.

"Demons! I saw my brother born, *of our mother*—ah, but your Church would say that was a sinful act too, wouldn't they?" The scorn in Marion's voice could have curdled new milk.

"I meant no discourtesy," was Alundel's soft protest. "I was just repeating—"

"Better than repeating foolishness," Gamelyn cut him short, also soft but laced with steel, "tell us why we're here."

They have made war against Us, Hob-Robyn. They have taken our stones and made of them a fortress, a barren temple with which to drain our magic from Us.

Robyn escaped to the only place he knew, and the Wode took him in, covered him in winter-grey and damp quiet.

The Horned Lord's voice, as his avatar went deeper into their realm, changed from nigh-mute whisper to hoarse growl to full-throated, furious howl. *You have but had a taste of it. They have never stopped. Taking.*

It echoed in his ears, scraped and stabbed into his already-bleeding mind. Robyn fled towards the impromptu camp they'd made, burst into it all panting and wild . . . and was sorry he had when he found Gilbert, Will, and John all gathered, weapons drawn, ready for the pack of wolves surely following him.

The only wolf was Robyn himself, the only predator lying in wait, his own spirit, and his only recourse flight, not fight, because Robyn couldn't fight this, couldn't make it right, couldn't even defend himself against it.

Mayhap it was no longer even safe to retreat to the only pack he knew, wounded and vulnerable. Mayhap he should slink off to lick his wounds in solitude . . .

Nay, dryw ardhu, *your coven is made of predators, but they will not turn on their Lord.*

"Robyn?" Will was saying, had said it twice, each one higher-pitched, louder with his concern. But it was John's hands cupping his face, cool and callused, and John's breath in his hair that finally pulled Robyn from the sodden shadows where his senses had fled.

He grabbed John's wrists, looked up, kenned he'd gone to his knees.

"Where's Marion? What's—?" Will cut himself off as John sloughed a level look in his direction.

"Hot drink, then," Gilbert suggested, purposefully bright, and bent over the hearth.

Will came over, put a hand to Robyn's back. "Rob?" It was gentle, worry transparent.

"They're all right," Robyn answered, a muted breath into John's palms. "They're with the minstrel . . . " And he couldn't help it, started to laugh.

"Rob?"

"He'd skelp me, Gamelyn would . . . 'trouvère', he'd say, all ponce and—"

"Bugger that bloody Templar!" Will expostulated.

"Aye, and I *do*. Every chance I have—who knows how many more we'll have left to us, aye?" And Robyn started laughing again, small uncontrolled snorts against John's hands. Felt more than saw John jerk his head at Will in a clear *leave off for now*, heard Will mutter about *bloody mad tossers* as he went back to the fire, and still Robyn couldn't halt the spasms. They tore at his chest, altogether akin to sobs, and all the while John just gathered him in, close as skin and bones beneath.

Earth magic, earth making. Calm. The stones were no longer shrieking here—couldn't, in his Wode, in his place, with his own. Not for the first time, Robyn was humbled by the simple power in his little John's great heart.

"I canna explain—"

"Then don't," John murmured against Robyn's ear, pulling Robyn to lean against him.

"No doubt you know by now our King is being held ransom by unscrupulous enemies. He is prisoned, with only his own songs to bear him company, against all decent—"

"No doubt you know by now my patience is limited, trouvère." Gamelyn put his shoulder to a pillar, crossed his arms. "As is our time. In another place you can regale us with a *lai*."

Their retreat was an alcove behind the black Madonna—chosen

upon Marion's assurance that none broached this area in the night hours. Alundel leaned against the far wall of the tiny alcove. He had traded gay clothing for plainer fare, braided his hair back from his face, and was bereft of lute. He seemed a bit naked without it. Indeed, he kept reaching for it and, when it was not there, smoothed his hair instead.

"This would be more a *chanson de geste*," Alundel parried. "But I take your point. Therefore, bear with me if I speak of events foreign to your experience." Said more to Marion than Gamelyn, the blithe condescension made Gamelyn want to do some damage. Anger cooled into amusement as he met Marion's gaze. She was tucked up, arms wrapped about bent knees, on another shallow ledge across from the trouvère. Her lips were curled in a tiny smirk. *Let him underestimate this renegade nun*, it said, and Gamelyn found himself relaxing against the column in agreement. He crossed one leg over the other, hands resting on his sword pommel, unflappable threat.

Alundel was not unaware of it, but his voice remained untouched: Scheherazade, exchanging words for one more living night. "My lady is at Blyth as we speak. She arrived there just before All Saints, to oversee the finish of the chapel she dowered—ah, you know of it?"

"Quite well." Gamelyn couldn't help the ironic tilt to his voice. "The Chapel of Saint Nicholas. Its construction began only a little while after my father received the honour of the castle. The Queen visited, once."

He had been not quite twelve, though he'd fancied himself nigh a man and used to all sorts of Importances in residence. Blyth was a major redoubt on the North Road, after all. Nonetheless, Gamelyn had been sideswiped by the sheer intensity in velvet and silk that was Queen Eleanor.

Even if the whispers in Cook's demesne told of how the Queen was still a prisoner because her sons had followed her to war with their lord father. Cook had glared at Gamelyn's elder brother Johan as she'd said it, and Gamelyn had not understood it—then.

Sir Ian had still been hale and whole, receiving his entitlement—*Boundys*, border lord—with humility and presenting his three strapping sons with no little pride. Gamelyn's knees had fair knocked as he'd knelt, displayed his fealty with a kiss upon the same golden signet he'd but earlier held, warm and weighty, in his palm.

"Indeed." Alundel smiled and touched at his hair. "She has that effect on many."

Marion looked sceptical.

"The stories of her are rife, some of them base and baseless both.

A woman to hinge an epic upon, she—" Alundel began a hint of rhyme-lilt; midbreath he eyed Gamelyn, cleared his throat.

Gamelyn was glad the trouvère could read what warnings flew, rampant, across his expression: *Get on with it, man.*

"Not long after your brother"—Alundel dipped his head to Marion—"laid Nottingham low, Count John descended like plague upon Blyth Castle. Fleeing the Wode's wrath, the old stableman swore."

"Brand. He aided you, then."

Alundel blinked. "Aye, that was his name. He took my horse and my measure all in one gesture, kenned my true duty was to my Queen and our rightful King. Not pleased with the turn of events, 'twas he who told me of the count's arrival and the changing of the guard. Said Count John had turned out the lord's wife and her retinue—the old one did not seem altogether sorry for that and mentioned how Lady Margaret did not mourn her husband's death overlong, merely took everything of value she could and departed."

His brother Johan, Gamelyn mused, and his brother's wife. It sounded as if Gamelyn had no cause to tender apology for making her a widow.

"It was quite plain to me, however, that this Brand was not pleased that a woman had been treated so. He warned me not to trust in counts and said the count's mother had done so to her incommodation. That," the trouvère added with another tug to his hair, "is where I come in."

"And where *do* you come in?" Gamelyn cocked his head. "You obviously have other uses than to sing your liege lady a pretty tune to ease her confinement."

"My truest skill, but not my only," Alundel concurred. "My eyes are keen as my voice, and those of my profession can go many places unhampered."

"You're a spy."

"Such a harsh word, my lord Templar."

"You assume the judgement, not I," Gamelyn replied, somewhat offhanded. His thoughts kept lingering upon a particular phrase, mayhap the most important: *changing of the guard.* "That's why Pontefract's men are sparse hereabouts. Prince John has taken the castle."

"Prince John has, in truth, 'had' the castle for several years. Can he 'take' what is by rights his?" Alundel pointed out.

"King Richard gave his brother the honour of Blyth and Tickhill, not the castle itself," Gamelyn retorted, just as blunt, and the trouvère smiled.

"For a monk, you are well informed."

Gamelyn returned the smile, albeit humourless. "Which you well knew when you made an offer I'm not sure you can deliver. Blyth Castle is 'by rights' beneath Baron de Lacy's jurisdiction, since de Lacy purchased those rights from a newly crowned King Richard and so rendered my father vassal of Pontefract instead of Huntingdon. If John has replaced de Lacy's men with his own, he's making quite the statement."

"But imprisoning his mother is an even bigger one," Marion voiced, and as Alundel peered at her, furthered, "That's what he's done, hasn't he?"

Approval crept into Alundel's smile, as if a new-bought horse had shown a pretty turn of speed.

"But why?" Marion was obviously not afraid to reveal her ignorance, even if a trouvère assumed it too readily.

"The down payment towards Richard's ransom has been raised. You might truly love that black-eyed brother of yours, fair maid, but the only fraternal affection Prince John holds for Richard relies upon the crown he hopes to inherit. Both old King Henry's remaining sons have proven as rapacious as their lord father. My lady's stay has been . . . lengthened, because her youngest son knows she was on her way to see to the second half of that down payment's disbursement."

Richard. Twice. All the formality the man obviously treasured, then this. Gamelyn shifted, giving another quick, defensive glance to all points.

"Second half. That implies a first," Marion prompted.

"Aye, it does. The first lies in London. Hubert Walter is waiting there, for the Queen's word." Alundel moved closer to Gamelyn, his voice even more muted. "I tell you as my lady told me, and gave me leave to use if I must. The second treasury is presently being held at Temple Hirst."

Gamelyn stiffened, nape hairs standing on end. Too many coincidences, all of them piling atop each other, almost eager . . . and was there, truly, such a thing as coincidence?

The dance was still ongoing. He was being dragged back in, and he wasn't altogether sure he was sorry of it.

"Your preceptory, Sir Guy." Alundel dipped him a nod.

Gamelyn was not inclined to return it—nor to correct the name despite Marion's bristling at it. "How much more"—a growl—"do you know of me and mine?"

"At first, not enough." Alundel was unapologetic. "I have spent my time wisely since our last impromptu meeting. I had heard of Robyn o' Wode even across the water . . . aye," he answered Marion's start, "your hooded brother is notorious, as I said. To my original chagrin, 'twas unknown to me that Robyn Hood lurked so far north—the rumours tell of Nottingham, not the Peak and Barnsdale."

"And why were you so far south, if you were looking for Pontefract?"

Alundel shrugged rueful acknowledgement of Gamelyn's query. "I was lost, I fear. When I left Blyth, it was with the understanding that Baron de Lacy bided at Peveril on business, so I hied myself there. When I found none there but Peveril's lord—none other than de Lacy's brother—"

"The Sheriff," Marion breathed. Gamelyn touched her arm; small comfort better than none.

"Aye, Brian de Lisle, Nottingham's sheriff. Former sheriff, I should say; I fear he was in no goodly mood for music. Mourning what he'd lost in his eagerness to pit himself against Robyn Hood. And when I made it known I was in haste to find the Baron of Pontefract, the route he gave turned out one fit to fall prey of Sherwood's wolves." He went silent, glanced around, wary, as a faint echo resounded through the chapel. There was a flutter and scratching, then an odd, muted moan.

Marion angled an indifferent eye upwards and twitched her shoulders, unconcerned. Gamelyn followed her gaze and spotted several doves roosting upon the thick rafters.

"The Queen trusts Baron de Lacy?" Marion asked. "He visited Nottingham before the tournament, to hear Count John's suit for power."

"How would you . . . ?" It was a pleasure to see uncertainty in Alundel's expression.

"I bided there, with t' Abbess of Worksop's retinue," she reminded. "You nobles seem to think your servants canna hear a thing."

Alundel swallowed this with another gesture to his fair head, then continued, obviously concerned. "My lady told me I was to go to either Pontefract or Doncaster, let either of those lords know how at her son's hands she was good as prisoner. She told me de Lacy had come to Blyth to see her before she found herself in such a plight. He told her what had transpired at Nottingham, and she gave a recounting to me."

"De Lacy has been fair in all his dealings." Gamelyn spread one hand with a shrug. "Many believe King Richard will never return."

"Treason!"

"Mayhap. But also expediency. De Lacy is no doubt hedging his bets upon the very real possibility that the count could well be his next liege lord—and who can blame him?"

Ah, but Alundel could. His pinched expression was yet another giveaway. A loyal hound, this; critical of pragmatism's fickle honour—Gamelyn knew the symptoms well. Had possessed them himself, once.

The question was, loyalty for whom? Eleanor? Richard, of whom he spoke with such familiarity?

"That there are factions cannot be denied," Alundel agreed, a bit sullen. "Even within your own order, *Chevalier*. Believe me, had I not heard of your loyalties—and your stakes—I would treat with you more carefully."

"You'd be wise to treat carefully with me, period."

"Prince John just let you leave after seeing his mam?" Marion tucked her chin against her knees, gave Alundel a wry twist of brow.

"I went in openly, you see, and claimed hearth rights for my talents. To Count John I remained nothing more than a trouvère making his way up from the midlands. There is ripe story fodder in this shire, as you might know." Another charming smile.

That smile pleased Gamelyn to no end. Alundel would underestimate this pretty peasant woman to his eventual undoing. He seemed ignorant of being well caught between not just one, but two hunting stoats.

"So you're the king's man, come to report to his royal mother," Marion said. "Happens you'll tell what any of this has to do with us?"

Alundel blinked. Gamelyn raised a hand to hide a smirk, pretended to smooth his moustache.

Marion glanced his way, mouth twitching, and persisted, "We've a right to know. Why would you think to hire wolfsheads and make promises to a Templar like you can keep 'em?"

Gamelyn had the urge to snog her, hard. Watching Madonna and all.

That one is of Me, is She not? the Lady breathed against his ear. *Your regard for Our Maiden is regard for Us, lordling.*

Gamelyn shook his head, saw Marion slide him a quick and curious look as Alundel protested, "Surely you realise what it means to carry the Queen's seal?"

"I ken how those in power make what promises they fancy, when they fancy, and in the end they're just as like to fancy not remembering they made 'em."

Again, the trouvère's affront told a good deal. Wily, a proper gamesman, a spy who could no doubt lie through his teeth when he must . . . but vulnerable for all that. Such resolution was altogether chivalrous—but unwise in enemy territory, to so give away the game.

"He well could mean to double-cross a wolfshead," Gamelyn told Marion without taking his eyes off Alundel. "But he'll think twice about doing so with Templars." He turned words as well to the trouvère. "Won't you?"

"I mean only this," Alundel replied, terse. "If you and yours help me to free Queen Eleanor from Blyth Castle, it could mean your lands. And"—he eyed Marion—"a pardon for your brother and his outlaw followers."

"*Could*," Marion repeated, with a negligent wave of one hand. "*If.* I'm all for freeing any woman from gaol, be it padded with purple cushions or crusted with muck. Me brother would heartily agree. But you're asking him to risk *his* brothers' freedom on nowt more'n maybes."

A heavy rattle resounded into the stillness. Marion's words stoppered as if choked. Another rattle, this one more insistent, echoing down the nave and up into the rafters. It was followed by a heavy slide and *clunk*. All three tensed. Dust motes danced through the dim. The front door burst open, with the scuff-slide and groan of heavy, warped carpentry, and above them the pigeons bustled into panicked flight.

With one hand, Gamelyn cut a rigid request for silence across his throat and quickstepped to the alcove's arch, peering around it.

For long moments, nothing. The remaining echoes died away into flat calm. The exhalations of his companions were barely audible from behind Gamelyn; nevertheless, he held his own breath and closed his eyes, listening.

Several murmurs from the entryway. The door was hauled shut; more groans of joined wood and metal fastenings pierced the stillness. From the echoes emerged the scuff of feet, soft-shod and measured, down the centre aisle. Light spilled around the stones, advancing on its own, it seemed, until two figures emerged: a black-clad figure followed by another, draped in grey.

Gamelyn belatedly defined the clench of his stomach as unease. Behind him, having crept close despite any imperative, Marion sucked in a tiny breath. Then the darker of the two figures halted, pulled the cowl back from his head—his. It was no enemy Abbess come back from the grave, but a black-clad priest. He moved to the altar, crossed himself, and knelt.

The other, grey-clad and stout, held the torch. As the priest made his prayers, the nun moved to light a sconce on the far side, then came and placed her torch into a second sconce, altogether close to the alcove hiding Gamelyn and Marion. Marion's breath escaped, silent and halting-heated, against Gamelyn's sleeve.

She knew this nun.

Gamelyn peered over his shoulder, made careful surety of the trouvère's whereabouts. Alundel had melted into the shadows of an alcove beside the one sheltering the black Madonna; he caught Gamelyn's eye and nodded, stayed put. Gamelyn turned back to Marion. She was still watching the nun with narrowed eyes and gave a start, albeit slight, as he reached down and took her hand.

It was not affectionate; a firm reminder, nothing more. His brows lifted a query; she gave a tiny nod and squeezed his hand in return.

"Will he come?" The nun's words were soft, yet travelled easily though the chapel as she turned back to the abbot: another reason to keep silence.

The priest didn't answer right away. Several more silent moments stretched out before he crossed himself and rose with a grunt. "He will."

The nun almost seemed to shrug, then made her own obeisance and approached the altar.

Gamelyn peered at Marion, then darted his eyes to all points of the chapel; another query. She shook her head, thankfully kenning it. No other way out, then—at least, not until these two had gone. Any movement in this silence would be . . . problematic. Being caught was no good option despite Alundel's reasoning that praying pilgrims would not be disturbed—the priest and nun were obviously upon some clandestine business, would likely not welcome any witnesses. Better to stay, chance their luck in the shadows.

Fingers touching the cross upon her breast, the nun rose, agile despite bulk. "You do trust him, then."

"Trust?" The priest gave a low laugh, mirthless. "His kind are never to be trusted, Sister."

"Then why—?"

Another loud *thunk* into the stillness, and its now-familiar accompaniment of creaks and groans: the main door opening and closing.

Marion's hand seized in Gamelyn's—for moments he wasn't sure why—as a shadow moved into the nave, glided down the aisle. Marion's apprehension transferred, as if by touch, crawling up Gamelyn's spine and to his nape, a skin of ice.

But neither reaction made sense. No ghost approached the altar, no like monster moved into the torchlight; merely a cloaked, cowled figure of medium height. Unremarkable, surely. Yet every instinct Gamelyn had was vibrating, furious and fearful. Marion's eyes had hardened into crystal beneath the faulty light of the torches; her hand sweated, quivering in his.

She felt it too. Whatever it was.

Halfway down the aisle, the figure hesitated. The cowled head cocked, first one way, then the other, the shoulders barely shifting.

As if it, too, sensed . . . something. Gamelyn had seen its like before: in the rise, sway, and rock of a desert cobra, waiting for its prey to panic so it could strike.

Against Gamelyn's arm, Marion sucked in a breath, and Gamelyn felt it nigh fill his own lungs.

A pale, gloved hand emerged from dark wrappings, extending to touch the sword at the figure's left hip. All the while the figure turned, slow, as if drawn to the wide stone against which Gamelyn and Marion clung.

"My lord." The priest, coming forwards. "I bid you welcome to Worksop Abbey."

The figure turned, so quick the priest recoiled. The ready hand alighted—habit, not reaction—on the sword hilt. It was plain, leather-wrapped, odd mismatch to the pristine, expensive gloves, one of which extended, expectant. A signet sparked upon one knuckle as a torch spat and flared on a pocket of pitch.

The nun folded her hands into her sleeves, waited.

The priest reached the figure, bowed over the gloved hand, and kissed the signet ring. Some church dignitary, no doubt . . . but no, Gamelyn reminded himself, not bearing a sword. And why meet now, in covert circumstance? With a priest who had no trust for . . . "his kind"?

Gamelyn angled forwards, ever so slight.

"What, then, have you for me, Anselm?" A nobleman's speech, well-modulated and betraying little regional accent. "I was preparing my way north when your missive was delivered, telling me you've found something of interest." The voice dipped, gave a hint of the dangerous edge that had announced the lord's presence. "I do hope it is more than merely 'of interest,' considering I'm neglecting welcome rest before the morrow's journey."

"You did ask, my lord, that I should send immediate word if I obtained any news towards those unholy events in Nottingham."

Gamelyn stiffened. Nestled against his spine, close as fur to skin, Marion gave a tiny shiver.

"I also advised you of my need for . . . circumspection." It was low, the cowled head turning to peer at the nun by the altar.

Aye, a cobra, this one. With a voice to snare the wits from unwary men. Yet again and unawares, Gamelyn's fingertips sought the sword strapped to one hip. Slow-sure, they caressed, then curled about the leather-wrapped hilt.

"Sister Deirdre is that, and more." The priest—Anselm—motioned the nun forwards.

Deirdre.

"She was seneschal and companion to the former Abbess, has kept the abbey in clear order whilst the bishop makes his decision. As you may be aware, my lord, there is talk of moving the sisters to another abbey, and re-establishing a priory of our brethren here."

Deirdre seemed more perturbed by having to make her obeisance to the lord than by the possibility of removal; her advance held as much distaste as trepidation. But she knew her duty, performed it with a silent dip of head and knee. The lord, just as unwilling, retrieved his hand to fist it atop the other, still resting upon his sword pommel.

Anselm continued. "I often come to Worksop to hear some of the sisters' confessions. In this time of upheaval, it is all the more necessary." He motioned to Deirdre. "Our Sister came to me only this evening—for confession, of course, and furthermore, advice upon a matter she feels has come to head."

"So, woman," the lord purred. "Amidst your bean counting and linen folding, you think you've something important enough to stay my journey to my own preceptory?" *Preceptory.* Gamelyn's breath hissed out from between his teeth, nigh silent.

The lord was a *Templar.*

As if he'd heard the breath—impossible, that—the lord half turned. Marion went rigid. Gamelyn's fingers tightened on his sword hilt, inclination pitting instinct against custom, obedience against perception. Warrior's loyalty nigh tipped the balance: this man was a Brother, one of Gamelyn's *own . . .*

Marion's fingers nipped Gamelyn's arm, sent shards of discomfort to stab at half-healed back muscles. It returned to Gamelyn not only the welcome and wary cool of consideration, but the realisation of what else was, perhaps even more powerfully, his own.

Aye, listen, my Knight, the Lady breathed, *and heed your Maiden. These stones embrace a madness 'twould not only take your wild leman. . .*

"Only, milord, if you're interested in the ones as *caused* the evil in Nottingham."

The lord had turned far enough so Gamelyn could catch a glimpse of well-trimmed beard and hawkish profile. At Deirdre's words, however, the lord angled back, took a step closer to her. "Caused." It was almost musing. "And how would *you* know such a thing?"

"I have ears, and a brain. Your like might have no use for women, my lord," Deirdre retorted—and was that a sneer in her voice? "I've no use for men, comes to it. But mayhap we have use, after all, for each other in this much."

Oblivious, Gamelyn considered, or just daft, this woman's attempt to charm the cobra.

The lord—*the Templar*, Gamelyn reminded himself—remained silent, unmoving.

Anselm looked anxious; Deirdre stolid, unrepentant.

Then the Templar lord gave a low chuckle into the silence. "My, my, Anselm. It seems you've brought me a she-wolf in sackcloth. What did these people do to you, dear *Sister*, to make you vengeful enough to try to use your betters?"

"They killed my mistress." Sorrow laced Deirdre's voice, but underlying that was hate, thick and strong and clotted dark as old blood. "When I saw what killed her, I knew. It was spelled."

"Spelled!" the Templar lord dismissed with a snort.

"Aye!" Deirdre retorted. "I know what rune-spells look like. I know what they *feel* like."

"Sister Deirdre was of the pagans, once." Anselm was respectful but insistent. "Which is why I took her word and passed it to you."

Again, silence. Marion's grip was abominably tight, sending spasms up and down Gamelyn's back. It was a relief, the discomfort. Something to hold his mind aloof.

The Templar lord's index finger tapped against his sword pommel. Then he shrugged. "Continue."

"They're here. Robyn Hood and his covenant. Here, in Worksop. And when I tried to have them arrested, the Hood set his spell about the whole tavern. There's still talk about it."

"And what interest should I have in some scruffy wolfshead?" The Templar lord's voice tilted pettish. Some underlying tone gave his disinterest the lie—and made Gamelyn's nape crawl gooseflesh.

"'Twas Robyn Hood's witch-sister killed my Abbess!" Deirdre told him. "Only this afternoon I *saw* her, sitting with her brother and their whoreson minions, watching the minstrel, laughing and carrying on as if they'd the right!"

"Minstrel."

"There's a troubadour here, my lord, holding court at the inn," Anselm supplied.

Trouvère, Gamelyn supplied with a roll of his eyes, and his thoughts fled, brief longing, to Robyn.

What had *he* Seen, here?

"And so?"

"That singer, he went over and sat with them too!"

Bugger. Gamelyn's next thought, just as furious, quickly fell upon how he could employ either of the shivs tucked in his bracers.

"Talked to 'em like he knew 'em!" Deirdre's righteous wrath, once unstoppered, quickly overflowed. "And then one of your men came over, and they were passing some—"

"One of *my* men?" The Templar lord stiffened—the cobra flaring his hood, deadly alert—and Gamelyn thought, again, *Bugger.*

"Aye. He wore the blooded cross on black. But he sat next to the Hood like a long-lost brother. And *her* . . . they were both too familiar with her. Not that it would surprise me—*that* one's traitor and spawn to witch-blood, nowt but a murdering temple *whore!*"

Gamelyn's fingers itched for a shiv. Just one. It would be so easy.

"Sister." Anselm was trying to soothe, in between vigilant glances to his master, who stood, unmoving as one of the chapel columns and about as malleable. Gamelyn could all but feel the gears turning beneath that cowl, the flare of . . . *something* unseen, heavy and bilious, slithering into the chapel and fanning outward, as if seeking.

Marion sucked in a noiseless breath, and Gamelyn shivered as she exhaled the heat of it across his back. Filled with intent, teasing the magic into being, and he could *See* it: familiar strands of glimmer-light and darkling, the warp and weft of *tynged's* time-pulse curling about them, about the dark Lady's alcove, up and over the curve of wall where they hid and back to encircle Alundel in his corner. A buffer, a shield . . . A protection.

Something within Gamelyn, sluggish and new, made to rise, respond, join. But just as firm, the dark Lady spoke to him, said: *Nay. Not now. Not here.*

As the flare of seeking power passed over them, it did not so much as pause. But that tiny, sluggish tendril deep within Gamelyn snaked upwards and reared, flared its own cobra-hood to sway in the dance, defiant.

The seeking sucked into nothingness, banished as surely as if Gamelyn had snuffed a candle. The Templar lord gave a jerk, a tiny sway and stagger.

In the space between breaths, Marion had laced tight fingers not only upon Gamelyn's arm, but into his mind. Unforgiving and stark, her grip, and the resultant, stinging throb of shock wisped Gamelyn's own response into guttered candle smoke, to waft where his Maiden's power gentled it still, invisible.

Again, silence; interior as well as outward. Then Anselm asking, hesitant, "My lord?"

The Templar lord did not answer, at first; merely brought a hand—shaking, ever so slight—to his cowl as if to throw it back.

Gamelyn watched, unable to prevent the snarl trembling his upper lip. *Do it,* he prayed. *Do it. Who* are *you, "my lord?" And what do you want with us?*

The gesture was abandoned, the change of subject perfunctory. "You brought the object, then?"

"I have kept it here, bound in God's sight." Deirdre peered at

Anselm, who nodded. Clearly controlling her own ire—through fear, mayhap, or circumspection—the nun moved past the altar and turned.

Padded towards their hiding place.

Gamelyn tensed, felt Marion's breath stutter against his spine.

At the last moment, Deirdre turned and disappeared into the alcove of the black Madonna and Child. Gamelyn wondered what she was after, and breathed silent relief that Alundel had chosen another alcove.

Meanwhile, the Templar lord paced, muttering to himself. It could have been prayer.

Gamelyn thought not.

Again, the *shush* of coarse woollen against the stones, and Deirdre returned, a cloth-wrapped bundle in her arms. Its length and bulk was suggestive of a short sword. She brought it before the Templar lord, but as she reached him, hesitated. Clutching it close for a long moment, as if she'd changed her mind, Deirdre gave a tiny shake of her veiled head and held it out.

The Templar lord did not take it. He made a curt gesture for Deirdre to place it at his feet. With another slight frown at Anselm, Deirdre did so. One hand lingering, she started to rise.

"Unwrap it, woman."

Deirdre peered up at him, truly wary now—though Gamelyn personally considered he'd be more wary of being on his knees before the Templar lord than unwrapping any artefact. But with a bow of her head, Deirdre set to her task, dutiful and once again oblivious. The wrappings were drawn aside. There were many of them, a thick shroud seeming unreasonable. It also seemed past reason how Deirdre was taking such care not to touch it.

Then it wafted over Gamelyn, a faint, sick-making wave that hollowed his stomach and set his nerves a-tingle. One altogether repulsive . . . but also seductive, and foreign . . . Nay, he had felt its like before, and more than once: when his master had made and bound the measure braided about his hips, in faltering attempts to call and cordon his own magic. Yet this familiarity—this *recognition*—etched a powerful, almost careless path through the protections Marion had woven about them. It smelt of blood and ash, wood sap and willow-green. It tasted of death, and vengeance, of . . .

Of *Robyn.*

Marion had once again gone taut as a drawn bow. Gamelyn's knees tried to buckle beneath an overpowering knowledge—confirmed by Deirdre's next words, a reverence that not only named it as weapon, but a tool of a magic old when the abbey was new-quarried stone.

"The Arrow, my lord. The evil and blighted thing that took my mistress's life."

"So much." The Templar lord's hissed inhalation could be heard throughout the chapel. "So *much*."

Gamelyn hoped, sane and abrupt, that Robyn was well away from here. In the Wode's shelter, with John's arms and the woodland magic holding him close-safe, with the others all wrapped in green and mist and well away from . . . from *this*. He didn't comprehend why he hoped—only that it was strong, and horrified, and innate.

With another action—and just as innate—Gamelyn slid his hand out from the press of his and Marion's bodies. Down the pillar, out of sight, then a twist and jerk of wrist.

Felt the shiv slide into his palm, deadly and familiar.

Felt Marion's grip tighten. Again, warning. Staying.

Felt doubt land upon him, a hesitant weight altering the light, perfect, *ready* balance of that shiv.

Brother. Templar. Of my own kind. . .

Then the cobra struck.

Deirdre was dragged sideways and away from the unwrapped Arrow, twisted around and yanked against the white-and-crimson tunic. She tried to struggle—brief and futile, for the grip was one Gamelyn well recognised. Pale-gloved hands braced against Deirdre's skull, jerked her neck sideways. There was an audible snap.

Anselm lurched forwards with a small cry. The Templar lord said nothing, merely turned upon the priest. Anselm staggered to a halt.

The Templar lord stepped back, loosed his grip. Deirdre's body dropped to the stone floor with a limp, heavy thud. Anselm's hoarse, terrified breaths tore into resultant quiet as the Templar lord peered down at his handiwork, pulling at the edges of his gloves, then smoothing at his cloak.

"My *lord*—!" Anselm's muffled squeak went mute as the Templar lord glanced at him, still fussing with his garb.

There was a growl building, low and muted-deep, in Marion's throat; Gamelyn could feel it in his own chest, burning.

"Those wolfsheads have gone too far, this time," the Templar lord remarked, toeing the nun's body. "Haven't they, Anselm?"

Anselm stammered something. More horror and dread than agreement, it was agreement nonetheless.

"You're such an old woman, Anselm. We couldn't let her spill any more tales to any more confessors. Besides, she died doing more important work than she would ever achieve alive. In grace, for you heard her confession only today. If you stop snivelling and give unction before she grows cold, surely God will understand."

Anselm's mouth worked for long moments. Then he knelt down beside Deirdre, made the sign of the cross on her forehead with shaking hands, and began murmuring in Latin.

The Templar stood there, hands folded and head reverently bent. Anselm seemed unwilling to hurry through his duties, but his hands never stopped shaking and afterwards he knelt there, chin tucked against his chest. Finally he said, more croak than whisper, "What shall we do, my lord?"

"I will take *this* thing"—the Templar lord jerked his head towards the revealed Arrow—"with me for study. The nun's sisters can discover her when they come for Compline. She won't lie here long, if that's what bothers you. I would suggest"— drawled, soft—"you let it slip she had some secret to incriminate the wolfsheads, though God knows how such scum could be incriminated further. Make it plain they saw her at the inn. Speculation should do the rest for us. Go."

Anselm rose with a quick, tight bow. He could not quit the chapel fast enough.

All of it seemed to happen between one breath and the next, and in the third breath, the Templar lord was stepping over the body in his way, cloak sliding, shrouding, then impatiently flipped loose. Two more long strides, and he came to stand over the Arrow.

He waited, however, until the opening and closing of the door signalled the priest had left. Only then did he bend down, cloak pooling around him. Drawing a folded square of cloth from his robes, he shook it out, his profile keen and absorbed. The cloth shimmered pale in the dim, fluttering with the weft of finest silk. Only then did he take up the Arrow—and that with utmost care, shrouding it in the silk cloth. He wrapped the provided woollen over that. Not so heavy, this time; only a few of those layers were necessary. The silk had already dampened the weapon's shrieking, bloody presence to a muted whimper.

Marion shuddered beneath Gamelyn's arm; with anger, or horror— or both—Gamelyn was not sure. As for himself, in this moment? He felt nothing. No hope or horror, relief or fury, only a strange combination of detachment and connection with the kneeling figure. Only the penetrative lack of affection he would direct towards anything he might have to label "enemy." Or "prey."

His grip tightened upon the shiv, slow, deliberate. He would never have a better chance.

The Templar lord looked up from his crouch on the chapel floor. Gamelyn froze.

The cowl still obscured the lord's features, but some trick of moonlight traced a sudden, silvery spill across the upper half of the Templar lord's face. Pale eyes gleamed, nearly crystalline as they fastened upon Gamelyn. For seeming aeons they peered at each other, some uncanny . . . presence lying between them, humming. The pale eyes lit further, with . . .

Acknowledgment? Concession? *Recognition?*

A flash of teeth, a dip of head. Then it vanished, all of it, into shadow. The Templar lord rose, put the silk-wrapped Arrow into his robes, and departed into the darkness.

The chapel door opened and closed, in a thick huff and shudder that echoed throughout the nave.

Marion was whispering against Gamelyn's ear, tugging at his sleeve, and when Gamelyn didn't answer—couldn't—she leaned in closer, said something that sounded like his name. Repeated it. "*Gamelyn!*"

Only then could he rouse himself from the spell of that cobra stare. The strange and humming *thing*, freezing him in place, made just as sudden a departure, sucking into the shadows and leaving him unhampered in voice or hearing.

"Did he, then?" Marion persisted. "See us?"

Gamelyn found himself shaking his head to Marion's query despite trying to frame the words. Trying, and failing, as if the spell—once cast—had bitten deep.

Aye, he saw. He. . .

He smiled, *and walked away.*

- VIII -

"My god!" Alundel stammered, breath steaming in the chill. "God in Heaven, what was that about?"

They had escaped the chapel. Slipping through the maze of back alleys, Gamelyn kept them going until they found some refuge against the walls of the inn and crouched there, panting.

Gamelyn eyed Alundel, gave himself a weary reminder—the man was musician, not soldier. "Lower your voice, man."

Marion had fallen to her knees, skirts spilling damp and dark over the ground. Trying to smother her gasps against her bent knees, her arms clung, crossed tight, to her breast. Her eyes, white-wide, were fixed to the abbey.

"What was that man doing there? Who was he?" Alundel kept babbling, though it had thankfully lowered to a hoarse whisper. "Why would he want something as inconsequential as an arrow—enough to kill for it? I don't under—"

"None of that needs be your concern." Gamelyn peered at the trouvère, deceptively mild, yet eyes hard as emeralds. "Go back to your lodgings. Keep your head down and don't do anything but entertain your audiences."

"But I cannot stay here for much longer!" Alundel hissed. "It will be suspicious if I don't move on."

"If you leave right away, 'twill be all the more suspicious. They might link you to the nun's death," Gamelyn shot back, gratified when the man nodded, seeing the sense of it. "You'll have word back before the sun sets tomorrow."

"I don't intend to take nay for an answer."

"I don't intend to give *any* answer until Robyn knows everything."

"Christ's blood! You're a Templar, and he's *wolfshead!* What sort of hold has he upon—?"

"You have," Gamelyn said between his teeth, "no idea. Don't push me, trouvère, or I swear—King's man, Queen's, or whatever you are—you'll regret it."

Alundel peered at him, then Marion, still wide-eyed. His fingers twitched, as if he longed for the reassurance of his own partner and paramour—his lute—against them. "I'll wait," he finally muttered and, shaking his head, retreated into the darkness.

Gamelyn didn't even bother to watch him go. He hunkered farther, sliding down against the wall beside Marion, silent. Waiting.

The trouvère was well beyond sight or hearing before she spoke, and that a bare whisper. "I know 't, like my own heartbeat. I used it. I bid its magic come to me, aimed it true, sent t' willow to do Her work. The willow can speak to me, but it canna *hold* to me, 'twere Robyn's making, not mine . . . sweet Lady!" It was a moan; Marion put her head in her hands. "That lord had the magic, could y' not feel it?"

"We don't know why—"

"There's only one reason sommun with the magic would kill for such a thing!" she shot back. "And we let him take it. We did *nowt.*"

"There was nothing we could do, not then." Gamelyn closed his eyes, leaned his head against the wall. "But we will." *I shall find you,* he swore into the black. *Brother.*

A bang-*clang* echoed down the line of the stone wall; a shutter thrown open, with the hurl and thick splash of a piss-pot being emptied into the dirt path. Gamelyn gave a jaundiced look above them—no windows, but people awake meant they could be overheard. He took hold of Marion's arm and dragged her up, pulled her along with him.

"Gamelyn," she protested, "that lord has sommat of ours!"

"That lord was a *Templar!*" he hissed back, was yanked backwards as she stopped, dead. Gamelyn turned, found Marion staring at him with an expression he couldn't fathom.

"Sweet Lady," she breathed. "Your like, one of the Temple Magicians, has the willow?"

"He won't have it long," Gamelyn growled, and tugged her on.

Marion tugged back with a muttered oath.

"Damn it, woman, we have to—"

"Y'r going the wrong *way,* you great pillock!"

Gamelyn gave her a harried—albeit chastened—look and gave way.

Marion's steps were rushed, her fists clenched; not finished with the subject, that was plain. But she waited until the buildings thinned, kept up a mix of mutterings and silence until they'd cleared the side postern that had been their original entrance. "Why didn't you stop him, if he's one of yours?"

"Marion, I . . . " It trailed off; he still wasn't certain of that himself.

"He has the willow! Blooded and bound and of *Robyn's making!* Don't you understand?"

Nay, he didn't. Not really, not in the horrified and bone-deep way she seemed to . . . and the lack was keen as the shamshir at his hip. He halted, looked out upon the ploughed section just past them, its furrows leading, as if by design, to the forest edge. Watched his breath exhaust, wafting and wasted into the cold, clear night, and thought *How apropos.*

Marion had begun to slog across the fallow, frosted ground, still muttering, angry. "I should have called down the . . . Robyn would have taken him where he stood, would have—"

"Robyn would not have." It was terse, stopping her in her tracks. "Marion, did you not *see* him? He was . . . incapacitated. As if that bloody trouvère spoke true and the chapel walls weakened him like—"

"*Gam*elyn!" Marion protested. "'Tis nowt to do with any deviltry and you know it! The Arrow—"

"Was not the whole of it. Not near the whole of it. I don't know how, or what, but it was there, *in* him," Gamelyn replied, his voice barely above a whisper. "That's why I told him to go. I . . . I heard it, somehow—couldn't not, really. If it was but a whisper of what he heard . . . felt . . . what *do* you call such a thing?" he asked, his voice quavering. "*Putain de merde,* can you not see, I don't know *enough!* My own master is one of those 'Temple Magicians' and he couldn't force my crippled talents—"

"You en't crippled, 'tis only—"

"Only nothing. *Less* than nothing. Better I be crippled, considering what I do See when . . . " He choked it off, veered the subject sharp and sideways. "I know a bare inkling of the Temple's secrets, and likely more than I deserve. I hear the Lady when she deigns to enlighten me as to some utterly mad and incomprehensible purpose; I hear the Horned Lord only when he wants to jab me with some verbal knife, only glimpse these . . . these *things* through a thick mist and comprehend *just enough* to be a danger to us all! It comes like pox—when *it* wills, not when I would command it— Hellfire, it did just that in the chapel, and if it hadn't been for you doing . . . whatever you did to quiet it?"

"Gam—"

"*Christ*, Marion! All I do know is the feel of rock against my knees in empty, unheard prayers and the clean edge of a sword—physical war, with *bodies*, not this . . . this fiendish dance of minds and powers and infernal spirits!" Gamelyn looked up into the clear night sky, clenched his being from teeth to buttocks, regained some control as the motion reverberated through his unhealed frame. Said, bloodless and measured, "So, Maiden, if I cannot understand what you took in with your mother's milk, pray forgive mine ignorance."

Marion remained silent for so long, Gamelyn angled his gaze sideways, wondering. A mixture of remorse and pity and self-castigation lay scrawled, naked, over her expression. Such amorphous things, all of them—and all of them had such power, as he'd just told her.

"I'm sorry." The words burst rapid, between the sudden chattering of her teeth. "I keep pushing, but we've lost so much time already . . . I've lost so much, and . . . bugger." Her hands had fallen against her skirts, palm up and curled open like wilting flowers.

They clenched. Marion took a deep breath, looked Gamelyn in the eye. "I'll explain as I can on the way," she said. "We need to tell the others what Alundel wants as soon as possible. And Robyn has to know what's happened here tonight."

"The Queen Mother, you say. Of England. Needs *our* help." The words came slow, as if Scathelock was having trouble rendering them into sensible or sane bits.

Robyn understood that. He felt as if words would never come easily again, as if that bloody, cursed chapel had robbed him of not only glib tongue, but any wherewithal to wield it.

Marion was the one speaking, quiet in the dark, seated on a tree root and explaining what she and Gamelyn had gleaned from the meeting with Alundel. Gamelyn leaned against the tree just behind Marion; Much also. He'd returned not long after Robyn had, and it must have been under orders, for he'd paced, a barely leashed hound, until his master had returned. Now he was a silent bulwark limned by hearth-light, waiting.

"There are those amongst us who know the castle better than any," Marion explained. "If we're careful, happens we can fetch her out with not even an alarm."

Yet something else lay beneath. A feeling skirting the corners of action's promise; something they were holding back. Marion kept avoiding Robyn's gaze, even as Gamelyn persisted in searching for it, a quiver of uncertainty beneath calculation. John propped behind Robyn, a breath in his hair and arms tight wrapped about him, steady earth upon which Robyn could sway and plant himself.

He wasn't, right now, sure of what else he felt. It set him totally adrift.

"Why would this . . . spy trust the likes of us?" Will's question was a good one, and Robyn wished he'd asked it.

"I don't think he has a choice," Marion answered, with a rueful smile at Will.

Will met her eyes for a long moment, then looked to Robyn. It was a prod, nothing less: *Say sommat. Anything.*

Robyn leaned against John just a little harder, stayed silent.

"Say, then, happens he's no choice," Will persisted. "I wain't believe a nobleman's about to tell us owt."

"He's not telling us everything." Gamelyn spoke for the first time. "Only a fool would think he'd tell us everything he knows."

"Are you calling me a fool?"

"William," Marion growled, "for the love of—"

"That would depend, wouldn't it?" Gamelyn replied. "On whether you do indeed believe he's told us everything."

This time, Gamelyn received Marion's exasperated look.

I have to do sommat about this, Robyn mused, *soon or late.* Still, he couldn't so much as speak.

It wasn't helplessness. Helplessness was when he'd emerged from the caverns four years ago with a withered arm and everything he'd loved rendered to ash—and even then, he'd stared it down, demanded its retreat. This was abandonment, and pain, and some inexplicable, overwhelming sorrow . . .

Was this what the fae had endured, faced with banishment by cold, hard iron?

"Say we fetch the Queen out of Tickhill," Gilbert interjected from his own cross-legged seat upon a deer hide. Those who weren't standing—including Robyn and John—had taken precautions against the chill ground. With no cloud cover, the temperature had dropped even as the moon had led them nigh to midnight. "Say we do," Gilbert continued, "and in the doing, don't fetch ourselves into Count John's hands. Whatever shall we do with her?"

"I'll take her to Temple Hirst," Gamelyn answered. "As Marion's already told you, the ransom's partially there, waiting. It also means safety. Not only for the Queen, but us."

Gilbert's gaze moved to Robyn, asking. When nothing was forthcoming, Gilbert took in a breath and studied the ground between his toes. "For you, certainly," he ventured. "But I think we all would like better assurances before we just walk into a Templar stronghold."

"Gilly's a point," Will added. "Why should we follow this Templar like little lambs t' slaughter?"

"This Templar," Marion's words were tight, "is not about to lead us to any slaughter, William."

"He's the only one as stands to gain from this, is how I see it."

"Happens you don't see so well, some days."

"Happens I en't the only one."

Robyn watched Much bristle, saw Will take notice with a sneer. And all he could contemplate was how Marion had bloody well asked for that one.

Fretting, she were. And it had something to do with that bloody chapel. "Rob?" Will prodded. "Surely you've sommat to say on this."

Robyn closed his eyes, put the heels of his hands there as if to scrub away . . . something. *Don't call me Rob, don't fetter me with another time, another life. I need to stay in thisworld, not any others, not now.*

"Don't be an ass, Will," Gilbert sighed. "Are you even bothering to pay attention? There was a pardon mentioned. For *all* of us."

What do I want with a pardon? Robyn thought, dully. *It en't my place or my world, in those dead and keening walls of stone, and they'll end up hunting us either way if we wain't bow down to their gods, be 't Law or their Christ.*

But this wasn't just his, this possibility. It belonged to all of them. Everyone had a right to this gamble; everyone a say—and the ones who would likely take it with both hands weren't here to speak.

John nuzzled into his hair with breath uneasy, troubled.

Will kept looking to Robyn, query plain: *Say sommat. Please.*

Gilbert said, as if his thoughts ran tandem with Robyn's, "You might not find the wager worth the marks when it comes to possibility of a pardon, Will. I'm not sure I can speak to it, either. I *chose* this life. But what of the ones not with us? You know better than most how Arthur'd like a wife and bairns and home, a fireside where he can prop his feet and tell stories—only he's marked a poacher, left with one arm for daring to hunt in the King's Forest. What of David? He'd escaped gaol in Strathclyde just to end up in one in Nottingham, a wife and three children, all but the eldest boy dying of fever because he was too poor to feed them properly. What d'you think *he'd* wager to be able to stay in Matlock with what's left of his family?"

Back to where more will starve, Robyn thought, sudden and numb, *as there's no help to be found in that world, is there? Just more of the same, ever on.*

Will fell silent, frowning, mulling it over.

"What we might gain from it en't the only point," Marion said into the silence. "It's wrong, that a woman should be locked up, is how I see 't. And, were all of you acting like the covenant of Shire Wode instead of a bunch of clots pissing out your territory, you'd see 't too."

Well, Charming William, our Mari has said sommat for me, and plainer at that. Fleeting-soft, it tipped a smile onto Robyn's face.

John kissed the edge of the smile before it retreated; Robyn trailed three fingers across his cheek, then shoved away, firm but gentle, and came to a crouch. "There's more, en't there?"

Will's relief was apparent; Gilbert frowned, folded his arms, and waited. Marion exchanged a glance with Gamelyn. Aye, they were both on edge.

"You called covenant." John leaned forwards, settling his knees into the fur next to Robyn, a light in the brown eyes Robyn well recognised. "Maiden."

Gamelyn looked away and refused to meet either John's or Robyn's eyes as Marion began, halting, to speak.

They make war against us, Hob-Robyn. They took our stones and made of them a fortress, a barren temple, with which they think to trammel Our magic, and take it from Us.

The Horned Lord's words, shoring strength into His soul-crushed avatar—and now that Robyn's nerves were regaining their steel and sinew, his heart expanding with every breath the green Wode gave him, he conjured those words over and over. With charge and charm came some understanding of what had so undermined him within Worksop's chapel, but it was not entire. No less inexplicable, or ominous.

And now, surrounded by his forest, shadowed by the ghostly presence of his god, Robyn walked the night alone. Once again was he taken by still and green, shaken by the Wode's living breath, the pulse of the darkening moon, the starshine as cold fire tearing through the thick, rain-heavy clouds: all of it, a silken rhythm runnelling through his veins. Considered, thought and thought-less, the magic—*his magic, blood, breath, and being*—held in a thin willow wand of death, fletched with cerulean and grey, and consecrated with his enemy's blood.

He had believed it destroyed in the rage of the Wild Hunt. He would not be so careless with his tools again.

If he was given the chance.

"Is it my time, then?" Robyn asked the presence just behind his Sight. As if voiceless query gave fruit then form, the great, dark silhouette—half stag and half man—began to manifest more clearly, pacing just beyond a stand of verdant, red-pocked holly and spiny fingerlings of gorse.

Nay, your time is not upon you yet, Winterlord. You have much left to accomplish. The Ceugant *has not even seen its first Summering, nor together danced a full ring of the Spiral.*

"And this . . . queen? This woman who holds such power in a golden ring, but can be prisoned by her own son?" Robyn agreed with Marion—it was wrong. What happened after would happen, but if they'd the means to free the goddess from her tower, they were bound to it.

Not only that. Robyn smiled. It would be proper satisfying to once again tweak the tail of that bum-boil Count John.

The Frankish queen is part of the puzzle. Her power cannot be denied, within ways Old and New. Through her husband has she borne children who carry ancient, hallowed blood.

Robyn snorted. "What Frankish king holds Old ways close? What Christian, warrior or woman, would stay slaughtering those as reject their god?"

She is a key; that is all I know. Bid Janicot throw the bones, make a Telling for your questions. . . but also heed your Maiden, for Our Lady and Her earthly avatar know female paths more than We ever shall, Hob-Robyn. Even your leman, who defies Me at every chance—an intemperate growl to set the wind swaying and clicking the bare branches—*will listen to Her. She makes many promises, courts him with Her knowledge.*

"Aye, well, She would, then." Robyn smirked again, but it turned fleeting as the Horned Lord purred, deep:

Trust to this queen. She embodies the Crone who spins the skein of tynged *to weave your time in thisworld. But you must also 'ware the Magician, my own. He too will court what is yours, seek to spell it, use it.*

Robyn thought of his men, of his Maiden and his Knight. Of thwarted powers locked in stone and bunged deep with pain. Of barren temples. Of Temple Magicians hunting the wolves of the Shire Wode . . .

That he will hunt you, there is no doubt. But we will turn it on its head. When time draws nigh, We shall Hunt him. Your Oak will coax him to the forest and we will take him. Break him.

"We have to find this Templar lord, first," Robyn muttered, knowing if it came to war within this war, they were not yet strong enough to stand. "We have to stop him, and owt he means to do."

"*I* should have stopped him. Somehow."

And bloody *damn*, but how had Gamelyn snuck up on him like that? Robyn had his answer as he turned to find John at Gamelyn's elbow, giving an unrepentant shrug and smirk. Both of them had halted by a coppiced elm; any footfalls silenced in the sodden, dead leaves. And the statement suggested they'd been there for at least a short time, watching Robyn mutter and pace and talk to wandering spirits.

Any others would cry Robyn mad. But not these two. John, of course, saw it all the more. He stepped forwards, lifted his hands to his face and blew a breath across the palms, mouthed the blessing words. They wafted across Robyn's cheeks like a kiss and, behind him, the Horned Lord took the magic in, wavered fully into thisworld. A long sigh gusted from him; his great head lowered. The sharp tines came to rest on Robyn's shoulders, a heavy weight curling about either side of his head like an ivory crown; Robyn reached up, rubbed his fingers upon sleek horn. Cozened, gentled, the Horned Lord retreated. There was a pull and dizziness within Robyn as his god stepped aside then . . . slipped, was the only way Robyn could describe it, out of thisworld and into the other.

Gamelyn looked disoriented. Aye, well, it meant he was at least feeling it, and that wasn't bad, considering. "I should have," he insisted.

John hiked himself up on the broad, coppiced stump, informed Robyn, "I told 'im, 'tis foolishness."

"I told him," Gamelyn countered, "Marion didn't think so."

"I told 'im, she was . . . mistaken."

"How can someone who barely puts five words together at a time still manage to out-argue me?" Gamelyn plainly wanted to know.

Robyn smothered a snort into a chuckle and tucked his chin to his chest, shaking his head. "When you find that out, tell me, aye?"

John shrugged and pulled his legs up to sit cross-legged on the stump. There was an amused glint in his brown eyes.

"What would you have done, then?" Robyn asked Gamelyn, advancing towards them. "Wrassle the Motherless git to the ground and run him through? You en't fit for fighting, not now. Particularly if those other Templars fight anything like t' you."

Gamelyn gave a growl to rival the Horned Lord's, looked aside. A stray gust of wind tugged a spray of copper from where it had been tied back, obscuring his expression.

Robyn looked up to find the treetops swaying, lithe and purposeful as dancers around the May-fires. But May was a season away, still, and this wind gusted bitter.

Aye, and what to expect, when Summer had slept, fevered and ill, through his birth?

"Nor," Robyn said, albeit with care, "are you fit for sparring with some sorcerer. Not yet."

Gamelyn stiffened. "I am," he answered, "all too aware of *that.*"

"He made a Thwarting," John said.

They both turned to see John bent over his thighs. A tiny smile tugged at Robyn's lip as he saw the worn, painted cloth spread on the broad stump between John's knees, and the bones there, marked and thrown.

Bid Janicot make a Telling, the Horned Lord had said, and John always seemed to know the need, even before Robyn made it plain.

"What are you . . . ?" Gamelyn cocked his head, a plain and puzzled *What the hell?* "A what?"

"A Thwarting," Robyn repeated, a grin tugging at his lips. "And aye, but you would, wouldn't you?"

Gamelyn spun on him, winced as the movement proved injudicious. "I would. What?"

"When someone reaches for you with the magic, and you deny 'em the right to bid you so, it's called a Thwarting."

The green eyes slid to John again, ill-tempered. "How do you know I—?"

A shrug, and a gesture to the bones.

Gamelyn uttered another intemperate growl.

Robyn reached out, tangled fingers in Gamelyn's ginger-gilt hair, and gave a sharp tug. When that didn't work, Robyn grabbed Gamelyn's chin, tipped his gaze upwards. "It en't easy, what you did."

Still, the green eyes chased away. "*Putain de merde . . .* I *did* nothing. It just happened."

"Let's be plain here, pet," Robyn murmured. "You're wanting their power, but you turn from ours."

"It's not that simple. I don't turn from it; I don't *know* it. I'm not like you and Marion. I'm no sorcerer, no magician or druid. Or priest."

"You *are*—"

"Balls! I'm *piss poor* at it, if I am."

"You thwarted a Templar," John parried. "Lord."

Gamelyn flushed. "And I did without thinking. There was no control to it, no direction."

"You don't have to control everything, pet." Robyn leaned close, whispered against the coarse fur along Gamelyn's jawline, "You have no trouble letting me have it when we tup, aye?"

Gamelyn obviously thought about pulling away, instead closed his eyes, gave a shivery exhale through clenched teeth. "That isn't exactly the point."

"You think it en't?"

"What I *think* . . . " Gamelyn shivered again, eyes darkening, and Robyn unsure whether it was because of some innermost contradiction or because John had snugged up behind Gamelyn, had begun running careful, light fingers up and down his sides. "I think you've rather put me between a rock and a stone wall."

Robyn found himself grinning, pushed in closer. "Which of us is the rock, and which the stone wall? There's measuring as needs done here, I'm thinking."

A laugh broke from Gamelyn, sun from behind sullen clouds, and Robyn had his answer. Genuine, the response, and no question it warmed lambent as a summer day. But edging it were those eyes, maintaining the frost, an invariable consideration behind the charm.

What, Robyn wondered, *are you so bloody afraid of?*

Then Gamelyn leaned in to kiss him, reached back and curled his good arm about John, and Robyn found himself . . . thinking.

Kept thinking as Gamelyn started unlacing his shirt and began trailing his mouth down Robyn's breastbone.

How some things hadn't changed, but the things that had . . . they had been truly surprising.

How the innocent lad from Blyth who had wanted to be a monk—*was* a monk—hadn't so much as batted a ruddy-pale eyelash the first time John had crawled between the furs—and between he and Robyn. It seemed more than a few things had become less *sin* and more *sod off* during Gamelyn's time with the Saracens, and whilst Robyn mourned the loss of his Summerlord's bright-hewn faith, he revelled in what had also been gained—and oh, but he'd wanted *this*, not just one or the other, which was lovely enough, but also both, together, since Gamelyn had recovered enough for it.

How fear could trammel things tight, how all that thinking—worrying—could cripple instead of just let a person reach out, do, follow instincts all eager as a horse to run full out.

How Gamelyn was willing enough to respond to this sort of magic, but disinclined to another at which he was just as bloody good.

And Robyn couldn't stop the thoughts flashing through his brain like ball lightning now, even in the middle of it, with John atop and Gamelyn between and Robyn's own body—*unthinking*—keen as a good knife in the rhythm whilst his mind harried and worried, darting along paths best left fallow, questioning the reality of everything he felt, and tasted, and touched.

And he lay there after, curled about soul's-mate and heart's-life, exhausted not only in body but mind, and *tynged* tangling past his eyes, making no sense . . . *no sense* . . .

"I love you," he breathed in Gamelyn's ear, and whispered down John's breastbone, but both of them were long asleep, buried beneath the furs.

The wind woke them about midnight, howling like a thousand damned souls, creaking the treetops with frigid blasts. They bundled up and headed back to camp, where the others had all huddled in a tight, fur-heaped cluster, leeward of a hedge near to their makeshift camp. Burrowed in with them just as Worksop Abbey's bells began to peal what Gamelyn muttered was more than just a call to Night Offices.

It kept ringing for the while. Robyn listened to it, thankfully muted and shifting with the wind, and hoped Arthur and David weren't out in this, had moved on to the caverns. He shifted—carefully so as not to disturb Marion against his ribcage, or John next to her—and turned to face Gamelyn. Robyn was unsurprised to find him wakeful, eyes gleaming as the clouds scuttered overhead, revealing and then obscuring the starlight. Not surprised at all, because now 'twas the burning of Gamelyn's thoughts that could have nigh well lit its own conflagration.

Robyn brushed a kiss to the corner of Gamelyn's mouth. It gave a slight quirk in response, tucked farther as a scraping snore reverberated through the furs. Not Much, back-to-back with his master, but just past Marion and John to Gilbert and Will. John preferred sleeping next to Robyn as he had done for years, cold or no, but was sensitive to both Much's and Marion's awkward positions when it came to having to choose sleeping partners or freeze alone.

Another mind-bending snore, then a stiff *thud* and an irritable curse from Will invoking Gilbert's name.

Robyn stifled a giggle into Gamelyn's front. His Gilly-lad snored for thrice his size, he did. He started to back away, found a sword-hardened hand at his nape, holding him there. Gamelyn kissed his temple, then released him and twisted onto his back. Much shifted, but otherwise did not stir.

Robyn crept closer, laid his head next to Gamelyn's and stole a hand across his ribs. "Marion's right," he whispered against Gamelyn's ear. "You *can* outheat damp compost."

A snort, nearly silent. "Is that supposed to be comforting?"

"'Tis for me," Robyn assured, falling into blissful silence. Then: "You want it, don't you?"

Gamelyn tensed.

"I don't think you even know why you want it, or how, but you do."

A silence, Gamelyn mulling over the words. "And what do *you* want?"

Still, it had the power to nigh slay Robyn in his tracks—that this noble's son would bother to ask. It was maddening . . . gratifying . . . and oddly intimate. "You make me think too much, y' allus have, allus will." It purled in Robyn's throat, near a growl, and Gamelyn's answer was a smirk and shrug.

"That could only be to some good."

"Nay, not really."

Gamelyn frowned, and Robyn—bugger, blast, and damn—started *thinking* again. *See, I'm not the only one holding secrets close, O Templar.*

The absurdity of it made him smirk again, and Robyn raised a hand to tap that copper-furred jaw, found his fingers riffling through it and up to Gamelyn's forelock. "You know what I want. What I've allus wanted, and 'tis here, in my reach. My men beside me, strong and untrammelled. My sister, alive and with me. *You.*"

Gamelyn muttered something, low and vehement. Robyn wished it was Arabic—likely 'twould end up in some sweaty, if clandestine, fun . . . but nay, no such luck.

"I distinctly heard 'shit' amidst that lot," Robyn whispered. "You really do have to teach me more."

"Give me what paltry weapons I have, Robyn Hood."

Robyn huffed a disgruntled breath. "Mm. You allus take y'rself too lightly. Wish I could meet what priest as first told a wee ginger-haired lad he were nowt—I'd show the Motherless sod nowt. Take his skull and hang it on t' Barrow oak."

Gamelyn snorted. "How . . . romantic."

"Aye, well, you'd do the same for me, pet."

The green eyes met Robyn's, sudden. Open and explicit, no parry or dodge. "Come with me to Blyth."

Robyn peered at him, thoughts whirling and gusting like the wind through the trees. Gamelyn merely leaned forwards and took Robyn's mouth with his, didn't pull away until Robyn was quivering.

Silence. Only the wind, tossing the treetops above them, buffeting the hedge.

"I guess," Robyn muttered, shoving and punching against Gamelyn's good shoulder like a recalcitrant feather bolster, "I'd best be sending Will, Marion, and Gilly back come morning. Seems we're mad enough t' storm a bloody castle."

- IX -

"So," Alundel said, far too cheery. "I've some ideas."

The day was fair, promising sun and a nip of warmth. Robyn strode a strong pace, but was taking in none of their glorious surroundings. Instead he stared, somewhat glassy-eyed, at John's brown mop of hair. John, who never missed a chance to enjoy the company of horsekind, led the small cavalcade at the nose of Alundel's fancy palfrey. He left off his silent communing with the mare to peer back at Robyn and cock an incredulous eyebrow.

"If I show myself for myself," the trouvère continued, "so soon after visiting Blyth last, it could mean suspicion. I should dress as a guide and man of the forest, even as you have."

Did Alundel actually intend for his words to tune themselves in the exact cadence of his mount's amble, or was it chance? Robyn borrowed John's twisty brows and raised them double, shared them over the mare's roan croup to where Gamelyn strode.

Gamelyn gave a roll of his eyes. The mare switched her tail as if in agreement; Gamelyn grabbed it just before it lashed his hip, ran his fingers through the coarse, blue-black strands.

Robyn's mouth tucked then tilted, amused. He'd seen the first impulse of those fingers, unconscious but telling, towards Gamelyn's sword hilt.

"I've not had to disguise myself overmuch before," Alundel turned in his saddle to tell Robyn, confident. "But I have done. Surely you know some hovel on the way that shall see to the care of my mount here."

"Surely," Much growled, very low, from his own place at Gamelyn's flank, "we en't going to have to listen to this all the way up Tica's hill."

Alundel, oblivious, kept talking some nonsense about a court in the Aquitaine where he'd dressed as a serving wench. The fellow might be good at spying his way through Frankish court gossip—though Robyn wasn't altogether sure of that, either—but if Alundel thought he was going into the castle with them? Not bloody likely. Robyn rested one hand on the mare's white-frosted haunch, followed the sway of it, to and fro, beneath dapples of shade and sunlight. He slid his eyes sideways to Gamelyn and winked.

All yours, pet.

Gamelyn's return smirk did not bode well for their earnest companion. He quickened his pace and, without taking his eyes from the road, put a deceptively gentle hand to Alundel's knee.

Alundel sank a full half head in the saddle throwing Gamelyn a look that somehow encompassed purposeful amiability, pain, and a touch of panic.

Gamelyn didn't take his hand away—or his gaze from the road. "You aren't going in."

The words weren't so far off from the ones Robyn had given the others only yester's eve—complete with the hint of evil temper. Robyn hadn't been about to entertain any more bloody debate.

"You'll stay at the new camp," Gamelyn informed Alundel, "and wait for the others."

Will, Gilbert, and Marion had headed back to their campsite in the glade by Barrow Mere with dual purpose: first to ensure the other two weren't sickening further, then to move camp towards Blyth. To Robyn's relief, everyone had consented. Even Will. No doubt Will was thinking upon pardons and gambles, knowing they would soon follow—and John accompanying Robyn, at least.

Unfortunately, when John and Much had delivered the outlaws' answer to Alundel, the trouvère had insisted on coming along. He had suggested they all meet well away from Worksop, which was all a-buzz. The bells night before last had indeed been tolling a grim announcement: the nun's murder.

"But"—Alundel was trying to be reasonable—"I can assist you—*ow!*"

"You aren't," Gamelyn repeated, "going."

"We didn't have to meet you on the North Road, you know," Robyn offered, giving the mare's haunch a fond slap. "If we'd known you as one of those fellows what hires a dog but does his own barking? We might've reconsidered the deal."

"We still might," Gamelyn added, scowling.

"My good fellow, it isn't that at all. I merely—" Another wince, and Alundel shot an offended look Gamelyn's way.

John, peeking over one shoulder, put a hand to his face, ostensibly to scratch his nose. Robyn knew it was to hide a smirk—he was having trouble concealing his own.

Much didn't even bother; he was out of Alundel's range of sight and grinning for all he was worth.

"We go in alone." Gamelyn spoke as if to a simple, captious child.

"There's several caves in the vicinity, far enough out for safety." Robyn peered at Gamelyn, making silent promise: *All save the one. 'Tis ours, and none else's.*

The slight flush against freckled cheeks hinted this journey might hold as much disquiet as comfort. Well, it was the way of such things. Robyn wasn't feeling too sound in his own mind, either. He wasn't fearful of what they would find there, more like what might be conjured of it.

Yours. They promise to make Blyth yours again.

And if they do, then what do we do?

"You sound as though you also know the area well." Alundel turned a quizzical frown upon Robyn, but Robyn was only half aware of it, still watching Gamelyn's profile, angular and hard as any copper idol.

"Aye." It was soft. "That I do."

Mayhap she just wasn't tough enough for this.

More than once she had witnessed the light in her brother's eyes at the promise of a set-to—and this morning had been no different. He and Gamelyn both, with Much and John nigh in tandem, all of them champing at the bit with a promise of action. She couldn't deny she'd had a tickle of it herself.

But just a tickle. Marion had frankly seen enough in the past few days to shake her confidence. She'd thought herself capable, ready, useful. Instead, it seemed she was more liability than asset.

Worse, she wasn't disappointed at being sent back to camp. Will had been disappointed. Irate, in fact, though he'd kept his mouth shut for a wonder. And Gilbert—well, Gilbert had such an even temper it was hard to tell with him. But he was a brave sort, seemed to love the interaction of the game. While herself? With shame, she pondered how relief filled her with every furlong they covered. Her hands were shaky with it, her tongue dry.

It *was* a game to them. Welcome, anticipated. Would it ever be so for her? Marion eyed the two men striding before her—nay, gliding, they were. Creatures of the forest, fine-honed weapons of stealth, survival, and cunning all rolled up into the packet known as Robyn Hood's Outlaws.

Of which she was not yet one—the past few days had but proved it.

She was worried more about David than the promise of skelping some deserving enemy. Worried Arthur too might have sickened. Neither of them that ill, to be sure, else she wouldn't have left, but still. Sickness could turn on a mark's clipped edge—would, in this oddling back and forth of weather. She was worried about Robyn's Arrow. They should have taken it back. Gamelyn didn't understand, not really, though he was trying. And Robyn had all but shrugged it off, said they would find it—or it would find him—and again, all the while, a blood-and-fire light in his eyes that suggested he might even welcome it.

Whilst all she comprehended was a deep, still fear.

Either Robyn was being a fool, or she a coward. And her brother was no fool. He had been wielding his magic, hard and fine, whilst Gamelyn had been learning war and murder, whilst she herself had remained bunged up in the convent, stagnating.

She *had* been in the convent too long, safe and cosseted as if wrapped in lambswool and leathern pouch. Been safe her whole life, really. Mainly because she'd gone along, followed expectations, done as she was told—mostly—and had expected no less—and no more—than to inherit her mam's place as wisewoman and priestess. Likely marry some fair-haired, handsome crofter—her eyes went to Will, regret and wistful memory—and, as Rob had once said, "*Raise up a passel of little fawns to sing the Horned Lord's name at night.*" Marion had been spirited as one of her like could be—a freewoman peasant surrounded by a Heathen existence in turn hemmed in more and more by newer gods and men's rule. But she had never gone seeking trouble. Never caused it. Never been the truly rebellious one, the firebrand.

That was her brother's calling. And now here she was, amidst it, and she was a disappointment, not up to the task.

An arm snugged through hers, tugged her sharply sideways, and Gilbert's voice sounded, light. "Are you besieged, fair Maid?"

Besieged? Marion frowned, peered into his grey eyes, and saw concern beneath cheer. Past him, just this side of a winding deer path leading into a grove of winter-naked birch, Will was coming back towards them. Attentive, but oddly accepting.

"If She's with you, we can wait," Will said, and took her other arm with such diffident courtesy that Marion wanted to pinch him to see if he was truly Will Scathelock, sparring partner and pain in the arse since they were bairns together.

If She's with you. . . Sudden understanding took Marion, explained

Will's solicitousness, Gilbert's care. They were of *dryw*, after all, and Will since boyhood, bound through his father's ties to the covenant of the Shire Wode. They knew such things, had observed the symptoms, rampant, in their leader. Since Marion had come, she'd herself witnessed Robyn . . . *leave*, eyes too full or altogether eerily vacant as the Horned Lord possessed and took him . . . else*when*, really. And all the while, Robyn's body still moving, knowing the woodland even without his mind fully attached.

Not that it was likely *that* would happen to Marion, even if the Lady was speaking to her. It was different. For everyone, really, but particularly upon the divide of man and woman.

Not that She was speaking. After all, what use had the Lady for a wilting flower of a Maid?

You judge harshly, girl. You are the one who sent the Arrow into your enemy's breast. The one who stood guard over her brother and his leman upon their escape from Nottingham.

That was . . . different.

As are you. Different. You are lioness, not pwca. *You have your own strengths—why seek another's?*

And if my own en't fit? Marion thought—to herself, but the Lady still heard.

They are fit for what you must do, and be. Otherwise you would not be Mine.

Will had moved closer during her inward occupation. He slid one arm about her waist. "Are you all right? It's been a rough couple of days for you, I ken."

And it had been. But Marion didn't like having it pointed out, like a leper's sore.

Aye, a lioness. And this one would be lion.

It made Will's arm, at first thought protective and welcome, seem heavy upon her skin. Presumptive.

"Go on, Gilly," Will said, pulling Marion closer. "You take point for a while, and I'll see to her."

The sudden, purposeful familiarity caught her off guard. Will hadn't tried so much since she'd come to the Wode. It had been all too easy to return to their previous relationship: close but at arm's length, circling the possibility of more without the complications of broaching it. A comfort, when she was but recently rediscovering who she was, trying to recapture what she'd lost.

Gilbert seemed taken aback as well. He started to say something, but Will's arm tightened upon Marion's waist and his frame stiffened, slight but there. Challenge.

Gilbert didn't answer it. He did slide a tiny frown Marion's way, but shrugged and turned away, walking on to take the lead.

And part of Marion—though it made her cheeks heat to admit it—was vulnerable to it, particularly now. She liked the feel of the male body against hers, broad and strong; moreover, was shaken just enough sideways by the past days to admit the weakness. Was hungry for *this* game if not the other; for this . . . claiming.

Fancied the warmth of knowing she could inspire it.

Whatever shall We do, Maiden? From cold stone walls of the convent, to the fecund forest and as many lovers as you could care to choose from.

Mockery slapped self-doubt and pity straight across their tender cheeks. Towards Marion herself or Will, Marion was unsure, but common sense came stealing back, abashed at deserting her. Drawing in a deep breath, she straightened, began to walk on.

In almost the same instant, Will's grip tightened, recognising the beginnings of rebuff. His fingers splayed against her ribcage and dug in, redirected onward movement sideways—and against him.

"Marion. Wait."

It was soft, purposeful—and set off an alarm bell in her skull to rival the clang of Worksop's. More fear—only this was a different sort, wasn't it? Mixed with resentment, at that.

"Gilly's leaving us—"

"We've time yet t' catch up. I want to . . . I've . . . " Sweet Lady, was Charming William actually stammering? "Look. I've barely had any chance to talk to you."

"We allus talk. Robyn'd say we yammer too much, most days." Marion tried to slip from his grip; he didn't let her.

"You know what I mean."

"Happens I mightn't." Though she was afraid she did. "Are you going to let me go, or am I going to have to skelp you one?"

"Marion."

"Will." As stern as his was coaxing. "I mean it."

He released her, somewhat grudging—but lately Will bided more surly than sensible. "Well, and 'twere you as started leaning into me."

"Aye, and now I en't." Marion didn't know what to do, what to say—how to retreat with some grace. She turned away and started after Gilbert.

"*Marion.*" Will's voice was slipping around the edges. "Once, Rob told me you wanted me back."

"I did want you back."

"But not no more?"

Marion halted. "That en't true. You and Rob . . . we're all that's left. You know that."

The amber eyes darkened and he took a few steps back. Aye, he did know, and all too well. It dogged every breath he took. It had layered complications atop a straightforward, rather cavalier lad and slicked fear-sown desperation beneath his skin. "Then why?" he shot back. "Why do you keep pushing me away?"

Because we en't right for each other. I don't love you, not like you want. And you really don't love me. The sudden surety of it made her mute, dry-mouthed past any relief or fear. *Only the wanting's left. I want what I had. You want t' same as allus—what you canna have.*

Everything's all changed around me. Including you. And the changes are hard, William, too hard to bear 'em all.

"Marion. Please. Just—"

"Just give me more time, Will."

"Rob says that. Keeps saying it. And I have done. It's been nigh t' several fortnights, aye?"

"Several fortnights," Marion retorted. "You think that's enough, do you? Whilst *you've* had several *years.*"

"I didn't mean it like that," he protested. "You know I didn't mean it like that. All I meant to say, 'tis done and ower, all of it. You're safe here. You're with us, where we can look after you."

Safe. Enough to make my own choices? I think not, Charming William. In frustration, Marion settled on the one thing she could say. "Look *after* me?" she repeated, soft and steely. "And y' think I en't had more than my share of *that?*"

She wasn't the only one wrestling with a proper bait of frustration.

Will protested, "You're taking everything I say and twisting it—"

"Nay, I'm taking everything you say just as you're saying it."

Falling silent, Will looked away. His ears were scarlet, his cheeks even darker, his fists clenched.

"William. Please." It was low. More desperate than she would like. "*Give me time.*"

He didn't answer, still looking down. About them, the woodland held quiet, spackled with waning sunlight and only the chill wind creaking the branches above. A small motion caught Marion's eye; Gilbert, a shadow in the birch grove, waiting.

Broad, callused fingers touched hers, making her start. Will didn't hesitate but took her hand, firm. Raised it to kiss her palm, and all the while, peered at her with eyes ill disguising a plea, deep behind grey-laced amber.

And still, try as Marion might, she felt nothing but frustration and a strange, sullen pity.

Thankfully, Will didn't see it. "Time's all we ever have, en't it?" Loosing her, he turned back to the deer trace and started following it. "Cept when we don't."

Ⓡ

Passing strange, to view Blyth Castle from this place in time. But even more so, to view it from this *place.*

Gamelyn sat just beyond, on a great, flat outcropping of rock, sword lying to hand, legs crossed long before him, face raised to the last fingerlings of sunlight. Smiling. No obdurate idol, this; instead the setting sun blazed copper from his hair, unplaited to feather across his cheeks in the breeze. Gleaning every scrap of light and warmth he could, no doubt.

Not a bad thought. Robyn pulled the hood back from his own cheeks and tilted his face skywards. With a shift to the longbow braced over his shoulders, he ambled over, considering both the burgeoning ache in his pectoral and the dark pewter clouds hunched over the horizon. The weather was plain chancy about now—blowing cold to freeze your knob off, then sunny and fair, and now, another cloud-edge on its way across.

They'd likely have the cover of rain for this bit of work. Again, not a bad thought.

Gamelyn didn't so much as twitch as Robyn hopped onto the great, flat stone.

"No spiced nuts left this time? Bugger."

Gamelyn snorted. "You're enough of both to go on." The smile stayed as he leaned back, drawing his knees up.

Robyn chuckled, lowered to a crouch beside Gamelyn, and followed his gaze down the low hillock to the only other rise amidst the forest-girdled clearing.

Tica's hill, Much called it, and John: a sandstone promontory long ago built up even higher with serf labour, first as a grazing hill and lookout, then into a great Norman motte. Blyth Castle looked every bit the formidable redoubt it was, flying crimson flags from top to bottom, hunched all white, sepia, and black at the fallow centre of green and fawn grazing-lands, dotted with dingy-pale clusters of sheep. The walls traced outward, a spider's web of protective mortar and stone. There were no weaknesses to be easily spotted.

Robyn contemplated it with a mix of fear and fury. Gave a tiny snarl and hurled thoughts like arrows at his god: *Will you abandon me here, like you did at Worksop? Leave me addled and shakin' in me boots, useless in those bloody stones?*

Such things have never been balm to our kind, the Horned Lord answered, muted. *The Christian place was. . . different. Cursed. By many things. In truth We were both hung between Arrow and Cross, trammelled by tamed and broken stone.*

Unease tremored about the edges of the normally powerful Voice and flitted a chill down Robyn's spine as He continued.

Their power grows, Hob-Robyn. Ours must meet it, match and vanquish it anon. Else soon it will be as the superstitious ones say, and the Church will have ensnared not only Us, but Our magic within its screaming stones.

"You don't have to go in, you know."

Almost nonchalant, the statement. Gamelyn was still peering at the castle. Robyn wondered if he'd heard any of the silent conversation. So many times Gamelyn seemed unaware of the ins and outs of consciousness melding Robyn and his god into one creature—until he would bring forth some suspiciously well-timed query.

"You asked it of me," Robyn said.

"Aye, but I didn't want . . . " Gamelyn took a slow, deep breath through his nostrils and let it out. Continued, somewhat hoarse. "I don't understand what happened, then. At Worksop. I . . . felt what was happening, but I don't understand, not enough of it, and I don't want it to happen again." Robyn started to protest; Gamelyn hurried on. "Not merely because it will compromise what we must do. I should only be thinking of that, I know, but I can't. I won't. I wouldn't see you . . . see you succumb to . . . " He ducked his head, cheeks blazing almost the hue of the fine strands blowing across them.

Robyn merely combed those strands aside, laid gentle lips against Gamelyn's temple, then straightened once more, peering at the castle. Robyn kept stroking the fall of hair, from temples to where it feathered between Gamelyn's shoulder blades. Gamelyn ducked his head, also staring out across the clearing. His gaze held there, ferocious.

It was so *quiet.* Even upon the castle ramparts, there were but inklings of movement, here and there. From this distance they looked more ants upon a mound than the soldiers they surely were. Impossible to tell if the gates were opened at all; the massive gatehouse sketched a deep, dark shadow. Then, activity: an odd shape wending its way across the pasture. A sharp whistle sounded and the shape segregated itself into two, one much smaller and faster, loosed like an arrow towards the sheep. The herder and his dog, come to put their charges into the night fold.

Robyn watched the elegant teamwork of man and dog and kept combing his fingers through russet silk. Moreover, Gamelyn kept letting him.

"We need Marion," Gamelyn said. "She has the longest eye of any of us."

"Mm. Anon. If me lads en't sickened for the worse. But John should be back even sooner, give us a feel for 't."

"I wish we'd some way of entering through the front gate. 'Twould make things simpler, to just have to sneak back out."

"Aye, well, your arse-rod Templar brass en't going to fetch us a pass from his Royal Prat-ness."

Gamelyn made a sound between a snort and a laugh. "It would have fetched us out of Worksop, had you not been so bloody impatient."

Robyn gave a sharp tug of protest at Gamelyn's hair, softened, and kept combing.

"Once we're in, though?" Gamelyn angled his head to peer at Robyn. "If John finds the old stable master, Brand, and he's able to assist—"

"Then we'll also know what sort of help we can count on," Robyn answered. "Who in Blyth as is still loyal to the Horns."

"And the Hood."

"Mm. It's all chancy," Robyn said softly. "What's passed, and what's passed us. But we're still here. It's still here." He wasn't speaking of the castle; looking down, he lowered one hand, smoothed it across the rock. Gamelyn stayed silent, watching. "Those castle walls will recognise you, know you. They'll welcome you and speak your name. In wake of 't, 'tis likely they'll speak softer to me. Like this rock. It . . . remembers us. Can y' hear *it*?"

"Would I know it, did I hear?" Bitter-soft.

"Aye, you would." Robyn kept the fingers of the one hand tangled in russet, with the other caressing the stone beneath them. "And do. You know you do. Some things are passing understanding, they're just meant to be. An' be *felt*. Aye? This stone lying beneath us, it en't been tamed, or hauled from its mam and moved to serve men's whims."

"But my people aren't the only ones to take stones, to use such things."

"Of course not. But those of the old ways know to ask before we take. We know honour must be done, and sacrifice. Our . . . penance, you'd say, and that's not far from the right of it. Everything's due a wooing and winning and t' be paid in kind. But your Church, it's altogether good at takin', aye?"

"'Fill the earth, and subdue it, and rule,'" Gamelyn whispered, then shook his head. "It's not my Church. Not anymore."

Robyn started to speak, didn't. The words said—and left unsaid— were too full and too empty both.

He edged close enough so his thighs nestled against Gamelyn's. Wanted to curl arms about him, spoon close and tight, but knew it wouldn't be welcomed, not now.

Instead, he said, light, "Want to go back?"

"We can never go back, even did we want to."

"I meant the cavern. See 't. Remember."

"I did too," Gamelyn replied. "I don't ever want to be that young again. That . . . ignorant."

"Aye." Robyn nudged him, raising his eyes to the sunset. "Though I'd not mind recapturing a wee bit of the stamina."

Gamelyn nudged back. "We're not so old, you and I."

"En't the age of me body, 'tis what it's lived through."

Gamelyn chuckled, reached down between his booted toes for a pebble, lobbed it down the hill to bounce through the winter-brown grass. A ways past that, the scattered sheep had submitted to the direction of dog and man to become an orderly mob. They milled through the castle's front gates—still open, after all.

"Speaking of what's lived through, how's t' back?"

Gamelyn shrugged. "Good enough. You're not the only one who's adequate with either hand."

"Fancy that." Robyn covered concern with a smile, all the while remembering. It had taken him nigh upon several years to regain his bow arm, and the great divot in his left pectoral still plagued him at times. Remembered Much on the way here, every step of the way an attachment to his master's flank, no less than that piebald sheepdog down the rise.

Aye, Much knew. And Robyn was grateful for it.

Beside him, Gamelyn tensed. "He's coming."

Another had exited the gatehouse even as the sheep had entered. With an all-too-familiar gait, a young man made his way across the fields, earth-brown hair and cloak tossing. The wind was picking up, the clouds looming closer, threatening, but John walked unhurried, a staff propped lazily across his shoulders. Another peasant on his way home from a day's work, nothing to see, no one of import.

Success.

Robyn stood, extended a hand for Gamelyn to haul himself up. "We'll meet him in the trees."

"So," Robyn said. "Brand's with us, and his lad."

"You're sure about the lad?" Alundel frowned, warming his hands.

"John's sure," Robyn answered, "and the lad's a good Heathen. That's enough for me."

Much fed up the small fire with no little expertise, garnering a warm and lovely light that reached for the ceiling of their narrow sanctuary. Outside, it was not so cosy. The bank of clouds had rolled in and delivered on their threat; rain was sheeting off the open entrance in torrents, blowing in the first several feet or so.

Thankfully the cavern was deep and dry. Robyn had found it years before whilst doing forestry duty for his father—and during a desperate courtship of a nobleman's son.

And hearken now to where we've come, Gamelyn mused, peering at his peasant lover who squatted across from him with wrists upon bent knees and fingers dangling, deceptively limp. Deceptive, for Gamelyn could see the tendons clenching in Robyn's jaw and neck—that, and John's eyes gleaming in the shadows behind, sullen mirror to his master's mood.

Not that John—or Robyn, for that matter—would ever consent to the use of "master." Gamelyn considered it accurate, nonetheless. His own sword-callused fingers traced lines in the sandy floor: curves and angles, a map of memory.

"I mean no offence," Alundel furthered, "but there's a lot at stake."

"More for us than you, I'd reckon," Robyn pointed out.

"More than a kingdom?"

"What kingdom do you mean?" Gamelyn interrupted, not taking his eyes from his sandy sketch-work. "There are so many, after all. Yet all those kings would claim God on their side."

Silence. Robyn ducking his head to hide a sudden grin, John's eyes still gleaming—this time, with appreciation—and Much sending sparks upwards, his own satisfaction measured in careful pokes with a suitable stick.

Alundel was peering at Gamelyn as if he'd sprouted horns. Well, Robyn would approve of *that.*

As do I, the Lady purred, with a waft of surely unseasonable—and desert-dwelling—rose. Gamelyn gave his head a tiny shake, bade Her quiet. Now was not the time.

Will it ever be the time, my lord, with you?

Robyn was peering at him, brows knitted. Gamelyn gestured at the outermost tracing, shaped like an egg spread to cook on hot iron. "The perimeter wall is nigh unassailable from here to here. The gatehouse is pure art, not only in the carvings upon it, but in defensive design. We shan't go near it. Entering by the front door isn't the best of ideas at present, anyway. Moat, of course."

"Of course," Alundel repeated, dubious.

"Old Brand says his lad's a little fishing punt?" Much suggested, leaning against the curved sandstone wall closest to the fire. "And he'll make sure the thing goes, eh, 'adrift,' t' our side?"

John nodded.

Much scratched his nose. "So's all we has t' do is find it . . . *How* old is this woman?"

"She is very lively for her age!" Alundel defended.

"Lively?" Much snorted. "Happens no aged noblewoman's about

to swim that moat. Bloody hell, *I've* no fancy to swim that moat. We'd best find t' punt."

John drew several airborne points above the drawing, from the back walls to the moat then back again, and lifted an eyebrow at Gamelyn.

"Aye," Gamelyn mused. "The visibility of a boat is . . . problematic."

"And no tree cover for a good sprint in all directions." Robyn had begun chewing on one thumb, scrutinising the sketch.

"I'd hazard the guards on that stretch of nor'east wall are bored," Much added, crossing his arms. "'Twere allus the new ones as drew duty there. Nowt to occupy y'rself but the back of the keep and a league of grazing. Goats are proper entertaining, but sheep or cows? No' so much." At Alundel's curious look, he explained, "I were milord's paxman, but I'd me other duties, after all."

"It'll have to be dusk or dawn, when the light's poor," Gamelyn suggested. "Or at night."

"Night's its own problems," Robyn pointed out.

"Then hope this foul weather eases just enough to be boon and not bane," Gamelyn replied. "Look. Bastions here"—he pointed to several outward curves bulging from the drawn circuit—"and here. These are the two exits I mentioned. The sally port past the outbuildings, and this one, the postern against Much's 'boredom wall'"—this with a grin to Much—"just past the chapel's line of sight beyond the dye stalls. It's the one that nigh collapsed whilst they were building the chapel. Brand's lad will see it's unlocked. It's our best recourse, with only the one window from the keep facing that way." This time he slid a glance to Robyn, saw an answering glint in the black eyes. Aye, Robyn well remembered that particular window . . . and well he should, since he'd once had to escape out it.

"That's"—Robyn stabbed a finger at the neglected postern—"our best entry pass, then?"

"It is, if it's still passable. Is it, John?"

John nodded.

"Passable to sommun who en't your size, 'little John'?" Much asked, smiling.

John grinned, nodded again.

"But that wall's what worries me." Robyn traced the curtain wall and the bastion an arrow's flight from the postern gate. "'Tis a blind alley, sure enough, so bored or no, 'tis likely peopled by more guards than we want. Assuming that bloody-minded count has any sense," he added.

"Count John is . . . mercurial," Alundel added, venturing closer. "But he is no fool."

Mer-cu-what? Robyn mouthed, brows twisting almost comically. *T' bloody fuck?*

A smirk tucking into one cheek, Gamelyn supplied, "No question Count John is unpredictable. And canny. But I'll warrant he also thinks he's no need to plan a strategy for anything he can't see coming for miles."

Robyn smirked right back, asked, "John? Mark it for us, aye?"

John lowered himself into the light, shuffled forwards on his knees, and began making little divots upon the sketch to represent what guards he had seen. More than would be optimal, but less than there had been in the time of Gamelyn's father. And fewer still, nigh to the neglected postern—indicative of Much's boredom assessment, as well as Gamelyn's that Count John was nowhere near the soldier his brother the King was.

In the end John placed more than a few touches to the bastions and the wall overlooking the chapel. *St. Nicholas*, Gamelyn mused, and considered they might need the saint's help.

"Happens I should ensure the weather," Robyn muttered, only half joking.

"Mm." Gamelyn studied the drawing. "Mayhap."

"It won't do us any good if you can't fetch her out of the castle unseen," Alundel reminded, after a curious look at Robyn. "You mentioned using the stables, but those are on the other side of the keep from the ruined postern."

"That isn't the pressing matter, truly. See here." Gamelyn drew two concentric rings, drubbed three fingers into one side, and pulled them outward. "Here's where the stables follow the motte's westmost curve. Well out of sight of the bastions—those made strictly for outer watch, not inner. The stable proper is dug into"— Gamelyn twitched a smile at John and Much—"Tica's hill."

"Dismal in the winter, I should think."

"But ingenious, and warm. All the animals' body heat, as well as security for the more valuable animals. Moreover, there are hidden entryways into the stables; all sorts of tunnels and escape routes from the castle, those known to none but the inhabitants. There are several in particular I'm thinking of 'twill service us, and John knows even more. All deep beneath the mound and into the bedrock, in some places as deep as the undercroft." Gamelyn exchanged a glance with John, whose brown eyes had dimmed, sombre.

Aye, John remembered: Gamelyn had been locked in the undercroft by his brother—supposed "protection" but more punishment than anything. They had thought him mad, ensorcelled by a pagan peasant into not only sins of faith, but flesh.

It had been the beginning of the end.

"John knows the hidden rooms and passages in the keep better than any of us here," Robyn told Alundel. It was soft, and bitter.

More memories. Gamelyn had to look down, forelock hiding his eyes from not only Robyn, but the others. He'd never quite absolved himself of his ignorance of those particular passages. His eldest brother, Johan, had known them all too well—used them to see and hear enough to set the trap.

Fire. Sculpting shadows in the trees, singeing a sullen, angry glow across the horizon.

The results? Loxley village had burned, and their lives with it.

A skin dropped into his line of sight, its unstoppered mouth scented with the spice and sweet of mead. Gamelyn looked up to see Much holding it out to him.

"We could all use a good drink 'bout now," Much offered, gruff.

Gamelyn took it, gulped it down; felt it slide down his gullet and spread welcome heat in his belly. Passed it on to Robyn with no less gravitas than Robyn himself, passing a blessing cup beneath the full moon.

Alundel watched, puzzled and aware of something personal being shared, and demurred when the skin was, in afterthought, offered. Instead he leaned to tap at the keep sketched into the sandy floor. "So you intend to use these . . . ah . . . secretive aisles, to make your way into and outward from my lady's gaol?"

Gamelyn nodded, more than thankful for the return to business. Robyn Hood might prefer to fight with emotions rampant, but it gave no comfort to Gamelyn himself. "You said you were allowed into the Queen's chambers, but you never said which. I assume the main solar?"

Alundel snorted. "You assume wrong, my lord Templar. Count John keeps himself in state, with plenty of bed warmers and servants in the main solar. They take up nearly the entire upper storey. His lady mother is relegated to a singular chamber on that level, off to itself without so much as a connecting alcove. It has a decent outlook, with a goodly window to the northwest, and is roomy enough for a singular occupant, I suppose. With several maidservants, however, there is hardly room to set up a decent seating area, let alone . . . " Alundel became aware of the gaze upon him: Gamelyn's, somewhat flummoxed.

"Bloody damn," Robyn said. "She's in *your* old chambers, en't she?"

Much gave a snort—pleased, not derisive. John rocked back on his haunches with a broad, brilliant smile.

Gamelyn's astonishment gave way to a smile nigh brilliant as John's. "You've just given us the best reconnaissance of all, trouvère." He slapped a triumphant palm down onto the drawing, displacing sharp lines into a blur of dust and sand.

A constant deluge of rain kept them hemmed all night and into the next day, foiling any hope of progress. Yet just as the cloud-obscured sun began to recede into crepuscular grey, the rain also dwindled, from downpour to a heavy drizzle. The four of them—two Templars, two outlaws—snatched the opportunity, leaving the caverns and Alundel behind.

The wet hung in the air, caught between falling and drifting, with a hint of ice upon its edges. Clinging to branches, it gathered in great, fat drops, then plummeted downwards to already slick earth and moss. Just as skilfully as a driving rain, the drizzle set any cloak or cowl, however well-oiled, to sodden—but this thick curtain was more forgiving. Moving through it was, indeed, possible.

Robyn sucked it in through flared nostrils, let it escape his mouth in a heated commingling of sigh and shiver, mist and blessing-breath. John kept a silent pace just ahead of him and to his right, Gamelyn just past. Much tailed them, so close Robyn could hear him breathe. They were all staying nigh, had emerged from the tree cover only a short while back. The bottomlands were a maze of shadow and mist, visibility poor and getting worse. The castle lay an arrow's flight ahead, invisible save for, here and there, the sullen spark of a torch upon the fog and gloaming. Truly, the only light to be found lay in reflections of wet ground against cloud-hung, darkening sky—but it was, after all, better than could be found in the middle of their Wode.

No drawn steel to catch any hints of light. No bows stepped and strung. Just stealth and slow advance, nigh-silent across the fields.

They left in their wake only the squelch and fill of bootprints in the saturated earth, only swirls and eddies of fog and breath.

Robyn smiled. He couldn't have wished—or witched—better. It was perfect weather for sneaking up on a great bloody castle.

Those gilt flickers brightened as they advanced, tens of fitful torches trying to pierce the murk. A mutter, fading and fetching, of voices seeming to come from the sky. The smell of excrement and rotting garbage—the moat's presence wafting, thankfully inconstant, upon the mists. Then it loomed up from the thick haze, dour and dark: the great white-and-black bastion of Blyth's outer walls.

A hoarse gasp echoed huge into the silence, and John tilted forwards with a wild and abrupt windmill of arms. Robyn lurched after, snatched John's cloak and hoisted him backwards, caught him as he stumbled, held him close. Neither uttered a sound. All four froze in place, looking up. Waiting.

But the "sky" voices did not change, in tone or timbre, and the fog seemed to breathe, a sudden lift to expose the deep gap lying in wait at their boot tips: the moat, ink-dark and swollen with the rain.

John had nigh gone in.

Shaking his head against Robyn's chest in a silent but vehement curse, John shoved back with an apologetic glance to his fellows. Much put a hand to John's shoulder, squeezed lightly. Gamelyn shrugged and, with a brief nod, turned his attention back to moat and castle. Catching his bearings, no doubt.

Robyn spared another glance upwards. The walls seemed to appear and disappear, nigh vanishing into the fog, as if Blyth hung between the worlds of fae and familiar; seen, then unseen. Good. It meant they themselves were just as invisible, unless some guard, patrolling the surround, rode right up into their laps. The likelihood of such a thing before dark truly fell?

Should be done, according to their soldier compatriots—but likely wouldn't, in this weather.

Gamelyn had moved—carefully—to the moat's edge, studying the castle walls as he could. It had been a while since he'd been a lad wandering his father's castle.

Robyn missed that lad sometimes. But the man before him, crouched all cold-fire, a raptor perched and intent on the hunt— aye, that one was proper fascinating.

Gamelyn rose, still looking at the walls, but grim consideration had given way to a satisfied smirk. He gestured them all close, made a few quick hand signals as they obeyed. They'd arrived just east of the outer sally port; next, to find the waiting punt, and cross the moat to the back tumbledown entry. John added a few gestures of his own, silent with a self-castigating reminder: it was a nasty drop into nastier water. They all should watch their step.

With a curt nod, Gamelyn turned on one heel and moved on, cloak swirling after like its own hank of darkling mist.

As Robyn followed, he reached back and rubbed a caressing thumb up and down the belly of the recurve loosely hitched at his shoulder blades. Not his lovely Welsh longbow, but a fine instrument of John's making, the magic fair humming from it—and easier to string and manoeuvre in close quarters.

John had breathed some magic into the bones he'd thrown last night after Alundel had fallen asleep. He and Robyn had both been satisfied with the outcomes—save one, an uncertain rift of future that even now sent a twirl of *tynged* dancing behind Robyn's eyes.

No question, in thisworld or another, the goddess must be freed from her tower. But what to come of it? Aye, *there* was a question.

David was nigh back to normal. Arthur had succumbed in the last days to the ague, but David had caught it in proper time, dosed him, and kept him warm.

Marion approved Arthur's well-being and David's care. She also made sure David hadn't fetched himself back into illness, checked his eyes and tongue and temperature. But nay, he even smelled healthy once again, with only the sniffly vestiges—and those, of course, would take time to clear off. 'Twas true, most wortwives—Marion reconsidered the title against David's sex with a grin—tended to be healthy. Her mam had always said it was due to being around the sick; one's own humours gained strength from them, like winnowing tiny bits of a poison to fashion a cure.

And even better, Will had been proper chivalrous since they'd arrived to the old camp. His affable nature had returned, and his cheer. He'd even sniped a tease at Marion when she'd shooed him away from the fireside. The pot was empty, and cold. Her mam had been right; men could be proper useless when it came to fixing a proper meal.

Not that they'd time for pottage. While Marion busied herself with a makeshift meal for them all, Gilbert filled the others in on what was happening. Will began packing the meagre belongings about their camp, and once Gilbert answered a few questions, Arthur started clearing away bedding, whilst David prepared what couldn't be taken for storage. He'd caches all over the place, David had, and a big one at the horse caves just south of Whitwell, deep in the Shire Wode. Robyn had already decided the latter as their destination, once this royal retrieval was seen to.

Will meandered over, nudged her arm. Marion let a smile tilt her lips as Will pretended to snatch at the venison she was carving into neat slices. "How long?" he wheedled.

"Not long. We've got to move on, aye?"

"You're in a hurry, then?" Phrased as merely another tease, there was a thread of something else beneath it. Marion slid her eyes to catch Will's; he dropped his own, but not before she'd seen a shadow, deep behind his gaze. It belied the grin he offered her, but didn't cheapen it, at least.

"Happens I am," she answered, easy enough. "Robyn needs us there."

"That's bloody true," Will agreed, and went to finish his packing.

Marion caught Gilbert's frown across the cavern. She shrugged and retuned her attention to her preparations. Nay, Will hadn't forgotten. Wouldn't forget, not this.

Some things you didn't forget, Robyn considered, just as some things you wish you could.

Like the comfort of the bow at his back, and the feel of soft peacock tufts and stiff goose fletchings occasionally brushing at his hood, arrows tucked, as usual, into a knot of unruly black hair.

Like the familiarity and ease of John beside him, tandem as two colts grown together in harness. 'Tweren't just the rutting to make such things, but its own kind of love, nonetheless: Gamelyn and Much had that same sense to them, that should one start something, the other would finish with nary a hitch.

Like the thrill runnelling down his spine—clear water from a sun-spangled rockfall—in the lovely tension of the stalk, the gratification of the hunt and the chase, with some of his best beloved at his side.

Like the pleasure of watching them work—all three so different, yet alike in their grace and skill and power. Particularly Gamelyn, who from the first moment they'd gained the other side of the moat and reached out, touched Blyth's walls . . .

There was no stolen/abandoned blood-magic weapon here, no cloistered and fetid not-magic to claw Robyn's senses or hamstring him. Yet a tiny wail had begun within Robyn's skull as they drew close to the keep—not unlike a neglected child realising there was finally someone near. It was more saddening than withering. However, as Gamelyn reached out and caressed the castle wall, it just . . . stopped.

Nay, not stopped, that wasn't the right word. It was still there. The sense of being, of biding and waiting, remained—a strange, hot glut simmering warning in Robyn's belly, emanating from stones given the taste of sweat and hot blood: hard work but no honour.

Gamelyn gave that honour. He courted the stone, coaxed it, a silent soothe of whispers he didn't even know he was uttering. And the keep, cozened, whispered back. Gave welcome to her Summering Lord.

It came to Robyn, sudden and surrounded by his lover's place: no wonder the Templars had failed with Gamelyn. They, too, had tried to set shackles on him, jess and hood him, hunt him only to a lure. As if they could deny the wind, like—not kenning it necessary, to lift and ruffle his lovely hawk's wings.

It was quiet, so quiet, with only the heavy drift of fog and the occasional snatch of voices, above and within.

The postern indeed lay in ruins, blocked to the outside by a slide of rubble. It had opened and settled with time, could now handily accommodate someone bigger than a twelve-year-old Gamelyn or John's slight frame. As they crept to the postern, kept watch, and one by one clambered in, Gamelyn hung back. He took Robyn's arm just as he started to pass through, leaned close, lips forming speech—

Bit it back and froze as lone bootsteps resounded against rock. A golden glow spattered down, vanished, and then glinted again, the wet not-quite-rain hissing against it. A sentry, on the parapets above. Silent, slow, Gamelyn leaned against the damp wall and just as carefully pulled Robyn into the wary curve of his body. No doubt Much and John, on the other side, were just as still and flattened, upon each other and the stone.

The sentry hesitated, held his torch forwards and down.

Robyn pressed closer, buried his breath in Gamelyn's hair.

"Hoy, Everard?" Another set of footsteps, coming their way.

"Over 'ere!" was the answer.

Another orange glow danced downwards. "Bloody weather!" groused the second voice. "Me for a warm fire and a willing wife when Vespers rings."

"Be a while yet," the first—Everard—said. "Seems later ... oy, hang on, 'ere—"

Torchlight reflected against fog, then spilled down upon them through a rent in the rain-mist. Gamelyn's breath rattled against the hollow of Robyn's neck. Both refused to look up—the glint of eyes would be a sure giveaway.

But bloody damn, if that breath heating his neck and their position against the wall didn't make Robyn proper aware of the fine erection he was beginning to spring. And the grin, ghosting against Gamelyn's freckled temple, for Will always did say how

Robyn's liking for a quick wank in the teeth of peril would do him, someday . . .

"What d'you see?" the second voice asked. "As if there's anything to see in this murk."

Everard didn't answer. Then he snorted. "That bloody punt, nowt more. It's drifted 'crost again—Christ!" This as the fading light gave an abrupt hiss and wavered into darkness. "Damn the rain! 'Tis my third torch t' die."

"Bloody weather," the other repeated, tired agreement, then chuckled. "The punt, eh? Who'd think the boy'd catch anything in this stinking moat?"

His voice was retreating, accompanied by two sets of boot-treads and the fade of the remaining torch.

"He does, though," Everard's voice was also fading as the two guards continued down the wall walk. "Big 'uns."

Big 'uns, indeed, Robyn thought with a sudden smirk. Gamelyn's anatomy was reacting to Robyn's own, a fair contest of butting knobs unfortunately confined by layers of woollen, linen, and well-wrapped braies. Robyn couldn't help the slight clench of buttocks, the slight push of pelvis. In response, Gamelyn's fingers dug into the small of his back, hard.

Robyn smirked. Was it full stop, or don't stop?

The guards kept going, only the sound of their voices floating behind their passing. And bloody damn, but Robyn wanted to shag Gamelyn cross-eyed, here and now.

"Wanker," Gamelyn accused.

"I prefer not, milord. Wanking, that is," Robyn mouthed back, gave another slow and grindy shove just for good measure, then pushed back.

"Funny, what a whiff of danger can accomplish," Gamelyn furthered, with the nigh-silent and practised lisp of one well-used to being in dodgy places and staying unheard. "I suppose it means you're . . . " Hesitation. "All right? No . . . " Again trailing away, as if Gamelyn really didn't know how to say it.

If only you knew, Robyn thought with a fond smile, *but then, maybe you don't need to, yet.* Leaning forwards, he nuzzled at Gamelyn's cheek and, in blatant demonstration, placed one hand flat against the curtain wall, smoothed it down. Gamelyn smiled back, brief but warm, and loosed him.

Some things you didn't forget. And some things you wished you could.

Gamelyn took a deep breath, considered how that was just the way of things, wasn't it?

Once within the walls, the way became easier. If things stopped because of damp weather, nothing would ever get done, this time of year. There were market stalls still open, errands and chores still to do. No one so much as noted the passage of several unsuccessful hunters headed to the stables.

Gamelyn was unsure whether his memories were too kind, or if Blyth had indeed suffered since his father's death. His elder brother had only recently met his deserved demise, after all—but surely would have ruled with a mailed fist until then. In fact, Johan had done even as their father's health had declined. If nothing else, Gamelyn had to admit he'd been capable.

Or perhaps it was one simple fact: the country was drowning in the wake of their monarch's monetary demands. First Crusade, and now the ransom . . . Gamelyn paused, ran a hand along the stones of the stable, a mute and musing apology to the place he'd grown from child to youth. True, it could be argued that Blyth hadn't endured siege or seen battle in some time—too long. The castle was being rendered unfit for her purpose—and through no fault of her own, one of many raw reminders of this peculiar tide swamping England.

Perhaps Count John had the right of it.

Treasonous thoughts, surely. *Yet after all,* Gamelyn mused, sardonic, *when one lies with wolfsheads. . .*

He'd do her proper honour, was he given the chance. The lord's sheltered third son might have lacked enough knowledge for such a thing, but the soldier and *Confanonier* knew better . . .

And in that instant, Gamelyn realised Robyn was right. He *did* want this. Even if still unsure of why, or how—or if it would ever come his way.

He shook his head, droplets of rainwater pelting his hand, then followed Much, Robyn, and John into the darkened haven of the stables. He'd no time for sentiment—but this wasn't sentiment, surely? Merely observations of a place they were invading; a reasonable care shown in enemy territory.

Nevertheless, inexplicable reactions waited everywhere he turned, shaking out his senses as if they were an unused and dusty rug. The nutty taste of hay and corn, the tart pinch of urine, the earthy-sharp reek of manure. The box of his first warhorse, inhabited by a coarse sorrel rouncey instead of grey Diamant, who had survived sand and Saracens merely to break his foreleg on the voyage back to England. Diamant would never see his old loose box again, and Gamelyn had thought he too never would return here.

Another box several rows back of that, where he had first espied John and Robyn . . . where he'd first discovered what two lads could do together . . . how his own mix of shame and wanting had given firm notice of things he'd never suspected.

The ill-used stair, concealed by cobwebs, dust, and dark, only there if you knew where to look, leading to his family's chambers atop the main tower.

At this rate, Gamelyn could only thank the God of his fathers that they would, in all likelihood, go nowhere near the chapel, and the library . . .

He jumped as Robyn's fingers slid against his palm; Robyn merely grasped his hand, squeezed. Said, "It looks different, aye?"

"Aye." And bugger and blast, but Gamelyn's throat tried to close up, making more words impossible.

"Much!"

Another start, this one also gentled by Robyn's fingers against Gamelyn's, light but there then releasing. They both turned, Robyn backing into the shadows and Gamelyn leaning forwards into the faint light. Shielded lamps and high window slits sketched a stooped, bandy-legged figure loping over to Much. Brand, the stable master Sir Ian had taken on when first bringing his family to Blyth.

Much met the old man halfway, hugged him hard and tight. John also had ventured close, smiling, one hand going to Brand's sleeve as Brand pushed Much back with a tiny shake and reached for John.

"Bloody damn, lookee the two of ye. Grown men, and all!" The old man was nigh babbling, tears in his eyes. "Glory, has it been so long since y've come tae visit auld Brand? I mean, I know times is changed, an' all, but . . . " Brand hesitated as he glanced towards where Gamelyn stood. He looked puzzled—and more than a bit worried.

"Do you remember," Much ventured softly, "milord of Blyth's youngest son?"

"Youngest," the old man muttered, and shook his head. "Can't be, Much-lad. Young Gamelyn's long gone, and this man's nowt like . . . "

Gamelyn stepped forwards, just as uncertain. Brand's hesitancy was one more sensory incursion in a vast sea of them, and Gamelyn himself less prepared for it than he'd prefer.

"It's as Much says, Brand. I am Gamelyn, Sir Ian's son."

Brand's gaze was milky even in the dim; already luminous, it widened, glimmered further. "Milord. Oh, milord, they told us you were dead, dead in the Holy Land!" He lurched forwards, grabbed Gamelyn's hand and brought it to his cheek. "You don't look yourself, lad—begging your pardon, milord—but you don't.

You've changed, sure enough, grown tae a man as tall and fine as my two lads 'ere . . . "

His voice warbled as he looked up, eyes going even wider as they focused past Gamelyn's shoulder. He stumbled back, just a pace or two, and went to his knees.

Gamelyn turned, saw only Robyn. He was still in the shadows, but by some trick of light, the peacock fletchings tucked into his hair reflected cerulean into midnight eyes, brought them gleaming 'neath his cowl. Then Gamelyn saw *more.*

The glint of horns, the rush, within silence, of a hot breath and canines bared beneath a snarl. The sense of something caged—but only just. Waiting for the chance to flee, or to strike. The jingle of gilt chain in a breeze that could not possibly exist in the protection of the stable aisle, and the flicker of lamps as if it could.

"Lord." It was a soft, hoarse breath. *"Bendith y mamau."* The old man lowered his head, half-afraid.

Gamelyn felt no fear, no insubordination; only a slow sense of dreamy abstraction. Curiosity—*Is this what it feels like? Is this it?*—then satisfaction purring, bone-deep.

Robyn's voice—with a startling hint of Gamelyn's own as the Horned Lord answered:

Stand together, My warriors, and none will stand against Us. . .

Then, an odd and fierce exhilaration as, amidst the waxing light of Oak and Summer, Winter's Lord glided forwards with a soundless grace and accepted Brand's blessing by giving his own, grave as any priest with the Host. *"Bendith y mamau, tad ceffylau,"* Robyn whispered, and placed both hands upon the white head, breathed a kiss there.

Gamelyn watched, still with that formless . . . fascination, was the only thing he could think to call it. John also was on his knees. And Much. Both of them, recognising what stood before them was Robyn, but also . . . *more.* Yet when uncertainty niggled at Gamelyn, the . . . *more,* sure and strong, reminded him he was one with the dreaming, not witness to it.

John's eyes rose to meet Gamelyn's, lustrous with consent.

Unreality faded, sucked into the shadows. Robyn knelt with Brand, took his hands and lifted him to stand. Repeated, soft, "Her blessings upon you, old horse father. Will you help us?"

Brand's ash-brown gaze wavered from Robyn to Gamelyn, then back to Robyn again before they lowered. "Be it Lord or land, I have allus been yours."

Brand proved good as his word. Not only through his lad lending them the punt, but with several of the house-bound villeins. To their god's avatar, they gave both obeisance and information, received his blessing with the same mix of love and fear. Robyn accepted it like the double-edged blade it was. It was too akin to what the nobles would inspire. Likely the day he was wholly comfortable with it would be his last—power wielded to no good end was suitable for blood sacrifice and little else.

What those villeins told them set a smirk upon Robyn's lip and lit wicked satisfaction behind Gamelyn's eyes, hearkening to that Templar assassin Robyn had, in his time, both loathed and lusted.

"Only four guards in the upper storey?" Much snorted his own amazement from where he leaned against a loose box partition. Beside him, scratching the ears of the box's occupant—an iron-grey filly—John also looked proper satisfied.

"Plenty below," replied one of the villeins, a short, stout lass with a mass of golden hair coiffed all neat. "Getting in our way all hours, playing knucklebones and eating the pantries bare. What with the Count's example, there's none of us women'll go down there anymore. A few of the younger lads en't safe, neither." A disgusted snort.

"His Prat-ness fancies lads?" Robyn couldn't believe it.

The description had everyone chuckling; the lass giggled a reply. "Nay! But anything as wears skirts en't safe, that's for certain. Some of the menfolk want to know what 'is cook makes, to keep Count John so able. As much as five, he's had in 'is bed!"

"I wouldn't mind the cook's secret meself," Much gave an appealing grin to the lass. "Should you find it."

The lass flushed, all pretty, and Gamelyn's mouth gave a tilt towards Much.

"And Herself?" Robyn prompted.

"None of us 're allowed to see to her," another put in. "Himself sent her ladies away."

"If he sent them home, they'd talk." Gamelyn frowned.

"He sent 'em, under guard, to Nottingham," Brand said. "In our fanciest covered coach."

"How'd we miss nicking *that*?" Robyn snorted, then shrugged his bow from his shoulders. He fingered one of the flax strings from its quiver pocket, twirled it between his fingers.

"But she has women with her, surely?" Gamelyn made it more statement than query.

"Oh, aye," was the answer. "But they en't hers, if you follow."

"We do." Robyn began stringing the bow. Four guards, more below—hopefully not even a factor—and several waiting-women who likely weren't to be trusted.

Oh, and Himself the bum-boil across the hall, shagging his way through the castle's female population.

Gamelyn drew a dagger from his boot sheath, inspected it even though he surely didn't need to. Much had been sharpening one of his own blades on a small stone—again, likely unnecessary. John kept murmuring to the filly. Unlike Much, who'd been Gamelyn's companion when Gamelyn had inhabited the chamber in which the Queen was now imprisoned, John knew little of the upper floors. He'd stay in his old demesne—here in the stables—be their eyes below.

"Then we go," Robyn said, and gave his bowstring a pluck. It hummed, sweet, into the expectant quiet.

"You do the talkin', pet. You know the language of her like, aye?" Robyn gave a tiny smirk, which Gamelyn answered. It vanished as Gamelyn drew his sword and ascended the narrow passageway. Robyn started up after, keeping an eye up and into the shadows. Gamelyn's cloak wafted, caught in a sudden draught of air; it trailed across Robyn's shoulder, then his cheek, and Robyn's step faltered as memory impressed itself onto the present . . .

Stone walls, heavy about him as he pursues a familiar, copper-haired shape up an unlit, narrow stair, and the hem of Gamelyn's cloak brushes his cheek as draughts puff downwards. . .

And those stones heavy upon him, tight and bearing down . . .

"Lord?" A soft whisper, and Much's hand upon his shoulder, literally pouring strength into Robyn's wobbly knees.

Robyn covered the hand with his own, nodded, then kept climbing.

Gamelyn waited for them at the top, backlit by torchlight—several of them, making the corridor brighter than the waning day outside. He held up five fingers—one more than they were counting on, and Robyn not sure of his senses. Then Gamelyn reached out, grasped Robyn's hand in his, and pulled him close. Those senses quickened, surging to the fore. Robyn shivered, then smiled. He only remembered one other time when he'd felt this powerful in any stone walls: the time he'd carried Gamelyn, injured, from Nottingham, and called the Wild Hunt from not only his own heart, but Marion's—and Gamelyn's.

His lovely Oak no longer needed to be passed out and nigh dead to touch his own power, even if he still wasn't aware of how or what . . .

A small roar upon the roof made them both start, then relax:

more rain, beating down upon wood and thatch. Gamelyn gave a nigh-silent, self-deprecating snort, then jerked his head towards the guards. As if to make things easier, they were clumped together around a warming brazier, trying to shake off the damp and chill.

"Can you take them?" Gamelyn mouthed against his ear. Again, this had been decided before. Was Robyn able for the magic, it would mean less struggle, less chance of being overheard.

Robyn nodded and squeezed Gamelyn's hand, released it and moved forwards. *Now I can.*

It was a bloody relief, actually. Something to do with his taut-twined senses, somewhere to funnel what danced, barely restrained madness, through his nerves. And easy—too easy, almost, to sneak up on the miserable guards and speak the words upon the hex breath, sing them all to sleeping.

Thankfully, not a one of them fell towards the brazier.

Gamelyn and Much ran up behind him, and they poured down the hall like water and rushed up against the door.

Opened it.

Again, Sense and Sight, memory laid open within Robyn. He didn't truly see the ladies in their corner, heads jerking up from the sewing tasks. Nor did he see the woman near the window, swathed in velvets and finest linen, inspecting an embroidery frame. When she turned, all he saw was . . .

Eyes. A mythic myriad of eyes, cerulean and emerald, peering at him . . . peering *through* him. Robyn pulled an arrow from his hair and nocked it, smooth and deadly instinct to deny the way his legs were wanting to give beneath him.

Eyes. The goddess's eyes upon his arrow. Her eyes imprinted on a royal bird, and the power behind them peering over a peacock-feather fan, and laughing . . .

Laughter sounded, soft and almost mocking, but stoppered itself as Robyn nocked and primed his arrow. There was a chorus of small gasps from the trio of girls huddled sewing in the corner; one sucked in a breath as if to cry out, choked it into a whimper as Robyn's bow lifted, creaked into the night-quiet. Much quickstepped towards them in Robyn's wake; a broad, dark-cloaked threat with knives naked in both hands.

"Bid 'em quiet," Robyn ordered, low, at the same time he bade his own senses do the same—surely he should be used to nigh walking over his own visions by now!

"Do be quiet, girls" came the obliging murmur from behind the peacock fan. "We don't want to wake our lord." A scathing under-current, only slightly modified as the voice lifted, ever so slight. "Or do we? Do you come to ransom, or as rescue?"

The peacock eyes turned fully their direction—these were not part and parcel of the elaborate feather fan, but grey ones lashed startlingly black, bordered by a green headrail that nigh blended in with the feathers. Robyn had the sense, again, of time dipping and wheeling as a bejewelled hand drew the fan downwards to reveal high cheekbones, a long, aristocratic nose, and mouth situated into sternness. The feathers smoothed over, then curled about the headrail, tucked snug beneath a jaw lax with age, but no less impressive in its set or sculpt for all that.

Despite any fore-Sight and warning, of the beings Robyn might have expected, all draped in one of the Lady Huntress's most powerful signs, a Christian queen was not one of them.

"That depends, my Queen," Gamelyn said, the words as fiercely contained as his body, taut-ready at Robyn's side, "upon whether your trouvère spoke the truth of your need for one more than the other."

There was a small, unwieldy silence. This was the turning point. They were in, or they were dead.

"My trouvère," Queen Eleanor said, considering, "is known to exaggerate upon occasion, but there is usually truth beneath his words. He is a dutiful man."

"My lady!" one of the maidservants protested. "I—!"

Much moved towards her, and the protest squeaked, warbled quiet.

"Shut," Eleanor said between her teeth, "*up*, girl."

Openly—and remarkably—sullen, the girl watched the three men with a mix of defiance, fear, and suspicion. The Queen also eyed the intruders, more curious than afraid. Dismissive of Robyn and Much, her gaze narrowed upon Gamelyn, pondering. Robyn wondered if she could see the gleam of the blood-crossed tabard beneath his turned cloak. No doubt it was plain who the nobleman was here, at any rate, and indeed the Queen spoke to Gamelyn in Frankish, her head cocking sideways like a hungry bird. Gamelyn, coiled into readiness beside Robyn, released it ever so slight, and answered her—also Frankish.

"My lady?" The one maidservant obviously didn't speak it—and was altogether too meddlesome for Robyn's liking. He shot Much silent command; Much raised his eyebrows and loomed closer to the maidens, contemplating the tip of his dagger.

"Aye, Madam, we understand. Sad, but true," Gamelyn answered in English. His eyes went to Robyn's, held. "Not all serve their master—or mistress—so uncompromisingly."

Kohl-rimmed eyes flickered to where the three maidservants stood against the wall. That lot was torn between watching their mistress and eyeing Much, who was making quite the show of twirling one of his knives between his callused fingers.

Well, and if they'd not known the maidservants' loyalties already, the Queen was giving them plain warning. Which boded well.

"That'll be you again," Gamelyn murmured to Robyn. "Can you?"

And aye, but he could and then some. Robyn gave a tiny smirk to answer Gamelyn's raised brows and relaxed the push on his bow. Drawing a soft, deep breath, he paced over to where the maidservants had huddled together against the farthest wall. They watched Robyn's progress with widening eyes, two of them drawing close. The third backed even farther, refused to meet his gaze . . . that one was of his people and recognised the wilding-light a-kindle in the eyes of her god's chosen. Robyn could smell her recognition, sweet as summer-plump grain, then the apprehension as he moved closer, sickening like that grain gone to mould.

Much too well recognised Robyn's intent, retreated with a deferential—albeit nervous—tip of his head.

"I'll not have them abused, mind." Eleanor's hiss of warning followed him, quiet with its own apprehension, and an edge of steel. "But a little fear of God and a gag might do them some good."

The maidservant who'd kept protesting narrowed her eyes and sucked in a breath to scream; the other made to join her.

Robyn didn't give either the chance. The charm was already on the back of his tongue; he breathed it out, spun it over defiance, and snapped it like a thin, dry branch.

"*Cysgwch yn dawel.*"

The first maidservant's eyes rolled up in her head and she dropped, limp as a rag dolly. The one alongside was but a breath behind and fell, just as unconscious, atop her comrade.

Gamelyn muttered something. A harsh, feminine intake of breath sounded behind Robyn, answered by a low croon behind his eyes, lighting flames there to dance and heat. *Good. Let Eleanor, by Grace of Her God Queen Mother of England, realise hers isn't the only power to reckon with* in *England. . .*

The remaining maidservant had also dropped to the stones, but her hands were clasped above her head, her voice thin-soft, beseeching. "Please, Lord, I dint mean it! I gots no choice, I—!" Her voice choked off into a phlegmy sob as Robyn bent over her.

"Which god do *you* fear?" he asked, ever-so-soft. "Look at me, girl."

She raised her eyes. Within them, Robyn Saw her sight: a black not-man with eyes of flame and, growing from hooded shadows, a rack of holly-twined antlers, dotted with crimson . . .

"Don't forget," the Horned Lord told her, taking her face in his palms. "Sleep, now." And held her as he breathed the charm, lowered her to the ground, gentle, as she went limp.

A wind sucked in through the window, guttering the candles into darkness.

Silence again, and as their eyes adjusted, the moon peeked from behind the clouds. The reflection shone off the wet cobbles and stones, bathed the chamber in silver half-light. It fingered its way through Robyn's hair, and he sighed, breathed it in. Stood.

Gamelyn knew the chamber well, dark or no; had moved soft-quiet to stand beside and take Robyn's elbow as he rose. "I didn't quite expect such a fine display," Gamelyn murmured. He gave a surprised blink as Robyn turned to him, and Robyn saw, again, the glint of fire-gold. This time it sank into shadows, reflecting in juniper green just before Gamelyn retreated, pale lashes touching freckled cheeks.

Robyn's lip tilted. "You want a bit of sun, pet," he said, leaning over to kiss Gamelyn's temple.

Sure enough, Gamelyn's eyes flew back open, and he hissed, "Why do you keep *doing* that?"

"You're just too pretty when you're all set t' sixes an' sevens."

"We *are* in the middle of a sodding castle raid, you realise."

Much cleared his throat. Loudly. Obviously trying his damnedest not to grin, he tilted his head towards the woman approaching them in the stark moonlight, skirts trailing a heavy, thick susurrus against stone.

Gamelyn turned to face Eleanor, flinging his cloak over one shoulder before he'd thought; Robyn also swerved his attention, dipping his chin more to hide the blaze still heating his Sight than any demanded respect in her presence. The latter merely reminded him of what she was—and Gamelyn, did it come to that—a dismissal, warning of what he and Much weren't. One bidding him duck his head, bend the knee, *crawl* . . .

The Horned Lord growled, soft mutiny, and Robyn picked up his black-scruffed chin to meet the Queen's gaze. A smile ticked his lip as kohl-lined grey reflected, for just the moment, the flame-eyed deity who had just bespelled her servants into slumber . . .

With a quick reestablishment of self-control that put Gamelyn to shame, the Queen lifted her own chin, then inclined it sideways, pondering her sleeping maidservants. "Spies, the lot of them. My son's creatures, particularly the pretty blonde. Young girls are so unfortunately . . . susceptible. To power and promises both." It managed scorn despite not rising above a murmur, mindful they were but a corridor away from her gaoler.

Eleanor nevertheless seemed in no hurry, taking in her would-be rescuers. The Queen was not as tall as one would first think; her head barely came to Robyn's chin as she considered first Gamelyn, then Robyn again, twitching the hem of her skirts close about her. The peacock fan, tied to one wrist, swung and fluttered against the wine-coloured fabric. "There's but one peasant who's rumoured to have the devil's own sorcery at his command. And how fascinating—" she lifted her fan, motioned with it to the goose- and peacock-fletched arrows cached in Robyn's knotted black hair "—that the notorious Robyn Hood should enjoy a bit of fancy and colour in his chosen murder weapons. But you're so young!" She chuckled, low and not unpleasant. "I'd not expected the notorious thief of Sherwood of an age to be my grandson. Or great-grandson, at that."

Brow furrowing, Robyn slid a bemused look towards Gamelyn.

"It would also seem the stories of Robyn Hood's curious . . . powers are not altogether exaggerated. Particularly"—the grey eyes moved to Gamelyn, whose tabard had been revealed, a scarlet-and-ebon beacon between Much's plain cloak and Robyn's dark cowl atop forest-coloured garb—"if he's a Templar at his beck and call. A young and handsome one, at that, even if baseborn."

"Milord is *not* baseborn, milady!" Much had obviously taken to heart one too many of such digs regarding his master. That this latest was delivered by royalty finally penetrated. "He . . . he is . . . " Much peered at his master, uncertain.

Gamelyn turned to the Queen and went down on one knee, sword point-down upon the flooring. The obeisance was that, but also held a fierce pride, a grace to make Robyn's heart hammer and his toes tingle.

"I am Sir Gamelyn Boundys de Blyth, *Confanonier* and *Templier* to Hirst Preceptory. This is my paxman, Much, and my other companion, as you guessed, is Robyn Hood."

Much had already gone to one knee; beneath Eleanor's raised brow, Robyn found himself doing the same. She kept eyeing him and Gamelyn, one and then the other, with a stern regard Robyn was sure he'd not endured since his mam had caught him, at the tender age of nine, sneaking out to the tavern in wee hours.

Copper-gilt head still lowered, Gamelyn lifted a hand, palm up. Gold glinted there, sharp between finger and thumb.

Eleanor, by Grace of God, Queen of the English, Duchess of the Normans, contemplated her ring. "So," she said, finally. "It is to be rescue."

"In which case, Madam"—Gamelyn rose, did not sheath his sword—"I would suggest haste."

"Aye," Robyn murmured. "The sleep'll only last for so long."

- XI -

Queen Eleanor seemed a bit dumbstruck as they herded her from her chamber and out into the hall. She might have hidden such when confronted with Robyn's method of dealing with the maidservants, but a cadre of guards laid out in peaceful sleep gave her pause.

Too much pause. Gamelyn had already made it to the hall's end and the corridor leading down. The castle breathed against him, updraught wafting across his cheeks, tugging at stray strands of hair. Distraction. Irritable, he batted at it akin to a bothersome fly.

And unfortunately, dumbstruck didn't last long. "Tell me again," Eleanor whispered, "how long this uncanny . . . lethargy will last?"

They hadn't *time* for this! As Robyn gave a shrug, Gamelyn rolled his eyes, strode back—silently—and took Eleanor's elbow.

Eleanor blinked, startled; he merely eyed her back, raised his eyebrows. "Not long, Madam," Gamelyn said, and the *Do you want bloody out of here or no?* must have been plain in his expression, for Eleanor demurred as he propelled her towards the stair.

Robyn followed, not bothering to hide a grin. *Cheeky sod,* it said.

Look who's talking. What else was there to be done? Here they were, in the middle of bloody enemy territory, and the one they were liberating chose *now* to start asking questions? Much, thank God, knew better, merely tucked a small box the Queen had refused to leave behind into a side pouch, and trailed after, keeping eyes open and knives to hand.

A sudden *thud* made them all freeze at the top of the stairwell.

Much met Gamelyn's eyes, a query. Gamelyn frowned, put up two fingers in warning. They heeded that warning, spent it in the wait: Eleanor's eyes going back and forth with her free hand at her throat; Much sliding slightly down the wall, blades ready; Robyn taking a few steps back the way he'd come, loose-limbed and ready for anything.

An irritated shout from what had been Sir Ian's quarters, and from behind the door adjacent, a low and urgent answer.

"It's a connecting chamber," Gamelyn whispered. "They shouldn't have to come out."

Nevertheless, Robyn pulled an arrow from his hair and into nock. He'd a half smile gracing his lips; that and the motion of arrow to string seemed almost lazy—did one not see the gloss hardening his black eyes.

"Wait," Gamelyn said.

"Aye."

More voices. One in particular, a shrill bellow recognisable to all: Count John.

"I do love my children" was Eleanor's sardonic mutter.

The voice from the nearest door sounded again, this time closer to the door. Robyn's bow creaked, soft, and he said, just as soft, "Take her on."

Gamelyn nodded, jerked his head at Much. Much also nodded, backing his way towards the stairwell as Gamelyn, with a tug at Eleanor's arm, started down.

Another shout, and an answer, this time moving away from the door. Gamelyn didn't question it further, just melted into the darkness of the stairwell. First Much, then—ah—Robyn's footsteps descended after as the darkness swallowed them.

"Nowt," Robyn said.

They took the steps downwards, rapid, hugging close to the wall. At the bottommost curve, a light came into view—the spatter-gold jerk and fetch of a torch. It moved at the stair bottom, held aloft by a slender figure. Brown eyes glinted beneath lit pitch, peering up the stair until John made sure of his leader's safe descent. Only then did he smile, a brilliant but fleeting thing, and with a sideways jerk of his chin, led them off to the right.

Gamelyn recognised it; a narrow, dark path behind a row of horse boxes, leading into an alcove. A round of demanding nickers started at one end of the boxes. Infectious, the throaty demands quickly made their way down the aisle, and Gamelyn cursed to himself. He'd forgotten the feed was kept in this room.

But John didn't stop, and Brand's voice sounded from the darkness.

"Cush, now," he said, and there was the rustle of hay being tossed, down the line.

Feeding time.

Eleanor halted, wary, as Brand came into the torchlight, still pitching fodder. John gestured reassurance, went over and put a hand to Brand's hay-strewn sleeve.

The old man sniffed, gave a curt nod, and muttered, "Mind t' torch, Johnny." He returned to his doling out of hay: nothing to see as far as he was concerned, move on, then.

The soothing rhythm of munching beasts filled the narrow chamber as they went deeper. Eleanor slowed again—again, understandable. They seemed headed towards a solid wall piled high with hay.

John put his torch into a rack in the wall, well away from the haystack, and started forwards. Gamelyn followed close—they both knew what lay beyond. John went first, diving into the hay like a salmon swimming upstream, then burrowing to the left. Part of the stack quivered, then slid forwards, a cascade of sweet-smelling fodder tumbling almost to their toes.

Behind it, there was a depression within the stones, and a dark chasm beyond. The entry was just over half Gamelyn's own height. He smiled, remembering the proud day he'd had to bend over to traverse it.

"Where is Blondel?" Eleanor suddenly whispered.

"Who?" Gamelyn nodded for John to go ahead, held his hand out for Eleanor.

Eleanor didn't move to take it. Robyn had started forwards and gave a soft curse as he nearly ran into her. "Milady, on with y—"

"Where is he?" Eleanor said, a tiny bit louder and still unmoving.

Gamelyn strode back the few steps he'd gained. "Madam, we haven't the luxury of—"

"Where is my man? Or I go no farther," Eleanor hissed back. "There is none other who could have given you my ring. He would have come with you, and when you said we had help in the barn . . . "

Gamelyn wondered, briefly, if Robyn should just set her to sleep as well. It might be easier to carry her if she was going to go on about some like nonsense every half furlong. Queen or no.

Robyn frowned. "If you're meaning that minstrel—"

"Trouvère," Eleanor corrected.

Robyn peered at her for a moment, brows knotted. Then he flung a glance at Gamelyn, gave a snort of laughter. "Poncy talk's catching, is it?"

Despite the darkness, Gamelyn could see the Queen shaking her

head and gathering up for another demand. *Putain de merde.*
Gamelyn rolled his eyes, started to take hold of her arm again, but
Robyn beat him to it, took Eleanor's elbow with a bow that would
have done credit to a courtier. She blinked, startled, and let him
move her on.

"I en't familiar with no Blondel, milady. If you're meaning t' singer
as gave our Templar there that shiny gold ring, well, he calls
himself Alundel so far as we know, and he's waiting for you in camp
with the rest of m' lads. T' tell the truth?" Robyn shot Gamelyn
another gaze, just as mirthful. "None of us thought he were up to
the likes of this sortie. He's a bit fussy, aye?"

"Fussy?" Eleanor, with a chuckle, proceeded to let Robyn pull her
along. "Well, that's one way of putting it."

Gamelyn peered back at Much, who shrugged and grinned. "She's
moving, 'tennyrate, milord."

Gamelyn gave a soft snort, then followed.

By feel and luck, John found another torch waiting on the far end.
It was dry from long disuse, but Much produced a hank of oil-
soaked wool from the bag slung over his shoulder. He stuffed the
wool onto the torch's prickly end and snapped a flint across the
steel of his dagger with the ease of long practise.

Down here, light was more than cheering; it was ease of movement, insurance that they didn't have to feel their way and—
possibly—follow the wall into being turned about and lost.

The Queen was still chuckling over the reference to Alundel. In
fact, Eleanor was taking this whole thing better than Robyn had ever
expected of a spoilt and elderly noblewoman. He let her spend a
little of what nervousness she did have in telling him a perilously
funny tale regarding said singer's fussy nature—in a subdued murmur, of course. They were, by John's reckoning, still beneath the keep.

Robyn found himself oddly thankful for the woman's soft chatter,
busied himself in keeping her on a steady course through the dark
tunnel. Were his men here, they'd be having a go at his expense,
but sod it, Robyn *liked* women. Despite rumour to the contrary,
and Eleanor's present and nervous example, the lasses he'd known
really didn't go on even half as much as some of his lads.

And it was bloody good to have a distraction from the ever-present
singsong whispering behind his eyes. Minimal, aye, and nothing
akin to the abandoned shrieks of Worksop's chapel. Moreover, the
deeper they went, the more . . . cozened the stones seemed, winding
down from urgent whispers to lazy hum. Of course, down in these

depths, the stones were more a cavern, carved by man with older prayers.

Striding behind Robyn, shoulder-to-shoulder with Much, Gamelyn seemed altogether comfortable and comforted in the darkness under the keep. Part of the comfort was in action, which Robyn understood all too well. Mayhap 'twas also because these passages were ones Gamelyn knew so well from boyhood. Almost as well as John did . . .

John certainly wasn't tumbled by any of it. It truly seemed John didn't hear what either Gamelyn or Robyn did, led them calmly upon a circuitous, ever-darkening route. Robyn could see John even when he closed his eyes, a steady beacon limned against his eyelids.

Your Janicot, the Horned Lord said, deep into the earth, *does not bear the Hood. Does not quicken the footsteps of Death as you must. It is not his to hold, even as the barren stones are not yours to sing living.*

Yet John's presence would bid the answers come; maker's heart teasing truth into being.

Summer still sleeps in the dark and cold. . .

John had Told it with the bones, and Robyn knew the truth deep in his own. It wasn't just the stolen Arrow, or the stones begging attention. It was also the vibrations—nay, the protestations—of a gift being trammelled sterile and silent.

The stone rumbled about him. Robyn at first didn't notice any difference, merely tucked his chin and gritted his teeth, kept going. But a hand gripped Robyn's arm, staying him. It was Gamelyn, coming up beside and speaking to Queen Eleanor in a quick smattering of Frankish. John had also come to a stop, looking ahead. His torch, held behind him, dipped and spat as if in reaction, sending molten flickers through the tunnel.

The stone cavern was still rumbling.

Eleanor, skirts fisted in one hand, gave a dubious look upwards. "Likely a waggon," Much murmured. "Aye, Johnny?"

John nodded, with a frown. It wasn't reassuring.

"A big one," Gamelyn concurred. "We must be beneath the high upper bailey." The ceiling shook, sent ghosts of dust from the overhead sandstone. "Not much longer. You'll need your hood then, Madam." As if following his own advice, Gamelyn shifted his own cloak forwards, covering his tabard, then moved to once more take the lead with John.

Eleanor watched after for a few moments, then turned to Robyn. "Very much the soldier, that man."

Robyn shrugged and took in a soft, dust-mote breath. Sure enough, visibility was improving beyond the reach of any torches. A soft grey philtred from ahead, and they were beginning to climb.

The stones, in the wake of Gamelyn's passage . . . purred, like a barn cat curled up on a horse's rump. Trailing a negligent hand along the wall as he ascended, Gamelyn was oblivious to his silent courtship. Unwitting that those stones would fain speak to one raised to their knowing as all those whispers slid around him like water over oiled cloth.

Robyn heard them. John too, a little. Yet Marion had been first to bring the knowledge into speech. If Gamelyn would not claim his own magic, then there could be no trine to gather all worlds as one. No gathering of talents and instincts, no Archer, Knight, and Maid to call the magic against the coming, sterile storm. There would be no *Ceugant*.

We have to speak to this, love, Robyn swore to Gamelyn's black-clad back. *Anon.* And as they turned the last corner, light streamed down into their earthen maze.

Gamelyn had missed this.

The thrill of the hunt, the chase, the dodge and parry. Like an injured warhorse who bit and tore at his tethers and bandages when the war-banner was set to fly over an encampment, he reacted to even the prospect of engagement. Horrific, but also beautiful, an instinct set free, mindless, and swept up in the use of honed talent and hard-won skills.

But here and now there could be no sublimation to impulse, no laxity of control. Gamelyn knew he was not up to his best. He needed more time, and application, and more practise. There was always satisfaction to be had in the practise—and he had not been able for enough of it so far.

But there was even more satisfaction in sinking into the familiarity of Templar assassin. There was reason, detachment, a calculative cool in this space. He was merely the weapon. He knew Guy de Gisbourne much better than he knew Gamelyn. In this function he wasn't sure he could trust Gamelyn.

Of course, the outlaws didn't trust Gisbourne.

The Queen had come up the small stair, eyeing him. And thankfully not prattling or demanding to know what was going on. Gamelyn's middle brother had often commented on his youngest sibling's resemblance to their mother; Gamelyn had been half-afraid Eleanor would prove to be the model upon which either of her sons had been moulded.

"You'll stay with John," Gamelyn said to her, curt, and motioned

Much towards the door. "If there's trouble, John will see you to safety whilst the rest of us hold the flank."

"You'll be with her as well, don't forget," Robyn voiced, a step down from Eleanor. "Me and Much'll hold up the rear."

"Robyn—"

"'Tis what we agreed, and I wain't argue this wit' you again." Robyn's face looked . . . drawn, in the half light. Gamelyn frowned at this, started again to speak, but Robyn cut him off. "I'll lay you out and Much'll carry you if needs be." From next to John, Much shrugged acquiescence as Robyn continued. "We en't after fightin' wars today."

Gamelyn had fought under worse circumstances, but . . . Robyn was right. Damn him.

Eleanor was quiet, eyes darting back and forth, trying to figure out what seemed a minor mutiny, no doubt. Her expression as knight conceded to peasant made black humour bubble up and tip a smile to Gamelyn's lip. Robyn no doubt would have had plenty to say on her assumptions upon noblemen naturally being in charge.

Now, neither of them had the temper for it. Gamelyn turned to her, held out a hand.

"We go."

Their door to freedom truly wasn't either; they still had to cross the bailey, and the "door" less than half-sized, more a sluice for possible flooding than anything else. They crawled up from there and into a small alcove, centre point for several storerooms long in disuse.

The rain had moved in even more, a hard patter that sent hanks of mist wafting thick across the path. It was nigh deserted—both from the hour and, no doubt, the small run of interference from their villein helpers. Across the way, steam billowed out around bright-hued ropes and tendrils, skeins of wool and flax sagging heavy on their lines and dripping pigments onto guttered ground. Voices rose and fell behind the sodden rainbow of swathes; the dye vats were seldom idle. But it was also seldom the workers peered past their barrier of steam and colour.

That steam wafted all sorts of oddities, stinging-sharp in the air: salt and stale, vinegar and plant matter. Robyn snuffed it, let it clear his head even as his hands were busy with his quiver, sliding a few more arrows from it to the knot of hair at his right collarbone. The bow—suspiciously strung, in town, in a downpour—couldn't be helped. A hand came to rest upon his back—John left it there, angled his head against Robyn's shoulder as Much stepped from their alcove and into the rain.

Much walked up the rutted path. He hesitated, gave a stretch and turned, as if looking for someone. He shifted his shoulders, pulled his cowl up farther, scratched at his nose.

Robyn met Gamelyn's eyes and gave John's hair a fond tug, took the proffered signal, and strode out to meet Much.

Nothing to be seen, and what few guards were visible on the wall were heading the other way, hunched and listless against the rain. Barrels were stacked several high not a stone's throw from where they had come, and just past the dye vats squatted a wide waggon, loaded high with fell wood. Mayhap it was the source of the rumbling they'd heard earlier. A horse stood, waiting in the traces and hunched against the wet.

As he and Much pretended to talk, Robyn gave the next signal—a hand to his nape and a nod. Gamelyn, cocking an eye towards the shield wall, emerged first. Then Eleanor, shrouded in her cloak with John beside her, dropping behind to tail. Quickly both Robyn and Much gained the point, keeping their eyes open.

The rain had intensified, the fog closing in on the heels of approaching darkness. They hunched against it, feet squelching upon first cobbled path, then grass, then mud and gravel as they made their way towards the back postern. No one so much as hailed them, and as Robyn glanced back, he saw why: past a stone's throw, nothing could be seen save grey hanks of wet.

He looked up. The wall walk, hidden here and there when they'd arrived, was now totally obscured. Robyn dropped back and put a hand to John's arm, asked quick and silent permission. John tangled his fingers into Robyn's hand and gave him what he needed: heat and breath and depth. With the last of Robyn's own Sight-strength, they gave the rain her due thanks and asked for more.

As they reached the ruined postern, Eleanor shook her head, gave a disapproving *tsk*. Over her head, Gamelyn smirked at Robyn.

Robyn, meanwhile, let the damp curl in his lungs, raised chill cheeks to the rain. It helped unclench expended Sight, sank into his blood. Almost. Home.

The Queen might be old enough to be their great-grandmother, but she was game as ferret Tess and just as quiet. Neither did she take offence when Much grabbed her velvet skirts just before she nearly slid down arse-first into the moat. She merely grabbed him back. Hard. They no longer thought of proprieties, just kept track of each other. Kept their voices down. And kept going.

It was strangely anticlimactic. Disappointing, even—though they had all bent themselves to just this outcome: a silent, darting steal inward and out to a clean getaway.

The quiet hung about them, eerie, as they boarded the punt; the water sloshing against the flat hull seemed loud as a shout, and the faint ripples as they pushed off the bank even more so. The water's surface was only visible within reach of the long pole before it, too, disappeared into the mists. Robyn heard John breathe a soft warding—not that Robyn blamed him for such a caution. This gloaming was ripe for a ride into the fae lands, perfect for mist-laced seduction into the otherworlds. But surely, in the fae lands, a punt wouldn't ride so treacherously low. Where four had been well enough, five was obviously pushing the little boat's limits—the aft end dipped with every shove of the pole in Robyn's hands, sending foul, fetid water about his heels.

So he poled less. And was mightily relieved when, with a *shuss* and *crunch*, the punt fetched up on the opposite side. A short ride, give the Lady grace.

Much clambered up the slick bank, began unwinding the rope from beneath his tunic. The Queen hadn't the upper-body strength for an arm-over-arm climb, but with a sling, Robyn and Much up top, and Gamelyn and John steadying her beneath, she dug her toes into the slick bank and "walked" the short ascent.

Game, no question.

They flanked close, had made it halfway across the rye-fuzzed and fallow fields when the bell started ringing.

Gamelyn started for his sword; Much turned to their flank and followed suit.

Robyn's hiss stopped them both midmotion. "Nay! Keep on!"

John slowed, waiting. It would not do for them to get separated now. Much looked mutinous, Gamelyn grave and considering; beside him, Eleanor looked distinctly on the verge of panic. Robyn understood it—aye, he understood all too well the horror of being nicked out in the open with no cover for at least another furlong and none even visible. Yet Robyn also understood—he and John both, better than any—how to disappear.

"Can you see the castle?" Robyn insisted, barely above a whisper. Sound would travel farther than eyes could see, in this murk. "Nay, y' canna see anything past your reach. And neither can they, aye? Keep quiet, keep together, and *keep walking.*"

Much was squinting back towards the castle—invisible save for, mayhap, a faint-dark shadow within grey—as if he could conjure sight of it by the bell's pealing alone. Eleanor too was peering back the way they'd come, relief beginning to light her eyes. Gamelyn lifted two fingers, saluted the hidden walls of Blyth, then met Robyn's gaze and used those fingers in another salute—this one to his lips, a kiss in Robyn's direction.

They kept walking, swift and shadowed. Only sound pursued

them—as close as their own breath, sometimes: the bell's flat clang, the shouts of men, the arrhythmic chaos of running feet against stone and wood.

It was too much to bear without some nerves; by the time they reached the trees, they were hot with sweat, sopping and panting and, if not running, at the very least showing a spanking good trot. Finally they slid into the trees, one with the ghosted mist. Eleanor again seemed dumbfounded, looking to each of her rescuers: the dawnings of respect. Gamelyn peered, keen as any hawk, back towards the castle—traceable only by the sounds following them. Much and John were exchanging soft murmurs.

Robyn merely took another breath, deep with relief, as he felt no more than the woodland about him, murmuring and tingling on his skin.

Home.

Queen Eleanor was to have a few more dumbstruck moments before this was done.

The forest must have been utterly foreign to her, impassable with dark and cold. Again and again she would catch her breath and hesitate as they'd round a tree to face a seeming mass of impassable grey mist.

To Robyn and John, however, whilst winter months meant brutal wet and cold, they also meant the deer paths and small traces were all the more visible. And a woodsman's familiar compasses: the moss thick as a lamb's hide upon the wood and stones, the reach and bend of limbs, scat and tracks, the runnel of water over earth. The rain had let up, but scattered evergreens and even the naked trees gave shelter, particularly the deeper the travellers penetrated. Deeper meant those mists all the more betrayed what air currents— and thusly, trails—lay amidst the overgrowth.

Deeper also meant they had more chance of avoiding the patrols surely being organised, announced by the bell's clanging. Though any patrols would pay hell getting more than two feet, in this fog.

The Queen didn't complain, not once, though her layers of skirts must be getting heavier with every step. But sure enough, her progress was lagging from purposeful stride to tiring slog.

They were closer now, though. Just to the inside of a died-back stand of brambles, Robyn and John halted. Robyn cupped his hands over his mouth, gave a trill, then an owl's call. It curled, soft echo, over the wet trees and inward. They waited. Then, into the silence, an answer: *Aye, friend, do enter.*

John grinned at Robyn, tossed the expression back to their fellows. Robyn clapped a hand to John's shoulder as they moved on, the others close after.

And then, there they were. The cavern entrance was lit from deep within, warm invitation. Not only that, but a smell drifted out that made Robyn's mouth water.

Will stood guard by the entry. He gave an awkward touch of his hat and a dip of the knee to Eleanor. Robyn smirked. Will had obviously been schooled, either by Marion or Gilbert. Only then did he tender an appreciative nod—if somewhat grudging—for the two Templars, as well as a fierce hug to both John and Robyn.

"David and Arthur?" Robyn queried into Will's fair hair, holding the hug a bit longer.

"Here. And better. The cough's hanging on t' David a wee bit, but Marion's setting it to rights."

"My Queen!" Alundel emerged, speeding over to Eleanor and going to one knee, drawing her hand to his cheek. "You're safe! And so very wet . . . Was it a terrible escape? You look dreadful!"

Bloody damn. Mayhap Robyn's bits didn't fancy lasses, but his brain surely knew better than to spout sommat like *that* to a woman.

"How . . . charming," Eleanor drawled, her eyes meeting Robyn's as if she read his thoughts, "of you to remind me."

Alundel blanched. "Madam, please forgive me, I only meant—"

"Oh, do get up. You're blocking my way from what looks to promise a goodly fire and the first hot meal I've had since morning porridge."

Alundel sprang up, held out an arm. Instead, Eleanor extended her hand to Robyn. Alundel blinked. Robyn peered at the gloved hand, wondering if an adder might bite him the less, and shot a swift glance over Eleanor's silk-veiled head towards Gamelyn. Who was smirking.

The sod.

Eleanor was giving him a level, too-patient look, her hand still outstretched. Uncertainty tumped satisfaction arse over tit, fierce and amused; Robyn tossed his head back, throwing hood and hair from his face with a grin. Aye, if this woman had the guts to gather the bones and hand them over, Robyn could certainly cast them into the wind and revel in it, flight or fall.

He took her hand, said, "Lead us in, Will."

Will was grinning; when Eleanor's gaze narrowed upon him, however, he ducked his head, meek as milk, and did as requested. "Aye. This way, milady."

Robyn motioned inward. "We're a bit rough about the edges, mind you, milady, but none sits to my hearth as wain't be fed and feted. Well come to my Wode."

"*Your* Wode?" It was amused. The hand in his had quite a grip, but when he offered the support of his forearm, she accepted it.

"Aye, who else?" Provocative, of course, and the grey eyes turned to him, chiding, even as a soft snort of amusement came from Gamelyn.

Alundel gave a half-muttered oath about cheeky ruffians.

Then the cavern widened out and upwards before them, bathed in golden light from not only the fire, but also several lamps and candles.

Eleanor halted, mute. Her reaction wasn't lost on Robyn—nor was it unusual. The few braving the Shire Wode in the past months had also been fair upskelled, not only by the doings at an outlaw's hearth, but how those doings were set in motion by a woman who obviously wasn't some whore or drudge.

It also helped that, in the short while Marion had been with the outlaws, she'd witnessed a few mealtime "invitations." In the doing, she'd decided upon her own methods. She waited, poised and reserved; the flush on her freckled cheeks and the frizz of her cinnabar hair, mostly confined by a neat coif, were the only signs she might be set awry by this particular guest. There was, surely, no sign of it to be gleaned from the cavern itself.

Their mam couldn't have done the place any more grace. It had been swept within an inch of its life, lain with furs, and made fair cosy. An impromptu board had been laid across two like-sized logs and spread with an old tapestry. Upon the thick weaving lay sprigs of yew and holly; several cheery lamps and an assortment of pewter and wood platters were set, waiting.

And the feast to honour such a lovely board: a small hind—*How fitting,* Robyn smirked, *to offer their guest royal meat*—as well as several coneys were set to roasting. What smoke spat and hissed from meat juices rose and lingered in the high ceiling, drifted out in lazy hanks. One of David's best cauldrons steamed to one side of the coals; its round belly simmered with something that smelt just short of heavenly.

Robyn grinned. If Robyn Hode was King of the Shire Wode, he'd a fine Queen in his sister; would back her any day against a spoilt noblewoman.

Marion's grey eyes—clearer and softer than Eleanor's—met Robyn's, dancing. Her lip curving, she gave a curtsey as graceful as any court lady would wish, murmured,

"I offer you guest-right, Royal Lady. Well come to our hearth."

Eleanor blinked. "And you are?"

Robyn opened his mouth, closed it again. Normally he'd scant patience with what was proper—but then, "proper" at his hearth oft meant to feed the mark stupid, then shake them down for some coin at meal's end. This was . . . well, it was different. An old custom, hearth- and guest-right; a welcome such as his mam and da would've once given.

Gamelyn was the one who strode forwards, took Marion's hand, and presented her to Eleanor with an artful flourish. "Madam. This is Marion of Sherwood, Robyn's sister and *our* lady."

Marion's vivid cheeks crimsoned further, but it didn't stop her from giving a curtsey that met and matched Gamelyn's civility.

Eleanor tilted her head to study them both, curiosity plain, then smiled. Her eyes sliding to Gamelyn, she spoke a few words of Frankish.

Over against the wall, Arthur and Will exchanged an uneasy frown with each other. David was seeing to the roasts, also frowning; it didn't set altogether right with Robyn, either. However, eyes dancing again, Marion answered the Queen—also in Frankish, her words soft and unhurried.

Eleanor blinked and, as Marion beckoned, she loosed Robyn's arm, allowed Marion to lead her to the fireside place of honour.

"Let me guess," Gilbert murmured, coming up behind Robyn. "She didn't think we'd any manners at all."

Robyn snorted. "Fancy that."

"Not many outlaws can claim they've had royalty as guests." Gilbert grinned and nudged him. "Willing guests, that is."

Robyn snorted again. Turning, he went over to the far wall, where a pile of furs lay warming, and began rummaging through them. Royalty, true enough, but the woman was no spring hatchling, had just taken a hike to fell any soft man, and was soaked through. Some warm furs would help set her to rights. He caught sight of John towards the back, filling a pot from the mead cask, and smiled. Even better.

Marion joined him, helping with the furs.

"Speak English, Mari," Robyn growled softly as she passed him and Gilbert, but she merely smiled wider.

"Nowt wrong with impressing a guest, Hob-Robyn," she murmured back, for the moment sounding so much like their mother it gave him a pang. Taking the armful of warmed furs, Marion headed back to Eleanor.

Much was digging in his pouch and, with an awkward bow, handed over the Queen's small casket. She received it with gratitude—and some surprise that he'd returned it so readily—which seemed to crawl up Much's pipe, just a little.

Aye, well, you run with thieves, Robyn smirked to himself. It turned into full-blown grin as John presented a pot of mead to Eleanor.

She received that with the same caution, took an experimental sip—
and smiled. The thieves had good liquor, at least.

"Right, then," Marion said, no-nonsense. "All you men, clear off.
Before we sit to any sup, there's comforts to be seen to."

Robyn, with a morning's trek behind him and enrapt with the
smell of food, felt the distinct urge to whinge. He wasn't the only
one, either—a quick look around revealed that much.

Marion puffed up like a goose. "Sweet Lady, how did any of you
not starve before I came? Take a hank with you, if you're so
famished, but our guest is sopping wet and needs some dry clothes
so she wain't take ague. You can all change t'wards the cavern's
back, but Queen Eleanor is our guest and deserves to shed the wet
by the fire. So, off with the lot of you until I sing out, and . . . you
too," she said as Alundel began to speak. "You're a man, en't you?
Out!

Much reached over, grabbed Alundel by the neck of his tunic,
and escorted him out with nary a word. The others were already
leaving.

Robyn grinned at his sister, tipped fingers to his pate, and
followed, leaving Eleanor once again bemused and Marion bending
to those sodden skirts.

- XII -

Of this Gamelyn had no doubt: if Robyn had been told, straight up by any but Sight or sovereign forest god, that he'd spend a winter's night drinking and feasting with royalty, he would have snorted his derision and said *Pull the other one, aye?*

The men too seemed staggered, eating with more reserve than Gamelyn would have frankly credited them.

But the true moment of astonishment for Gamelyn had come when the King of Sherwood had challenged the Queen of the Angevin to a drinking contest.

More, Eleanor had *accepted.*

Of course, this was the woman who'd ridden on Crusade with her maidservants, the lot of them dressed as Amazons. Should it be so surprising that the same woman, dressed in borrowed clothes and wrapped in wolfskins, should sit to sup with outlaws and drink their liquor?

Particularly once Much, John, and Arthur had come back from their own sweep of the fog-shrouded trees and announced the patrols had become hopelessly lost just a brace of furlongs past Blyth's gates.

Aye, time to play. At least until morning came and the fog began to clear.

A shriek of laughter rose into the caverns—was that Marion? Gamelyn hadn't heard her laugh like that since they were children, and it put a fair, lovely warmth into the pit of his belly. The mead— brewed by David, with a subtle but mighty kick—wasn't hurting, either. For either of them.

Will, meanwhile, was goggling at Marion, and no wonder. Marion had spilled mead on her fingers and was licking it off, still giggling. Gamelyn found himself just as riveted by the sight.

It was rather a surprise . . . well, perhaps not that surprising. He'd never been as unresponsive to females as Robyn or John, and Marion had always warmed a part of him none else could. But the way his belly quivered and tightened caught him unawares. Gamelyn gave his head a tiny shake to stop such daft mooning, turned to say something to Much . . .

Much was mooning even worse.

Good humour restored shaken equilibrium. Gamelyn chuckled and took another drink. The mead burned, thick-sweet and pleasant, all the way down.

The contestants had downed two drinks already, with John pouring Eleanor a third one. Marion had left off her fingers, peering over towards Gilbert, who was leaning against the far wall of the cavern in earnest conversation with Alundel and David. Much snickered and nudged Gamelyn, pointing out Gilbert—was he? Bloody hell, but he was!—proposing a wager with Will. Not only that, but damned if Alundel wasn't getting in on it, and David.

"Had I good Bordeaux with me," Eleanor was saying, "we'd see who could outdrink whom, messire outlaw."

"Well, you en't, and I en't yet seen you tuck away that cup o' mead, there." Robyn tapped at it, on the board between them, then tapped at his own cup for John to refill—which John did, grinning. "Are you still in, milady, or nay?"

Inconceivable. Preposterous. And so . . . Robyn.

Gamelyn downed his pot, let John pour him another, and gave a comfortable hove against Much's shoulder.

This should be entertaining.

"Blondel!" The Queen flung an expansive gesture towards her trouvère. "Come here, my lad, play for us. If this bold outlaw is to lose our game—"

"Lose!" Robyn snorted and knocked back his drink.

"*Lose*," Eleanor emphasised, "then best we have some music to soothe his temper." She drained her own cup and leaned forwards, set it on the board with a decided *thunk*. "For I'd wager you've a temper, Robyn Hood."

"I'd not bet against you on that, ma'am," Will put forwards.

Alundel obeyed his lady's summons—but not before secreting a few coins into Gilbert's palm, Gamelyn noted with another small chuckle.

Robyn gave Will the archer's salute—two fingers jabbing upwards. "Never mind me lads," he apologised to Eleanor. "They're cheeky buggers."

"And they've no"—Marion put in with an elbow to Will's ribs as he tried to curl an arm about her—"proper example of *that*, do they?"

"Aye, you'll note me sister is proper dead bossy," Robyn pitched right back, and smiled wide—that brilliant, charming-rare expression that banished all others to shame in purgatory.

Add the power of Robyn's smile to the amount of mead Gamelyn had on board, and the possibility of later stealing Robyn off to shag him voiceless . . . nay, there was nothing more Gamelyn wanted in this moment of time.

First, though, Robyn needed to win this drinking game. Send Her Royal Majesty to a mead-induced sleep and spend the rest of the night in lovely exercise—for the morrow certainly brought with it more work than play.

"Carefully darkened, my dear. Of course, your brother's no need—hardly fair, is it, how men have all the luck with such things?—but you understand." Eleanor leaned sideways, allowed Marion to inspect her half-closed eyelids . . . Bloody hell, were they really discussing cosmetics? Eleanor's next words confirmed it. "Why trudge through life with pale lashes if one can help it? The East has given us many lovely things . . . Surely you know of what I speak, Templar?"

Gamelyn agreed, bemused, wishing he'd a bit of lovely Eastern hashish, about now. And wouldn't that make his black-lashed Robyn all the more willing . . .

Mayhap the hashish wasn't necessary after all—David's honey brew was very fine, indeed. The timbre of Gamelyn's thoughts and the knot in his braies attested to it.

Ah well. The drinking made some mean, others morose, some silly or sleepy . . . As for himself, Gamelyn took some care where he had a good piss up, for it made him relaxed and very, very susceptible. To whatever. Whats'mever. Gamelyn smirked.

Much kept watching Marion. Odd. Not that Marion wasn't pretty; she definitely was, pale eyelashes or no. At least she'd stopped licking her fingers.

"You keep calling him Blondel." Robyn's acknowledgment interrupted meandering thoughts; not altogether unwelcome, since Gamelyn himself had wondered.

Alundel, walking from the back of the cavern with lute in hand, gave Eleanor a slight frown.

She didn't seem to notice. "With such fair hair as my *trouvère* has, what else?"

"And here I thought it were all lime paste, like Scathelock," Much murmured. It was more than a little unfriendly, and Gamelyn chuckled, sliding his gaze over to where Will was busily telling Marion another tall tale.

Robyn downed his drink, waggled his eyebrows at Eleanor. "How many names does the man have, then?"

"Less, surely, than the Green Man." Alundel brushed at said blond hair and tipped his head to Robyn, fingers limbering up over his lute strings. "Or Guy of Gisbourne, known as Gandelyn."

"Gamelyn." It was a bit sharp, the correction—sharper than Gamelyn had intended. The other sounded too like one with which his elder brother had taunted him. *Gadelyng. Gipsy's bastard.*

Alundel peered curiously at Gamelyn. "Pardon my error, my lord. Blondel is one of several names I've borne. Nothing more or less."

And you don't like it, either. Gamelyn peered at Alundel until the latter dropped his gaze, and wondered from where such certainty had come.

Drink has a way of loosing tongues, the Lady breathed in his ear. *And talents.*

And what in hell was that supposed to mean?

Get out, Gamelyn told her, *of my drunken reverie.*

She gave a soft laugh and retreated. The concession was almost as inconceivable as Queen Eleanor downing . . .

Christ's blood, was that her fifth?

"Got to give it to her," Much remarked.

Maybe Gamelyn had just imagined his paxman goggling at Marion, because now he was avid upon the drinking contest.

"This mead is fine stuff, en't just horse-piss ale," Much continued, with a nudge at Gamelyn. "Mebbe you 'n me should have at that wager . . . ah, happens not. What should happen did Himself find you gaming his loss?"

"He'd demand a tithe of it, likely." Gamelyn's lip tilted again, more mirth.

Much snorted. "Well, should I leave, you'd fall over, anyroad."

Gamelyn merely leaned harder, and Much laughed.

"How many?" Gilbert also had more than a few on board, but it wasn't slowing his calculation of the odds.

"If she downs this one, it makes six," Will put in, looking smug.

"But she's slowin' down." Arthur sounded worried. He'd been chatting up David—who'd gone to sit closer to Much and Gamelyn—and had come back to crouch beside Will, a nondescript brown crock in his hands.

Eleanor was indeed starting to slow. As if to assist, Alundel's tuning took an abrupt swerve into vigorous, a dancing jig resounding through the caverns.

It warmed the mead in Marion's belly, coaxed her toes to tap, filled her with the lurch and lilt of music made solely for pleasure. It had been . . . Sweet Lady, how long had it been?

But there was a protest to be made, in all good conscience and despite any tipsy longings. Marion peered sideways at Arthur, likewise eyed Gilbert and Will.

"Don't tell me you made book *against* your leader?"

"Give ower, lass." Will gave her a too-patient look. "Robyn en't never had no head for drink."

"Bloody . . . traitors!" Marion protested. "He's all right with the mead!"

"Aye, but should sommun bring out whiskey?" Will shrugged, then waggled his eyebrows at Arthur.

"Robyn loves a good shot o' whiskey." Arthur grinned and gave a fond pat to the crock, which he put down to rest between his knees. "The whiskey loves him, too, aye and she does." He gave a touch of his pate to Marion, and the grin widened.

"Bugger!" Gilbert swore, then began running sums across his palm again. "That changes the odds, lads."

Marion started to giggle. "Ohhh, y' wouldn't. Couldn't."

"'Couldn't'"—Will grinned—"implies honour 'mongst thieves, love."

"At least David's having none of this!" Marion felt she should keep up her protest—even though all she wanted to do was giggle like a fool.

And dance. She wasn't the only one, either. Gamelyn's eyes were closed; leaning against Much, he mouthed silent accompaniment to Alundel's song, body swaying— slight, as if unwilling to admit to it, but just as unable to resist. Much's toes were also tapping; he seemed to feel her eyes upon them, gave her a quick and damnably aloof smile, then returned his attention to Robyn and the Queen.

She'd fancy Much was a fine dancer. Or mayhap as not. Mayhap he couldn't yank that rod from his arse enough to dance a step.

"David's already made his bet," Will protested.

"'Tis been too long since we've had a good wager," Arthur defended. "How can we let such a sure one pass by?"

Marion laughed, couldn't help it despite slapping her hands over her mouth.

"Come on, then!" Will demanded, springing up and pulling her along with him. "I want to hear you laugh again."

A good thing the cavern was large, for though Will was an able dancer, he was a bit less than careful *where* he danced. He whirled Marion around, and Robyn yipped as her overkirtle slung close, nearly took out his drink and Eleanor's as well.

Will was also a bit tipsy—enough to remind Marion of one of the things about him she'd never cared for. Drunk, he got angry, and aggression only the soft beginnings of it. For now, the music worked its magic, swooning him into some sweet moves, but once she relaxed against him, he started to hold her just that much too tight and close.

"Mind yourself," she hissed at him, "or I'll find sommun else to dance me."

He grinned and shook his head—again, just tipsy enough to be more oblivious than usual—and kissed her cheek. Held her tighter. Marion grinned back. Spreading one hand upon his ribs, she grabbed the loose flesh over them, and twisted. Hard.

Will let out a yelp and loosed her. Before anything else could be done or said, Marion dove for her brother and dragged him up.

Robyn was surprised—he'd been paying attention to his drinking game, to be sure—but neither did it take much to coax him. He sprang to his feet, gave a cheeky little bow to his royal drinking partner, then grabbed Marion and skipped her around the cavern.

Aye, Robyn loved to dance—and Charming William couldn't be getting too arsy over her dancing with her brother.

As if he had a right to be arsy. Her own ire, unfolded by drink and warmed with her brother's laugh as she whirled him around, heated all the more.

Will had no right. No rights at all, no say over who or what she chose, particularly after all they'd spoken of. Agreed to.

"—cheating, to work off some of the drink!" Eleanor rose to her feet in protest—though the twinkle of humour in her gaze belied indignation.

Gilbert was in full agreement as Robyn sashayed Marion past. Muttering to himself—loudly—he once again began refiguring the odds on his palm.

"I might be a thief and a liar, but never let it be said I cheat at me own fireside!" Robyn vowed, tugging Marion back over. "And if we're both dancing, milady, then how can it be a cheat?"

Robyn loosed Marion and held out his hand to Eleanor.

The music gave a squawk and yammer, subsided. Alundel stared at Robyn as if he'd lost his mind. The others were still clapping— sort of—and Gilbert was still counting—sort of—and Will was still fuming—though that was anything but ambiguous.

Eleanor's pale cheeks flushed nearly crimson. But it was from drink, not any presumptuous wolfshead—even if he was presumptuous. She laughed, more canny mare's snort than any girlish giggle, and took Robyn's hand. "Keep playing!"

Robyn led her in a willing jig around the cavern, accompanied by shouts of encouragement. Alundel, after a small jolt and pause, started up again. The more he settled into the music, the more he watched his lady laughing like a young girl—and the broader his smile became.

Marion kept clapping and calling; laughing, too—until she saw Will heading her way. With an oblivious pretence to his just-as-oblivious determination, she spun and made the safest—or so she imagined—retreat possible next to Robyn.

Gamelyn stared up at her outstretched arms, green eyes sprung wide.

Gilbert left off his odds with a long, low whistle—obviously a monarch dancing with Robyn Hood was nothing, but a monk dancing—this monk dancing . . . well. Fodder for the fire.

"Can y' dance, Brother?" David called out, and next to him, Arthur snickered.

"Well," Marion challenged. "*Do* you know how to dance?"

"I—" Gamelyn seemed flummoxed.

Beside him, Much wasn't even looking at Marion—which *was not* vexing her, even if it made her doubly glad she'd not arsed herself to ask *him.*

Will shook his head, moved towards Marion with an outstretched hand, and Arthur hooted: "That 'un's arse is too *tight* fer dancing!"

"Hoy!" Robyn protested over one arm, the other occupied with sending Eleanor into a swung circle. "I beg to differ!"

Gamelyn shot him a glare yet, unaccountably, laughed.

It stopped Will in his tracks. "He's laughing. The bloody stone-faced sod is *laughing.*"

Which just brassed off Marion all the more. She leaned closer, put her hand on Gamelyn's chest, and said, her gaze holding his, "Dance with me. *Now.*"

Gamelyn stopped laughing, eyed her, then Will, the smirk still chasing about his lips. Taking her hand, he brushed a kiss across it and said, "As you wish, fair Maid."

Whatever Marion had expected, this wasn't it. And neither had she expected the slip-slide and shudder of her heart against her breastbone as Gamelyn leapt up with the quickness of a cat, pulled her close, and moved her across the cavern just as quick and light.

"Y-you can dance," Marion stammered.

"Of course I can," Gamelyn replied. "Were you hoping I couldn't?"

"I weren't expecting—hoy!" This as he skipped her altogether close to Arthur and his crock of whiskey; she leapt it—and Arthur, who'd crouched protectively over it.

Gamelyn really *didn't* laugh all that much anymore. Because now he was, and so hard he gave a tiny wince as they neatly avoided Robyn and . . . John?

Aye, if John couldn't dance very well, he nevertheless cut some wild capers next to Robyn. And also had obviously cut in on Eleanor, who looked miffed as only a somewhat tipsy queen could.

Which only prompted both of them to laugh all the harder. Gamelyn winced again, gladly leaned against Marion's offered support. "Bloody back." But he was still chuckling. "My swordmaster was my dancing instructor. 'Tis very similar, you know."

Eleanor had cut back in. Robyn didn't miss a step. Marion could hardly dance, she was giggling so hard.

"My turn now, Templar," Will said at her shoulder.

Gamelyn started to ignore him and push past. Will's hand landed on his shoulder—his weak shoulder, at that. Gamelyn gave no hint whether the grip was painful, or not. But his eyes turned to jade; with a distant bow, he backed away.

It knocked a hole in Marion's composure for no good reason. After all, what was Gamelyn supposed to do? Cause trouble for no more purpose than some amorphous, unreasonable pique of her own?

Like she needed any man's help to handle Will Scathelock, drunk or sober.

As Will took her hand, mannerly enough, Marion called herself ten kinds of names, none of them pleasant and most of them having to do with cowardice.

"Don't push me away this time, aye?"

"Don't maul me like a prize hog, then, William," she answered, tart. "I didn't mean—"

Gamelyn sauntered over and cut in on Robyn's game. Instead of taking Robyn's arm, as Marion half expected, Gamelyn bowed to Eleanor and took her hand.

It should have been uproariously funny. Everyone else fell about, hooting and snorting with laughter. But Marion wasn't, and Will wasn't either, leading her through the steps to Alundel's jig.

"You don't push the others away." It was sullen. Then, with a quick glance to where Gamelyn had started squiring Eleanor about the cavern, "There's sommun else, en't there?"

Someone else . . .

But there wasn't, and the reasons for that were slapping her in the face right now, frustration yanking fury along behind, like a disobedient hound.

There en't, because I didn't want to hurt you. I didn't want to be the cause of more trouble. There's enough of it now, and. . .

But she, too, had had enough.

I'm as Heathen as any of you, free to make my own choices and take my own lovers as I see fit. You've no call to make me feel any of this, make me once again that bloody novice, untouched and hiding. . . like it's my *fault you want me and think it means you own me!*

"There is, en't there? Sommun else?"

"And if there was, 'twould be *my* choice!" she shot back. "Not yours. Not Robyn's. Mine!"

"But I have t' rights t—" His voice had started to gain some volume. He pulled her closer again; Marion brought a sharp elbow against his ribs, made him huff.

"And they're more important than mine?" she hissed. "Is that what you're saying? Is it because I'm newly come here, or because I'm a woman?"

Will was silent, peering at her, morose and angry and entirely too pissed up. Before she'd come, and Gamelyn, had he drank like this?

It softened her, just the little, and she tried again. "Will. Would you have our world become like theirs?"

"Our world *is* theirs!" he hissed back. "They took it, long ago!"

"So that makes it all right when you act like them?"

This didn't so much as penetrate, Will intent on making his own point. "It makes it all right they should come into our places, aye? Be given guest-right at our hearth?" His gesture took in Gamelyn first, then Much, but also Eleanor and Alundel. "They don't belong here! And *that* one"—he jerked his head at Gamelyn—"has *no* rights t' be courting you!"

"He en't courting me, Will."

"En't he? En't it what you and Robyn and John keep *not* saying, even if it's fair plain on the ground?"

Plain on what ground? Marion felt she had walked out into the Mere and found the footing disappeared beneath. She shot a quick glance about. Alundel's music still filled the cavern, Gamelyn and Eleanor still danced, the other lads still were haggling over their bets. Robyn was sharing a drink with Much . . .

Those two were watching. Robyn's eyes caught hers, a question.

Marion shook her head. "Will, you're drunk. You en't making any sense!"

His grip tightened. "You said, give y' time."

"Which you en't giving me!"

"I'm surely not going to just crouch down and do nowt whilst sommun else walks over me and takes what's allus been mine! Their like has taken enough!"

"William, there's none in this cavern as means to take anything."

"If they're here, in our place? Taking. Did our people die for nowt, Marion? Yours. Mine. His like killed them!"

"His like"—this through gritted teeth—"but not *him.*"

He yanked her close and held her there, the mead stale upon his breath and the anger lying just beneath it. "You don't see what's happening, do you? Neither of you will see it—!" It travelled upwards into a yip even as Will suddenly went down to one knee.

Robyn was there, one hard hand at Will's nape. Much lurked at Robyn's elbow.

Marion shot a swift and mortified glance around. Gamelyn was glaring at them past Eleanor's turned-away shoulder, but he was the only one paying attention. The music hadn't stopped. The others kept on laughing and drinking, fully fascinated by a queen who danced with monks and outlaws.

Then Arthur's eyes cast their way, and he frowned.

Robyn smiled at Marion, used that insanely strong grip upon Will's nape to drag him back up. He claimed, just loud enough, "You're drunk, Scathelock. No more dancing for you, lad—y' canna even stay on your own feet."

"Rob," Will started, looking guilty as murder.

Robyn jerked him close. His face was still pleasant, but his voice hissed cold. "If you make any more from this, by our Lady I'll smack your great fair head from your shoulders. You've no call to fetch y'rself this drunk when there's outsiders here and you know it. Out."

Will's face crumpled, remorse and resentment both. With a vicious glance towards Gamelyn—who'd surely done nothing to deserve it—he spun and left the cavern.

The music had stopped. Gamelyn still glowered at Eleanor's side. Eleanor's expression was much more astute than Marion cared to think upon.

"Hoy, Will!" Arthur called after him.

"He's drunk and a bit queasy," Robyn answered. Well, it wasn't a lie.

Arthur seemed satisfied; with a shrug and a knowing snort, he turned back to another haggle with Gilbert.

Marion felt another set of eyes upon her; she turned to find Much watching her. When she met his gaze, however, he merely gave a courteous dip of his head and turned away, going back to his place. *Holding up the wall,* Marion scoffed to herself, and controlled the impulse to kick his backside as he went, just to see if he'd notice.

Before she had the chance, Robyn took her arm and steered her back to the fireside.

"Rob—"

"Aye, well, Mari." A sigh. He knew the problem as well as Marion herself—and had no more answers than she.

"'Tis true, some men can't hold their drink." Eleanor eyed Marion, then Robyn, then motioned to Alundel. "Another tune, my dear. It still remains to be seen if the king of outlaws can hold *his.*"

It went into the night, shadows spasming across the cavern walls as they caroused, and drank, and sang bawdy tunes, and forgot ills both new and old. Robyn—sneaky sod that he was, Marion grinned—came off with the evening's honours. He even danced with Gamelyn—then won the drinking contest to top it. This despite the addition of whisky and the chagrin of his men, and accomplished purely by wearing Eleanor out with dancing.

The Queen of the Angevin ended up snoring, padded and swathed in a heap of furs, beside her trouvère, who kept playing. Surely 'twere a lullaby, it sounded so soft-sweet. Will had come back, bundled into his pallet, and not emerged. Others soon followed: Arthur, Gilbert, David, Much. John, still wakeful, tended the fire. Outside, the rain had finally stopped.

The trouvère kept a covert eye to Robyn and Gamelyn, Marion noted. She too had retired to her own pallet, but wasn't sleepy. Instead, she listened to the soothing music, and watched. Alundel kept up his ever-present accompaniment, but there was an almost imperceptible frown twitching his brow. His fingers faltered upon the lute, a tiny dissonance shivering into the cavern. None of the others seemed to notice, but Marion kept watching the trouvère, curious, as with one hand he reached for the pouch that never strayed too far from his side. His other hand kept tracing the lute's neck until, with a grimace, he pushed the instrument over on his hip and rummaged in the pouch.

Still, the others ignored him. Marion rested her chin on her folded hands. What was Alundel up to?

Her question was answered as he drew out a tiny pot and a small scroll. There were several quills wrapped in the latter; with some care, Alundel revealed this, unrolling the parchment. After a thorough inspection of each quill's business end, he chose one and unstoppered the ink. He never stopped his glances towards the fire and the men there, lips vibrating as if words hummed just beneath the surface. Flattening the parchment roll against his thigh, he dipped his chosen instrument into the inkpot and started to write.

Marion frowned. She could make out, just barely, the marks Alundel's quill left behind on the crème-hued skin. They didn't look like any words she'd ever seen.

John left off his tending and sidled close to Robyn. Cradling his head into Robyn's shoulder, he raised a hand, smoothed the black fur along Robyn's jaw.

Alundel had looked up from his writing, fingers pausing. His frown went from subtle to overt, and troubled. Gamelyn took in that notice and gave a soft murmur to Robyn: warning, mayhap. Robyn shrugged, then raised his gaze, met Alundel's with open, almost-bland challenge. Marion could all but hear his thoughts. John preferred touch to talking, and Robyn wasn't about to shrug his loved ones' affection away in his own place, his own camp.

Marion found herself in defiant agreement.

Gamelyn started to speak again; Robyn covered his mouth with his fingers, leaned in, and whispered against his ear. Gamelyn's lip curved as Robyn took his fingers away, and he nodded, rose. Padded from the cavern.

Robyn kissed John's temple and spoke—a query, likely, for John shook his head. Then John smiled and nodded, as if he kenned something none of them had yet fathomed. Gave Robyn a small push.

Robyn kissed him again, then stood and meandered from the cavern after Gamelyn.

All the while, Alundel watched. When Robyn disappeared into the black night, he kept his gaze on John. Puzzled more than angry, Marion would swear to it.

John kept his own gaze upon the cavern entry long after Robyn had exited. Next he angled that gaze upon Alundel, held for long moments, then turned away, as if the trouvère wasn't there. Alundel's lips quivered—again, as if words demanded speech. Instead he turned to the parchment and began scribbling those strange not-words with something akin to contained fury.

Marion got up. Conscious of John's eyes upon her, but more so that Alundel didn't heed her, bent upon his writing. Careful not to block the sparse light from the torch beneath which Alundel had settled himself, she padded closer, silent as a bitch fox. Unnoticed. Except for John, of course, watching with a slight smile. She shared it. At least her own stealth hadn't deserted her.

She didn't, however, want to scare Alundel juiceless—or mar his work. She stopped and waited, just within the periphery of his vision, until he looked up. Towards John, to be sure, but he started upon seeing how close she'd come.

The . . . not-words? Well, they looked even stranger at close range.

Marion moved in, pointing at the parchment spread across his thigh. "What are those?"

He'd the impulse to pull the parchment into shadow; it was written in the faint dismay upon his expression and hands, which trembled, wanting to clench. But she'd fair caught him. The ink wasn't dry. Alundel gave a tiny smirk, and his next words betrayed a sudden superiority.

"It's called writing. Words on paper. You see, our spoken tongues can be marked down, with symbols—"

"Oh, aye, that's plain enough." Marion pointed to the top lines. "Robyn and Gandelyn,' it says here in Frankish—only as he said, his name's Gamelyn, not Gandelyn—and here, between these marks as look like bird tracks:

"Gandelyn looked east and then looked west
"And searched under the sun;
"He saw a little brown-haired boy,
"Whose . . . "

Alundel's eyes widened as she began; her effortless reading left him gaping. So much she wanted to chuckle.

"You can . . . *read*." It was flat. Incredulous.

"Me mam taught me," Marion said. "Frankish, Anglic, and Latin. I used to write, too. First at our hearth, when the weather kept us bunged in, then at Worksop. I wrote many a letter. One of the few there as could, and nowt as is useful gets shunted aside in the abbey, believe me."

"Read and write," Alundel muttered at his parchment, as if it were someone. "Remarkable."

"I miss it. En't had much chance to fetch paper hereabouts, or books." Marion shrugged off the sudden melancholy the thought gave her, pointed to the unfamiliar writing. "So. What are those marks?"

Alundel's condescending tone had been whacked down a few levels; his reply was gentle. "They aren't words, they're notes. Symbols for music. See?—each one has its place on this." His fingers lightly brushed the lines upon which the little tracks sat, and the gesture made Marion blink, sudden insight.

"They look like the strings on your lute, almost."

A smile softened Alundel's face. "Ah, they do. It's called *pneuma*—"

"That means 'breath,' aye?"

The smile broadened. "You know Greek as well?"

"I know words for the magic," she murmured. Glancing for permission, Marion hunkered down and peered at the tiny squares, now dry, dancing up and down the lines.

Alundel demonstrated, softly, the run of notes, finger tracing over as he sang.

Breath, indeed. Its own magic, written down like words and just as powerful. Marion wrapped her arms about her knees and rested her chin there. "Why are you writing music about Robyn and Gamelyn and . . . John, I'm guessing?"

He stiffened, then shrugged. "I write what plays itself in my head. Most of it is rubbish. Only special tales end up being written dow . . . " He trailed off, aware of the unintentional confession.

Marion rocked back and forth. "Seems to me what's happened these past days is well worth ink and parchment."

Alundel was looking aside, lashes making shadowy crescents upon his cheeks. It hearkened Marion back to her discussion with the Queen. It *wasn't* fair, how men got all the luck with lashes. And there was a distinct, discomfited flush edging down from Alundel's.

He rolled up the parchment, put away his things, and began strumming his lute once again.

Marion took the hint and rose, going back to her pallet. John was already there. She gave a caress to his brown curls as she crawled in. He smiled, a faint flash of white in the dim, and sighed as Marion set herself, back-to-back, against his warmth. Alundel kept playing, until Marion drifted into sleep.

"You sure you want t' go? You keep making these little detours"

"You insisted on the first one, 'checkin' t' bounds.' The second one I nigh lost you in this bloody be-damned—" Gamelyn cursed as a root appeared in the bottom mists and tripped him "—fog!"

Robyn chuckled. "And the third was to rid ourselves of excess mead—hoy, did you hear sommat?" Robyn paused, started to turn around, but Gamelyn grabbed him, pulled him close.

"Ghosts," he murmured. "I hear ghosts."

"Aye, and what else does the like of us hear?" Robyn bent close, nuzzled Gamelyn's cheek.

What else? Robyn's voice, only not, and eyes gleaming a-gilt in the shadows.

"The likes of you, maybe," Gamelyn said, sly against those presences, and Robyn kissed him.

"Us," he insisted. "But then, we wain't have to go to the cave, if you'd rather not," Robyn breathed in his ear. "We can fuck right here, an—!" It escalated up into a yip as Gamelyn gave a sharp tug to black hair.

"Tease." A growl, then Gamelyn murmured a few other choice ones against the long tendon in Robyn's neck—in Arabic.

Robyn threw his face to the sky and juddered to his toes. Gamelyn smiled. Tugged Robyn's tunic open. Said more words, sweet and silk-thick as honey, down the fur of Robyn's chest and belly.

"Any more of the like, and I'll be having me way wit' you here and now," Robyn whispered. "D'you want the cave, or nay?"

"I want . . ." Gamelyn's voice betrayed him, hoarse. He twined his hands tighter in Robyn's tunic, layers of linen and wool twisting in his palms.

Robyn merely stayed silent, waiting, stroking Gamelyn's hair. Gentling a beast . . .

"We can't go back," Gamelyn whispered. "But . . . " He fell silent, nudging harder against Robyn's belly. It quivered, muscles taut, a tiny push-pull against Gamelyn's cheek. And all the while Robyn stood there, still silent, still *touching* him.

"But?" Robyn prompted finally, still gentle.

"God," Gamelyn said. "Just tell me again. Who am I, here? Just tell me who I am."

"You're Gamelyn." Robyn's voice slurred with drink, but remained defiant. "They can call you what they like, or me. The wolfshead, the witch, the crazy bastard out runnin' t' Wode in his skin. Guy t' noble-bred bastard, or Templar, or bounty hunter . . . " He grinned. "Whats'mever. Names are power, and we'll take the power from those names and all the while know who we are."

"Will we?" A mutter into Robyn's hair.

"You're my Summerlord lover. You're what you are, what I want. Life's too short, and we've wasted too much of it already."

"*Robyn—*"

"Bloody . . . " Robyn tugged Gamelyn's hair, pulling him upwards. "Shut t' bloody fuck *up*, Gamelyn."

Then led him deeper into the trees and the mists.

Fog, thick and closing in, tried to tease them lost. Woodland inevitably changed, expanded and died back. But no question remained in them; the direction, burned into both their brains.

And other parts of their anatomy, at that.

The cave was damp and overgrown, and were the trees burgeoning with summer, they might indeed have never found it. No longer simply their place, but it still, unfathomably, welcomed them. It might have been the forest welcoming her lord—or it might have been those ghosts: two boys, nearly men, who'd dared to dream of a world where they *could* dream. Together.

And after all, damp earth could be cushioned by a thick-woven cloak, and had there been some legendary, hibernating bear spirit . . . well then, Robyn could gentle him too.

Gamelyn pulled Robyn down on the cloak.

Robyn rolled atop him.

They rutted each other breathless, and remembered, and held it for a brief, sweet time. Then had another good rut to stop the remembrance; not so sweet, swift and brutal . . .

Then they curled up on that oiled woollen cloak and fell asleep in each other's arms.

- Entr'acte -

He'd no intentions of following, at first
There was puzzlement, certainly, about everything he'd witnessed from the outlaws so far. A tangled web of personalities and opinions, jealousies and passions . . . but not a treacherous one. Nay, quite the contrary. There was much honour to be seen in this peasant rebel and his band of followers, much beauty held within this green Wode—one to which could be sung a grand *geste*.

Alundel had mulled over his puzzlement, turned it into tuning and song as his liege lady and most of the outlaws had fallen asleep. Had watched, whilst notes and phrases flitted through his brain, instinctive response to make sense of what he saw . . .

The two of them, outlaw and Templar, facing off across the coals. The way their eyes had met over the fire, too intimate. And the understood intimacy of the two beside them—both paxmen in their own rights. One a brawny Templar lieutenant who slept, separate yet there, at his master's side. And the other—Little John, had Robyn called him? And so he was, the slightest of any outlaw, yet none even thought to cross him—John had been clinging so close to Robyn. Yet however Alundel had looked for it, there had been no signs of resentment when Robyn had left his side. Nay, instead there had been an odd . . . encouragement from John as the other wakeful two had risen and left the fireside. First Templar, then outlaw.

But what was he encouraging? Surely not what Alundel suspected. His own sins were ramping things out of proportion. A kiss here and there was certainly nothing to prompt such insidious speculation.

Indeed the girl, Marion, had been watching as her brother and the Templar left the cavern, had merely turned over to her own slumber. And all this time—up until this moment, in fact—Alundel would have wagered a fortnight's lodging on not only the Templar's passion for Marion, but its reciprocation. Even Queen Eleanor had come to the same conclusion. A woman alone in a band of men usually played a simple role: whore, property, or sacrosanct.

Yet this wasn't so simple. This woman—this peasant—could read more than her name and her own rustic speech. Could *write*.

It had almost swayed him from the purpose to which his lady had bidden him: to watch the Templar closely even as she tested the Hood's mettle. Was the Templar false to his Order? After all, a man who'd played false to one oath would likely break others. They had to know what weaknesses their rescuers might hold. His liege lady had not lived the life she had to ever be easily fooled.

How, then, had *this* escaped her canny notice?

You're the fool, Alun. You know *why.*

Alundel lay his instrument on his cloak and crept from the cavern.

The thick fog should have made impossibility out of following anyone. But Alundel could hear them. Robyn and Gamelyn had imbibed more than their share of both mead and whiskey, were ambling in an unsteady perimeter about the cavern campsite. Alundel waited not far from the cavern mouth, ready to dart back inward, but the two showed no sign of heading back to where their comrades slept. Indeed, they ventured out into the mist-shrouded forest.

Alundel followed, cautious. He daren't go far in this fog. It roiled around him, insubstantial yet thick as hanks of combed wool. Reaching into his purse, Alundel silently pulled out a few pennies and began sowing them every other stride, just to be sure he could retrace his steps.

"You sure you want t' go?"

Alundel nearly stumbled in his haste to halt—he'd almost run atop them!

"Did you hear that?" A hiss, from Robyn, not a stone's throw beyond.

Gamelyn's voice was a bare whisper, unintelligible, as was Robyn's reply. Then a grunt, a laugh, and a rustle from the branches of the yew beside Alundel—he'd blundered too close. Frozen like a coney run to ground, barely willing to draw a breath lest the predators hear him . . .

Another laugh, this from Robyn, softening into a purr. It shivered alarm down Alundel's spine. "We don't have to go to the cave, if you'd rather not. We can fuck right here an—!"

Startling, to hear his suspicions confirmed so matter-of-fact. Alundel wasn't sure why he was so surprised. Such things were said of Templars—of any monks, truly—and he had heard pagans would rut anything including, it was said, their beast god . . .

Gamelyn growled an answer, and Robyn laughed again. The laugh trailed off as Gamelyn kept speaking—in what sounded like the Saracen tongue.

Alundel chanced a look from between the thick branches of his evergreen sanctuary. He'd wager neither of them were paying heed to anything but each other. And they weren't.

And it was . . . beautiful.

There was a fierce . . . joy? on Robyn's face, held up to the night sky with his mouth open, panting, and his strong fingers twisted in the ginger-gilt hair of his lover . . . his *lover*, who traced tongue and foreign endearments along Robyn's neck, pulling his tunic open to then trace them upon moon-pale skin . . .

Alundel froze, closing his eyes, once again hardly daring to breathe. He shouldn't be here. Was trespassing where he'd no rights. And when he'd the courage to open his eyes, look once more, they had disappeared into the night.

Alundel fled in the opposite direction, back towards the cavern camp. He knew what he had to do—but there was no joy in it. There never would be.

Not for him, at any rate.

- XIII -

"Sun'll be up anon," Robyn said, and it echoed softly through the little cave. "But the fog wain't be burning away so quick. We've time yet."

The fire they'd kindled midnight had burned to embers, but they were warm, all wrapped in Gamelyn's cloak. And Gamelyn, Robyn amended, nuzzling closer. "It really must be all that red hair."

"What?" Gamelyn was still muzzy, half-asleep. Worn out from . . . four times, was it? And here they'd both been pining for boyhood stamina.

"Red hair. What makes you stay so warm."

Gamelyn snorted his opinion, gave a vigorous scrub over his face with the palm of one hand. "I know your mother did her damnedest to educate you properly. You do her no justice by saying such barbarously ignorant things."

Robyn laughed, soft, into Gamelyn's neck. "You're still warm, en't you?"

A grin stole its way into one corner of Gamelyn's mouth. "And hungry. I suppose we should head back."

Was there a sigh in those words? Some regret? Aye, it *was* there, lingering in juniper-green eyes.

"We've time yet," Robyn repeated, and scooted even closer. "Happens I like a good rut first thing in the morning."

"Before breakfast? Have the fae come in the night and stolen the Robyn I know?"

In answer, Robyn trailed one hand down, tickled at belly fur, then lower. Aye, those bits were pliable and sleepy, but all it took was another tickle and squeeze to make them shiver and stretch, eager to meet the dawn.

Gamelyn gave a humming sigh against Robyn's hair. "And what of our guests?"

"What of 'em? They're well taken care of, should we arrive after they wake."

"I meant how we need to see they aren't our guests overlong. And avoid giving them suspicion of anything up between me and you."

"Anything up? Aye." Robyn grinned, curled his fingers around Gamelyn's promising erection, and began stroking in earnest. "That'd be you."

Gamelyn smirked and tilted his chin. Said, the smile broadening, "So you don't mind if the Queen of England—our *Christian* Queen, mind—figures out how Sherwood stands for sin, sodomy, and sedition?"

Robyn blinked at him. Gamelyn opened his eyes, kept grinning. Robyn shook his head, grinning back.

"You clever boots—an' how long did it take you t' think that one up?"

Gamelyn chuckled. "Not too long."

Robyn traced a kiss along his chin, then nipped, gentle. "Sin, aye? I'd call that . . . *merde.*"

Gamelyn rolled his eyes.

"What?—I pronounced it the way you allus do. As to sedition . . . aye, that we've brought, and more coming. And sodomy? Mm. Y'see, I'm not sure the word means what you think, clever boots."

One pale eyebrow arched, offended.

"Nay, hear me out. 'Twere Marion as told me sommat stuck with me. She read some of your holy book, not long after we met you. Most of it proper horrified her—but that word made no sense, the way the Church used it. Nowt surprising there, they twist everyt—*oof!*"

Gamelyn had poked his ribs. "Come to the point. For someone who wanted a rut before breakfast, you're talking overmuch."

"You started it, you and your 'S' words." Robyn grinned. "From what Mari kenned, that village—Sodom, right?—well, 'twere punished for breaking hearth law. Not because the whole bloody village fancied boys."

"If I'm too clever for my boots, you're too big for yours." Gamelyn chuckled. "Tell it to the Church. I'm sure they'll be receptive."

"Aye, right before they hang me." Robyn pushed up, made sure he gave a roll of his hips whilst doing so. "T' hell with 'em all. Let's have another go before we start back, aye?" He bent his arms, nuzzled at Gamelyn's cheek, his voice going even deeper, softer.

"Because soon you'll be going, wain't you?"

The green eyes met his. "I have to."

"Happens you don't."

"Happens I do." It was soft, resigned. "Rob, I'm sworn to them. I owe the Templars everything I am. They . . . own me."

"Not here." Robyn lay full atop him, nipped at his ear. "I've told you before, milord, this is ours, here, this place. And in this place, you're mine. Mine, and none else's."

"I thought no man belonged to another, in the Shire Wode."

"Gam—"

"If you own me here, and the Templars own me elsewhere, where do I own myself?"

"Stop twisting me words so," Robyn growled. "That weren't my meaning and you know it."

"But words *are* twisted, Robyn Hode," Gamelyn whispered. "There's those who say—quite rightly—how words were given to us, not to express, but conceal our thoughts. Words trick us, snare us, blood us. Even here in our once-Eden, where there is no right or wrong, no knowledge of opposites, no fetters of 'shalt' or 'shalt not' . . . One way or another, the words will betray us like jealous gods."

Aye, betray us. Robyn pondered how when Gamelyn was like this, he was as spellbound-mad as Robyn himself clad in sky and horns and hood—and only the way to bring either of them down: fierce, with caress and nip and breath, skin against skin.

I weren't meaning it, not that way.

Even if something in Gamelyn, because of or in spite of never having truly *been* property, yearned for the bonds.

No bonds this time.

Gamelyn flipped Robyn over, aggressive, worked him slow and thorough-hard; this time their loving held no faded-sweet memory of boys' discoveries, but the inexorable prerogative of men grown and passion known.

But there was gentleness afterward, and the words Gamelyn whispered against Robyn's spine—from the steel of Frankish to the fire-silk of Arabic—rose and fell in tandem with the heart hammering close. One sword-hard arm wrapped tight-wound about Robyn's own ribs, callused hand splayed to feel Robyn's own heart knocking, fit to burst, and the breath coming spare.

"What," Robyn panted, "are you saying?"

Gamelyn tensed, then breathed a small chuckle against Robyn's left shoulder blade. "I said, bloody damn, my ribs are killing me."

"Pull the other one . . . wait. Now I think on 't, that might well kill *me . . . Ow!*"

This as Gamelyn nipped at the soft skin just behind Robyn's armpit. Hard. But the support of Gamelyn's good arm was indeed beginning to shake, more with every passing moment. Robyn twisted, kissed the clutch of freckles sprayed on the shuddering bicep, and pulled forwards, away. Turned over onto his back, squirmed and grimaced as he held out his arms.

Gamelyn had risen to his knees, rubbing at his arm. "What?" Then, as Robyn squirmed farther sideways, "You didn't."

"Like I could help it!"

"It's my warmest cloak."

"'Twill wipe dry. And 'tis on the inside. Wain't show," Robyn insisted. "If you weren't about bein' so bloody good at the poking, milord . . ."

Someday Gamelyn's eyes were going to pop out from all that rolling. "Stop calling me 'milord,' you wretched wolfshead."

Robyn pulled him down—careful, for now the blood-heat had ebbed, Gamelyn was indeed moving a bit tenderly. "I'll stop calling you 'milord' *if* you'll tell me what you said."

A wry chuckle, this against Robyn's chest. "Nay, you really won't." Then, as Robyn opened his mouth, "And I shan't, either."

Robyn smirked and shifted sideways, trying to make himself into a somewhat-less-bony pillow. They lay quiet, gathering both thoughts and breath.

"Fog'll cling to the bottomlands, and the lower pastures. T' moat'll hold it all the more close. They wain't come into the trees until it starts to fade . . . I'm thinking afternoon. We'll have a good start, and keep to the Wode."

"Count John is arrogant, but no one's fool. He'll bring hounds."

"We'll split up, if that happens. Use some of Madam Herself's clothes for drags, lead 'em a merry chase deep into Peak and down t' Shire Wode, if needs be."

"I would pay good marks"—Gamelyn traced a deliberate finger across Robyn's chest—"to watch you talk Eleanor of Aquitaine out of her skirts."

Robyn snorted. "I'll have Marion do it." Then he grinned, cut sly eyes to Gamelyn. "How many marks, then?"

Gamelyn laughed, soft.

"I wish you would stay," Robyn said abruptly into Gamelyn's bright hair. "Stay here with me, and damn 'em all."

Another smattering of Frankish, this obviously a curse, the breath of it lifting and heating the fur along Robyn's breastbone. Then, "Robyn, I must. I've put it off as long as I can, and now . . . " Gamelyn sat up, peering into the dark hollows of their haven, one hand lightly—almost absently—running up and down Robyn's pale thigh. "Now it's all come to roost on our step. We knew this time would come. We knew I couldn't just vanish into the Wode like a spirit." He chuckled, but again, it was rueful, light. "That's for you, Green Man. Not for the likes of me."

"Summer comes. The Maying comes. You're Summer's lord, and—"

"I don't know what I am."

"I know. Marion knows. The men—"

"Don't want to know."

"They're coming 'round."

"Even so, it doesn't matter, Robyn. Won't matter until *I* know."

"Know what? What chains you prefer?" Robyn snapped. Gamelyn's hand nipped at his thigh, whilst remorse popped Robyn behind the eyes. His next words were softer, half apology and half hurt. "Don't you *want* to stay with me?"

"Of *course* I—!" Gamelyn hissed in a breath, contained it.

Stop strangling it. Just this once, Robyn begged, silent. *Just tell me.*

Gamelyn remained quiet—so quiet, and for so long, Robyn began to despair of the begging.

"My heart," Gamelyn finally said, soft, "wants nothing more than to stay. But my head?" He shrugged, leaned his forehead against Robyn's, and said, heavy with meaning, "You always say I mix you up . . . D'you truly think it's any less the other way around? Only you don't make me *think* too much."

"Aye, you already do that," Robyn murmured.

Gamelyn closed his eyes, huffed a wry breath. Paused, as if trying to test and taste his words. "You . . . you make me *feel* too much. You always have. And so, Winterlord, the *tynged* which would weave itself about us holds this much truth: we have, you and I, the power to destroy each other."

"D'you think I don't know it?"

Gamelyn's hand began again to stroke, back and forth, so gentle along Robyn's thigh. "And you revel in it. While I . . . I don't know how. I've spent too much time and effort hacking my way back from oblivion. And now, to turn to it and just . . . embrace it again?"

Robyn fell silent. Within him gathered a whirlwind of . . . *too much thought* . . . not instinctive, not *now,* but a place holding no answers, no possibilities—no darkling glimmers of *tynged* beckoning—just a void, impenetrable, spilling yearning and confusion.

He needed to do. To move, to act, to . . .

Rolling to his feet, Robyn began gathering his discarded clothes. The air bit against his flesh; without Gamelyn against him, it was cold. Bloody cold.

Yet Gamelyn's eyes weren't, when Robyn looked to them. They were pensive. Soft, as Gamelyn spoke.

"Say you understand." It was a plea.

"I do," Robyn said, shivering as he layered into his clothes. And he did, but it was cold, and he needed to *do*. Something.

"Then stay with *me*," Gamelyn said, sudden. "Come with me."

It brought warmth; heat into the chill. There was nothing like it: the simple-pure rush of standing back-to-back with one of the few Robyn knew would *hold* that back. *Back-to-back, none shall stand against you. . .*

Aye, the Lady had said it, and what of Marion? What of the rest he trusted—and who trusted him? And not only that, there was the Shire Wode. His Wode. *His* way, what needed him all the more, and now. Robyn turned and steadied himself against the cavern wall. Felt the grit of sand made stone, shaped by wind and water. Tasted the thick, heady power of it—tamed only by itself, and time.

"Robyn." Gamelyn lurched to his feet, started towards him. "Hubert invited you, remember? He said he wanted to speak with you. No doubt as he spoke with Cernun before you, and treated with him." A pause, then, low: "Please. Come with me."

Robyn wanted it. Wanted to turn around, to go and wrap his body about Gamelyn and never let him leave. Wanted to go with Gamelyn, ride into the wind and the rain and the danger flexing its wings towards them. But something within Robyn faltered, rumbled warning:

Would you, then, willingly march into more stones bled sterile?

It sounded like the Horned Lord. It sounded like *himself.*

You are the Green Man, the Hooded One who bears the Horns. Your tynged *will never belong to the stones and the iron bells. Hob-Robyn, you are the last of Us!*

Gamelyn heard it too. They were still too tangled in each other. Robyn slid a gaze at him; too late. Gamelyn's own had flickered away, down, cheeks flared crimson.

Robyn started to walk on, trailing fingers along the stone in echo of his slow progress outward. Halted.

"Are you coming?" he asked, quiet. Desperate.

Gamelyn's answer was no less of either. "I shall. Anon."

And, fingers still trailing on the stones, Robyn left him there.

His forest took him in. Wrapped about him, whispered his name— or mayhap whispers were just the wind, tickling at the fur slung over his shoulders. Nay, no tickle; it stung his cheeks, bitter. After this bit of work was over—this proper balls-up, more like—he and his band would have no choice but to burrow in, abandon the wandering for some warmth and safety. The caves here were unsuitable for long habitation and too close to danger. The horse caverns deep in the Shire Wode were better, large and dry—though by the end of a long winter, they always closed in smaller. Of course, they'd have two less to worry over . . .

Robyn stumbled, wondered how the stumble could have possibly happened, and looked down. Before him lay a stream, and on its bank a wooden bucket with water still spilling from it, kicked over. He'd kicked it over. Someone had left it there, half-filled; 'twere one of their buckets, at that. Robyn bent to pick it up, realising he'd done what Gamelyn bloody well excelled in. Not paying attention to what was around him, because it bided too full of things he didn't want to notice. Like pain, and loneliness.

He cannot go. You cannot let him go, not like this.

"Do I have a choice?" he growled back. "Should I tie him like a boar for roasting?" Then thought, *Aye, and he might like it. . .*

The laugh tore at his chest, more rue than honey, and he pressed on. Realised he was sort of heading back towards camp, but mostly not; had been circumnavigating it in a wide arc until he'd smacked into the bucket, still dangling from one hand.

"Robyn?" From behind him, a worried, harried voice with its telltale, slight lisp.

And Sweet *Lady*, but if there were any he weren't yet prepared to face this morning, it was Will Scathelock.

"Later," he growled, and kept walking.

"*Robyn!*" It was urgent. Full of reproach, and insulted injury, and regret . . . always, the regret. Will was never sorry he'd said any-thing, but he was very sorry when it gave offence, as if the two were somehow disconnected.

Will caught up to Robyn, half skipping beside him in earnest need to be noticed, to be *heard.* And aye, well, wasn't *that* over half the problem? "Robyn, *please.*"

The quaver in Will's voice always got to Robyn, because he knew it wasn't practised, or put on. It was real, and Robyn knew it. It was why he halted.

Took a deep breath. Turned.

"I were hoping . . . hoping to find you, but I weren't sure . . . " It wavered off. Will obviously knew where Robyn had been—and with whom. "Since that fever, sometimes he en't in his right mind when he wakes, like . . . " Again, it wavered off; this time because of Robyn's glare. "You know 'tis true! I've rights to worry!" Will defended. "And sure enough, you look . . . erm . . . poorly. Are you all right?"

'Twere all genuine, to be sure: the worry, the attentiveness, the affection prompting it all. The ties, bone-deep for both of them, to what was gone.

It didn't make it any less overpowering. It didn't make it right . . . or even all right.

"Will." Robyn threaded warning into it: *Back off, damn you, not now, let me breathe!* "What do you want?" Even though he knew.

Sure enough, Will's broad, handsome face pinked. He dropped that contested bone merely to gnaw at another one. "I've been trying to apologise to Marion. But she wain't talk to me."

"Aye, and do you blame her?"

"It were the drink, you know 'twere. The drink, and I didn't mean nowt by it, it's just—"

"But the drink looses the anger, Will, and you should know better by now than—"

"So everyone's allowed to have a good drunk but me?"

Bloody damn. "I thought you were sorry, Scathelock? When did this become about *you* bein' the wronged one?" Robyn shook his head, started to walk on.

Will grabbed his arm, strong enough to bloody well stop Robyn. And did. "I'm trying to tell you I didn't *mean it.*"

"You didn't mean for it to go so far, aye." Robyn knew he was too close to every edge he possessed to be having this out, here and now—yet it was a relief. "But you did mean it, and you bloody well know it."

And Will had the brass to look *surprised.*

It pushed Robyn just a little further, teetering over those edges. "Arthur warned me. Months ago, he warned me—"

"About what?" Will paled, and Robyn wondered what he was so worried about.

It didn't matter. Not now. "He said one woman in a bunch of men is nowt but trouble, and I told him to belt up, 'twere bloody disrespectful, not only to Marion, but to all of you. He weren't weaned to our ways, thinks too much like the damned Church, assuming women no better than slaves, and men having the right to stick their knob even in sommun as en't willing. But mayhap he were right, because it's slunk into our own band like fever pox—and *you* should know better! I wondered if me sister had been too long in that bloody sterile convent, why she hadn't so much as sought to lie with anyone—as she is free to do, in t' Shire Wode—but after last night, I think I know."

"It en't like that. She—"

"The only reason you've ever wanted Marion is because she's only ever said nay to you! You want Gamelyn gone—"

"That one's name," Will snapped back, "were Guy of Gisbourne. In case you've forgotten."

"*Were*, Will. Just as me own name *were* once Rob of Loxley. But Loxley's gone. Rob died in a cave from a crossbow bolt t' the heart. Gisbourne were beheaded on Samhain."

"And grown another to spit poison! No matter what he's decided to call hisself, it don't mean he en't still a murdering nobleman. One of *them!*"

"Aye, and there's a finger in a festering sore, en't it?" Robyn took a step towards Will. "You don't see straight when it comes to him. You never have!"

"It en't me who en't seeing things what are—"

"He's some . . . some bloody icon of everything as threatens you!"

"The only reason he threatens me is because he threatens *you!*" Will stood his ground, just as angry.

"Bollocks! How 'n bloody fuck does he threaten *me*, then?"

"I keep telling you. Keep telling, and you en't *listening* to me, Rob!"

"Sweet Lady, why does it allus come back to this? Why are you allus *at* this?" It was raw. Robyn was well over the edge, now, but instead of fury, a black, bleak chasm of misery loomed. "Why wain't you just *leave it be?*"

He'd taken more time dressing than normal. With each bit of clothing Gamelyn donned, he armed himself with vagrant thoughts, tried to make sense of each one.

Foolish to have even asked. Not after what had happened at Worksop—though the power of it had likely been brought on by that damned Arrow, as Marion had suggested. Robyn had been all right at Blyth, after all. But last night—with Will, and Marion . . . nay, Robyn couldn't leave.

And so speaks the noble-born. It was chiding, the Lady's voice—with a tinge of Eluned of Loxley lurking in the corners. *Do you speak in protection, or in man's pride? Do you not think Our Maiden has the ability to care for herself?*

"There are things," Gamelyn replied, lacing up his tunic with uncommon ferocity, "that anyone can be made prey to. And women most of all."

In your world, O man. Not in mine.

"Well, unfortunately this world is the one in which we must walk."

Is it?

Gamelyn shook his head, small and irritable, and began gathering his knives. Only the three—he'd gotten used to carrying fewer when knocking about the forest, and his sword still bided with Much in the cavern. That would have to change. Like everything else . . .

Misery swamped him, brought a hot surge to his eyes and made his hands shake. He forced them still, strapped his knives into their places. Contemplated the dawning, and the plans to be made.

Mayhap it is well, after all, for you to leave. You are still the snake with two heads, Templar. You threaten Eden, after all.

Gamelyn gritted his teeth, the familiarity of anger rising to deny melancholy. "I think you should look to your own people for the true threat."

Thus saying you are not? Of my own?

Cheeks burning, Gamelyn went to reach for his sword belt, remembered he didn't have it. Instead, he snatched up his cloak. Saw the small, dried stain upon it. Rolled his eyes—only partway—before he closed them and lifted the cloak to his face, breathed it in.

It still smelt of Robyn. Leaf-mould, moss and clean sweat, the musk of sex, the tang of earth and well-oiled yew and alder . . .

Those who would walk nothing but their own small path, who bend to see only their own reflection in the pool? Those have strayed. They will either retrace their steps and find the many paths leading to the otherworld, or they will continue, lost.

Breath at his temple, riffling his hair, the impossible every day becoming more possible, *real.*

Will you also continue, lost?

"Why are you here? To torment me with riddles?" Gamelyn swung the cloak about him, tied it secure. "I thought that more your Consort's line of work."

Why are you here, proud one, and arguing with Me?

Gamelyn started to give a hot retort. At the last moment he bit it back, smiled—though it was far from pleasant—and bowed. Flipped the cloak that still smelt of his lover over one shoulder. Quit the cavern.

Aye, you could never go back. It was impossible.

But there had to be *some way* . . .

Gamelyn was beginning to feel like a quintain sparred by three inexpert squires: fury and fear and desolation. He stalked through the naked trees, breath exhausting behind in thick, misted bursts. The cold wind set his eyes to watering, but he didn't feel it; more from sense than any sensation did he pull his cowl forwards for protection. And kept going. Up one small hillock and down another, careful over wet moss and stones, through bare trees, evergreen shrubs, and down into a small ravine—

"Bollocks!"

Gamelyn dropped to a crouch, had drawn the curved knife from his belt before he recognised the voice, wafting and falling on the chill wind.

Robyn.

He started to rise and sheath his knife, halted midmotion as another voice sounded. "—and you en't *listening* to me, Rob!"

Gamelyn rolled his eyes. Why was it inevitable he would wander in on conversations he had no right to—and no good temper for? Gritting his teeth, Gamelyn put one hand against the damp earth and started to push upwards, make a silent return back the way he'd come. There was another path, longer but . . .

"—does it allus come back to this? Why are you allus *at* this?"

The raw misery in Robyn's voice hit Gamelyn like a flail in the belly, immobilised him.

"Why wain't you just *leave it be?*"

Will didn't answer right away, and for moments Gamelyn had a spark of hope. Might Scathelock show the man he surely must be, the friend Robyn so loved? Might he *see* what this was doing to not only Robyn, but all of them?

Of course, that hope was destined to be disappointed.

"I en't the one who's bellying 'is own death! I en't the one who's letting Marion flirt with it!"

"Letting? I'm *letting* . . . Will—!"

"For pity's sake, Robyn, have y' forgotten what he *is?*"

"You've *no* pity, that's for certain!"

Footsteps, clumsy and rushed, splashing through the stream and up through a stand of trees—Gamelyn could see the two of them, shadows upon grey and faded green. Making entirely too much noise for hardened outlaws.

God! He hissed out a breath through gritted teeth. *Why now? We have the bloody Queen Mother of all England waiting in our camp, and. . .*

"Bloody fucking hell, Rob! He's a murdering Templar, and a noble, and of their be-damned Motherless Church!" Will's voice followed, just as raw and furious, and Gamelyn slid slow against a sheltering elm as Will continued.

"If . . . *If* he's the Summering Lord, as John keeps insisting . . . well, I en't the most powerful or gifted of our covenant, but I know what such a thing means. *Winterlord.*"

Robyn started to laugh—and there was absolutely no humour in it. "Sweet Lady, William, but you sound like me da."

"And your da *died* because of what he is! *My* da died because of that bloody Templar's kind, and our mothers as well—but he's to be the Summerlord? *Him?* He's no true rights, but he's taken 'em.

He's taken you and he's looking to Marion now, en't he?—and this can't go on, Rob! It—*uh!*"

Robyn had been holding something heavy—but no more; he flung it at Will and hit him, hard, in the solar plexus. It bounced away and went clattering to the ground, rolled back down the slight slope towards the stream.

A bucket. It skipped over the stream and skidded to a halt against a large rock, not three strides from Gamelyn.

"Well then," Robyn spat, "happens you'll be pleased to know he en't staying, then. And if it weren't for all the shit you slung about last night, I'd as lief go with him!"

That, finally, shut Scathelock up.

"Don't make me choose." Robyn's words were a hiss. "I'm warning you, don't you dare, because you . . . you . . . damn you, Scathelock, why wain't you just *leave it be?*"

And instead of pounding the bloody-minded stuffing out of Scathelock as he bloody well deserved, Robyn backed away, shaking his head.

Spun around. Retreated—and it was a retreat, nothing less.

Will stood there for long moments, and Gamelyn could only hope Will had sense enough not to go after. To both Gamelyn's horror and undeniable satisfaction, Will instead turned and started marching his way.

Will was so brassed off he didn't even see Gamelyn until he was almost atop him. First mistake. Bent on retrieving the bucket, when Will did see Gamelyn, he started, opened his mouth as if to say something, then peered back the way he'd come.

Second mistake. Gamelyn let it pass. Despite the knife in Gamelyn's hand, Will bent to reach for the bucket. Third mistake, that.

"What're *you* doing here?" Will growled, snatching up the bucket.

"Scathelock." Gamelyn returned the greeting—such as it was—with a deliberate and slight lean, sheathing the knife back at his belt.

Yet Will didn't so much as tense at the motion. The mistakes were indeed mounting up.

"You might need that, Red." Will jerked his head to the sheathed knife. "If happens you're lookin' to finish what you really wanted to start last night."

Gamelyn hadn't truly felt the temperature's descent thus far; now he felt a chill at his spine, was wary of and yet welcomed it. A quirk teased itself onto one side of his mouth—just as icy, Gamelyn was sure.

"I mean to finish something, all right. But *happens*"—he rose, still deliberate, and let his voice slide into a scornful rendition of Will's Yorkshire purl— "it en't quite in the way yer thinkin'."

Will didn't have the freckles, but *my*, if he didn't have the same Saxon-fair cheeks—and the telltale flush Gamelyn also found a handicap when concealing his own emotions.

"You . . . you . . . !" Will stepped forwards, then once more glanced back the way he'd come, hesitated.

Fifth mistake. Charming William was fast running out of them.

"Yes. Me. It seems you have several things to say to me." Gamelyn shrugged, pretended to look off into the trees. "Don't be shy, Scathelock. If you have something on your mind, I suggest we discuss it—"

"You *suggest*, do you?"

"—instead of skulking about and refusing to face me with it."

Will's face flamed once again, and he lurched forwards, fists clenched. Gamelyn didn't so much as move. At this Will halted, visibly took hold of himself. He allowed another, tiny step towards Gamelyn, and deliberately hawked, spat on the ground between them. Then, just as deliberately, he turned his back on Gamelyn and started for the opposite end of the hollow.

Last mistake. A quirk lifting one side of his mouth, Gamelyn lunged forwards. Silent and quick as a sand viper's strike, he grabbed Will, spun him around and slammed him against a handy tree. Dry, bare branches shuddered with the impact. Gamelyn felt it through his ribs and up into his shoulder. Refused to heed it.

"You poncy ginger bast—!"

Will's protest went from snarl to squeak as Gamelyn's fingers dug into his throat.

"You seem to have some familiarity with this predicament," Gamelyn ventured, almost pleasant. "Let's revisit it, shall we?"

Snarling, Will tried to shove back. When that didn't work, he swung his fist at the side of Gamelyn's head. Gamelyn ducked, snatched the fist midair and, with a shift and heave, had Will face-first against the tree, offending arm twisted up behind his back before he could so much as draw breath.

It hurt. But not enough to loose the angry bear.

And, like an angry bear, Will didn't submit. Likely he wasn't used to losing—taller, a lot broader—and quite the dirty fighter, Game-lyn discovered as Will drove an elbow backwards, then flailed a fist into the space where Gamelyn's testicles should have been. They weren't. Gamelyn merely danced sideways and gave an upwards crank on Will's arm. Said a silent prayer that he was using his good arm. He'd curled the other one tight against his ribs, Gamelyn noticed—when had that happened?—but he didn't need it, not now. And the inward pressure helped him breathe.

"I don't believe you're listening to me, Scathelock." The words clipped themselves close, quite soft and even more reasonable. "I'll make it more . . . simple, shall I? If you have something to say about me, mayhap you should say it *to* me."

"I've nowt to say to you!"

"If"—Gamelyn's voice revealed nothing; not pain, not fury—"you can't be arsed to face me like a man, then mayhap—"

"Face *you*? I'd think you'd be t' one who'd want me arse facing, you boy-buggering piece of—!"

This time Gamelyn yanked Will's knuckles nigh up to his skull. Will gave a hoarse yip, muffled by rough bark and thick moss, and nearly went to his knees.

God, but Gamelyn wanted to kill him for that alone. Really, truly, wanted to hear him scream. Not for what it said about Gamelyn himself—he'd heard worse, after all, and from experts. Nay, it was what it betrayed, about the edges, in Will.

Gamelyn leaned even closer, pleased his voice didn't so much as tighten as he whispered, "And wouldn't Robyn love to hear you say just that?"

There was a strange sense of relief at the sudden tremor in Scathelock's frame—and what *it* told.

"Are you so stupid, Scathelock? You really think you know best? You bloody thick-witted *peasant*, would you take a blade to your own just to get to me?"

"You're nowt!" Will was nigh frothing against the tree. "I'm thinkin' of Robyn, *nobleman*. Not you!"

"You're not thinking of Robyn, or you'd leave him be. You'd trust him. Instead you keep gutting him, and it stops. Stops now, do you understand?"

Will slackened against the tree. Gamelyn wasn't fooled. He yanked Will from the tree and, before he could lurch about and fight back, flung him sideways. With a yelp, Will hit the dirt like a tun of ale and sprawled there.

"I've killed men for less!"

"So have I," Gamelyn purred, and began to back away. "But seeing as it's you, it'll take more. Don't think I've gone soft. It's for Robyn's sake, not yours."

"Don't do me any favours, nobleman!"

Gamelyn rolled his eyes, kept backing away.

"You think I'll hurt Robyn?" Will didn't give it up. "It en't *me* who keeps putting a knife to his throat!"

A knife, all right, and one slipping unaware past Gamelyn's considerable defences. Thank God Will remained unaware of how insidious it truly was. Gamelyn tilted his head, insult and acknowledgement both. Turned his back—with as much insolence as Will had earlier displayed—and started walking.

Slowly. There was a distinct and sharp edge of discomfort flirting about the edges of his consciousness.

It was a mistake. Will saw the weakness. Like a challenged wolf, he leapt on it.

Gamelyn shouldn't have been there when Will finished that leap. But reflexes, normally tight-honed, betrayed. He did manage to whirl around just as Will barrelled into him and knocked him a full ell sideways. They went down in a tangle of flailing limbs and grunted curses, kept rolling down the small hillock, towards the stream.

The bucket stopped them. Gamelyn slammed against it with all the momentum of charge and fall. Will cursed, heaved against Gamelyn again. Gamelyn heard his spine pop—or did he dare hope it was Will? The bucket?—as he half rolled atop it, arched and bent backwards, arms flinging upwards like cut ropes.

They lay there for a smattering of heartbeats—nay, for hours, surely?—then Will cursed. Shoved upwards, pushing off Gamelyn and mashing him against the bucket. Knotted fingers in the oiled-wool cloak that still, impossibly, smelt of Robyn, and shook Gamelyn like Tess would shake a rat.

It was then Gamelyn knew the bucket, not his spine, had broken. The pain hit.

"Y' say Robyn matters to you?" Will growled, shoved him down.

A gasp tried to burst into air and light; Gamelyn bit it back with a sound that, remarkably, escaped more a return growl than the whimper it had surely started as.

"*You're* the liar." Will shook him again; again Gamelyn gave the strange, agonised growl, which seemed to only make Will more furious. "If you truly cared for anything but your own Motherless hide, you'd leave and never come back! You've only ever given Robyn misery from the day you both met."

Will stuck his face closer—too close, and Gamelyn should kick him into next week. Instead, he let out another growl/mewl.

"*He* en't listening to me—you've bewitched him, but you en't going to work your ways on Marion. I'll bloody see you dead before you so much as *touch* Marion!"

Marion? What?

Will dragged him up by his tunic again, and Gamelyn braced himself. He was going to have the shit kicked from him and there wasn't a damned thing he could do about it.

Will gave a strange sound, like a sob or curse. He loosed his hold, so abrupt that Gamelyn flopped back down against the smashed bucket. Gamelyn felt his legs drawing up of their own accord, like a babe curled in its dam's womb, and tried to stop them. Straighten them. If Will saw . . .

Will wasn't watching. He'd turned away. He made another odd sound, stumbled away on legs that didn't seem to want to hold him up.

Gamelyn well knew what it felt like. His own legs curled tighter, his arms wrapping close. He rolled off the bucket with a gasp, and though only a matter of several inches, the jolt of contact with the ground sent a horrific flash of pain from thighs to nape. Finally it escaped his throat in a long, shuddering groan.

He was, suddenly, bloody *cold*.

He pulled his cloak close, shut his eyes, and found his nostrils filled with Robyn. Found his mind going muzzy. Found himself praying—praying!—*Lady. Help me.*

And time . . . *Slips*. . .

"I have him!" Much snaps, but it is Robyn's hands Gamelyn feels upon his face, Robyn's voice murmuring a soft cadence. Words, their meaning unfathomable, but the spell of them breaks the remainder of Gamelyn's dream, sends it peeling from him in thin shards, like a film of ice shaken from a tree branch.

"Milord?" Much murmurs, soft, and Gamelyn well recognises the tight grip—two stout arms and one hard-muscled leg—wrapping him close.

"I'm all right," Gamelyn husks, forces himself to the humiliation of opening his eyes, finds the outlaws in a wary, loose semicircle— not too close, mind.

"When it's like this?" Much chides Robyn—low enough to not be heard by the others, thank God. "Y' wain't be cozening him through. Tie a knot and hang on, more like."

Robyn nods, listening and clearly unruffled—unlike the others, particularly Will and Marion. It is no comfort to understand how Marion's concern comes from a very different source than Will's.

Will has a knife in hand—but then, somehow, so does Gamelyn.

Gamelyn says, a murmur of apology to Robyn, "I don't know why now."

"Don't you?" Robyn asks, then shrugs. "I do."

Gamelyn starts to ask *You do? How?* But Robyn heaves up from their furs, shaking a white cloud of snow from them.

Wait. It hasn't snowed all winter . . .

The snow cloud floats upwards, shimmers against grey and green, begins to coalesce into . . . something. Like pictures in stars or clouds, he has to look very hard to make sense of it.

It forms, shifts, forms again to become a white hart. It starts towards Gamelyn, with every deliberate step becoming more real, more *here*—yet still, all Gamelyn can do is lie on the frigid ground, panting.

The stag bends his ebon-tined head, nudges Gamelyn. It is not gentle. Gamelyn gasps as the tines poke him, lets out a harsh grunt as the stag butts even closer, the enormous rack lifting him, rolling him over to lie, spread to all points and vulnerable. Then the stag breathes on him.

It is warm as new-drawn milk, thick as frost-mist, and fills him with a tingling, stinging, almost delirious heat.

And Sight. For suddenly he can see—*See*—the shimmering pathways of *tynged* stretching out before him, a multicoloured tapestry still upon the loom and not even half-finished, patterns forming, being woven and set . . .

Aye, there you are. Reach for it.

It is Robyn's voice, but it is the stag's horns that tilt, roll beneath, then lift Gamelyn to his feet. The tines are sharp and curved as his best Damascus knife, but there is no pain even when red furrows trace across freckled skin. There is only the bliss and strength as he grasps the base of the great horns, only the heat and magic of that voice.

Take it! Take the horns and breathe it all in, my lovely Summering storm. You cannot curl back to sleep and death. Anadlu eich tynged. *Breathe your destiny.*

The latter echoes in his skull with Robyn's deep-smooth baritone.

See it. Tynged, *upon the Lady's loom. You understand frost; you must also brave the fire.*

His grip falters. Fire. He fears it. Craves it.

Aye, you would. For Oaks burn long, and strong, and what is fire if not the wild way inward?

Fire, in the woodland. Scorched trees, and despair hanging over the place, part and parcel of the thick smoke, and memories edging closer still, as Queen Eleanor moves her horse close to his, says, *A shame, but such things happen. Mayhap you will do better, my lord Templar, when King Richard returns and you are rewarded for all you have done. . .*

Fire, in the blood. Bonfires—Bel-fires—and the dancing, drums and pipes into the night, and challenges met in moonlight. Robyn's laughter beside him as Marion paces slowly to them, ivy in her hair and bearing the horn-crown in her hands . . .

Fire, in the mind. Promises whispered in a honey-fire voice, and hands beside it, pale and somehow . . . twisted, as they wind a braided, shimmering cord about a blackened, bloodstained arrow . . .

Fire, in the heart. Warming stone and bringing strength, and a hearth and home thought ever lost is once again filled with family— safe here, all of them, they are safe . . .

Nothing is safe. Nothing easy, never easy with you, pet.

Mockery? That he understands—but this is tinged bitter-cruel, changes to a voice he does not recognise—but has come to know in dreams: *You will betray him, you know. You must. It is what you are meant to do, were born to do,* will *do, within this little Dance in which we've found ourselves.*

It is every nightmare Gamelyn has feared, a backdraught to twist and take him, then reach for the brightest flame of them all—for surely 'tis the hottest fires that die the fastest—as his soul burns to ashes, turns to death . . .

Hold me. . . I must. . .

And Robyn in his arms, loosing a golden, peacock-fletched arrow from his bow, and it flies, a flame over Barrow Mere as Robyn collapses against Gamelyn's breast. The delicate, sharp beauty of the quillion dagger, glinting in the arrow's wake as he brings it to Robyn's throat . . .

With a choked cry, Gamelyn shoves back.

Falls.

Sees it, over and over *and over.*

"No," he growls into the frosted loam. "No, I will not. You cannot make me see it waking as well as—"

Can I not?

It flashes through his mind: the Horned Lord standing across the Barrow Mere, forcing Gamelyn to his knees . . . nay, it is *Robyn,* clad in sky and the horn-crown, and in his hands he holds his longbow, nocked with a flaming black arrow . . . nay, not, for as Gamelyn watches—

Lies helpless, blinded by sense and Sight in the green Wode. . .

—the figure blurs, fire-flung and crossed by longbow, into a scarlet form that retreats, once more, into the man. Into the Templar.

His Master stands above him, a flaming cross upon his snowy-white tabard as he kneels beside Gamelyn.

Mask forever marked, no longer merely Guy de Gisbourne, Templar weapon. You are no good to me now; beheaded—humiliated—by a wolfshead witch. . .

"Your oaths are rusty, are they? Sherwood has killed Guy and stolen Gamelyn. Ah"—Hubert *tsks*—"but then, Gamelyn was never fully mine. He was the one I could never trust."

"That isn't true," Gamelyn growls.

"Ah, but what is truth? What happens, Templar, when you give to Sherwood what belongs to us? Whom do you serve?"

No answer, only fire, raging through his mind and into every breath he takes, until he clutches to the ground and begins praying—praying!—to the only one he still knows will hear him, as he has heard Her.

And She gives him silence. Blessed, blessed silence.

Then, into the silence . . .

Dreaming, it is dreaming waking—can you not be hearing it? Wounded and sore cold.

It is being cold, aye, cold iron is lying at its hip, and to defy Sire's will it is using colder heart. It is wounded, it is killing the dreaming.

Gamelyn tries to open his eyes. Cannot.

Mother voice be bringing us here, he is invoking Her. Hearing *Her. Happens this is being the one?*

Nay, fool, this one is not being the one. Not one who would be wearing the iron and the stolen scarlet rune.

Not this one. The oddling whisper echoes behind his ears. *It is belonging to the iron and the bells. Its time is not thisnow. It would be bleeding, but not for the Horns, not thisnow. . .*

Bleeding?

Gamelyn shot upright and was sorry—oh, so very sorry—he had. But his world was no longer tilting about him. Slowly, he found the pain ebbing further and further into bearable proportions.

He wasn't bleeding, body or—worse—mind. There were no waking nightmares whirling about him, no fractured futures—nay, not futures, they *would not be*—playing out behind his eyes, and . . . O *God!* How did Robyn stand it?

Gamelyn crouched there a while longer, head in hands, forcing his mind into black, black ice. Making sure. Moved first his neck, then his limbs. And, when those proved relatively sound, moved to stand.

There was pain, yes. Particularly when he breathed too deep and incautious. Likely the ribs. A sticky-wet portion of undertunic clung to the scar beside his shoulder blade where the crossbow bolt had been dug out. Likely torn open again. All along his shoulder and arm tingled, half-numb. But only that—not limp, not broken. Nothing seemed broken—save perhaps the rift only just healed across his rib cage.

Save, perhaps, the rift in Robyn Hood's band.

If he is *the Summering Lord. . . I know what such a thing means. Winterlord.*

It was reminder of the dreams. Over and over, confirmation skulking from the darker reaches of his mind, reminder of what he and Robyn truly were.

Well. Gamelyn lifted his chin, started a careful, almost delicate pace forwards.

There was only one thing to be done.

He'd been in worse straits, after all.

- XIV -

Marion stirred at the cooking porridge and gave a soft sigh. Finally, silence.

Her bed had been chilly—and unfrequented—when she'd woken. Even John had been gone. Of course, she had not expected Robyn's or Gamelyn's return. Much had been awake, and Alundel, who had both risen not long after herself and exited. Neither had yet returned. The others still slept, including their guest of honour.

At least David's breathing was easier this morn. Amazing, how good whiskey could clear out a clogged windpipe. Unfortunately, it had other consequences.

Her lips tightened. Will had been missing when she'd awakened— the discovery had held some awkward relief—and he, too, had not returned.

Or so Marion had believed, until she'd gone out to fetch fresh water and found Will waiting, spilling over with low, stammered apologies. Marion had merely shoved the bucket at him and marched back into the cavern, ignoring any further protests.

She had cobbled together some grain porridge—oats and barley— with what water she had, sliced some apples, measured out some nuts and dried blueberries. It began to bubble and stew long before her own stewing had abated.

She hadn't escaped one imprisonment merely to find another. She *hadn't*. Mayhap she should speak to Robyn. The moment she considered it, humiliation stung her cheeks. She shouldn't have to speak to Robyn. She should be able to deal with this herself.

Thought she *had* dealt with this herself.

Maybe everyone would stay asleep or lose themselves for a while.

"The tales make no mention of a woman amidst the wolfsheads."

Well, the silence had lasted a short while, anyway. Marion tilted her head to see their royal guest sitting up, albeit slow.

"But then," Eleanor considered, soft and wry, "they never do. Do they?"

It was in Anglic, companioned with a just-as-rueful, if friendly, smile. Marion found herself responding to it, mayhap more candidly than she should, considering.

"Aye, well, mostly men are the ones as tell 'em."

"There are a few women. Too few, but they are, in their own right, powerful talents. We must be twice as loud to be heard in this man's world, *non*?" Eleanor's smile broadened. "Several I have known quite well. There is one—ah, but Marie can spin a tale worth the telling." Brushing at her clothes, Eleanor gave a small laugh. "Marie is one who would delight in an adventure such as this. Particularly considering your brother's . . . ah . . . abilities?"

Marion frowned, ever so slight. Careful.

"Marie is one for the . . . what is the best word for it . . . the *merveilleux*?"

"The tales of magic?" Marion asked, still careful.

"She would do such things justice." Eleanor nodded. "She is, after all, of the old blood."

"The . . . old blood?" Definitely wary, now.

"I named the wrong son after that old warlock," Eleanor muttered, almost to herself, but her eyes returned, keen, to Marion. "My youngest son finds almost unseemly fascination in such tales."

The habits Marion had developed in the abbey—both unconscious and aware—served her very well now. She'd no veil to tuck her face into, true, but she lowered her lashes until she saw the gilt of them against her own cheeks. Lowered her head and said, dutiful, "Can I offer you some warmed cider, Madam?"

Eleanor didn't answer for moments; Marion could feel those slate-grey eyes considering her. Then Eleanor gave a soft huff and said, just as muted, "Anon. Is there, mayhap, a piss-pot handy?"

Aye, well, and wasn't that the last question Marion had expected? Which was just bloody daft—but nowhere near as daft as expecting a fancy piss-pot in the middle of an outlaw camp. Marion denied the tilt of her lip, said, "I'm afraid not, Madam. But rain's stopped, so you're in luck there. And I know a prime spot for a bit of privacy."

His insides were crawling—not with the Horned Lord's ire, but his own.

Mayhap he should just go with Gamelyn. Not that *that* would do either of them any good—it was a bloody monk's hall, weren't it? All right, so it seemed they were monks with the magic—but it weren't no proper magic, bugger it sideways, if they'd failed to teach it to one as had it filling him from nose to toes. Mayhap what the head monk had wanted with Robyn was some of the wild magic, the woodland ways, but the head monk'd have to hike his robes, first, and leave off all this chastity nonsense.

A chill twitched at Robyn's nape, shuddered all the way to his tailbone. He frowned, hesitated, then rolled his eyes fit to best Gamelyn's expression of choice. He'd be seeing ferlies and boggarts next, drooling mad—more than normal—whilst shoving meaning into every little twitch and shivery chill.

It was *winter*, after all.

Then, like a dog worrying a bone, his thoughts slipped back into the same groove, the same dance. Winter, so he could go with Gamelyn; there wasn't much to be done this time of year but burrow in and try not to do murder to each other out of boredom. He'd take Marion with him—that'd show bloody Scathelock, it would—and then they'd all three be together as the Lady said, forge the *Ceugant* strong, and come back with the spring, start over . . .

Aye, start over. Go with the Oak, bide close in Barnsdale. Reclaim what once was Ours, the Horned Lord whispered, always spoiling for action.

Robyn smiled, let it slide into a snarl.

What is lost cannot be won until We have fully claimed what is Ours. The Lady, so sudden, and Robyn stumbled again, this time to a halt. *The old magics are strongest here, upon the edge where Shire Wode commingles with Tor, gives way to Peak and feeds Barrow Mere. This is where We must stand, and stay, and raise the power of the* Ceugant.

"How can I do that if he en't *here?*" It was desperate.

He has been *here, weak yet still unbending.*

You are too lenient, the Horned Lord growled. *Put the Oak on his knees and keep him there.*

"Aye, and that's done so well for you," Robyn snapped back, and a soft breath chuckled against his hair.

She was . . . laughing.

Time slows to a crawl, or catches Us up. My Knight is filled with time, indeed.

More nonsense. "Back-to-back, you said. If we stand together, you said." The weight of both of them, fully focused and *present*, was not too much for Robyn's strength of will, but his body all to the sudden went wobbly. He stumbled again, this time went down into a crouch.

Our lovely Oak has too many leaves still clinging from Autumn, She whispered, edged with soft mockery. *Ah, but he has always been a late bloomer.*

"And how can he shed those leaves *there,* where they make of him a barren *shell?"*

You said it yourself, O Virgin Consort.

Robyn snorted; he couldn't help it.

Have you touched a woman, in thought or doing? Have you taken a Maiden to the fires? Have you wanted Me in your bed? You are My Virgin Hunter, love, and therefore can be ignorant of My ways even when a wisdom dwarfing the power of opposites falls from your mouth.

The Lady leaned closer; he could smell the green-wild moss of Her hair, feel the heat of Her body against his, and aye, only comfort and closeness settling into his belly. And fear, a tiny thrill and curl that made him shiver, then smile.

What wisdom, the Lady persisted, *did you spout, O Hunter, in the barren press of their unholy stones? You quailed—and who could blame you?—yet kenned your lover's strength despite infirmity.*

"I said," Robyn whispered, "they were his. Those stones know his name, call it, sing it, scream it. I saw it at Blyth, too. He *gentled* them."

He closed his eyes and put both palms to his temples. The memory. Her. And the Horned Lord, lurking, never far from his awareness, as if Robyn's own measure—like the one girdled against Gamelyn's hips and that, unlike Gamelyn's, lay deep-hidden in the Shire Wode—bound them, an umbilical between.

Indeed. For not even the Green Man, Horned and Hooded, has all the knowledge We must possess to win this war.

The Horned Lord, steaming in contemplative silence, gave a satisfied breath. *Aye. I see it.*

Fine, Robyn thought to himself, etched in acid, *and will sommun arse themselves to explain it to me? He's leaving, is all I know, and what if those old oaths grow tendrils, keep him there?*

The Horned Lord's tines came to rest upon Robyn's shoulders, weight and comfort. *Rest assured, our mistletoe vine has taken fiercer hold. It will but twine the tighter as he leans into the wind.*

And, the Lady said, fading into the black, *mayhap others will grow in barren stone, to speed him home.*

Robyn started to question, but She was gone.

When Marion brought Queen Eleanor back to the cavern, Much was standing there, lone sentry; he bowed them in. John had also returned, warming his hands over the flames. Still no sign of Robyn or Gamelyn, but Gilbert and Arthur were eyeing the porridge and David bent over it, stirring. They all gave way as Marion offered Eleanor the best seat by the fire.

"You don't cook for these knaves *all* the time?" Eleanor passed a gimlet eye over said knaves, who promptly found things to do.

"Often enough," Marion said. "But then, I like cookin'."

"I despise it," Eleanor proclaimed.

Nice to be able to have your druthers, Marion thought but did not say. Though she wondered if Eleanor kenned it anyway, from the arch of eyebrow she threw Marion's way. The woman was too bloody canny by half.

"Come on, then," Marion told Alundel, who had returned and was sitting against the far wall, tuning at his lute. "Have a bite."

"Nay," he said, soft. "But I thank you."

David brought a stack of crocks and began dishing up hearty portions. Eleanor accepted hers with graceful thanks, but it didn't stop her from sliding a curious gaze to Alundel.

The man did seem morose, Marion considered.

John wasn't much better. He ate, all the while watching the trouvère. A definite threat lingered behind those soft brown eyes.

David took a bowl of porridge to Much.

"We seem to be missing a few of our members," Eleanor said. "Do you think they'll be long?"

"I'm surprised they've not come back yet," Marion answered. "My brother likes to hunt with the dawn, but he can smell porridge miles away."

Eleanor chuckled. "Tis true, the lean ones always manage to out-eat the paunchy ones."

"Johnny?" Much leaned inside the cavern, gestured to John, who set his bowl down and went out.

"Looks as if one's returned," Gilbert murmured to Marion; she followed his gaze and saw, sure enough, a dark cloak topped with a glint of copper. As John exited, there was a small exchange of murmurs, and then they moved away.

Marion felt a twinge of worry and curiosity combined, but Eleanor spoke and drove both from her thoughts. Completely.

"What would you say, girl, if I asked you to do me the favour of accompanying me to Hirst?"

"Tis an old rag, milord, nowt but," Much temporised, with a brandish of faded and worn linen. "See? Already I've ripped a few bits from 't. And you know should I go rummaging in the cave, Herself will be all over it, wanting to know what's happened."

Gamelyn shrugged acquiescence, grimaced at the injudicious motion, then continued angling—carefully—his tunic over his head.

"Mightn't be a bad thing," Much considered. "Herself wain't knock the daft git for her own sake, but she'd give him what he deserves and more for sommat like this." On a rock half again as high as himself, John gave a reproving hiss at Much.

"Well, 'tis true and you know it, Johnny. First last night, the cheek of the bastard!" Much was winding up the more he unwound the linen about Gamelyn's ribs. "He should keep his place. Going for you like he's sommat. I'll wager he en't drunk this morn. And you en't recovered from nigh *dying!*"

"I did start it," Gamelyn reminded, glad he'd not elaborated further than the barest of explanations for his trouble: a bit of a set-to with Will.

Much snorted, soft, then wisely changed the subject. Asked John, "D'you want I should tell him what you told me, about that singer?"

Gamelyn frowned. "The trouvère?"

"Aye, milord. He followed you, last night. You and Robyn. John saw him, went after."

Gamelyn's eyes went to John. "Why would he?"

John tilted his head: *Why, indeed?*

"Johnny weren't trusting, at first, that the man didn't mean some mischief. But he stayed close. Only sane to, in last night's murk."

Gamelyn peered into the trees. The fog was only now beginning to lift.

"How much did he see?"

"Enough, it sounds, to be going on," Much groused. "As wild as you and himself can be, I'm surprised you en't cocked up your ribs before now."

Maybe he should have gone with that explanation for the re-injury after all. Gamelyn wanted to chuckle—but it would hurt, and this wasn't all that funny. In fact, it wasn't funny at all.

"Why would the trouvère bother following us? He knows nothing."

"His kind, they don't like knowing nowt," Much pointed out, and John nodded agreement. "'Tis but more fodder for those tales of his, nosy bastard . . . beg pardon, milord," he apologised as he peeled the last layer away and Gamelyn winced.

"En't his t' know," John growled.

"There's nothing he can do," Gamelyn replied, though, aye, the thought of someone watching even a bit of what had passed between he and Robyn last night . . . *Mine,* he snarled, silent. *Mine.*

Not altogether yours, "milord," if you would ride away with your kind and let them lock you back into your barren stones.

The Horned Lord, anger escaping, steam from quenched steel.

Gamelyn put both hands to his face, wishing the Lady would talk some sense into her Horned Consort . . . something . . . just *leave him be*, because he was tired of his brain feeling like the raw, abraded flesh on his back.

"Aye, and this en't good," Much muttered. "A fine mess, more like. Your ribs are bruising up again. The scab's all ripped up—the oozing's what stuck the bandages to ye. How's this, then?" Much probed up and down Gamelyn's back—gently, to be sure, but it felt like a swarm of angry bees was nesting in his ribcage.

"Could be—uhn!—worse."

"Could be better. Johnny, have you any help to offer?"

"I've no healing." John was rueful.

"We need sommat for this."

Gamelyn shook his head, grimaced as, again, discomfort jangled down his spine. "God, I could use a smoke."

"I've none left of that neither, though I've a few other things in me pouch. But those wain't settle things like the hashish, or Herself's medicaments."

"Use what you have, and bandage me up nice and tight. Marion doesn't need to know this. Nor Robyn." Gamelyn peered at John. "He really doesn't need to know this on top of everything else, not now."

Though it was plain John wasn't best pleased, he seemed to ken the sense of it.

Much rummaged in his pouch, found what he needed and, humming a tiny, tuneless refrain beneath his breath, began medicating.

"So far"—Gamelyn sucked in a breath as the ointment stung—"I've heard no patrols this morning." It was only then he realised he'd been listening. Of course he had, but he was thankful for the proof—he wasn't flat useless yet.

The fog had forced a wait, given them some respite—but not for much longer. The patrols would come. After all, something had been stolen out from under Count John's nose. He'd undoubtedly want his mother back, and revenge against the ones who'd taken her.

Gamelyn smirked. *Bring it.*

"Aye, well." Much started on the bandages. "Johnny, Arthur, and I went to have a listen when we woke. There's no lack of activity. All of Blyth's champing t' bits. 'Tis nobbut a matter of time."

"Mm. And at this point, if they're smart, they'll use hounds. But not until this fog begins to lift, which should give us a head start." Gamelyn stood, testing the bandages. They were tight, restricting his movement but not overly so. If he took care, he could likely conceal it well enough—from ones who would scent the weakness as well as ones who could be weakened by the knowledge of it.

"You're going," John ventured, low, "en't you?"

"It's what I must do," Gamelyn answered, just as low.

"You must *come back.*"

"Very few of you feel that way."

John looked away, into the thinning fog. "Y' only choose your way."

"Do we choose, John?" Gamelyn said, and he couldn't help the scorn of it. "Really? Robyn would say it was a nobleman's luxury."

"Aye." John was still looking into the trees. "Nobleman."

Gamelyn blinked. John putting more than several words together was unusual enough without him deciding to spout cryptic nonsense as well.

"John." Much shook his head. "You just en't understanding."

John shrugged, then peered at Gamelyn. "You can. Go back." Another shrug, and John shoved off the rock to stand. "*Should* you?"

"I am all too aware," Gamelyn answered, clipped, "of what I should and should not do, believe me." He turned away but didn't miss the silent look Much and John exchanged; Much warning, John woefully unimpressed.

Moving became easier with every step; by the time they reached the cavern, Gamelyn felt close to normal. Well, as close as one could be to normal with an angry wound and cracked ribs.

There were voices wafting from the cavern, hanging in the fog's layers; one a deep baritone they all recognised. John turned from disapproving uncle to eager lad, ran ahead. For moments Gamelyn also wanted to sprint forwards, spend the lurch of his own belly in like enthusiasm.

He made himself walk. It wasn't that far. Anyway, he'd just anger his injuries more than they already were, and he was going to have to get used to not being with Robyn, wasn't he?

You are so wonderfully apt at penance, my Oak. One would think it had some purpose, the way you turn to it. The Lady, mocking.

He was getting used to that, as well.

"—the sooner we have you safe away, the better." Robyn was crouching at the fire. He'd a smile for John and Much both, but the one he sent Gamelyn's way slipped at the corners, his eyes deep with both wariness and wanting. "'Tis good you're here, Gamelyn. John's already sent Gilly away up Conisbrough. You'll be meeting him by Cadeby."

Robyn slid his gaze back to where Eleanor lounged, well-padded with furs a-plenty, between Marion and Alundel. Marion flashed Gamelyn a quick smile.

"Cadeby?" Alundel asked. "There's nothing there but a broken-down stone henge."

"Which means none'll tarry too close, fearing what ha'nts might be waiting." Robyn smiled. "Gilly will have horses waiting."

"Stolen horses are better than walking the entire way, I suppose" was Eleanor's wry comment.

"Stolen!" Robyn looked offended, as if he wasn't called the Thief of Sherwood for a very good reason. "Nay, borrowed, 'struth. If you walk the way, 'tis likely you'll be fetched back to Blyth, and Gilly has . . . an arrangement, with a lass he knows."

"Say no more." Arthur was chuckling. "If Gilly knows a lass, that lass'll do owt for Gilly."

Beside Arthur, Will sat at the fireside as if he belonged.

Well, of course, he did belong, didn't he? He was one of them, even if he tortured his leader with words like blunted, cruel knives, even if he got drunk and groped that leader's sister like some tavern wench.

Whilst Gamelyn did not. Belong.

Surely the tally of his own sins wasn't any worse than what the outlaws had already forgiven others. They had a displaced noble-man in their midst; several of their members openly professed a preference for lads.

Ah, but Gamelyn had done the unforgivable: taken the role of Guy de Gisbourne, Robyn Hood's deadliest enemy. It made no matter it had been unawares, in some blinded game of foxes and hounds.

And now, that role was more and more sliding back over his shoulders, a comfortable—and comforting—cloak. It was Guy who eyed Will, all stone and smoulders, and oddly enough, it was Will who looked away first—or, mayhap, not so odd. It was a pretence, nothing more. The set, broad shoulders and the sneer touching one corner of his lip gave testament.

Another testament: he was not sitting close to Robyn. Or Marion.

"Scathelock ran across a patrol," Robyn was saying—yet another testament, the formality of name and the way those black eyes acknowledged its bearer, but did not hold, and dead giveaway to any who knew him. Fortunately their guests did not.

Unfortunately, all the others did.

"They were wet and miserable and more full of mutiny than finding us," Robyn said. "But I canna imagine your son just letting you waltz away without doing sommat."

"Your imagination is guiding you well." Eleanor nodded. "My

youngest would pay dear to see me never reach the continent. I fear the sons of kings are born competitive."

"We've a few hours more," Robyn offered. "Then they'll likely set their dogs on us, two- and four-legged." He grinned. "Aye, but we're a sett of foxes. We'll outwit 'em, see you safe to Hirst."

Eleanor's eyes narrowed, studying him for long moments; then her gaze broadened, swept bright and birdlike over the outlaws and their snug, sandstone nest. "They may hunt you now, and for the near future, but trust me in this. King Richard will return to his reign. You will not regret having aided me. I will see to it, person-ally. And you, Templar"—her eyes turned to Gamelyn—"I will charge with ensuring it."

For—it was unspoken—*if all goes well, you will once again be lord of Blyth.*

Unspoken, but every one of them heard it. And everyone in the caverns had their own reactions, from scorn to worry to satisfac-tion. All, in silence.

All because Gamelyn had let himself keep the most ridiculous of hopes alive, guttering like an ill-wicked candle, but there regardless. He hoped Eden might still exist. Not merely within the cave they'd hidden away last night, but outside it. A place for them. Somewhere.

And he was not the only one with such hopes, Gamelyn reminded himself as Robyn's eyes gravitated to his.

Robyn looked away, slapped his hands together. "Aye, well, here's what's what. I'll stay here, play drag with milady's overskirts—"

David hooted, made a kissy face Robyn's way. Everyone laughed, and Gamelyn thanked God for David.

"Not *that* kind of drag, you wanker—mayhap you're t' stay with me and you might be wearin' em yet!" Robyn corrected, with a grin, then sobered. "Will, you'll go north, with Arthur and milady's shawl."

Will started to reply; Robyn slid a black glare his way, and Will shut his trap *that fast.* Robyn kept talking, of plans and details and what part each of them would play to enable the rest of this escape. His eyes moved to Gamelyn's, held.

Gamelyn broke the gaze when he saw not only Will watching, but Alundel.

Well, the latter was his problem, from now on, and he'd see to it if he must. The former remained Robyn's, and ah, he didn't envy him. Forlorn and foolish hopes didn't just belong to Gamelyn . . .

Stay with me.

It was not only the voice of a tall, bearded outlaw crouching at the fire in a shape worth mortal sin; but a lanky, lovely-strange peasant boy, sideswiped enough to chew his pride and swallow, beg, *Please, don't leave me.*

Foolish boys, he told them. *Have you learned nothing yet?*

Obviously not, if Robyn's gaze was any clue, if the heat behind Gamelyn's own eyes gave any indication. Gamelyn lowered his gaze, let his lashes catch the moisture that sought escape, watched the flames swim and shatter into prisms through a hot, gilt-edged glimmer.

✠

"Watch Alundel," Robyn said, as Gamelyn snugged the catch strap of his scabbard about his thigh.

He'd tried to bend too far over, and it had sent stars dancing behind his eyes. Then Robyn had appeared in a swirl of mist, and what he held made Gamelyn's breath catch again, no less painful.

The quillion dagger had been the first bit of weaponry a young Gamelyn had bought with his own means. He'd left it with Rob, first by accident and then by design and then as the destruction of Loxley had sent them all into the winds of separate fates.

How many strands of *tynged* could such a blade sever, in the wrong hands?

Gamelyn wasn't about to take the dagger from Robyn now. Or ever.

"Keep it for me." It was quiet, almost nonchalant.

Robyn shrugged, sheathed it at his hip. "What will I do for a dagger when you do finally take it with you?"

"You likely won't need one anymore," Gamelyn replied, light, before he kenned what he was saying.

Thank any gods who would listen that Robyn's return gibe was just as trivial. "Aye, 'tis the only way you'll have it back is ower my body at this point. I do fancy this pretty dagger."

He moved closer, and Gamelyn threw a quick glance towards the others. Their voices were plain, but the fog still hung in thick, opaque hanks.

"The fog's our friend this morn. And Marion's got their attention." Robyn grinned. "My sister loves us, aye?"

Gamelyn didn't know what to say. What to do.

"I might come visit you," Robyn said, sliding close. "If you canna return before spring. You can teach me some more Frankish. But I en't gonna pray wit' you."

It made sense Gamelyn should raise a hand, tuck one of Robyn's long curls behind one ear. Quite natural he would bend, kiss that ear, linger and breathe his lover in. But it was beyond any understanding that he would lean in and whisper, soft as swan-down:

"Within my heart, my lover returns again and again,

"Transitory as the waves surging against the winter's shore.

"He leaves me shaken as the sea when the east wind blows.

"How empty thus, O love, my spirit without thee . . . "

Robyn stiffened as Gamelyn spoke the first line. Stayed there, stilled and hardly drawing breath, as Gamelyn continued. Then turned to peer, wide-eyed and more than a bit speechless, as Gamelyn trailed off, retreated ever so slight.

More voices, drifting through the fog. Robyn's eyes piercing his, wondering.

Silent.

Gamelyn had to break the silence before it broke him.

"'Twas a bishop wrote that." Defensive, no question, but Robyn was still *staring* at him, so Gamelyn continued, a bit stupidly, "Another monk who preferred lads."

Robyn blinked. Opened his mouth once, then twice. On the third time he gave a croak, and on the fourth managed, hoarse, "Gilly said it, once. Said he'd warrant you'd fancy a bit o' poetry."

Gamelyn's cheeks were tingling, no doubt darkening.

"I never thought *I'd* fancy it." Robyn leaned close, whispered, "Knock me for six and more. Say it again. In Arabic."

Gamelyn laughed outright. Barely managed to not wince, covered it by drawling, very soft, "I'll never leave if I say it in Arabic. You'll trip me on the forest floor and rut me in front of Queen and country and your bloody band of outlaws, most of whom are ecstatic to see the arse end of me, mind—"

"You exaggerate, pet," Robyn drawled back. "*I'm* the one as is allus glad to see the arse end of you." He hesitated. "So were 't what you said to me before?" A hint of tease had entered the soft, hoarse voice—Robyn was regaining composure from being "knocked for six." Capricious wanker.

Gamelyn shrugged. "You'll never be sure, will you?"

A snort, and Robyn began to pull away. "Never sure with you, pet."

Gamelyn's hand shot out, almost on its own, and stayed Robyn. "Not yet," he whispered. "Not just yet . . . "

He left off more words, even in Arabic—no time, too unwieldy, they'd already wasted enough on them—and yanked Robyn close. Robyn's arms snaked about him; the pressure stabbed iron into Gamelyn's side, but he pushed into it, welcomed it. Held Robyn brutal-tight, kissed him even more so, and when Robyn groaned and opened his mouth, Gamelyn plumbed him, teeth and lips and tongue. Tangled his fingers in coarse-soft ebon—tighter, tighter— refusing to let go, of pain or passion, until they both were trembling and panting like trapped hares.

Agony was fast overtaking bliss, but Gamelyn merely let his hold falter as if he'd intended it, tried to soften his breathing, and trailed his lips, damp, across Robyn's cheek, to halt in the curve of his neck.

But Robyn wasn't totally fooled. "Are you all right?"

"Same damned thing," Gamelyn muttered—and no lie, at that. The band of pain loosed, random as it had taken him, finally allowed Gamelyn to nuzzle into Robyn's hair, breathe him in, let out a sigh.

Robyn shivered again, lifted one hand to rake through Gamelyn's forelock, then framed his face with both hands, lifted it. Breathed, heat and hex-magic and soft, unintelligible words, across Gamelyn's cheeks. Eyed Gamelyn, tiny witch-lights dancing in a starless night.

"Come back to me," he said.

Then pulled away. Backed away, black eyes never leaving Gamelyn's. And disappeared into the mists.

- XV -

The fog curled down from the parapets of Blyth's tower first; from a distance, Robyn and David bore witness, perched in a tree up the small hillock towards their temporary shelter. That shelter had been cleared of any signs, and Will and Arthur sent north and south, one with a velvet bliaut and the other with a woollen kirtle, both belonging to Queen Eleanor.

Robyn and David waited upon their lookout, chewing on some cheese and venison, sharing a skin of ale, until the bell had resounded, harsh and carrying. More noise— bedlam, more like, to carry all this way—and the gates were all flung open, the patrols scurrying in the wake of the receding fog, eager to make up for lost time.

"Eagerness"—David *tsk*ed, feeding little Tess a titbit— "should be a sin in their Church, aye? Eager mons make sorry mistakes."

Then another bell; but this one crooning, ending with a yelp. Dogs.

"Time to go hunting," Robyn said, and smiled.

That afternoon, they heard the hounds.

It came and went, mayhap merely a trick of wind and the clearing fog—or more so, a trick of overwrought nerves, Marion considered, when it faded. They'd spent most of a day, after all, slogging after John on deer tracks almost too small to see, doubling and backtracking and leaping fallen logs. The fog was so thick in the lower woodlands, just walking through it left them soaked as a powerful rainstorm. Normally a morning's delight—moist upon the skin or a cleansing, pipe-opening rite of breath and waking—all it did now was chill inside as well as out.

She had heard the hounds—or not-hounds—even before Gamelyn, which surprised her. But then, he'd been . . . preoccupied, ever since they'd left. Marion thought she had some understanding; had glimpsed his and her brother's leave-taking, seen Robyn's face when he'd appeared back amongst his outlaws and started giving curt directions with the Templar a distant, shifting silhouette, left behind. Even now that held true; Gamelyn stood a careful distance from his charges, chill as the fog clinging to them. Watching the wheels turn so careful behind those flattened green eyes—every step considered, every outcome planned—Marion couldn't help but wonder if her understanding was as complete as she thought.

And she found those thoughts turning to her rescue from the Nottingham gaol.

This man was in truth the one who'd made that happen: a grim, resourceful revenant. Not Gamelyn. Not the youth who'd persisted in befriending peasants. This man was once again the Alamut-trained assassin, the defrocked Knight Templar. Sir Guy de Gisbourne.

It made the past months seem a fog-shrouded dream.

"Did I hear dogs?" Alundel said. He sat next to the Queen on a huge, rotting log— the small party had stopped to give their charges a breather. Neither of them was used to this sort of going, though Eleanor had discarded her heavy skirts—not only for dog-bait, but practicality. She was garbed in plain woollen hose and leather leggings alike to Marion's own, much more suitable for a scramble through soggy forest.

Gamelyn, shrouded once again in the stark black, scarlet, and grey of his Templar habit, put curled fingers to his lips and let out a short, low whistle. From just north of them, scouting with John, Much's answer came. Whatever it was, Gamelyn seemed not best pleased. He cast an eye over their two seated companions, frowned.

"Robyn will set them all to sixes and sevens," Marion reassured Alundel and Eleanor, her eyes on Gamelyn as he slid his gaze skyward, cocked his head. Closed his eyes. Aye, and it was proper difficult to gage direction in trees and fog . . .

Gamelyn opened his eyes, glared southeast just as Marion heard it again. Several bell-like, canine voices, floating into hearing, then gone. No question of illusion, this time.

John, closely tailed by Much, came gliding back into the small clearing. "Milord," Much began.

"I heard." Gamelyn's reply was terse, his next order no less. "We go. Up."

Alundel started to object—on his liege lady's behalf, to do him justice—but Eleanor saw the look on her Templar guide's face. She touched Alundel's arm, shook her head, asked, "How much longer, *Chevalier*, 'til we reach Cadeby?"

The use of Gamelyn's rank not only gave due, but reminder: his liege lady demanded information. It reminded Marion of more: this small, aging woman had gone on Crusade, had fomented rebellion amidst her sons against her husband and endured exile for it, had been one of few stabilising forces in a country thrown political arse over financial tit by its king's wars and resultant abduction. Aye, Eleanor of Aquitaine knew soldiers; had manoeuvred and manipulated as well as bedded and bred her share of them. The result was this perfunctory understanding—nay, appreciation—of Gamelyn's diffidence.

Marion had a lot to learn, there.

Gamelyn took the hint with a flare of nostrils and a brief quirk of lip, shot a muted query John's direction. John answered with a few hand gestures; Gamelyn translated. "At this pace? Another hour, Madam, likely two."

"But my lady is—"

"Grateful for the opportunity to elude those hounds," Eleanor overrode Alundel's protest. "Both four- and two-legged. And whilst not looking forward to exchanging sore feet for a sore arse, resigned. I assume we shall be moving on soon as we meet your man with the horses?"

"I hope for the chance to give you a well-deserved rest there."

"But hope is a fickle bitch."

Gamelyn's lip twitched again, approving. "Aye, Madam. For now, we move."

Eleanor nodded, began to rise.

"See to your mistress!" Alundel snapped at Marion, just that much slower than he at assisting Eleanor.

It was a mistake. Gamelyn took a step towards the trouvère, hand going to his sword hilt. Much and John bristled. Alundel halted midmotion, taken aback by the sudden ring of snarling wolves about him.

Marion couldn't blame Alundel overmuch. He was a lord himself, used to the company of royalty, and peasants were made to serve, were they not? But the defence was warming, particularly Gamelyn's. Another proof of the sense in their struggle: that a nobleman's son could learn, even in instinct, to treat a crofter's daughter as equal.

"She is freeborn, and is my companion," Eleanor chided, "not my servant. She is sister to the man who wields the power that presently matters in these woods. Mind that, Alundel."

"Or mind your head," Much muttered—his own crofter's upbringing rampant in it: just low enough to be heard, but not enough to be given overt notice.

Gamelyn broke his own carapace long enough to tic another smile, this in Marion's direction. Almost immediately it hardened. He turned and started off, John beside him.

Much took up his place at flank, but not before shooting Alundel a surly look that melted into a head-dip of respect to Eleanor. As he took his place a few paces behind Marion and out of their noble companions' range of sight, he treated Marion to a reassuring grin. It made her stomach lurch and dip and, once again, twist in a confusion she didn't at all care for.

It was like the old days, Robyn considered. When they were small and wily foxes instead of significant and nigh-fearless wolves. And setting all the old traps: fording streams in a zigzag, coloured smoke wafting on the mists, rags fluttering in the breeze. The testicles and musk glands of the deer they'd roasted the previous night had been stowed in a meandering, inward path, as well as pissing out the skin of ale they'd drank, then taking to the trees with rope and agile limbs, not coming down until they were at least a furlong away. All of it, a game with serious intent: confuse their pursuers, both canine and man, and send them in circles until they could run no more.

The only thing missing was their little John's presence, stealthy and steadfast companion for the game, and Gilbert, whose unerring aim with darts of belladonna or monkshood would crease the skin and cause delirium. There had been no Guy de Gisbourne slowly throttling the "sin" of Gamelyn's innocence, no nun likewise smothering Marion's consciousness, bunging it deep within sterile convent walls. Only Robyn Hode and his merry band of thieves: setting chaos in the Wode, taking revenge for a multitude of injustices with a random strike, then a swift disappearance into the depths of their sanctuary.

Yet here they were again, giving the archer's salute to the noble-bred bastards. Even if they were rescuing some of the noble-bred bastards amidst brassing them off.

Four men, carrying long knives and axes. Despite frantic calls and whistles, their dogs had all run off, crazy upon some other trail. Only one of them had a bow—a crossbow, at that.

Robyn grinned, locked his legs about the limb of the stout oak they had climbed—considered he'd as lief be locked about *his* Oak, at that—then raised his longbow and pulled an arrow from the cache of his hair.

"I'll bet you can knock that ugly hat from here!" David's soft challenge came from the neighbouring limb.

Robyn grinned wider, took aim upon the man's hat—yellow as strong piss and proper ugly—and loosed.

The hat went sailing, and its owner let out a screech, went diving for the dirt. The others likewise, scattering for what cover they deemed suitable—which, as usual, meant it wasn't.

Foresters? More like bloody daft sods. His da would have sent them home. Or proper lessoned 'em with a boot to their sorry, useless arses.

The one with the crossbow scrabbled for the quill in his hip quiver—he hadn't so much as armed the bloody thing! David pushed his own bow, sent an arrow whistling past the man's ears. Crossbow Man tried again—full marks for him, but no mercy; this time David shot the crossbow from the man's thick hands. Meanwhile, the now-hatless one rolled over and started scooting backwards, frantic, on his backside. Robyn *tsk*ed, gave a swift nock and loose of his own second flight; the arrow impacted the dirt exactly in between the man's legs. He froze.

"I fancy you know where the next one's going!" Robyn called, pulling another brace of arrows from his hair.

David fisted two arrows and nocked a third, chortling to himself.

"It's Robyn Hood!" one of the men hissed.

Wellaway, fancy that! David mouthed Robyn's direction, and Robyn laughed again. Aye, this sort of lark had been too long in coming.

"And who did y' think 'twould be? What are the lot of you doing in my Wode, with your dogs and your smell and your great daft clumsy feet?"

"A prisoner escaped!" Crossbow Man blustered.

"Aye, and they're in my Wode, now. My prisoner. You tell yon Count that. On second thought"—Robyn pretended to ponder it—"happens you shouldn't. I hear His Royal Jumped-Up-ness has a fearful temper. You might be better off as outlaws, man."

There was a quick buzz of murmurs and whispers. The one with Robyn's arrow at his crotch, however, still was loath to move however his gums flapped.

"Not that a one of us would give any room in your hell for the lot of you. Noisy as browsing cattle!" Robyn growled, and pushed against his bow. In the sudden silence, the creak of it echoed like thunder through the trees. "You know what that is. You know I can shoot you where you stand, curse your shades to walk unquiet, and hang your skulls on the Horned Lord's Oak. So do as I say! Take my message back to your master." Robyn hissed it, scornful, then took a breath, spun the magic through the trees to make them judder and creak as he ordered:

"And stay *out* of my Wode!"

"Word's already coming up the North Road. They seem to think we're making for York. I was stopped once and let pass, frisked and questioned the second. I didn't wait for a third, took to the woods. The roads are piss-poor with the past days of rain, anyway."

Piss-poor roads, beneath a midday sun rendered invisible behind thick clouds anxious to make the roads even muddier. Lovely. Gamelyn's frown took in the horses picketed past Gilbert's shoulder, greedily tearing at the thick, dried grass within the ruined stones that were once a ring. "Only three, then?"

Gilbert shrugged. "'Twas all Dagrún had. She says Conisbrough sent extra mounts to aid Pontefract barely a week ago—none knows why—but this might interest you. Some Templar Master and his brethren had a lame horse, took the two 'twould have given us five mounts."

It was not untoward—many Templar brethren travelled the North Road on business and between preceptories—but it was inconvenient. Gamelyn spent a few curses, dismissed it. Became aware of the dull throb reverberating from lower back to right pectoral, and how he kept collapsing into it in response, hunching just that much too far. He needed to have Much wrap it again—had hoped to pretend a call to nature and have it done here, but . . .

The low clouds, sullen and waiting, spat fitful bursts of wet. At least the fog had cleared, sinking into lowlands and hollows— plenty of which they'd have to traverse before this day was done. Gamelyn straightened, carefully, and rested a hand to the sheath at his right hip, cocking the wrist so he could snug his arm hard against his ribs . . . ah. Sweet pressure, its own sting easing the greater ache. Walking had become misery; riding would be easier, thank God. The lankiest of the rounceys had long pasterns and a good shoulder, looked to be fairly smooth-gaited. He'd ride that one, could brace and sink his hips loose from his torso . . .

Gilbert spoke again, and Gamelyn forced himself back on task.

"I told Dagrún to say the Master of Temple Hirst was the one in need of these three, did anyone ask. She didn't believe me, of course— she's one of ours, knows who I run with—but she's too nice a lass to throw into trouble head-first. And this means trouble, my friend."

The affection warmed an otherwise chilly statement. Gamelyn kept scanning their surroundings. Trouble, indeed. All of it, setting his nape hairs erect, with no logic or reason to soothe the unease.

And this place.

They'd but a few moments previous emerged from the trees south of the henge; John and Much were circumnavigating the area, trebling Gilbert's assurances as to the place's security. A few ells away, Marion assisted Alundel in seeing to the Queen's comfort upon a fallen perimeter stone—and it seemed awkward. Almost sacrilegious, somehow.

But Marion knew much more than he about such things. She seemed as unconcerned with resting upon a sacred stone as with her semisubservient role in seeing to Eleanor's needs on this ride . . . and Gamelyn no more comfortable with that, come to it. Preposterous—what else would be expected? She'd agreed to it. And she'd been servant to Worksop's bitch of an abbess for how long?

That was it, he decided. That, and . . .

This place.

The ring of stones was indeed broken down. Torn asunder by misplaced fervour, worn by wind and water, neglect and time, nevertheless it possessed an eerie, fragile peace. Abandoned, like so many of its kind over this isle of his birth. But not forgotten— the very dance of avoidance afforded this and other ancient circles remained, proof of their remaining power.

Power. Yes.

Gamelyn had never seen this place, never known of its existence. But he could *feel* it, humming in his bones. Somehow.

Aye. It knows you, Oakbrother. The Horned Lord, this time, a shadow framed against the farthest, still-upright stone.

Not now, he growled back. *Go plague Robyn; he'll be more receptive.*

My avatar is. . . busy, the Horned Lord answered, and Gamelyn's neck hairs lifted even further, desperately wanting to ask how and why. But he didn't, was taunted further. *You prefer the ice of the convent to this?*

A rash of heat filled him, stiffened him from nape to knees even as it sent a soft, forlorn wanting through his vitals. *It's a preceptory, not a convent,* he chided, trying to regain control.

Robyn's voice answered him, mocking and fond. *Whats'mever.*

You, he told the Horned Lord, *are a bastard.*

Bastard? Laughter, full of scorn and velvet thunder. *You think to insult Me by claiming Me fatherless? I am Father. Son and Grandfather. Sire and Sired. Which means I have a Mother, unlike you, little monk.* It further stabbed a heated dirk into Gamelyn's composure. *Is that why you hide behind Her skirts? Do you think She will save you? Nay,*

Gamelyn Oakbrother, if you keep to this ridiculous path, She will but toss you at My feet and watch the rendering.

A hand touched his sleeve and Gamelyn jerked away, turned with shiv in hand. Was sorry he had, a scant intake of breath later—not only from the pain sparking from tailbone to shoulder, but the looks upon their faces. Gilbert was peering at him, concerned, and Marion's hand still outstretched.

Composed, she dropped the hand, said, "I see Him. Don't let Him sway you, injure you. You are no less than He."

And she glared—glared!—towards the Horned shadow, a tiny crescent of moonsilver lighting her cloud-grey eyes.

It will take a Mother's power to sway Me in the springtide and the summering, little virgin Huntress, the Horned Lord crooned, unimpressed. *And more desire than one who willingly dons a monk's skirts will ever find within himself.*

"He's . . . here, isn't He?" Gilbert whispered, sliding his eyes towards the stone.

A smile tilted Gamelyn's lip. "He's just leaving." *Aren't you. Lord.*

And for a wonder, the Horned Lord listened. He bared canines—more snarl than smile, to be sure—but dipped His great head and faded into the mists.

"He fears you'll forget." John had also somehow come up to where they were standing without Gamelyn's notice—and God, but Gamelyn could not *afford* this! Would not, not now! It would have them fetched back to Count John's little private gaol faster than they could spit.

"I forget nothing," he said, grating. "That's the true problem, isn't it?"

John closed his eyes, shaking his head, and Marion looked stricken. Gamelyn decided he wanted a good flogging for the unkind reminder of what they, too, had endured. The pain was getting to him.

Instead he flogged himself back to task, let it override everything else. "How looks the way?"

John answered with a shrug, pointed to the south and held up four fingers, then just to their east with another three. He turned away, ambled over to the horses.

"Sounds about like what I found south," Gilbert said. "But if they're this far up the North Road?"

"More trouble," Gamelyn concurred, eyeing John in the stones' midst. The horses had pricked their ears; one was creeping over in its hobbles, another already nuzzling down his front. John was as irresistible, it seemed, to animals as Robyn. "We can take the Selby Road. Smaller, but Much and I know it well, and it seems our tail is expecting us to make for Pontefract or York."

"And not likely as a Templar and his escort," Gilbert added.

Gamelyn nodded, asked Marion, "How goes Queen Eleanor?"

"She's bloody good, considering. But even a short time of rest would help." Marion flicked her eyes back where, past her right shoulder, Eleanor slumped on the upturned rock. At her side, Alundel was, from his gestures, telling her some improbable tale. It must have been a good one; Eleanor's eyes were closed, but she was smiling.

"We've a short time here, not much more. And will likely be forced to a swift clip after," Gamelyn said. "Not to mention there's still Doncaster to go around, after all. And another problem—"

"The horses." Gilbert grimaced.

"You did your best, and they look in good nick, but none of us are small enough to triple up and expect a mount to keep pace."

"Even with our Johnny putting a wee hex in their ears" was Gilbert's wry agreement as he glanced to the circle's midst where John was, indeed, still chatting up the horses. "Should he, Marion, and I return to camp, then?"

"We've little choice." Gamelyn gave another quick skim of their surroundings, saw Much approaching from the west. Meeting his lord's gaze, Much made a few sharp gestures. Gamelyn responded with his own: *Understood. Watch.* Much ambled over to their most exposed side—giving the stones a respectful berth, Gamelyn noted— and settled in to do just that.

Thank God. If he had to explain anything else to anybody else *and* keep tabs on his throbbing ribs much longer, he might explode.

"I promised to accompany Queen Eleanor to Hirst," Marion said, then as Gilbert and Gamelyn exchanged sideways looks, furthered, "It en't like that. I don't mind. Doing sommun a service doesn't have to be demeaning—and all of you should know that better than most."

"She has treated you kindly, but Alundel takes far too many things for granted," Gilbert protested, soft.

"She *is* the Queen, after all," Gamelyn reminded, a bit sharp. "I'm not sure Alundel is the only one taking things for granted. You've been in the Wode too long, Gilbert." *And so have I, to forget, even for an instant, who has the true power in this group.*

So sure, the Lady murmured behind his eyes, *you are.*

And the wind whistled up through the stones, a frigid gust sending the horses wheeling and wide-eyed.

"Brilliant! It were bloody brilliant, Robyn!"

Arthur and Will had returned to the cavern, full of brass and balls and tales the minstrel would have loved to snag for one of his lays.

Trouvère, Gamelyn's voice chided, clipped, and Robyn smirked, then told it, *Shut t' bloody fuck up, Gamelyn.*

David was grinning to match them. "Same for us—here!" He tossed a skin of ale to the newcomers. "The Wode's clean of those bloody sods, and dinner's nigh ready."

"Aye, and it's been too long"—Will was practically dancing in place during thirsty pulls at the skin— "since we've had a good rout, like."

"Just like old times."

Arthur's toast prompted them all to follow suit, passing the skin. But it also twitted at Robyn as he raised the skin and drank, reminded him of his own earlier, somewhat traitorous thoughts.

Arthur boasted further, "They thought to make rabbits outta us! Well, we hunted 'em proper!"

"We'd have a few skulls for t' old Barrow Oak, did we have a proper mad on."

Will grinned, peering around the cavern. "Hoy, where's Marion and John?"

"You'd already gone when we decided on who were going and staying." *And a-purpose, that were.* "John took 'em through the Wode, and Marion's with Queen Eleanor, who asked for her company." Robyn was curt.

"And you *let* her go?"

"'Tweren't mine to consent"—Robyn looked up and caught Will's gaze, plain warning through his forelock— "but Marion's."

"Robyn—"

"Plague take you, Scathelock, don't even *think* to start," Robyn growled, "or I'll hang *your* skull up on t' Oak. I've had about all of this I can stand from you."

Will's mouth opened, but his brain seemed to finally kick in. Plus Arthur had grabbed at him. Arthur might only have one arm, but he'd quite a grip in the one. What came out of Will's mouth was a meek "When're they comin' home?"

"When they've done t' job."

David brought crocks over, started ladling pottage into them. Will took up a stick, started poking at the fire, desisted as David shot a warning look: *Don't mess with my heat.* Then said, awkward, "I'm glad you stayed, Rob."

Looking up, Robyn peered at Will for long moments, black eyes holding amber-brown. Then he nodded. Will dropped his gaze back to the fire.

"Dinner's nearly ready," David said, and a comfortable silence fell.

Robyn eyed the others, then leaned over, took up a wooden bowl.

Simple in shape, it was marked about its rim with Barrow-marks. All of them fell silent at this. David quickly finished passing out portions as Robyn rose, taking the bowl to the cavern's back. A bucket sat there, brimming fresh—a different bucket than the one he'd only a day previous lobbed at Will. As he bent to dip the bowl into the water, his reflection danced in the ripples left behind, strands of *tynged* flying separate on a sea of tiny waves . . .

Anon, he told it and, cupping the wet wood in both hands, took the blessing bowl back to their fireside. The others watched his slow progress, expectant and sombre.

"'Tis the dark moon in two nights." Robyn's voice lowered further, into singsong rhythm. "I'll be travelling t' Mam Tor. Stronghelm, you shall take our covenant to the horse caves."

Will both softened and straightened beneath the trust, *drywdd* to *drywdd* and charged beneath his covenant name. He answered in kind. "Aye, Hob-Robyn."

"The others know to meet us there." Robyn stopped when his boot toes met the embers of their hearth and crouched there. Lifting the bowl to his face, he breathed across it.

This time, *tynged* knotted and sought to reach up from the water and pull him in. "Anon," he whispered again, this time with lips as well as mind, and the breath of it combed tangles smooth as he held the bowl aloft.

Rite and reminder—and promise. The old ways needed them to thrive, and they needed each other to stay alive.

"We will wrap our woodland about us, burrow into her depths. Lady, upon my blood, give us leave for this, allow us entry, shelter our spirits."

Will reached out across the heat, held the bowl as Robyn took Gamelyn's dagger from his belt and laid it across his palm. Fisted it. Sliced.

It went deep, this time—not the cut, but the sensations: metal sharp-sour in his mouth, rush of blood-pound in his temples, hoarse whispers flitting just out of hearing and echoing in his skull. All consequences of the power rising within him—from him—as droplets of blood dribbled between clenched fist and fingers, escaped to drip and puff dark clouds into the water.

And more ripples. More *tynged,* beckoning, but cozened by blood-rite from howls to soft mewls.

The small sacrifice, accepted.

Aye. The Lady trailed cool fingers across his blooded fingers, sighed warmth at his nape. *It grows stronger, this gift. Heed it, Hooded One. 'Ware it. Draw down the moon into your spirit and let it hallow you, well come to My deep places. Sing the Barrow further into the light, and there wait for your Maiden and Knight. Prepare. For as Summer takes up his crown, shadows fall upon Winter.*

More than She usually shared with him. Robyn sensed the layers beneath it both cryptic and plain, woven strands of a warm cloak. Beneath welcome, a warning.

Things, said the Horned Lord, *are set in motion. There is no going back.*

Is there, ever? Robyn replied, and passed the bowl so all could drink.

The journey north should have taken a day at most, a-horse. Unfortunately the short amount of daylight, two of their mounts carrying double, the slop that sporadic and driving rains had made of the roads, and the circumnavigation of Doncaster proper—peppered with quick detours to avoid the Count's soldiers—meant they barely made five miles the entire morning. And most of it in circles or sideways.

Thankfully the horses were stout rounceys; rougher of gait than the Queen and her court singer were used to, but more than capable for a hard day's work.

The heavy cloud cover was darkening, admitting dusk if not yet succumbing. Gamelyn had hoped to reach Hatfield, at least; he was beginning to jettison such hope. Instead, he set his sights upon a small village not too far from here—*very* small, it would not boast any of Hatfield's comforts, but anything with a roof might be wise, from the look of those approaching clouds. They were thick, dark as pitch hanging in the winter-bare trees, and would no doubt make the road more miserable than it already was.

Nay. That was no weather-hung cloudbank. A grit-sharp tang wafted on the wind, filling Gamelyn's nostrils. Burnt chaff and wood, scorched meat . . . more telltales of battle's aftermath than any farmsteading, rising the blood and ruin of undying memory.

Gamelyn slowed. Marion's chestnut mare had crept up, her nose at Gamelyn's stirrup. Much's gelding crowded close on the opposite side. All of them chary, in one way or another, of what waited around the bend.

The trees gave way, too sudden for any natural breach. The land had been cleared for the plough several furlongs wide against woodland—but it was more. Much more.

A blackened scar seared past them, as if some biblical retribution had smote the village to char and cinders. The surrounding trees were black, had only been saved by the wet weather. But there were lumps and piles of smoking brush, flames quenched but still smouldering . . .

Nay. Gamelyn's guiding hand fixed, went hard, and his grey lurched to a stop.

Those were not brush piles. They were *cottages.*

Had been cottages. Had been a village.

The ploughed earth was smudged black. A well, tumbling and scorched, stood in the middle of the ruined cots. What looked like a dead draught animal lay, still and crisp amidst the wreckage of the closest cot, and what looked like a bare human leg stuck out from the fallen timbers of what might have been a door. Crows were already busy at what they could reach. It seethed like some level of Hell, edging the road with scorch. It was a visitation from every battle ever fought, ruin in the aftermath of pillage and slaughter.

Gamelyn had seen it all before, in various incarnations. Yet all he could think, in this moment and this place was: *Loxley. Oh God, it's like Loxley. . .,*

Much gave a curse. Marion shuddered and turned away; Gamelyn saw the glitter of tears upon her cheeks just before she pulled her hood closer, concealing them.

"A shame," Eleanor said, and crossed herself. "A pity, truly, that such things happen."

None answered her. Marion hunched down all the farther. Gamelyn sidled his horse closer, reached across, and took her hand in his.

Eleanor watched with a pensive frown. Gamelyn didn't care. Aye, such personal attention challenged every oath and stricture of a Templar Knight travelling with company—yet he could do no less, not now. Not in sight of this.

Marion's hand quivered in his, then squeezed back. Gamelyn released her, peered back at Much. Much's concern was written in twist of brow and darkened gaze. Alundel looked conflicted as well.

Good. Someone should feel something at this.

"It is a waste." Eleanor's voice, pensive, reached Gamelyn through a muddle and haze of uncertain emotion. "Mayhap, my lord Templar, you will do better, when King Richard returns and you are rewarded for all you have done."

The words shook from Gamelyn another memory, just as painful but in a different fashion. Lying in the forest after his tangle with Scathelock, when the world had, for a time, *gone away.*

When he'd heard those strange, inexplicable voices. Envisioned this very scene.

Fire, in the woodland. Scorched trees, and despair hanging over the place, part and parcel of the thick smoke, and memories edging closer still. . .

. . .fire is what he covets. Fire is what he fears.

"*Chevalier?*" Eleanor's voice brought him back. No less contemplative, but there seemed a daunting edge to it. "I do not think this place is overly safe."

And that edge, thankfully, lanced the wound and let healthy blood. Gamelyn repurposed his attention, gave a brief nod, and touched spur to his horse's side.

Fire, in the woodland. Scorched trees, and despair hanging over the place, part and parcel of the thick smoke, and memories edging closer still. . .

Dark moon brought dark memories. It was the way of things. Death, and rebirth, and Robyn could no more shrug its calling aside than he could stop the clouds tearing open to reveal a fiery sunset, red as blood and fire, philtring through sodden trees.

He stood at the cavern mouth, watching. Preparing.

Behind him hummed a small hive of industry; the finishing touches of leave-taking. Robyn knew from long practise he fared better out of the way—Gilbert and John had returned just in time to help David, and all three got arsy if their routine was interrupted. Will and Arthur had already gone on, a wide sweep and scout ahead, ensuring Count John's pack had indeed abandoned their hunt. No doubt ranging farther to the North, following a more expected—and less affrighted—trail. Though did the unlikely happen and those patrols catch up to the two Templars and their charges, Robyn wagered said patrols would learn a new kind of fear.

If they survived to feel it, that was. A grim smile quirked at Robyn's lip, slipped as he contemplated hunted instead of hunters. The isolation of their circumstance stole over him, sudden, cold, and ultimately foolish. He gave a tiny shiver, tugged closer the wolf fur thrown over his shoulders, then caught a movement from the corner of one eye. His smile returned, slight but no longer so grim, as he peered down to see a lithe bit of fur undulating over his boots. Tess reared up on her haunches, propped her forefeet on the top of his boots, and peered right back with beady, black eyes.

"Well, come on, then," Robyn murmured, and the ferret climbed him like a favourite tree, chittered and chided—for what, he wasn't sure—then settled into the wolf pelt with satisfied, purry noises.

Absently Robyn stroked her, staring into the sun's waning light.

The moon was waning as well. 'Twas no doubt that spawned his bleak mood, nothing more; he could sense it, just as obvious as the fading sun. Not as palpable, mayhap—no warm brush upon his cheeks or pricks of blinding-bright against his eyes—but just as steady within his consciousness. A reminder. Tomorrow would be moon-dark, and Robyn had an obligation. Now, more than ever. No time for moping, or wishing on . . . well, the moon.

Robyn closed his eyes, entertained the sparks zagging and darting against his closed eyelids, then twitched his shoulders beneath both fur and ferret. He retreated back into the cavern, striding over to his meagre pile of belongings. "Well. I'm off, lads."

The others made some response, busy with their own things. Robyn gave a curious frown—everything looked tidied to him—then set himself to unclenching little paws from fur and hair. Tess was rather unwilling. Finally he was able to set her on the ground—with a tiny admonition when she would have climbed back up. As the ferret gave it up, humping back over to David, Robyn took up his longbow, strapped his quiver between his shoulder blades, and slung a wallet of supplies over his head. John moved to do the same.

"Nay, love. You en't going with me."

John ignored him.

"John. I said you en't going."

That was ignored, too. Sticking his knife in his belt and hanging his sling from the pommel, John ambled to the cavern mouth, where he set himself in a comfortable lean, arms folded, looking outward. Waiting.

Gilbert's and David's industry made abrupt sense. Robyn shot a glare at them.

"Did you put him up to this?"

"Nay," Gilbert said, then in response to Robyn's look of disbelief, "We didn't!"

"You know as well as I, Robyn, there's nae stopping Johnny once he sets his mind," David chided, then added, "Be careful, now."

Bloody damn. Robyn blew out a fierce breath, merely said, "See you soon."

"Aye."

"Aye, Robyn," Gilbert added. "Safely home."

Robyn went to the cave mouth, put a hand to the stone just above John's head. Contemplated the tilt of that head, the firm press of lovely bottom lip below the sharp-angled nose, the large, peat-brown eyes nearly shadowed by darker curls, all thrown into gilt by the last of the sunlight.

Found himself tangling his fingers—not gentle—into those curls.

"You wain't go into the stones. You didn't witness what happened. Even I canna gainsay your presence. It en't safe, you know that."

John's eyes slid to him, a wry chide obvious as his thoughts. *Of course I know that. But I'll be with you until then.*

His tight fingers relaxed, stroked, then trailed down to linger at John's cheek. John turned and kissed them.

And suddenly, having John at his side was very important.

They were forced to move on. There was no other village for several miles. But as if the Wode was angry for their hasty departure, more clouds came roaring in from the southeast, bringing a driving, bitter rain. It slowed the three horses to a grim trudge, their riders hunched beneath their cloaks, water shedding off in thick sheets.

Thankfully the rain dampened the smell of smoke and charred carrion.

Marion's little mare, still clinging at the hip of Gamelyn's grey, gave a sudden grunt and fishtailed, scrambling in the slick footing. Marion grabbed the saddle's wet pommel and threw the reins; Eleanor, a-pillion, gave a shout and grabbed at Marion's belt. The others could do little more but watch for agonised moments as the mare floundered and heaved and skidded as if treading ice. By the small miracle of capable riders who didn't interfere, and a final lurch against Gamelyn's grey, the mare found some purchase, set her feet and halted, blowing, rain pouring over her stretched out neck and head.

They had all come to a halt. Marion's eyes sought Gamelyn's and clung, cheeks pale beneath the wet. But her hand, reaching forwards to pat the sodden chestnut neck, and her voice, speaking a soothing cadence, refused to project any fear to her demoralised mount.

"Mary, Mother of Christ!" Eleanor made the sign of the cross against her breast. Her other hand didn't loose Marion's belt. Gamelyn started to twist in the saddle to grab the mare's bridle rein; a shock of pain flared up and down his spine, freezing him in place.

"All right, then?" It was Much, half shouting in the rain from his tail position. He dismounted—throwing the rein to Alundel, straddled pillion on their gelding—and slogged up to retrieve Marion's slack rein.

Marion took it with a grateful sigh. Much nodded, gave the mare a once-over—difficult in itself, considering the downpour.

Gamelyn hugged his free arm tight against his side, felt the pain subside once again to a dull throb as Much straightened from inspecting the mare. "She's all right?" They were in truth all shouting beneath the pelt of rain.

"Aye, milord!"

Gamelyn slid his attention back to Marion and Eleanor. "And you?"

Eleanor nodded. Marion's smile was wan, but there.

"That's it. We're losing what light we have. We'll stop, find shelter for the night."

"I saw an overhang, milord," Much put in. "Only back a furlong at most. A good, deep one. Assuming there en't no wolves with the same idea."

The relief was palpable.

"We'll take the chance," Gamelyn said, "and hope this blows through."

The overhang proved thankfully deep, more a shallow cavern than a cliff, and tall enough to bring the horses in for shelter as well. No wolves, though there were bones scattered, here and there, suggesting some predator used it as a dining board on occasion.

Best thing to banish all of it was a fire. And the best thing to make that happen, in the wet, was old deadfall, split open with the dry heartwood dug out for fuel. Much had insisted on gathering it. Gamelyn had propped himself against the curved, root-laced wall and let him.

From her pack, Marion produced a cheese, some dried venison, and a skin of David's mead. They fell to like a royal feast.

"Gilbert and John should be back with the others by now," Marion said, her toes close to the heat, leaning against the wall beside where Gamelyn had settled himself and not moved since. They had shed the wettest layers and all huddled together beneath several furs and a cloak that had somehow managed to stay reasonably dry, packed fortuitously deep in a satchel filled with emergency fodder for the horses. Everything else was sopping. But the fire, with Much's ministrations, burned hot.

A soft snort came from the back—one of the horses, hobbled next to the same fodder that had helped save the furs and cloak. It almost—but not quite—disguised the snore emanating from Alundel's cowl. He'd ensured his lute case had kept the instrument reasonably dry, then eaten, then fallen asleep sitting up.

"Aye, well, here's to Johnny and Gilbert being well out of this weather," Much said.

Gamelyn agreed. Better they were out of this, going back home. And John would watch after Robyn better than anyone.

There was no doubt but with the intruding forces away—himself in particular, and Much, but also Marion—the outlaws would fall back into former habits, former roles. They would stop testing pack order, find comfort again, and hopefully by the time Marion returned . . .

And your return, Oakbrother?

The words were faint and faraway; Gamelyn had closed himself off to anything but the path ahead of him, and the purpose. He didn't even want to contemplate the possibility of his own return. Didn't dare to hope. He'd been too long away, after all, and while Master Hubert had been apprised of his pet assassin's condition—or lack thereof—Hubert might just decide to ship Gamelyn back to Outremer just to remind him where his true duty lay.

"How did a man like you come to the Templars, Brother Gamelyn?"

And aye, but Gamelyn had felt Eleanor's gaze on him for some time now. He'd been wondering how long it would take before the questions simmering behind her eyes found voice. And had hoped—admitting the cowardice of it all the while—Eleanor would pick on Marion first.

But Marion didn't even seem chary of the prospect. Perhaps Eleanor had already quizzed Marion to her satisfaction.

Or perhaps Marion was just as weary as the rest of them.

"Necessity," Gamelyn answered, easily enough. "I am a late-gotten son, Madam. The monastery was a given."

Until Robyn. . . happened. And then after—Loxley burned, Rob and Marion left for dead, me chained to a buttress in Blyth's hall until they could get rid of me—there was nowhere else.

God, but he hurt. Must be why he was so bloody ripe for maudlin thoughts.

That, and the reek still pervading his nostrils: char and cooked flesh.

Marion was shivering beside him, inching closer. He wasn't cold. Why wasn't he cold, damn it?

"I see. But to choose the Templars? A somewhat more . . . extreme decision, yes?"

Gamelyn shrugged at Eleanor's query. He could still feel her eyes upon him, knew she hadn't finished. He wasn't sure, however, what she was on about.

"You're a young man. You must have been quite young when you joined. Do you regret it? I don't mean to pry, of course."

Of course. The poor light was fortunate—it masked the inevitable roll of his eyes. No doubt rolling one's eyes around royalty could result in them being put out.

Much peered at him from Marion's other side. It seemed . . .

chiding. But surely Much didn't give a damn if he rolled his eyes at any queen.

"I'm tired, and not expressing myself adequately." Eleanor did not sound overly apologetic. And experience had proven a tired and frustrated Eleanor would chat. And *chat*. "What I'm trying to say is, I understand extremes. Or I certainly thought I did. No question I've been faced with some new ones over the past days, enough to puzzle over. This one, however, intrigues. You see, I also know walls better than most," Eleanor continued. "Having spent more than my share in them. So forgive me the surprise that anyone should *choose* to closet themselves. You're no young woman anxious to escape a marriage bed. You're young, healthy, and more than capable of wielding that sword. You've been away from this lovely if dreary island, known the spread of other lands beneath your feet. Known the taste of other cultures, sailed both flat calm and tossing seas and"—her eyes met his, grey and keen as steel—"and yes, even the vast darkness of English forests."

Gamelyn blinked at her, waited for her to finish. When it became clear she was waiting for a response, he made some attempt. "Madam, I am merely a sworn Knight of the Temple."

"Who wears the black of the base-born and half-sworn as if a challenge, and tests his fetters—and no doubt his master's patience—by lingering in the greenwood with a wild peasant green man. And a maiden who is not *your* sister."

Marion tensed against his arm. Gamelyn tossed a look to Much that was nigh to panic. *Set the cavern on fire, will you? Something?*

Much, however, paid no attention, chewing on some meat, expression suggesting he was miles away. Their impromptu hearth had started to dim; he rolled upwards to tend it.

Eleanor had noticed. A smirk touched her lips. "Whatever are you afraid of, Templar?"

Gamelyn answered before he thought. "What any man, monk or otherwise, should fear in an out-of-the-way cavern, surrounded by temptation on all sides."

Eleanor's laughter filled the narrow stones. "How bloody marvellous." Her head tilted, slight but definite bequest of the point. "And spoken with the confidence only founded in one who finds himself rarely so tempted. I imagine, however"—this time her eyes slid to Marion—"that icy blood you've cultivated so might warm with proper . . . inducement."

"I could use some warming of me own blood," Marion said, and reached from beneath the furs for the wine sack. "More mead, Madam?"

As interventions went, it was better than most. Gamelyn wished he could kiss Marion. But Marion was looking at him with . . . well, the look on her face suggested she might be figuring out how much he was hurting, and if he kissed her, she'd damn well figure it out. Not to mention, the Queen would keep on drawing her conclusions . . .

"Thank you, girl, but nay." Eleanor leaned forwards, chewing on a bit of dried meat.

How apropos that it was royal meat. But what could she do—lock them up for breaking forest law?

"There," Much said. "Is the fire better now?"

"Twould be better if you'd come back," Marion said, tart. "Y' keep flinging the furs aside and lettin' in cold air."

Much frowned, then stood. Gamelyn noted how he moved back to his place with all the eagerness of a man going to be interrogated. What in bloody hell was that about, anyway?

"Is it why you agreed to Blondel's—Alundel's—bargain?" Neither did Eleanor relent in her interrogation.

"Alundel made the bargain," Gamelyn pointed out, "not you, Madam. Not the King. I took a bet, nothing more."

"I think it is rather more than 'nothing,'" Eleanor retorted. "It brought you from Sherwood, after all, and your wild fellowship."

Rather more than you've guessed, also. Comforting, to realise Eleanor hadn't comprehended the full extent of what Robyn was to him.

Which meant the trouvère had followed them, *seen*, and disclosed . . . nothing?

What did Alundel mean to do with what he knew?

"An odd thing, that fellowship. One of God's most holy warriors, biding amongst pagan outlaws. I cannot approve, of course, but I can understand. There is little law in a land without a king, and little regress save retreat." A rueful smile. "After seeing but a part of the wood and *its* peasant 'king,' I fear we could send an army into Sherwood and they would never come out alive."

Marion was casting a beseeching eye upon Much, no doubt hoping for some help with the intervention. Much seemed to be on the verge of some important decision, then offered an arm to her.

Oh. That was why Much had been eyeing Gamelyn. But Gamelyn was unsure he could even raise his arm, at present. He shifted, tried to find a more comfortable section of cavern wall.

And. Bloody. *Ow.*

"You stand to gain much from this. But I'd dare to guess personal gain is merely one layer atop many—"

I wouldn't dare to guess anything, right now.

"—and there are more layers to you than a tree has rings. So, why? Why *do* you return to the Temple?"

Silence. Marion had nestled her head into Much's shoulder, whilst Much truly looked as if he feared Marion might bite him at any moment. They were both peering at him, a bit wide-eyed. Alundel still snored, albeit quieter.

"I go back because it is what I am," Gamelyn finally said.

Eleanor sat back, brows knitting. "Loyalty is a rare commodity, Brother Gamelyn. Lucky any man—or woman—who holds it or inspires it. The price, however, is high." She held bony hands to the fire. They trembled, albeit slight. "And what of your loyalty to the wolfshead?"

Indeed, what of *that, my Knight?*

Oh God, leave me be! Just for a while, until I sort this out!

Gamelyn didn't allow anything to show in his face, just peered across the fire, unblinking.

Queen Eleanor nodded. It seemed . . . satisfied? Whatever it was, she left off her questions, pillowed her head on Alundel's haunch, and closed her eyes.

- XVI -

The heart of the *Ceugant* had been forged here, in death and blood and fire.

Aye, Robyn considered. Fire, above all else.

"How long?" John murmured, looking about him with wide eyes. "Four years."

The first time Robyn had returned to Loxley, the village had been in ruins. The cots, home and hearth of any community, had been mouldering lumps, recognisable only by placement and the bits of stonework and timber sticking up like charred skeletons. The fields were still a relentless and hopeful break in the soil, if straggled with weeds and creepers, soil lumped in tussocks where wild pigs had rooted out what was left.

The second time, the Wode had started to encroach upon what men had sought to take from her. Suckers of alder had eagerly crisscrossed the furrows, and outcroppings of yellow broom and brambles had begun to crawl over the fertile ground.

But now . . .

The Wode had fully reclaimed her own. If Robyn hadn't been born and lived most of his years in this particular patch of forest known as Loxley Chase, he never would have found it. Left fallow, beneath occasional sun and thickening clouds, the village's ruins had been hallowed with young trees, the buildings collapsed beneath the weight of hedge and winter grass, the crumbling well wreathed with ivy. No doubt summer's wild growth had—and would—further strangle any sign men had ever been there. Sacrifice had done its work, blood and bone; the ground breathed . . . hummed . . . sang . . . and Robyn swayed with the sheer power of it.

Power, bought with fire and soaked in blood. Sacrifice. *Beauty.*

The ultimate mystery, the Horned Lord whispered. *You know this, all too well.*

"And the ultimate answer," Robyn murmured. It met and matched, tandem with his own heart's beating, wound about him in a singsong lullaby whispering his name. Breath, and blood, and the Wode promising pleasure to her lover.

With the boneless grace of silk fluttering in a breeze, Robyn knelt, then folded forwards upon the dirt. Chest and cheek upon the wet loam, he twined long fingers in damp ryegrass, closed his eyes, and sank into the wild and ever-present rhythm of his first and truest love.

If he could sprout and take root, likely he would, just on the force of this alone. This magic, this power . . . this *breath* . . . it filled him and runnelled skeins of brilliant-dark behind his eyes, wove them complex and delicate, a spider's web of *tynged* pulsing through him and out, beyond . . .

Slender, callused hands slid up his spine to tangle in his hair, and a lithe form curved against his spine. "Coom tha' by," John whispered, and kissed Robyn's left ear. "Look."

It took some effort, but Robyn backed out from under the thrall of sensations, found another waiting. Bits of white were dancing on the breeze.

Beside him, John put out a hand, watched the snowflakes disappear upon his fingers. Already tiny flakes dusted his brown head like jewels.

You are welcome here, Winterlord. Remember your people. Hallow your place.

Temple Hirst was a beautiful—and subtly ferocious—place.

The sun had hidden itself all day, yet, as if in league with lofty first impressions, had finally decided to grace the small band of travellers with its presence. It peeked from behind the clouds and slatted sideways across the fields to set fawn-coloured grass from sodden into shimmering. It turned the path's muddy puddles into orange and crimson, scattering back to murk as the horses sloshed their weary way along.

"You have never been here, have you?" Queen Eleanor murmured at Marion's shoulder. Cheeks warming, Marion realised she'd been gaping like any peasant first come to market fair. She wasn't sure what she'd been expecting—mayhap a steep and sinister cliff redoubt comparable to Nottingham, or a martial border crossroads like Blyth—but this wasn't it.

The preceptory itself was situated on a small rise, just up from flood plain, bordered on the near side with steep dykes. Such delineation did not, however, render it inaccessible from the vast network of well-drained fields and outbuildings. Claimed from marsh into fertile meadow, those fields were dotted not only by the furry hides of horses well-clad for the cold, but the smaller, dingy-white clusters of grazing sheep. Shards of light were reflecting across the holding from the west, sure telltale to another landmark dominating the countryside: the River Aire, turning back on itself, tranquil and wide.

"I forget," Eleanor continued, her voice a thin thread of its normal timbre, "that travel, so commonplace to myself, is truly not so for all. A fair setting, is it not?"

In truth, their destination did seem more some large and prosperous manor estate than any warrior's redoubt.

Almost.

Fair, yes. But such simple and agrestic beauty was deceptive. The preceptory's riverfront façade, from singular tower to nave-like end, was of mortared stone, imposing not solely through height, but also spread. Those cleverly fashioned dykes were not only protection against flooding, but steep ramparts to thwart any invasion. The sole visible entry was a narrow earthwork arch that looked to barely admit one person a-horse. A quay hunched on the river bank flew the piebald banner of the Templars, well-buttressed with several sleek boats docked. And while there was no doubt the topmost walk of the preceptory's east boundary and singular tower possessed a stunning view, said fortifications, as well as the moat fed from river drainage, made it obvious that severity lay in wait amidst the scenic.

Gamelyn paid their surroundings scant heed. Even as their approach led them past various outlying buildings—some with cot-holders who gave greeting, or followed their passage with curious eyes—he kept his mount moving forwards, seemingly fixed upon their destination. When Marion's chestnut mare lagged a bit, wanting to glean every bit of that sunny warmth into her sopping coat, Marion let her, pulling her own cowl back to feel the light on her sodden curls. She didn't have the heart to press on until Much pulled up beside—and it seemed, from the murmur of disappointment from her royal passenger as Marion urged the mare to walk on, that Eleanor felt likewise.

No wonder, after the ride they'd had. Two days of misery, all told.

But they were nearly done. They followed Gamelyn as he kept to the road, heading for that eastmost stone boundary wall—and the road wound itself through several tree copses, then a meadow, then to what looked to be the front entrance. No single-person postern, this: across the moat was lowered a stout wooden bridge leading to an arched entry gate, with a squat barbican hunched to one side. From that a fenced, narrow lane of cobbles extended, and upon it a string of horses stood, saddled and waiting.

And—hoy!—a small complement of soldiers poured from the barbican and mounted those horses. As one, they swarmed down the road towards the intruders in their territory, the lead one unfurling the same piebald banner adorning the river quay.

A shrill and sudden whistle resounded, high then low, from just behind Marion. She flinched; Eleanor, still mounted pillion, also winced as their mount sidled sideways. Much rode up beside them, fingers still to his mouth and a grin on his face. A short distance ahead, Gamelyn had halted. Waiting, stiff in his saddle as a fighting cock.

The company of horse responded to the whistle. Several peeled away and headed back for the gate at a brisk canter, whilst the others slowed to a trot, coming to meet them. The lead Templar—clad in white as opposed to the black and brown of his fellows—dipped the banner he held thrice, then twirled it in a fashion that seemed almost joyous. His horse responded to this with a leap sideways and a burst of speed forwards. The banner bearer almost careened past them but regained control, his teeth flashing in a wide, white grin as he directed the horse's speed into a layback spin and a dancing halt.

"So, Brothers!" he crowed. "You have finally returned from the wild places! How does . . . " Both smile and voice faded away as the Templar fully beheld the strangers following.

"Quite a greeting, Brother Elias," Gamelyn answered. "I see you've still not managed to accustom your stallion to our banner." There was a hint of a tease in his voice—but he sounded weary to bone, worse than Marion had heard in a long time. Small wonder, she rebuked the worry, with what they had ridden through, and how.

"Half the fun's in the training, Brother Guy, you know that." Brother Elias's use of the name bore as much reminder of what the fortress facing them truly was—a monastery—as the tone of Elias's voice, pitched to Gamelyn alone. The other Templars had halted a full horse-length behind Elias, just as subdued. Marion was tired and arse-sore enough to yield to a moment of panic—were they going to be turned away after all?

"Brothers—"

"Wait," Eleanor interrupted Gamelyn. With a slide and thump of one heel, she cued the mare sideways, exposing both women fully to the surrounding Templars. "We are Eleanor, by Grace of God Queen Mother of your Sovereign Liege Richard." Her voice rang into the crisp air; despite cracking with fatigue for the past half day, it did not so much as quaver. "Do not stare at Us like peasants at a coronation as opposed to the holy warriors you assuredly are, nor take to task one who has so graciously led Us here for sanctuary. Do not even bother to kneel." Eleanor made the hasty and necessary addition as several of the Templars shook themselves into action and started to dismount. "Instead We would implore you, in all haste, to take Us to your Master, in order We might make him known to Us."

Silence.

Brother Elias gave a stiff nod and a just as stiff dip of the banner he held, with a curt "Follow me, I pray you all."

If it was more to Gamelyn than the rest of them, Eleanor didn't seem to care. In fact, Marion heard her tiny snort of satisfaction. There was also an approving twinkle in Much's blue eyes—Marion saw it as she peeked sideways—though Gamelyn's rigid posture didn't ease.

Elias spun his fine black horse on its equally fine black haunches and, with the others fanning out to flank them, led his visitors to the gates.

A tall, middle-aged man waited, framed by a massive oak door and flanked by several black-clad sergeants with pikes. Arms crossed over the crimson cross upon his white tabard, his close-cropped head was bared to the setting sun. As they drew closer Marion's lips quirked, ever so slight. She remembered Hubert de Gisborough. With any luck, Hubert would also remember her—and hold to the fealty he'd done to the Lady through her.

The Master of Temple Hirst showed no emotion whatsoever as the cavalcade came to a halt at his gates, his brethren filing to their visitors' flank. Gamelyn rode a few paces forwards, braving his commander's chill blue eyes—and was there a hint of thaw there? Nay, not really. Master Hubert's gaze brushed over Marion. Again, little to be garnered. Hubert then took in Marion's passenger. Still, nothing—unless a tip of the chin might be considered.

"My lord Commander," Elias began, waved silent as Hubert paced to the bottom of the stair and knelt, with all the grace of a leashed panther.

All the Templars immediately followed suit. The mounted ones held their positions, but bent their heads respectfully low.

"Help me down, girl," Eleanor murmured. "You first, if you'd be so kind, in case my legs aren't so steady?"

Marion wasn't sure hers were much better, then told herself to buck up—the Queen was nearly thrice her age. Flinging a leg over the mare's red mane, Marion slid down and found her legs not as clumsy as she'd feared. She turned to thread the rein over her horse's head as well as hold a stirrup for Eleanor. Much, however, was already there, grasping the bridle with head solemnly bowed.

Eleanor took Marion's hand, descended with remarkable ease—if one didn't take in the clench of the hand upon Marion's, or the grind of teeth as Eleanor willed her legs straight. One breath, then another—and upon the back of her tongue, Marion gave covert shape to a silent *Nerth*. She smiled to herself as the tiny blessing-breath followed its intention, filling Eleanor with some strength. Expression reflecting her surprise, Eleanor straightened beneath the damp shoulder of her cloak and eyed Master Hubert.

"Chevalier." Eleanor held out a hand and rattled off a few more words. Marion was unfamiliar with the dialect, though it seemed Frankish.

Master Hubert answered in kind, too swift to follow, and touched his lips to the golden ring upon Eleanor's finger. He rose, his next words pitched to all. "You are most welcome here, my Queen. What sanctuary you and your party have need of, you shall be given. If you and your . . . maid"—a hint of smile and dip of grizzled head as he continued—"will follow this man?" He turned, motioned, and spoke. This tongue was even stranger than the first, clipped and guttural.

A small, elderly man answered, coming forwards with a bow.

"Confrere Otto," Hubert said, "shall be happy to see to your comforts."

"Comfort would be most welcome," Eleanor replied. "But there are messages to send. Matters to see to."

"But of course, Madam," Hubert acknowledged. "My schedule is yours."

Eleanor smiled. "We are too wearied to frame thoughts properly, but a good meal would set much to rights. Say an hour? And after we convene, a bath and sleep will be most welcome."

"As you wish. I have already ordered food sent to my lady's chambers, and preparations for a bath."

"After Our trouvère pens Our letters"—Eleanor held out a hand to Alundel, and Marion was that tired, she had nearly forgotten him—"if there is a chamber, close to Our hand, where Our lord of de Nesle can also find some comforts?"

Hubert's eyes widened as he took in Alundel's filthy cape and the lute 'crost his shoulders. He knew the name, it would seem. With a definite respect in his tone, he tilted his head to Alundel.

"The name of Blondel de Nesle is known to me, my lord. Can I hope that, during your stay, you will honour our humble preceptory with some music?"

"I have many suitable choices, my lord *Chevalier.*" Alundel gave a bow. "Your notice honours me."

Marion wondered what would be suitable in a monastery. Likely the same sort of dreary hymns she'd known in the convent. Though Gamelyn had been right—Solomon's songs were full of passion—and therefore, little doubt as to why the Abbess had forbidden them.

Hubert gestured to the old *Confrere,* waiting upon the stair with hands folded into his plain woollen sleeves. "Otto will see to your comfort as well, my lord. All of you"—his eyes took in Marion, a brief softening—"be welcome to Temple Hirst."

Alundel held out his arm for Eleanor, with a nod to Marion. "Let's have you over this moat, my lady, and mayhap some music for your supper?" He lowered his voice, chatting Eleanor up even as he rated his steps to hers.

Marion was fair glad of the slower pace, particularly as Hubert turned from them. The pleasant, opulent baritone went hard as good iron.

"And now I would speak with my wandering *Confanonier,* who dares bring women, unannounced, to our gatehouse." Hubert spoke English, but his Norman Frankish drawl merely sharpened underlying scorn. "That is, when he finally deigns to return to the preceptory which made him."

"My lord Commander." Gamelyn's voice tilted slightly, almost a crack but not allowing it.

Marion slowed, turned to see Hubert walk over to Gamelyn and stand there, arms once again crossed, forbidding yet expectant.

Gamelyn's head dipped, lank ginger hair falling into his eyes as, respectful and obedient to the unvoiced command, he dismounted. It contained very little of his usual ease; in fact, he almost seemed to stumble as he landed . . . but nay, likely nowt more than a skipped step as he knelt before the Master of Temple Hirst.

And that Master did nothing to assist or dissuade. Marion could only see a bare profile of Hubert's bearded, angular face. Of course, the man had seemed fond enough of his *Confanonier* when last they'd met and had been very interested, according to Much, in the reports of Gamelyn's health. Mayhap Templars acquired the forging of an iron will as part of their training. Mayhap Hubert de Gisborough had bequeathed a stony carapace along with a name-right to Guy de Gisbourne.

All Marion knew was she didn't care for it, not at all.

"No doubt you have an explanation for this, even as I am sure you can explain your, ah, sudden decision to return to your preceptory." Hubert started a slow pace, back and forth before his kneeling protégé. "Despite the obvious fact: you are not back to your full capabilities."

Eleanor, too, had paused, a frown quirking her brow. Alundel as well. Then Eleanor shrugged, gave a tiny grin that again bespoke understanding of soldiers' ways, and started up the walk again. Again, Marion paid heed, stayed quiet when she wanted to intervene. But she walked slowly, listening.

"Many things have come to pass here, these past fortnights. Business of much import, *Confanonier*, upon which I could have used your skills," Hubert continued. "Where have you been? Ah, I remember. Lazing about in the woodland, indulging sloth and pride. Living *soft*." This, it would seem, was even worse. "And smoking the hashish, no doubt."

"It was mushrooms, my lord Commander. The hashish is . . . hard to come by, in the Shire Wode."

Marion blinked, indulged curiosity with a quick glance. Had Gamelyn truly said what she'd just . . . ?

Hubert gave a loud sniff, glaring down the bridge of his hawkish nose at the kneeling Templar, who was the very appearance of contrition and humility.

"I have much to confess, my lord Commander. Much to atone for, I know. I can only offer illness as excuse. Though"—Gamelyn paused, ducked his head lower—"I do not doubt it is very important business, indeed. To contemplate raising . . . sheep."

Marion blinked again—she recognised the tone, tinged with wry-soft mischief.

"It was deemed quite a lucrative venture to take on. Have you seen the price of good English-grown wool of late?" Hubert riposted, curt. "Ah, but of *course* you haven't. You've been too busy keeping company with ragged miscreants!"

Marion slid a worried gaze to Much and found him remarkably unworried, patting her horse's neck.

"'Twas with the help of those ragged miscreants our visitors were retrieved," Gamelyn offered. He still did not raise his head, seemed to be leaning against his bent knee more than usual. But the parry of tone remained, his next words aid and abetment. "Sometimes risks must be taken. Outlaws must be . . . persuaded."

And oh, but wasn't there a wealth of meaning there? Marion tilted her head down to hide the sudden dancing in her eyes.

"I would have advised against the sheep, however, my lord Commander."

"You never have been any good at hedging your bets," Hubert

growled—and aye, there was fondness in his voice, at last. "Oh, get up. Go have a bath and change before I throw you into the river. You smell like a dung heap. And look worse."

Marion's arm was tweaked; she turned to find Eleanor watching her, an eyebrow lifted. Marion found herself flushing for no good reason, looked down, and mumbled, "Apologies, Madam."

"*Kommen sie, gnädige Königin,*" Otto told Eleanor in a soft and creaky voice, gesturing them farther into the preceptory.

It was a measure of Hubert's approval—whether at Queen Eleanor's rescue, or mayhap, Gamelyn hoped, some pleasure at his own return—that they were allowed a hot bath. The large tub, only hauled out for important visitors, had been set up in the small common bath, where all the Templars, from Master down to the lowest-ranking attendant, would endure a communal sluice and scrub with the aid of several unheated buckets of water. Often followed with a good steam sweat, then another bucket poured overhead.

Indeed, a group of Templars was murmuring amongst themselves in the quiet cell of the steam bath. Another "immoral" comfort brought back from the East, but a useful one for working men in its ability to combat soreness and sickness, as well as sweat away ill humours. Hubert had suggested it as well as the bath. He had also requested their presence in the Planning Hall after Compline.

"Bliss, this is." Much sighed, hunkered down across from Gamelyn, and submerged to his collarbones.

It was.

Other than the men partaking of the steam, Gamelyn and Much were alone in the baths; an unusual occurrence, but one for which Gamelyn was grateful. He stiffened, swore at Much, who had left off his soak to crouch behind Gamelyn and peel away bandages. Despite a good soaking, the thin linen adhered fast to Gamelyn's ribcage, taking plenty of dried matter along in the process of removal.

The slow ooze after, at least, gave some relief.

Save to Much. "This looks proper angry, milord." He traced exploratory fingers, too light to be felt save by the tingle of raw sensitivity following them. "Too much pus amidst good blood. Should have let Herself tend it before we left. She'd have seen to the rights of it."

"And worried the entire way. And given Robyn cause for worry . . . *putain de merde*" Gamelyn hissed as Much began laving water over his back.

"Aye, I don't doubt it stings like hot iron. You've more bruising down your back." Much's voice was threaded with concern. "Travelling, like."

"Likely because I had you tighten the bandages so." It was true, now that the wrappings were loosed, Gamelyn felt as if his back were afire. Added to the warm water soak, no wonder he felt so light-headed.

Much, of course, noticed. "I think you'd best forego a good sweat until you've had a bite. Don't need you a-swoon with more heat on an empty stomach."

That just made good sense.

"First, let's have this clean." Heaving up from the water, Much padded, naked and dripping, over to the cabinet where such minor medicaments were kept.

Gamelyn cupped his hands in the water—dingy, and no wonder, what with soap and two road-filthy Templars—to splash his face.

Much was *tsk*ing and growling over his choices in the cabinet. He offered over one broad shoulder, "The lads at t' stables say a Visitor's here."

A Visitor. Gamelyn noted the emphasis, considered the water dripping from his face into the tub. No mere guests, Visitors were missionaries, mouthpieces and overseers of the Grand Master himself. Sometimes not much better than toadies and sycophants, sometimes good men doing a tough job.

Much was, as usual, proving himself the latter, muttering as he lifted several pot jars and opened them to squint and sniff within. Gamelyn smiled, then sobered. No wonder Hubert seemed . . . harried. The timing was not at all fortuitous: for a Visitor to be in residence at the same time as the women Gamelyn himself had brought?

Or perhaps it was intentional. The ransom funds were—partially— here. And whilst the earthly feminine was frowned upon, the divine was another matter entirely. Most preceptories had altars dedicated to the Virgin. Temple Hirst followed older ways, in that and several more: a shrine to the Magdalene as well as homage to ancient predecessors left unspoken—save in proper rites, of course. Hirst also had a place, properly set aside, for visitors as well as *confratres* like Otto, and what had once been called the *consorores*, the Templar affiliate-sisters. Of course, the Temple itself was prone, as any governed body, to differing factions with differing opinions, moods, and motivations.

It was part of why the hierarchy held so strict to obedience; the primary of its demands. The Rule.

Surely this Visitor, no matter his political or social leanings, could not object to the English Queen Mother and her attendants claiming sanctuary?

Much, for whom there was no greater problem at present than seeing to Gamelyn's reopened injury, padded back over. He'd obviously decided if one jar would not do, two might be better.

"Let's have this cleaned and salved, then."

"Mayhap I should just have done and tump a cold bucket over my head before . . . " Gamelyn reconsidered as a careful rotation of his arm made the entire side of his body throb and sting like a swarm of angry bees. "Or mayhap have you wield the bucket, if you would. Wake me up, at any rate, enough to face Master Hubert without swooning like a fool."

"En't foolish to swoon if you're ailing," Much chided. "Mayhap 'twere better if I went to t' Master and explained—"

"Explained what? That I got into a tussle I knew damned well I wasn't ready for, with a brassed-off wolfshead who outweighed me?"

Much gave a growl, something about his fingers and Scathelock's throat, and Gamelyn grinned.

"Get in the queue, my friend. But our Master would knock me to the floor for being so stupid, and I'd deserve it. Nay, I'll go to the infirmary in the morning, have it seen to. We're back in our preceptory now, Much. Rule and Duty first, aye?"

"Aye," Much sighed, and began carefully cleaning the irritated wound. "The Rule. Duty first."

A bucket of icy water, along with salve and fresh bandages snugged beneath the grace of clean, stark-black garb, did much towards improving Gamelyn's outlook.

Mealtime was, of course, over, but Gamelyn's appetite had shrunk since the bath. Food sounded decidedly unpleasant now, on his knees at Compline. Not to mention the fact of being blasphemously unfit for prayer by any lights of his youth—it had been a brace of months since he'd received confession or communion. Unless one counted the blessing cup Robyn passed the night Gamelyn had been pulled back into thisworld, racked by magic and his fever finally broken . . .

Utter blasphemy, that.

Only now, not so much.

We're hard to kill, remember? Gamelyn didn't recall much of that nigh-deadly, delirious night except Robyn's voice, repeating those words to him over and over. Remembered being able to finally drink of that blessing cup and husk the only reply he could: *"Beauséant."*

To be whole. It was all he'd ever wanted, *to be whole*—and there was that here, in this community of warrior monks. Not altogether unlike the rebels of the Shire Wode.

Save for the no sex. Robyn's voice sounded in Gamelyn's skull, as close as if he knelt there, beside. The thought of Robyn kneeling, let alone praying, in any chapel tilted a brief smile to Gamelyn's lip, quickly hidden by folded hands.

Marion, of course, was not here, nor were Queen Eleanor or Alundel. Guests had their own chapel.

Around him, his Brother Templars murmured responses, rote; first call and answer with the leader of prayers, then the Psalms themselves. Gamelyn's responses were tardy, warbling, and not only because his thoughts were wandering where they should not.

"In manus tuas, Dómine, comméndo spíritum meum. In manus. . ."

There was none of his normal comfort to be found in the familiar rise and fall of the Latin cadences. In fact, Gamelyn was feeling decidedly light-headed. Found himself listing slightly sideways—away from that damned shoulder—and leaning heavily on the rail. *Grown unused to being penitent and on your knees, have you?* Hubert would accuse, dry—and likely not far from truth. Another truth: Gamelyn should have eaten of the apples and cheese Much had produced from his bags after they'd bathed.

"Redemísti nos, Dómine Deus veritátis. In manus tuas, Dómine, comméndo spíritum meum. Glória Patri. . ."

Hubert would likely have something edible in the Planning Hall after Compline. Gamelyn would force it down, if need be. And then have the bloody sodding shoulder seen to, first thing in the morning.

"Noctem quiétam et finem perféctum concédat nobis Dóminus omnípotens."

"Amen," he whispered and, for the moment, believed it.

There was food. And wine, warmed at the hearth in a small and round-bellied pot.

Much tailed Gamelyn until the door, where he took up position with a swart, brown-clad sergeant—Hubert's guard, who greeted both Gamelyn and Much cheerfully enough and did not seem overly dismayed by how Hubert's preferred bodyguard had finally returned from the Wild.

Hubert watched, even more reserved than normal, as Gamelyn approached the long, broad map table. The room spanned large enough to easily accommodate a full council of three-and-ten. It was heated only by a hearth at the far end and thick, unadorned tapestries on the arched wood-and-stone walls, but it felt . . . too warm. Too close, as if shades filled the corners, spectral presences lurking behind the pillars and within the alcoves. As if the presences Robyn had heard in Worksop had followed Gamelyn here, muttering and pleading.

Gah, he had been in the forest too long, no question. To imagine he had even a tenth of Robyn's uncanny abilities; that without Robyn here as fulcrum and focus, these stones should sing Gamelyn himself welcome or plaint.

"I trust the others were gracious with their welcome?" Hubert asked, and still it sounded careful. "Not too intrusive?"

"They were . . . gracious," Gamelyn replied, thinking of his progress back to the dormitories after Compline. Hubert had not yet called him by name, Gamelyn noticed, even as his Brother Templars had approached with muted welcomes, acknowledged him with a name he'd not answered to in months: *Guy.*

"You have been missed." It was gruff.

No hint of the last time they had laid grateful eyes upon each other, in the Wode and in the wake of Robyn loosing the Wild Hunt's madness upon Nottingham. No query after Robyn, whom Hubert had invited to come and treat with him, *dryw* master to Master Templar. Not a word of Marion, whom Hubert had acknowledged as an avatar of their Lady's form upon earth. And still, no name—either Gamelyn, devout nobleman's son, or Guy, bitter-forged in penitence and fury. No claim.

Who am I, here? Just tell me who I am.

You're Gamelyn. Robyn's voice drifted, defiance and entreaty. *You're what you are, what I want. Life's too short, and we've wasted too much of it already. . .*

But had it truly been wasted? Surely it had made them what they were, given them things past measure even as it had taken. Amongst the tally: the Temple and this man, a mentor he had never before possessed. Things had been so . . . simple, here.

Aye, and only fools believed in simple *anything.*

Hubert's omission of any name was an identity crisis for which Gamelyn found himself ill prepared.

How it waged numerous tiny battles within his being.

How Marion kept insisting *Guy is dead,* against his own silent, blunted dissent: *Nay, he really, really isn't.*

How only a few of the outlaws had called him Gamelyn, despite Robyn's quiet, matter-of-fact insistence: *You're the only one as wants him dead,* anwylyd.

Just tell me who I am, he begged of Hubert. *Here.*

"Eat," Hubert ordered. "You'll need your strength for the morrow. From the looks of it, you didn't spare yourself on the journey here."

All the way around and back, all within a brace of heartbeats, and the small, private war had exhausted Gamelyn past reason. He stared, a bit stupidly, at Hubert and the table between them.

"Don't you want my report first, my lord Commander?" God, even his voice sounded thin.

Hubert hesitated—the briefest of pauses, and had Gamelyn not known his Master so well, it would have passed him by.

"That is why you are here, of course. But sit, first. Eat, I say. Then we shall talk of your journey. And what comes with our important visitors."

Visitors. Plural, unstressed. It twinged warning, just below the surface; thankfully Gamelyn was not so far gone as to be deaf to it. Neither was he hungry, not in the least. But food was necessary. His knees were starting to wobble.

Hubert had started to pour wine into a pewter goblet; his fierce blue eyes reflected just-as-fierce approval as Gamelyn first saw to Much's repast, taking him a plate piled with salted fish and fresh bread. The elder sergeant gave polite refusal.

Hubert met Gamelyn halfway back from the door, goblet outstretched in one hand. "A hearty vintage," Hubert remarked, "to put some colour back in your face. Your eyes look like piss pools in the snow . . . aye, Much, I know you try to look after him, I meant no criticism." Over by the door, Much had no doubt twitched in protest or defence. "Kindly leave us for now, both of you. If you like, Much, take your meal right outside the door. We shan't be too long, and then you shall see your tired master to his bed."

"Aye, milord Commander."

The sergeant bowed and repeated Much's words, opened the heavy door. Much gave the briefest of smiles to Gamelyn as he exited, still holding his platter and cup, and as Gamelyn turned back around, Much began a soft exchange with the sergeant. The door closed.

Hubert still hovered with the wine, insistent. Gamelyn took it, drank a slow third as he took the few steps to the waiting bench and sat at Hubert's behest. Carefully.

Hubert wasn't looking, thank God. He'd taken Gamelyn's cup and was pouring more wine.

And it was indeed good, red as blood and tasting of earth, dates, and sun-dried apricots. Gamelyn drank more, and the wine settled his stomach, began to slacken the thick feeling of his tongue and brain. Hubert busied himself with heaping a plate with fish, dried apples, and bread, setting it on the board. Gamelyn peered at it, still apathetic but resolved. Obedience did have its merits. Bread first, mayhap.

"I've a few matters," Hubert said as Gamelyn began working away at the bread, "of, ah, a political nature—ones with which to acquaint you before the morrow. Missives have been sent, via pigeon and mounted messengers. There shall no doubt be even more visitors come the morrow, for a meeting with Queen Eleanor, and you will need what information I can give you. Keep silence," he furthered as Gamelyn started to speak, "and eat whilst you listen.

"During your . . . leave of absence"—Hubert's stress upon the words was light, but apparent—"you might not have been conversant with happenstance. And I did not wish to overburden Much with news to only make your enforced absence and convalescence more difficult."

The bread washed down well enough with plenty of wine, but the fish was not so biddable. Gamelyn chewed it to mush before he attempted to swallow.

"As you no doubt know by now, Count John might be called Lackland, but through the virtues of massed troops and more than half of England's barons having given him either monies or fealty, he is making up for the, ah, lack. He has taken hold of not only Blyth's castle"—Hubert nodded at Gamelyn—"but Nottingham's. You might have heard how Brian de Lisle had the shire-reeveship stripped from him? *C'est ça*, and he has been replaced by two less-empowered castellans, by name, Murdac and de Weneval. Both fiercely loyal, of course, to Count John."

Gamelyn had encountered Murdac briefly whilst at Nottingham; another of Count John's toadies, short and stout and, as oft common with men who lacked stature, mean as hell. The confirmation of Sheriff de Lisle's fall from grace—mostly for being the one who'd been in command of Nottingham whilst a wolfshead had humiliated Count John—afforded him a small smile.

Hubert snorted. "Neither am I brokenhearted, after what happened to you. My lord count will not lightly tangle with us again. But de Lisle has retreated to his Peveril holdings to lick his wounds—and heed me, my *Confanonier*, he is not finished in this business, not by a long shot, though he and his brother are at odds . . . Don't speak," Hubert insisted when Gamelyn would have tried. "Eat. Listen."

Odd. In these sorts of conferences, Hubert usually wanted exchange, the back and forth of ideas. The wine was heady, to boot. Gamelyn slowed down, took on more bread to help sop it up. His hand, as he reached out, trembled.

Hubert took due note of this, nostrils flaring, but continued. "De Lacy and several other barons have been duly convinced of the inevitability of Richard's return. De Lacy has wisely distanced himself from John's attempts to woo him. And now, with the ransom amount accounted for and their lady mother newly free and capable of directing the disbursement?" Hubert shrugged.

"I—"

Hubert motioned to the goblet, didn't let him finish. "Grand Master Erail agreed to aid in the transaction some time ago. As our Provincial Master hails from Birkin, along with our convenient connection to the coast via the Aire, we were designated as the secondary funding receptacle, with London the first. We are, as ever, honoured beneath and obedient to our Grand Master's commands. We were making preparations when Queen Eleanor was . . . ah . . . detained. In fact, I had plans to send for you—you know Blyth, as does your paxman—but?" He shrugged. "It seems my plans were upstaged by the King's . . . friend."

The inflection was all too familiar; Gamelyn frowned. As with the nature of Lionheart's fierce faith, of the nature of his bedroom preferences there had also been little doubt, particularly amongst the soldiers who had been with him on Crusade. But this particular one Gamelyn could scarce credit. "The trouvère? *He* is—?"

Hubert gave a shrug, started to pour more wine. As Gamelyn made to refuse, Hubert peered at him, poured anyway. "You will need a good night's sleep tonight. Indulge me in this, my *Confanonier.*"

Abandoning any more thought towards Alundel's rather unconventional connections, Gamelyn drank. A good night's sleep, indeed. The wine was affecting him more than usual; he was becoming pleasantly muzzy.

The small of his back itched. It felt damp, sweated. No doubt there . . . it was bloody *warm* in here.

"I must say, before you tell me of your journey, I spoke briefly with Queen Eleanor. She has nothing but praise for my Templars, undisguised admiration—amidst amazement—for a band of notorious wolfsheads, and disparagement for the roads you were forced to take."

"The Queen was an admirable traveller, my lord Commander." Even his words were beginning to show the wine, coming thick and slow. "The Selby road was, unfortunately, our only option."

"And normally a fair choice. The rain has been passing south of here in torrents, unfortunately. I, for once, consider—"

"Let us more consider these wolfsheads of which you speak." The new voice echoed through the hall, soft. Alarming. *Familiar.*

Alarming because Gamelyn had not so much as suspected there was anyone else here.

You heard the shadows against the stones, speaking, a feminine voice whispered behind his eyes. *And heeded them not?*

Alarming because She then faded to nothingness.

And *familiar*—it was the voice accompanying the worst of his nightmares.

It is what you are meant to do, were born to do, will *do, within this little Dance in which we've found ourselves. . .*

Gamelyn tried to lurch up from the table. Failed. As if his legs were weighted to the bench.

Hubert, on the other hand, did not seem alarmed. He rose, all the while peering at Gamelyn, and gestured towards an alcove.

"I believe, my *Confanonier,* you have not been formally introduced to our distinguished Visitor. Wymarec de Birkin, *Templier,* our lord Master of England."

From the map alcove he came, gliding silent as a serpent against the flagstone floor. His bare head was iron grey, as were his boots, but the rest of him was pale: spotless cloak, the blood cross splashed broad on a snowy-white chest, a white-gloved hand resting on one hip. His eyes were of a blue so pale they looked golden against the light of fire and candle. They strafed Gamelyn head to foot, and teeth flashed in the well-trimmed, salt-pepper frame of moustache and beard.

The Templar lord smiled.

But this time, he did not walk away.

Unthinking, Gamelyn heaved up from his seat and halfway over the table. His wine cup went flying one way, his platter the other, and the bench yet another. All his brain could process was: *The Arrow. . . found him.*

Enemy.

Our lord Master of England.

It staggered him as he leapt up—first the realisation, then pain. Something ripping across his back and up through his skull, which sent him hurtling headlong upon the wide expanse of wood. Gamelyn again tried to rise, instead floundered like a drunken sot.

They merely peered at him, as if in dismay: both his Master and his Commander.

The sick and impossible thought came to him: the wine. He had been drugged. Then immediately after, contrition: why would Hubert bother? He could have openly held a poisoned cup out to Gamelyn and demanded he drink, and every vow Gamelyn had made would hold him to it.

But Guy had made those vows, hadn't he? Why should Hubert trust Gamelyn?

Two heads. You are a serpent with two heads. . .

I am not the serpent here!

This time Gamelyn managed to heave up from the table. It meant he merely pitched sideways to the flagstones. There was a grunt and muffled shriek—was it himself?—and the ringing cry of his knife—he'd drawn a knife?—as it clattered upon the stones beside him. Then pain put a sharp-edged knee to his back and held him there, helpless.

There were voices around him, but nevertheless faint and faraway beneath the agony.

"Christ's blood, what is wrong with him?"

"I don't know. Guy? Guy, what is—?"

And others too. The stones upon his cheek, whispering his name—and he knew it was his, even as he knew it was one he'd never before heard.

"Was it the wine? Mayhap something—?"

"Only wine, my Master." Unfailingly polite—and cautious as one addressing a cobra.

A *cobra.*

Contact broken, then, soft welcome overruled by harsh and human voices, by hands upon him. The lifting was more cautious than their demands—but not cautious enough. Agony flared up and down his spine, encircled pale fingers about his throat, and began to smother him, hot-white.

"*Sacré tête!* Look here . . . Much! *Much!*"

Running feet, heavy, and a familiar voice: "Bloody *hell* . . . Milord? Milord, please. Talk to me."

And in the confusion, one voice above all.

"Now," Hubert hissed against Gamelyn's ear, "you will be wary, *non?*"

Then, nothing.

- ENTR'ACTE -

"I am grieved by this news, my lord. I will confess, I had hoped your fierce young *Confanonier* could be amongst those to accompany me across the sea."

This took Hubert aback. But then, his fierce young *Confanonier* did have a way about him.

Of course, therein lay much of the problem. Not only with Queen Eleanor, but with Hubert's own Master. Wymarec de Birkin was pouring from a pewter pitcher, filling three goblets. His eyes were downcast upon his task, pale and opaque glass—yet Hubert could sense the gears clicking and spinning behind them.

"I perceive Marion, too, shall be grieved at this," Eleanor continued. "I shall tell her straightaway—is there any way she can be permitted to see him?"

"Why," Wymarec de Birkin asked, handing first Eleanor, then Hubert a goblet brimming dark, "should a maidservant be interested in one of my Templars?" The words held utter respect, but nevertheless quivered with the tiniest of threats: disapproval, unravelling across a sharp-honed edge.

Eleanor accepted the goblet, gave first a sniff, then a slow sip. With a nod of satisfaction, she slid a gimleted eye towards her benefactor.

"Whyever not? From what I gather, they have known each other long, my lord de Birkin. Marion is of the outlaws, Robyn Hood's sister, in fact. Moreover, she is a woman, and your *Confanonier* is not unpleasant to look upon. Dangerous yet safe, all at once; a perfect receptacle for gallant romance."

Not at all subtle; in fact, provocation. Not at Hubert—Eleanor had tested his mettle last evening and obviously been satisfied. Nay, England's matriarch had played the game long enough to see in Wymarec's expressionless face what Hubert already knew as fact: the lord Master of England found womankind not to his taste, in any fashion whatsoever.

Any other time, Hubert would have enjoyed the diversion—particularly as it was not aimed at himself. But this time, he wished this particular maiden had not been brought to Wymarec's attention.

"Robyn Hood's . . . sister?" Wymarec repeated, as if curious. "From what I've heard, the Hood all but has horns and a tail. Surely such a one could have no earthly connections."

"You'd be surprised." Eleanor took another sip and smiled. "This is indeed fine, Master Templar."

Wymarec toasted her with the goblet. "I understand you enjoy a good Bordeaux, Madam. This was brought in from York's cellars—am I right, Hubert?"

Hubert nodded, hoping that would be the end of it. He had already played his hand almost to a loss—but curse it, he'd had no idea Gamelyn was so sore wounded! Had Hubert known, he certainly would have taken more care in doctoring his wine. A clumsy effort, true, but Hubert had been desperate to hold Gamelyn's tongue towards any of his time in Sherwood—at least, until Wymarec played his own hand and Gamelyn's wary reticence shut his mouth tighter than any vault.

Now it seemed the two had crossed paths already, God knew how.

As to tongues, the Queen unfortunately made no effort to hold hers as Wymarec began another foray.

"Little surprises me, Madam—though I do pray one of our Order has not acted at variance with his oath."

"Actions can be deceiving." Eleanor parried and added, "No fear, good Brothers, I would swear to his virtue. He is an . . . interesting young man. I find myself liking him despite . . . well, I suppose, despite how the lad rather reminds me of Louis. Not his fighting ability, of course—My Dear Annulled was no soldier, ever. But Louis found it easy to disregard what comes natural to most men, and would have no doubt been happier a monk—no slight intended, my lords. No man who does not enjoy a marriage bed should try to broach a wife. It only makes for misery."

"Indeed," Wymarec said, smooth, but again with disapproval threading about the edges. This time the distaff spun distaste.

A slight grin quirked upon Eleanor's lips as she raised her goblet to drink. "I would see to Brother Gamelyn's welfare personally," she added after another sip.

Very neat, this particular snare. Hubert approved.

Wymarec shrugged and turned to Hubert. "It is yours to say, Commander, as he is your man."

So now he's mine? Hubert tipped his head, distant respect to first Wymarec, then Eleanor. "Of course, Madam, as you wish. Upon our first convenience, I will have Much take you and your hand-maiden—it is not seemly you should go alone, if you understand."

"Of course," Eleanor conceded. "I would—"

A tap at the door—the sharp ring of dagger or sword pommel. Company.

"You may enter!" Hubert called, and the door swung open to admit a squire, somewhat out of breath.

"My lords?" The boy bowed, then noticed Eleanor, hastily added, "My lady? My lords the Bishop of Durham and the Earl of Conis-brough have arrived."

"See them in, immediately," Eleanor strode forwards and de-manded, just as Wymarec opened his mouth. With a slight smile, he closed it and gave a nigh imperceptible nod as the squire threw him a glance of panicked *Whom do I obey, Master?*

As for Hubert, he was heartily thankful for the interruption and its reality of more pressing political matters. It merely bought more time, of course—the matter of Sherwood would not lie fallow for long, not with de Birkin sniffing after it. And Hubert's own hands were tied, not only by obedience of arms and Rule, but the inflexible hierarchy of the Great Work, humming and swirling at the Temple's nexus. Like—yet very unlike—the mystic heart of the forest that had sheltered Guy—*Gamelyn*—these past months.

Wymarec's gaze slid from Eleanor and the squires to take in Hubert; it pondered, conscious of every intention, however slight. Hubert dipped his own head— acknowledging his superior, kept his thoughts his own.

He'd his own talents, after all.

- XVII -

Robyn had long ago learned to scale his longer legs to John's pace ... or John had learned to step it up; they'd been together for so long neither was sure of anything but the silence in which they travelled, the animal nearness of body and intent in tandem harness. The *comfort*. The thick trees were behind them and, like animals, they kept scanning the horizon, wary with lack of cover yet resolute upon the scattered hills of the Peak. The wind had died. Snow was falling in earnest, dusting their hair as well as the furs slung over their shoulders, leaving a pristine carpet snugged to the moors. Beautiful, but also treacherous. New snow slid underfoot and, moreover, left traces of passage.

Well, few dared Mam Tor. Particularly in winter. Robyn himself always made a careful gage of time during the longest and coldest nights. David had tales of such things from the northern lands. They called it "the snow sleep" there, would find victims frozen—no sign of struggle, just fallen asleep in the endless white. But a man didn't need snow to die of exposure, and quicker than one would think.

They'd make camp in the caverns footing the Tor—no less sacrosanct, but less forbidden than the ruined stones upon the Tor itself, where the original Shire Wode covenant had been murdered during their rites by the Christ's followers. 'Twould be four years ago this coming Beltane and, in accord with the Lady's sorrow, none save himself, Marion, and Gamelyn—the ones who had been there upon the slaughter—were permitted passage within the stones upon moon-dark. Not even John, who had witnessed what had been left.

They made their way down the trails, rounded the last bend to find a huge, dark maw yawning before them, edged here and there with new snow. Called simply the Hermit's Caverns, they had been in use long before Robyn himself had first been brought, blindfolded and bound, before the old *dryw* Cernun for initiation into his parents' covenant. He'd fancied himself quite a man—but that night of ritual had convinced him he likely needed to reconsider.

John gave a touch to the runes and pictures drawn on the entry to their right; Robyn gave similar reverence to the ones on their left and said, to John's look, "Aye. 'Twould be a good time to make the wards again. And none better to do it, *anwylyd.*" The endearment echoed, a soft murmur going deep. John smiled and pursed his lips, breathing across the runes as Robyn went ahead, then following.

Aye, they both knew these caves like the breath in their lungs. Here, too, had Robyn been brought after Loxley's ruin, to lie in his blood, die and walk the otherworlds to return, Horned and Hooded. And John had been here, with him.

A short distance by memory and feel, then slow even more, for the ledge waiting would tumble you arse over tit if you weren't minding for it. The torches were there; Robyn reached into the waterproofed pouch where he kept chaff and flint as John took up the two near torches with a sniff and shrug—the latter more felt than seen, in the cavern's dark. Robyn scraped his dagger against the flint, caught the chaff, and with a bit of coaxing, had a tiny fire upon the rock ledge. The torches took a bit more than coaxing; finally John breathed across them, called the flames into full life with a soft "*Llosgwych.*" He knew Robyn would need all his own endurance for the coming moon-dark.

Each holding a torch that gleamed with silvery hints of flame-magic, they went deeper; through grottoes and alcoves and finally past a many-fingered branch of gilt and crystalline, gleaming within the rock like the veins upon an archer's forearm. It meant they were nearly there—and sure enough, within another ten breaths, they were entering the main cavern.

There was the constant trickle and seep of water into deep, milky pools, the inaudible, indescribable *purr* filling Robyn's chest as the cavern opened out beyond and above. These stones were where they belonged, where their Mother had borne them; they were . . . content. Wrapping about Robyn and John, the stones welcomed their *dryw* to the old places, whispered the way to the Barrow Fortress where, long ago, the Old Folk had thrived before their disappearance into the otherworlds. Said, *You are of us, sing our memories alive once again.* Anadl 'n tynged. *Breathe our destiny. . . and live it.*

"We shall," Robyn whispered into the dark corridors.

John echoed, even softer. *"Anadl dy tynged."*

Their words wafted into the deep and disappeared; their torches flickered over crags and juts of rock, but would never pierce or describe the heart of it. It had been overlong since Robyn had lingered here for longer than a day and night. Mayhap he'd come, take the Hermit's guise, did he live to such a grand age as Cernun had . . . but given Robyn's life, 'twasn't likely. Regardless of stay, the main cavern constantly seemed unchanged. As if little fae kept house here, danced around the fire pit beneath the drawings both ancient and new. Even the floor seemed swept—though not to Marion's standards, granted.

Robyn smiled. Aye, what if this wheel's turning saw his sister coming here in her time, old and wise? Mayhap 'twere time a goddess spread her kirtles upon the god's fae-swept floor.

A rustle sounded—no louder than a whisper, but unusual. Robyn alerted. John was gathering wood from a goodly pile to one side of the cavern; likely nowt more than that. Only . . .

Only John's head was cocked as he returned, one arm piled with faggots and kindling. He didn't slow, continued to the fire pit and unloaded his burden. But his eyes sought Robyn's, curious.

"Likely vermin," Robyn said. An inward query to his god would do no good—upon such times the Horned Lord lay tight-wound within him. There was no need for query. Robyn *knew.*

It wasn't vermin. It was . . . older.

"A bear," John suggested, teeth gleaming in the torch's light as he wedged it upthrust between two rocks and bent to make the fire.

"One the bloody Franks didn't catch, aye?" Robyn played along. Nevertheless, his fingers traced a warding sigil, and he started to walk the fire pit widdershins—another warding.

In such a place of old magic, there were too many possibilities— and no Hermit, now, to keep the place cozened.

"Old bear," John suggested, one eye on Robyn's spiralling steps and the other upon his fire-making.

"Like t' be bloody ancient, more like . . . " Robyn hesitated. Definitely a rustle, this time—then, an abrupt and small cascade of shale and stone, as if someone had brushed against a pebbled ledge.

John's eyebrows rose again, but he merely put torch to kindling, coaxed the flames larger. He was aware, but not afraid. Neither was Robyn, truth be told. Wary to be sure, in strange circumstance—aye, that was only sensible. But the taste of it was . . . exhilaration, not fright.

Well, then, he and John were both of the Old Blood, weren't they?

Robyn completed his circuit, breathed the finish upon it, then came to crouch across from John. Around them, the spiral had sunk into the stones; not warning but reminder, gentle-firm, of their right. The flames were licking upwards, fire-magic remainders burning into warming result.

The cavern lay quiet about them, and did not stir again.

"*Stroppy* old bear," John elaborated, and Robyn snorted.

A good night's sleep had done much towards setting Marion to rights. She'd woken at a pounding upon the door—old Otto, bearing a goodly platter to break their fast with. Alundel didn't join them—Marion discovered during breakfast that he'd been sent to York, envoy to the Archbishop.

Eleanor's expectations had Marion falling back into old habits like a retired draught beast into harness. She assisted, silent and capable, and that help was accepted—Eleanor being the Queen—but there was a little surprise, Marion fancied, within acceptance. Perhaps Eleanor didn't imagine an outlaw woman would know the slightest about being a suitable maidservant.

It must surely be some great meeting, with all the care the Queen gave her appearance.

It took Eleanor's absence and Marion's near finish with tidying the small chamber before she realised exactly what she was doing. And even then, growling a soft, deprecative curse against ingrained habit, she finished making the Queen's bed.

Sommat to do, after all. She was a crofter's daughter, unused to being idle for long.

They had been housed, not within the visitors' dormitory outside the eastern boundary wall, but in the wall itself, a set of rooms cunningly devised within a small barbican. The chamber was simple but eased with some luxuries, the latter of which Marion suspected Eleanor's rank had gained her. Marion's own alcove, just off her lady's as befit a maidservant, was not quite as well-appointed. But the clothes found for Marion—two underkirtles soft and warm as a lover's sigh, with a brushed-woollen bliaut in sumptuous dark green and a thick grey cloak with rabbit-fur hood—were the finest she'd ever worn.

All of it brought to the fore memories both comforting and cruel. It hadn't been so long ago Marion had lived in such arrangements—not so grand, but near enough like. A servant to a powerful woman, her former life forgotten, in innocent sway of one who'd murdered her family.

The Abbess was dead. But the memories would not fade. Marion welcomed them, held them close, no matter the pain. They were hers, again.

But it was when she'd started to drag the straw-laced besom across the well-sanded oak floor for the third time that Marion found her teeth were chattering. Nervousness, and chill. She snatched up the fancy new cloak from her temporary cot and flung it about her shoulders. Ambling over to a shaft of roseate sunlight coming in from the east windows—several higher up, but one at waist height, looking over a pasture full of those sheep Gamelyn had ridiculed—Marion took in the warmth with a soft sigh.

Daft git of a nobleman's son, to scorn good sheep. And these were some proper northern-bred ones: Rough Fells, hardy with lovely, thick wool. She wished she had their pelts, considering those clouds edging to the southeast. It looked like snow.

Couldn't help but ask, in worry's wake, *Is Hob-Robyn all right?*

Nothing, at first. Marion shivered, tugged her cloak closer, and watched the sheep nibble at the lawns. Finally the Lady's voice sounded, but it was pitched . . . differently. Higher, softer, with a stern benevolence as She answered, *Your brother is well.*

Mayhap the odd inflection was merely due to Marion being deaf-mute to her own talents far too long. Before Loxley's destruction, before the slaughter of her family and everything she'd ever known, she had only just begun to hear what voices her brother had from childhood been subject to,

Loxley. And the village on the way here. No wonder she bided uneasy.

Just be. . . present, Mari, Robyn had told her, more than the once. *'Tis the only way you'll come out the other side with your own thoughts still attached.*

Aye, well, in this much Robyn had always been eldest.

Be present. The sun felt delicious upon her head and upturned throat, ran copper and cinnabar through the curls finally grown long enough to tumble over her collarbones. By the spring 'twould be grown to a length more respectable to the Shire Wode's Maiden . . .

Again, an odd shiver threaded up and down her spine. It was not yet spring, and the sheep grazing Hirst's fertile river bottom had, by the look of them, some time before they began lambing. Marion smiled, remembering the lambing times south of the River Loxley, and reminded herself *No countin' t' increase before the dams start swellin', mind.*

A quick *tap-tap-tap* at the door made her jump, and a familiar voice called her name from the other side.

Much. What was . . . ?

Inexplicable worry ramped into alarm. Marion strode to the door and pulled it open.

"Let me in," Much muttered, leaning against the door. "I en't got very long."

"Where is he now?"

"In our place, nigh to t' Commander's chamber. The doctor's looking after him— 'twere the only way I felt right t' leave him, you understand." Much had put his back to the wall in more ways than one. He was uncombed and, though clean, looked as if he'd not slept at all. His tunic hung unlaced halfway down his chest, the sleeves carelessly rolled up, and only a dagger at his belt. "And I wain't be staying long away, 'case he needs me. But I knew you needed to know, and figured none'd tell you."

"A doctor," Marion gritted out.

"Aye, but this un's different." Much was quick to put any fears to rest. "Learned his craft away t' Outremer, where they en't so bloody ignorant 'bout things."

"Will they let me see him? Tend to him?" Even as her mam had done, Marion never travelled far without her bag of medicaments.

Much's expression was uneasy. "Truly, I en't sure they will. Hubert would, I know—he kens things. But we've a Visitor, one who's also new-made Master of all the Templars of England, and 'tis sure I don't know what he'll allow. That, plus all the messages sent, and the Queen's men t' come here."

"But they let you come see me."

"None let me, 'cause I didn't ask. Neither have I taken all the vows milord has. And with everyone so busy with councils and t' like?" Much shrugged, then reached out and took her hand, his eyes open and searching hers. "I'll do me best, to see you should see him. But I'm nowt in the scheme of things."

"You en't nowt." Marion said it before she thought; embarrassed, she pulled her hand from his. His fingers clenched in reflex, only to release. When she peered upwards, his face was once again unreadable, eyes shadowed.

I'm sorry. I didn't mean it was what she wanted to say. Instead, "Gamelyn truly rode all the way here with his wound reopened?"

"Aye." Impassivity slid into wretchedness.

"You should've told me *then*."

"Nay, Maid, I should mind as milord says—and he didn't want to worry either Robyn or you. Though if I'd dreamed for a moment it'd go this way . . . " Again, Much looked miserable.

Marion clenched her teeth, crossed her arms, and retreated over to the window. At present she wasn't sure whom she wanted to roast over slow coals the more: Gamelyn, or Will.

Damn William, anyway, for offering the fight to Gamelyn—and bloody well damn Gamelyn for taking it . . . and moreover, for being such a hard-headed, prideful git who'd refused to let on what had happened until they were here where she couldn't do a damned thing . . .

And damn this place. This comfort, this gaol, this . . . this *place.*

"This seemed a good idea at the start," she murmured. "But now it's all gone wrong. It's cold here, cold with reverences that begin and end in restrictions . . . no wonder Robyn hates 'em. This preceptory of yours en't for the likes of us . . . of me. Women have little place here. Oh, mayhap on some pedestal of stone, all lofty and *untouchable.*"

Much kept up his lean against the wall, gaze averted.

"Even to the point you Templars prefer lying wit' your own rather than allow a mere *woman* to sully you."

"I've no interest in tupping lads," Much said, so sharp and quick that Marion turned to him, surprised. He continued, with a rueful shrug, "I've nowt against milord's preferences, mind, but I don't share 'em. Never have. Though I can say for a fact milord likely shares a few of mine—he en't as blind to women as he'd prefer." The blue eyes lifted to hers. "Some women, leastways."

Marion's brows quirked.

"See here. I told the doctor of you. He said 'twere likely a wise-woman'd be more use in stewing frogs or sommat." A smirk as Marion's nostrils flared. "Aye, but he changed his mind proper fast when I told him more, like how you was the one as healed milord's crossbow wound so clean and quick. It proper impressed 'im. May-hap betwixt him and milord Commander, we'll have you in there."

"I'll ask the Queen," Marion added. It could do no harm and might do a lot of good. Eleanor certainly had treated her kindly thus far.

"Aye, do that. For now, I'd best go." Much uncoiled himself from the wall.

Marion found herself lurching towards him, grabbing at his tunic. "Please, don't leave me here to wonder."

His hand covered hers. "I wain't." And he was gone.

Marion turned back to the window and found the sun muted. Just outside, on the green ryegrass and the grazing sheep, snow was beginning a sparse and silent fall.

When the Horned Lord went quiet, his possession merging with Robyn's own voice . . . those were the times Robyn felt the most isolated.

It was daft, surely. He wasn't alone; he was part of something greater. But he wasn't . . . himself at such times. Or mayhap he was. 'Twas sure those about him distanced themselves—or he made the distance, however slight, to protect himself and them.

He wasn't sure which plagued him most—that the god would stay away, or settle in for good. There was always an oddling relief/grief when the Horned Lord finally *was* separate again, and Robyn's thoughts once again his own. Those times, he would wrap himself in the warm cloak of his men's company or, perversely, go deep into the woodland and wallow in solitude.

The latter made no sense. His people had, for time upon end, lived in these caves and forests together, tribes bound by blood and oath. He had clannishness bred into him bone-deep. But the solitary wanderings calmed him. Hunter became Hermit, in the end. Robyn was beginning to understand it, more and more.

Mayhap it was the real reason why he didn't mind being alone. Because with all the spirits and voices oft writhing within his own being, he rarely *was* truly alone.

Or mayhap he was just light-headed. The climb up the Tor seemed more a trudge than normal, what with the wind bitter through bare trees and crusting snow over the fur covering his hunched shoulders.

"And sod you, Gamelyn," Robyn muttered as he slid on a particularly slippery patch—ice beneath the snow—and kept on through the gloaming, "but here you have me thinkin' too much on things as wain't bear thinking."

The circle, ruined as it was, thankfully was not along the bare ridge but down from it, sheltered from the wind's full brunt. The opposite side was not so lucky; the Tor liked to roll in her sleep, and her east face was pocked with landslides, some ancient, some not so.

Altogether a forbidding place to the unwary. But the Tor did not forbid one who wore the Horns and knew the sacring of Her.

Even as John was doing in the caverns, Robyn went to each of the fallen stones, made the marks, spoke the protections and the wardings until he could see the stones glowing again with blue-white magics. A cry lingered in them not unlike the stone of Worksop's church, or Blyth Castle—yet this cry Robyn could ease. This was a language he could speak, a magic he could make and bring, in rites close as instinct and old as time.

Robyn wore no antlered crown on such occasions, but he felt its weight. Felt the changing in his blood, akin to a drug in his drink or spread upon his flesh, but *more*—as if he could take wing and fly, or leap into stag-form and bound uphill, or duck into a burrow and defend it with temper and sharp-white teeth. It shivered him separate, in a solitude that paled all others—yet nevertheless brought him *in*, consort and counterpart within a nexus: the stones, the god-form, and his own frail-potent being.

He knelt upon the frozen altar stone where his mother had last called his father to the Hunt, where the rites of spring had become death, not life . . . and for the first time felt something, deep within the broad, flat altar, quiver and quicken.

Curious—compelled—Robyn bent down and let the heat of his own breath gust across frosted stone. In response, the film of ice cracked and curled. Danced, making pictures against indigo veins and dark grey, runnelling outward to every edge.

It was then he heard it . . . nay, felt it. A soft, hesitant thrum against his chilled fingers and knees, a breath against his cheeks to answer the one he'd given. A tremor of blood-beat.

A tremor of *life*.

His own blood quickened; his heart lurched in his chest. Flattening his hands against the frigid stone, Robyn felt it warm to his touch. Reacting. Quavering, new-come . . . but old, old as the earth beneath this altar. It whispered to him, recognition and claim, with old tongues that vibrated through his bones.

You are the Hooded One, Horned and Hallowed, flaming Arrow-point of the Ceugant. *You are Her brother. You are lover to your iron-clad brother-king, the touchstone 'twill ere bring him home.*

And then Robyn heard something else.

A rustle. A sigh. It was behind him, not beneath him. Not within him.

And just like that, his senses went taut—ready as dagger to hand, arrow to string. Robyn gathered his limbs, in the process also gathering the bow he had dropped moments before. The movement was all too casual, the longbow not suggesting a weapon, but merely a support to gain his feet. Robyn took his time, allowed his knees to wobble and seem weak. Between grappling with, leaning against, and bending over his longbow, had it strung and ready. In another half breath he had an arrow in his fingers, whirled and aimed.

There was nothing there.

No shadows on the edge of sight, no odd ripples of mayhap-voices. Only the snowy moor, and the trees beyond, snow dusting from them in the wind.

Robyn didn't loose. Neither did he relax his push on the bow.

His eyes darted about, his breath held in his chest, disallowing so

much as an exhale into the quiet . . . and it was quiet. *Too* quiet.
No birds, no branches creaking, no winter-dried leaves shirring
from a careless step. Even the Horned Lord's presence had
shrunken to a mere sigh within Robyn's consciousness, still one
with it, also holding His breath on the edge of listening.

Still, nothing. Only the throb of his own heartbeat behind his
ears, and the wind moaning through the stones. One by one, the
normal woodland sounds resumed, filling silence. Robyn waited,
nevertheless. Let a warm breath roil from his nostrils and travel
outward. Let his senses travel with it, taut and contained and
seeking.

There were tales of ghosts, here; ones from the old hill fort atop
the Tor. Could their spirits be waking as well, roused by whatever
was stretching its limbs along the backbone of Mam Tor . . . ?

But, nothing. Only his own magic hummed about him, and of
anything else, inward or out, there was no sign.

What was it? Robyn asked his god.

But the Horned Lord had no answer.

Confrere Otto stood waiting, as Marion answered the knock upon
her door, with an apology for the disturbance and a request: the
Queen required her cloak and her jewel casket.

Marion gathered both, fully assuming she would merely hand
them over; as she made the attempt, he shook his head, motioned
for her to follow.

She made him wait a few scant moments more whilst she made
sure of her own comportment—veil secured over her hair and her
own cloak fastened at one shoulder— then followed. *Confrere* Otto
didn't waste any time, led her quickly from the barbican chambers,
down the steps and into the snowy courtyard. There, against the
massive stones of the preceptory's main hall, Eleanor stood talking
with a lord whose stooped shoulders didn't quite fill his fur-lined
surcoat. They were flanked by several Templars, two of whom Marion recognised as Master Hubert and the fellow who had met them
at the gate upon his fractious black. *Confrere* Otto led her over.

"Ah, lovely." Eleanor halted as she spotted Marion's approach. Letting the tall nobleman reclaim what seemed to be his cloak, Eleanor
gratefully hugged her own close as Marion draped it over her
shoulders. "Thank you, my lord. Open the box if you would, girl."

Marion did so, allowing Eleanor to claim what she wanted: the
signet ring, a-glimmer even beneath a cloudy sky.

"Not a good idea to attend even a council with my stepson without this little reminder," she said, wry, to the lord beside her.

Marion's eyes had gone to Hubert, found him returning her gaze. It decided her next action—and to make it before she was dismissed back to her chamber. Tucking the box once more against her ribs, Marion took the few steps over to Hubert, went down on one knee in the slush.

"My lord Templar," she said. "With my lady's grace, I would beg your leave to speak."

Hubert frowned and retreated a tiny pace. Beside him the tall lord gave a small mutter—amused or surprised, Marion wasn't sure. Nor did she care. Neither did she give them time to reconsider—or to have her dragged away before she could speak.

"I beg you, my lord Templar, before witnesses. Please, if you have any pity or mercy, let me see him."

Hubert looked at her, made as if to speak. Instead his gaze took in their company, and his frown deepened. Down the length of the wall behind him, a door shoved open, with a creak and growl of metal hinges. Whatever decision Hubert was contemplating, that seemed to seal it. He gestured to Queen Eleanor.

"Master Wymarec signals the room is ready, Madam."

Then, without so much as a glance, he strode past Marion's kneeling form.

Cheeks stinging as if the rebuff had been a slap, Marion didn't turn. Didn't look up. Heard the feet crunching—departing—in the snow, yet even then Marion remained where she was, humiliated, and merely glanced sideways around the curtain of veiled curls.

It had been a long shot, but she knew enough of the game that surely . . . *surely* . . .

Hubert reached the door, speaking to the man there—another white-clad Templar. The tall nobleman had followed a short ways, with a gesture indicating the Queen should precede him. The Templars were patiently waiting, not looking at anyone. Eleanor let them wait, peering down at Marion, her expression unreadable.

"Go back to our chambers." The dismissal was curt. "I shall speak with you anon."

Eyes stinging, Marion rose and made a hasty retreat.

"You were bold, girl."

Eleanor's preamble wasn't exactly complimentary, but neither did it sound angry. There might have even been a tiny bit of admiration.

Or, maybe not. The next words were flint to steel. "Well? Has your tongue uncharacteristically decided to lie still, or do you have an explanation?"

"I had to . . . to ask."

"You should have asked me, first."

They were walking the east wall, taking in the fresh, cold air and the spectacular bend of white-edged river. What snow had fallen was turning to slush, here upon the parapet stones and anywhere, really, the Templars trod their duties. Eleanor had made this pilgrimage, Marion dutifully trailing, every day after the first set of interminable councils since their arrival . . . when had it been? Marion was fast losing track of time. The bells rang, shaking the stones—and her memory as well, giving it notice. Those bells had thrice pealed notice of Sext since they had ridden into the gates of Temple Hirst.

I'm allus up for bein' Sext, her brother teased, another memory bubbling to the surface.

Marion missed him. She wanted to go back. Wanted to assert her own rights, her own place. Not be humiliated, or defined ever again as "someone's." Was sorry she'd come, to bide here, in this rigid place of Men, useless save as thrall to yet another noblewoman—and that's what it was, no matter her respect for the Queen.

Who was still rather intemperate. "Well?" Eleanor demanded.

There was no choice. Marion had to make sure of her stay. There was *Gamelyn* . . .

Marion's step faltered, slipped a little in a patch of dirty, grey slush. "I did not want to trouble Madam with such a thing."

"Instead you 'trouble' a Templar Commander in his own preceptory, in the middle of a courtyard next to a hall where some of the greatest powers in the land were waiting for a council to convene—a council gathered to rescue their liege lord from foreign bondage! And over a wounded companion who, by the Rule of this preceptory, you have no rights to even acknowledge!"

I have every right, Marion seethed—silently. *He is ours. And Hubert* knows *it.*

Gamelyn and Much would both be proud. She didn't allow even a hint of mutiny to show upon her face.

"Did you honestly expect him to recognise you, speak to you as if you matter? Good God, girl, women *don't* matter here. I know as much, and I'm their Queen!"

But Hubert had spoken as if Marion mattered, once. Bare months ago, when he had ridden into Nottingham to retrieve one of his own, merely to find Gamelyn in the Wode with outlaws, sore wounded but alive. Why had Hubert so refused her now? *Was* it pride that a peasant—nay, a *woman*—had dared to speak to him whilst his men were watching?

There are undercurrents you do not yet understand, the Lady whispered.

Even She remained remote, often absent. As if hidden.

The problem with having memories? One always knew when one was truly alone.

Marion halted with a jolt. Lost in thought, she had almost run up Eleanor's heels; indeed, she had trod upon the embroidered hem of her skirts. But Eleanor ignored it, looking out over the river. The least of breezes set the boats rocking gently in their moorings at the quay. One bustled with activity as supplies of some kind were unloaded, the men's voices travelling upwards. Not Templars. They were too boisterous.

"Another se'nnight, and I shall be taking a long journey. I hope I am up to the task."

"Is there none you can trust this to, Madam?" Hesitant. Properly subservient.

"He is my son."

They fell silent, watching the boats. The breeze wafted chill upon Marion's cheeks, holding the promise of more snow.

"I assume you, like your Templar Knight, will be constrained to not make the journey with me. Albeit for differing reasons."

It sounded . . . wistful. It came to Marion: Eleanor, too, was lonely.

"But nay, you cannot leave him thus any more than I can leave the ransoming of my son to another." Abruptly Eleanor turned. Her hands were still deep within the fur ruff she carried, her hood drawn close, more warm fur. From the shadow of it, those grey eyes were piercing. "It is a tale worthy of Blondel's—Alundel's—telling, is it not? So much happening within the nexus of a forbidding Temple. Layers upon layers of plots and plans . . . and yet in the midst of it, brought in by chance, is a peasant girl who merely wants to see the man she loves."

Marion peered back, unsure of what to say.

Eleanor shrugged, started to walk back down the parapet. Her voice, strong and carrying, floated behind her on the winter air. "Before I leave, I will see what can be done."

<h1 style="text-align:center">- XVIII -</h1>

The Queen was as good as her word.

But Gamelyn looked . . . horrible.

The surroundings did him little justice: a stark grey chamber in the centre of a maze of hallways just as stark and chill, with only a few plain hangings to leaven the monotony. There was no hearth, though a brazier had been brought in and well stoked, and the narrow cot upon which he lay was propped and padded on one side with woollens and furs. His hair was flung over the head of the cot, lank, and in the grey light seemed more faded straw than gilt-edged copper. Pale as thin milk; even the overlay of freckles on his face and along one exposed arm were faded.

Marion took several quick steps into the chill, spare room before she thought. Forcing herself to a halt, she spoke his name, muted into the fetid stillness.

"Gamelyn?"

No response—not so much as a quiver from those closed, sunken eyelids—but from across the tiny cell a voice came, imperious. "What are you . . . ? Woman, you should not be here alone."

"She is not alone, Brother Physician."

Coming to stand just that much ahead of Marion's shoulder, Eleanor halted; hands clasped, head tilted with a graceful, artful lift. Marion hadn't even seen the man until he'd spoken—and he was somewhat remarkable. Not for his garb—plain, floor-length black robes with their small crimson cross over the heart—but the hue of his skin, dark as fecund earth. He stood before a squat table, holding a flask of pale liquid to the one window's light. Marion knew of such people, of course, but she had never seen one this close and couldn't help but stare.

Not that he noticed. Still holding the flask, the physician started forwards.

"And *neither* of you should be here, unescorted in a Templar's cell." Annoyance fuelled his words, already clipped with the accents of Outremer. "By what right do you wander our halls?"

"But I *am* escorted, by this handsome paxman here." Eleanor gestured to the entry. Much lingered there, clearly wanting to defuse the situation but respectfully silent. At such complimentary notice, he met Marion's eyes, openly startled, then looked down, as if to hide not only that but the sudden flush suffusing his cheeks. He looked like a lad still unbroached, and Marion fought a smile.

"Moreover," Eleanor continued, "plainly you do not recognise Us. We are Eleanor, Queen of England, wife and mother to kings; as such, what We *can* do is oft directly and thoroughly divergent to what We *should* do."

The physician's expression suggested he was hoist between a choice of axe or hanging. He went down on one knee.

"Forgive me, my Queen. By chance . . . " He paused, considered his words carefully. "Does Commander Hubert know of your visit?"

"Of course he does." Eleanor looked as if she might take pity upon the kneeling physician. Instead, she went on tour. "I have been in the chambers of kings, emperors, and archbishops. But until now, I must confess, never have I seen a Templar's cell. I thought you all slept in mobs."

The physician shot a glance after, then transferred it, not to Marion, but Much, nearly at her shoulder. The physician mouthed, silent: *What in Hell?*

Much merely shrugged. Marion left off such silent undercurrents with scarcely a thought, focused on Gamelyn. She wanted to rush over, touch him, ensure for herself it wasn't as bad as it looked. Had she been in the Wode, she wouldn't have hesitated.

However, as she'd had pointed out to her more than once, this wasn't the Wode. And if she made some wrong move, said the wrong thing, she might find herself outside the gates with no further chances to see to Gamelyn. Not to mention, the added burden of going back and telling Robyn . . .

Much was waiting. If Gamelyn looked any worse, then Much would not be so patient. Marion clenched both her teeth and her fists and awaited the Queen's pleasure.

It seemed to take forever, though it couldn't possibly have done. First Eleanor glanced into the darkened, adjoining chamber—Marion couldn't see anything from where she stood, though she guessed it to be Hubert's. She remembered Much saying he and Gamelyn were quartered off their Master's chamber. Eleanor gave a shrug and continued, wrinkling her nose at nearly all of it: the scrubbed-pale, plain wooden floor, the far walls bare save for the plainest of warming tapestries, the relentlessly clean but dull pewter of the washbasin upon its equally pristine bench.

"Impressive, for a gaol."

Again, the physician and Much exchanged a wary glance.

"Oh, do get up, Brother Physician. We have interrupted your duties." An apology, of sorts, though Eleanor didn't stop her slow pace upon the flooring—that is, not until she came to the small cell's singular adornment: a small altar against the eastmost wall laid with cross, candles, and brass burning bowl. There were daggers placed—not haphazardly but with form and intent—next to the bowl. Dipping her head and making silent reverence to the cross, Eleanor went on to inspect the deadly curve of the sword hung above. Marion recognised it as the one carried when she had first encountered—and not remembered—Sir Guy of Gisbourne. She didn't recognise the broadsword beside it, sheathed in plain leather with one adornment: the Templar crest. Next to it hung the banner of Temple Hirst in its holder, a drape of piebald emblazoned with the scarlet cross; Eleanor scrutinised it for long moments before she turned to Marion.

"*Beau Séant*," Eleanor ventured, sudden. "Are you, then, girl?"

Marion wasn't sure what to say. *Beauséant*. The word meant several things, and not only to the Templars—she knew that, at least. Also knew Gamelyn used it like a prayer towards myriad ends and meanings, one being the banner itself. To be brave, glorious, magnificent. To be as one with the piebald banner, or his brothers-in-arms.

And knew, but would not say, what meaning lay beneath every time Gamelyn whispered it, invocation and entreaty: *To be whole.*

A shift from the bed, accompanied by a creak of bed strings and a hoarse-soft groan from Gamelyn, arrested all their attention. Marion made a step forwards, halted. The physician also angled towards his patient but hesitated at the Royal Presence. Eleanor gestured him on.

At least the man was attentive. But . . .

"Madam?" Marion implored, and hated the begging in her voice. Hated worse the necessity for it, and chafed as a horse would, bitted too harsh.

Again Eleanor gestured assent.

The physician was not so willing. He stepped between Gamelyn and Marion.

"Madam, please understand. I mean no disrespect—"

"But?" Eleanor's mouth curved in what could have been either smile or scorn. "Whenever I hear the words *I mean no disrespect*, they are inevitably followed by a *but.*"

The physician was adamant. "Madam, this is all most irregular, and this"—he frowned at Marion—"*woman*—"

"*This woman* is the one as mended milord's wounds before he reopened 'em." Much's slight growl suggested he and the physician had already not seen eye to eye on several things. As Eleanor shot a glance at Much, he flushed again and fell silent.

But the statement flared a tiny dawning of understanding—and respect—in the physician's eyes. When they widened, it was quite noticeable; the irises were black as Robyn's, and the surrounding whites made sharp contrast to the man's face, as well as the wiry black beard.

"When the request was made," Eleanor put in, "for we the forbidden sex to wander your sacred and masculine halls, the condition was given how Marion must keep a proper place with me, should Master Hubert grant her request of an audience at your Brother's sickbed." The smile reappeared, knife-sharp. "And so, my children, there indeed are times when queens heed the bidding of peasants."

"Please, Madam," Marion began, "I only meant—"

"Be quiet, girl," Eleanor chided. "I know exactly what you meant. I don't know, however, if you fully understood the consequences of what you asked, or you are merely arrogant past your place. Either I find likely, considering."

Marion's nostrils flared, but she had learned much in the convent; lashes lowering on her cheeks, she looked down, away.

"Master Hubert," Much offered, "says she has t' right, Brother Diata."

This seemed to tip the physician's verdict. He gestured assent—but stayed close as Marion lurched forwards and knelt beside the cot.

"Gamelyn?"

No response, not even a twitch, and the answer was teasing at her nose, dull-sweet. Poppy. It also explained the sweat-damp streaks upon bed and bandages—he didn't smell feverish. "He's been violent?" she asked, looking upwards at the physician. "Brother . . . Diata, is it?"

One eyebrow arching upwards, Diata nodded and answered, "Thus the poppy. Many of our Brother Knights do not take well to . . . enforced confinement."

"Who would?" Marion stood. "May I, then?"

"As my Commander says." It was bland.

Marion ignored it. She mightn't have another chance, though she was bloody intent on trying for one.

Gamelyn should never have come back to this horrid, unnatural place.

Guy's province. Gisbourne's place.

No wonder such things laid Robyn low. Marion's uneasy grasp of her brother's weakness in the chambers of Worksop was pooling into sick comprehension. For here, in this place, there was a hint of it, quelling fingers reaching, trying to . . . to pull her under, somehow, sap her vitality. Unlike the abbey, however, this didn't seek to deny. There *was* magic here, of a kind, but its taste was younger than the ancient strands of *tynged* so familiar to Marion. It . . . consumed, asserting itself as brash as a new convert to any cause.

But it did not change Marion's mind. Gamelyn should have stayed in the Wode, with them, where they all belonged.

Aye, where the wolves of the Shire Wode take down the weakened ones. The Lady's voice still sounded odd. Reserved. But the power of sarcasm was plainly at hand. *Some would claim it all in the name of Love.*

Back-to-back, you said. None can stand against us, you said.

Again, all in the name of Love, you speak. As if healing hands upon an arrow wound and a few bouts of energetic tupping can so easily unsnarl tynged's *strands. Our Oak is despoiled, not only in body but in spirit—and more, Maiden, you* know *it.*

The sharp rebuke silenced Marion, sent her widdershins with doubt.

A wounded king cannot hold the land, much less wield the fires of Ceugant. *So better he lie, a kennelled dog in his own sterile, unchanging place. If the Shire Wode cannot heal this oddling chancre within Gamelyn, mayhap here will he find the strength to take what is his. We have time. . . but only so much. Summer will come.*

Marion gritted her teeth. To cover it, she reached forwards, pulled the covers from Gamelyn's bandaged torso. In doing so, her fingers nearly snagged in the thin cord about his hips. Deft—unthinking— she avoided it.

Diata noted this with a slight frown—which said mayhap he knew the significance of the thin measure. Or even what the significance would be to someone with the magic. He was Templar—did they all know of such things? Were they all sorcerers?

If they were, it was a sorcery well practised. One that thrived in containment, concealment.

"You, then, originally treated the crossbow wound?" the physician asked, in his soft-clipped voice—and was it courtesy she heard?

"Aye," she answered.

"A neat job." The black eyes met hers, a familiar and cool consideration behind them. Marion was beginning to think all Templars had that, as well. Mayhap it was necessary, when you'd stones and brass enough to wear your measure about your hips and so dare anyone to handle it.

"I must confess, most of the women who claim to be healers in this country are anything but," Diata offered. "I've come to expect ignorant and dirty slatterns who have no knowledge of anything resembling sound medicine."

"Funny, that," Marion replied. "I've come to 'spect the same from jumped-up gits of men who claim they know healing."

Was that a . . . it *was* a smirk, crinkling the dark face. "Often England is a barbarous country."

She couldn't argue, so bent to inspect the bandages. They stank, but with normal ooze, not infection. With all they'd done over the past days, that alone was a miracle. Another . . . *neat job.*

"I was preparing to change the bandages." Diata was still at her side. "It will enable you to see everything."

"I'll help, if you'll allow," she answered, and started unwinding the thin linen.

Gamelyn lay unresponsive and limp, in heavy thrall of the drug. Much came over, helped shift his master upright. A twitch and a small sound came from Gamelyn as Much held him close—but it was not anxious. Soothed, more like.

The sight of the wound was not soothing. An angry swath of bruising and inflammation spread from the reopened injury and down.

"There's sommat there," Marion said, before she thought better of telling the physician his business. Likely he'd see it as threat, or insult.

But Diata was nodding. "I have seen it more than I care for, and often in injuries such as this."

It was why any healer had to take such care when removing a projectile—though Marion had, thankfully, not had an overabundance of experience with the like.

"You were the one who cut out the arrow, then?"

"Aye, I did, and it came clean. 'Twere all there, unbroken."

"So likely bone, then. Mayhap part of a rib, the shoulder blade . . . some fragment displaced by the force of entry has worked its way down. Better down than inward, to pierce the vitals."

Marion nodded agreement, though she couldn't help a small shudder.

"I've been trying to sweat it to a head—yes, see the black paste there? I fear the fragment shall have to be cut out. Which I would of course prefer not to do until absolutely necessary. Better a shallow cut than deep."

Again, Marion nodded. She tried to meet Much's blue eyes—

unsuccessfully, for they were closed. His cheek lay against Gamelyn's sweat-lank hair, lips vibrating in a small charm. That it was a charm, Marion had no doubt; she could feel the faint tremolo of intent and fondness and worry. She'd not known Much had any affinity for such things, and it warmed her heart. She let out her own breath, nigh-silent whisper to add to his.

Eleanor stood across the room, looking out the narrow window with nostrils pinched. The discomfort was a surprise to Marion—surely she'd seen worse.

Gamelyn suddenly jerked in Much's arms, gave a hoarse murmur.

Diata frowned. "He should still be drugged quiet."

Marion reached out, pushed back a strand of russet forelock. "Shh, pet. We're trying to help you."

As if her fingertips had been spark to tinder, Gamelyn's eyelids fluttered open. He blinked once, then twice—likely trying to focus, his eyes wide and black with a mere thin ring of jade.

Much had a grim look on his face; he stayed silent but didn't loose his grip. *Tie a knot and hang on*, Marion remembered him telling Robyn once.

Marion gripped Gamelyn's chin—his beard had grown rather scruffy of late, was adequate hold. "Gamelyn—"

"No!" Vehement. "No . . . Gamelyn is . . . " The words stumbled, beginnings sharp but endings trailing. "Gamelyn died."

"Bloody hell," Much murmured, then raised his voice. "How much did ye give him, Brother?"

"Not enough"—the physician had returned to his table of medicaments, making a quick mix in a small pot jar—"if he's waking this soon."

Marion wondered if, unintentional-like, she and Much had conjured the waking. No matter, now. Gamelyn's eyes weren't seeing what was in front of him, and he was starting to fight Much's hold. Much's response was to keep murmuring—and keep hold.

"Much?" After that, a few words strung together, which Marion couldn't recognise, then in English, "Are we caught? Where are w—?"

Much murmured more of the language—Arabic, Marion suddenly realised— against Gamelyn's temple, soft as a mother to her child. And in English: "We're both here. The Temple. Here."

Only Gamelyn was not eased. As if the word had triggered some wild spark, he repeated, "*Here?* Oh, God, *he* is here. He's—!"

"Gamelyn," Marion tried again.

"*That's not my name!*"

"Here, Brother, have a bit of this," Diata said, appearing beside them with calm insistence. He extended a small stoneware pot.

Gamelyn froze, peered up at him for one breath, two. Then he twisted, lashed out with the speed of a striking snake. The pot went sailing, its contents splattering an arc of wet over the physician's black robes and halfway across the wooden floor.

Much growled—some foreign curse, from the sound of it—and wrapped both arms tighter.

For a man with a bunged-up back, Gamelyn was giving a fine imitation of a mad ferret. Furs and woollens went flying. Several of the bed strings popped. On one pass Gamelyn's left hand smacked against Marion's arm. He took hold and refused to let go.

"They're drugging me. *Drugged. . .*"

Marion did the only thing that made sense; she grabbed Gamelyn's arm right back and shook it. "Of course they're drugging you!" Worry made her voice sharp—the tone seemed to penetrate, for he stopped struggling. "You're hurt, you great pillock, and no wonder, you riding over the countryside with an open wound!"

"Remember your wound, milord?" Much asked. "The crossbow bolt you took for Robyn? D'you remember Robyn?"

Again, the start of panic. "Robyn's *dead!*"

"Nay, milord, he en't. Think."

Gamelyn blinked, repeated, "Think. I can't . . . think. Drugged. So I can't . . . "

"So you can't what?" Much's voice held nothing but reason. "*Think,* milord."

Gamelyn's eyes seemed to focus, then widened on Marion. "*Putain de merde* . . . Marion? Is it you?"

"It's me," she answered, at nearly the same time Much affirmed, "It's her."

"Here . . . both here . . . here at the end of things." Gamelyn slumped, slinging his head back and forth, muttering, "I won't. Won't survive this time."

"Gamelyn."

"Dreams. I *remember!*" Gamelyn rocked forwards—tried to, Much still held him tight. Gamelyn's fingers dug into Marion's arm. She bit back a gasp.

"Give over, milord." It was sharp, but Much remained reasonable. "We en't able to help you should you hurt sommun."

"Hurt . . . no one . . . but he's here, and he can hurt—Marion, you have to *listen* to me!"

"I'm listening." She leaned closer. "I hear you, pet. Tell me."

Gamelyn's grip eased, but his eyes narrowed, peering to where Diata had just risen and, past Diata, Queen Eleanor. "No. I . . . they'll . . . "

His struggles had lessened—not because Much had clutched him even tighter, but because pain seemed to finally be slowing him.

Marion threw a pleading glance to both Diata and Eleanor; incredibly, they both seemed to understand.

"If it quiets him, we'll go into the Commander's cell," Diata said, and looked to Eleanor. "If Madam will permit?"

Eleanor seemed eager to retreat; she snatched up a candle and led the way into the chamber. It was not, however, without an uneasy glance towards the bed. Gamelyn watched the candle flame as it passed, then spilled into the dark adjoining chamber, then disappeared as the connecting door shut.

"They're gone, milord," Much told him, but Gamelyn knew.

"You have to tell him." He tried to lurch up. "Marion, he's *here.*"

"Gamelyn." Marion reached up, gripped the tight-clenched forearm, and when he seemed to not respond, said, helplessly, "*Guy.*"

"Tell Robyn." It was a hiss, and his fingers once more clenched upon her forearm, stark-white. Marion couldn't stop the gasp this time. Much seized Gamelyn's forearm, his own fingertips digging in.

"Sir Guy!" This time it snapped. "Stand down!"

The fingers loosened, but didn't let go. Gamelyn kept struggling to sit up—not a good idea from the way his entire body shuddered—but Much let him, supported him as best he could on the uninjured side.

Not that it would matter—Gamelyn was pie-eyed as a peregrine stalled and preparing to stoop. "He's here. You have to listen. He's *here!*"

"Who's here?" Marion demanded.

"The Templar!"

"Milord, we're at our preceptory, there're Templars everywhere. You're makin' no—"

"No! The Templar! Marion, the Templar lord! *The Arrow!*"

Marion froze.

"He's here. He's Master! He's *here!*"

"The Master? Hubert?"

"Nay, the *Master!*" Gamelyn insisted. "The Visitor . . . he's in the west dormitory, th . . . th . . . castle." His voice was wavering again, his frame taken with shudders. "You have to find it . . . find . . . take it, you—!"

Gamelyn paled, collapsed against Much. But he held, frantic, to consciousness. Still dogged in his hold to Marion, he slapped his other hand against Much and clutched, fingers snarling in the brown tunic.

"See to her," he commanded. "Much. No matter what happens . . . to me . . . you . . . you'll . . . *stay* with her."

"Milord—" Much was interrupted by another hard knock of Gamelyn's fist against his chest.

"Order!" he grated. "Don't . . . leave her. 'Ware the Master! Take . . . *care* . . . !" His voice rose up to a choke. His hold faltered, he shuddered, went white. Collapsed again, senseless, heavy and unwieldy as a too-large burlap stuffed with roots.

He nearly pulled Marion down with him. Much managed by some phenomenon of muscle and madness to catch them both. Pushing Marion gently aside—even as she disentangled her arm from Gamelyn's now-lax fingers—Much wrangled his master down onto the cot.

The physician must have heard the struggle, came bursting in. Halted.

"He's all right." So gentle, as was the hand Much placed to the back of the russet head in a caress. "He'd a wee fit, is all."

Marion backed away, rubbing her arm. She couldn't stop staring. Not at Much's care, not at the ugly, inflamed expanse of Gamelyn's back, but into air, her ears ringing with what Gamelyn had spent himself saying.

The Templar lord. He's here. The Arrow. . . you have to find it. Take it. . .

"It's been a while," Much was saying to Diata, laconic as if what had just happened was nothing. "But he was used t' poppy before. Only lately that he en't used it overmuch. Happens the dosage mightn't have done after all?" It was respectful, a proper peasant's *I en't meaning to suggest anything about your job, milord. . .*

"Of course." Diata nodded. "We'll take care of it now, before he wakes."

He's here. The Arrow.

And Gamelyn was here. Helpless and drugged and wounded.

Marion realised she was shaking about the same time she realised Eleanor had also emerged from Hubert's chamber, peering at her with some concern.

Clenching her fists, Marion remanded herself to some control.

"He'll be all right, won't he?" Eleanor said. Still, the concern.

Why should the Queen Mother of Christian England feel any concern about a renegade Templar, his paxman, and a Heathen cunning-woman?

"Let me help you!" It burst from Marion. "When you take the thing out, let me help!" Eleanor started forwards. Diata frowned, began to speak. Marion, afraid either might be a refusal, continued, "I've also brought some things. I'd like to offer 'em to you, if you'll take them. These are some of the medicines I used on him before."

The physician's frown changed to curiosity as Marion threaded her satchel over her head.

"I beg you, Brother. Me mam were a cunning-woman, and she

taught me all she could before she w . . . before she died. I truly mean to help. I know my presence here is awkward, like, but I've known him since we were bairns, if you understand?"

It was hard—so hard, to know she'd no rights here, no recourse. She was alone. Her Summerlord lay wounded, and Winter's Arrow lay in the hands of an enemy.

The physician's dark eyes had softened as she spoke. "I would never scorn valuable tools. Including the offer of your assistance. What you did before, as I said, was remarkable—"

"For a native wortwife?" she finished, forcing a small smile. "Well, then, there en't many leeches as put off cutting and spilling blood, so I guess we've surprised each other."

Digging into the satchel, she went over to the table. Much came over to help, his eyes searching for hers. She refused to meet his gaze, afraid she would start bawling like a hysterical lass if she did. She swiftly busied herself with placing a small assortment of jars and packets upon the board.

Diata had come beside her as well, lifting the jars, one by one, and peering at them. Marion opened one for him to smell; he blinked, it was that pungent, then smiled. More relief, nearly prompting another rash of inexplicable tears; he recognised it.

In the Temple tower, the bell began a soft peal—not call to prayer, but to supper.

"If you could keep us appraised, Brother Physician?" Eleanor said, making her way to the door.

"I will, Madam." Diata bowed. "And I will send for you when it is time," he told Marion.

Marion couldn't speak; instead she dipped a grateful curtsey and hoped it was enough.

It seemed to be. Diata smiled, then turned back to the jars.

"See them to their refectory, Brother Much?"

Much was no longer trying to catch Marion's eye. Impassive, he motioned the women on.

- XIX -

"We find ourselves in a delicate situation, my *Confanonier*."

Snow tips the forest edge, drifts to mantle the fields and stones. It's an unreal snow, more than he has ever seen here, and it keeps snowing, peppers of ice that somehow do not melt upon his cheeks or in his upturned palms. Gamelyn stands upon the parapet of Temple Hirst, looking out over a demesne blanketed white. Watching. Waiting . . .

For what? There is no breeze. No murmur of river, no sway of trees. All of it, unnaturally hushed, icy snowfall the only sound, the singular movement within a stillness that seems forced.

Strange. It is not unlike an overlong prelude to an anticipated and bloody battle.

"Hearken to me in this." Hubert is beside him; his tone barely scratches at the stillness, so quiet-calm. "Within our Temple are two powerful women—one to whom the laws of this land seek our obedience, the other of whom the altar of our own law demands veneration."

Finally, movement. One snowflake too many falls upon a too-heavy branch; with a dusting of white mist it gives way, tumbles, and melds into the thick drifts below.

Leaves still cling to the branches of that tree, more stubborn than snow. They are desiccated, gold and brown stark against white and grey.

It is an oak tree. This is important, somehow.

"I tried to warn you," Hubert reminds, reasonable. Of course,

Hubert worships reason almost as much as he does knowledge. "You have brought change into this place."

"Change must come," Gamelyn murmurs, and places his hands upon the parapet wall. They are blue with cold, but he does not feel them; indeed, when he looks down at himself, he is clad in nothing but thin braies, bare feet planted firm against stones and snow.

"Aye, even the Rule endures that inevitability. And the Great Work is ever changing."

"The Rule," Gamelyn whispers. "And the Great Work." This, too, is important.

"There is one who would be the instrument of that change," Hubert warns. "He will not take a challenge lightly."

The oak sheds another snow-clad branch, creaking beneath winter's weight. Mayhap Gamelyn shouldn't be able to hear it, this far from the trees, but in this hush, he can.

"Neither," says Gamelyn, "do I."

"I've never enjoyed seeing what wars do to men." Eleanor sat at the scarred, well-varnished dressing table, contemplating the small box where she placed her rings and bracelets, one by one. "But then, I used to be younger. Stronger. Willing to pay the price." She shook her head. "It is high. And I'm no longer strong enough."

"Is that such a bad thing?" Marion was lighting several lamps. It was nigh to sunset, and she and Eleanor had returned to their provided chambers after supper.

"For queen or king, a lack of strength—of purpose—stands to take from you what is yours."

There had been no further opportunity to speak to Much. Someone had pulled him away to some other task as they were leaving the hallways to his cell, had taken his place as escort to the supper board. There had been only a few others, including *Confrere* Otto, and the meal had been silent, thankfully, each lost in their own thoughts. Eleanor's—who knew? But Marion's own thoughts had wound and curved about a spiral spun with *tynged*'s possibilities. She was not yet as capable as Robyn at the kenning of such things. But . . .

Tis no time to doubt, Maiden, she had told herself, and heard the Lady's voice in echo. *Danger lurks here, in every corridor. You must protect the fallen Oak. You must find the Arrow.*

Do you know where it lies?

Silence, long and disturbing. Then, even more disturbing, *I cannot feel it. I . . . do not know.*

And all the while Marion had chewed, dutiful—she would need her strength, though happenstance left her with little appetite.

For now, she was glad to busy herself with the small chores of readying a noblewoman for bedtime. It came early, this time of year—and while Eleanor seemed devout, she also seemed willing to leave off the dark hours of chapel observances for much-needed rest.

Marion finished lighting the lamps, padded over—she'd gladly slipped from her boots to bare feet; the room was reasonably warm from the hearth—and began tending Eleanor's coif, brushing out the silvered bronze hair for braiding. The duty, despite its similarity to ones she'd done for the Abbess of Worksop, did not, in this place and for this particular woman, gall or sting.

It was . . . comforting. Like when she and her mam would brush and braid each other's hair for bed. So much that, as she tied up the braid and dropped it to hang down Eleanor's back, Marion's tongue was not as wary as it should be.

"Why would anyone *want* to be strong enough to sit by and watch their men suffer?"

Eleanor had been idly fanning herself. The gorgeous peacock fan was a bit bedraggled by their torrential journey, but still more than useful; it stilled as Eleanor turned to peer at Marion. The searching quality of it reminded Marion of her lapse in assumptions: this woman was, after all, not Marion's mam in any form or shape. Only a fool would tread so familiarly with a powerful noble—particularly this one.

But Eleanor smiled, folded her fan, and tapped it at Marion's cheek. "The inevitability of fire, my dear girl."

"Fire, Madam?"

"It burns. Whatever it touches. Including itself."

Marion frowned.

"You keep company with men like those two Templars, or your brother, and you'll have to come to some understanding of it. One could become an anchorite, I suppose. But if the fire—the hunger— if it's also there, in you?" A small shrug, and another tap of the fan, this time to Marion's chin. "Retreat will leave you . . . empty. Even if it's your only option. All you can decide is what price you're willing to pay." Eleanor's hand dropped to the table. "I'm no longer young, am barren of any fire to heat my belly. I've paid my dues."

"But you still . . . " Marion closed her mouth and looked down, eyes lowering.

"I still what?" Eleanor asked, flaring the fan and resuming an idle wave towards her neck. As Marion remained silent, Eleanor prompted, quick-sharp, "Speak your mind, girl! As of now, you and

I both stand, maiden and crone made sterile in this Temple of Man and his God. We are rendered . . . even."

Not likely, milady Queen of the Normans.

Soft laughter, from the other Lady behind her eyes. *As We are. . . Quean of the Shire Wode.*

The ancient term, both sacred and profane, tilted a quirk to Marion's lip and finally, *finally* eased the burning behind her eyes. *Happens it wain't matter here, Lady.*

You would be surprised, Maiden.

"I see no retreat in *you*, Madam," Marion braved, muted but firm. "You might be a grandmam, but you en't lost your . . . fire, even if you say 'tis guttered. You still involve yourself in matters of state—'tis my understanding you're t' only thing holding what remains of this country together. You're even contemplating a sea journey to see to the ransom of your son. You use your power."

"Because I *am* Queen." The grey eyes, bordered by the cerulean peacock tufts, bored into Marion. "And I am a mother. You have not known the latter, I perceive. So you cannot yet know the burning *it* incites."

"That explains why we're here." It was slow, feeling her way. "You want to set your son free, and I mightn't have no bairns, but I proper understand seeing to your own. What it en't explaining is . . . well, *this.*" Marion gestured about them—the preceptory, the chambers they inhabited, even the dress she wore—all provided by the Queen's grace.

Eleanor shrugged. "I believe in repaying debts. I owe you and your two cross-caste suitors quite a lot."

Cross-caste. . . suitors? Marion wondered.

"At this point, in fact, my Richard owes you his crown. He will likely be insensitive to it, but I am not."

If that was surprising, Eleanor's next statements, as she folded her fan and set it on the table with a small *smack*, were astonishing.

"Neither will I say I am . . . unsympathetic to the old ways. This was once a dark land of even darker magic, rising up from the bogs and woodlands. Parts of it still remain wild and ungovernable. The priests would claim what cannot be controlled is dangerous—and they are correct, I suppose, in so much—"

Marion bristled—she couldn't help it.

"—but life is danger. Legends are oft more reliable than any supposed rote 'truth,' and myth is as gold within the dross of history. We forget such things to our detriment." Eleanor sat back in her chair, eyeing Marion. "If we women are indeed the ones who led Adam astray, then what does it make of us? Twice as intelligent and, therefore, dangerous.

"Neither am I ignorant of what tales the crofts tell. My own trouvère has spun some fine greenwood tales, has through chance found himself amidst even more. Yet . . . " Again the fan spanked the dressing table. "I warn you, girl. There can be but one king in English lands, and it is *not* your black-eyed brother. And my eldest, unlike his younger sibling, is Christian. Inconstant, mayhap, but fervent."

Uncertain of what to make of any of this, Marion murmured, "My lady, I—"

A hard, swift knock upon the door, and a voice, strong but flawlessly polite. "My Queen?"

"I am readying for bed." Eleanor rose with some resignation, as if she knew the man's response before he spoke.

"I bring the Master's apologies, Madam, at such an ill-timed intrusion, but he requests your presence."

Eleanor slid an expectant look to Marion; belatedly Marion remembered a queen didn't just up and open her own doors. As she trotted forwards, the preceptory bells began to intone Vespers.

The man at the door was no youthful squire, but a full-fledged Templar. "My lord of Pontefract is here, Madam," he announced as he knelt. "He has urgent news. My lord de Nesle accompanies him."

Alundel. Marion kept her head respectfully lowered, but slid her eyes back and forth, from knight to queen.

"I will come with you," Eleanor said. "Marion, if you would be so good as to help me replace my coif?"

Not only the coif, but the jewels and a bit of kohl and the long, fur-lined cloak. A queen didn't do anything, it seemed, by halves.

However, Eleanor's urgent business with Pontefract and her returned trouvère couldn't have come at a better time. Marion had her own tasks to see done, in privacy.

Preparations were rather skimpy and in haste: the door bolted to ensure solitude, some nicked salt from the cellar at supper spiralled on the floor about her, and one hoarded candle to centre and illuminate it. Of course, her mam would have said a cunning-woman who couldn't make the magic without a bunch of trappings was like an archer who needed a warm-up before he shot. Both of them would be caught empty in a pinch.

But these seemed . . . well, right. Marion unbound her hair and belt, shrugged from the green bliaut, and stepped into the tiny circle barefoot, wearing only her linen underkirtle. The Temple welcomed the scant ritual and wished for more, spreading beneath her feet like good, ploughed earth.

Not for the first time, Marion wondered what else went on, deep in the stone tunnels below the keep. They were there—she could feel them, lines and leys of fierce and controlled magics. And a whisper of the Lady's influence, heady as the scent of Eleanor's Eastern cosmetics.

Lowering to kneel in the circle's midst, Marion reached out, placed the objects for the working between her knees: a tiny silver cross on a narrow chain, and a bodkin.

The cross had belonged to Gamelyn's mother. Kept close, as he could not the one who had died birthing him, he had worn it when baptised, when given his first sword and sworn to his father's fiefdom; even after that father had died and Gamelyn had gone to war to come back as Guy de Gisbourne, it had been still bearing his mother's cross.

Until the previous waxing of Samhain. They had both been in Nottingham, then; Marion still trapped, unknowing and unknown, as novice to Worksop's Abbess, and Gamelyn as Guy de Gisbourne, hired by the Sheriff to kill a notorious wolfshead known as Robyn Hood. He'd laid a tiny blood spell upon the cross and gifted it to Marion. For protection—yet it had been the beginning of her awakening: Gamelyn's blood upon the little amulet, and Robyn's upon the altar at Mam Tor, where Templar and Outlaw had met and matched each other . . .

Her turn, now, to spell it—for awakening, aye, but more for protection. How apropos, that it had been his mother's, bequeathed to one she'd died in birthing.

"Protect your son," she murmured to the otherworlds and to that woman, tracing a light finger over the tiny object. "He's much yet to do before he journeys back to Her womb."

Such womb-shed blood was, of course, preferable for this sort of thing. But though Marion's body vibrated with the telltales of her courses, it was not yet her time—and there was no time to wait. She pulled up her kirtle, all the while forming the hex-breath behind her teeth. Taking up the bodkin, Marion made a tiny nick to the inside of her thigh. Blood welled, slight but enough.

On the edges of her sight, at the edges of the salt-laid circle, the air . . . juddered.

And the ground fell away.

Marion sprawled forwards, at the last moment stayed her limbs from broaching the circle, caught herself from planting her face into the hard planking. A wave of sound—only it was *not* sound, not truly—rose from the stones, enveloping her with a power laid hard and fast. Protection, indeed—a cordon of the impenetrable, it asked her right to work her secrets in their midst. She tried to lurch up, but fell back, crouched obdurate beneath it. The reverberation sought to cow her; it sank deep into her chest, timing heart and breath, seeking control by pinning her within her small, hasty circle. Marion gave, but only so far. She pressed her cheek to the ground just past her bent knees, released a mist of breath out and over the tiny silver cross lying across her open palm.

Sweet Lady, she'd been foolish. Arrogant and daft and not given suitable consideration to the possibilities of other magics . . . worse than any Christian conqueror, assuming she had the right without giving due. And now this magic, affronted, sought battle.

What were Templars, after all, if not warriors?

And what are We, if not the Mother of Warriors? the Lady murmured. *You have lived in barren stone—you know the secrets. Get up, girl. You are the Maiden and you kneel to no man's whim.*

It warmed her, skin and down to soul. She sucked in a deep breath, spoke the words of claiming and giving, let them mist over the cross lying beside her cheek.

Again the not-sound; hesitant, this time. Not penitent, not at all, and asking her right.

Surety filled Marion. *I am Maiden to the Shire Wode, recognised by you and yours.* She stood, feeling the Lady's presence settle over her like a cloak. *I stand here within the rights of the Magdalene and to tell you this working is mine, done for one of yours, to protect him in his blood. You will have your due from it, I promise.*

And, as swift as it had risen, the indefinable puissance gave way, ebb tide beneath a gravid moon.

It left Marion panting, sweating with effort. Slowly she knelt, once again bent to the line of scarlet upon her thigh.

It had closed. She made another, let the blood bead on the bodkin like a scarlet pearl, then moved it, quivering and alive, to the cross that had been Gamelyn's. Smeared it there, spoke the words— a heavy-soft exhalation. Felt the vortex about her own small protections whirl sunward, then sink, along with her workings, back into what lay below. Marion could nigh See it beneath the glint of lash and lowered eyelid: a fortress foreign in so many ways to everything she had known, yet with a subtle, oddling kinship.

Her mam would call such things nonsense. Would remind Marion that sorcery was rampant in the Christian teachings, aye— sorcery by men. For men. Not woman's spinning of warp and weft, or the wild god's Wode magic. Eluned's cautions were sound ones, and well-remembered in a place where secretive men worked a clandestine magic that, while it might venerate women, allowed them no admittance or true power.

Marion rocked forwards on her haunches and, with one flattened palm, smeared the westmost quadrant of the faint, salt-soot ring. Taking up the necklet and cupping it in her hands, she rose. Her legs were amazingly strong, steady. The slick of blood upon the tiny cross was already beginning to dry. Another breath saw to it: more power, more protection. As Marion stepped from the circle, the Lady's presence sucked away, leaving her wobbling in its wake and suddenly wary.

There was something else here. Something . . .

Marion glanced at the door—still bolted—then whirled to see a figure just inside the pulled window drapery. Broad, silent, the sombre-clad silhouette stood in profile to her, quite intent upon not looking.

The oddest things came to one's mind at such times. Marion wasn't disturbed to be caught amidst the conjuring, or how Much had managed to fetch himself in without her knowledge. All she was conscious of—sudden and bloody *daft*, actually—was how close-damp her thin kirtle clung, and how it was a bloody good thing she'd decided to not do the conjuring in nowt but her skin.

"What are you doing here?" she hissed.

Still in profile to her, he answered, seemingly unruffled, "The door were bolted."

"So you snuck in the *window*?"

"I knocked." A laconic shrug. "There were no answer. It fretted me, like."

Fretted him? Hardly. "What if sommun had seen you, climbing in the Queen's chamber?"

"There en't many as pass by that window at night. I knew *she'd* gone, and all, so I let meself down the wall and over the ledge." Suddenly he did look at her, eyes still shadowed and expressionless, but with a white flash of grin against the candlelight. "'Tis getting to be a habit with you, that."

Marion found herself grinning back despite wanting to march over and smack him one. She controlled the latter, being as how the Temple was all over control, aye? But another impulse claimed her—worthy of Robyn at his worst—to just drop her kirtle, walk over mother-naked and kiss the man. See if that wouldn't put an expression on Much's careful face, or pop those pretty blue eyes!

Hardly. The impulse dwindled beneath abrupt insecurity. After all, Much would likely just push her away and cover her with his cloak, mutter about her taking cold. Not that she wouldn't admit to a shiver or two—her kirtle was wringing wet with sweat, after all.

"What," she gritted through teeth she refused to let chatter, "are you *doing* here?"

"Brother Diata sent me for you."

She stilled, realising what he meant, then gave a huge shiver.

Sure enough, Much came forwards, shrugging from his cloak and flinging it about her shoulders. The heat from the thick woollen—from his body—curled around her, stifling any objections, even when his voice sounded against her ear, all hearty and supportive and pure, aggravating, Loyal Brother Much.

"I'll turn me back, or hold the cloak, but you need a change of clothes, lass." His next words belied the mild tone. "We'll have our lord set to rights, sleeping and safe, then'll we find it."

"Find . . . " Marion had tiptoed over to her bed and snatched up both her second underkirtle and the green bliaut. She started to shrug from the cloak, found Much there already lifting it, holding it up so she could change with some dignity.

"Aye, 'tis plain enough," Much said, and now his voice was hard as the dagger at his belt. "That thief is here, I wager you know who he is, and we're t' fetch back what's ours, en't we?"

We. She wasn't alone. It curled a warmth in her belly that had little to do with desire and everything to do with the sudden knowledge: even if Loyal Brother Much wasn't the least bit interested in shagging her stupid, he *would* hold her back in another fashion. With his own head, if necessary.

But . . .

"Nay." Marion began peeling from the damp kirtle and ducking into the other. It fell about her toes, longer and slightly thicker. Warmer. Then the woollen bliaut, definitely warmer, though it gaped in the back. She reached around, began groping between her shoulder blades—the beautiful, if bloody, thing was made for one who could count on servants. Marion had managed so far by leaving the laces hanging loose. Sort of.

The blissfully warm cloak was pulled aside, tossed on her bed. Fingers brushed the small of Marion's back, making her jump, but Much merely set himself to lacing up the bliaut.

"You didn't really just tell me nay?" he asked.

"There's no sense both of us fetching trouble," she shot back. "If I do this on my own, then it's just me as stands to be caught. I risk nothing but that. You'll risk . . . " *Everything,* she thought, solemn.

His fingers had stilled upon the lacings. With a small huff, he resumed the task.

Said, matter-of-fact, "I've my orders. I'm to stay wit' you. Help you."

"Orders given by a delirious man!" she protested.

"I note you're taking the rest of what he said fair serious." Much nipped the laces tight—a little too tight and on purpose, she was sure.

"*Much—*"

"I've my orders, Maiden. So milord has said, and so I intend to do." Another hard snug, and Marion gave a tiny squeak.

Almost immediately the lanyard was eased and quickly knotted in place. "Sorry," he murmured. "But you en't going alone. That's all there is to 't. But first"—he bent over, snatched up his cloak and hers as well— "we've to go, now. Brother Diata is waiting."

Marion grimaced at the salt and soot on the floor. "I'd best clean this up, first."

A small sound came from Much—Marion peered at him, recognised it as a chuckle. "What?"

"You womenfolk. Wain't leave a burning house 'lessen it's clean."

With a small growl, Marion went for the besom and started sweeping. "Leaving this sort of mess is likely to fetch me for burning. Again."

Much sobered at the reminder, silent while she swept the circle's remnants into a tiny pile. He waited until she'd scooped it up and tossed it out the window for the wind to scatter, then, "Brother Diata has to wait for me, leastways." Even more sombre: "I'll likely be the main one holding Himself down for the knife."

It was a dismal thought. Marion quickly finished up, peered at him, then held up one hand. The cross dangled from her wrist, quivering and dull with the blood smear. His breath drew in, held.

"Before we do anything, I need you to put this about Gamelyn's neck."

Much studied it, then a smile twitched his lip. "Aye, well. That'll be the easy part."

The first time they'd had to cut into Gamelyn's back, he had been nearly dead, unresponsive until the last agony of removing the crossbow quarrel. That agony, in truth, had been part of what brought him back from death's edge—and the magic Robyn had pulled from their souls into the Wild Hunt.

This time, things were not so simplistic.

Gamelyn was drugged nigh senseless, but his body still knew what was happening even if his mind was absent. It took both Much and the squire—a cheerful, burly youth, poignant reminder of a younger Will—to hold him down. Not for the first cut, which gushed blood and pus and must have been more relief than any pain, but for the prodding that followed. There was more than the one fragment. Diata had to do some searching.

Gamelyn finally went limp in Much's hold as Diata straightened with the final culprit—a half-inch splinter of bone. He tossed it in a pewter bowl at their feet; the bowl already held two others, sticky with discharge.

Marion, steady as the rock surround throughout, found her fingers shaking as she'd mixed up the same medicine paste she'd used on the quarrel wound—and likely with a few salt-hot tears in the mix.

She was just glad there'd been no difficulty in Much fastening the cross about Gamelyn's freckled throat. After tonight, its tiny, powerful spell would likely be the only presence and protection Marion could give. She intended to vanish into the forest with the spelled Arrow. The Templar Master wasn't stupid; he would know who'd taken it. But if she left on her own—one of the Shire Wode thieves—they would likely think she'd acted alone.

She'd not confided this to Much, wasn't prepared to argue the point. He needed to stay with Gamelyn.

If only they could get word to Robyn. Somehow. But she couldn't even glimpse him in dreams—as if he wandered deep in the caverns, so much a part of the Tor and the stones there. Marion'd had no hint of the Horned Lord's presence, not even lurking nigh to Gamelyn—and the Lady was not one to conscript as messenger.

Particularly not the Lady who inhabited Hirst, Her aspect as inaccessible and frosty as any of Her Temple.

"Sommat's happening, John."

Dawn was casting sullen fingers of grey-rose over the eastern horizon. A beauty worth taking in, coming from the highest peak and down into the snow-frosted valley—but Robyn hadn't been intent upon sightseeing.

It had been a wary, watchful trek back, every sense honed to the possibility of being followed. By whoever—*whatever*—it was. Robyn's limbs still quivered, as wearied by the tension as if he'd run ten miles instead of quick-stepping half of one. And he'd felt no cessation of it when he'd descended into the Hermit's caverns. Those quicksilver presences had followed him.

John's hands covered his. It made Robyn jump, ken he was staring into the flames and rubbing his own hands together, over and over. Looking up, he met John's eyes, saw only puzzlement in earth-brown depths, and worry.

John wasn't feeling it. That was either proper good or dead wrong.

"Gamelyn?" John asked, and after a squeeze of Robyn's hands, turned back to the fire where he'd spitted a rabbit and set a few gourds to roasting. "Marion?"

"I en't sure, I . . ." Robyn's mouth went dry as he came to the abrupt realisation: he *didn't* know.

A frown quirked John's brow.

"It . . . *teases* me, John. Here there's us, and our magic. There's the magic earthed and bedded around us, part of us and part its own. But outside our ken, this place—this *here* . . . it's distance, but it's sommat else as well." He shook his head. Words remained inadequate with this, but he had to try. "I'm Sensing nowt but a faint sort of . . . covering, like. 'Tis like when me mam used to cradle eggs in combed lambswool for taking t' market. There were a whole new existence in those shells, aye? Life waitin' to be seeded into being, its own world . . . shielded, like, from crackin' too soon. Only now, the lambswool is about us and we're—"

"Eggs." John's frown had deepened, and Robyn heard his thoughts, surely as if he'd spoken. *Protection, then? Or a. . . trap?*

And wouldn't Robyn like to know that.

John leaned back and snatched up a small doeskin bag, breathed a soft blessing across it, shook it. There were pale *clinks* and hollow rattles as John set it on the ground between them, untied the string, then scooped up the bones and let them fall on the hide.

Eyes closing, head tilting, John loosed his own sensibilities. He'd no godling possession to release or channel his Sight—he was a maker, used tools and talent to pluck at *tynged*'s strands. Robyn could feel it, sure enough—a familiar presence of velvet-soft earth, fed to full-blooded potency by both nurture and strength of nature—but moreover he Saw it: a soft-fierce outward rush, quest and question; a swift in a barn rafter, or a mouse darting across straw. John was going to penetrate the dullness, and . . .

Hesitation, sudden. The multihued, strong warp of *tynged* seemed to . . . unravel, the end strands to waver and lose shape and then thread back amongst themselves.

This time Robyn was the one to take hold of John; both hands about his face, fingers tangling in brown hair, a kiss to bring him back.

John opened his eyes. Puzzlement had trebled to patent mystification.

"Aye," Robyn murmured. "It en't . . . normal, whats'mever it may be. 'Tis something I've not felt before, not even in the Church stones. But nowt or owt to do wit' their like," he added as John frowned again. "Those want to take what's ours, like. Or see it crushed. This just . . . is. It en't against us. But it en't friendly, neither."

"*Fae.*" John whispered it into Robyn's hands, and those hands quivered. A tingle and hum penetrated the air, releasing a soft breath through the cavern. The flames danced, more confirmation. John whispered again, the Barrow tongue in a grave and powerful warding; syllables of protection wrapped up in the music of the hex-breath.

They knelt there, communing silent for long moments, with only the susurrus of air against rock and the eternal *drip-drip* of moisture into dark pools.

Robyn's stomach gave a sudden grumble, loud, into the quiet.

John grinned, reached forwards to cup Robyn's face as well, and kissed his nose.

Then he backed out from under and started seeing to the rabbit once again.

Aye, well, no use cogitating impossibilities on an empty stomach.

"Today?" John asked, starting to slice meat from the rabbit carcass. More than ready to be gone—and no wonder. Robyn felt it himself.

However.

"Tomorrow." Robyn went over to John's pack, rummaged there. "The clouds are heavy with snow, and 'tis a fair jaunt to t' winter camp. But if we can spare the day, we should. There's things to be set to rights here, other than t' runes." He paused. "Those you've done are proper beautiful, John."

A pleased smile replaced the look of trepidation begun in John's expression, and his lashes brushed his cheeks.

"Twould take a se'nnight, in truth, to hallow this place as it needs. Deserves. We've neglected it ower the past months."

"For good reason," John reminded. "There's no anger here." He peered at Robyn. "You're only one. There should be three."

John was becoming downright garrulous in his disapproval of Gamelyn and Marion's absence.

"'Back-to-back,'" John added, fierce. "She said."

"You and I, love, have each other's backs."

"I en't *them.*"

"And they en't *you.*"

John met Robyn's eyes. They peered at each other, a glance emotive as a caress, then Robyn went back to searching the pack. "There's some wild magic waking in the Wode, no question. And no surprise, I should think."

John still peered at him whilst portioning out the rabbit.

"Watch what you're doing, love. I don't want you losin' fingers."

John chuckled, returned his attention to his hands.

"Where is . . . ? Ah." Robyn pulled out a small hand-axe. "Cold iron, to make your sleep sounder. And our bellies happy." Tossing the small hatchet into the air and catching it as he returned to the fire, Robyn knelt and considered the gourd John had just shoved from the coals.

"Daggers," John suggested. "I've salt."

"Happens a bit of sexing's like to keep the fair folk happy." Robyn gave a suggestive grin at John, then brought the hatchet down in a precise *whack*. The gourd split open; steam rose, and its nutty-sweet smell made both their stomachs protest the long moon-dark of fasting.

"We'll do honour, and watch our backs," he continued. "But we'd best leave come tomorrow's sunrise, aye?"

John's nod was vehement.

They finished portioning the meal, and fell to.

Much could roam the halls of Temple Hirst with some impunity, but for Marion it proved more a challenge.

Particularly since they were set on wandering where no outsider was allowed—the inner chambers of the Temple, set aside for the highest dignitaries, for meetings and, should they choose, to stay.

It was what Gamelyn had called the "Castle." Much explained how the nickname was somewhat disparaging; the accommodation was very grand by Templar standards. No less spartan than the other dormitories or cells, but it was spacious and solitary, set up at the top of the west tower, with both a view of the river and the comfort gained by windows both east- and west-facing.

Most Templars made it a matter of pride to stay with their fellows, accepting meaner placement as not only Rule, but true solidarity. Like any closed community, they depended heavily on each other; like any healthy one, they had their strictures, good things shared and savoured, grudges called out and dealt with, both harsh and fair.

Much, however, didn't seem surprised that this Templar Master—Wymarec, was his name—was staying in the tower. The "Castle."

"He fancies himself, no question." Much shrugged. "But 'tis his right—he's second only t' Grand Master."

'Twere the secondary wolf in a pack, Marion mused, as bided most dangerous. There was only the one above them, after all, and very few were content long with being next best.

Hadn't Count John made himself adequate proof of that? It was, after all, why they were here. From what Marion had gleaned—not much, granted—Eleanor's youngest had managed to suborn quite a few of the lords. Now Eleanor courted the rest, buying, bargaining, and otherwise insuring loyalties that had proved supple more than once. All that amidst making plans to leave before week's end and ransom her eldest. Even now Eleanor sat in council again, behind closed doors with several notables including the Archbishop of York, the lords of Pontefract, Hallamshire, Conisbrough, and Durham, the Templar Masters of Hirst and Newsam, as well as, thankfully, England's Master. All of them, making ready plans to free a king.

Aye, well, Marion meant to free hers, as well.

Footsteps sounded from down the corridor, hurried. Ahead of Marion, Much froze, listened until the steps retreated the other way. Likely a squire, late for Vespers. Even at night, even during offices, there were constant comings and goings. Marion was cloaked and hooded in the same type of voluminous robes Brother Diata preferred, but better they not be seen together any more than already had been necessary.

"Can you . . . feel it, like?" Much's voice came so soft as to be barely heard, all sibilance purged.

Marion shook her head, tried to do the same. "Not yet. It en't being . . . used. 'Twill bide quiet—sh—" She broke off as the slight "s" sound carried farther, muted it. "Bide quiet 'til I'm near. Likely wrapped up as he did at t' abbey, loath to touch it." *Aye, this man knows what he's doing.*

Much slid forwards and around a corner. No more communication save with gestures for a few taut-strange moments, as voices echoed from other cells and Much ducked from alcove to hall with Marion his shadow. He stopped in an alcove, waved her in and followed, motioned for silence.

It was then she heard the boots, a soft tread coming from the very hall they had been ready to broach. The hall to the stair, and the Castle at its landing.

The steps were quiet, but rhythmic and slow. The one making them hummed tunelessly to himself—Psalms, Marion recognised, though the voice was unfamiliar.

Much, however, knew the voice. He had nearly stopped breathing next to her.

Marion realised with a sick thrill, *It's him.*

The bootsteps slowed as they passed their hiding place. The half-murmured Psalm went quiet.

It all stopped.

Unthinking, Marion used the same weapons she had used against this man at Worksop. The Thwarting gathered, swift and efficient, on the back of her tongue. In the next breath, she loosed it, silent but *there . . .*

Nyd wyf yma i.

You cannot see us. We are not here.

Silence, still. Then the Psalm started up once more. One boot dragged forwards. Another. And soon the rhythmic, barely audible tread was moving on, heading for the preceptory's depths.

They waited some moments to be sure. When nothing more was forthcoming in either direction, Much jerked his head and led them on.

It had to be here.

The Arrow had to be here, and she had once held it, used it; therefore, she must be able to feel it. Yet Marion felt . . .

Nothing.

She had roamed the chamber thrice now.

Much had heard talk in the dormitories—the Templars, it seemed, were as prone to gossip as any nunnery—as to how Master Wymarec had come directly here from Worksop. He'd only the stop-off at Conisbrough—the lame horse and Templars Gilbert had mentioned, Marion concluded, when her own party had stopped at Cadeby. Surely he still had the Arrow, hadn't rid himself of it?

Nay, he'd handled it with such care, as if it were treasure indeed. He'd not lightly cast it away.

Marion clenched her fists on the bedpost—no cot, this, but a noble's bed, with feather tick and tall posts and curtains against the cold—then rested her head against them, gritting her teeth.

"Mebbe it en't here," Much muttered.

"What about below?"

No response. Marion turned to him, found his cheeks damp beneath the dark curls of beard. Noticed, as if for the first time, how his forelock had grown enough for a slight fall over his forehead. It also emphasised how he'd paled.

"How d'you . . . ?" He trailed off, as if answering his own question, then tried again. "There's no speaking to below."

"Much—"

"There are those as know what might be below, but I en't one." It was still quiet, but rushed and as close to unnerved as she'd ever heard him. Much seemed to realise it, took a quick breath before he next spoke. "I know once milord were taken, to a secret place, like. Just the once, and never again. He didn't speak of it, neither would I. There's no speaking to below."

"And what if the Arrow is down there?" she demanded.

"If there's anything down there—and I en't saying there is—'tis sure neither of us'll get to it."

She started to question, saw the grim negation. Marion started to search again, hands out and palms down, as if she were blind and feeling her way.

"We have to find it!" Low, panic curling about the edges.

"We could do what we should have from the going," Much said, soft. "Go to Master Hubert, tell him."

Marion shook her head, said the same as she had earlier, when both of them were trying for solutions other than broaching a cobra's den. "This man is Hubert's Master, Much. Can we truly trust Hubert to not go to de Birkin?"

It had been the deciding factor then, both of them familiar with the unbending nature of Church obedience. But this time Much protested.

"Milord trusts Hubert."

"Then why didn't Gamelyn tell Hubert? Why did he tell us?"

Much had no answer for that, either.

"Gamelyn trusts Hubert with many things, of that I've no doubt. But we canna trust *anyone* with this, Much. Not with my brother's ma—"

A rattle at the door, and voices.

As one, Marion and Much dropped to the wooden floor planks and scooted, silent-quick, beneath the bed.

"—only a moment, I'm sure," sounded as the door swung open, then back. The door didn't close all the way, or latch. But after a moment, the exact measured tread they'd heard earlier, whilst hidden in the alcove, came across the floor. A wooden floor board squeaked. The reverberation travelled to its other end, fluttered against Marion's ribcage and spread-flat palms. Boots came into view, long strides deeper into the chamber, then across.

The boots were grey, brushed clean, well-kept. They progressed to the bed, paused midstep. A mutter.

Neither of them dared take a breath. Much's arm stole about her, protection and support. She gave her own; again she breathed denial, silent breath curling over her.

We are not here. You cannot see us. . .

The boots went around the bed's foot and moved over to the far wall, shorter strides, but no less measured. They stopped. There was a whisper—a mutter, really—and one would think it nothing, save for the white singsong beginning to escalate behind Marion's ears.

She didn't know what the man was doing, only she had to shut it out, refuse it even as she kept the breath swirling-silent, repeating the charm: *Nyd wyf ymi i.*

You cannot see. You. Will. Not.

A creak of wood—the table on the far wall—a rustle of fabric and sword-harness, and a soft *scuth* as one grey boot crossed over the other.

"I know you're here. Whoever you are."

"Stay *here*," Much mouthed against her ear, then shoved away, rolled out from under the bed.

What are you—No!

Marion made a snatch at Much, missed as he rose, slow, on the opposite side of the bed from those boots—and the sorcerer who wore them. Said, quiet: "Tis only me, Master. You've gave me a start, like."

"A . . . start?"

"I weren't thinkin' anyone t' be back this way for a while."

Silence. The strange white-hum faltered, then increased. Marion looked out from between Much's worn brown boots, smothering a sudden terror into the clench of her hands against the flooring, the repeat, over and over, of the charm . . .

"I'm here under milord's orders. He says he left sommat important here."

A sound echoed through the chamber, soft at first, then increasing by degrees, covering Much's words. Cloying and ominous. Laughter.

Just as abruptly as it had begun, it was stilled. "Did he, then?" The voice was deep and quiet. Unthreatening—was one not noticing the slight quiver of malice threading its edges. "Do you have any idea what it is you're looking for? Or did you just intend to ransack my quarters?"

"Milord is sick, Master de Birkin."

"Of that I'm well aware."

"I just came up here to peer about, like. I meant nowt by 't, just meanin' to look about and go back to him, be able to tell him the truth that I'd done as he'd asked."

Much was doing Thick Clot of a Peasant to bloody perfection; Marion wanted to laugh herself. If she weren't so horrified.

Maybe the ruse would work . . . though it was a sword-thrust through Marion's heart at what this ruse would undoubtedly cost Much.

She took the chance he was giving, flattened against the flooring. Took in a long, soundless breath and began to weave it: something more than a Thwarting.

If she could, this deep within the enemy's place.

A knock on the door. "Master?"

"In a moment!" was the response. The boots uncrossed, then crossed again—casual. As were de Birkin's next words. "I see." It sounded almost indulgent. "Then I've truly a quandary. Should I call the guards and have you put in chains for this intrusion? Or should I just release you, then? Back to your . . . master?"

"I were obedient to his command, milord, nowt more. I'd no thoughts anything like this would come of 't."

"I'm sure of *that.*" Another silence, and Much not even shifting from foot to foot, standing firm.

And every time Marion tried to gather strands of the magic towards her, they would wisp away, more smoke than strands. Unbending. Hostile.

"So, what would your master have you look for, in the Master of England's quarters?"

Much started to answer readily enough—de Birkin cut him off.

"There are only a few—very few—in the entirety of Temple Hirst who have any idea what Brother Guy might want from my chambers. One stands before you. One lies—nay, not as you lie, and I know you're lying, man—"

The lazy menace of it sent gooseflesh down Marion's haunches and up the small of her back. She gritted her teeth, dived deeper, inward and out.

"—nay, he lies in some discomposure—bloody and not quite sound, body or mind. *His* physical well-being—indeed, his life—is not only due to Brother Diata's skills, but more . . . abstruse ones. I've no doubt the one possessing those skills also put you up to this. Typical."

Silence. Marion knew it wasn't confusion at Wymarec's complex vocabulary—anyone who had spent years as Gamelyn's constant companion would have become used to such.

Wymarec knew. *Knew.* And she was getting no more from her conjurings than a lot of sweat, wrath, and a mouth dry as if she'd been sucking on wool. *Lady, help me.*

"Where is she, man?"

"Milord, I don't understand."

It is not here. You have failed, Marion.

Help *me!* It was a demand.

The Ceugant *is torn apart, crippled. Without it you haven't the power here, and neither. . .*

It dipped, then feathered away.

Neither do I.

It left Marion gasping on the wooden floor, stunned and desolate.

"Where *is* she?" The Templar lord's words were white-hot, furious.

And Marion rolled out from under the bed, stood.

- Entr'acte -

The quillion dagger glinted, rose-gold in the fire's light. Glinted and held, iron-sharp compellence, in myriad soft-shadowed eyes lurking deep in the caverns.

Come no farther, it exhorted, charm and barrier.

And the wild things obeyed.

John was proper glad the old tales held that much truth. Glad Robyn slept beside him, a lax hand upon John's knee to ensure they stayed within each other's reach. Even drained and wearied with the obligations—not only to Tor, but this the Old One's cavern—Robyn's instincts never slept as deeply as Robyn himself.

The dagger was powerful. Gamelyn's dagger. Robyn's dagger. Of them, each and both, consecrated with despair and passion. John passed it through the flames: once, twice, thrice. Whispered a breath and tangle of words, binding more protections about the blade. Let them waft upwards on shifts and shimmers of heat, curl into faint smoke that spread into the cavern like bottom mists. Heard the words pass, a bare breath echoing through the watching presences, ripples in an oh-so-still pool.

They knew him. His father's dam had carried the blood, a tiny seed sprouted in none but the smallest and youngest of her grand-children—John himself. But they kenned Robyn even more. 'Twere Robyn's mother, the *si* woman, who'd been kith and kin to the Old Blood, an unbroken trail branching from the Barrow Lines, plucked and grafted into thisworld . . . who knew why?

It didn't matter. All that mattered were this making, this protection, in this fae place amongst spirits who were starting to slip in and out of existence, waking even as his love and leader slept.

They wanted something from him. From Robyn. But they weren't going to claim it tonight.

- XX -

"Now that you are back, whatever shall we do with you, my *Confanonier*? Have you returned to take the white? Or have you merely come to seek your oath undone?"

"What oaths I have made, I will keep." It is resolute, but nonetheless Gamelyn feels his voice quiver, threading shaky against the parapets.

"Of that I've no doubts," Hubert answers, soft. "But what oaths are those? See."

At the gesture, Gamelyn turns to peer at the trees once again. There are shadows flitting around the snow-clad oak, glimmers within the dark woodland: eyes, waking wet from an endless sleep. Forms creep towards the parapets, not unlike an ambush of outlaws—but nothing like, in ways he cannot seem to ken.

"Mm." There is a nod in Hubert's voice. The satisfaction of solving a riddle. Gamelyn wishes Hubert would share the answers.

But nay, only more riddles. "They come to take you back, my *Confanonier*. Ah, but you're already gone, aren't you?"

"My lord, *you* are my Master!" Gamelyn whirls. Halts.

Marion, not Hubert, stands there, clad in all the colours of spring and summering, cinnabar hair escaping the fur hood pulled to shadow her face. Her hands are clasped before her, deceptively demure . . . aye, deceptive. For there are budling horns amidst her curls, and she holds his quillion dagger, point down, in her hands.

His dagger. Robyn's dagger. Down its fuller trails a thick skim of blood.

"What of your master within the Wode? What"—her voice dips harsh, even as her head rises—"of Me?"

There is a crescent glimmering, silver in grey eyes.

Gamelyn shivers. Whispers, "Lady, you do not understand."

"I think I do. And can only pray that one day soon you shall understand the difference between self-indulgent guilt and the sacrifice of true obligation."

Sacrifice? He wants to accuse, but cannot. Can *not*. Instead, he retorts, "Obligation? I have too many obligations—oaths of head, of heart. Can't you see, I need to sort this. I need *time*."

"Time." It is drawn out, with a *tsk* as punctuation. The dagger drips upon his naked feet, sheds carmine into grey-white slush. "You have spent overlong in rage and slaughter, denied and drowned yourself in it. Have you not yet had enough of *time*, my lord?"

"You say that like you think I want this!"

Another droplet hangs. Falls. "Do you not?"

"*No!*" It rings, fully voiced, across the parapets, and in its echoes, they peer at each other. Lady and Lord, Maiden and Knight, both barrened in stone and waking to spring.

Then why are you here, my Oakbrother? No Lady, this, but Her Lord, breathing at his neck and running familiar, sinewy hands through Gamelyn's hair. *Why are you not with me?*

Gamelyn steels himself—it is not hard. It is not Robyn: merely his form and illusion, nothing but.

"You *know* why!" Thunder, cold and stark. "You would see it set in motion! You play with it—with *us*—as if we're nothing but mummers dancing, puppets beneath your twisted dominion of life and death!"

So certain, are you, the Horned Lord sneers. *Summerling, you persist in mistaking Our ever-spiralling Dance for the jealous machinations of your desert-bred god. I do not. . . "hold dominion"*—it curls, sibilant and rife mockery—*over my Wode. I am the Wode.*

Gamelyn's own breath exhausts into the frigid air. It surrounds him, prickling against skin, punctuation to the squeak and squash of his bare feet treading upon snow and slush. Beneath that the stones hum, a peculiar warmth. *Sleep,* they say. *Stay. Sleep with us. Sing our name to us and we will give you yours. . .*

You already have a name, Gamelyn Oakbrother. Another sneer—a goad, really. *Or do you prefer the barren chill of anger, "Sir Guy?"*

Drifted snow blusters up from the parapet edge, thick-white into his eyes. Cold; Gamelyn is abruptly as cold as he's ever been, staggering half-naked on the parapets.

Nay. There are no stones about him, no high wall from which to look down, observe. He is alone, wandering in the forest. Searching for something he's lost, and found, and is terrified of losing again.

The trees arc over him, creaking with snow, little whirls of powder-dust dancing about him. Dancing about the oak.

This time will end. The Lady is once again a whisper behind his eyes. *Summer will come despite its lord hiding his light in sterile stone. And should you let it pass you by again, 'twill burn itself through the Wode. Do you not understand, My Knight?*

A memory that never dies: the conflagration through the trees, lifting to a summer-black sky, and a lone figure standing amidst the flames, defiant, arrow at nock. Gamelyn is afraid he does understand, all too well.

You must feel the fire, let in the heat of Summer. You must use all *of what you are, or you will have none of it.*

Ice is his shield, but fire is what he covets. Fire is what he *fears.*

Gamelyn walks around the oak, shivering, but before he's halfway around, he halts. Stares at the arrow buried, point-first, into the oak's gnarled roots. It is black with soot, fletched with the goddess's eyes. Blood magic writhes through it, setting the runes to dancing.

The tree is bleeding. And Gamelyn should know that arrow.

It is important.

Only blood can loose the nock, the Horned Lord says. *Blood, and fire, and wild, wild magic. You are not one third of the* Ceugant *for nothing.* Think, *Gamelyn.*

"Think, Guy. Attend me, and consider this," Hubert says, once again at his elbow, patient sage and stern taskmaster. "We must be observant. Cautious. We can hold nothing higher than our own. Thus do we bear witness to our Brotherhood and the sanctity of our oaths; thus do we protect the Greatest of our secrets. Obedience *is* our love, marked with our blood and honour. It is a weight we must bear even as Christ bore the cross from both duty and love. Even as the Holy Mother bore the love and pain of Sacrifice with Her Son's birth and death."

The Eternal Return. Death and rebirth. The White Christ is but another King who gave his blood and life to His people. And what shall you sacrifice, Summerling?

Not this. *Never* this.

"Think, Guy. Only you can claim what you are."

Nay, he cannot think, not on this. Will not consider *this,* even in the cold light. They do not understand. None of them do. The dream keeps coming—its own Eternal Return—spiralling to an end that plays out behind his eyes, over and over.

Battle.

Enchantment. Betrayal. *Death.*

From the moment we first met, leading to this.

The arc of that one last arrow, black flaming into green. Holding a battered, blooded Robyn in his arms, unable to do anything but watch as a fierce glee past any understanding blazes in ebon eyes, and as cracked lips shape one word: "Free. . ."

Has to watch, hopeless and helpless, as the dagger does its work. As the fire in Robyn's eyes dims. Dies.

Has to see it, over and over and. . .

A soft crack, then a thick *shuss* as a huge blanket of white cascades down upon him, burying him in cold and quiet. It happens so fast he cannot so much as struggle.

So you will sacrifice thisnow to your fears? Nay, my lord, my Knight. You must use all *of what you are, or you will have none of it.*

Enough of this, another voice murmurs, beloved and faraway. *Everyone dies, soon or late. Let me hold it for you, just for the while longer. Hold it, let you heal. Lie easy, love, and rest you quiet.*

Ice-white gives way to heavy grey, and grey to an envelope of darkness curling about Gamelyn; deep as a woodland night, black and wiry-soft as Robyn's hair falling about him, bending for a kiss.

"Sleep," Robyn tells him, alive and vital, warm and *there*.

And Gamelyn does.

They were escorted through a labyrinth of corridors to the far side of the preceptory compound. The guards accompanying them had many a sympathetic glance for Much— clearly one of their own, and well-liked. But for Marion—obviously at the heart of their comrade's inexplicable behaviour—they'd merely a stone-faced glower.

Wymarec didn't even bother to accompany the guards.

Such progress led them to another small barbican, not unlike the one Marion had recently occupied with Queen Eleanor. That was the only resemblance, however. No door, no stairs to upper chambers, only several narrow openings laid into the back curve of the empty, circular hollow, furnished with thick doors and impressive locks. Much and Marion were gestured towards the rightmost of these.

There was no fire. There were three cots in one corner, a piss-pot in the other— more a pail, really—and another pail next to it: water, icing about the edges. A scarred bench lay overturned against the far wall, with one end looking as it if had been hacked off. The verdigris of mould skimmed corners and seams, the packed earth of the floor dank and bloody cold, and illuminated—barely—by an ill-trimmed lamp and several openings nigh to the high ceiling.

In essence, a gaol.

Marion halted at the threshold. And, try as she might, she couldn't make her feet move any farther.

This seemed to flummox their guards. One, without meeting her eyes, gestured into the cell. Not that it mattered; she might as well have been frozen in place.

This is not Nottingham, she reminded herself, almost angry. *Not the oubliette. Not dark, or inescapable, with rats that will take what's left of you when you die here, all alone. . .*

"Marion." Much's voice in her ear, close. "We've t' go in, now."

Still, she couldn't make herself move.

This time Much cupped a gentle hand at her back, urging her forwards like a spooked horse. The heat of his strength penetrated the icy numbness in her belly, and Marion wanted to lean back against him, give in to it . . . only that would mean weakness, wouldn't it, in this cold Temple of stone and ice . . . ?

Angry pride gave her the wherewithal to shrug off assistance; sheer will made the first step, and after that pride bid her take another, then another. Behind them, the solid wood closed, quiet but firm. Templars, it seemed, didn't slam doors.

Much came around but kept his distance, wide as the cell would permit, wary. "All right, then?"

She didn't answer. Couldn't.

"Marion?"

Both wariness and concern tilted his voice, and put the frown on his brow. Mayhap it should have been comforting, but wasn't; all it made her feel was vulnerable, humiliated. Marion turned away from his gaze. Rubbing at her chilled arms, she forced a slow circuit around the cell, spoke of inconsequentials.

"Why would they quarter us together?"

Those high openings were more arrow loops than any window. A child wouldn't be able to squeeze through, could one make the sheer climb.

Silence. She turned to peer at Much, found him looking, it seemed, at the mould in the corners. As if he felt her query, he shrugged.

"I'm nobbut a lay Brother, sworn as paxman, not monk. I en't the strictures of the true Brothers." It was flat. "Mayhap 'twas merely convenient."

"Then they don't mean to keep us here for long." Relief swamped her, with a faint, foul hysteria peeking over its edges. Sternly, she bid it to heel. Much shrugged again, and went to examine the door.

Three Templars came and took Much away the next evening, leaving Marion with a platter of food and a sense of panic that, with every solitary moment, scratched harder beneath the surface of any control. It wanted escape. Expression.

She didn't allow it so much as a whimper, refused to contemplate anything save homely things. They'd slept well, considering, dragging the cots together the previous night, back-to-back for some warmth. The Templars hadn't taken Much away in chains. Neither did they intend to starve their prisoners; the food was simple, but there was plenty of it. And several blankets—thin, but no less than any given to the preceptory's residents, considering Much's gratitude upon finding them folded upon the cots.

Despite such a game try at distraction, anxiety lingered. It kept Marion circling, over and over, around the same thoughts:

What did the Templar Master want?

And what would the Templars do to Much for what they surely would view as betrayal?

She was not alone. Marion reminded herself of this. There were others about, particularly when the Hours were called. Three of them had been called so far. The accompanying sounds were becoming quite familiar: the stride of shod feet filing from dormitory to chapel, the crunch and slosh of snow, fresh and half-melted, the loft and song of Latin through the cold air as they passed.

Yet it was so *quiet*. Marion hadn't imagined that a horde of men possessing such excessive skills in killing and maiming, as well as no regular access to sex, could be so lacking in vocal noise. It was strangely soothing—though in no way did it lull her into any false securities. Or ease the waiting. Or dispel the panic lying in wait, searching for the slightest hint of surrender.

She flung herself onto the cot and wanted to groan aloud. If only she'd something to *do*. A book to read. Some wool from those lovely sheep to spin and keep her hands busy. She'd already tidied the small cell and wished she'd a ladder and a good soft besom to reach those cobwebs in the corners.

Instead exhaustion finally took its toll and she slept, at least for a while, and woke before dawn the next morning. Not this time to the telling of the Hours, but to the ring of bootheels and shod hoofs upon the cobbles. Overlaying that was the rattle of equipment and harness, and voices raised not in ire or impatience, but merely to be heard above such preparations. Several men and horses, readying for travel—explicit, by the sounds alone—and soon verified. With impressive speed, the small cohort gathered. The gate was opened. Hoofs and feet set off, faded into the distance.

Then, again, the quiet.

Marion lay there for some time, her nose and fingers cold from where they peeked beneath the woollen blankets. Two of them—she'd cadged Much's. He'd not yet returned.

Panic, wishful and insidious, slid sideways into worry. And that disallowed any further sleep.

Dawn had begun to finger its way through the high, narrow window when more voices, muted against the thick door, invaded the quiet from outside Marion's cell. Shoving upwards from the cot, puzzled and wary both, Marion gained her feet, silent. More voices. She did her best to shake out her skirts, running quick fingers through snarled curls; half a moment later, she chided herself for caring. 'Twas sure that none who'd visit this cell would.

The iron latch rattled, then released with a dull *clunk*. The door swung inward on heavy, well-oiled hinges. Backlit by torches from the circular entry were three figures: two guards—boys, really—and another woman.

The Queen. Marion gaped for a full four heartbeats until she remembered that fact and lowered her head. She also dipped to her knees, green woollen pooling about her and clenched tight in her fingers.

Silence. Another several heartbeats pounded in Marion's ears, overloud in the stillness. Then a *shuss* of heavy draperies against hard-packed earth, and Eleanor's voice, languid but commanding.

"You may leave Us."

A stillness, heavy in the air. Marion lifted her gaze just enough to peer past Eleanor's velvet skirts and cloak to the two squires beyond. They seemed uncertain, but even more so at the possibility of disobedience to their monarch. Particularly once she turned on them, folding her hands before her. Waiting, overly patient.

They bowed out—though "took flight" might be a more apt description, Marion thought with a tiny grin. That grin also fled, however, as Eleanor turned back to her. Marion dropped her gaze, said nothing.

"We-ell." Eleanor drew it out, flat and with a click of tongue as punctuation. "I return to my chambers from a series of absolutely interminable meetings. I find those chambers spotlessly clean—well done, you—whilst the one who cleaned them?" A pause. "Disappeared. Seemingly without a trace . . . and why should I expect otherwise, from the like of outlaws?" The skirts again made a heavy drag across the floor, a sure telltale even if Marion hadn't dared to peep upwards to see the back and forth progress.

"Or so I was informed."

"Milady, I did not—"

"Be silent, girl, whilst your betters are pontificating!" was the sharp rebuke. "The man seems reasonable, self-contained—which should have been my first warning. One does not rise to his position by being reasonable. I'm sure the self-containment is more than genuine, however."

Puzzled, Marion peeked again, found Eleanor across the chamber, peering back with eyes of unreadable rainwater.

A bare breath later, Eleanor resumed her stalk, back and forth. "There are more mummers' plays being held here than at a May Fairing, you see, so I'm afraid it took me more time than usual to ferret out that my handmaiden's disappearance did, in fact, have an explanation . . . and all my suspicions, uncharitable as they proved, diverted and *contrived* with!" She made a hasty halt before Marion, snapped, "God's *teeth*, but do get up, girl! I'm seeing enough red without having to stare at the top of your head."

With a tiny frown and a tinge of heat pinking her cheeks, Marion obeyed. She was abruptly conscious of topping the Queen by nearly a head—not that it mattered to Eleanor, not one bit. It merely made Marion feel more awkward and provincial.

Eleanor resumed pacing. "That bloody-minded, puffed-up, arrogant . . . *tosser!*"

Marion blinked. Of all the words she'd imagined to emerge from the royal mouth, "tosser" hadn't even made the list.

"That insufferable monk lied. Lied! To *me*! And thinks he can have done with it. Only he hasn't thought it through, not at all, and if he has allies and the blessing of our Holy Father"—she crossed herself—"neither am I without resources, or hallowed friends. In Rome and indeed here, in *his* precious preceptory."

Marion kept blinking and watching, mute. She wasn't sure what she could say, or should. But she knew, beyond a shadow of a doubt: *She's speaking of him. The Templar lord. Wymarec de Birkin.*

"What did you do?" Eleanor whirled, strode forwards until she trod nearly upon Marion's toes. "What could a peasant forest woman do that the Master of the English Templars should lie to keep her from my notice? That one of his ilk should even deign to notice *you*?"

Disarmed by the direct question, Marion gave just-as-direct answer. "He has something that belongs to my brother."

Eleanor's eyebrows rose. Again, Marion gave frank reply.

"It is an arrow."

"An . . . arrow." Eleanor's tone was dry. "One would think, considering your brother, that he should be in possession of enough of *those*."

"It is . . . different."

"Ah. A relic, then," Eleanor guessed, and as Marion shrugged, unwilling to divulge any further, continued, "Some pagan thing, no doubt. That explains much. In this age, a pagan has little *but* relics left to them—and Templars possess overt interest in the trappings of faith." Her eyes met Marion's own, and there was something in them—something benevolent, *malleable.*

"Help me," Marion blurted out. "Please, Madam, I beg you—"

"Do not beg," Eleanor growled. "There are few things upon this earth that are worth the price of begging—and none will honour you for it."

Face burning, Marion looked away.

"Better to take the reins yourself when you can, and seek help from none you cannot afford to be indebted to."

Chin lifting, Marion said before she thought, "And your debt to us?"

Silence. Yet Marion kept her chin high, refused to look or to back down.

What more could they do to her?

You have no idea, the Lady whispered against her temple, the sudden presence filling Marion with hope and despair both. Hope, for it was Her . . . but despair, for Her mien did not seem at all helpful, or even friendly.

The laughter that answered flushed Marion's freckled cheeks even more. Belatedly she realised it was not the Lady, but Eleanor, low and somehow not at all mocking.

"Christ's blood, but I detest spineless girls." Eleanor's eyes were twinkling as Marion finally turned to peer at her, cautious. "Are you sure you have no inclination to travel with me, Marion? You're clean and neat, even if you're too quick for your own good. 'Struth, but your impertinence is damned refreshing after the hordes of whey-faced, would-do-well *pucelles* that the finest families of England and the Continent would inflict upon my household."

An unspoken *but* edged the words. Marion waited for it, folding her hands before her.

"And manners when they suit you, as well as patience to try a nun."

Marion twitched; surely Eleanor didn't know that as well?

"Still. I have more weighing upon me than the fate of one headstrong peasant woman. I cannot tarry to untangle this." Eleanor shrugged, the gesture saying, plain as plain: *Did you expect otherwise? Would you not, in my place, do likewise?*

Her brother? Her son, had she one? Marion knew she would, and smile in the doing.

"My dear girl, you have gambled and lost. Fallen afoul of Templars. I warned you, yes? How little power women have in this place?" A shake of the greying-fair head. "Or anywhere, in truth. We have only that which we take . . . and even then, as you're beginning to find, a woman is altogether likely to reap a stone gaol as reward for her presumption. But?" Eleanor tossed back her splendid cloak and began unfastening a small satchel, which Marion could now see hung from across one shoulder. "Even stone cannot silence us, unless we let it."

Marion extended her hands as Eleanor handed over the pouch to her. It was not very heavy, but filled with things that gave a rustle and mild clink. She couldn't help a swift glance at the closed door.

"They cannot object to this. It is not, I fear, anything to aid physical escape. But Blondel fancies the escape yon tools offer as one adequate to cast away whatever chains bind us. 'Twas he told me the Hood's sister possessed a remarkable ability for letters and learning. That, indeed, she missed the comforts of such." Eleanor shrugged. "I prefer reading or needlework, myself."

Blondel. It was hard to think of Alundel so; particularly when he seemed to . . . "Why does he dislike the name so?" Marion asked, opening the pouch.

Eleanor shrugged. "His whims upon it shift with the wind, since 'twas Richard who bestowed it. Their . . . relationship"—a small grimace, almost not there—"is somewhat tempestuous. And not mine to speak upon, other than it has proven useful more than once. My trouvère is faithful and true of heart, but I refuse to keep track of what day he likes his name or not."

There were sheaves of flat parchments within the pouch, and a handful of goose feathers, and—the source of the small clink—two small, tightly corked pots, wrapped in lambswool.

"Enough ink there for several months—though I have doubts you'll languish here that long. Of course, you'll need to trim the quills to your own satisfaction. I should hope they left you some sort of blade? If not, I—"

"I've my eating knife." The words were somewhat shaky. Marion placed the writing things one at a time on her cot, scarcely knowing why tears were burning, all to the sudden, behind her eyes. Only . . . only . . .

Surely it is not so difficult, the Lady whispered. *After all, you have been winnowed of your memory and will, left voiceless far too long.*

Marion clenched first her fists, then her throat against the sudden sob trying to escape. Her expression was not so biddable. Marion wasn't wholly sure of what shone in her eyes, but Eleanor's face softened and her lip tilted in a tiny smile.

"I have also ordered your cloak brought, and some extra hose. It's bloody cold and dank in here. Much more I cannot—"

A knock, soft but insistent upon the door. "Madam? My Queen?"

"Ah," said Eleanor, and called, "Enter!"

It was the two youthful squires, this time accompanied by *Confrere* Otto. He gave the two squires a severe look, then turned a more respectful gaze upon the Queen. With a small bow, he spoke in the same guttural speech as before. German, Eleanor had said it was.

"Alas, they are looking for me. Again." Eleanor answered Otto in the same tongue. Back and forth several times; some conclusion must have been reached, for *Confrere* Otto bowed and backed against the door, waiting.

"I hope we shall meet again, girl." Eleanor took the remaining steps to the door, started to cross the threshold. Hesitated. She turned back to Marion, ever so slight, and gave a small nod.

"Take heart," Queen Eleanor said, and departed.

Robyn woke, as usual, with the dawn-tide, pillowed on the furs that still smelt of his John. He lay there for moments, blinking at the cavern ceiling, the crackle of a new-stoked fire in his ears, the smell of cooking porridge overtaking the lovely heartwood-and-beeswax whiff that Robyn had buried himself in last night. Two things came to him: they were in the Hermit's caverns, and . . .

And last night, he'd had no dreams.

Not a smell, not even a taste of one. It was so quiet—sated, almost—as to make his chest all tight and full. Robyn felt more rested than he had in well over a fortnight. And—lovely!—there was one part of his anatomy proper responding to a good rest.

He rolled in the furs, stretched, and sat up. Where was John, anyway? No use to waste such a well-strung bow with his own loose.

There he was, seated not far from the hearth, watching the fire's light play over the blade of Robyn's long dagger. Gamelyn's dagger. Sobering, Robyn rolled from beneath the furs and stood. First he checked the porridge—just beginning a roiling boil, so he moved it to a cooler spot in the coals. After, he padded over, feet soft against the stone floor and skin rashed with prickles and shivers at the chill.

"You weren't going to burn our breakfast, were you?"

John gave Robyn a slow smile and shook his head.

"Have you been up all night, love?"

A shrug, then a jerk of John's brown curls to the cavern depths.

"I know," Robyn admitted. "One of us needed to be watchful. I never meant to sleep so long. You never should've let me."

"But?" Another slide of eye and gentle tuck of lip.

Robyn chuckled, knelt by the rock upon which John was seated, and nuzzled his head against John's shoulder. "I've to admit, 'twere the best sleep I've had in some time. Thank you."

John's lip tucked further, pleased.

Robyn leaned in, purred against his temple, "So come back to bed, then, and let me send you to sleeping. Aye?"

A grin appeared, swift, then just as swiftly faded. "First," John murmured, "go look."

Robyn frowned, hesitated. John gave him a gentle push towards the cavern entrance.

He took a torch to light the way, yet it proved necessary only for a short time. More light than a normal winter's dawning could promise was philtring around the corners, and when Robyn rounded the last bend to the up-and-out, bright white filled the caverns, brilliant as summer sunlight. That, and a howl of cold air buffeting his frame, peppered with tiny, icy pinpoints.

It wasn't just snowing. It blew sideways, mixed with sleet; had blown into the cavern mouth and deposited a fat, white cushion.

One thing was sure: they weren't going anywhere in this mess.

Robyn wove his way back through the caverns. John knelt at the hearth, stirring the porridge as Robyn crouched to warm chilled bits.

"Good thing we brought food to last. Nothing'll be moving in this. On the other hand?" He grinned and shot a winsome look John's way. "No reason not to go back to bed and stay warm."

A soft chuckle. "After breakfast."

"Aye, allus."

They sat on the furs, side by side, waiting. John still held the quillion dagger; its tip resting on the floor, he angled it back and forth, catching the light and reflecting it on the ceiling above. The runes and pictures he'd traced into newness seemed to dance around the reflections. But it wasn't only the walls he'd reconsecrated.

Robyn reached out to touch the dagger, to stroke the soft tingles of magic spiralling about it like a lovely golden-copper serpent.

"Against Them," John murmured.

"Good thing, that," Robyn said. "We'll be here for a little while longer, it seems."

John dipped his head, cradling the quillion dagger in his arms like a bairn.

"I know. I miss him too. I just wish"—Robyn looked out towards the storm-wracked entrance—"wish we could spell it t' tell us what's happening. I en't used to this . . . fog. Like all of our *tyngeds* . . . standin' still, though *that* makes no sense. Even the least of sommat would be better than nowt."

Marion had begun fashioning one of the goose feathers into a quill when, not long after the midday meal, Much was brought back to their cell.

As the door rang shut behind, he stood there, expression blank. His eyes surely took in the sight before him—Marion, the oddly precious pouch beside her, knife in one hand and bits of feather vane dusting her lap—but he displayed no reaction. With an abrupt shudder—it could have been cold, or an attempt to shake off happenstance—he ambled over to the bench against the opposite wall. He gave it the same, blank stare, then turned and eased himself down, moving like a man who'd been through one too many tourney bouts.

"They . . . brought you back?" Marion asked. Stupid question, but it was the only one she could voice. The other one begging for utterance—*Are you all right?*—was even more stupid and thrice as obvious.

"I asked to be put back here" was his answer. "Told 'em milord had given me a task, and I would see it through."

And if milord told you to fling yourself from the highest turret, would that be done as well? Then, just as tart but even more humiliating, *Would you even be here if he'd not told you to?*

Marion bit that back as well, merely said, "I'm sure he didn't mean to put yourself in such jeopardy with—"

"I'm not fancying talking 'bout it now." Much cut her off, curt. "I've been standing, waiting Commander Hubert's pleasure since sun-up, like, and . . . " He closed his eyes. "Milord's doing well enough, at least. Commander told me that much."

He looked . . . grey. Worn out. More than anything else, it shut Marion up, prompted her to rise. Shaking her skirts, she put down the feather and knife, took up the unfinished platter the two squires had brought her a scant hour previous. Much's blue eyes opened and followed her, listless and bloodshot, as she brought the platter over.

"There's plenty still. I can recommend the cheese particularly. And the bread's right fresh."

Much closed his eyes again, shook his head. "There's no call you waitin' on me."

"There's every call."

"Save me . . . " It petered out as his eyes opened and met hers. Behind them was a wretchedness to sink Marion's stomach. It smothered the last, whimpering vestiges of her own panic, made her want to kneel and take his hands in hers, lay her head in his lap, and tell him it would be all right.

Only, likely it wouldn't be. Nor would, she was sure, such an action be well received. Instead, she set the platter on the bench next to him. "Eat, lad."

His eyebrows rose. "Herself's calling me 'lad,' now," he said to the wall.

"I thought you said you didn't want to talk anymore." Marion pointed to the platter. "*Eat.*"

Much fell asleep on the bench and didn't wake even when Marion covered him with one of the woolsey blankets, then crawled into the bed farthest from the frosted wall. She woke the next morning to not only the ubiquitous bells, but a repeat of the day before. Hoofs and boots upon the cobblestone path—twice as many. Much shot bolt upright on the bench, flinging back the blanket and leaping up. He halted halfway to the door, blinking and staring at it, then Marion.

"Sommun's leaving," he said. "A large party."

The Queen, Marion thought but did not say, as Much put a hand to the door. Listening, trying to glean what he could.

Not that it mattered. Some hours later, after the call to midday prayer, guards came again. This time, they took both Much and Marion from the cell.

The inner bailey spread before them, all tromped-over slush, but the surrounding buildings were still edged with a thin white coverlet. The sun peeked from scattered clouds, giving at least the sensation of warmth. Marion lifted her woollen skirts from the wet, her face to the sunlight, and tried to ignore the four guards surrounding them.

They were young men, two of them the squires who had haunted the cell door, and the other two a brown-dressed lay brother and a black-clad sergeant. They had treated Marion with courtesy, albeit aloof and silent, and had brief speech with Much. In fact, the lay brother—an obvious compatriot of Much—had given some earnest information, low-voiced, when Much had asked after Gamelyn. Marion heard bits of it, was satisfied Gamelyn was well cared for and doing adequately. But it only eased her wariness a little—where were they being taken?

First, to a small alcove behind the kitchens, where the four young

Templars waited until Marion and Much had eaten. Then, to the stables.

The four guards halted at the great doors to the stables; the sergeant motioned for Much and Marion to go on in.

After the bright-white of sun glinting off sparse snow, the stables were dark, indeed. Marion's eyes took a few moments to adjust; it was with a bit of a stumble that she nearly ran into Much, who had stopped in the middle of the aisle. His hand went to her arm—absently, it seemed.

Marion saw it, then. Clad in motes of sun and a white tunic, grey cloak falling to booted calves, the figure at the end of the stable aisle would have been quite imposing—had he not been crooning and handing over treats to the three horses there beside him.

The rounceys they'd ridden here were tied to a post, saddled and seemingly waiting. The stoutest had a saddle festooned with several loaded-down bags.

"My lord . . . Commander?" Much ventured, approaching. All of it, hesitant.

Hubert turned to them, wiping bits of carrot from his hands. "Ah, there you are. Have you eaten, then?"

Marion peered at Much, mystified. He gave a tiny shrug in response, then said, "Aye, my lord Com . . . my lord."

It was odd, the sudden stutter of title, but Hubert continued, almost jovial. "*Bon!* It will be a damnably cold ride, but any break in the weather is a good one, eh?"

"Ride," Marion repeated.

"No doubt you heard the commotion earlier this morn. Queen Eleanor has left our walls and started her own journey—one to ransom her son and our King. We wish her Godspeed." Hubert genuflected, fingers touching all points of the scarlet cross upon his white tabard, but the blue-grey eyes did not leave Marion's. If they weren't exactly benevolent, neither were they unkind. "Our Queen did ask after you, Maiden, as she left."

Maiden? Marion frowned, started to speak, then just as suddenly quelled the impulse.

Those eyes noted it, lit with something Marion wasn't quite sure she wanted to label as approving . . . yet neither was it *disapprov*-ing, that was sure.

"Master Wymarec left several days ago for the mouth of the Humber, preparing not only a way, but a company of Templar horse and men as escort down the coast. They will see our Queen and her treasury safely south to a waiting ship, which, along with the remainder of the gathered ransom payment, shall set out across the sea. Once those duties are discharged, our Master shall return. Of course, by then you will be gone and—" Hubert shrugged "—Master Wymarec's assurances to Queen Eleanor as to your, ah, whereabouts? They will be . . . accurate."

Much seemed at bit staggered; Marion no less.

"My lord, Com . . ." Much started, then trailed off as Hubert shifted, frowned, then reached into his sleeve and pulled out a sliver of carrot. With a lift of silver-dark brows, he shrugged at the new find, broke it into three equal pieces. At the telltale *snap*, the rounceys' ears nearly touched at the tips, nostrils flaring, eager. With a slight smile, Hubert fed the titbits, the horses making quick and greedy work of them.

"My lord," Marion said, feeling her way, "I don't understand."

"It is quite simple, really. My men have gathered your belong-ings—yours as well, Much. All of it lies neatly packed in your saddlebags, including the cloak the Queen insisted you should have, Maiden. And thus you shall return to Sherwood. Much will take you there. Such was the order of the Queen, so has our Master said"—a tiny, wolfish smile and a pat to the nose of the nearest horse—"and so it shall be done. A noble thing, to ensure one's superior does not, ah, perjure themselves."

Marion slid her gaze to Much. Several emotions were playing across his face— relief, then frustration, then resignation sliding into determination. Another surprise, that, as he was nigh as bloody capable at concealment as Gamelyn . . .

Oh.

Nay, this wouldn't do. Queenly assist or no, Masterly *faux pas* or no, this could not be.

"My lord, please." Marion stepped forwards. "Much mustn't leave here. He shouldn't leave Gamelyn behind. Surely you can't . . . you wain't make him—"

"I cannot go against my Master's orders," Hubert replied. "And from what I understand, Much has, ah, likewise been compelled to several tasks by *his* master. One of them being how he will guard you with his life." Hubert's eyes went abruptly dark and half-mast; his voice dipped. "And believe me when I say you could well spend that worthy life to no purpose if you refuse to depart these gates this afternoon."

Much stiffened and his hand, almost of its own accord, curled about the pommel of his sword. Hubert was watching him, nod-ding. The wry, wolfish smile never left his lips.

Marion's stomach lurched.

"The Solstice comes, all too soon." Hubert's comment seemed snatched from the air, a soft inconsequential—yet his gaze, glinting in the stable dim, was a rasp of steel. "And this object you were seeking? It is not here. It is unlikely—though not impossible—that it could be hidden from me in my own Temple. Neither do I want to know what it is," he added, holding up a hand as Marion started to speak. "Suffice it to be said he knows who—what—you are. He does not want to admit it—you and your brother are not what he expected, not at all. But the Lady of the Wild Things and Her Consort do things in their own fashion, with their own folk. That demands respect." To Marion's surprise, Hubert knelt and took both her hands in his. "I cannot give Her obedience—that is already sworn—but I can give fealty to Her through you, Her Huntress and Virgin *Quean*."

Upon Hubert's lips, the archaic inflection twisted from subtle insult into an ancient reverence. Marion's response was just as primordial and intuitive. Sliding her hands from his and onto his head, she bent and exhaled a tiny blessing-breath over the short-cropped grey locks. As Hubert looked up, she could see the moon-bow reflected, gleaming, in his gaze from her own.

"You *must* look after Gamelyn!" The words escaped, a knot of emotion she didn't truly want exposed. The *Solstice*, and they had to leave him here. Here, with . . .

Much looked down and away. Hubert rose to answer just as sombre—and just as revealing.

"He is the son I never had. And there are other things he, ah . . . is. Could be. Even as you, and your brother. That will protect him, Maiden. Believe me when I say to you: Gamelyn is valuable to us. None of us wish any harm to come to him. Not I and"—a shrug—"certainly not Wymarec de Birkin."

Marion wasn't altogether sure she believed that. Much gave a growling mutter, fingers not leaving his sword pommel.

"You've seen to some protection already," Hubert added. "A Mother's breath is puissant, and so will help until Gamelyn regains his own strength."

Marion blinked at him.

"Do you think you can weave a spell about my protégé and me not realise it?" Hubert chuckled. "Nay, Maiden, you are talented, yet neither am I without resources. And my Master"—another frown—"is even more powerful. We must take him at his word. I will guard the coming light and we must see you gone."

Much had moved to the horses, was already bridling the two readied to ride.

"*Allons!*" Hubert turned and spoke to Much, another quick Frankish mutter Marion didn't catch.

Much ducked his head lower, nodded, said, "Aye, my lord Com—my lord."

Then Hubert was striding away, down the stable aisle, and a sombre Much held a stirrup for Marion to step up.

It wasn't long before they were riding out the gate, their horses' hoofs a sullen, wet rhythm against slushy cobbles. Marion looked back at the Temple Hirst, her sharp and giddy sense of freedom tempered with reluctance.

"We'll fetch Robyn, come back. We'll come for Gamelyn as soon as he can travel."

"I can't come back," Much said, and put spur to his horse. "Master de Birkin's banished me from the Order."

- ENTR'ACTE -

"You . . . let them go."

"I saw no reason to keep them further. You had already passed sentence on the lay brother, Much. You told me the girl would be sent back to Sherwood—"

"After—" Wymarec bared his teeth and pretended it a smile "—I questioned her."

"You did not mention any questioning. Ever." Hubert's reply was smooth, pleasant—and just as subtly barbed. "I knew you were interested in the wolfshead's cult, but as you've said more than once, she is not the wolfshead, merely his sister. A peasant. A woman."

His own words. Wymarec smiled just that much more, hiding the slow seethe, and raised his arms at the soft "Master?" that prompted him.

It was Hubert's secondary bodyguard who assisted Wymarec with his garb—the primary one, of course, lying senseless in the adjoining chamber. Other than the one prompt, the young sergeant made no entry into, or note of, the conversation. Nor was he allowed to, being assistance, no more and no less. The sergeant dutifully unbuckled the chainmail tunic and leggings, then laid them carefully upon a nearby press where the rest of Wymarec's travel garb awaited cleaning.

Once Wymarec had found the outlaw woman and the paxman gone, he'd sped to Hubert's chambers without so much as time to change. Hubert had offered the comfort of relinquishing his travel armour—no doubt in hope of leavening his Master's disposition. Wymarec accepted the former, but refused to submit to the latter.

Hubert offered, appropriately meek, "I merely thought to observe your will, Master. They were incarcerated for several days, after all, and you only spoke with the paxman once."

"I was tied hand and foot by the Queen's demands, as well as those overdressed popinjays tumbled arse over tit as to whether they're backing the right horse!" Nay, not good, Wymarec realised; his voice was scaling upwards and betraying his agitation.

But . . . *damn* Hubert! The man had no imagination—surely if he'd more of it and less stubborn mulishness, he would have seen the opportunity.

Again, Wymarec cooled rising ire. Opportunity, indeed. Better Hubert had not seen it. He would prove too potent an adversary should he start thinking outside his own little cell of a mind. Might think to challenge his betters. Hubert was considerably gifted himself, after all. It was merely lack of imagination that kept him in his place. With it, Hubert could be a threat.

Like the ginger-haired young man with his several names.

Sir Guy de Gisbourne, once Gamelyn Boundys de Blyth, *Confanonier* to Temple Hirst, defrocked of the white—a penance for sins Wymarec had not yet been able to fully ascertain. Already possessing a reputation for ruthlessness and cunning despite his youth, Guy was bruited to be quite dedicated and—the most important—circumspect. Devout young men with an allotment of bloody purpose made for excellent Templars, no question. Easily channelled into proper uses, once they saw the paths of righteousness, they usually found obedience a relief and good work invigorating.

This one was powerful, as Hubert had said. But more intelligent than was preferable. And—obviously—conflicted. Too busy dancing avoidance with his own demons, instead of claiming and directing them. Too distracted with outside ties, Wymarec snarled to himself, where there should be none.

"Enough," he told the bodyguard. "Go."

The man bowed to both provincial Master and preceptory Commander, then exited, his arms full of chainmail and leather.

"Might there have been other methods to punish the paxman outside banishment?" Hubert had gone over to the candlelit board, poured wine into two goblets. More . . . leavening, and the words were phrased with the most respect possible. There was no excuse whatsoever for Wymarec to take umbrage.

But the fact Hubert had even *said* it . . .

"It was not permanent, Hubert."

"Six months away from the side of one's master," Hubert cradled one goblet and extended it, "can be bedevilled purgatory to an honest man."

Wymarec took the offered cup. "Good Christ, man, one would think the man was *your* shield brother!"

"I merely remark upon how my *Confanonier* will not be, ah, happy with circumstance."

"Your *Confanonier*'s happiness is of little concern, as long as he does as he is told." Wymarec went over to the main table, pondered the goblet Hubert pushed his way, then the wooden platter a servant had brought in moments after his arrival. Some slices of pork, bread, several apples. He chose an apple, drew his eating knife, and began paring it in thin, exact curls. "And if he does not, that also will be dealt with."

Hubert shook his head. "You are often cruel, Wymarec."

"Not unnecessarily, I trust. We all must use the weapons we have. I—" Wymarec shot a glare at Hubert, glad to see the other man give before the gaze "—have more powerful ones at my disposal than a short-term reprimand of banishment."

"Of that," Hubert murmured, "I am well aware. I am merely pointing out the reality of the bond between Brother Gamelyn and his paxman. It will not well dispose him to you."

Wymarec couldn't help a tiny smile. "He does not have to like us to do as we require. To respect what we wield."

Again, Hubert shook his head. Stubborn as a mule. Or he loved this ginger-haired young man more than he was letting on.

Taciturn, as well as mulish. It was hard to read Hubert.

Wymarec made his way from the private chamber, out to where the injured Templar lay. Hubert followed, silent, stood with hands clasped behind him as Wymarec peered down at the stricken man, noting every detail. The too-long coppery hair and scraggly beard; the sunken, bluish eyelids and the lax form—slightly muscle-wasted, suggesting he'd been ill and out of training for a few months at least— propped with furs and bedding. A tiny cross nestled at the pale, freckled throat, glinting dully with every hoarse breath. A mother's, no doubt. Young men took much stock in such homely things.

"Since we are speaking of your *Confanonier*, Hubert, let us continue in that vein." Too much flesh came away with the apple skin; Wymarec adjusted his angle. "You have called him Gamelyn more than once, now. I thought his name was Gisbourne, akin to yours. Guy de Gisbourne."

"A name he took in penance, along with the black. Mayhap now he has done penance enough."

Wymarec cut a quarter of flesh from the apple and ate it slowly, watching Hubert with eyes narrowed. Hubert did care for the young man!

Ah, such things were understandable. All too easy, in a world of darkness, to draw close to anything promising fire, and heat.

"If he survives this latest trauma—and I think he will, Hubert, our Brother Infirmarer is one of the best to come out of the African north—then young Guy could prove quite an asset."

"So I have said, more than once." Hubert shrugged agreement. "Yet obstacles remain. He wears the black for several reasons. One being that his soul is not merely of the Temple."

"Yet *that*," Wymarec countered, nipping another apple quarter from his knife, "is what most intrigues me. He is of us, yet there are also these ties. Such a deep and powerful attachment to such . . . primitive forces."

"I would also"—Hubert's words were respectful, but too firm—"warn against holding such wild magic too lightly, Wymarec."

"I do not take it lightly, Hubert. Not at all."

"Contempt has many faces," Hubert persisted—and while Wymarec didn't like his tone before, now it was flat annoying. "I myself knew the old man who came before this wolfshead hero, this Robyn Hode." He used the old inflection with purpose, Wymarec noted. With respect. Hubert had been born in Normandy, but he loved England no less than Wymarec, whose family had been Saxon thegns. "The old one too had powers the likes of which I've not seen. They won him the leadership of the Shire Wode covenant when he was not much older than this successor of his, and that back during the Anarchy. To underestimate that successor—or the girl who has gone back to his forest—would be a grave mistake. It is that I warn against."

Wymarec devoured the last quarter of apple, kept every bit of ire tight-leashed. "I appreciate," he said, clipped, "the warning. However." He looked over, held Hubert's gaze. "You seem . . . somewhat noncompliant, Hubert. About much surrounding this subject."

"You misconstrue, Master." The address was adroit; reminder, perhaps, to both of them. "I exist to serve our Order."

"Good. We shall both see to this latest important service, Hubert. The Temple cannot afford to lose such a talent."

"I have attempted to bring my *Confanonier* into the arms of the Inner Temple," Hubert countered. "It has been . . . difficult."

"Then we must overcome the difficulty."

"Ah." Hubert took a drink from his goblet, peered at Wymarec. "Do you think I have not already tried?"

"I think you have." Wymarec smiled and tossed the apple core into a tip at the bed's foot. "I, on the other hand, have not.

"Leave us."

Hubert hesitated—only slight, but there. Then, without looking at Wymarec: "As the Master commands."

As Hubert retreated into his own chamber, closing the door firmly, Wymarec started to uncover one hand. He hesitated, put cautious fingers to the young Templar's head and brought them back for inspection. Nodded. The girl must have washed it after the surgery, or else the man's paxman. Ex-paxman.

So reassured, Wymarec peeled the glove from his left hand, touched fingers once again to the ruddy hair. Twirled it, idly, in his hands.

The longest night, tonight. There would never be a better time.

With his other hand, Wymarec yanked the woollens down. Slid flat eyes over the fresh bandages, the fair skin prickling with the sudden chill, eyed farther down . . . there. Smiled again.

Ah, Guy. Or is it, indeed, Gamelyn? You remembered, didn't you? Despite the ban I laid, you remembered. And I remember you, very well. Before this is over, we will know each other better, you and I.

Wymarec closed his eyes, opened his arms, and stood. He kept the Working close about him, nigh invisible, and with one raised hand traced the sigil into the air above the solitary cot. His lips moved, sounding silent placations and prayers to the lords of the four quadrants, invoking their names, their beings. And when, finally, the sigil glowed, five points and all fiery angles behind his eyes, he opened those eyes and raised his voice for the first time—albeit a soft hiss, the final paean of a litany:

"*Agla*, O Bornless One, Manifestor and Begetter, He of Many Names, *Iao!* Shield my works and my way." Even softer, "Amen."

And Wymarec reached out, took delicate hold of the narrow cord girdling Gamelyn's waist.

- XXI -

M arion shot bolt upright, her hoarse shout still echoing in the rafters.

A rustle, the feel of things quaking and shifting about her, and a shadow hurrying over. Strong hands grabbed at her arms, pulling her. Still caught in the formlessness of dreams—nightmares—Marion struck back, loosed a kick, and twisted nearly free.

A grunt, a vehement string of soft curses, then Much said, "Faith, woman, but you kick like a jenny ass, see if you don't."

And the quaking, shifting something came cascading down, in a slick-dry, sweet-smelling avalanche of dust and prickles to nigh bury them both.

They dug to the surface, literally swimming in hay, and it all came back to Marion. They'd found the small village just as they thought they were going to have to risk freezing to death in some shallow cavern off the road. Moreover, the villagers had honoured hearth right, given space for two travellers and their horses in the common hayshed. Much had put a few silver pennies in the headman's hand to make up for the trouble, as well.

The longest night of the year was not one to spend out, particularly when it was stacking up to also be one of the coldest.

Much came breasting through the hay, shrugged free of the fallen stack, and started picking bits of chaff from his beard. "I hope," he said, eyeing the stack where it had fallen, "they en't expecting us to shift it back."

Marion waded free, brushing at her fancy green bliaut. Little better than a hay magnet, it was. She grimaced and bent over, tossing her hair forwards to shake it, too, free of hay. The air upon her nape inspired a sudden shiver, and with it came memory: the tenor of her dream . . .

A burning brand, five points of a star hanging in the black, thick air, and the lurch and shift of a strong will being thwarted. . .

"Are you all right?" It was low, troubled.

Marion looked up to see Much eyeing her, also half-bent, shifting hay from beneath his tunic. She didn't know what to answer; felt as if she were indeed cocooned, and not in hay but wool batting—the same sort her mother used to cradle eggs in to keep them from breaking in the market baskets.

"All right, then? Marion?" Much came over, arms folded over his broad chest, concern plain. It was nigh bright as day with the full moon shining through the high loft opening, and reflections from the snow outside.

"Just a bad dream." Even though it was more, she was sure of it—but it was also fleeting, the notion, and darted out of reach even as she thought to test it.

He peered at her for a moment more, then gave a flash of teeth amidst dark beard and shadows as he went to go ensure the horses—supposedly in their own corner by a pair of stalled dry cows—hadn't been the cause for their bed to collapse.

"At least none'll take you without missing some bits in the doin'."

Marion grinned despite herself as he ambled over and started fussing at the chestnut rouncey, who had been bullied away from the best of the allotted fodder. In consequence, the little mare had decided all that piled hay was too tempting, and untied her lead to creep over in her hobbles.

Much didn't act a man bereft of purpose or torn from everything he'd known. He seemed to have even more of one, grimly driving himself and Marion both as hard as was safe or feasible along the snow-lined roads.

At least those had so far proven solid, not a wash of mud and slop. But such had its own difficulties. Driven to reach their destination or no—and before more snow would fall and perhaps trammel them in an unfamiliar place, beholden to who knew—considerable care had to be taken with their mounts. The roads were treacherous after another fashion: rutted hard with the cold, all too easy to bruise a hoof, turn a fetlock, slide sideways if one wasn't paying serious attention.

Marion and Much both paid attention. They'd made it their business to stay out of the main road ruts; the swarded sides were easier going, almost soft in comparison. But that meant more loose snow, which meant more time ensuring it didn't pack solid in their horses' hoofs and lame them that way. Slowed travel and the bitter weather meant shelter had to be found more often.

Which had brought them this far at least. Owston was a small village, claimed from Royal Forest, but it was a prosperous one. The size of their overnight shelter—the village's hay shed—attested to that.

Marion had almost expected pursuit, after the way Hubert had let them go. But, nothing. She wasn't sure if it made her feel any easier in her mind, though.

"The dream," Much said, pulling Marion from her backwards musings. "It weren't nowt to do wit' . . . ?" It dragged off midquery; Marion made a silent finish for him.

Gamelyn? I fear it is, but I fear more if it en't.

Silence. "I'd know," she said, low, "did he worsen. I don't think I could help but know."

"The cross." It was a breath, almost of relief. "I'd forgotten." Another pause. "I'm glad. Glad one of us . . . "

Again, the pause, this one more than telling. *I should know. Should be there.*

And Marion couldn't order him back there, not now. Wouldn't be able to even when they did reach their cavern-camp in the Shire Wode. Assuming they did reach it.

"This is no time for travelling," Much said, as if he'd heard her thoughts. "I were thinkin' on that, all the way here, and the weather just looks to worsen as we go south." His face was hidden as he turned to her, moonlight spilling over his hair and shoulders, fetching forth glints of stray fodder. "The headman here, he were talking of snowstorms and drifts high as a man's head, goin' into Peak."

Summer sleeps, in the dark and cold, and Winter trapped overlong. It was lethargic, the Lady's puissance lulled to a soft sigh. As if She would lie down and sleep with them.

"We have to try to reach our people." It was higher than Marion liked, reedy-thin as any girl with breasts unbudded.

"I know. I know it en't right to burden any other than our own wi' more mouths to feed through winter," Much agreed. "Which is what I were thinkin' on. See, Auckely's a mite closer than the horse caves and t' Shire Wode. I've people there—family, like—who wain't begrudge us a place 'til weather shifts to better. Particularly as we can pay our way," he added, a bit wry, and Marion remembered he was the fifth of eight children, the youngest son, at that.

He looked so tense, she felt she had to answer. Unfortunately what came out was not what she expected.

"You're taking me to meet your family?"

And oh, but blast, *bugger*, and damn, what a thing to blurt out!

Much went so abruptly and unnaturally still, Marion was afraid she'd turned him to stone. She was wishing she had the power, about now, and over her *mouth*.

"I'm ower chancy," he admitted, still unmoving—and his voice seemed forced, grating outward, "at durst bringing the likes of *you* home to me ma."

Mortification twisted into confusion. "What is that supposed to mean?"

"What d'you *think* I mean by it, woman?" Intemperate, the query—but somehow more to himself, more inward than outward. "My people are good Heathens. Auckley has a sacred spring up from t' mill. D'you think they wain't know you?"

"So I en't common *enough*?"

"That en't—!" Movement, finally. Much wrenched around so quick he skated sidewise on the loose hay underfoot. Cursing, he caught his balance, skipped a few steps away, arms flailing and spooking the little mare.

Who had crept back over to the hay pile and was snatching from the bottom, sly and quick between munches.

"None o' that," Much growled, ostensibly to the mare, but more than a little at Marion as well. He made a feint for the mare; she pinned her ears, sidled crossways.

Marion went after, cutting the mare off. "You are bloody *impossible!*" She was, most definitely, not talking to the horse. "You en't making any sense!"

"I'm making sense, you just en't wanting to hear 't, is all I can figure," Much growled right back, sliding on the hay as he tried to catch the mare. "You are as you are, and I am as I—*bugger* you, you silly bitch!"

The little chestnut was having a proper game of it, hopping around in those hobbles like some dancing trickster of a jongleur, the chewed-off end of her tether like a mocking tongue waggling at them.

"You're used to your brother, who hangs his heart behind his eyes. Or milord, who's too concerned sommun'll find he actually has one. You ken nowt to do on a man who likes his heart just where it is."

"That's you all over!" Marion sniped back. "Just where it is, all fine and rock-solid . . . and sodding *impenetrable*, like! You'd not even be here if your master hadn't ordered you to—ah!" Marion snatched at the half-chewed lead attached to the mare's head collar. "Caught you, little vixen!" With a sniff in Much's direction, Marion began to half skate, half slide over the hay, leading the mare to the other side of the shed. "Coom by, lass. We'll go ower here, so all these evil-tempered geldings wain't bully us from t' fodder."

The words were proper shot from a mocking bow, as was the pat and croon to the little chestnut as Marion started to lead her to the opposite wall. The mare walked a few steps, halted all bug-eyed, and shied back as Much cut them off. The small spook nearly yanked Marion off her own feet.

Nearly. Much had grabbed Marion by the other arm, and before she could think, he'd one hand curling around her nape. Before she could as much as say a word, he'd bent in and kissed her. Broke it to say, swift against her mouth, "I might've been of t' Templars, but I en't no bloody *gelding.*" Kissed her again. Hard.

Her arms almost flapped. She didn't know what to do for a wild spasm of heartbeats. Couldn't believe what *he* was doing.

And Sweet Lady, was he *good* at it.

Her lips parted beneath his, and Marion let out a soft, aching gasp into his mouth, and her brain went into rampant, blissful dormancy.

But her arms were still *flapping.*

Are you daft?—use those hands to grab *him, you idiot!* something carped at her, *before he changes his mind!*

One hand found purchase—but in her own kirtle. The other one did better; it slapped flat against Much's broad chest, fingers starting to dig in as Marion finally— *finally*—was able to convince enforced chastity instincts that four years was just three sodding years and eleven months plus twenty-odd days too *long.*

Blast and bugger, but he *did* change his mind. Shoved away from her, backing like a well-trained destrier. Somehow her hands finally got the message, the one tangling in his tunic and refusing to let go even when he kept up the retreat.

They ended up against the far wall with a proper stiff *thud* and a grunt from Much, and he stammered, "I . . . I'm sorry. I'm—"

"I'm not," Marion said, and leaned in.

And bloody *damn,* but he was fast. He'd ducked, grabbed her wrists, twisted, and had her up against the wall, nearly on her toes, before she could blink. Then he started to lean in, and as her body arched a bit mindlessly, she smiled, considered mayhap this posi-tion was a fair one. Unfortunately, just before their bodies aligned, he ducked his head and held her at arms' length.

"I en't just here because of me orders. That's t' problem, and . . . and I'm *sorry.* I . . . I've no excuse. This en't my right—"

"Your *what?*" she snapped. "What are you—?"

"I've no rights to this. No right t—and sod me, woman, but there's neither of us thinking straight, bloody tired and nerve-raw—"

This time Marion slapped both hands against his chest. Hard, and fancied she saw the Great Templar Paxman wince. "Rights? Your *rights?* You mean to *me?*"

"You know what I mean, an—"

"I know what you said, but the meaning's nowt but gibberish—"

"I'm speaking plain as I can, and nowt but truth!" His voice had scaled upwards, tight and frantic. Not that neither of their voices had gone much above a frantic murmur, and no less vehement for that. His hands, still on her wrists, were brutal, tight and quivering.

He meant it, no question.

Marion lifted her chin, nostrils flaring, spoke with clipped calm. "Let's talk about 'rights,' then. What you're saying, plain as you can. Like it's yours to say, yours to decide who's *allowed* to say. Or that I'm already deeded to sommun like I were nowt but *property!*"

"That en't my meaning, woman!" Much protested.

"Then what, exactly"—still flat, still furious, and if she could have wrenched her hands free and slapped him again, she would have—"is your meaning, *man?*"

"Bloody . . . d'you truly need me to spell it out, wallow in it? En't this humiliating enough for the both of us?"

I only see one of us being humiliated here, you sodding daft bonehead of a soldier, and it en't you.

Much was still stammering, still low and earnest and blurting out words as if they might bite him. "I'm no . . . I en't t' Summerlord. I en't King of the Winter Wode. I'm nowt, and I've no rights to even touch the hem of your kirtle, let alone thinkin' what I've thought since the moment I saw you in *his* arms."

His arms. *His.* . . Marion mired in a hot wash of humiliation and confusion, then suddenly, understood.

Filthy, lousy, with a torn dress and bloody legs from her stay in the Nottingham oubliette, they'd come for her, not *left her there* but taken her up and out and away, but not before Gamelyn—Guy, then, *Gisbourne*—had held her, rocked and comforted her so close-tight she thought she'd fall into a thousand pieces of need and desperation and gratitude.

And somehow, Much followed her, either with his own bit of magic or she was blasting it like an unshielded lamp against a gaol wall, for he shook his head, fingers tightening against her, said, low and vehement, "*Nay.* 'Twasn't just that. If I'm no gelding, you en't no fair victim t' rescue neither, no matter what auld bloody Scathelock would like. But it . . . it's only . . . " He fell silent, and for so long, Marion was afraid he'd say nothing more.

Then, "'Tis what's meant. And just that obvious. Wit' every glance you give him. Every word you speak with his name following. And he's one I wain't cross, even could I." His hands had loosened, slid down to hold at her elbows, lingering, thumbs rubbing back and forth, back and forth. "Y'see, we *both* love him that hard and fine, Lady."

Marion didn't know what to say, how to form the words.

Until he said, again, adamant: "You're Maiden t' Shire Wode. It en't my right to win and woo you."

"'Tisn't Beltane, this night, but the longest of nights," she said back, sudden-soft. "And whether I'm Maiden of t' Shire Wode with the Maying blood running in hot rut, or whether I'm Marion of Sherwood, the lone bitch in my brother's pack of Heathen wolves, seems to me 'tis *my* right to say who'll woo or win me." She bent closer, whispered, "Not yours. Not any man's. *Mine.*"

He was the one, now, all mired uncomprehending. Or mayhap he comprehended just enough, for as she leaned even closer, he loosed a tiny, halting breath. She took that breath, then with a flick of tongue and a tiny press of teeth, took his mouth with hers.

The hands holding her own against the wall quivered. Tightened.

Then he was kissing her back, rough but sweet as stolen honeycomb. Leaning into her, pressing her spine to scrape against the rough-hewn wood of the shed wall, and her hair to catch in the grain and edge of his beard as he left her mouth to trace his lips up to her temple, hanging there.

And Much *stayed* there, for three, then four deep breaths, as if mapping the scent of her, or unsure.

Her left leg was plenty sure for both of them; knee hiking up, lower leg curling up and around his right buttock. His body, too, seemed to have its own ideas, listing inward.

"*My* right," she whispered in his ear. "So do you want to fill me, pet?"

Another shudder, yet there was nothing hesitant about the sway of his hips as she curled both arms around him, hands pressing against the small of his back and urging him closer. He obliged, with a sound deep-kindled in his throat and one hand sliding across the wall to tangle in her hair . . . and Sweet *Lady*, but what a haunch he had on him, solid with muscle rippling against her thigh as she tightened against him. And *that* too, with a skinning knife's graceful curve, but blunt-thick, and lurching all sudden and importunate to butt against her belly.

A soft growl vibrating her own throat, Marion reached down, but Much was too quick for her, already on another trail. He ran his lips down her throat, lightly skimmed the freckles smattered there, then dipped lower, tongue and heat of breath tracing the curve of one breast, around and up, lingering at the nipple risen hard beneath linen and woollen.

Her free hand, thwarted of grasping that lovely not-dagger, tangled in her own skirts, hiking them up to further free the leg curling snug at his arse. His hand loosed her hair, with a slight pull of her head sideways, and slid down to grasp her bared thigh. Marion gave a gasp, haunches tightening, hips rocking forwards, and the sword-callused fingers spread, clutching her even closer, if it were possible. With a shake his hand gentled, smoothed upwards, mapping more freckles and fine, gilt hairs. Gripping into her haunch, curving around, lifting her up on the very edge of her toes. Sliding knowing fingers down the cleft of her buttocks, and down.

Breath rattled against her breasts as he found what he sought, chill fingers diving into warm-slick willingness. She echoed his rattle and raised it a gasp as he stroked, slow and maddening.

Marion pulled her other arm free from the wall, tangled her fingers in dark hair—it was long enough, now, to clutch and tug—and this time when she reached between their tight-hoved bodies, she bloody well *found* him. Well, he was coming up to greet her, no question, and she smiled, clutched, and tugged a bit more. Then it was only the small matter of tunic yanked upwards and a duck beneath linen braies, before Marion wrapped long fingers about him and played him like a reed pipe. With almost the same breathy sounds, only an octave or so lower.

Aye, there was something to be said for knowing what a lad liked. Even if she was proper out of practise.

She must have said it aloud, for Much chuckled against her, said, "Tis like riding a horse, aye? Once you know the rhythm, you en't forgettin . . . " It trailed off, a groan replacing the chuckle, and a soft "Ah, pet, much more of *that* and I'll not be filling anything but your hand."

"That'll do," she said, soft.

"But it en't what I were hoping for."

"Twere more, either way," she said as he lifted her, and locked her firm against the wall, "than I ever dared t' be hoping for."

Robyn couldn't sleep.

The emptiness had, for nigh onto several days, been a blessing. A soft blank that had allowed him ease both waking and sleeping, a cocoon of blissful comfort, without the constant writhe and com-mingle of danger and hardship. A space of nothingness, biding where the Horned Lord would normally rake velveted tines, forging edges of razor-sharp bone and will.

Gamelyn would have called it: *Eden.*

Robyn smiled. Even John's croft-bred apprehension of fae doings had mellowed, in the soft pale of this cocoon. The smile gentled as Robyn nuzzled a warm breath into brown hair, then slipped. From the depths of the caverns came a flutter. Moth-wings in the dark, contemplating a fired candle.

Robyn wasn't that far gentled. He reached out for the quillion dagger, smoothed his fingers over the tang and down the blade. Breathed the charm of iron into the cavern, felt it vibrate into rock and air.

The flutter stilled.

Robyn waited a short while, to be sure, then shrugged and pulled his arm back beneath the furs, easing it once more around John's ribs. John murmured, curled closer to Robyn. Fingers splaying against warm, pale skin, Robyn peered at the stony ceiling, frowning.

The heart beating within John's ribs and against Robyn's palm seemed . . . slowed. As if a false shot had winged time to drag itself, wounded, between one blood-thrum and the next. And against all sense, for the previous night that same, lovely-steady heart had seemed too swift, beats pressing together with hardly a pause.

Even accounting for the fact that John really, *really* liked being tupped into the next fortnight.

And there was something beyond the caverns, something *happening*. Robyn merely suspected, where in truth he should be able to reach out, find out, *know*. Yet it lay just out of reach, a mere itch, and one Robyn couldn't so much as scratch. It wasn't eased with food or befuddled with sleep. It couldn't even be sated against John's warm body.

Another rustle, deeper, this, but louder. And murmurs, this time— he'd swear it.

Robyn rolled to his feet, naked with dagger in hand. The heat of his body steamed into the chill cavern, but his low voice frosted the stones.

"What do you want, then?"

But of course, there was no answer.

"Have you been growing your hair for me?"

"Um. Mayhap."

Marion gave the brown forelock a tug. They were lying in the hay, padded and swathed in furs and one corner of Much's cloak— save for one of Marion's legs. She was on her belly, propped on her elbows; Much lay on his side, and seemed fascinated by that leg. He kept tracing his fingers back and forth.

"You said it," he deferred, with another of those laconic shrugs. "Whilst milord lay so ill. 'Twere the only row you and yer brother had in that dreadful moon, and 'twere about milord's hair. Robyn, well, he were willin' to owt, would've spilt his own blood t' see Gamelyn well again, and whole, and he said when he were sick, auld Cernun had cut off his hair t' cool the brain fever. The two of you, snapping at each other, worn out, and you wouldn't back down. You said you knew how much Robyn loved his hair, and that you loved it just as much and you'd save him without that sacrifice, see if you wouldn't." His voice shook, dipped, and he raised his hand to cup her face. "And you did. You saved him."

She nuzzled her face into his palm, kissed it. There were tears, fresh and fat, in his eyes.

"Aye," she murmured against his wrist, "I know what to do with a man who likes his heart just where it is. Just ride beside him during the day, and atop him at night, is what I'll do."

And it looked like she'd finally found a way to broach Templar Stone. Much looked quite fetching with a rose bloom upon his brown cheeks. Even in moonlight. He bent to her thigh, nipped it.

Marion snorted. "Aye, well, an' change the subject—"

"Aye, well, an' I'll do just that. For I've never seen so many freckles on sommun." There was a distinct smirk playing wry with the curve of his lip. "Cept milord, mayhap," he added, flipping her skirt higher to expose one milky-pale buttock to the moonlight. "Only he's got 'em on his arse."

"I've not been bare-arsed in the sun for a long time," Marion defended, flipping her skirt back. "Brrr!—quit staring at my arse and warm me up a bit, wain't you?" A chuckle, fond. "Me mam nigh had me ears when I were a barely ripe lass and fetched a few freckles in places she thought me a mite young for yet."

"It's a proper lovely arse," Much said, still grinning, then pulled her closer, yanking up the cloak.

"Mine or Gamelyn's?" Marion cut grey eyes at him, all innocence.

"What do you think?" Much snorted, mock-stern, and gave another yank at his cloak to cover her further. "I fear I en't the best authority on lads' arses. Happens your brother'd be the one to ask."

Marion sobered, snugged closer. "We'll have the chance, sooner than late."

Both arms curled about her, stout but gentle, as Much buried his cheek in her hair and breathed her in. "For one, if not the other."

"We *will*," she insisted, but he wouldn't meet her eyes.

She spoke no more of Temple Hirst, but it *was* sooner, rather than late, they were able to ride into the Shire Wode.

Instead of the weather they'd been expecting from the headman of Owston's dire predictions of snow and ice on the way south, the waning Solstice moon brought sunny skies and clear, if cold, travel through Yorkshire on the King's Road. Snowy patches, to be sure, and firm roads slowing them with due caution—and caution to be shown, as well, in which villages they took shelter at night. Much's purse found them several warm meals and spare cots—once another barn, where they felt at liberty to share more than a cloak and a few kisses in the dark. On the road, if there were any outlaws who thought to brave the cold or Robyn Hood's territory, none wanted to brave the set of Much's shoulders, the light bow strung ready at Marion's back, or the fine steel sheathed at Much's saddle cantle and belt.

A stop at Auckley was no longer deemed necessary, but at Marion's insistence, they stabled the horses at an inn in Whitwell, with coin to feed them for several fortnights. She intended to have a swift way back to Hirst; was sure Robyn would, as well.

Even if Much still refused to speak of it.

They walked the rest of the way, a steady pace over thawing snow and through bare, wintering woodland. As they drew nigh to their destination, the signs were clear, to those as knew how to read them—and those who did would either know they were welcome, or would be wary enough to stay far away. While Robyn had been fair specific of which cavern, there was the possibility plans had changed, and shifting might have been done. But the runes led Marion and Much to a place fond-remembered from girlhood: a deep, beautiful sink of rock, cool in summer and warm in winter, with ancient pictures drawn upon the walls depicting wild horses and a different sort of horned one long disappeared from these lands: the aurochs.

When she gave the signal, the answer was immediate, and it wasn't too long before golden tongues of light marked the ascent of torches from the depths to the snow-fringed entry.

"*Marion!*" Will came running up, grabbed her in a hard hug and swung her around several times before he set her down. She hugged him back, turned to greet David, then Arthur and Gilbert—more hugs.

Happy to see her, yet . . . there was a thread of tension beneath. Marion frowned.

Will put her off such thoughts by slinging an arm over Marion's shoulders, drawing her close with a tiny shake. His eye was on Much, who had stayed a small distance back of her, watching the reunion.

"I thought you were staying longer, and I sure wain't 'spectin' you to bring comp'ny back."

"Hullo, Much." Gilbert strode up, one arm outstretched. "Don't mind him, he's no manners."

"Well, I didn't *know* he were coming back," Will shot back as Gilbert and Much clasped arms. "Marion, there's sommat as—"

Marion was watching Much, not liking the tense diffidence she saw in his expression. She started for him.

Will hung on. "Marion—"

"Let go, Will."

"Nay, but—"

Gilbert was speaking quietly to Much, whose frame had stiffened. Marion knew he was nevertheless watching; she gave a shrug, and when Will still didn't release her, growled to herself.

Aye, not this time. Not again. We're done, lads.

She pushed at Will. "Let me go, William, or I'll do you one." The soft snarl was altogether reminiscent of her mother on a no-non-sense tear; Will remembered Eluned well enough. With a tiny start he released her.

"Marion." David reached for her arm, this time, and Will's repeat urgent upon her heels. "*Marion*, you need to listen!"

Gilbert turned from Much. Much's eyes went to hers, with a concern mirroring the warble in Will's voice, the frown upon Gilbert's face.

"Will's right, lass," David agreed, and it was then she saw—truly saw—how it wasn't just Will who bided tense as an unbroken colt, but all of them.

"The weather's been so bad, until just yesterday," Gilbert said, "and the thaw."

"We couldn't so much as go look for 'em," Arthur added, miserable.

Look for them.

"Where's John?" she asked, her voice scaling suddenly tight. "Where's Robyn?"

"They both went to Mam Tor upon t' moon-dark," Will said. "You know he don't like it when we come after him, but . . . "

"But." Marion felt her knees go wobbly. Much came up behind her, put a hand on her shoulder, and she gave a sudden and heavy lean back against him, uncaring of the looks garnered or the sudden pinch to Will's face. "But that was—"

"Over a fortnight ago," Much finished. It was low, but it echoed past the rest of the outlaws, poured down into the caverns and came back, mocking.

For'nigh o . . . for'nigh o . . .

- XXII -

At first, it is like an itch he cannot scratch. Then it graduates to the tingling of a blood-starved limb waking from numbness.

Gamelyn growls in sleep, turns over, refuses to hear.

And though he well knows what will happen next, somehow he cannot make himself react—as if it is happening to someone else, somewhen else. Some*when.*

A snarl in the dim—"I told you to get up!"—and the shock and disruption of peaceful, warm slumber, bedclothes flung back, dragged up by the hair across cold stones to an ice-encrusted washtub. Shoved in headfirst and held there by a hard hand at his nape. Gamelyn struggles, bubbling and gurgling and trying not to suck frigid water down his windpipe.

Drowning. He is *drowning.*

The panic is very real, still has the power to set lightning through his nerves. With a strength Gamelyn knows/did not realise he had, he twists, ducks . . . Escapes.

Turns on his elder brother as panic boils itself dry and into fury. Gamelyn knows he will win this bout, will manage to fetch his own, silent and unexpected blows before their father comes down the hall . . .

But there is no one there. Only the stone walls around him. And the water bucket is smaller, dry with dust and cracking in the heat.

An abandoned keep in the desert, only Much is not at his side and where is . . . ?

From behind him it comes, a loud *shuss* and slide across the dry stones, and a huge, rattling hiss.

Gamelyn does not move, slides his eyes to see what he knows/did not know would be there. The cobra is bigger, somehow, than he remembers—

Remembers?

—rearing up, hood flared, swaying. He will feint with his left, use the sword in his right, and—

The cobra goes for his eyes. Gamelyn has no time to consider any conundrum; he dances out of reach, unthinking, and manages to grab the serpent behind its flat, dusty head. With a sculpt and whistle of thin, hot air, he swings his sword.

Halts, just before the sword hews the snake's head from its body. For the cobra is gone, and Gamelyn now holds a man by the throat, wheezing in the iron-hard cage of his fingers, kneeling on the sandy floor.

"You have won this bout, my *Confanonier*," Hubert concedes, then growls, "But you have failed to return what I asked, eh?"

"F-failed?" Gamelyn stammers, loosing his hold. Almost immediately, something at the hollow of his throat starts to sting. Raising a hand, he bats at it, wonders if the cobra managed to spit at him after all.

"Where is the goddess's Arrow? The Horns of the god?"

"But you . . . you *know* . . ."

"What"—Hubert's eyes gleam, too pale in the dusty keep—"do I know, then?"

The sting heats to burning. Gamelyn curses, drops his sword, and reaches for his throat, merely to find a chain there, and a small talisman. No venom, no threat—nay, this soothes. Croons, and wraps a soft-steel protection about his name.

Gamelyn.

Oakbrother.

The room goes dark and cool, then goes . . . away. Instead, there is a faint patter of rain against leaves, and the taste of tree-wet dripping upon his lips.

Then hands, long and callused and *familiar*, curling around his waist and tangling—delicious, half-painful—in the cord at his naked waist.

So—a breath against his ear—*that is how it is with you, eh?*

Gamelyn stiffens.

The voice is not Robyn's. Neither is the hand, twining in the cord at his waist. Twining in his *will.*

Again, the burning at his throat: warning. Redoubt.

For this is a siege. He is under siege.

Soft mockery answers. "Indeed, my lord. But you hold well. Despite the ban I laid, you remembered me."

Remember. Aye, the memory was there. The sense, the . . . *taste* of this will. The voice hangs midair, shifting into silence to hang within his *mind.*

And this ability of yours. This remarkable strength. You parry as skilful with your mind as with a sword. You. . . intrigue me.

It probes for weakness, seeking entry through some magic of memory—or trying to, anyway. But Gamelyn is somehow not weak, here, and the talisman nestled at his throat means to protect what might weaken. Things shift and shimmer about him as if the weaving of his own threads, the shape and weft of fate—*tynged*—hangs in stasis.

Now is here. Or there. Tomorrow is . . . Yesterday. Or a fortnight's waiting.

I also remember you. Before this is over, we will know each other better, Templar.

Nay. The negation fills his breast with blood-heat, spreads, then sinks. It purls into the deeps: a predator's rumble, the rank scent of must and a gleam of teeth and eyes against torchlight, the rasp of horns being sharpened against an oak branch, to come away tangled with mistletoe. *I don't think we shall.* Gamelyn reaches up to the talisman at his throat, cups it.

How disappointing. You would use women's *tools against me?*

His mother's cross, Marion's blood, the Lady's mark upon him. Gamelyn smiles, grim. *Oh, I shall. And more.*

Good. The Templar lord glides from the darkness, gives a graceful, nigh-mocking bow. *That shall make our little interactions fascinating, indeed.* Then he smiles, and . . .

And walks away.

"Bloody damn," Will muttered. "This makes no sense."

They had halted in sheer consternation, gathering together uneasily: a small and ragged group of fur-wrapped searchers broaching the dips and slopes of the Peak. Beneath their feet crunched cold, winter-leached grass. The wind was harsh here, blowing down through the valley, and bitter with the tang of snow, which still lay upon the upper elevations.

The long fur of Marion's wolf-lined hood tossed in the wind, slapping and stinging despite her numb cheeks. She had pulled the outlaws from a mire of indecision—indeed, had the rights to approach the Tor as much as Robyn—but she'd not expected to lead them into such as this.

Across the valley it meandered, pristine and sparkling, through some chance that couldn't have been mere chance. Snow had retreated from the remainder of the lowland moors. The ground beneath their feet squelched soggy, bespeaking the thaw and warmer air that lingered despite the bitter wind. Yet before them lay a thick, uncanny swath of snow, cascading down the hillside and towards the entrance to the Hunter's cavern like a frozen river.

Arthur made a warding sign. Much whispered a small charm, shook his head, and looked away.

No wonder, the closer they had come to this place, the more Marion had felt that sensation again, of wool and soft chains.

She didn't care for it, not at all.

Will came up the slope to stand beside Marion. "No wonder they en't come out. If they think it's like this all the way out . . . damn. No wonder we en't seen 'em. What sorcery is this?"

"No sorcery."

"Marion—"

"This en't sorcery. Nowt made by man or woman. 'Tis deeper, and . . . " Marion shivered.

"Deeper?" Will's hand touched her elbow, asking. Marion turned to him, found no high-handedness to the gesture, merely concern. Not that she could see much of his expression; he'd started a beard for the winter, and all that was visible beyond that and the woollen wrap snugged about his head were narrowed amber eyes, fair forelock, and reddened, broad nose. Plus a frown etched above the bridge of that nose.

"Aye," she answered. "Familiar. Somehow."

The frown turned thoughtful, and Will squeezed and released his hold, considering the terrain ahead.

"You sure they're in there, lass?" Arthur, on the other hand, was sceptical. "We'll pay some hell digging through that drift."

Marion looked to Arthur's right hand, where Much stood, once again composed. Willing to the wait, his eyes on her, all comfort and confidence.

Her mouth twitched his direction, and she turned back to the snow. "Then we'd best start breaking trail."

Robyn crouched, looking down a narrow, dark tunnel. With the tip of his dagger, he drew shapes in the dust just inside the salt traced in a half arc against that tunnel's entry. He was careful not to disturb the warding—John would have his ears, should he.

There was an allure, there, in the tunnel depths. Something that was Robyn's by rights, should he choose to reach for it. A power that sang behind his ears, and drove his fingers to make sigils in the dust in a language his brain didn't know but his heart kenned. And his lips, tracing the sounds of the marks . . .

A hand came down into his vision, with a swift scuff smeared the tracings. Robyn started. He hadn't so much as heard John approach. That in itself was unsettling.

Too close! John signed, vehement. *They're too close to you. They'll sing in your blood, and you'll go—*

"D'you think I'm daft?" Robyn huffed, and started to brush at his dusty hands.

John grabbed Robyn's fingers, forestalling him, using both their hands to point at what Robyn had been tracing. Old marks, pictures of ancestral talk long before letters and words had begun. Learnt from an old man by two lads—one nigh mute, the other sore wounded from an arrow in his breast named Sorrow—over a long and bitter season spent underground in a battle with Death.

John's fingers trailed up Robyn's arm and gripped the curls of his beard, yanking his chin upwards. "*I* hear it." His fingers tightened, nigh painful. "In *my* blood. Through yours."

Robyn held the brown eyes with his own for long moments. John remained adamant, grip and focus. Finally Robyn looked down, muttered, "M sorry."

A kiss against his temple, gentle acceptance.

"We're both a bit daft, bunged up in this cavern," Robyn furthered, rising from his crouch, sticking the dagger in his belt and dusting at his hands. "Surely t' weather's to break soon. Another three days, we'll be down to lean rations."

"En't soon enough," John growled, soft against the dark tunnel. It almost seemed something echoed back at him—soft murmurs, footfalls?—and they both alerted. Silence. Then, again, the echo.

"It's echoing off the back," Robyn declared, "but it en't coming from there, I'd swear to 't."

John nodded. His head was cocked, listening.

Voices. Human *voices.*

Then a whistle, echoing against the rocks. John grinned at Robyn, who put fingers to his mouth and answered Will's query: *Right here, you daft pillock!* And Marion's voice, full of relief. "*Robyn?*"

They didn't even bother to ask how it was possible, just darted for the upper caverns.

⊠

"A . . . fortnight."

Marion nodded, and Will put in, eagerly, "The thaw happened

half a se'nnight ago, Robyn. Upon the Solstice, at that. Another day at the most, then Arthur and me were coming."

"A *fortnight*," Robyn said again.

"And then comes Marion, with Much," Arthur put in. "She led us in."

"Snapped our heels, more like," Will said, wry. "Said we'd waited too long."

"Well, you had," Marion retorted.

And aye, but that sounded more like the sister Robyn had once known. His eyes went to Much, clad plain as plain, with no Templar's garb in sight—and no Gamelyn. Robyn wanted to leap up, grab both Much and Marion, and shake what had happened from them. Something had happened, he knew, and . . .

But a *fortnight*.

Robyn peered at John. John peered back, eyes wide and white-rimmed in the dim. Winter had turned, and bowed to the light, and neither of them had felt the stirring of it, only the lengthening dark.

"Three days," Robyn insisted, just as Marion started to continue her explanations. "It's been more like three days."

Will snorted. "More like losing track of time! It's been ower a fortnight, I tell you, and us worried to death whilst the pair of you knackered yourselves eating 'n sleeping 'n shagging your silly knobs off—!"

John rocked forwards, quick as a stoat. "*Three days.*"

An uncomfortable silence.

"We'll ponder on the way," Robyn said, curt. "Though I'm thinking there en't no explanation—not one that makes sense, leastways. For now, we fetch ourselves out of here, soonest's best."

Robyn and John didn't even bother to hide the fact they were both fair staggered. Marion watched them as they emerged from the cavern, trudged through the broken trail through snow piled to the waist, merely to find the ground thawed to slush and mush a good arrow's loose away from the cavern mouth.

She also didn't miss the glances Robyn kept giving Much—or the questions begging to be uttered.

"Uncanny, aye?" Will had insisted upon carrying both Robyn's and John's packs. "But we've found you, and that's what matters."

John was looking back at the caverns, wary and worried—and that convinced Marion more than anything. John knew these caverns better than any of them save Robyn. These had been the caverns where the old hermit Cernun had brought a dying Rob of Loxley; where John had stayed at Rob's side through death and life again. Yet John now eyed those caverns with apprehension, turned away with a furtive, fearful sign.

Marion saw it, knew it. A ward against the fae.

She stumbled. Gilbert reached out, instinctive and polite, but Much was quicker. His hand scooped beneath her arm to right her, lingering to curl around her elbow, a subtle and covert caress.

Robyn saw it, and his brows drew together all the more. Much saw *that* and immediately released Marion's arm.

Oh, *bloody* bothering damn!

"Best we stop in Hathersage for the night," Robyn said, meeting Marion's gaze. "The wind's too bitter to sleep out on the moor. An early morning's start will see us home, whilst an early night will catch us up together."

Gunnora had been headwoman of Hathersage since a nine-year-old John had been taken to Blyth and apprenticed to the old horsemaster, Brand. Gunnora had also been cunning-woman and village priestess for twice that—ensuring, whilst she courted the goodwill of the parish priest, that she also did her duty by the Lady, Her Horned Consort, and the covenant of the Shire Wode to which the people of Hathersage had given oath.

She never asked why or what-for when the outlaws came—it didn't matter—and there was no doubt of her welcome when they did come. Neither was there any doubt she'd refuse the coins Robyn offered for the stay. The brace of rabbits, however, was another matter; quickly accepted and whisked into hiding—out of reach of several dogs who obviously thought rabbit stew a waste of good raw meat.

The villagers gathered about the outlaws, friendly and curious as a litter of puppies and just as welcoming as their headwoman. But the sun was setting, and the cold biting, and all had tasks to see done before the remaining light faded. Gunnora opened her own cot to them. Built by her man, dead these past ten years, it had housed up to twelve and now sheltered only Gunnora and her eldest daughter's family—all but one boy up to Peveril for the season, it seemed, doing their tithe of smithy work.

"No worries there, though. We've my grandson"—Gunnora nodded to the lad, about fourteen with a set of shoulders any youth would be proud to sport—"who's learned his da's trade well. The village en't suffering any lack."

The boy's shoulders broadened even further with the compliment, but he quickly ducked his head again, shy in the presence of such important guests.

"We should have some fine news for ye when the fambly returns, aye? Talk is, Sheriff de Lisle's holed up in Peveril, licking his wounds." Giving Robyn a meaningful look, Gunnora picked up a tallow-lamp bowl and took it over to the hearth. "Ex-sheriff, I mean. That one'll bear watching, so close to our doins."

She had a point. Robyn considered not only the past fortnight, but how the whole bloody winter had so far been spent in a strange . . . hibernation, almost. And the goddess's face at every turn, be She commoner or queen.

Lamp kindled, Gunnora brought it to the board in the room's centre. It, plus the warmth of the hearth at one end, gave faint light against the early dusk; reminder of other times, hearth and home and family.

"Sheriff or no, everyone is eager for t' Maying. Everyone's sure 'twill be worth the wait." Gunnora's smile was aimed at Marion. "We've a Maiden born and bred t' her duty—which *you've* sadly neglected, Hooded One."

And there was Her face yet again, chiding him. As usual.

"Aw, Gunna—" Robyn was surprised to find a hint of a whine in his voice, and wondered how Gunnora unfailingly brought out the ten-year-old in him.

Marion was smirking. Will was chuckling, damn him, and even Much was hiding a twitch of lip behind a hand. And Gilbert . . .

"*Je t'adore!*" Gilbert hooked his arm in Gunnora's, swung her in an impromptu jig about the small cot. "How I've missed you, Gunna!"

"Huh!" Gunnora snorted. "Don't be chatting me up in Frankish, you! 'Tis certain did *you* wear the horns, Gilly-lad, we'd fetch more bairns and corn than we'd know what to do with!"

"Gilly has enough horns without adding those!" Will quipped.

"Jealous?" Gilbert wrinkled his nose at Will, who snorted a laugh.

"Faith, let an old woman go before you dance her over the moon!" Gunnora protested as Gilbert tried to take another turn. She held out a hand to Marion. "Do me t' honour of takin' my place, Maiden. Boy, see to your da's duties and fetch the blessing bowl!"

The lad, respectful to his grandmother's wishes, poured from a corner cask into a wide wooden bowl. He brought it to Robyn with black-lined, powerful hands, chin still nearly touching his chest.

Robyn took the bowl and set it before him, then reached out and lifted the lad's chin, grinned thanks into the blue eyes. The boy's complexion betrayed a rash of blushes that made Robyn want to pinch his cheeks—and likely either set of cheeks would be welcome, if blushes were any clue.

Instead, he took up the bowl again, raised it to the ceiling, and spoke the Lady's blessing.

"Bendith y mamau."

There was little talking to be done in front of their hosts, though the wishing nigh burnt Robyn's tongue.

Once everyone had gone to bed, however . . .

"What's up with you and Much?" Robyn cornered Marion as soon as the chance came. They were hoved close to each other, watching the hearth-coals dance, and wrapped in an ancient bearskin that surely had been in Gunnora's family since before Willy Bastard had brought his Franks a-pillaging.

Marion smiled, peered over at the broad silhouette standing against the doorway. Much was unable to resist the habit of watch even when unnecessary.

"Just what you think."

Robyn grinned back. "Was he good, then?"

A nod, Marion's smile broadening.

"Took you long enough."

Marion shrugged. Robyn kissed her temple, acknowledging the reasons.

One of the main ones was, thankfully, not in earshot of this particular conversation. Will had gone for a piss after sitting and sharing the fire with them long enough to fill Robyn in on how the new camp was going. Growing up as son of a farmer—who'd also helped run the market at Sheffield—had made Will the best amongst them with inventories. He could rattle off stocks and stores and how long they'd last without thinking.

Robyn also had a wager on with himself that Will had succumbed to that young widow who'd been making eyes at him since the autumn. Hoped, anyway—Will needed something to take the edge off.

No question where Gilly had gone—there were two lasses here who fancied him, and neither minded sharing. *Lucky Gilly*, Robyn thought, and peered over to where John sat, courteously out of earshot, whittling away at another tiny wooden charm. John felt Robyn's eyes upon him, looked up, and smiled—but it was shadowed with concern. Aye, well, John felt Robyn's worries as his own.

And read his intent. John put aside both knife and wood—it looked to be some sort of tiny arrow, skilful hands filling it with curves and hollows—and went over to the doorway, speaking quietly to Much.

Much nodded, came slowly over whilst John stayed at the door.

The outlaws spent the night warm and well-fed on Gunnora's hospitality. Robyn, Much, and John had still been catching up as Marion had fallen asleep, head pillowed on her brother's lap.

Dawn saw a quick breakfast and an early departure before the rest of the village was stirring. John had dragged Gilbert out from beneath three lasses—Marion's smile was that admiring—and, even better, claimed Will from the widow's bed. Both of them moved with some care, sotted on too little sleep.

Marion decided she was going to kiss that young widow when next she saw her. So far Will wasn't biding overly attentive; mayhap all he'd needed was his wick fair dipped.

Loping cross-country, swift as hunting wolves, Robyn led them past thicket and marshlands, navigated iced fens and frosted ploughlands, and kept mostly to the woodland. His feet seemed to have eyes in them, finding paths where most men would see nothing. They moved more swiftly than Marion would have thought possible. No doubt this route was long familiar to the dog-wolves of the Shire Wode. It was still being learned by one newly come russet bitch and a battered ex-Templar outlier.

Marion's smile slipped as her eyes once again went to Much. Outlier, indeed. He followed them, holding the flank with Gilbert, there but . . . separate, somehow, as if some ghost of Gamelyn's own place with the outlaws—or lack thereof—had settled about him.

Preoccupied, Marion reminded herself, as much as Robyn and herself, and no wonder to any of it, with what had happened.

They returned to the horse caves on the heels of darkness, another storm blowing in behind them.

David celebrated their arrival by dumping the small crock of pottage into a great kettle and adding more water, barley, and an assortment of roots. Instead of salting a haunch of the deer he'd taken the day before, he portioned it for the kettle. Arthur was so pleased to see them, he broke out the whiskey. They all got mildly pissed, made many a toast to how they were all together again, cordoned against the winter.

Only Marion saw the look passed between Robyn and John, shared with a sombre Much. The latter drank himself wobbly, set up a solitary bed in the corner, and took to it without even a look to Marion.

Marion slept with Robyn and John, as if nothing had changed.

Over the next several days, the wind turned from insistent to fierce, cold enough to freeze off a Church gargoyle's respectable knob. The proof of that was in the first time David and Will went for water; they had to chop ice several inches thick to get to it, and came back with frosted patches on their cheeks, fingers, and toes.

Marion had managed to save David's two smallest toes. Will's cheeks had peeled and bled, and one fingernail had sloughed away. Robyn decided there would be no more lengthy jaunts out, for water or otherwise. They'd use ale and the water barrelled in the storage caverns below until the wind died down.

So they all burrowed in. There was nowt else to do, truth be told.

Robyn spent too much time sitting by the hearth, eyes bleak and blacker than normal. It didn't help that every time John threw the bones, nothing Told from them. The others stayed clear of their leader. Marion knew from a lifetime of experience to do likewise; she shoved food at her brother and otherwise left him alone.

It was harder to do the same with Much, though.

The others treated him with a fair respect. Even Will. The young Hathersage widow's attention to his virility had no doubt helped—but Marion wagered Much's peasant status didn't hurt. There was also, unfortunately, the undeniable fact that Much showed no interest in taking anyone's perceived place. In anything. He'd been acting strange—distant—ever since they'd arrived back to the Wode. Courteous, aye, but irritatingly diffident. Particularly to Marion.

It sent a tickle of disquiet, tiny and somewhat forlorn, along Marion's nerves. Of course, they'd made no promises save the sharing of pleasure . . . but Marion had hoped it might lead to more. Thought Much had, maybe, held the same hope.

A man loses his livelihood, he feels himself less t' man. Her mam's voice whispered to Marion from memory. With this, as with so many homely and common things, Eluned was right. Too tempting to take it personal, to feel jilted or foresworn . . . but Marion had to be honest with herself. This part, leastways, wasn't about her.

Or was it?

From boyhood had Much set his rights and boundaries in a life of doing service—as a soldier, as his lord's paxman. Now he was neither, and even doing service to his woman—be she his Lady's face or no—couldn't fill the rent. Much had left his lord behind—and his world. He'd been given no choice, but the fact remained: he had left Summer in the clutches of cold stone and sickness. And now he walked, numb, as if only beginning to comprehend what he'd done.

For her.

Marion could only hope it wouldn't fester into resentment. Only wanted to make it right, somehow. Not only for Much, but her brother. For herself.

They wanted—no, *needed*—Gamelyn back.

- XXIII -

"I warned you, my *Confanonier*, to take care. You did not heed me."

I... did... heed you.

"I do not believe you did, Gamelyn. Not enough. Our Master is powerful. He is ambitious." Hubert moves closer, whispers against his ear, heady-dark, "Only blood can loose the nock. Blood. And fire. And wild, wild magic. *Mon Dieu*, are you nothing? *Think*, Gamelyn . . . "

And Gamelyn woke, with a start and a fetch and a rusty groan that began in his chest merely to retreat from his lips as a mewl.

He rolled sideways on the narrow cot—only he was already sideways, so he nearly fell out, saving himself only by a prop of arm and another pained hiss.

Bloody buggering damn, his back was . . .

Paused, the consideration rising within; what his back was *not*. It was not a burning brand thrust between his ribs and slashing back and forth with every breath. It was not filling his lungs with a heavy, hot-thick weight that felt more akin to drowning in his own skin.

It felt . . . like he could move.

Gamelyn tested the possibility as he would any theory put forth by his Master: a puzzle for which, with some caution, he could arrive at a solution. First a cautious glance about his cell—for several raspy breaths he hesitated, unsure it was his cell, so strangely barren of any presence within sight or sound. But nay, there was the door—firmly shut—to his Master's chamber just past the head of his cot. On the opposite far wall the altar still sat, festooned with sword and banner and objects. And there, at his foot, Much's cot sat crossways to his own.

It was empty. No blanket, no sword hung athwart one post, no belongings stacked carefully beneath. There was not so much as a straw-stuffed tick; only the bare strings held taut by the wooden frame.

Puzzles, theories, and possibilities abandoned, Gamelyn lurched upright. Pain felled him before he made it halfway up, flung him sprawling and naked to the chill planking. It was only by the virtue of his mouth shoving up against his forearm that his cry didn't ring through the chamber and alert everyone within earshot that he was awake and couldn't even make it to the piss-pot without falling.

"Good Lord."

Gamelyn peered up through bleary, swimming eyes to see a tall black man. Not like Robyn—this man was truly dark from the hem of his robes to his shaved head, and his eyes, gleaming against the lamp he held, were black as Robyn's own.

Memory flooded through Gamelyn, then, sending him reeling against the stones, this time with another kind of agony. Saying farewell, and the road, and coming here, face-to-face with the one who'd taken Robyn's Arrow . . .

A *shuss* of fabric, a waft of clove and anise dipping deep into his nostrils, and firm, cool hands lifting him, pulling him against voluminous midnight. His hands splaying then clenching the thick, coarse woollen—close to its breast-sigil of crimson—reception and rejection in strange conflict.

The man didn't seem to care, merely murmured, almost conversationally, "*So you are back amongst the living, fire-hair.*"

It was in the Berber tongue; unthinking, Gamelyn answered back in same. "*Who are you?*"

"*I am your physician, Brother Guy.*"

Again, unthinking, but this time a denial in English: "That is not my name . . ." He stopped. For it was his name, here in the Temple's heart.

"I see." English, now, and a flash of pale amidst all that dark. Teeth, gleaming against the lamp, which had been set on the floor carefully out of reach, Gamelyn noticed. The lamp flame reached upwards in the still room, brought some colour to Gamelyn's own skin, also shrouded in black woollens. His limbs were tangled in an ungainly sprawl upon the wooden floor; they looked spindly and bloodless, prickled with chill. "The other fire-haired one—the *shawafa*—she gave you a different name, true. Your man said it was your birth name."

Shawafa. It meant . . . witch.

Marion, then. And . . . Much. *The Arrow.*

"She is gone, I am afraid. A sorry business." A *tsk*, then a grunt as the physician started to lift him from the floor. "You must lie back down. And take the draught I'll mix for you. It is good you want to be strong, but you should not waste such strength fighting. Or wake enough to wander and injure yourself fur—"

"Where is she?" A sorry business, the physician had said. Though Gamelyn's realisation was delayed, it was no less anxious. "Where is Much?"

"Master Hubert knows of your paxman, Brother." The physician draped him back onto the cot, and gave a brisk tug to unclench Gamelyn's hands from his robes. He turned away, headed for the table Gamelyn normally used for scribing duties. It was presently occupied with jars and vials, two of which the physician lifted, swirled about, then poured, first one, then the other, into a pot jar. "For now, you must drink this." With another rustle of thick black, the physician advanced, holding the concoction.

He looked . . . wary. But no less than Gamelyn, who, after fighting for consciousness so fiercely, was loath to give it up.

Even if he did hurt like hell.

Drugged. Marion and Much. The Arrow, and dreams of Robyn . . .

The physician frowned, no doubt reading the mutiny of Gamelyn's body cant. Despite the damned shakes.

"Consider, Brother. This is administered in compliance with not only your Commander's orders, but the Master of England's."

The former he would have swallowed without a qualm; the last nigh sewed Gamelyn's mouth shut.

The Master of England. Wymarec de Birkin, who entered dreams with the ease of breasting a shallow pool.

"You will take this, insolent one," the physician said coolly, "whether you do it of your own will, or I call in men to hold you down. Will you yield, or shall I humiliate you further? Obedience, Templar."

Obedience, Templar. A breath along his nape: the Lady's voice, soft and mocking. *Hold out your hands for the chains, scarlet dog.*

Gamelyn relented, even let the physician hold his head and tip the cup to his mouth. He drank, made passable imitation of a swallow.

"Excellent. I will go find the Commander, tell him of your waking."

Gamelyn watched the physician retreat. Watched the door close, heard steps echo a retreat down the narrow corridor.

The Master of England recognises you for what you are. Therefore you must fear him, surely. Still mocking, the Feminine Divine—but with a hint of approval about its edges as Gamelyn inched onto his side. He listened again, heard nothing for long moments. Then and only then did he lean over and spit the bitter stuff into the piss-pot. Afterward, he used the piss-pot as it was designed, not only for further concealment, but because he really had to.

Aiming—or frankly, trying to—at a pot the size of one's spread-out hand was not easy with the tremors that continued to plague him.

Another breath—his name—and intangible fingers stroking fierce approval through his hair as the Lady's murmurs crooned into a lullaby.

In quivers and starts, the shakes began to leave Gamelyn. Hubert did not come, but finally, slumber did—undrugged and undreaming.

The morning the wind finally—finally—died, it took with it Robyn's sullen lethargy. He went out into his Wode and wandered.

Thought too much.

Combated thought with action. Pretended to race Gamelyn up a hillock and down through a bare, open field, slowed to enter another thicket that grew into dense woodland, travelled the deer paths with a steady, mile-eating trot and circled back around. Climbed an old elm and snuffed the wind, strung his bow and drew sights on an old stag grazing the bark of a neighbouring tree. At the last moment relented to creep down and sneak up on the old one, slapping his haunch. Robyn narrowly escaped being kicked into the next fortnight.

By the time Robyn had his run, the rampant, too-filled thoughts were wonderfully silent. Only intention remained. In a copse bordering a deep, fast-running rill, he went to his knees on the frosted earth. Propped on his hands, hair falling to cover his face, and asked the first thing that came to his being—the first thing, really, that had been in his heart since . . .

Since forever.

Since he'd caught his first glimpse of Gamelyn over eight years ago, addled and upskelled against an oak after being thrown from his horse.

Will he come back? Is he all right?

He is safe.

Which was no answer, not really. *Would you tell me if he wasn't? Surely you would know if he wasn't.*

Would I? I canna. . . feel him.

Your Maiden worked her spell to protect him, did she not? the Horned Lord countered. *One to shore up his own powerful gifts, guardian against any intrusion. Small wonder even a lover cannot pierce the veil, save when he lifts it, even for a heartbeat.*

That explained the small glimmers Robyn thought he'd felt, all the while wondering if they were nowt more than—

Wishes? Of course they are. But it does not make them less real. When he is able to know you, you see him.

The frigid ground sapped warmth and strength, and the weight of the god's presence was heavy. Robyn stood, broadened bow-hardened shoulders beneath it. Felt fur tickle his cheek, and Horns adorn the Hood.

Saw, through his lord's eyes, and his own.

Our Consorts worry over the Arrow, but it will find Us. And when it does, We will find in it another purpose. Blood, and fire, and wild, wild magic.

Robyn smiled, breathed a stag's gust of challenge into the waxing day and lifted his arms, palm up, to wreath the breath upon his wrists like bangles. Or bindings, shivering his skin into gooseflesh.

Still, he had the presence of his own mind to ask: *And the fae?*

ilence, long and considering. Then another *shift-slip*, the Horned Lord's presence fully crossing the threshold of worlds. Possession in full; a gasp pulled from Robyn's throat and vibrating into the stillness, as he Saw . . . *Everything.*

Time unwound, spilled over—thisworld, otherworlds—and Robyn let it take him. To not surrender threatened its own madness; to fight it meant he would lose, to think upon or ponder what passed through him would lose him in that moment, that place . . . mayhap never to escape.

From his throat the words came: whisper-growl of otherwhen. *Nowt and owt are ours. . . but 'tis long past time for Holly and Oak to twine in Ivy's Dance, and call the music of Mistletoe conjuring. The worlds are ever-shifting, but at times we must draw back the veil, light the welcome fires. So must it be.*

The wild god left Robyn then, pulling from his consciousness with a tug that left him reeling, tottering once more to hands and knees in the sudden stillness. The forest held silent to her lord's passage; only Robyn's panting breaths exhausting into the damp and cold.

Then . . . another.

Robyn whipped his head around, every muscle tensed, snarling-ready.

No danger, no otherwhen presences seeking to call his name;

only a tall, broad shadow stumbling away, clumsy with affright. Much had followed, had seen . . .

Well, there was no telling what he had seen.

A grin, somewhat ruthless to be sure, tilted Robyn's lip. May 't happen Much might consider harder, next time he thought to follow.

Robyn was not the only one who used the break in the weather to roam. Most of the men scattered to all points of the compass; even a short wander from the caverns would do.

Marion could scarce believe her good fortune. She wasn't complaining overmuch, but they were all a bit growly, being in such close quarters. Not to mention she was unused to biding with a group of men who were well-used to behaving . . . well, like men did when left to their own devices. She wasn't desperate enough to go back to the nunnery—'twas all too true living with nowt but women had its drawbacks—but come spring, she would hie herself off to Hathersage to spend some time with Gunnora. Or sommat.

For now she'd take this little break in routine, and fair welcome. Garbed in layers of furs and cloak and head-scarf, breath hanging in hanks about her head and freckled cheeks flushed with the cold, she went hunting. Not for game—though did she see some, she'd her bow across her back and arrows in her quiver. More important for now, she had her thick, dull dagger and a carry sack over one shoulder. If the ground hadn't thawed enough to dig winter roots, there were still resins to be found, hardened-thick, this time of year.

And other finds made her smile. A lot of rosehips, and a patch of nettles not far from that, though the latter she took care gathering, looking for the dock never far away. She dug a sunny, thawed patch with red-numb fingers to find some dandelion root, as well as a few fat parsnips that demanded a bit of work whilst taking as penance a ripped and bloodied fingernail. And a stint of putting frigid fingers in her armpits.

It was warmer, aye, but not spring yet by a long shot.

All the while, Marion thought. There had been plenty of time for thinking, these past fortnights—but not much room, in a crowded cavern hollow that stayed warm but gave none of them enough space to swing a cat, much less so much as change their mind. Of making one's way in a divisive, contrary world.

Of men's ways, and women's ways—or gods and goddesses, did

it come to it—and how the earth's rhythms both made sense of and senseless the divisions of anything.

Of the Wode's confines, home and succour. No less a protection than a nunnery or preceptory . . . yet neither was it less a hardship.

Of stone walls and gaols—and gaols that had no walls but, nevertheless, imprisoned.

Given that, likely it was not at all surprising that it wasn't her mam's voice she heard, but Queen Eleanor's.

We have only that which we take. . . and even then, as you're beginning to find, a woman is altogether likely to reap a stone gaol as reward for her presumption.

"Us and them." It was a mutter as she sawed away at another patch of resin. "Tis allus one or t'other. Forced that way like bairns set young t' plough or sword. Taking or giving, making or breaking, none exists without t' other . . . Robyn's right. The changing has to happen. We canna just knuckle under, let it all die. And it'll be worse, much worse, before it gets better."

For queen or king, a lack of strength—of purpose—stands to take from you what is yours.

Aye, and Marion'd had everything taken from her that mattered. Her family. Her home. Her unlikely comradeship with a nobleman's son. Her mind, her memory, her . . . *voice.* Even the songs and the singing—the magic of the tiny blessing-rhymes her mam had taught her and she now hummed as she took up root and scraped at tree bark—they faltered occasionally with lack of practise. But they grew stronger each time she sang them, more sure. Women's magic, women's tales, women's tools with so few hands, now, to tend them. Even John, taught by women, with a power of making many women didn't possess, hadn't the full way of such things. John could not have fashioned the charm that now lay at Gamelyn's throat.

Marion gave the yew a thankful pat, thinking on that charm and the one it protected. Of Much, solitary and impotent, lost and looking . . . and *that* was sin, if there was such a thing! Of Robyn, determined upon his path, walking over the precipice and glorying in the flight to come even if it meant a fall . . . yet all the while hoping, somehow, that path and his lover's would conjoin again, for longer than a few breaths, and he and Gamelyn walk together—*love* together—hand in hand.

Back-to-back, none shall stand against you.

The Lady's words, and it was wrong that they were separated, wrong! Marion knew that in her bones. Heard her mam's lessons as if Eluned stood beside her, speaking as they gathered their needfuls from the forest:

Abred, *thisworld,* Annwn, *otherworld, and* Gwynfyd, *lands of undying. . . linked and unlinked, all wrapping our tiny existence. Yet they'll be like us in this much: they yearn to be part of sommat, straining to be together. To be blazing with the power of the bringing together—the* Ceugant—*to tip or right the balance. But such powers ne'r start the merging without consequence. Oft-times* cythraul—*evil and cruelty—lingers, starting the cycle. And bringing great change.*

Her mother had spoken of change with the white roil of fear in her eyes. Marion understood that, well enough. Yet . . .

The inevitability of fire, my dear girl. Eluned's memory shifted, gave to Eleanor's. *It burns. Whatever it touches. Including itself.*

It was not in Marion to shrug away the changing, good or ill. And she no longer could give room to fear or doubt.

Aye, my own. The Lady this time, the arrow-point of another *triskele,* this of Woman. *Fear is what stands to disarm the* Ceugant *now walking thisworld. If doubt and denial of what comes should conquer, then the bringing together would never happen, and the balance rocking widdershins, spreading ripples into the worlds that would last eternities.*

Arrow-point. The willow Arrow in the Templar lord's hands. Another wild-cruel toss into the game, and who knew when that throw would be made? Robyn seemed unworried . . . well, if not unworried, accepting. Marion had done as well—he'd fashioned it, after all, he knew it best.

But that was the problem, wasn't it? This acceptance Robyn affected. This *waiting.*

Even stone cannot silence us, unless we let it.

Let it.

Let it.

"It en't to be borne," Marion whispered to the yew, and the stubborn resin gave to her hand, as if in accord. She peered at it, and smiled.

She was tired of waiting. Tired of Winter's stasis. The longest night had passed. Summer was coming. Something needed to be done.

Marion had a dirty apron and a full pouch as she made her satisfied way back to the cavern.

The men had all returned, save Robyn and Much. And when Will thought to query her overmuch, she cut his worries off with a fierce look, not of a mind to explain herself, not now.

Not anymore, really.

Will gave, with a readiness that would have been suspicious had she been willing to entertain suspicion. Instead, she hoped he'd visit that lovely widow a bit more often, and the weather would hold fair and ensure it. Marion distributed her finds: the resin to David, who wanted to learn the ways of its use; several small stones and a discarded branch from the yew for John to craft and charm; and the rest of her bounty to the stores.

Robyn returned on the heels of that, with water in the large skin he'd carried, and dinner.

"Fresh meat!" Marion couldn't help the pleased cry, and smiled as Robyn flung the hare towards the stone arc of their hearth.

Will snatched the furry body midair. "Wherever did you snare such a big lad?" Will held the hare up by the hind legs, admiring. "Tis nigh large enough to ride, were y' more our little John's size and less all stretchy-lanky."

John, against the far wall and busy inspecting Marion's gifts, snorted and grinned.

"And *fresh*," Gilbert repeated Marion's invocation, winked at Robyn. "I suppose letting you out for a run now and again is useful."

It was Robyn's turn to snort. He flung himself down on a pile of furs and gave a huge stretch. "So I'm useful, aye?"

"Occasionally." Gilbert came over, toed Robyn's arse. In quick denial of sudden lethargy, Robyn grabbed Gilbert's foot, yanked it out from under him. Gilbert yipped and went down—atop Robyn.

A wrestling match ensued. Marion chuckled, danced deftly aside as she went to relieve Will of the hare's carcass. Will presented it to her with all the ceremony of a courtier to his queen, and she patted his cheek.

Aye, no question but since she'd returned from Hirst, he seemed more like the William she'd known.

Much, on the other hand . . .

Marion's smile faded as Much came in from wherever he'd been— slunk in, more like. A smile tried to quiver at his mouth upon the sight of Robyn and Gilbert still piling into each other—with plenty of vocal, well-salted commentary—then disappeared as he met Marion's eyes. Dropping his gaze, Much went over to where John was still whittling away and slid to seat himself beside, leaning against the wall.

"Dried peas and leeks with the coney," David opined. "Plus the parsnips you found, all crisp and sweet with the cold, and a good shovel-in of oats. We'll have a few days off that."

"You bloody . . . *bugger!*" Robyn said—into the cavern floor, as Gilbert was atop him. "I fancy *this* en't wrestling!"

"I fancy it does the job, aye?" Gilbert mimicked Robyn's accent with a grin—and rightly so, Marion thought, as he rarely won a bout. "Mayhap you should pay more attention to our newest member, brother-mine. Much has a few, erm, 'not wrestling' tricks up his sleeve."

Much's gaze had once more gone to them, the smile flirting about his lips. But as Gilbert allowed Robyn up, the latter's next words put a pallor to Much's cheek.

"Aye, I'm paying attention to that one. He's full of soldier's tricks. Sneaky. I'm eyeing you, Much."

Much wasn't eyeing Robyn back; he was studying the floor. Next to Much, John slid a curious glance Robyn's way.

Marion also glanced at her brother, found a rather pitiless grin quirking his mouth.

Asked, with her eyes, *What?*

Nowt to worry, Mari, he answered, plain as spoken.

"So did *you* bring some game, O Templar Hunter?" Arthur's dig was sly—no worse than he gave any of the men, truthfully.

Much nevertheless seemed pinked by it. "You lookin' for one?" he growled back. "A game, leastways?"

Arthur's eyes widened and he held up his hands.

"Nay," Robyn said—and again, to Marion's ears it sounded ruthless. "He en't the one crossing lines, here."

Anger disappearing behind wide eyes, all blue and white, Much jerked his gaze to Robyn's.

Robyn crossed his arms and raised his eyebrows.

"'Bout time," Will muttered, with no little satisfaction. Just as Marion started to ask him what in heaven's name he meant by that, he grinned, once again the charming boy, and held out his hand for the hare. "Here, pet, I'll help you with the skinning."

"Time?" Robyn asked, and his voice turned inexplicably gentle, as were the eyes that met Much's and held. "We've all had to learn, in our time. Some *don't*."

Much had gone after Robyn, Marion realised. Gone after, and likely seen something he shouldn't have done.

"Those as don't learn," Will added, "don't stay."

Much slid his eyes to Will. They flickered with something distinctly unpleasant—just that flicker—then, nothing.

Robyn laughed out loud. "That's rich, coming from you, Scathelock!"

Will's turn, now, to have conflicting emotions play across his face. It took him longer than it would have in the old days, but he joined the laughter. That hadn't changed either—Will had always been keen for japes and jokes, and if they turned and bit his arse, all the better for a laugh.

"I'll let you skin that hare," Marion agreed, with a light slap to Will's cheek.

"*Let* me? How bloody good of you!" he retorted, still grinning.

"Thinking of you, all the time." Marion left it wide open—a thrown line, bait, a test.

But Will didn't so much as bite. He took the hare and blew her a kiss, sauntering out to do the deed.

Later, full of warm pottage and tired from the day's jaunt, they were all lounging about. David was dozing—and snoring. Tess lay curled up on his chest; occasionally the little ferret would reach out, tap David's mouth as if in commentary on the volume. Will, Arthur, and Gilbert were playing knucklebones. Marion had shaped the quills Queen Eleanor had given her, was using them to ink the cork tops of the herb stores, taking inventory. She'd thought to ask Much's help, decided that was beyond pathetic, begging like an anxious girl. Much seemed more willing to tend his steel than his lover . . . honestly, did the man do anything else?

Aye, pathetic. Marion gave a soft growl and slapped pique across its snippy, whingy nose.

A flash of gilt winked; firelight against Much's knives, no doubt—but, nay. Robyn had his quillion dagger point down in the dirt, spinning it like a whirligig. He'd sprawled with his head pillowed against John's thigh. John was still busy with the bit Marion had brought him, heeding little else. Robyn's eyes were dark, unreadable—not that Marion had to read anything. The dagger had been Gamelyn's first, after all.

Both her men, pining—but unlike Robyn, Much didn't have his closest comrades nigh to spend it on. Trouble was, she'd no idea how to fix *that* without dragging Gamelyn back by his coppery, stubborn head—and why Robyn hadn't yet done was beyond her.

Marion paused in her writing and luffed the quill feather across her lower lip, pondering. Fear. Was Robyn afraid to go after Gamelyn? And if so, of what? The Temple's power? The Templar who had taken his arrow? Or . . . denial. Aye, it remained altogether possible that Gamelyn would, once again, indulge his particular choice of barren poison over Robyn, and the Wode.

And Us, the Lady echoed Marion's sudden forlorn anger, and Marion demanded:

Why? Why is he doing this?

You know why. And indeed, what is there not to be afraid of, Maiden? A ghost of a smile. *With such men, denial can become a drug. Forcing action is better than leaving them to stew in their own dreamings.*

Just as Marion thought to query, She faded. Marion peered at her ink-stained thumb and forefinger, with quill firmly nestled and the inkpot balanced on a tun of cider.

Mouth set, she tidied her doings, took the writing things back to her corner, and settled down there. The pouch with the parchments still lay half-open; she dragged it closer and pulled into her lap the small, thin board she often used to measure herbs with.

It took two rushlights, a fat lamp, and one of the precious candles Robyn had stolen off the Abbot of St. Mary's to properly illuminate the corner. Marion settled cross-legged on several furs, found herself scrutinising her quill, a bit daunted. It had been too long, in truth, since she'd indulged in this sort of writing. She had written the Abbess's letters for her, of course, after the Abbess had by sheer accident learned Marion could not only read, but pen a fair hand. But since then?

So she took her time, spending some effort on a smaller piece, reacquainting herself to the feel of sharp quill on fine parchment. Her mam'd had bits of skin, Marion remembered, though nothing so fine, upon which her children could practise. Robyn had never graduated to the larger pieces; as soon as Eluned had released him from the requested drudgery of nibs and ink and reading "squiggles on skin," as he'd constantly disparaged, he would be out in the Wode and away. Marion had persevered—and prevailed.

"What's all this about, then?"

Marion looked up to meet Robyn's curious gaze. Her hair was escaping her coif to crinkle about her cheeks, her back kinked all stiff, and her nib finger reddened, trying to blister. David was snoring louder and Tess had given up on him, also snoozing. The lads were still at knucklebones—with Arthur losing and Will winning, both badly from the sound of it—and John and Much intent upon their own tasks.

"I think John wants a piece of that yew resin you found, for the making he's thinking on." Robyn stuck the quillion dagger in his belt and folded his legs to sit beside her. He was careful not to jar her work, and she smiled at the thoughtfulness.

"Of course."

"I en't seen you after this since you came back from Hirst. Those monks a bad influence?"

She wrinkled her nose at him. "Nowt bad to writing, you clot."

"As long as it's you and not me, pet. That's the lot what Madam Herself gave you, aye?"

She nodded. "I'd no thought to need it. Until now." She leaned against the cavern wall and gave her brother a level look.

He peered back, one eyebrow lifting. "You've a need. Now."

"I think we both do." Marion reached out and took up a clean sheet of vellum, spread it on the board, and pinned it. "You can help me."

"Help you?" The eyebrow was all but disappearing into his fore-lock, and a tiny, intrigued flame had begun to kindle behind his dark-dark eyes.

"This needs straight talk as well as fancy." Not that Robyn didn't have his own vocabulary—their mother had done them both that service.

He murmured a colourful example of that vocabulary as she put a formal address at the top of the page. Eluned would have clipped his ears for it, grown man or no. Marion simply grinned, and began to compose the beginning sentences of the letter. As he followed the strokes of the pen, he grew hesitant—anxious, even. But she kept poking at him—with words, not gestures—insisting he help.

Insisting this needed to be *done*.

Resistance began to fold like an ill-propped tent as she kept it up, and her brother began, despite himself, to lean in, intrigue flaring hot with the challenge. Together they parsed and pondered and wrangled. Robyn began to proffer his own language. Marion listened, mused and judged, replaced more than a few, but there were just as many altogether bloody perfect to the task.

By the time they got to the end of the letter, both of them were broadly smiling— and sweating, to be sure. Marion looked at the finished letter with some satisfaction— only a few mistakes, and those easily scraped away—then blew lightly across it. The inked words quivered and drew up beneath her drying breath. Marion kept smiling, watching it then Robyn as he gave a satisfied grunt and, abruptly, stood.

It was hardly possible, but Marion's smile widened even more as Robyn paced to stand over Much and spoke to him.

Much's brows drew together; still puzzled, he rose and followed Robyn back over to where Marion sat with the still-drying parchment.

- ENTR'ACTE -

Nowt were right.
Not right that the outlaws should be so willing to welcome Much to their place without his lord—all right, mayhap Scathelock were a bit less than "willing," but, well. *Scathelock.*

Not right that, even as Much were of them, peasant and pagan, they should scorn his lord so. Didn't they see what Gamelyn *were?*

Not right that he'd left his lord behind. You never left a downed comrade behind, never!—though he'd had no choice, and his like never had choices, did they?—but he'd left Gamelyn there and wouldn't know if he died, even though Master Hubert loved him and would take care of him best he could.

Not right that life should just . . . just *go on* like this, with no purpose or sense to it. Everything that mattered, all of 't ripped from him just for doing what his lord and his heart had demanded. Though the livin' did, didn't it, allus coming around and going again, the Return and the ways of the Lady being what they were, unfathomable and stubborn.

And oh, but *Lady* . . .

It surely weren't even close to right that Much should look at Marion—lovely, unfathomable Marion—after what they'd shared and feel nowt but . . . hollow. Wonder at the wrong of that, freezin' him so in his tracks, useless as a hamstrung deer confronted with torchlight and dogs. Wonder if pride kept her at arm's length, or the reality that he weren't meant for her, never meant for her; the Lady's avatar in thisworld, after all. But he couldn't help but wonder if she understood how their few, hard-sweet tups had been something more than a few nights of pleasure, at least for him.

Much did his share of work, ate what was put before him, drank more than he should, minded his tongue and his doings, and felt . . . nowt.

His lord would be right proud of him . . . only Much knew that his lord weren't always so pleased with feeling nowt. Gamelyn felt things for Marion passing understanding—though Much kenned them, true enough—and Gamelyn loved Robyn so deep and fierce it liked to rend him to pieces, all that feeling.

And considering that, it were particularly wrong how Robyn should up and leave, what with the weather just broken and no one so much as wondering or worrying. Aye, Robyn were the god's face, Hooded as well as Horned, but Much knew damn-well *that* only meant 'twere likely he'd run into more trouble than most.

So it seemed the only right thing in a bloody sea of wrong that Much should do what he would have done for Gamelyn—and couldn't, and had done for Marion—and couldn't . . . and, in its place, fasten that rightness into tailing Robyn.

Much knew he was good at being invisible, had wagered his life on it more than once. Now he wagered Robyn wouldn't see him, even though it was likely the cheekiest flutter he'd ever had, that the Shire Wode's uncanny lord shouldn't know he was being followed in his own place.

Uncanny, but mad as a buck in rut. Much knew Robyn talked to spirits, that the Horned Lord would possess Robyn to make of him the Hooded One, the Green Man. Much had heard of how Robyn could call—had called!—the Wild Hunt, and nigh t' fae as anything of thisworld. Much had seen that power—reverenced it—upon Marion. Had known, deep down, that Gamelyn had sparks of the god behind his eyes—banked different, but just as deep and powerful.

But *this* . . .

Where did the Horned Lord end and Robyn Hode begin? Forest and fae lord, all one. Madness, surely. But a divine one.

Much lowered his head beneath the weight of it and slipped away. No wonder the outlaws left their leader to roam. There were some things only gods should know; some things only gods' sons could endure.

And knew, later in the caverns when Robyn spoke to him all sharp, that Robyn kenned he'd been followed.

Mayhap it had been a trespass beyond sense or forgiveness.

Much writhed—beneath a calm face, to be sure—when he saw Robyn and Marion seated together, curly heads nearly touching. Close as twins they were, but Marion kept writing something; she'd pen and a long scrap of parchment spread on a small board in her lap.

Much set himself to tend to his steel—it had been over a week since he'd done so, and he might need it. Particularly if he'd trespassed too far and Robyn decided it was Much's time to leave.

Where would he go? Much knew he could hire his sword, no question—any guard post would be glad to have a skilled warrior, even if temporarily. Because it would be. He'd another five months of this aimless hell . . . but at the end of it, who knew if the Templars would take him back? Gamelyn would, he knew that, but what if Gamelyn were . . . were . . .

He wouldn't think it, much less say it.

He had to do sommat. He couldn't just sit here and *wait.*

"Much!"

He looked up with greasy hands and faraway, grim eyes that belatedly focused. Robyn stood above him, bending to take Much's steel away with gentle-firm fingers and an expression that brooked no argument when Much thought to voice one. Before Much could balk, Robyn pulled him to his feet.

"Coom by, lad."

Who are you callin' lad, leastways? Much thought, but did not say—already in enough trouble as it were.

Robyn heard it anyway, snorted a chuckle, then hauled Much like a recalcitrant pony to where Marion sat over her papers and quills, watching them the whole way. She'd sepia smudges on her fingers, and one on her nose that Much yearned to kiss away.

"Sit, now. Been too long since you've sat with me sister, anyway." Robyn kept up his chuckling, bugger him sideways . . .

Only he'd probably fancy it, that one.

And *owt*—but for being such a skinny lath of a fellow, Robyn had a grip that put a wobble to Much's knees and sure enough, had him shoved and sliding down the cavern wall beside Marion.

"We've sommat you may fancy hearing." Robyn crouched down, his knee brushing Much's and effectively cutting off any hope of escape. He still had that puckish, daunting gleam to his eye. "Read it to him, aye, pet?"

With a smile on her face—and faith, but she were proper lovely when she smiled, like an autumn morning, crisp and colourful— Marion lifted the parchment and began to read.

Penned words were arcane magic to Much, but Marion parsed them effortlessly, and the eager, easy shapes made Much want nothing more in that moment than to kiss the lips forming that magic. But Robyn kept up wit' watching him, still with that *light* in his eyes and lip tilting—he knew damn well what Much were thinking about his sister—so Much set himself to listen, determined.

Blinked. Began to *listen*, rapt and bug-eyed—not merely because of Marion saying the words, but the words themselves.

Now there bided no doubt in Much's mind at all: Hob-Robyn were bloody proper mad—but mad as a fox, more like.

Much met those wild, soot-black eyes, and smiled.

- XXIV -

Come by, then.
Not yet.
Lazy bugger, you canna sleep all day. 'Tis time to wake, Gamelyn.

And, as the preceptory bells began to ring, Robyn's voice faded into the dawning.

This time when Gamelyn woke, he was warm from that whisper, aloft on sweet tones and morning light, without a hint of dreaming, or drugged fugue.

He could breathe, somewhat. He could move, somewhat. His thoughts were vague—but they were his own.

Testing the second possibility, Gamelyn reached out. Smooth-worn linens and woollens met his quivering, questing fingers. Lank hair hung over his eyes, clinging to his cheek and vibrating with every shallow, careful breath. He made that another test, raising his hand to rake it back.

A throb of discomfort, but not so far as to be called pain.

He was on his uninjured side, propped by several bolsters. The room was quiet, still. He saw and heard no one; better still, no one came, attentive, to pour noxious draughts down his throat.

Good.

Careful, considerate, Gamelyn rose. Discomfort flirted with pain, gave stabs of warning. Gamelyn breathed through them, kept moving. With a tight grip and lean against the wooden headpost, he managed to drop his legs over the side of the cot. Stayed there for moments, panting and uttering soft oaths against the twang of outraged nerves and sinews.

He was stiff, and thought for moments he was going to vomit—but soon the urge subsided and, with it, the anticipation of agony. An odd feeling—he'd become altogether used to chronic endurance. His breath hung, frosted, about him, and his thighs prickled with chill. Still careful, Gamelyn dragged one of the blankets to him, shrugged into the warmth still impressed there, and wondered if he had clothing that could be easily retrieved.

More abstruse senses, rested and eager, told him quite abruptly he was not as alone as he'd believed.

One hand started for his hip, instinct.

A combination of sharp pain and Hubert's lush baritone soothed that instinct, stood it down. "You are up. Good."

Boots striding from the Commander's private chamber, brisk, and Hubert gained Gamelyn's side. A hand came to rest, albeit brief, against his jaw; the fond gesture made sudden, illogical heat swim behind Gamelyn's eyes. Then Hubert crouched next to Gamelyn's pale, chill-pocked knees and fished beneath the cot, with a small grunt yanking a long, squat trunk into what light philtred from the overhead window. "Let us have you dressed straight away. No sense you catching a chill after all this."

Nonplussed, Gamelyn watched as Hubert selected suitable items, stayed silent as Hubert, quite matter-of-factly, helped him dress. He was unsure he could say anything past the tightness in his throat, at any rate. But soon he was warmly clad and standing on legs that grew stronger with every totter and sway.

"*Bon!* Better to be upright, is it not?" Hubert stepped back and nodded, crossing his arms. "Would you care for some food? Mayhap a few sips of good red wine. Brother Diata says you must go slowly, but—ah, see?" This as Gamelyn's knees tried a sudden buckle. "We have poured broth into you, but you need more."

"Brother . . . Diata?" Gamelyn husked.

"Ah, but of course, you do not know him. He came to serve as our Infirmarer whilst you were in Nottingham . . . *sacré tête*, has it truly been nearly a year's half since I sent you there?" Hubert shook his head. "Whatever I thought would come of *that*, never did I imagine the outcome."

Guy of Gisbourne, sent to Nottingham to hunt an outlaw. A will o' wisp would-be spirit known as Robyn Hode, who ended up being exactly that, and more . . .

Gamelyn squeezed his eyes tight-shut. Robyn. Robyn's Arrow. Faint heat akin to a stag's blast echoed behind his gaze—it made no sense; surely the Horned Lord was as ill-suited to bide here as

Robyn. An accompanying trace of moonsilver danced back and forth across his closed lids, quelling, and runnelled down like fire-warmed water to encircle his throat. The cross. Marion. Then his gaze fell upon the empty bed adjacent to his own.

Much.

"Where is Much?" Gamelyn was mortified how his voice quavered, and bid it strong. "He would not have left—"

"He is following your orders." Hubert went over to the table. To one side of all the pots and potions were a pitcher and a cloth-covered platter.

"My . . . orders." Gamelyn found his tongue slow, flailing in its attempts to catch up with mind and body. He took a step, found it not as difficult as he'd feared. Straightened, and when pain whinged in the background, he slapped it like the recalcitrant laggard it was. Took another step towards Hubert, then another. "Where is Much?" Gamelyn said, again. "Where is Marion?"

There was a quick *tap-tap-tap!* of fingernails upon the wooden door, just the thrice, then silence. Hubert stiffened, waiting. Gamelyn started to question, but the sound of steps, ringing down the corridor in the silence of the keep, gave him pause.

As did Hubert's hand alighting on Gamelyn's good arm, with a swift lean in and mutter, "I warn you. He will be Grand Master, if he can." And before Gamelyn could form any sort of reply, Hubert drew away and said, quite normal, "I am very glad to see you so soon upright. You have been very ill, eh?"

Gamelyn was dazed enough—confused enough—to heed no more than the briefest of cautions. All he wanted to know—

"Much. Marion. Where *are* they, my friend?" It was a plea. "You are my friend, aye?"

"You know the answer to that!" Hubert hissed. "I—"

But the sharp, swift footfalls grew louder, silencing anything further Hubert meant to say, and the blue eyes went to frost as voices sounded outside the door.

A knock, and a voice muffled through the thick door. "My lord Commander? Master de Birkin wishes your presence."

De Birkin.

Gamelyn slid a gaze to Hubert, but Hubert was not even looking at him, calling a courteous and carrying "Enter!"

The door was flung open, a white-clad figure filling it.

"Master Wymarec," Hubert said, and gave a small bow.

Gamelyn followed suit, found his balance not adequate to the task, not yet—and more, the resultant wobble and sidestep reverberated a flash of pain up his spine and into his skull.

Hubert gripped his good arm again, tight. A support. A reminder.

"Ah, Commander." Wymarec gave a nod in return, his eyes sliding to Gamelyn. "And a pleasant surprise, Brother. I did not imagine I would find you so swiftly on your feet."

Gamelyn's tongue finally decided to outpace his brain—abrupt and likely ruinous, but he cared not. "A surprise," he answered, through his teeth but just as soft. "Why that? Other than you didn't expect me to pour your drugged draughts into the piss-pot?"

"*Confanonier!*" Hubert snapped, and his grip upon Gamelyn's arm turned from snug reminder to white-knuckled warning. "Master Wymarec, you must excuse him, he is—"

"Entirely too intelligent for his own good." Wymarec was laughing. A soft concurrence—indulgent, almost. As if a favoured dog had been first to the kill, or a sullen haggard had flown unexpectedly well. "Ah, well. There was little hope such a thing would work for long, eh, Hubert?"

Complicit, no question. Gamelyn slid his eyes to take in Hubert, a query.

"Of course he agreed, lad," Wymarec supplied. "Of course we kept you drugged. Had to, you were thrashing about so. Surely the damned don't have such nightmares. Whatever could such a young man have done to earn such nightmares?" A shrug. "Ah, but war's fortunes visit us each our own Hell."

The words were so reasonable, so grave; they threw Gamelyn sideways. He frowned, considering, and Hubert's grip loosed, once again plain support.

As if the return of blood flow to his forearm clustered his thoughts as well, Gamelyn set his jaw and persisted. "Much. Where is Much? Where is Marion?"

Hubert's grip tightened again.

"Surely you realise they are gone." Wymarec folded his arms, cocked his head.

"If you will allow me?" Hubert's grip tightened once again, halting the impulse Gamelyn only then kenned was there. "He is, after all, of my preceptory."

"Which means he is mine as well. Are not services done to all English preceptories done to me, and in turn all preceptories to our Grand Master, whose representative I am?"

"But where have they gone?" Gamelyn's skull felt empty, unable to *think*, to come up with anything . . . ah, yes. That. "The Queen—"

"Favoured you, no question—and no wonder, with the service you did *her*. But she has other matters to tend. The Queen has already set sail, her son's ransom in hand and an escort of Templars at heel." Wymarec crossed his arms, one gloved finger tapping against a white woollen sleeve. His pale eyes were keen upon

Gamelyn, with a slight frown that radiated concern. "Take heart, Templar, that Eleanor of Aquitaine's favour would have requested your company upon her voyage. Alas, you have been too ill."

"Much!" Gamelyn grated out. "Marion. *Where are they?*"

A sigh. "I understand you are not altogether coherent at present, but this grows tiresome." Wymarec's expression flattened. "Your peasant companions bide with us no longer. Your paxman has been dismissed from the Order."

"*What?*" Again, Gamelyn lurched forwards. Again, Hubert's grip tightened, stayed him. This time Gamelyn rounded on him and jerked away. The pain it caused was almost worth it. The conflict in Hubert's gaze, however . . .

"Why have you dismissed him? What have you done with them?"

"Nothing has been done *with* them." Hubert's tone was plainly reassuring. "Much escorted Marion back to the forest, nothing more."

"They were caught snooping in my chambers," Wymarec added. As Gamelyn turned back to him, the pale eyes showed no malice, no glee . . . nothing. Flat as a cobra's, before the strike.

Yet if Gamelyn struck first?

"You banished my paxman for obeying my orders?"

"Your orders." Wymarec smiled. It was almost . . . fond.

Again, Hubert grabbed Gamelyn's arm; this time it was the injured one, in a grip not merely strong, but bloody painful. "What have you done?"

Gamelyn refused to heed it. It was not his, this pain. Mayhap he would claim it later, but for now?

Instead, he kept his gaze, unblinking—*reptilian*—upon Wymarec, as he answered his Commander. "Had I been able, I would have done. He has something that belongs to me."

"Nothing belongs to *you*, Templar, but your order and your oaths." It was almost lazy—almost. There was a tiny telltale a-gleam in the pale eyes.

Gamelyn once more jerked his arm free from Hubert's grasp, once more was nearly staggered by the pain. He disguised it as a step towards Wymarec.

"You know why my man did as I asked. As *she* asked."

"She?" Wymarec was still smiling. *Smiling.*

How stupid. Didn't the bastard comprehend he was about to have the life choked from him?

"*Confanonier!*" Hubert growled, jerked Gamelyn back. "Heed me! Disengage!" The language of war—a master snapping the chain upon his vicious hunting lion. "You will *stand down!*"

"Hubert"—Wymarec didn't take his eyes from Gamelyn—"leave us."

"Wymarec, you cannot—"

"I can*not?*" Wymarec shot back, quick and vicious. "Do you think to challenge *me*, Hubert de Gisborough? Or shall I make you watch as I take down your little pit dog? Be obedient, *Templier*, to the Rule and the Great Work!"

The first was surely adequate; the second made Hubert . . . quail, was the only way Gamelyn could describe it. So rarely seen, Gamelyn was fairly gobsmacked to describe it.

"Leave us, Hubert. Your quarters will be sufficient."

Hubert gave a nigh imperceptible shake to Gamelyn's arm.

Without taking his gaze from Wymarec, Gamelyn said to Hubert, urgent, "*You* are my Master." *He is an enemy.*

"Nay, he is not," Hubert murmured, as if Gamelyn had spoken aloud. "And he is mine." He loosed Gamelyn and retreated to his quarters.

"Mayhap I am," Wymarec admitted as the door closed, making Gamelyn wonder if he had indeed said it—enemy—aloud.

Or had it been just that bloody obvious? He must be slipping.

"But I would rather we did not oppose each other," Wymarec continued.

Gamelyn merely peered at him. "Did they fetch it?"

"What do you mean, Guy?"

"My name is Gamelyn." It escaped as a growl. Gamelyn took another step. "And you know exactly what I mean."

"I also know you are *of* us." Without taking his eyes from Gamelyn—merely wise, that—Wymarec tugged at one glove, inspected it. "More than you can possibly understand at present. Enough of this foolishness."

He held out the gloved hand, palm up.

Gamelyn gazed at it, unmoving.

"Take it, *Confanonier*."

Still, Gamelyn did not so much as twitch.

"Know this: I do not often extend my hand. Certainly to none I would not consider either threat or"—a smile, brilliant as the sun beginning to edge the high, narrow window—"*possibly*, an equal."

How . . . disturbing. Not the hand itself, smoothed in snowy perfection, but that Gamelyn wanted to reach out, take it. And, just as unsettling, a dark and strangely passive strength . . . *shivered* about him, humming in his ears and reverberating through the stone surround with soft, familiar accord.

Gamelyn gave a tiny shake of his head and persisted, stubborn,

"Did they? Find it? And you cannot convince me you don't know what I'm talking about."

Still holding out his hand, Wymarec said, almost musing, "You mean the thing that tiresome nun found and gave to me? The arrow that killed her mistress?"

So calm and matter-of-fact, and surely the man had not made Hubert leave the room because he didn't want Hubert to know. Surely he knew Gamelyn would tell him.

"Nay," Wymarec said, with careless ease. "This is between us, don't you think?"

Control yourself. It was abrupt against Gamelyn's senses, faint but there and draped with starry indigo. *You denied him once,* the Lady hissed. *Do it now. Or do you intend to drop your braies and bend over for him next, as he's already in your mind?*

In his mind, parcelled with the soft hum of stone and sorcery that Gamelyn had always feared/yearned for. Yet the *Magister Militiae Templi,* did not—could not?—hear the Lady's voice. Nay, the man merely walked over to the table, grasped the sweating pitcher's handle, and took his time pouring two goblets of wine.

"Tell me this, my Templar. How is it that the thing is yours? I was of the understanding that it belonged to one they call the King of Sherwood. A *peasant* king"—a curl of lip—"named Robyn Hode."

It was napped with velvet, the old inflection, drawn out into a darkling sound-shape, layered with a type of magical biddance Gamelyn himself had long ago despaired of ever achieving. It roused several emotions—alarm, vigilance . . . *envy*—and also provoked in Gamelyn what even the Lady's withering taunt had failed to inspire.

Robyn would have made a lithe disentanglement of any mental fetters. Stroked them sated, no doubt, merely to steal out from under with the barest of smirks. Gamelyn swung denial with all the force of a mace, entangled chain around sword, yanked it free, and slammed his opponent with a battle-scarred shield.

The riposte held no grace, but of its innate power there was no doubt. The strange hum sucked itself from behind Gamelyn's ears and into nothingness.

Wymarec gave a shudder, nearly stumbled. The wine slopped over twin goblet rims; a quick motion saved one but left the other to splash a blood-hued stain upon one pale glove. Nevertheless, the man's ability to recover was impressive. Wymarec peered at Gamelyn, then grimaced at his stained glove.

"Clumsy of me. And of you. You can do better . . . *did* do better, in the chapel at Worksop. Of course"—a *tsk,* accompanied by a tilt of the dark head—"you aren't up to much of anything yet, are you?" Wymarec started to hold out one of the goblets, then reconsidered—it was the one that had "blooded" him. He passed the other goblet. "I think this one, for the now."

Gamelyn didn't move a muscle, to refuse or accept. "Is it drugged?"

"If it was, I could still make you drink it," Wymarec chided. "Obedience, Templar."

Obedience! Surely 'twas some hellish imp that made Gamelyn hear Robyn's chuckle, as surely as if he were there beside him. *That'll have you proper. Tied like a boar for slaughter. But then—you might fancy it, aye?*

Not now, he wouldn't.

Still, he drank.

Noted that, before Wymarec drank, he peeled off the soiled glove. Noted further the scar tissue, thick and roped, upon that hand, before Wymarec tucked it in a nonchalant but telling gesture within his snowy tabard. Tipping his goblet to Gamelyn, he quaffed a full half, to show no fear of what it contained.

As if Gamelyn didn't know that a common source had no relation to a poison slipped during the pour.

Wymarec smiled, put down his own goblet, and glided over. Held out his gloved hand and, when Gamelyn peered at him, jerked his fingers towards the goblet.

"Give it to me."

Gamelyn did so.

Another tiny smile. "Excellent. You have been obedient. Now I shall put your mind at rest." He tipped the goblet to his mouth, and drank.

Well, Gamelyn supposed, that was one way to prove a point.

"Now." Wymarec handed back the goblet, went over to the table and took up his own, dandled it as he sat in the room's singular chair, crossing his legs at the knee. His bare hand was still hidden within his tabard, the other occupied with his wine. A comfortable posture. An arrogant one. "Sit. You've been on your feet overlong for one just on them. Tell me of this arrow that is not yours. Oh," he continued as Gamelyn started to protest, "I did sense your presence upon it—but you were part of the intention, not the making. That much was obvious."

"By those lights," Gamelyn growled, "the Arrow is most certainly not yours."

"Too true," Wymarec acknowledged, wry. "I could not make such a thing so crude and simple, horrific and effective."

Gamelyn's outraged stiffen was so slight as to almost not be there . . . but the cobra had noticed.

"I meant no criticism, my Brother. Believe me. For the power in that arrow?" Wymarec made a toast with his goblet. "Pure. Astonishing . . . Sit, I tell you," he ordered. "You're shaking and not in control of yourself, and no wonder. The physician dug out a sizeable splinter of bone barely a fortnight ago. It had travelled down your back. You were bleeding out, slowly, from the inside—for several days, the physician believes. No wonder you fainted. How you managed to ride as hard as you did . . . ?" Another toast of the goblet, this time to Gamelyn. "You are truly a Templar Knight."

First the slap, then the kiss. Robyn's memory again—only where once it had shivered weakness along his nerves, now it set them into steel. There was nothing to be said; Gamelyn dipped his head in stiff acknowledgement.

"Had the shard gone sideways instead, or into some vital organ? Well, you would not be standing here, defying your betters as if you are, indeed, someone." No more admiration, real or feigned; Wymarec's voice sharpened, dipped with irritation. "Humility, *Confanonier.* If you wish to rise amongst us as you deserve, you must first bend that proud, stiff neck. Sit. *Down.*"

It was England's Master who spoke. Again, rote and Rule took over, bending Gamelyn's knees before he could so much as think and enforcing a seat on the edge of his narrow cot. But Gamelyn took a large quaff of wine after, to wash down risen bile.

"I would like to know more," Wymarec ventured, once again pleasant, "about this wolfshead who can fashion such a primal and powerful object. Particularly since one of my own has become so . . . intimately acquainted with the man." Gamelyn didn't like the sound of that, not at all, as Wymarec gave another smile and tilt of his own goblet. "But first, let me ease your mind. I will not—cannot—return the object to you. It has been neutralised."

"What?" Gamelyn knew his voice rang flat with disbelief. Wasn't sure he cared, except . . .

Except every little tic, every small slip, be it contempt or drug-befuddled wits or weakened body, was a luxury he knew, deep down, he could ill-afford.

'Twas a serf gave me this most excellent advice, Hubert had once told him, long ago. *Never let one's masters know too much.* Then, as if musing, *I do not imagine such will be a problem with you.*

Gamelyn had then been young enough—naive enough—to feel some guilt over it. Now?

Hardly.

Wymarec shrugged. "There was no choice, I'm afraid, but to release the object from this world. Such things are beyond any control . . . save, mayhap, of the one who fashioned it." He leaned forwards in his chair, cupped his goblet with both hands: one gloved and one finally laid bare, exposed. The scars were thick in places, in others paper-thin, travelling up beneath Wymarec's sleeve. Several fingers were affected. The marks of burning. Torture, mayhap?

Gamelyn did not let his eyes remain there, merely sipped at his own goblet, considering. Wymarec was, for the moment, more intent on words than watching.

"You seem quite intelligent, so I've no doubts you've gleaned a hint of what goes on in the innermost Temple. Indeed, Hubert tells me that at one time he thought you would share in our Great Work, forged with the most elite of our talents. You might yet, Guy-who-is-also-Gamelyn, so this much I shall share with you. That arrow was forged with a will and power beyond our understanding. There is no place within our Temple for such . . . wild magic."

He speaks truth. The Lady, again.

Ah, but what is truth? Gamelyn returned, swift as thought. In the next breath, he wondered how an adept such as Wymarec did not feel Her presence.

Wondered further: why She chose now to be here, with him.

It is the time of the Summering, is it not?

The cold leeching through the stone walls would say otherwise. But Gamelyn seized the opportunity. *Is it here, then? The Arrow? Does he lie?*

You know the taste of it. Of its maker, our forest pwca, *your Winterlord leman. Do you feel it?*

What if—?

Be silent. Feel *it.*

All of it, in the time it took him to take a breath, with Wymarec heeding nothing, speaking again. And in the next breath, Gamelyn cast about, instinctive, scenting and seeking.

" . . . are welcome to search my chambers. As your man and the girl did. They too found nothing."

Aye, and Gamelyn *felt* nothing. No traces, not even a whiff of Robyn's presence.

Though would he know it did he feel it?

And that, the Lady sighed, *is why you do not.*

Wymarec seemed to know Gamelyn was not wholly attentive; his next words were goading. "The girl has her own talents, no question, but nothing of significance, surely. Is she Robyn Hood's whore, then?"

Again, reaction claimed him—a lurch upwards, threat and defence. This time his body betrayed him; agony snagged his back, a giant raptor fastening talons into his spine.

"So." Wymarec's eyebrows rose. "You have some sort of fondness for the woman? Her affection for you was obvious"—a sneer—"but then, women incessantly want what they cannot have. They will go to great lengths to suborn a strong will. Heed your vows, Brother Templar. Hubert led me to believe you were"—another smile, sharing secrets—"not a man for women."

Gamelyn concentrated on attempting breath, watched with eyes going flat as any cobra could wish as Wymarec rose, made his leisurely way to the table where the physician's medicaments sat. Leaning one buttock against it, he contemplated the banner hanging across the small chamber, eyes tracing the piebald lines. Said, "You should have taken the Infirmarer's draught after all, Brother Guy. Hubert also led me to believe you were much more self-possessed, more . . . equipped for siege than the man I see before me."

Siege. He is under siege.

Gamelyn drank the last of his own wine and did not bother to amend the name. Wymarec was correct—in his weakness Gamelyn had already made too many blunders this day.

No doubt Wymarec had planned on that. He hadn't become Master of England by being kind or equitable.

He will be Grand Master. . . Hubert's warning tickled at the back of Gamelyn's skull, moved from cryptic to sudden sense. And, of course, not until Gamelyn was in the middle of it.

Sometimes Gamelyn wished all his mentors, goddesses, and god-plagued lovers would just shut the bloody fuck up.

"Ah, but I make judgements that are, considering your state, mayhap unfair." Wymarec slid a glance his way, then picked up the pewter pitcher, busied himself with taking Gamelyn's goblet from him in a purposeful—and pointed—service. "I must say, the physician was truly surprised when Hubert told him how you had originally been injured. Usually a crossbow injury comparable to the one which struck you would prove crippling, if not fatal. More wild magic? What price, I wonder, does such power claim? I'm hoping that, in time, you will share more with me about this wolfshead of yours."

Almost a tease, and again, Wymarec touched his own mouth to the cup. This time not merely a sip, he ran his tongue along the edge, tipped and took a goodly swallow, then passed it to Gamelyn, all with that slight, edgy smile. "Ah, but that is for another time, yes? When we know one another better."

Gamelyn knew refusal would be another admission. He took the cup, tipped both it and his head in thanks, and drained it.

Wymarec's smile slipped, ever so slight. He covered it by turning away, pacing back to the table and pouring another for himself.

By the time he curved back around, he'd regained the tiny loss, indeed spoke light as if discussing the weather.

"So, Brother Guy. If you wish to redon the white and take your rightful name and place amongst us, then you must regain your control. The best way to do that is by regaining your health and strength. A faulty vessel holds nothing overlong." He sipped at the wine slowly, mulling it over his tongue as surely as the thoughts behind his pale eyes.

"Do you agree?"

Redon the white. . . take your place. . .

"It is sound advice," Gamelyn ventured, whilst his mind spun, furious, to his rescue. "There is one problem, my lord. I can have no place here if my paxman is banished."

"Your paxman made a mistake." The pale eyes went even more so.

"At my orders."

"Another mistake. Pray yours does not prove as damaging as his." Wymarec turned away, raised his voice. "Hubert?"

The door remained closed. Wymarec's mouth tilted—satisfaction—and he peered at Gamelyn, expectant.

The fact that Gamelyn considered throwing the wine cup at him instead of dutifully opening the door as he should? It was both satisfying and unnerving. He wouldn't have considered such mutiny even six months ago, before . . .

Before you woke, and found yourself no longer merely a Templar. The Lady was smug, no question. *This ambitious magician knows it. He courts you, Oakbrother.*

Gamelyn hoisted himself to his feet and went to the door—inward mutiny, this time, even if it hinted at a mewling, angry child.

So a good fuck or two from your resident sodomite outlaw, and you think I'll discard the only life you left me?

And what life is that? the mewling child within insisted. *I want to go home.*

Abrupt and capricious, the Lady cuddled it close, whispered lullabies even as She curled against Gamelyn's still-healing back, breathed protections upon his nape. *Yes. You will have your home, and more. Your leman awaits you in the green Wode, and your paxman, and your Maid. I will be waiting, my Lord.*

But Robyn is your—

Aye, also my Lord. But he is irksome. Stubborn.

And I'm not? he retorted, wanting to laugh and daring not.

About this? Not overmuch. Again, Her breath tickled his nape, heating his spine and quivering in his belly . . . and he was rising against the loose confinement of his braies like a stallion scenting a mare.

Our Hob-Robyn does not possess the necessary passion. But you? You are more. . . flexible in your needs.

My vows—

What of the ones unspoken, and all the more powerful? What of your vow to Me? And it was abruptly Marion's voice he heard, Marion with a moonsilver reflection in her grey eyes, slicing his resolve keen as any dagger. Then, a further twist of blade: *You belong with Robyn. With us. Find a way. Come home, Gamelyn.*

And the entire conversation had taken no more time than Gamelyn moving the several steps towards Hubert's door and raising his voice against the hard oaken planks.

"My lord Commander?"

Again, no response. Gamelyn wondered if Hubert knelt in prayer or meditation; just as he lifted his hand to tap at the door, it pulled inward. Hubert's face was composed, but the keen eyes searched Gamelyn, head to heels.

"My task here is nearly done," Wymarec said, and Gamelyn whirled, grimaced from not only the sudden movement, but at finding him merely an arm's reach away. "There is only tonight, and the working to be done."

Hubert's eyes flicked slightly towards Gamelyn. Surprise. Gamelyn was no less taken aback. One did not speak openly of what passed beneath—not, at least, to ones who were not worthy of its secrets.

He courts you.

Yet Wymarec didn't so much as look at Gamelyn, speaking solely to Hubert. "Upon the morrow, I ride for Temple London, to confer with our Grand Master. There are plans to make for the King's return, and Hirst's information shall be invaluable to him. Much of this is your doing, Hubert, and that of your *Confanonier.* I shall tell Grand Master Erail so."

Hubert inclined his head in silent acknowledgment.

"As for that *Confanonier . . .* " Wymarec did turn to Gamelyn, then; his smile was slight, and cold. "When Brother Guy is well enough for travel, let him be of further service. Even as we have discussed."

Another nod from Hubert. This one held a satisfaction that was less than reassuring; more so as they both turned to peer at Gamelyn.

Wymarec's gaze in particular held to Gamelyn's. "I warn you, Templar. Mind your oaths. Take care not to choke yourself upon what leash we deign to give you."

- XXV -

There was little pleasure to be had in the practise, these days. To the contrary, it remained a bloody painful and aggravating business, this rehabilitation of muscle and bone. It was even worse than the first time.

Gamelyn had been up and attempting to regain his strength since Wymarec de Birkin had left for London nigh onto a month ago. Brother Diata disapproved, calling such exertions "ambitious, bloody-minded pride." The good Brother Infirmarer had the rights, certainly. It was he who kept having to repair things if Gamelyn overstrained. But Gamelyn kept at it.

Hubert was pleased, and that mattered. The cross warmed Gamelyn's throat when a hint of his former strength and skill pulsed through him, and that mattered.

Hefting the sword again, he tried another exercise. It was pathetically simple, but nonetheless a useful drill. He had to get well. Had to be whole. That, too, mattered.

But his mind far outpaced his body, and dreams sped his sleep with yearning. Gamelyn felt in himself a wing-strained hawk, blinkered and jessed to his perch for just that much too long. Whether the hawk would be allowed to fly again?

You know you must tend the muscles, Hirst's wrestling master kept reminding, *before you think to ask them to raise a sword overmuch. You must have patience, hold to the wait. The body remembers its purpose, but your body is not ready to meet that purpose.*

A soft, baritone laugh from memory: *The body remembers, aye?*

There were other things . . . waiting. Voices in his heart. It made convalescence bearable. Even his dreams had turned to soft, waiting things. No more drugs. The Horned Lord had retreated, as if He could only broach preceptory stone when Gamelyn was at his most vulnerable. But the Lady . . .

She was waiting, as well. But not over-softly. Never had She before this season's waxing left Hirst's Lady chapel. She had taken their honour and radiated demure comportment. Now, however?

Now, She followed him, gliding through the spartan halls of Temple Hirst, inhabiting the peripheries of his vision. And She was *beautiful*. Wild, with dark hair tinged scarlet and tumbling about naked brown shoulders, silver bangles at wrist and ankle, robes of indigo rustling against stone and wood, wafting the heady, commingling scents of rose, of frankincense, of greensap spring.

Ah! The sun has burnt me. . .

"My lord?"

Some squire, no doubt, and it brought Gamelyn's attention to the hourglass at the practise area's east entry. It was nearly spent— as he himself. The bells would soon ring Nones, fill the stones with sound.

As if there wasn't sound enough, those stones *breathing* against his feet in fierce inhale and soft release.

Robyn would know what they were saying, Gamelyn was sure of that, as sure as Robyn would smother, here.

"Confanonier!"

At this Gamelyn did turn, only the use of his rank allowing him to recognise the voice. A squire running up—*his* squire, out of breath and a flush suffusing winter-pale skin. Too eager, perhaps, but the lad was skilled.

And noisy. Gamelyn put a finger to his lips, tilting his head towards the others in the armoury; not many at present, but . . . still. Quiet comprised a huge part of the Rule, even if young Stephen was finding it onerous.

But then, Stephen had been assigned in place of Much, so mayhap Gamelyn's selective hearing was more refusal than lack of recognition. Unfair, but there it was. Gamelyn felt like he'd lost his good arm. Had tried more than once to persuade Hubert to ameliorate Much's dismissal—particularly since the one who'd demanded it wasn't likely to return until well past the six months sentence. Of course, Gamelyn knew better. Hubert was sympathetic, but indomitable as ever, and rightly so. Insubordination was anathema, mutiny the first steps along a path of self-destruction. In the Temple must all things, disagreeable or no, run their course.

So, a hound denied the hunt, Gamelyn fastened his rebellion and resentment upon Wymarec de Birkin.

"Brother Guy?"

"What is it, Stephen?" Gamelyn asked, soft, and tried to not exhibit undue relief as his swordpoint tipped to rest against the floor.

"Sir." Chastened, Stephen had choked his voice down to a nigh-whisper. Thankfully it could be heard in the quiet. "There's a stranger at our gate, and Master Hubert wants to see you right away!"

A . . . stranger? Gamelyn's heart gave an odd shiver and thud, and it was only then he realised what he hoped—and how truly absurd that hope was.

"Master Hubert said to tell you . . . " The boy paused, no doubt making sure his words were accurate. "That *an old friend has returned home, but not in a manner either of us expected.*"

Gamelyn frowned, then handed his sword to the lad. "Kindly return this to our cell. I'll change and go from here."

With a duck of his wheat-coloured head, Stephen cradled the shamshir and scooted away.

Of all the hopes he'd entertained the past, drawn-out month, this was both greatest and least. Unexpected. Gamelyn's feet faltered upon the stones, just as unsure as his gaze. The duty guardsmen were there, of course. Hubert waited this side of the opened gates with several lay brothers at heel.

Just past Hubert waited Much. Standing a proper distance of two paces outside the preceptory, one hand on his sword hilt and the other holding the rein to a stout, iron-grey rouncey, Much looked well—if a bit thin—and hard. His sudden, brilliant smile upon Gamelyn's approach belied that hardness.

A warm surge of affection filled Gamelyn's belly and he quickened his pace, didn't stop until he was past the gate and grasping his friend's broad shoulders. "*Putain de merde . . .* you're *here!*"

Much wasn't so constrained. He nearly hoisted Gamelyn off his feet with a huge, hard embrace, chattering as eager as Stephen had ever done.

"Sweet Lady, milord, 'tis good to see you!

"I never thought—"

"Feels like a year, 'stead of a month!"

"Marion. Did you fetch her back safe? Is she—?"

"She's well. She's with t'others, and Himself." An inexplicable tint rising in his cheeks, Much pushed Gamelyn back. His blue eyes were swimming wet. "*You* en't looking so well. You're awful pale."

"It is still winter, after all," Gamelyn said, wry, and cuffed a hand at Much's temple. "Have you joined the outlaws, then? Look at you, a proper wild man with all that hair."

"Whilst you're a bloody rack of bones . . . begging your pardon, milord!" Much apologised as his hug turned to a shake and Gamelyn winced, ever so slight. "You're overdoin' it, en't you?"

"As usual," Hubert drawled, and they both started like guilty boys, turned to make quick, belated acknowledgement. Hubert paid little attention. He was eyeing a rather-fine sheet of parchment, unrolled in his hands. "But he would not be your lord and my *Confanonier* if he did not always push, pace, and push, like a caged lion." A shrug, and Hubert twisted the parchment back into its snug roll, handed it to Gamelyn.

Gamelyn peered at it, brows quirking.

"Well?" Hubert seemed impatient—or bemused, Gamelyn wasn't altogether sure. "Take it. See what your paxman-turned-messenger has brought to our gates."

Turned . . . messenger? Gamelyn took the parchment roll and eyed Much, who gave a laconic shrug. All sorts of questions begged utterance; instead, Gamelyn opened the missive. The moment he glanced at it, he knew Marion's hand. It answered no questions, and surely the thrill-chill that roiled in his gut then settled in his chest was untoward. Commanding himself to some sensibility, he read. Not once, but thrice over, a tiny smirk begging, then tugging his lip.

> To my lord Hubert de Gisborough, Master and Commander of Temple Hirst:
>
> Greetings.
>
> It was my old and beloved mentor, Cernun, hailed by the Wise dryw ardhu, and now taken to the Lady's embrace in the otherworlds, with whom you first treated in peace and wisdom and for the understandings of pleasant intercourse. Indeed, in the time after this past Samhain, you declared your willingness to extend that same courtesy to my self, upon whom is bestowed Horns and Cup, and the Maid, my sister-consort who wields the Arrow of Our Lady.
>
> At present you have within your ranks and fealty one who also bears his own honours, and therefore, is sworn

*and dear to us. If my lord de Gisbourne, known to those
of the Shire Wode covenant as Gamelyn, is held within
his own consent, then we have no reason to disagree.
Indeed, I would have us, for his sake as well as good will,
clasp hands and reaffirm the accord of Cernun. In truth, it
has become necessary to speak of many things.*

*Yet if my lord de Gisbourne is not held within his own
consent, then I pray you reconsider your charge. It should be
taken into account whether any covenant of the White Christ
has the rights to claim or hold what is ours by right, be it
hallowed artefact or sworn consort. Nottingham is testament
to what can be laid upon those who scorn the ancient ways.*

*Much better, then, that we meet in amity, one with
another, in a safe and mutual place upon which the bearer
of this message has been empowered to agree.*

*For the thawing is now upon us, my lord, and he who is
dryw ardhu of the Shire Wode covenant would fain claim
his Summerlord home.*

Robyn Hode

The first thing that came to Gamelyn's mind was how no doubt
Robyn had put that bloody "intercourse" in there on bloody *purpose.*

The second was outrage—how dare that arrogant, buggering *sod*
of a wolfshead . . . *treat* for him? Like he was some well-landed
widow?

The third was a self-conscious, silent curl of satisfaction. Robyn
was coming. Robyn wanted him back, and badly enough to throw
a veritable gauntlet at the whole of Hirst to see it done.

You have sommat as is mine, Templar. Robyn's voice purled from
the missive, and then Marion's. *Summer must come to the Shire Wode.*

Summer must claim what is his by right. The Lady, at his shoulder.
*The Maying comes, and the stones must let you go. Set them aside,
lovely Oak, in places of honour, to make room for Plough and Seed.*

Gamelyn shivered. How apropos, that She whispered at his *left*
shoulder.

"Well?" Hubert demanded.

The voice was soft, yet still a whipcrack into stillness. Gamelyn
looked up, found the guards dismissed to a discreet distance,
Much watching him with a mix of concern and conviction, and
Hubert . . .

"Well?" Hubert said. "What is your opinion to this?"

Gamelyn blinked.

"Yes, yes!" was Hubert's demand, pettish. "I am asking your opinion. You know these outlaws better than I. There is no reason we cannot meet with them . . . despite the arrogance of *this*"—he reached out, took the parchment—"which is, given circumstance, not entirely unjustified. So. Are you, ah, 'held within your own consent'?"

"Commander!" Gamelyn protested.

"I am impressed by the way this peasant frames a letter," Hubert mused, looking over the missive. "It shows a remarkable presence of mind. He believes we have something that belongs to him, so in true chivalrous process, he has demanded either hearing or confrontation. I've no doubt the Maid at his elbow has her own . . . agenda." His eyes rose to Gamelyn's, then slid sideways and took in Much, waiting stout as any oak and just as deliberate.

A frown twitched at Much's brow, and he seemed chary as to whom he should look to: first Gamelyn, then Hubert, and back again.

Hubert stepped closer, laid one hand upon Gamelyn's shoulder— light, with some consideration of weakness—yet forcing Gamelyn to return his gaze to Hubert.

"We will speak of this in private," Hubert told Much, a benign dismissal, but one nevertheless. "You may wait, or return to these gates before the sun sets behind the trees, there." A wave of one hand towards the grey silhouettes of elm and birch near the river's bend.

"I'll wait." Much's answer was firm, but he caught Gamelyn's gaze again, a plea.

Hubert saw it, ignored it, and gestured Gamelyn back through the gate.

"He looks to have settled well enough in Sherwood," Hubert mused, looking out the window of his chamber. Beside him, Gamelyn had to agree that Much did, rather.

Leaning against the stones, giving his horse enough rein to graze the commons just past the gate, Much was engaging in spare speech with young Stephen, who had been assigned watch upon— but was more curious about—the man who had previously served the *Confanonier*. It was obvious that Robyn—or Marion, now Gamelyn thought on it— had possessed enough sense to give Much some sort of purpose. The trust implied in this errand eased Gamelyn's heart, yet also gave an ever-so-slight twist of rue. Would Much return when he could?

Unworthy, the thought. They had seen too much together to doubt what each owed the other. Even if it became a fond fare-you-well.

"He will fare well there, serve out his time into the new year and the spring rising." The dwindling sun spilled past Hubert, glimmering the silver in his beard and slatting into the dim-close stones. It made a lamp unnecessary and left murky shadows in the far reaches of the chamber. "And how would you fare, my *Confanonier*," Hubert continued, still looking out, "at the side of your brother-in-arms? In the spring's rising, running with your wild wolf, his pack, and his, ah, vixen?"

Gamelyn slid his gaze to Hubert's profile, breath escaping in a long hiss.

"Would you choose to return your oath, should I offer your release from it?"

Like our kind ever has choices.

Shut up! he told the memory, merely thankful it didn't clothe itself in Thorn and Rose, or Horn and Holly . . . but then She ran fingers of mist and new leaves down his spine, hummed, *Come to Me.*

Why, so you can use me to betray him again?

Nay, so We can make of thisworld more than forgetfulness, betrayal, and death!

He almost—*almost*—wanted to believe Her. Gamelyn hardened his heart and mind, seeing blood seeping through his fingers and a black arrow flaming, arcing against the green.

"What oaths I have made, I will keep." Started firm, it faltered beneath the memory: those very words, vibrating cold in the depths of fever dreams.

And Hubert's gaze, never leaving him. As if Gamelyn were himself some unique and troublesome artefact.

"My lord Commander," Gamelyn finally murmured, looking down. "What would you have me do?"

"I would have you," Hubert said, curt, "for once, admit your will in this matter. England's Master has noticed you and made many plans upon your dispensation and shall have you do his bidding regardless. Yet I, Hubert de Gisborough, Master and Commander of Hirst Preceptory? I would know this much about the man with whom I have fought and bled, shielded and prayed—the one who carried our banner beside me for the past four years!" He leaned closer, until his breath stirred the hair at Gamelyn's temple, a gilt flutter at the edges of their sight. "What is in your belly? In your heart?"

"Neither are the same as what my will would see done." Quick, almost furtive, the answer—but undeniable.

"Ah, then," Hubert murmured, not moving away, "but our will is not our own. Is it? So, what is your will? *Whose* is yours?"

Gamelyn met his mentor's eyes, was held there, writhing through a glut of foreign, fatal emotions.

Hubert's grip tightened, painful, then he bent closer and kissed Gamelyn, first one cheek, then the other. He pushed back, blue eyes suspiciously a-glimmer. Peered at him, moments stretching long, then nodded. Turned away. Clasping his hands behind his back, Hubert paced into the murky shelter of those shadows lengthening across the chamber.

More interminable moments, each one nigh swallowed in silence. Hubert finally spoke, soft against the shadows.

"Master Wymarec has given us our charge, *Templier*. Where our Order demands us, we will go. Be it to Outremer and the caravanserais of the East Road beyond, to the keeps of our fathers in Normandy and Anjou, or"—a shrug—"even the sweet green Wode."

Gamelyn's heart shuddered against his breastbone. He did not drop his gaze from Hubert. In truth, could not.

"Mayhap," Hubert ventured, "there is a way you can keep to all your oaths . . . ah, I neglected to inform you." He turned. "Speaking of oaths, your paxman brought not just the one, but two messages."

And if Gamelyn's heart had given a hard twist as Hubert had kissed him, it lurched and jerked and fell downwards as Hubert came from shadow into a shaft of fading light. As Gamelyn saw what was hanging almost negligently between the callused fingers of his master's right hand:

Gamelyn's quillion dagger. Robyn's dagger. *Their dagger.*

Hubert forgot little, did nothing that was negligent.

"Much said you would recognise it," Hubert continued, still so quiet, so . . . *casual.* "Said he'd been requested to tell you that you would know why it had been sent."

Why it had been sent . . . why Robyn had sent it. Surely he didn't know what Gamelyn had dreamed, over and over and over . . .

Why?

Challenge? Another gamble, another game for the Horned Lord's own *pwca*? A gauntlet thrown?

A . . . good-bye?

A swift lurch forwards, with unhealed tendons snatching a grunt from Gamelyn, bringing him back to sanity. At the last moment he kept himself from seizing the blade from Hubert. But his fingers gave an angry, thwarted tremble as Gamelyn contained them to measured-slow acceptance, curling about the dagger's oak pommel.

All the while Hubert watched him, just as measured, just as slow. Taking it all into account.

Then, again, turned away.

"I think we shall meet, you and I alone, with this *dryw ardhu* . . . this black druid." Hubert translated the Barrow Talk effortlessly. "An ominous title, eh? We shall see what choices—or challenges— he would offer."

Like our kind ever has choices, the Lady whispered, mimicry from the shadows just beyond Hubert.

It sounded all too satisfied.

Robyn half expected the proffered meeting place to be refused.

So when Much came riding into the forest overlooking Blyth— carefully, for even if the rumours held truth and Count John had fled, he'd left behind enough troops to hold the place—and deliv- ered Master Hubert's agreement, Robyn was thrown for six.

But only for a span of heartbeats. He had, after all, issued another sort of challenge by sending along the dagger with Marion's letter.

"How is he?" This from Marion—and wasn't she more anxious than she wanted to let on? Lit with sparks to set the entire woven swath upon *tynged*'s loom aflame.

So many kinds of love. All this wealth, waiting, and only a fool would refuse it.

And it is past time for your leman to shrug aside the mantle of the Fool, the Horned Lord muttered.

Robyn quieted him with a soft breath as Much said, mostly to Marion, "He's well enough. Though he looks like bloody murderin' hell. Been pushing too hard."

"They'll be here tomorrow, then," she murmured, frowning as she looked down.

"Aye. As y' asked for: when the moon begins to rise, a few hours past noon-tide, in this place." Much gestured to the tiny cavern where he, Robyn, and Marion had stayed the night. He didn't know the place, only that it lay close to where they'd camped with the Queen and her trouvère. But Robyn and Marion did.

And Gamelyn sure as bloody hell did.

Robyn wished he could have seen the cant to those juniper- green eyes when Much had asked, oblivious to what he was asking.

Much reached out, albeit gingerly, to brush back the fat curl fallen over Marion's scrunched brows. Marion looked up, slight surprise levelling into a dollop of gratification as well as a liberal helping of *about bloody time, you daft bugger.*

Aye, Robyn had to agree, *'tis about bloody time. You should've been the one as kept her warm last night, not her brother. Damn me, but you'd better find some sort of compass in this, and right quick. Else I'll pound you into butter for hurting my sister. You and your bloody Milord the Stubborn Arse of a Bloody-Minded Templar.*

All kinds of love, and they'd trammel it in stone. Fearing it, all of 'em, and passing that fear on like pox, or leprosy.

Robyn walked a few paces away, pretending to ponder but in truth letting his two companions have some kind of moment, whatever it might end up being. Not for the first time, he was satisfied with his insistence upon the others staying behind. As usual, John had taken charge—and John's relief as to why and whatfor had seemingly infected the others. Gilbert and David had openly professed their support—Gilbert with a sly, fond dig at how Robyn kept moping like a silly twelve-year-old lass over "that scarlet knight of his." Arthur was resigned, nowt more, but agreeable for all that.

The odd thing? There hadn't even been a peep of *I'm going with you* protest from Charming William.

It niggled behind Robyn's eyeballs, an itch he couldn't so much as scratch. Will was being too biddable, too quiet. Biding his time, he was . . . but for what and why?

Hoping that Gamelyn wouldn't return to the Wode; that he was, finally, gone?

Not if I can help 't, Robyn swore. The Horned Lord growled soft agreement/threat as Robyn cleared his throat and spoke aloud.

"The dagger?"

Marion's hand was in Much's—promising, that. Much started, tried to pull away. Robyn smirked as Marion didn't let him.

"The—?"

"Dagger," Robyn repeated. "Does he have it, then?"

Much nodded. "I didn't see Master Hubert give it ower, but when they came back, milord had it stuck in his belt."

A taunt lay sheathed with that dagger, lacing the quillion's keen edge like salt and lye.

Assuming, of course, Gamelyn didn't just bind up whatever painful slice it gave, let it sting and seep more ice into his heart.

It's what I'm best at after all, isn't it? Feeling nothing?

Then why are you staying, milord? Duty? Love? Fear?

Tomorrow. They would see each other tomorrow, and Robyn would need nothing more than the look in Gamelyn's eyes to guess at the game.

We will give the Temple sorcerers something to see, well enough, the Horned Lord promised. *We will be waiting.*

It tilted a ruthless, satisfied smile to Robyn's lips.

All kinds of love, waiting.

Marion's right, Robyn thought, grim. *'Tis time to throw the bones again. To know, win or lose, whether we* will *win. Or lose like bloody damn.*

Once, there had been three children in the green Wode. Two lads and a lass, altogether naive, and a little too eager to think they could escape the realities of their existence.

They'd learned. O, had they learned.

But until they had, they'd made their own world in a tiny cave beneath the very noses of the ones who'd thought to teach them their place.

Here, it had been.

If he blinked, Gamelyn wondered, might the Wode's magic take him back?

Nay, he decided, closing his seat in the saddle and his fingers on Falcon's rein. There was no magic left to thisworld so powerful, to set time to naught.

He didn't even notice that the word ran together—*thisworld*—like *they* would have said. Not for a few heartbeats, anyway.

Time. Thisworld, and thisnow, and still no hope of any existence where they could just *be.*

Only four years ago.

Only a lifetime.

Robyn and Marion were standing in the cavern's mouth, waiting. For him. With a fire blazing behind and the ghost of a new moon wafting over, framed by bare trees and wisps of grey sky.

Everything had changed, and nothing.

No choices.

Only the knowledge that, once again, his feet were set upon the path of betrayal and destruction.

This time, however, he could see it going in.

He'd surely known the power this place, this moment, would bring.

Yet Robyn had woefully underestimated its power upon his will and heart.

It did not stagger him. Instead, it fed the flames with pitch and alder.

He heard them before they saw them; two horses picking their way through deadfall and brittle-dead bracken, with that peculiar blunted and prickly *thup* of hoofs upon thawing ground. Then two mounted silhouettes upon the small, overgrown path. The sun rippled, then broke fully from behind a thin cloud, limning tunics of white and black with scarlet breasts, catching a glint of bay hide and black mane, and the ultimate telltale: a gleam of autumn splintering gilt against cold, heavy grey.

Robyn had, and more than the once, told Gamelyn that his fair head was a liability, did he want to not be seen in the woodland.

Not that two Templar Knights were worried on *that*.

As they rode ever closer, Robyn let his senses spill out behind them, around them, was satisfied this much of the bargain had been kept.

"They're alone," Marion confirmed, putting her hands on his shoulders.

"Aye." He covered her cold fingers with his. "Waiting is done."

Aye, and he'd been proper willing to the wait. Robyn had curled protective arms about his wounded consorts, cosseting their unhealed hearts, sheltering their tender powers, carrying the burdens. Because he could.

No more. His Mari had shouldered her own bow; Gamelyn would do no less.

You'll give him back to me, he swore to the Templars. *You'll honour my place and let loose of what's mine, or I swear by Horns and Arrow, what I brought down on Nottingham'll be nowt to what I'll bring upon you.*

Surely her heart shouldn't be in her mouth, seeing the two Templars ride in all calm, piebald-garbed, and seeming more at-odds chess figures than compatriots.

Yet compatriots they surely were; strung together tight as a good Welsh longbow by their god and their shared battles. Hubert and Gamelyn halted their horses together, dismounted together, advanced together—albeit Gamelyn hanging a slight and proper stride back—all as smooth as her mam's spring butter. It proved there was every reason, did Robyn put it to a choice, for Gamelyn to choose what he was—not what he'd been. Not what he could be.

But there was *every* reason to choose this. Her brother beside her, tall and lithe-strong and all but vibrating with the vitality of his place, his god. Much, who had left them to it and disappeared into the woodland, loyal paxman and willing sacrifice to the choice Gamelyn had, in truth, already made. That woodland, beginning to wake, burgeoning with the coming rebirth. Vibrating through every fibre of being Marion possessed.

She was also a reason, and had her reasons to call Gamelyn home. To fence with the Master of Temple Hirst—or his Master, did it come to it. And it would.

You need t' be chilly, like, when you strike the blow.

Marion wished, for a split intake of breath, that Much was here, with her. Then realised it was likely better that he wasn't.

There were things, hot-sharp and replete, that none but the *Ceugant* could hold.

- ENTR'ACTE -

Power dwelt here, here, raw and hot-sweet, on a fine-spun thread
of control. Hubert could nigh taste it. It clung in his nostrils and
lay thick in the back of his throat; he swore if he bared his arm and
smoothed a hand over skin, he would come away with a glimmering of it, marking his palm.

The lanky, black-haired peasant had more magic vibrating wild
behind his eyes than most Temple Magicians could summon with
an hour of incantations and blood and sweat. There was no doubt
that, with a flick of his bow-callused fingers, this *black druid*—and
how apropos was that?—could summon angels or demons . . . and
need neither.

And the girl, with her demure calm that hid living flame. Behind
storm-sea eyes lay a power no less wild than her brother's, but
more . . . considered. If Robyn Hode could call the wind, his Maid
would be able to raise a hand to calm it—or direct it to level a
village. She held a grace both savage and cultivated, and met
Hubert's gaze like an equal.

Wymarec would have been furious. But misogyny was a blindness
Hubert did not share with his Master. Masculine oaths of life and
living were not compromised by swearing fealty upon the altar
of the Magdalene—which Hubert had done, long ago. The godling
man, Horned and Hooded, Hubert understood, respected, and did
not fear. The Divine Feminine, however . . .

Even her name: *Marion.*

She would have Her due, that one.

And together? Lord and Lady, both winnowed into avatars of

chaos, seeking what fate would demand of them. Aye, worthy of respect, and care.

Hubert could also See—did he shutter his eyes and let the appeals for such come, half-swallowed and silent, to his tongue—what They meant to demand of him, this day. Their consort, wearing the tabard of his father's god, but in whom the old Saxon gods of his mother pounded through his veins with undeniable talent and the sap and salt of Summer's coming.

Nothing but some unspeakable fear of that same destiny, which Robyn Hode and the Maid Marion were speeding towards with opened arms, had stayed Gamelyn this long.

Fear and—Hubert amended, and hoped—love for his Master and his Order.

Wymarec's instincts had been true. Again. Thankfully Hubert had leave to grant this Maiden and Archer what they sought—if not quite in the way they sought it.

After that, he mused, he would merely close his eyes.

- XXVI -

The mead blessed in its wooden bowl, Marion took it from her brother and passed it to a seated Hubert across the fire, with Her own blessing. "*Bendith*, milord Templar. I bid you welcome to our place."

From stubborn pique alone—or so it seemed to Marion—Gamelyn had chosen to stand just behind Hubert's left shoulder. He seemed willing to take up the diffident cloak of lackey or guard, determined not to be present unless called upon as shield or threat. His eyes were just as opaque, giving nothing away.

Stubborn bastard.

No less a stubborn bastard, her brother refused to sit. Robyn crouched on his haunches like a wolf, looming close to the hearth. His eyes were as naked as Gamelyn's were not: wary upon his lover, watchful upon the Templar Master.

Marion took the blessing bowl over to Gamelyn—since he didn't look as if he was coming closer—and held it out to him. "Will you share this much?"

Stern, it dared refusal. Gamelyn didn't rise to it; he took the bowl with steady hands and drank. As he handed the bowl back to her, mead glistened on his upper lip—or was it sweat? He wiped at it with the back of one hand before she could confirm or deny, and gave a small, tight dip of head. Nothing else; his face might have been of stone.

Or might not. Another voice, faint behind Marion's eyes, made answer to some internal dialogue: Lady and Knight. *Fie. If you* were *given the choice, whatever would you do with it?* It was mocking, but with a soft, fond overlay.

"Come sit," Marion implored.

Gamelyn's gaze rose to meet Marion's. Just as swiftly he looked down, away, his cheeks ashen. He followed her, closer to the fire—but he did not sit. He maintained his guard's position, his face in shadow. One hand hovered at his hip—ready or uncertain—to a metal hilt, half shadow and half spark.

It wasn't his sword, still slung in its scabbard across his back, but the quillion dagger.

Marion gave it up and went back to the fireside. She knelt at her brother's right hand, across from Gamelyn, then dipped her fingers into what mead remained in the blessing bowl. As she flicked it at the flames, Robyn's lips vibrated, breathing the charm even as she did. The fire took breath, offering, and due with a hiss and flare.

Gamelyn's eyes were closed—either refusing or overwhelmed, she'd no way of knowing. Hubert was watching, curious. Intent.

Only then did Marion rise again, taking up the wine sack sitting at Robyn's hip. She made herself busy with taking smaller bowls from the supplies they'd brought—to serve mead for the enjoyment, this time.

"A fine, snug place." Hubert motioned about the little cavern. "I imagine you have many such hideaways, tucked away across your territories."

"Not many hold up to this one," Robyn said, with a glance upwards at Gamelyn. If her brother had winged by sending the dagger, now he was going for the kill. "Happens I've heard it likened to your god's Eden, a time or three."

Not that Gamelyn was about to react to that, either. Tucking his chin, he met Robyn's gaze with cool, practised consideration. But there was no victory in the green eyes when Robyn turned aside.

What are you trying to prove? Marion implored. *Eden, remember? Your Master is here, treating with us. He is willing to give you leave!*

Or mayhap not. The chill was sudden. Mayhap that was why Gamelyn stood so remote and angry.

Again, Marion occupied herself with host duties, pouring mead.

"Gods. Yes." Hubert nodded. "It is why we are here, *non?*"

"And goddesses," Robyn put in. "But happens your god en't so fond of the Lady's face."

"Of which god do you speak?" Hubert accepted the bowl of mead Marion handed him with a grateful smile and nod.

"Mayhap my ignorance is speaking," Robyn conceded, "but I thought your like refused any god but the one."

"Such readings of the original text can be argued. The insistence upon certain, ah, tropes?—well, such things rise and fall with the aims of those in power—and in direct correlation with *their* ignorance." Hubert shrugged. "Or should I say, wanton stupidity? After all, ignorance can be levied, taught. As to the God of Jerusalem, He is known by many names, with many forerunners and aspects. Some of them female." Another dip of his head to Marion.

"I've only tangled with the one." Robyn slid another dark glance at Gamelyn. "And that one has done his best to take what's mine."

"Is anything, truly, ours?" Hubert riposted, and Robyn blinked. Marion was no less surprised by the sentiment—a question of the Eastern faiths, and the Gnostics. Hubert's eyes twinkled in due note of her understanding. In the next moment, he took a drink of mead and broadly grinned. "Ah! But I must say *this*"—he held up his bowl—"is wonderful. Never have I tasted honey wine so brilliantly brewed. Usually it is raw, too sweet, *non?*"

One of Robyn's eyebrows lifted as he took his own bowl from Marion. "I'll tell the man you're grateful for his craft. 'Tis to be hoped the Church won't take more of the lands as—how'd you say 't?—*en't his?* But the Church seems to think it's theirs, and've already come in like carrion birds, turned out half the cots and caused a proper swarm of Wulfstan's bees, halfway to Derby."

Oh, Hob-Robyn. Are you trying *to annoy the Templar?* Marion hid a quirk of lip that was more admiring than chiding, and poured more mead for Gamelyn and herself. Across the fire, Gamelyn was trying—and failing—to stop a roll of his eyes.

Hubert, to his credit, refused such annoyance. "That would be a great shame, indeed. It is lamentable, how such things happen in war—and it seems to me this lovely island has been in a strange and subtle war for a very long time, *oui?*" Taking another appreciative sip of mead, Hubert smiled, swallowed, and continued. "I must say, though the God of my fathers is a vengeful sort, formed of a young and downtrodden people, I think His Son would weep tears of blood to see what wrongs are done in the name of the Christ."

If Marion was liking this Hubert de Gisborough all the more, Robyn was frowning more with each word spoken. Marion could only hope Hubert would not construe it as weakness.

"Retribution is, sometimes, necessary. Justice will not stake itself. I believe you and yours understand this." Hubert gave a courteous tip of his mead bowl first to Marion, then to Robyn. "It is why we are here, why I treated with your wise predecessor. The . . . coalescence, eh? Merging our struggles and faiths."

A sudden hope filled Marion's belly as that word—*coalescence*—

vibrated upon Robyn's lips so slight. The taste of it seemed to agree with him, though he didn't fully comprehend it, that much was plain.

"We." Robyn's voice was flat as he once again lifted his gaze to take in Gamelyn. Hubert's eyes, taking in Robyn, widened. Marion sensed the cause; Sensed it, actually, tugging at her even before the fire pulled it into full illumination. The Horned Lord's beast-eyes challenged, gold within jet, and His growl, couched itself within Robyn's voice, tilted musical, all spun cobwebs and blackest earth. "Does he speak for you, then? Oakbrother?"

"Do you speak for Marion?" Gamelyn shot back.

Aye, well, and that was enough. "When I've need to speak, I will," Marion's gaze tried to pin Gamelyn to the wall as she approached and extended his bowl of mead.

Gamelyn took the drink but refused to be so pinned. He answered Robyn, terse. "Hubert is Master of Temple Hirst. You asked to treat with the Master of Temple Hirst. About my . . . disposition, as I recall, among other things." Then, lower and no less a growl than Robyn's own query: "What is between us is another matter. We will speak to it, anon."

"That we will, pet." Robyn turned his full attention back to Hubert, eyes now reflecting more the hearth than any internal flame. "To treaties and talks, then. You do your damnedest to dance around it, but you're a Templar Knight, of the Church and empowered by the Crown. I've learned a wee bit about your Order in these past months." It curled, ironic. "Monks and nobles are what's set against me and mine. To say that nowt is ours is an inner truth, fit for the otherworld, but we're living thisnow, in thisworld. And what claims our heart or hand can be taken, destroyed. Has been, more than t' once, and by your like. Why should we trust you?"

Aye, Marion considered, *trying* to brass off the Templar, no question. Gamelyn refused to rise to that bait, but peered at his Commander. Would Hubert take it?

"Mayhap not I," Hubert conceded. "But I have brought one you have come to trust. Nobleman and Brother—and more, so he once told me."

Robyn was giving nothing away; but neither was Gamelyn, his face shadowed.

Then Gamelyn made soft admittance. "I told no lie. But to trust me is a fool's bargain." The last words hardened. Marion put down the mead sack, would have retorted.

Robyn beat her to it. "The Fool makes no bargains." It was not angry, but gentle. "He *is* the bargain."

Again, nothing from the shadows, but Marion thought she saw Gamelyn's fingers tighten on the dagger's hilt.

"A powerful figure, the Fool," Hubert concurred. "Even more when combined with the Hanged Man."

A strange chill-thrill raced up and down Marion's spine. She took up her own bowl and drank from it, long and warm. Robyn kept looking to Gamelyn, expression unreadable, the fire-and-ice of the Horned Lord rampant in his gaze.

Hubert cleared his throat, continued. "You are correct—somewhat—in assuming the Temple's alliance with the Church. But not all of us are born to vast honours. And power—true power—comes to who it wills, and when." He straightened. "Let me explain. My Order is, ah, separate from the Church, answerable only to the Holy Father, with whom we have an . . . understanding. We are more than monks, by our very existence and creed. Of course"—a wry smile flitted across the grey-bearded face—"this often is not agreeable to the Church. Thankfully we possess much knowledge that is . . . useful. Those in power need us, but they do not trust us. And they should not. We know too much. About many things."

Gamelyn seemed more surprised by the revelation itself than of what it told.

Robyn's mouth fell open but no sound came out.

Marion found herself murmuring, "You're . . . a threat."

"I believe the proper term would be *coercion*," Hubert offered, helpful. "But *oui*, knowledge is always a potential threat to those fearful and jealous of power. Alas, that a few men have turned a serpent's wisdom into an avatar of evil."

"We were speaking to truce," Marion retorted. "Not threats."

"Ah, but is not any good truce backed up by threat?" Hubert countered. "Is it not true that any treaty worth having is met and matched by each side having damned fine weapons they'd rather not use?"

Marion frowned, mulling it over.

Whilst she did, Robyn found his own tongue, addressed Gamelyn with a rueful smirk. "Now I see why you like this Commander of yours." He sat back on his heels. "Hearken the pair of you, clever as old dog foxes . . . and me sister as well. Thinking on things as don't need so much thinking."

Marion was abruptly weary—weary of it all, spoken and unspoken—and they seemed no closer to their purpose than when the two Templars had first ridden up. She busied herself with refilling cups, thought upon how her mam would approve her attention to host-duties. More so, certainly, than making pacts with noblemen. "More mead, *Chevalier?*"

Hubert smiled and held out his bowl. Marion poured, did likewise for Robyn, then walked over to Gamelyn. She poured a generous libation into Gamelyn's bowl, found her frustrations pouring just as freely.

"Drink up, pet, and we'll hope another draught or three will help unclench that iron jaw. Or whats'mever needs it, aye?"

She hadn't meant it to be heard save by Gamelyn, but in the small cavern, sound travelled all too well. Robyn snorted up a laugh that nearly sprayed good mead all over Hubert. Hubert raised his brows, tilted his bowl to them both, and took another drink.

"What in hell is that supposed to mean?" Gamelyn hissed, his face blanching even more.

Mayhap it was the mead as well as frustration. Or mayhap she was just wanting to see something—anything—on that too-composed face. Marion shrugged. "I've no understanding of why you're just standing back and waiting. Like you've no say or stake in this."

"What makes you think I have?"

Nay, no need for the honey ferment; Marion snarled a soft curse and flipped a smack to the russet pate. Gamelyn didn't even see it coming.

"Ow! *Marion—!*

"Bloody damn but I've just about had enough of this! You rode with a nasty barb in your back for how long?" she snapped, shoving the stopper back into the wine sack's mouth. "You stand here like you don't give proper sod-all about any of it, but I smack you like you damn-well deserve and *then* you yip like a bairn!"

"For Christ's sake, Marion—!"

"Nay, for *our* sake! *All* of us, and what's left of the Wode. Or if you en't caring about that, then think of *Robyn!*"

"Bloody sodding . . . !" Gamelyn trailed off then tried again, prodded just that much too far. "Think of us? The Wode? *Robyn?* Like you think I'm not? What do you think all of this is for . . . *putain de merde,* woman—this *is* for Robyn!" It rang into sudden, keen silence.

Gamelyn's face splotched, pale and crimson flaring through the half shadows. Marion angled forwards; it was then he actively panicked. No thought to it, just a lightning-quick whirl of escape. But the cavern wall foiled him. Lurching to another swift halt, he stood there, staring into nothing.

Marion wanted—really wanted—to follow. But from the iron set to those broad shoulders, it was likely the worst thing she could possibly do. She clenched her hands tight in her green kirtles.

Come home to us, Gamelyn, she wanted to say and dared not. *Please. Stop all this.*

As if she'd spoken aloud, the answer came, just as choked-silent. *Oh, I'll come. I've no choice, heart or head. But I won't stop it. What's meant. Fate.* Tynged. *Hell, all of it. Forever and ever shall be, end without end, amen.*

The trace of uncanny contact shut itself down.

Forever, end without end. How true, for always, the Lady inserted into the muddle that abruptly comprised Marion's thoughts, *has our Summerlord caged himself with his own doubts.*

Then help *him!* Marion pleaded, silent into the black. It vibrated behind her eyes, as if in consideration.

Ah, Maiden-sister. That is not mine to do. Or yours. The god must claim his own strengths, his own place.

Marion eyed that black-clad back then, hands still twisting in fabric, turned back to the other two men. Hubert's gaze openly brushed hers, cool and, oddly enough, approving. Robyn's was the worst—watching Gamelyn, dark and disquieted. A stricken *knowing* lurked there, as if in that scant and scared moment he'd ferreted every secret Gamelyn possessed.

Yet he broke the silence almost carelessly. "I have t' say, milord Templar"—and his words were just as heedless, were one not watching his eyes—"there's sommat about your god that makes a man willing to martyr himself for the chanciest things. Aye?"

"That is not the subject of discussion here," Gamelyn growled to the wall—and if he knew it was desperate, he didn't seem to care. "We were talking treaties."

"My *Confanonier* is correct." Hubert's concession was dry; he leaned forwards, eyeing Robyn. "To you, *dryw ardhu,* I would say that we of the Temple have no wish to be at war with those of the Heath. Indeed, we have many things in common."

"And what would celibate monks have in common with us?" Robyn's tone still held challenge, but it had lessened.

"Just as there is power to be had in release," Hubert spoke to Robyn's query as if nothing else had entered his mind, "there is power to be had in, ah, containment. I think you understand this more than you know."

Robyn was frowning.

"Have you never lain with a woman?"

Not that it was a wise confession to make to any of the White Christ, but then, her little brother had never been one to hide when pinned. "Nay."

"Are your gods happy with your . . . celibacy?"

A snort. "Happens I en't celibate."

"I'd wager in *their* eyes, you are. The Horned Lord and Lady Huntress are consorts, partners. Harvest and fertility deities, aye?"

Was Robyn looking . . . uncomfortable?

"So in a way, you are *Their* sacrifice."

Over by the wall, Gamelyn had stiffened. His hand, resting on the quillion dagger, curled about it in absolute and mindless reaction to the words.

Robyn had noted everything. His gaze held to Gamelyn as he spoke—ostensibly to Hubert. "There's no 'in a way' to't. Only a daft fool'd not ken what my price will eventually be—and one I agreed, long ago, to pay."

"The price," Hubert mused, "of a strange and subtle war."

"'Tis a war *we* never asked for," Marion said, abruptly. "But we're in it, nevertheless." And all the while she made silent entreaty against that broad, black-clad back. *Turn around. Please. . .*

"War is a hideous business," Hubert agreed. "The things to which it drives men, even more so." His eyes lingered upon Gamelyn, then Marion, as if curious. "Ah, the avoidance of it would seem merely sensible. But there are also times it is of divine purpose."

"Only a man would say so," Marion retorted. "One with no bairns to lose and no home to be burnt."

"Yet the face of the goddess can be cruel, can punish, *n'est-ce pas?*" Hubert countered. "There is, in truth, little mercy in a life spent in service to the divine powers. Whoever may wear that face, and how." Hubert met Marion's eyes, silent communion—and daunting acknowledgement. "I pray you keep to mercy, Maid. Love your consorts, and let us in our own time face our fears, and desires."

Silence.

"But 'tis also the Mother who watches her sons do battle." Robyn broke the quiet, an eerie, singsong murmur that again sent the chill and thrill zigzagging down Marion's spine. "The Mother who knows the balance must be held. Summer and Winter, at odds and allus together. And so the Maiden takes the victor—for he has proven his place and right."

As Robyn spoke, Gamelyn slowly turned back to face him. The gaunt, freckled cheeks were no longer so pale, and his green eyes almost glittered.

Marion was unsure she could process the extent of what had shone from Gamelyn's eyes—and what Hubert had just admitted. Openly making accord with the old gods, honouring Robyn's power . . . and in the doing, venerating Hers. Inexorably, Marion found herself drawn to the desperation, lying hectic and insubordinate—and how it told tens of tales by the fear lurking behind it.

Fear. Denial. *Desire.* All echoed in Gamelyn's face, like a mirror of Hubert's words.

We are lovers. We are rivals. What it has already done to us, this tynged, *this fate. What will it do to us, in the end?*

Yet he was *here.*

"I know what I am, milord," Robyn broke the silence. His words seemed pitched as much to Gamelyn as Hubert. "I see the warp and weft of m' *tynged* . . . m' fate," he clarified at Hubert's puzzled look, "stretching out before me, different strands like a half-set loom. My battle's still to come and all but lost. But I'll defend our world to my last breath. There's no doubt in me to the meaning of sacrifice. I live it, every day.

"And as you say, there's nowt of sacrifice in the taking of sommat that en't valued or even needed. So I told Cernun, long ago. 'Twere why I made the bargain with my god, to be His in every other thing save this. For me to lie with a woman . . . it would mean nowt, bring the rites all hollow, a soulless rut. But if I *did* want, and held meself apart from the wanting?" Robyn tipped a nod to Hubert. "I see the power in that. I wain't hold to 't, not as your like does. But I think, at last, I begin to understand what the purpose of such a thing might be."

"I say to you, it would be well to understand such things. There could come a time when you'll need such." Hubert lifted his bowl. "But for now, it is enough we understand each other. We shall look to each other, aid each other, and protect what we are and what we hold. Protect it against all who would see such arcane knowledge subdued. Suborned. Chained. That we make what sacrifices we must so we shan't be suborned. Or bound. Or wiped from our Mother's face."

"Aye." Robyn's voice was hoarse with emotion. Then the daunting, gilt light rising in his dark eyes once more, Robyn leaned in. "And Gamelyn . . . *Guy,*" he murmured to Hubert. "He's *yours,* en't he? Your . . . sacrifice."

Hubert stiffened. Marion sucked in a breath through her teeth, held it prisoned there.

A tiny smile graced Robyn's mouth as his gaze moved to Gamelyn's, pinned and held. "So do you come here, freely, to the appointed place? What will *you* sacrifice, Summerling?"

And beneath that voice was the Horned Lord's promise/threat, spun out honeyed as the mead.

But His Summerlord refused to be bent, or bowed.

"Haven't we all," Gamelyn said, deadly soft, "sacrificed enough?"

Robyn rose from his crouch, sudden enough that Hubert blinked. Stepping over the fire, Robyn then padded towards

Gamelyn, measured-slow. He looked more a stalking predator than any lovesick suitor. And Gamelyn some resolute illumination from a manuscript of St. George, hand on hilt, ready to slay any dragon.

"That depends on what you want," Robyn growled. "And if you're wanting it bad enough."

"*Wanting* isn't the problem!" Gamelyn snarled back.

Another whip-quick motion—this one forwards. Gamelyn jerked back, ever so slight, as Robyn grasped his shoulders, sidled close. Heedless of any other presence, he bent in, kissed Gamelyn's cheek. Lingered. Gamelyn quivered, and his eyes closed.

Robyn pushed back, gave him a tiny shake. "Then enough of this." Another growl—but scaling up, beseeching. "Please. Come back to me, Gamelyn."

- POSTLUDE -

F ate sealed—or if not sealed, at least delivered and bargained for. Home regained. Eden within his grasp . . .

Only not.

Gamelyn walked between Robyn and Marion, between the reaching fingers of evening fog and a copse of tall, spidery willows, between thaw and misted bottomland and the arch of grey sky, between sunlight and shadow.

Between.

You will be, in a very real sense, an ambassador, Hubert had said before they left Hirst. *Our Master has assigned you this task, to take up your place amongst them, be as one with them.* Then Hubert had added, with a peculiar and earnest candour, *This is the one chance I can give to you, Gamelyn. Take it.* Use *it.*

His Templar garb left behind at Hubert's request, with the exception of shamshir and knives, a few necessities—and his warmest cloak, its palm-sized cross turned to lie, hidden, against his heart. *Turncloak,* a spiteful inner-self jeered, but wisped into nothing as a slender arm slid into the warmth of that black cloak.

"You seem," Marion murmured against his shoulder, her arm curling into the crook of his, "unhappy."

"I'm not un . . . It . . . " Gamelyn tried, failed, tried again. "It's not . . . easy to explain."

"Nowt's ever easy with you, pet." Robyn, a bare pace ahead with longbow propped across his shoulders, turned slightly. There were arrows tucked into his black curls, damp with the bottom mists;

his hood slung back, body lithe and strong and arrow-straight . . . All of it, added to the fond mix of chagrin and chiding upon Robyn's expression, nearly undid Gamelyn then and there.

God! Gamelyn thought. *If only I could save you by hating you! But that didn't work either, did it? Instead what lies between us, burning, will merely beguile us back into the trap. Hunted wolf and leashed hound.*

Another taunt surfaced—the bearer of whom he was no more free. *Take care you do not choke yourself upon what leash we deign to give you.*

That, he snarled back, *would solve all of this!*

It would solve nothing and would only bring more chaos. No Templar Master this; 'twas Her, lingering within the indigo-black of a *tynged* he could not see past. *Everyone dies, Gamelyn. In their time.*

You will not use me to betray him!

So many assumptions.

It is what we are, he growled into the black, heard its echo, repeated in Wymarec de Birkin's too-reasonable voice: *It is what you are meant to do, were born to do. . .*

And he's right! Isn't it what we have always been? Rivals for your hand!

And surely as your Master Templar is of the Wise, it is true that cobras are also the most poisonous of serpent-kind.

"Gamelyn." Marion, grey eyes serious and searching. She hadn't heard, thank God, though she no doubt knew whose voice plagued him. "You're home. 'Tis all that matters, wain't you see?"

"All that . . ." He halted, pulled his arm from Marion's. "You don't understand."

"Then make us understand."

Robyn had also halted, head cocked. Curious.

Gamelyn tightened his jaw, said, "The Templars have sent me here, you know."

"Aye, well." Robyn shrugged and kept walking. "Whats'mever."

The answer was so . . . ludicrous. Gamelyn stared after Robyn, watched him glide farther in, then lurched after. He snatched at Robyn's tunic and yanked him about, grabbed both arms and hoisted him close.

Robyn let him, even if that made Gamelyn even more aware he'd a bit of healing yet to do. Chest tight, breath even more so, his words rasped harsh. "Look, you stroppy git of a peasant, this is no game, no jape. I've been *sent* here, don't you see? By my Masters."

"Whats'mever," Robyn said again. It was maddening. "If it fetches us what we want—"

"My Masters don't care what we want."

"I'll wager your Master Hubert does," Robyn pointed out. "He loves you, you daft sod. Canna you see that?"

"What I see is . . . That isn't . . . it isn't the . . . the underlying purpose, can *you* not see? Bloody hell! He was under orders, Robyn, and we both knew that before ever he met with you. Orders. And who gave those orders? The Templar Magician who took your Arrow . . . we can only hope it is gone."

"You said he destroyed it," Marion pointed out. At least she'd the grace to look somewhat concerned.

"I know what I said, bugger it! But what if he didn't?"

"He didn't." Robyn revealed this with an utter lack of the concern his sister held.

Gamelyn shook him—or tried to, best he was able. "That just proves how powerful he truly is! I tangled with him—"

"And thwarted him, as I recall."

"Only just. Hubert warned me. De Birkin means to be Grand Master—"

"I like your Master Hubert," Robyn inserted. "Despite meself."

Gamelyn shook him again. "—and I'd wager my shamshir de Birkin is up to something. I think he intends to find what he can about the Wode's magic."

Robyn merely shrugged again. "He can try. Happens that one'll find sommat he wain't fancy, if he does."

"*Damn* it, Robyn!" Gamelyn kept trying, though he was nigh to frothing. "Don't you understand? I'm here to *spy* on you!"

And good *Christ*, but was that a smirk tugging at Robyn's lip?

It was! And a scant breath later, Robyn was sliding his longbow, gentle, to the ground. Sidling close, then closer still, nipping at Gamelyn's lip, then his ear, with a breath against that ear.

"Spy, you say? Fancy that. Happens we'll give 'em sommat to spy on, you 'n me. Aye?"

Another nip, one that melted Gamelyn's bones to butter and drove every sensible thought from his head but *Oh God*, and *It's been too bloody long*, and a final, fatal *Yes, now please—the harder the better.*

As if he heard the inner whimper, Robyn gave a chuckle—and damn, but he likely had, he was Robyn Hode after all, wasn't he? Heathen priest, *dryw ardhu*, Winterlord . . .

Aye, he'd heard, all right; teeth flashing in a wide, sly smile. "That's more like my poncy ginger paramour. Been too long, has it, in that solitary Templar cot?"

"You . . . *sod*," Gamelyn managed.

"I'm your sod, now. And you're ours." Another chuckle. "By order of the Temple." Robyn pronounced this last with relish, then kissed

Gamelyn again, long and hard. With tongue. And just enough teeth.

All *right*, then, mayhap Robyn did have a good argument. Marion, damn her eyes, was *smiling*—Gamelyn saw it, just before his brain melted into dormancy and his eyes closed. A bow-hardened hand slid into the small of his back. Serious, this kiss, and it *had* been too long.

The hand smoothed down, squeezed his arse and tickled its way back upwards . . . then, with an abrupt jerk and snatch, nicked the quillion dagger from Gamelyn's belt.

"Hoy!" A twist then a hiss, stiff muscles betraying him, but Robyn had eluded him, lithe and swift, and was backing away with the quillion dagger in one hand.

Robyn's smirk did not belie the tiny question, deep behind black eyes.

Nerves primed for action wibbled beneath that gaze, still blissfully— ridiculously—dormant. Gamelyn bid them heel with even voice and raised eyebrow, held out his hand. "I rather fancy that dagger, you know."

"Half as much as I?" Again, the question.

And Marion watching them, still grinning like a fool. It came to Gamelyn that too long had passed since he'd seen her lovely smile. Infectious, teasing and coaxing, and Gamelyn realised that his answer to it also felt foreign.

Encouraged, Marion sauntered over and took Gamelyn's outstretched hand, snugged up close. "Happens you'll take it from him? I quite fancy watching handsome men wrestle."

"He'd stand no chance," Gamelyn heard himself saying. "A scrawny archer against a trained Templar? Not likely."

"You're still not healed up," Robyn protested. "I'd stand a chance with those odds!"

"'Tis all about odds with you," Marion sighed.

"Aye. And your point?"

"The point is, you nicked my dagger," Gamelyn reminded.

"Aye, well. Y' lie with thieves . . . " Robyn flipped the dagger midair and caught it again, all in one effortless motion. Dangled it, questioning.

Gamelyn shrugged and pulled Marion closer. He knew his meaning was plain.

Moreover, Robyn knew it too. Smile widening, he flipped the dagger again, then stuck it in his own belt. Skipping sideways a few steps, he scooped up his longbow from the chill ground, slung it across his shoulders, and started off again. "If we get on, we'll make it home by morning and keep ourselves warm in the doing."

Gamelyn couldn't help either the shake of his head or his own smile, broadening as the lean shadow disappeared, one with the mists and the winter-bare willows.

Marion kissed his cheek. "Twill be all right, Gamelyn. Remember: *Back-to-back, none shall stand against you.*"

The Lady's promise, spoken so long ago. And, miracle of miracles, She repeated it, soft against Gamelyn's nape.

Marion must have heard. She smiled, then kissed him again, this time full on the mouth. "All that ever matters are things bein' as they should be, here and now. Aye?"

He nodded. Marion laid her head against his shoulder, then loosed him and headed off into the trees after Robyn.

Those trees were budding. New growth, into the crisp air, and Marion, clad in all the colours of spring.

The smile came to Gamelyn's lips, both rue and sweet flooding his senses. No choice, mayhap—and this time, no choice but to follow. Not that Gamelyn was sure he wanted a choice. Better to take this with both hands, follow Robyn's example, and live for *now.*

All that ever matters are things bein' as they should be, here and now.

Only . . .

The thought curled in, like a cobra beneath an Eastern altar, glutted sleepy on honeyed milk:

Only you've not had the dreams I have. . .

Gamelyn gave a growl, shook his head. Followed his Maiden and his Archer, into the waking Wode.

- END BOOK THREE -

KINDLY TURN THE PAGE FOR A
PREVIEW OF BOOK FOUR

Candles, everywhere.

Full dozens of them illuminated the east-facing solar, commingling with the roaring hearth to banish murk from stubborn corners. Nevertheless, shadows lingered. In alcoves they tarried, and from without the light-filled sanctuary, they crept over stone walls into the stair beyond, dispersed only by an inadequate spatter of gilt to mark comings and goings.

And when the candles thought to gutter, Count John, Count of Mortain and Lord of Gloucester, demanded more.

Nightmares lingered in Nottingham Castle.

He knew why. Comprehended the realities—all of them—as few others might. Still, he craved light even as he nursed its reminders. The possibilities. The impediments . . . aye, the impediments.

It had been a right bloody bastard of a fortnight.

One of his favourite castles invaded—not by storm and fire, but by a horde of savages who'd stolen his best piece in a crooked, desperate game. The hunt after, a failure. The removal from Blyth Castle to here in Nottingham, a dogged try at reestablishing what political ties he could . . . and to dispel an enduring terror of spectres from a hellish Hallows. And then, this.

He'd known it was coming. But, still.

John gave the fire a savage thrust with the iron poker. Sparks fled upward and flared, albeit cold, against the emerald adorning his left hand. The centre log collapsed with another burst of light. Spilled gold over the clenched parchment.

"My lord, I—"

"Count. You will address Us as Count John. Or my liege." Poker still in hand, John put his backside to the fire, contemplating both the hastily vacated bed and the figure to whom he spoke, standing shadowed by the post drapes. "For despite circumstance rendering Us low, We are nevertheless the latter. Yes?"

"Of course, my liege," the figure soothed. "I was merely—"

"Questioning me. And what else would you have seen me do? Just knuckle under whilst my brother beggars England? First his be-damned holy war, and now this!" Rage nearly choked him; he gave another savage poke at the fire, showering sparks. "God's teeth, but more than a king's ransom is worth! All for my mother's precious and shining idiot son!"

Over by the open door, Nottingham's newest castellan inched towards escape, gaze equally held by his liege lord and by the one still lurking in the shadows.

Bloody annoying, that.

"And always, your like in the midst of it! Riding in mid-night, upsetting everything, dragging me from my bed and scaring that poor maid so."

The castellan started to make excuse, realised the words were, again, not for him, and continued his steady creep.

"It took well over a se'nnight to cozen her from her shift, and now your dour manner and that bloody cross on your chest has no doubt set me back another!"

Silence. John gave a fleeting grin—he knew exactly with what weapons to pink his visitor—and rounded on his retreating castellan. "Murdac!"

The man froze in place, his broad, bewhiskered face nigh white with both fear and regret. He had nearly made the door.

John let him bask in both for a full intake of breath, then snapped, "Wine! Mulled hot and sweet!"

A flush this time, dark as the man's beard, and Murdac wheeled, making a grateful escape into the shadows.

It was humiliating, but John didn't envy him.

The candles glimmered, warm sanity, over the draperies and tapestries. John stretched a hand out towards one, flitting his fingers through, back and forth. "Of course, you and your like always are. In the midst of things."

"It is the way of our Order, my lord Count. It has, I would suggest, in its time served you well."

The shadowed acknowledgment was silk over steel, but concilia-tory. As it should be. Along with his other titles, John was overlord of this bloody castle beneath their feet and regent of England— well, to be frank, his mother had been that for the past several years—but no matter. He was damned determined to be more. Was more.

"And as to my precipitous entry, I fear I'd little choice." A pale flicker in the shadows, the heavy shush of a cloak being flung back.

A gesture towards the parchment clenched in John's fist. "Particularly once my agents delivered *that.*"

Rage swelled, humid heat, and John lurched forward. In the next moment, dread choked the furious outburst, roiling in from the shadowy stones. John scooted back for the fire—for the light.

Had John been his father, he would have stomped and bellowed, rolled on the floor, and chewed the rushes. His brother Richard would have laughed, then led his mercenaries to burn a few towns in retribution. No fear in them . . . no imagination. They'd no need for it. They'd never been the least of anything.

They didn't know. Hadn't seen. Hadn't . . . Seen.

"My lord?" It was rigid with calm.

As if that calm were contagious, John turned, took a deep breath, and met the Templar's gaze.

"You must take care, my lord Count," Wymarec de Birkin counselled, low. "He is, after all, our king."

"He is, after all, our king.'" Mockery curled upon John's lips. "Is he, then? Truly?"

The pale blue eyes shifted, uneasy.

"And what sort of king? Barren as his sodding marriage—taking, always taking! From the moment I stood on my own and reached for what was mine, he was set to take it. Or had it given to him as if by right! Even now . . . " Dropping his gaze to the parchment, John refused to unclench his stiff fingers. The emerald ring glittered, hand atremble.

Shadows in Nottingham. Ghosts in the Wode, and a power called from it to eclipse his own. And now, one line—just one line, set with ink and careful quill. One line, to inspire more dread.

Look to yourself—the Devil is loose.

No signature or felicitation. None was needed; John recognised France's hand. Lovely, treacherous Phillip had penned this himself.

Wymarec was frowning. Or was he? Damn Templars, anyway, they'd no fear of shadows—they captured and set them to their bidding with countenances of iron and ice.

"Master of England, eh?" John growled. "You, Master de Birkin, mouth promises of powers and unholy Kingships, yet all the while, you play Us with this game of yours!"

"It is no game, my lord. Surely—"

"Game. You bluff keenly as any dice peddler, claim to wield things which you do not yet possess, whilst my brother beggars the country, blind to any might save that of mace and chain, sword and cross. And wins. Whilst a wolfshead rides with demons, calls spirits down upon my people and my lands, takes my forest and my crown! And wins!" It was ramping up into a scream, and he didn't care. "He is mocking me, and you give him aid?"

"Not aid, my liege. A spy. Gisbourne will find what needs be known."

"So you say?" John snorted. "Unless you're keen to know the size of the wolfshead's prick, I doubt you'll gain much from your precious Sir Guy."

"A small price to pay, lying with animals," de Birkin insisted, albeit cautious, "if one can learn secrets thought long lost to us. Such a power, my liege! It still lingers in Nottingham Castle, whispering within every shadow of the stones beneath our feet."

The sentiment sank home with a barbed and poisoned crossbow bolt. John shivered, inched closer to the fire. Realised the parchment remained, clenched, in his fist. A talisman of ruin—or mayhap just of patience.

All he could hope for now was escape. He might have the blood-right, but Richard had the devil's luck, always had. What was there for John to do but let his brother further plunder the kingdom? He could hardly stop him. Could do little but wait.

But the waiting? Interminable.

With a snarl, John threw the parchment into the hearth. It flared, brief brilliance to shame the tens of candles. Dread retreated, banished by scorn even as light chased shadow and nightmare into their corners. And suddenly John found himself laughing.

"My lord?" De Birkin looked puzzled.

"What a homecoming our lovely King shall have! A country drained of its resources, nothing more to give him. A brutal winter, poor hunting, meagre crops. And an eldritch power that Richard could never wield or understand, coiled in wait for him."

Upon the hearth the parchment roiled, curling into sullen embers. Still chuckling, John shook his head.

"The devil is indeed loose—in Sherwood Forest! And I daresay my dear, lumbering brother has no idea."

Find this and the rest of the series
(in trade paper, ebook, & audio)
at your favourite retailer
&

FOREST PATH BOOKS
https://forestpathbooks.com

Moments come to us, a gift; we snatch at them, try to hold them, stay them. And it's those moments—those *memories*—that either stand in our way or make us appreciate it all the more. But we only ever have this moment—*thisnow*, as the Heathen of the Wode would say.

Winterwode, as the sort-of beginning of a new trilogy and the third book in the overall series, (and how magical is that?) is in the very midst of *thisnow*. It speaks to the distinct curse/blessing of being unable to let go of *then*, and *soon*. All of the characters in the Wode books bear this to some degree, but it lies particularly upon Marion, Gamelyn, and Robyn. The Maiden, the Knight, and the Archer will each have their own journey towards the final act.

As has their amanuensis. It's always a journey, the writing and finishing of a book, but *Winterwode* required a bit more from me. You see, a very specific chain of events begins here, the proper telling of which meant a return journey to my sources for some very specific information. I've travelled to the UK before, but this was one of the most fruitful research trips in my experience, particularly in terms of surround. "Write what you know" has a lot of baggage, but also some essential truths: if you want to have any sort of authority or fluency with your subject, there must be kinship and understanding with it. The time in the UK was bliss, first with Amazing Spouse and then on my own; a process of both reacquainting myself with and discovering places that have, in a very real sense, *been* home for several books and many years.

There is never enough time for such things, no.

So this became my mantra: *Be present. Be in thisnow.*

And I was. Even taking all the pictures I needed for research sometimes grated, interfered with experience. Never mind, go on, *be present*. The caves at Nottingham. (Finally!) Riding an ex-steeplechaser through Sherwood Forest. Hiking the North Country. The B and Bs and YHA hostels, which rarely disappoint. The YHA at Hathersage was particularly notable, with delightful roommates and absolutely gobsmackingly gorgeous scenery. No wonder little John has such a beautiful soul, growing up in such a place. I didn't want to leave. But I had a date with a Yorkshire town and its castle: Tickhill, aka Blyth. I've met some fascinating people in my travels, but it's to the folk of Tickhill in particular I've some thanks to tender, for this book would not be the same without their help.

Dorothy Bradley of the Tickhill Historical Society, who corresponded with me via e-mail, opened her home to me for an afternoon, took me on a fascinating tour of her town (and gave me some invaluable knowledge in the doing). She also set up my day with one of the leading authorities on the castle at Tickhill and Senior Lecturer of the Hallamshire Archaeological & Historical Association.

And to that lecturer, Lloyd Powell, I offer sincere and avid thanks for his understanding, knowledge, and time. The map accompanying *Winterwode* uses as its basis a sketch he made for me (as well as my own photos and measurements from a book entitled *Old Yorkshire* by William Wheater). I'd not yet had my knee surgery, so it was a job and a half and lots of painkillers in keeping up with him ;)—but every bit of it was amazing. I will *never* forget being able to actually touch the Norman tomb in St. Peter's at Conisbrough and speculate (all right, geek out) over the carvings upon it. Seeing the charcoal-burner sites along Loxley's river and walking what was Loxley Chase. Sharing a mutual discovery of a brilliant Templar church replica near Hirst. The long talks, whilst hoofing it across various old mottes and graveyards, about history; especially the history of the ruined Norman motte and bailey castle at Tickhill, where Lloyd worked for many years.

Indeed, all of Tickhill, from the amazing staff of the town library who not only gave this Yank a library card but helped her find a new source for used books, to the lovely proprietor of Hannah's B and B, whose establishment was a quiet and cosy home for my stay and who did me the simple kindness of fresh laundry, to expat Americans Sandy and Gordon who invited me not only to an archaeological dig at Clipstone (that I was forced by circumstance to miss, damn it!) but to a bell-ringing practise up the ancient narrow stairway of St. Mary's Church, to the lovely man there who showed me those bells and mechanisms with all the justifiable pride of a new father . . . indeed to *all* the people of Tickhill, who welcomed me graciously to their lovely town.

I also must give several shout-outs to this side of the Pond. First to Tali, who gently reminded me that sometimes what you think is an ending to a story arc, well, isn't. To Carole, who listens even when I've had too much wine or too little sleep. To the original editors of *Winterwode*, who understood my wish to make this story pertinent to *this* moment—thisnow—and hopefully into the future. I'm reaching for other chances, now, but no matter the circumstances or passages, it's nice to have someone believe in the work.

Any errors—either purposeful in service to Story or accidental through memory—aren't due to any of these lovely people, but are solely my own responsibility.

All the moments shared, snatched at, held, stayed, *cherished?* For all the necessity to be present, here, in thisnow, we still have the need—and the privilege—to hold those moments close and let memories both burn and warm. It is my hope, through the next several Books of the Wode, that those who share *thisnow* with the outlaws of the Wode will find in that experience a memory worth keeping.

Bendith— JTH
Autumn, 2015

- ABOUT THE AUTHOR -

J TULLOS HENNIG

has always possessed inveterate fascination in the myths and histories of other worlds and times. Despite having maintained a few professions in *this* world—equestrian, dancer, teacher, artist—she has never managed to not be a storyteller. Ever.

Given a heritage of forest-dwelling peoples—Choctaw, Chickasaw, and Scots-Irish—the decision to make a home base in NW Washington State with the Amazing Spouse was a no-brainer. They live alongside an equine 'pasture potato' on a retirement pension, a wolfhound who alternates between leaping over the sofa and snoozing on it, and a press gang of invisible 'friends' Who Will Not Be Silenced.

Active in conventions and genre literature in the 70s/80s/90s, Jeanine returned to the authorial fold with the publication of an award-winning series of historical fantasy novels She is a member of the Author's Guild, the Historical Novel Society, and SFWA. In 2018 she was presented with the Speculative Literature Foundation's juried Older Writers Grant.

Her historical series *The Books of the Wode* presents a truly innovative re-imagining of the Robin Hood legends, giving emphasis and reality to both pagan and queer perspectives.

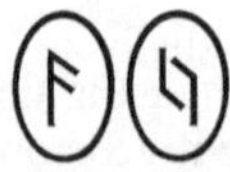

http://www.jtulloshennig.net